The Saint

FIVE COMPLETE NOVELS

ABOUT THE AUTHOR

LESLIE CHARTERIS was born in 1907 and attended Cambridge University. His most famous literary creation is Simon Templar—the Saint—the handsome bon vivant who excels at taking the law into his own very capable hands. Charteris has written more than fifty novels featuring the Saint, and his books have been translated into fifty languages. The ever-popular Saint novels have been made into a radio show, a television series, a comic strip, and several feature-length films.

Charteris has served as supervising editor of *Saint* magazine for many years, written for *Gourmet*, worked as a film writer, and contributed pieces to leading English and American magazines. Charteris is a fellow of the Royal Society of Arts and now lives in Englefield Green, England.

The Saint

FIVE COMPLETE NOVELS

by Leslie Charteris
with a new introduction by the author

The Man Who Was Clever

The Lawless Lady

The Saint Closes the Case

The Avenging Saint

The Saint vs. Scotland Yard

AVENEL BOOKS · NEW YORK

This 1983 edition is published by Avenel Books,
distributed by Crown Publishers, Inc., by arrangement with
Doubleday & Company, Inc.

This Omnibus edition was previously published in separate volumes under the titles:
Enter the Saint copyright MCMXXX, MCMXXXI by Leslie Charteris
The Saint Closes the Case (formerly *The Last Hero*) .
copyright MCMXXX, MCMXLI by Doubleday, Doran & Company, Inc.
The Avenging Saint copyright MCMXXX, MCMXXXI by Leslie Charteris
The Saint vs. Scotland Yard copyright MCMXXXII
by Leslie Charteris, copyright MCMXLV by Avon Book Company

The Man Who Was Clever and *The Lawless Lady* were
previously published in MCMXXX as *Enter the Saint*.

Manufactured in the United States of America

Library of Congress Cataloging in Publication Data

Charteris, Leslie, 1907–
The Saint: five complete novels.
Contents: The man who was clever—The lawless lady—
The Saint closes the case—The avenging Saint—
The Saint vs. Scotland Yard.
1. Detective and mystery stories, English.   I. Title.
PR6005.H348A6   1983   823′.912   82-20656
ISBN: 0-517-403048

h g f e d c b a

CONTENTS

Introduction

WHEN A PUBLISHER asks me for an Introduction to a volume like this, I feel much the same as if I had been asked to write my own obituary, because I can't write an introduction without going far back into my own vintage years.

The first "Saint" book (of which I am not particularly proud) was published in 1928, which is fifty-five years ago as I write this. The first stories in which I began to develop the Saint as a series character were written two or three years later and came out in book form as *Enter the Saint*,* the first in the present collection, and comfortably more than half a century ago. The dates of the other titles in this omnibus can be found in the copyright notice behind the title page. I have to mention this because many readers of this compendium might not observe it themselves and would be puzzled by not a few details and references in the text.

So what you will be reading is in fact a collection of period pieces. Not, perhaps, set quite as far back as the Sherlock Holmes or Raffles stories, but already getting on that way. When I was writing them, it seemed only natural to be specific about current motoring conditions, for instance, and amusing to take sidelong digs at contemporary personalities and events. It never occurred to me that such topical allusions might be totally baffling to another generation of readers. If I had thought about it at all, I should probably have found the very idea that I might have a future generation of readers quite hootably hilarious. Indeed, having since extended the span to at least two generations, I still find the idea as hard to grasp as the reality of my own age.

Short of an annotated edition ankle deep in footnotes, I can only offer this general explanation, with my apologies, and perhaps some humble suggestions. If some details seem incongruous to life as you know it today, be assured that they were congruous in the days I was writing about. If anything sounds "dated," that is exactly what it is. If you don't understand a joke, or a reference to someone you never heard of, skip it. I hope you will still find yourselves left with some good entertainment.

Englefield Green, England   L.C.
1983

*Listed in this edition as *The Man Who Was Clever* and *The Lawless Lady*.

The Man Who Was Clever

1

MR. "SNAKE" GANNING was neither a great criminal nor a pleasant character, but he is interesting because he was the first victim of the organization led by the man known as the Saint, which was destined in the course of a few months to spread terror through the underworld of London—that ruthless association of reckless young men, brilliantly led, who worked on the side of the law and who were yet outside the law. There was to come a time when the mere mention of the Saint was sufficient to fill the most unimaginative malefactor with uneasy fears, when a man returning home late one night to find the sign of the Saint— a childish sketch of a little man with straight-line body and limbs, and an absurd halo over his round blank head—chalked upon his door, would be sent instinctively spinning round with his back to the nearest wall and his hand flying to his hip pocket, and an icy tingle of dread prickling up his spine; but at the date of the Ganning episode the Saint had only just commenced operations, and his name had not yet come to be surrounded with the aura of almost supernatural infallibility which it was to earn for itself later.

Mr. Ganning was a tall, incredibly thin man, with sallow features and black hair that was invariably oiled and brushed to a shiny sleekness. His head was small and round, and he carried it thrust forward to the full stretch of his long neck. Taking into the combination of physical characteristics the sinuous carriage of his body, the glittering beadiness of his expressionless black eyes, and the silent litheness with which he moved, it was easy to appreciate the aptness of his nickname. He was the leader of a particularly tough race-course gang generally known as "The Snake's Boys," which subsisted in unmerited luxury on the proceeds of blackmailing bookmakers under threat of doing them grievous bodily harm; there were also a number of other unsavoury things about him which may be revealed in due course.

The actual motive for the interference of the Saint in the affairs of the Snake and his Boys was their treatment of Tommy Mitre on the occasion of his first venture into turf finance. Tommy had always wanted to be a jockey, for horses were in his blood; but quite early in his apprenticeship he had been thrown and injured so severely that he had never been able to ride again, and he had had to content himself with the humble position of stable boy in a big training establishment. Then an uncle of Tommy's, who had been a publican, died, leaving his nephew the tremendous fortune of two hundred pounds, and Tommy decided to try his luck in the Silver Ring. He took out a licence, had a board painted ("Tommy Mitre—The Old Firm—Established 1822") and enlisted a clerk. One day he went down to Brighton with this paraphernalia and the remains of his two hundred pounds, and it was not long before the Snake's Boys spotted the stranger and made the usual demands. Tommy refused to pay. He ought to have known better, for the methods of the Snake had never been a secret in racing circles; but Tommy was like that—stubborn. He told the Snake exactly where he could go, and as a result Tommy Mitre was soundly beaten up by the Snake's Boys when he was leaving the course, and his capital and his day's profits were taken. And it so happened that Simon Templar had elected to enjoy a day's racing at Brighton, and had observed the beating-up from a distance.

Snake Ganning and a select committee of the Boys spent the evening in Brighton celebrating, and left for London by a late train. So also did Simon Templar. Thus it came to pass that the said Simon Templar wandered up the platform a couple of minutes before the train left, espied the Snake and three of the Boys comfortably ensconced in a first-class carriage, and promptly joined them.

The Saint, it should be understood, was a vision that gave plenty of excuse for the glances of pleased anticipation which were exchanged by the Snake and his favourite Boys as soon as they had summed him up. In what he called his "fighting kit"—which consisted of disreputable grey flannel bags and a tweed shooting-jacket of almost legendary age— the Saint had the unique gift of appearing so immaculate that the least absent-minded commissionaire might have been pardoned for mistaking him for a millionaire duke. It may be imagined what a radiant spectacle he was in what he called his "gentleman disguise."

His grey flannel suit fitted him with a staggering perfection, the whiteness of his shirt was dazzling, his tie shamed the rainbow. His soft felt hat appeared to be having its first outing since it left Bond Street. His chamois gloves were clearly being shown to the world for the first time. On his left wrist was a gold watch, and he carried a gold-mounted ebony walking-stick. Everything, you understand, quietly but unmistakably of the very best, and worn with that unique air of careless elegance which others might attempt to emulate, but which only the Saint could achieve in all its glory. . . .

As for the man—well, the reputation of the Snake's Boys for toughness was founded on more substantial demonstrations than displays of skill at hunt-the-slipper at the Y.M.C.A. on Saturday afternoons. The man was tall—about six feet two inches of him—but they didn't take much count of that. Their combined heights totted up to twenty-four feet three inches. And although he wasn't at all hefty, he was broad enough, and there was a certain solidity about his shoulders that would have made a cautious man think carefully before starting any unpleasantness—but that didn't bother the Snake and his Boys. Their combined widths summed up to a shade over six feet. And the Saint had a clear tanned skin and a very clear blue eye—but even that failed to worry them. They weren't running a beauty competition, anyway.

The important point was that the Saint had a gold cigarette-case and a large wad of bank-notes. In his innocent way, he counted over his pile before their very eyes, announced the total at two hundred and fifty pounds odd, and invited them to congratulate him on his luck. They congratulated him, politely. They remarked on the slowness of the train, and the Saint agreed that it was a boring journey. He said he wished there was some sort of entertainment provided by the railway company for the diversion of passengers on boring journeys. Somebody produced a pack of cards. . . .

It can be said for them that they gave him the credit for having been warned by his grandmother about the danger of trying to find the Lady. The game selected was poker. The Saint apologetically warned them that he had only played poker once before in his life, but they said kindly that that didn't matter a bit.

The fight started just five minutes before the train reached Victoria, and the porters who helped the Snake and his Boys out of the compartment were not thanked. They gave the Boys a bucket of water with which to revive the Snake himself, but they couldn't do anything about his two black eyes or his missing front teeth.

Inspector Teal, who was waiting on the platform in the hope of seeing a much-wanted con-man, saw the injured warriors and was not sympathetic.

"You've been fighting, Snake," he said brightly.

Ganning's reply was unprintable, but Mr. Teal was not easily shocked.

"But I can describe him to you," said the Snake, becoming less profane. "Robbery with violence, that's what it was. He set on us—"

" 'Sat' is the past tense of 'sit,' " said Teal, shifting his gum to the other side of his mouth.

"He's got away with over three hundred quid that we made to-day—"

Teal was interested. "Where d'you make it?" he enquired. "Have you got a real printing-press, or do you make it by hand? I didn't know you were in the 'slush' game, Snake."

"Look here, Teal," said Ganning, becoming more coherent. "You can say what you like about me, but I've got my rights, the same as anybody else. You've got to get after that man. Maybe you know things about him already. He's already on a lay, or he's just starting on one, you mark my words. See this!"

Mr. Teal examined the envelope sleepily. "What is it?" he asked. "A letter of introduction to me?"

"He gave it to Ted when he got out. 'That's my receipt,' he said. Didn't he, Ted? You look inside, Teal!"

The envelope was not sealed. Teal turned it over, and remarked on the flap the crest of the hotel which had provided it. Then, in his lethargic way, he drew out the contents—a single sheet of paper.

"Portrait by Epstein," he drawled. "Quite a nice drawing, but it don't mean anything to me outside of that. You boys have been reading too many detective stories lately, that's the trouble with you."

2

THE SAINT, BEING a man of decidedly luxurious tastes, was the tenant of a flat in Brook Street, Mayfair, which was so far beyond his means that he had long since given up worrying about the imminence of bankruptcy. One might as well be hung for a sheep, the Saint reflected, in his cheerfully reckless way, as for a foot-and-mouth-diseased lamb. He considered that the world owed him a good time, in return for services rendered and general presentability and good-fellowship, and, since the world hitherto had been close-fistedly reluctant to recognize the obligation and meet it, the Saint had decided that the time had come for him to assert himself. His invasion of Brook Street had been one of the first moves in the campaign.

But the locality had one distinct advantage that had nothing to do with the prestige of its address; and this advantage was the fact that it possessed a mews, a very small and exclusive mews, situated at a distance of less than the throw of a small stone from the Saint's front door. In this mews were a number of very expensive garages, large, small, and of Austin Seven size. And the Saint owned two of these large garages. In one he kept his own car; the other had been empty for a week, until he had begun smuggling an assortment of curious objects into it at dead of night—objects which only by the most frantic stretch of imagination could have been associated with cars.

If the Saint had been observed on any of these surreptitious trips, it is highly probable that his sanity would have been doubted. Not that he would have cared; for he had his own reasons for his apparent eccentricity. But as it was, no one noticed his goings-out or his comings-in, and there was no comment.

And even if he had been noticed, it is very doubtful if he would have been recognized. It was the immaculate Saint who left Brook Street and drove to Chelsea and garaged his car near Fulham Road. Then, by a very subtle change of carriage, it was a not-nearly-so-immaculate Saint who walked through a maze of dingy back streets to a house in which one Bertie Marks, a bird of passage, had a stuffy and microscopical apartment. And it was a shabby, slouching, down-at-heel Bertie Marks who left the apartment and returned to the West End on the plebeian bus, laden with the packages that he had purchased on his way; and who shambled inconspicuously into the mews off Brook Street and into the garage which he held in his own name. The Saint did not believe in being unnecessarily careless about details. And all these elaborate preparations—the taking of the second garage and the Chelsea apartment, and the creation of the character of Bertie Marks—had been made for one single purpose, which was put in execution on a certain day.

A few hours after dawn on that day (an unearthly hour for the Saint to be abroad) a small van bearing the name of Carter Paterson turned into the mews and stopped there. Bertie Marks climbed down from the driver's seat, wiping grimy hands on his corduroys, and fished out a key, with which he opened the door of his garage. Then he went back to his van, drove it into the garage, and closed the doors behind him. He knew that his action must have excited the curiosity of the car-washing parade of chauffeurs congregated in the mews, but he wasn't bothering about that. With the consummation of his plan, the necessity for the continued existence of Bertie Marks was rapidly nearing its end.

"Let 'em wonder!" thought the Saint carelessly, as he peeled off his grubby jacket. He switched on the light, and went and peeped out into the mews. The car-washing parade had resumed its labours, being for the moment too preoccupied to bother about the strange phenomenon of a Carter Paterson van being driven into a garage that had once housed a Rolls. The Saint gently slid a bar across the door to shut out any inquisitive explorers, and got to work.

The van, on being opened, disclosed a number of large, wooden packing-cases, which the Saint proceeded to unload onto the floor of the garage. This done, he fetched from a corner a mallet and chisel, and began to prise open the cases and extract their contents. In each case, packed in with wood shavings, were two dozen china jars.

As each case was emptied, the Saint carried the jars over to the light and inspected them minutely. He was not at all surprised to find that, whereas the majority of the jars were perfectly plain, all the jars in one case were marked with a tiny cross in the glazing. These jars the Saint set aside, for they were the only ones in which he was interested. They were exactly what he had expected to find, and they provided his entire motive for the temporary and occasional sinking of his own personality in the alias of Mr. Marks. The other jars he replaced in their respective cases, and carefully closed and roped them to look as they had been before he tampered with them.

Then he opened the marked jars and poured out their contents into a bucket. In another corner of the garage was a pile of little tins, and in each jar the Saint placed one of these tins, padding the space that was left with cotton wool to prevent rattling. The jars so treated were replaced one by one and the case in its turn was also nailed up again and roped as before—after the Saint, with a little smile plucking at the corners of his mouth, had carefully laid a souvenir of his intervention on the top of the last layer of wood shavings. He had worked quickly. Only an hour and a half had elapsed from the time when he drove into the garage to the time when he lifted the last case back into the van; and when that had been done he unbarred the garage doors and opened them wide.

The remains of the car-washing parade looked up puzzledly as the van came backing out of the garage; it registered an even greater perplexity when the van proceeded to drive out of the mews and vanish in the direction of Bond Street. It yelled to the driver that he had forgotten to close his garage after him, but Mr. Marks either did not hear or did not care. And when the parade perceived that Mr. Marks had gone for good, it went and pried into the garage, and scratched its head over the litter of wood shavings on the floor, the mallet and chisel and nails and hammer, and the two or three tins which the Saint had found no space for, and which he had accordingly left behind. But the bucket of white powder was gone, riding beside Mr. Marks in the front of the van; and very few people ever saw Mr. Marks again.

The van drove to an address in the West End, and there Mr. Marks delivered the cases, secured a signature to a receipt, and departed, heading further west. On his way, he stopped at St. George's Hospital, where he left his bucket. The man who took charge of it was puzzled, but Mr. Marks was in a hurry and had neither time nor the inclination to enlighten him. "Take great care of it, because it's worth more money than you'll ever have," he directed. "See that it gets to one of the doctors, and give him this note with it."

And the Saint went back to the wheel of his van and drove away, feeling that he was nearing the end of an excellent day's work. He drove to the Great West Road, and out of London toward Maidenhead. Somewhere along that road he turned off into a side lane, and there he stopped for a few minutes out of sight of the main traffic. Inside the van was a large pot of paint, and the Saint used it energetically. He had never considered himself an artist, but he man-handled that van with the broad sweeping touch of a master. Under his vigorous wielding of the brush, the sign of Carter Paterson, which he had been at some pains to execute artistically the night before, vanished entirely; and the van became plain. Satisfied with the obliteration of the handiwork which only a few hours before he had admired so much, the Saint resumed the wheel and drove back to London. The paint he had used was guaranteed quick-drying, and it lived up to the word of its guarantee. It collected a good deal of dust on the return voyage, and duly dried a somewhat soiled aspect which was a very fair imitation of the condition in which Mr. Marks had received it.

He delivered it to its home garage at Shepherd's Bush and paid twenty-four hours' hire. Some time later Mr. Marks returned to Chelsea. A little later still, the not-so-immaculate Simon Templar turned into another garage and collected his trim blue Furillac speedster, in which he drove to his club in Dover Street. And the Simon Templar who sauntered through to the bar and called for a pint of beer must have been one of the most impeccably immaculate young men that that haunt of impeccably immaculate young men had ever sheltered.

"We don't often see you as early as this, sir," remarked the barman.

"May it be as many years before you see me as early as this again,

son,'' answered the Saint piously. ''But this morning I felt I just had to
get up and go for a drive. It was such a beautiful morning.''

3

MR. EDGAR HAYN was a man of many interests. He was the proud
proprietor of ''Danny's,'' a night club in a squalid street off Shaftesbury
Avenue, and he also controlled the destinies of the firm of Laserre, which
was a small but expensive shop in Regent Street that retailed perfumes,
powders, rouges, creams, and all the other preparations essential to modern feminine face-repair. These two establishments were Mr. Hayn's
especial pets, and from them he derived the greater part of his substantial
income. Yet it might be mentioned that the profits of ''Danny's'' were
not entirely earned by the sale of champagne, and the adornment of
fashionable beauty was not the principal source of the prosperity of the
house of Laserre. Mr. Hayn was a clever organizer, and what he did not
know about the art of covering his tracks wouldn't have been missed
from one of the microscopical two-guinea alabaster jars in which he sold
the celebrated Créme Laserre.

He was a big, heavy-featured man, clean-shaven, pink complexioned,
and faintly bald. His name had not always been Hayn, but a process of
naturalization followed by a Deed Poll had given him an indisputable
legal right to forget the cognomen of his father—and, incidentally, had
eliminated for ever the unpleasant possibility of a deportation order, an
exercise of forethought for which Mr. Hayn was more than once moved
to give his sagacity a pat on the back. The police knew certain things
about him which made them inclined to regard him with disfavour, and
they suspected a lot more, but there had never been any evidence.

He was writing letters at the big knee-hole desk in his private office
at ''Danny's'' when Ganning arrived. The knock on the door did not
make him look up. He said, ''Come in!''—but the sound of the opening
and closing of the door was, to him, sufficient indication that the order
had been obeyed; and he went on to finish the letter he had been drafting.
Only when that was done did he condescend to notice the presence of
his visitor. ''You're late, Snake,'' he said, blotting the sheet carefully.

"Sorry, boss."

Mr. Hayn screwed the cap on his fountain-pen, replaced it in his pocket, and raised his eyes from the desk for the first time. What he saw made him sag back with astonishment. "Who on earth have you been picking a quarrel with?" he demanded.

The Snake certainly looked the worse for wear. A bandage round his head covered one eye, and the eye that was visible was nearly closed up. His lips were bruised and swollen, and a distinct lack of teeth made him speak with a painful lisp.

"Was it Harrigan's crowd?" suggested Hayn.

Ganning shook his head. "A bloke we met on the train coming back from Brighton last night."

"Were you alone?"

"Nope; Ted and Bill were with me. And Mario."

"And what was this man trooping around? A regiment?"

"He was alone."

Hayn blinked. "How did it happen?"

"We thought he was a sucker," explained Snake disgustedly. "Smart clothes, gold cigarette-case, gold-mounted stick, gold watch—and a wad. He showed us his wad. Two-fifty, he said it was. We couldn't let that go, so we got him into a game of cards. Poker. He said he didn't know anything about the game, so it looked safe enough—he struck us as being that sort of mug. We were geeing him along nicely right up to ten minutes or so before Victoria, and we'd let him take fifty off us. He was thinking himself the greatest poker player in the world by then, you'd have said. Then we asked him to be a sport and give us a chance of getting our money back on a couple of big jackpots with a five-pound ante. He agreed, and we let him win the first one. We all threw in after the first rise. 'What about making it a tenner ante for the last deal?' I said, tipping the wing to the boys. He wasn't too keen on that, but we jollied him along, and at last he fell for it. It was his deal, but I shuffled the broads for him."

"And your hand slipped?"

Ganning snorted. "Slipped nothin'! My hand doesn't slip. I'd got that deck stacked better than any conjurer could have done it. And I picked up a straight flush, just as I'd fixed it. Mario chucked in right away, and Ted and Bill dropped out after the first round. That left the mug and me, and we went on raising each other till every cent the boys and I could find between us was in the kitty. We even turned in our links and Mario's diamond pin to account for as much of the mug's wad as possible. When we hadn't another bean to stake, he saw me. I showed down my straight flush, and I was just getting set to scoop in the pool when he stopped me. 'I thought you told me this was next to unbeatable,' he says, and then he shows down five kings.''

"Five?" repeated Mr. Hayn frowning.

"We were playing deuces wild, and a joker. He'd got the joker."

"Well, didn't you know what he was holding?"

"It wasn't the hand I fixed for him to deal himself!"

Mr. Hayn controlled his features. "And then you cut up rough, and got the worst of it?"

"I accused him of cheating. He didn't deny it. He had the nerve to say: 'Well, you were supposed to be teaching me the game, and I saw you were cheating all the time, so I thought it was allowed by the rules!' And he started putting away our pile. Of course we cut up rough!"

"And he cut up rougher?" suggested Mr. Hayn.

"He didn't fight fair," said Ganning aggrievedly. "First thing I knew, he'd jabbed the point of his stick into Ted's neck before Ted had a chance to pull his cosh, so Ted was out of it. Bill was all ready for a fair stand-up fight with the knuckle-dusters, but this man kicked him in the stomach, so *he* took the count. Mario and me had to tackle him alone." The Snake seemed disinclined to proceed further with the description of the battle, and Hayn tactfully refrained from pressing him. He allowed the Snake to brood blackly over the memory for a few moments.

"He wasn't an amateur," said Ganning. "But none of us could place him. I'd give the hell of a lot to find out who he was. One of these fly mobsmen you read about, I shouldn't wonder. He'd got all the dope. Look at this," said the Snake, producing the envelope. "He shoved that at Ted when he got out. Said it was his receipt. I tried to get Teal to take it up—he was at the station—but he wouldn't take it seriously."

Hayn slipped the sheet of paper out of the envelope and spread it out on his desk. Probably he had not fully grasped the purport of Ganning's description, for the effect the sight had on him was amazing. If Ganning had been disappointed with Inspector Teal's unemotional reception of the Saint's receipt, he was fully compensated by the reaction of Mr. Edgar Hayn. Hayn's pink face suddenly turned white, and he jerked away from the paper that lay on the blotter in front of him as if it had spat poison at him.

"What's it mean to you, boss?" asked the bewildered Ganning.

"This morning we got a consignment over from Germany," Hayn said, speaking almost in a whisper. "When Braddon opened the case, there was the same picture on top of the packing. We couldn't figure out how it came there.''

"Have you looked the stuff over yet?" demanded the Snake, instantly alert.

Hayn shook his head. He was still staring, as though hypnotized, at the scrap of paper. "We didn't think anything of it. There's never been a hitch yet. Braddon thought the men who packed the case must have been playing some game. We just put the marked jars away in the usual place."

"You haven't had to touch them yet?"

Hayn made a negative gesture. He reached out a shaky hand for the telephone, while Ganning sat silently chewing over the startling possibilities that were revealed by this information. "Hullo. . . . Regent nine double-o four seven . . . please." Hayn fidgeted nervously as he waited for the call to be put through. It came after what seemed an eternity. "Hullo. . . . That you, Braddon? . . . I want you to get out the marked jars that came over in the case with the paper in—you remember? . . . Never mind why!" A minute ticked away, while Hayn kept the receiver glued to his ear and tapped out an impatient tattoo on the desk.

"Yes? . . . What's that? . . . How d'you know? . . . I see. Well, I'll be right round!"

Hayn clicked the receiver back and slewed his swivel-chair round so that he faced Snake Ganning.

"What's he say?" asked the Snake.

"There's just a tin of Keating's powder in each," Hayn replied. "I asked him how he knew what it was, and he said the whole tin was there, label and all, packed in with cotton wool to make it fit. There was ten thousand pounds' worth of snow in that shipping, and this guy has lifted the lot!"

4

"YOU MAY DECANT some beer, son," said Simon Templar, stretched out in an armchair. "And then you may start right in and tell me the story of your life. I can spare you about two minutes."

Jerry Stannard traveled obediently over to a side table where bottles and glasses were already set out, accomplished his task with a practised hand, and traveled back again with the results.

"Your health," said the Saint, and two foaming glasses were half-emptied in an appreciative silence.

Stannard was then encouraged to proceed. He put down his glass with a sigh and settled back at his ease, while the Saint made a long arm for the cigarette box. "I can't make out yet why you should have interested yourself in me," said Stannard.

"That's my affair," said the Saint bluntly. "And if it comes to that, son, I'm not a philanthropic institution. I happen to want an assistant, and I propose to make use of you. Not that you won't get anything out of it. I'm sufficiently interested in you to want to help you, but you're going to pay your way."

Stannard nodded. "It's decent of you to think I'm worth it," he said.

He had not forgotten—it would have been impossible to forget such an incident in two days—the occasion of his first meeting with the Saint. Stannard had been entrusted with a small packet which he had been told to take to an address in Piccadilly; and even if he had not been told what the packet contained, he could not have helped having a very shrewd idea. And therefore, when a heavy hand had fallen suddenly on his shoulder only a few minutes after he had left Mr. Hayn, he had had no hope. . . .

And then the miracle had happened, although he did not realize at the time that it was a miracle. A man had brushed against him as the detective turned to hail a taxi, and the man had turned to apologize. In that crisis, all Stannard's faculties had been keyed up to the vivid super-sensitiveness which comes just before breaking-point; and that abnormal acuteness had combined with the stranger's apology, so that the stranger's face was indelibly engraved on Stannard's memory. . . .

The Saint took a little package from his pocket, and weighed it reflectively in his hand. "Forty-eight hours ago," he murmured, "you assumed, quite rightly, that you were booked for five years' penal servitude. Instead of that, you're a free man. The triumphant sleuths of Vine Street found nothing on you, and had to release you with apologies. Doubtless they're swearing to make up for that bloomer, and make no mistakes about landing you with the goods next time, but that can't hurt you for the moment. And I expect you're still wondering what's going to be my price for having picked your pocket in the nick of time."

"I've been wondering ever since."

"I'm just going to tell you," said the Saint. "But first we'll get rid of this." He left the room with the packet, and through the open door came the sound of running water. In a few moments he was back, dusting his hands. "That disposes of the evidence," he said. "Now I want you to tell me something. How did you get into this dope game?"

Stannard shrugged. "You may as well know. There's no heroic or clever reason. It's just because I'm a waster. I was in the wrong set in Cambridge, and I knew most of the toughs in Town. Then my father died and left me without a bean. I tried to get a job, but I couldn't do anything useful. And all the time, naturally, I was mixing with the same bad bunch. Eventually they roped me in. I suppose I ought to have fought against it, but I just hadn't the guts. It was easy money, and I took it. That's all."

There was a short silence, during which the Saint blew monotonously regular smoke-rings towards the ceiling. "Now I'll tell you something," he said. "I've made all the enquiries I need to make about you. I know your family history for two generations back, your early life, your school record—everything. I know enough to judge that you don't belong where you are now. For one thing, I know you're engaged to a rather nice girl, and she's worried about you. She doesn't know anything, but she suspects. And you're worried. You're not as quiet and comfortable in this crime racket as you'd like to make out. You weren't cut out for a bad man. Isn't that true?"

"True enough," Stannard said flatly. "I'd give anything to be out of it."

"And you're straight about this girl—Gwen Chandler?"

"Straight as a die. Honest, Templar! But what can I do? If I drop Hayn's crowd, I shan't have a cent. Besides, I don't know that they'd let me drop out. I owe money. When I was at Cambridge, I lost a small fortune—for me—in Hayn's gambling rooms, and he's got IOU's of mine for close on a thousand. I've been extravagant—I've run up bills everywhere. You can't imagine how badly in the cart I am!"

"On the contrary, son," said the Saint calmly, "I've a very good guess about that. That's why you're here now. I wanted an agent inside Hayn's gang, and I ran through the whole deck before I chose you." He rose from his chair and took a turn up and down the room. Stannard waited, and presently the Saint stopped abruptly. "You're all right," he said.

Stannard frowned. "Meaning?"

"Meaning I'm going to trust you. I'm going to take you in with me for this campaign. I'll get you enough out of it to square off your debts, and at the end of it I'll find you a job. You'll keep in with Hayn, but you'll be working for me. And you'll give me your word of honour that you'll go straight for the rest of your life. That's my offer. What about it?''

The Saint leant against the mantelpiece languidly enough, but there had been nothing languid about his crisp incisive sentences. Thinking it over afterwards, it seemed to Stannard that the whole thing had been done in a few minutes, and he was left to marvel at the extraordinary force of personality which in such a short time could override the prejudice of years and rekindle a spark of decency that had been as good as dead. But at the instant, Stannard could not analyze his feelings.

"I'm giving you a chance to get out and make good," the Saint went on. "I'm not doing it in the dark. I believe you when you say you'd be glad of a chance to make a fresh start. I believe there's the makings of a decent man in you. Anyway, I'll take a risk on it. I won't even threaten you, though I could, by telling you what I shall do to you if you double-cross me. I just ask you a fair question, and I want your answer now.''

Stannard got to this feet. "There's only one answer," he said, and held out his hand.

The Saint took it in a firm grip. "Now I'll tell you exactly where you stand," he said.

He did so, speaking in curt sentences as before. His earlier grimness had relaxed somewhat, for when the Saint did anything he never did it by halves, and now he spoke to Stannard as a friend and an ally. He had his reward in the eager attention with which the youngster followed his discourse. He told him everything that there was any need for him to know.

"You've got to think of everything, and then a heap, if you're going to come out of this with a whole skin," Simon concluded, with some of his former sternness. "The game I'm on isn't the kind they play in nurseries. I'm on it because I just can't live happily ever after. I've had enough adventures to fill a dozen books, but instead of satisfying me they've only left me with a bigger appetite. If I had to live the ordinary kind of safe, civilized life, I'd die of boredom. Risks are food and drink to me. You may be different. If you are, I'm sorry about it, but I can't help it. I need some help in this, and you're going to give it to me; but it wouldn't be fair to let you whale in without showing you what you are up against. Your bunch of bad hats aren't childish enemies. Before you're through, London's likely to be just about as healthy for you as the Cannibal Islands are for a nice plump missionary. Get me?''

Stannard intimated that he had got him.

"Then I'll give you your orders for the immediate future," said the Saint. He did so, in detail, and had everything repeated over to him twice before he was convinced that there would be no mistake and that nothing would be forgotten. "From now on, I want you to keep away from me till I give you the all-clear," he ended up. "If the Snake's anywhere round, I shan't last long in Danny's, and it's essential to keep you out of suspicion for as long as possible. So this'll be our last open meeting for some time, but you can communicate by telephone—as long as you make sure nobody can hear you."

"Right you are, Saint," said Stannard.

Simon Templar flicked a cigarette into his mouth and reached for the matches. The other had a queer transient feeling of unreality. It seemed fantastic that he should be associated with such a project as that into which the Saint had initiated him. It seemed equally fantastic that the Saint should have conceived it and brought it into being. That cool, casual young man, with his faultless clothes, his clipped and slangy speech, and his quick, clear smile—he ought to have been lounging his amiable, easygoing way through a round of tennis and cricket and cocktail-parties and dances, instead of . . .

And yet it remained credible—it was even, with every passing second, becoming almost an article of the reawakened Stannard's new faith. The Saint's spell was unique. There was a certain quiet assurance about his bearing, a certain steely quality that came sometimes into his blue eyes, a certain indefinable air of strength and recklessness and quixotic bravado, that made the whole fantastic notion acceptable. And Stannard had not even the advantage of knowing anything about the last eight years of the Saint's hell-for-leather career—eight years of gay buccaneering which, even allowing for exaggeration, made him out to be a man of no ordinary or drawing-room toughness. . . .

The Saint lighted his cigarette, and held out his hand to terminate the interview; and the corners of his mouth were twitching to his irresistible smile. "So long, son," he said. "And good hunting!"

"Same to you," said Stannard warmly.

The Saint clapped him on the shoulder. "I know you won't let me down," he said. "There's lots of good in you, and I guess I've found some of it. You'll put out all right. I'm going to see that you do. Watch me!"

But before he left, Stannard got a query off his chest. "Didn't you say there were five of you?"

His hands in his pockets, teetering gently on his heels, the Saint favoured Stannard with his most Saintly smile. "I did," he drawled. "Four little Saints and Papa. I am the Holy Smoke. As for the other four, they are like the Great White Woolly Wugga-Wugga on the plains of Astrakhan."

Stannard gaped at him. "What does that mean?" he demanded.

"I ask you, sweet child," answered the Saint, with that exasperatingly seraphic smile still on his lips, "has anyone ever seen a Great White Woolly Wugga-Wugga on the plains of Astrakhan? Sleep on it, my cherub—it will keep your mind from impure thoughts."

5

TO ALL OFFICIAL intents and purposes, the proprietor and leading light of Mr. Edgar Hayn's night club in Soho was the man after whom it was named—Danny Trask. Danny was short and dumpy, a lazy little tub of a man, with a round red face; a sparse head of fair hair, and a thin sandy moustache. His pale eyes were deeply embedded in the creases of their fleshy lids; and when he smiled—which was often, and usually for no apparent reason—they vanished altogether in a corrugating mesh of wrinkles.

His intelligence was not very great. Nevertheless, he had discovered quite early in life that there was a comfortable living to be made in the profession of "dummy"—a job which calls for not startling intellectual gifts—and Danny had accordingly made that his vocation ever since. As a figure-head, he was all that could have been desired, for he was unobtrusive and easily satisfied. He had a type of mind common to his class of lawbreaker. As long as his salary—which was not small—was paid regularly, he never complained, showed no ambition to join his employer on a more equal basis of division of profits, and, if anything went wrong, kept his mouth shut and deputized for his principal in one of his Majesty's prisons without a murmur. Danny's fees for a term of imprisonment were a flat rate of ten pounds a week, with an extra charge of two pounds a week for "hard." The astuteness of the C.I.D. and the carelessness of one or two of his previous employers had made this quite a profitable proposition for Danny.

He had visions of retiring one day, and ending his life in comparative luxury, when his savings had reached a sufficiently large figure; but this hope had received several set-backs of late. He had been in Mr. Hayn's service for four years, and Mr. Hayn's uncanny skill at avoiding the attentions of the police were becoming a thorn in the side of Danny Trask. When Danny was not in "stir," the most he could command was a paltry seven pounds a week, and living expenses had to be paid out of this instead of out of the pocket of the Government. Danny felt that he had a personal grievance against Mr. Hayn on this account.

The club theoretically opened at 6 p.m., but the food was not good, and most of its members preferred to dine elsewhere. The first arrivals usually began to drift in about 10 p.m., but things never began to get exciting before 11 o'clock. Danny spent the hours between 6 o'clock and the commencement of the fun sitting in his shirt-sleeves in his little cubicle by the entrance, sucking a foul old briar and tentatively selecting the next day's losers from an evening paper. He was incapable of feeling bored— his mind had never reached the stage of development where it could appreciate the idea of activity and inactivity. It had never been active, so it didn't see any difference.

He was engaged in this pleasant pursuit towards 8 o'clock on a certain evening when Jerry Stannard arrived. "Has Mr. Hayn come in yet, Danny?"

Danny made a pencil note of the number of pounds which he had laboriously calculated that Wilco would have in hand over Man of Kent in the Lingfield Plate, folded his paper, and looked up. "He don't usually come in till late, Mr. Stannard," he said. "No, he ain't here now."

Danny's utterances always contrived to put the cart before the horse. If he had wanted to give you a vivid description of a deathbed scene, he would have inevitably started with the funeral.

"Oh, it's all right—he's expecting me," said Stannard. "When he arrives you can tell him I'm at the bar." He was plainly agitated. While he was talking, he never stopped fiddling with his signet ring, and Danny, whose shrewd glances missed very little, noticed that his tie was limp and crooked, as if it had been subjected to the clumsy wrestling of shaky fingers.

"Right you are, sir."

It was none of Danny's business, anyway.

"Oh—and before I forget . . ."

"Sir?"

"A Mr. Templar will be here later. He's O.K. Send down for me when he arrives, and I'll sign him in."

"Very good, sir." Danny returned to his study of equine form, and Stannard passed on. He went through the lounge which occupied the ground floor, and turned down the stairs at the end. Facing these stairs, behind a convenient curtain, was a secret door in the panelling, electrically operated, which was controlled by a button on the desk in Hayn's private office. This door, when opened, disclosed a flight of stairs running upwards. These stairs communicated with the upstairs rooms which were one of the most profitable features of the club, for in those rooms *chemin-de-fer,* poker, and *trente-et-quarante* were played every night with the sky for a limit.

Hayn's office was at the foot of the downward flight. He had personally supervised the installation of an ingenious system of mirrors by means of which, with the aid of a large sound-proof window let into the wall at one end of the office, without leaving his seat, he was able to inspect everyone who passed through the lounge above. Moreover, when the secret door swung open in response to the pressure of his finger on the control button, a further system of mirrors panelled up the flight of stairs gave him a view right up the stairway itself and round the landing into the gaming rooms. Mr. Hayn was a man with a cunning turn of mind, and he was preëminently cautious.

Outside the office, in the basement, was the dance floor, surrounded with tables, but only two couples were dining there. At the far end was the dais on which the orchestra played, and at the other end, under the stairs, was the tiny bar. Stannard turned in there, and roused the white-coated barman from his perusal of *La Vie Parisienne.* "I don't know what would meet the case," he said, "but I want something steep in corpse-revivers."

The man looked him over for a moment with an expert eye, then busied himself with the filling of a prescription. The result certainly had a kick in it. Stannard was downing it when Hayn came in.

The big man was looking pale and tired, and there were shadows under his eyes. He nodded curtly to Jerry. "I'll be with you in a minute," he said. "Just going to get a wash."

It was not like Mr. Hayn, who ordinarily specialized in the boisterous hail-fellow-well-met method of address, and Stannard watched him go thoughtfully.

Braddon, who had remained outside, followed Hayn into the office. "Who's the boy friend?" he asked, taking a chair.

"Stannard?" Hayn was skimming through the letters that waited on his desk. "An ordinary young fool. He lost eight hundred upstairs in his first couple of months. Heaven knows how much he owes outside—he'd lost a packet before I started lending him money."

Brandon searched through his pocket for a cigar, and found one. He bit off the end, and spat. "Got expectations? Rich papa who'll come across?"

"No. But he's got the clothes, he'd pass anywhere. I was using him."

"Was?"

Hayn was frowningly examining the postmark on one of his letters. "I suppose I shall still," he said. "Don't bother me—this artistic hijacker's got me all ends up. But he's got a fiancée—I've only recently seen her. I like her."

"Any good?"

"I shall arrange something about her."

Hayn had slit open the letter with his thumbnail, but he only took one glance at what it contained. He tossed it over to Braddon, and it was the manager of Laserre who drew out the now familiar sketch.

"One of those came to my house by the first post this morning," Hayn said. "It's as old as the hills, that game. So he thinks he's going to rattle me!"

"Isn't he?" asked Braddon, in his heavily cynical way.

"He damned well isn't!" Hayn came back savagely. "I've got the Snake and the men who were with him prowling round the West End just keeping their eyes peeled for the man who beat them up in the Brighton train. If he's in London, he can't stay hid for ever. And when Ganning's found him, we'll soon put paid to his joke!"

Then he pulled himself together. "I'm giving Stannard dinner," he said. "What are you doing now?"

"I'll loaf out and get some food, and be back later," said Braddon. "I thought I'd take a look in upstairs."

Hayn nodded. He ushered Braddon out of the office, and locked the door behind him, for even Braddon was not allowed to remain in that sanctum alone. Braddon departed, and Hayn rejoined Stannard at the bar. "Sorry to have kept you waiting, old man," he apologized, with an attempt to resume his pose of bluff geniality.

"I've been amusing myself," said Stannard, and indicated a row of empty glasses. "Have a spot?"

Hayn accepted, and Stannard looked at his watch.

"By the way," he said, "there's a man due here in about an hour. I met him the other day, and he seemed all right. He said he was a South African, and he's sailing back the day after to-morrow. He was complaining that he couldn't get any real fun in England, so I dropped a hint about a private gambling club I might be able to get him into and he jumped at it. I thought he might be some use—leaving England so soon, he could hardly make a kick—so I told him to join us over coffee. Is that all right?"

"Quite all right, old man." A thought struck Mr. Hayn. "You're quite sure he wasn't one of these clever dicks?"

"Not on your life!" scoffed Stannard. "I think I know a busy when I see one by now. I've seen enough of 'em dancing here. And this man seems to have money to burn."

Hayn nodded. "I meant to come to some arrangement with you over dinner," he said. "This bird can go down as your first job, on commission. If you're ready, we'll start."

Stannard assented, and they walked over to the table which had been prepared. Hayn was preoccupied. If his mind had not been simmering with other problems, he might have noticed Stannard's ill-concealed nervousness, and wondered what might have been the cause of it. But he observed nothing unusual about the younger man's manner.

While they were waiting for the grapefruit, he asked a question quite perfunctorily. "What's this South African's name?"

"Templar—Simon Templar," answered Jerry.

The name meant nothing at all to Mr. Hayn.

6

OVER THE DINNER, Hayn made his offer—a twenty per cent commission on business introduced. Stannard hardly hesitated before accepting.

"You don't want to be squeamish about it," Hayn argued. "I know it's against the law, but that's splitting hairs. Horse-racing is just as much a gamble. There'll always be fools who want to get rich without working, and there's no reason why we shouldn't take their money. You won't have to do anything that would make you liable to be sent to prison, though some of my staff would be jailed if the police caught them. You're quite safe. And the games are perfectly straight. We only win because the law of probabilities favours the bank.''

This was not strictly true, for there were other factors to influence the runs of bad luck which attended the players upstairs; but this sordid fact Mr. Hayn did not feel called upon to emphasize.

''Yes—I'll join you,'' Stannard said. ''I've known it was coming. I didn't think you went on giving and lending me money for looking decorative and doing an odd job or two for you now and again.''

''My dear fellow—''

''Dear-fellowing doesn't alter it. I know you want more of me than my services in decoying boobs upstairs. Are you going to tell me you didn't know I was caught the other day?''

Hayn stroked his chin. ''I was going to compliment you. How you got rid of that parcel of snow—''

''The point that matters is that I did get rid of it,'' cut in Stannard briefly. ''And if I hadn't been able to, I should have been on remand in Brixton Prison now. I'm not complaining. I suppose I had to earn my keep. But it wasn't square of you to keep me in the dark.''

''You knew—''

''I guessed. It's all right—I've stopped kicking. But I want you to let me right in from now on, if you're letting me in at all. I'm joining you, all in, and you needn't bother to humbug me any longer. How's that?''

''That's all right,'' said Mr. Hayn, ''If you must put things so crudely. But you don't even have to be squeamish about the dope side of it. If people choose to make fools of themselves like that, it's their own look-out. Our share is simply to refuse to quibble about whether it's legal or not. After all, alcohol is sold legally in this country, and nobody blames the publican if his customers get drunk every night and eventually die of D.T.'s.''

Stannard shrugged. ''I can't afford to argue, anyhow,'' he said. ''How much do I draw?''

''Twenty per cent—as I told you.''

''What's that likely to make?''

''A lot,'' said Hayn. ''We play higher here than anywhere else in London, and there isn't a great deal of competition in the snow market. You might easily draw upwards of seventy pounds a week.''

''Then will you do something for me, Mr. Hayn? I owe a lot of money outside. It'll take three thousand flat for the first year, to pay off everybody and fit myself up with a packet in hand.''

"Three thousand pounds is a lot of money," said Hayn judicially. "You owe me nearly a thousand as it is.''

"If you don't think I'm going to be worth it—"

Mr. Hayn meditated, but not for long. The making of quick decisions was the whole reason for his success, and he didn't mind how much a thing cost if he knew it was worth it. He had no fear that Stannard would attempt to double-cross him. Among the other purposes which it served, Danny's formed a working headquarters for the Snake's Boys; Stannard could not help knowing the reputation of the gang, and he must also know that they had worked Hayn's vengeance on traitors before. No— there was no chance that Stannard would dare to try a double cross. . . . "I'll give you a check to-night," said Hayn.

Stannard was effusively grateful. "You won't lose by it," he promised. "Templar's a speculation, granted, but I've met him only once. But there are other people with mints of money, people I've known for years, that I can vouch for absolutely. . . .'' He went on talking, but Hayn only listened with half an ear, for he was anxious to turn the conversation to another topic, and he did so at the first opportunity.

Under pretence of taking a fatherly interest in his new agent's affairs, he plied him with questions about his private life and interests. Most of the information which he elicited was stale news to him, for he had long since taken the precaution of finding out everything of importance that there was to know about his man; but in these new enquiries Mr. Hayn contrived to make Stannard's fiancée the center of interrogation. It was very cleverly and surreptitiously done, but the fact remains that at the end of half an hour, by this process of indirect questioning Hayn had discovered all that he wanted to know about the life and habits of Gwen Chandler. "Do you think you could get her along here to supper on Thursday?" he suggested. "The only time I've met her, if you remember, I think you rather prejudiced her against me. It's up to you to put that right.''

"I'll see what I can do," said Stannard.

After that, his point won, Hayn had no further interest in directing the conversation, and they were chatting desultorily when Simon Templar arrived.

The Saint, after weighing the relative merits of full evening dress or an ordinary lounge suit for the auspicious occasion, had decided on a compromise, and was sporting a dinner jacket; but he wore it, as might have been expected, as if he had been an ambassador paying a state visit in full regalia.

"Hullo, Jerry, dear angel!" he hailed Stannard cheerfully. Then he noticed Mr. Hayn, and turned with outstretched hand. "And you must be Uncle Ambrose," he greeted that gentleman cordially. "Pleased to meet you. . . . That's right, isn't it, Jerry? This is the uncle who died and left all his money to the Cats' Home? . . . Sorry to see you looking so well, Uncle Ambrose, old mongoose!"

Mr. Hayn seemed somewhat taken aback. This man did not wear his clothes in the manner traditionally associated with raw Colonials with money to burn; and if his speech was typical of that of strong silent men from the great open spaces of that vintage, Mr. Hayn decided that the culture of Piccadilly must have spread farther abroad into the British Empire than Cecil Rhodes had ever hoped in his wildest dreams. Mr. Hayn had never heard of Rhodes—to him, Rhodes was an island where they bred red hens—but if he had heard of Rhodes he might reasonably have expressed his surprise like that.

He looked round to Jerry Stannard with raised eyebrows, and Stannard tapped his forehead and lifted his glass significantly.

"So we're going to see a real live gambling hell!" said the Saint, drawing up a chair. "Isn't this fun? Let's all have a lot of drinks on the strength of it!"

He called for liqueurs, and paid for them from a huge wad of bank-notes which he tugged from his pocket. Mr. Hayn's eyes lit up at the sight, and he decided that there were excuses for Templar's eccentricity. He leant forward and set himself out to be charming. The Saint, however, had other views on the subject of the way in which the conversation should go, and at the first convenient pause, he came out with a remark that showed he had been paying little attention to what had gone before.

"I've bought a book about card tricks," he said. "I thought it might help me to spot sharpers. But the best part of it was the chapter on fortune-telling by cards. Take a card, and I'll tell you all your sins."

He produced a new pack from his pocket and pushed it across the table towards Hayn.

"You first, Uncle," he invited. "And see that your thoughts are pure when you draw, otherwise you'll give the cards a wrong impression. Hum a verse of your favourite hymn, for instance." Mr. Hayn knew nothing about hymns, but he complied tolerantly. If this freak had all that money, and perhaps some more, by all means let him be humoured.

"Now, isn't that sweet!" exclaimed the Saint, taking up the card Hayn had chosen. "Jerry, my pet, your Uncle Ambrose has drawn the ace of hearts. That stands for princely generosity. We'll have another brandy with you, Uncle, just to show how we appreciate it. Waiter! . . . Three more brandies, please! Face Ache—I mean Uncle Ambrose—is paying! . . . Uncle, you must try your luck again."

Simon Templar pored over Hayn's second card until the drinks arrived. It was noticeable that his shoulders shook silently at one time. Mr. Hayn attributed this to repressed hiccups, and was gravely in error. Presently the Saint looked up. "Has an aunt on your mother's side," he asked solemnly, "ever suffered from a bilious attack following a meal of sausages made by a German pork butcher with a hammer-toe and three epileptic children?"

Mr. Hayn shook his head, staring. "I haven't any aunts," he said.

"I'm so sorry," said the Saint, as if he were deeply distressed to hear of Mr. Hayn's plight of pathetic auntlessness. "But it means the beastly book's all wrong. Never mind. Don't let's bother about it."

He pushed the pack away. Undoubtedly he was quite mad.

"Aren't you going to tell us any more?" asked Stannard, with a wink to Hayn.

"Uncle Ambrose would blush if I went on," said Templar. "Look at the brick I've dropped already. But if you insist, I'll try one more card."

Hayn obliged again, smiling politely. He was starting to get acclimatized. Clearly the secret of being on good terms with Mr. Templar was to let him have his own irrepressible way.

"I only hope it isn't the five of diamonds," said the Saint earnestly. "Whenever I do this fortune-telling stuff, I'm terrified of somebody drawing the five of diamonds. You see, I'm bound to tell the truth, and the truth in that case is frightfully hard to tell to a comparative stranger. Because, according to my book, a man who draws the five of diamonds is liable at any moment to send an anonymous donation of ten thousand pounds to the London Hospital. Also, cads are unlucky for him, he is an abominable blackguard, and he has a repulsively ugly face."

Hayn kept his smile nailed in position, and faced his card. "The five of diamonds, Mr. Templar," he remarked gently.

"No—is it really?" said Simon, in most Saintly astonishment. "Well, well, *well* . . . There you are, Jerry—I warned you your uncle would be embarrassed if I went on. Now I've dropped another brick. Let's talk of something else, quickly, before he notices. Uncle Ambrose, tell me, have you ever seen a hot dog fighting a cat-o'-nine tails? . . . No? . . . Well, shuffle the pack and I'll show you a conjuring trick."

Mr. Hayn shuffled and cut, and the Saint rapidly dealt off five cards, which he passed face downwards across the table. It was about the first chance Mr. Hayn had had to sidle a word in, and he felt compelled to protest about one thing.

"You seem to be suffering from a delusion, Mr. Templar," he said. "I'm not Jerry's uncle—I'm just a friend of his. My name's Hayn—Edgar Hayn."

"Why?" asked the Saint innocently.

"It happens to be the name I was christened with, Mr. Templar," Hayn replied with some asperity.

"Is—that—so!" drawled the Saint mildly. "Sorry again!"

Hayn frowned. There was something peculiarly infuriating about the Saint in that particular vein—something that, while it rasped the already raw fringe of his temper, was also beginning to send a queer, indefinable uneasiness creeping up his back. "And I'm sorry if it annoys you," he snapped.

Simon Templar regarded him steadily. "It annoys me," he said, "because, as I told you, it's my business never to make mistakes, and I just hate being wrong. The records of Somerset House told me that your name was once something quite different—that you weren't christened Edgar Hayn at all. And I believed it."

Hayn said nothing. He sat quite still, with that tingling thrill of apprehension crawling round the base of his scalp. And the Saint's clear blue gaze never left Hayn's face.

"If I was wrong about that," the Saint went on softly, "I may quite easily have been wrong about other things. And that would annoy me more than ever, because I don't like wasting my time. I've spent several days figuring out a way of meeting you for just this little chat—I thought it was about time our relationship became a bit more personal—and it'd break my heart to think it had all been for nothing. Don't tell me that, Edgar, beloved—don't tell me it wasn't any use my finding out that dear little Jerry was a friend of yours—don't tell me that I might have saved myself the trouble I took scraping an acquaintance with the said Jerry just to bring about this informal meeting. Don't tell me that, dear heart!"

Hayn moistened his lips. He was fighting down an insane, unreasoning feeling of panic; and it was the Saint's quiet, level voice and mocking eyes, as much as anything, that held Edgar Hayn rooted in his chair.

"Don't tell me, in fact, that you won't appreciate the little conjuring trick I came here especially to show you," said the Saint, more mildly than ever.

He reached out suddenly and took the cards he had dealt from Hayn's nerveless fingers. Hayn had guessed what they would prove to be, long before Simon, with a flourish, had spread the cards out face upwards on the table.

"Don't tell me you aren't pleased to see our visiting cards, personally presented!" said Simon, in his very Saintliest voice. His white teeth flashed in a smile, and there was a light of adventurous recklessness dancing in his eyes as he looked at Edgar Hayn across five neat specimens of the sign of the Saint.

7

"AND IF IT'S pure prune juice and boloney," went on the Saint, in that curiously velvety tone which still contrived somehow to prickle all over with little warning spikes—"if all that is sheer banana oil and soft roe, I shan't even raise a smile with the story I was going to tell you. It's my very latest one, and it's about a loose-living land-shark called Hayn, who was born in a barn in the rain. What he'd struggled to hide was found out when he died—there was mildew all over his brain. Now, that one's been getting a big hand everywhere I've told it since I made it up, and it'll be one of the bitterest disappointments of my life if it doesn't fetch you, sweetheart!"

Hayn's chair went over with a crash as he kicked to his feet. Strangely enough, now that the murder was out and the first shock absorbed, the weight on his mind seemed lightened, and he felt better able to cope with the menace. "So you're the young cub we've been looking for!" he rasped.

Simon raised his hand.

"I'm called the Saint," he murmured. "But don't let us get melodramatic about it, son. The last man who got melodramatic with me was hanged at Exeter six months back. It don't seem to be healthy!"

Hayn looked round. The diners had left, and as yet no one had arrived to take their places; but the clatter of his chair upsetting had roused three startled waiters, who were staring uncertainly in his direction. But a review of these odds did not seem to disturb the Saint, who was lounging

languidly back in his seat with his hands in his pockets and a benign
expression on his face. ''I suppose you know that the police are after
you,'' grated Hayn.

''I didn't,'' said the Saint. ''That's interesting. Why?''

''You met some men in the Brighton train and played poker with them.
You swindled them right and left, and when they accused you you attacked
them and pinched the money. I think that's good enough to put you away
for some time.''

''And who's going to identify me?''

''The four men.''

''You surprise me,'' drawled Simon. ''I seem to remember that on that
very day, just outside Brighton racecourse, those same four bums were
concerned in beating up a poor little coot of a lame bookie named Tommy
Mitre and pinching *his* money. There didn't happen to be any policeman
about—they arranged it quite cleverly—and the crowd that saw it would
likely be all too scared of the Snake to give evidence. But yours truly
and a couple of souls also saw the fun. We were a long way off, and the
Snake and his Boys were over the horizon by the time we got to the
scene, but we could identify them all, and a few more who were not
there—and we shouldn't be afraid to step into the witness-box and say
our piece. No, sonnikins—I don't think the police will be brought into
that. That must go down to history as a little private wrangle between
Snake and me. Send one of your beauty chorus out for a Robert and give
me in charge, if you like, but don't blame me if Ganning and the Boys
come back at you for it. Knowing their reputations, I should say they'd
get the 'cat' as well as their six months' hard, and that won't make them
love you a lot. Have it your own way, though.''

The argument was watertight, and Hayn realized it. He was beginning
to cool down. He hadn't a kick—for the moment, the Saint had got him
right down in the mud with a foot on his face. But he didn't see what
good that was doing the Saint. It was a big bluff, Hayn was starting to
think, and he had sense enough to realize that it wasn't helping him one
bit to get all hot under the collar about it. In fact—such was the exhil-
arating effect of having at last found an enemy that he could see and hit
back at—Hayn was rapidly reckoning that the Saint might lose a lot by
that display of bravado.

Clearly the Saint didn't want the police horning in at all. It didn't even
matter that the Saint knew things about Hayn and his activities that would
have interested the police. The Saint was on some lay of his own, and
the police weren't being invited to interfere. Very well. So be it. The

cue for Hayn was to bide his time and refuse to be rattled. But he wished the Saint hadn't got that mocking, self-possessed air of having a lot more high cards up his sleeve, just waiting to be produced. It spoilt Hayn's happiness altogether. The Saint was behaving like a fool; and yet, in some disconcertingly subtle way, he managed to do it with the condescending air of putting off a naturally tremendous gravity in order to amuse the children.

Hayn righted his chair and sat down again slowly; the alert waiters relaxed—they were a tough crowd, and selected more for their qualities of toughness than for their clean finger-nails and skill at juggling with plates and dishes. But as Hayn sat down his right hand went behind his chair—his back was towards the group of waiters—and with his fingers he made certain signs. One of the waiters faded away inconspicuously.

"So what do you propose to do?" Hayn said.

"Leave you," answered the Saint benevolently. "I know your ugly dial isn't your fault, but I've seen about as much of it as I can stand for one evening. I've done what I came to do, and now I think you can safely be left to wonder what I'm going to do next. See you later, I expect, my Beautiful Ones. . . ." The Saint rose and walked unhurriedly to the stairs. By that time, there were five men ranged in a row at the foot of the stairs, and they showed no signs of making way for anyone.

"We should hate to lose you so soon, Mr. Templar," said Hayn.

The Saint's lounging steps slowed up, and stopped. His hands slid into his pockets, and he stood for a moment surveying the quintet of waiters with a beatific smile. Then he turned. "What are these?" he enquired pleasantly. "The guard of honour, or the cabaret beauty chorus?"

"I think you might sit down again, Mr. Templar," suggested Hayn.

"And I think not," said the Saint.

He walked swiftly back to the table—so swiftly that Hayn instinctively half-rose from his seat, and the five men started forward. But the Saint did not attack at that moment. He stopped in front of Hayn, his hands in his pockets; and although that maddening little smile still lurked on his lips, there was something rather stern about his poise.

"I said I was going to leave you, and I am," he murmured, with a gentleness that was in amazing contrast to the intent tautness of his bearing. "That's what I came here for, ducky—to leave you. This is just meant for a demonstration of all-around superiority; you think you can stop me—but you watch! I'm going to prove that nothing on earth can stop me when I get going. Understand, lovelines?"

"We shall see," said Hayn.

The Saint's smile became, if possible, even more Saintly. Somehow that smile, and the air of hair-trigger alertness which accompanied it, was bothering Edgar Hayn a heap. He knew it was all bravado—he knew the Saint had bitten off more than he could chew for once—he knew that the odds were all against a repetition of the discomfiture of the Ganning combine. And yet he couldn't feel happy about it. There was a kind of quivering strength about the Saint's lazy bearing—something that re-minded Edgar Hayn of wire and whipcord and indiarubber and com-pressed steel springs and high explosives.

"In the space of a few minutes," said the Saint, "You're going to see a sample of rough-housing that'll make your bunch of third-rate hoodlums look like two cents' worth of oxtail. But before I proceed to beat them up, I want to tell you this—which you can pass on to your friends. Ready?"

Hayn spread out his hands.

"Then I'll shoot," said the Saint. "It's just this. We Saints are normally souls of peace and goodwill towards men. But we don't like crooks, blood-suckers, traders in vice and damnation, and other verminous ex-crescences of that type—such as yourself. We're going to beat you up and do you down, skin you and smash you, and scare you off the face of Europe. We are not bothered about the letter of the law, we act exactly as we please, we inflict what punishment we think suitable, and no one is going to escape us. Ganning got hurt, but still you don't believe me. You're the next on the list, and by the time I've finished with you, you'll be an example to convince others. And it will go on. That's all I've got to say now, and when I've left you you can go forth and spread the news. I'm leaving now!"

He stooped suddenly, and grasped the leg of Hayn's chair and tipped it backwards with one jerking heave. As Hayn tried to scramble to his feet, the Saint put an ungentle foot in his face and upset the table on top of him. The five tough waiters were pelting across the floor in a pack. Simon reached out for the nearest chair, and sent it skating over the room at the height of six inches from the ground, with a vimful swing of his arms that gave it the impetus of a charging buffalo. It smashed across the leader's knees and shins with bone-shattering force, and the man went down with a yell. That left four.

The Saint had another chair in his hands by the time the next man was upon him. The waiter flung up his arms to guard his head, and tried to rush into a grapple; but the Saint stepped back and reversed the swing of his chair abruptly. It swerved under the man's guard and crashed murderously into his ribs. Three. . . .

The next man ran slap into a sledge-hammer left that hurled him a dozen feet away. The other two hesitated, but the Saint was giving no breathing space. He leapt in at the nearest man with a pile-driving, left-right-left tattoo to the solar plexus.

As the tough crumpled up with a choking groan under that battering-ram assault, some sixth sense flashed the Saint a warning. He leapt to one side, and the chair Hayn had swung to his head swished harmlessly past him, the vigour of the blow toppling Hayn off his balance. The Saint assisted his downfall with an out-flung foot which sent the man hurtling headlong.

The last man was still coming on, but warily. He ducked the Saint's lead, and replied with a right swing to the side of the head which gingered the Saint up a peach. Simon Templar decided that his reputation was involved, and executed a beautiful feint with his left which gave him an opening to lash in a volcanic right squarely upon the gangster's nose. As the man dropped, the Saint whipped round and caught Stannard.

"Fight, you fool!" the Saint hissed in his ear. "This is for local colour!" Stannard clinched, and then the Saint broke away and firmly but regretfully clipped him on the ear.

It was not one of the Saint's heftiest punches, but it was hard enough to knock the youngster down convincingly; and then the Saint looked round hopefully for something else to wallop and found nothing. Hayn was rising again, shakily, and so were those of the five roughs who were in a fit state to do so, but there was no notable enthusiasm to renew the battle. "Any time any of you bad cheeses want any more lessons in rough-housing," drawled the Saint, a little breathlessly, "you've only got to drop me a postcard and I'll be right along."

This time, there was no attempt to bar his way.

He collected hat, gloves, and stick from the cloakroom, and went through the upstairs lounge. As he reached the door, he met Braddon returning. "Hullo, Sweetness," said the Saint genially. "Pass right down the car and hear the new joke the Boys of the Burg downstairs are laughing at."

Braddon was still trying to guess the cause for and meaning of this extraordinary salutation by a perfect stranger, when the Saint, without any haste or heat, but so swiftly and deftly that the thing was done before Braddon realized what was happening, had reached out and seized the brim of Braddon's hat and forced it well down over his eyes. Then, with a playful tweak of Braddon's nose, and a cheery wave of his hand to the dumbfounded Danny, he departed.

Danny was not a quick mover, and the street outside was Saintless by the time Braddon had struggled out of his hat and reached the door.

When his vocabulary was exhausted, Braddon went downstairs in search of Hayn, and stopped open-mouthed at the wreckage he saw.

Mr. Hayn, turning from watching the Saint's triumphant vanishment, had swung sharply on Stannard. The Saint's unscathed exit had left Hayn in the foulest of tempers. All around him, it seemed, an army of tough waiters in various stages of disrepair were gathering themselves to their feet with a muttered obbligato of lurid oaths. Well, if there wasn't an army of them, there were five—five bone-hard heavyweights—and that ought to have been enough to settle any ordinary man, even on the most liberal computation of odds. But the Saint had simply waded right through them, hazed and man-handled and roasted them, and walked out without a scratch. Hayn would have taken a bet that the Saint's tie wasn't even a millimetre out of a centre at the end of it. The Saint had made fools of them without turning a hair.

Hayn vented his exasperation on Jerry, and even the fact that he had seen the boy help to tackle the Saint and get the worst of it in their company did not mitigate his wrath. "You damned fool!" he blazed. "Couldn't you see he was up to something? Are you taken in by everyone who tells you the tale?"

"I told you I couldn't guarantee him," Stannard protested. "But when I met him he wasn't a bit like he was to-night. Honestly, Mr. Hayn— how could I have known? I don't even know what he was after yet. Those cards . . ."

"South African grandmothers," snarled Hayn.

Braddon intervened. "Who was this gentleman, anyway," he demanded. "Gentleman" was not the word he used.

"Use your eyes, you lunatic!" Hayn flared, pointing to the table, and Braddon's jaw dropped as he saw the cards.

"You've had that guy in here?"

"What the hell d'you think? You probably passed him coming in. And from what the Snake said, and what I've seen myself, he's probably right at the top—he might even be the Saint himself."

"So that was the gentleman!" said Braddon, only once again he described Simon Templar with a more decorative word.

Hayn snorted. "And that fool Stannard brought him here," he said.

"I've told you, I didn't know much about him, Mr. Hayn,"Stannard expostulated. "I warned you I couldn't answer for him."

"The kid's right," said Braddon. "If he put it over on the Snake, he might put it over on anybody."

There was logic in the argument, but it was some time before Hayn could be made to see it. But presently he quieted down. "We'll talk about this, Braddon," he said. "I've got an idea for stopping his funny stuff. He didn't get clean away—I put Keld on to follow him. By to-night we'll know where he lives, and then I don't think he'll last long."

He turned to Jerry. The boy was fidgeting nervously, and Hayn became diplomatic. It wasn't any use rubbing a valuable man up the wrong way.

"I'm sorry I lost my temper, old man," he said. "I can see it wasn't your fault. You just want to be more careful. I ought to have warned you about the Saint—he's dangerous! Have a cigar."

It was Mr. Hayn's peace-offering. Stannard accepted it. "No offence," he said. "I'm sorry I let you down."

"We won't say anything more about it, old man," said Hayn heartily. "You won't mind if I leave you? Mr. Braddon and I have some business to talk over. I expect you'll amuse yourself upstairs. But you mustn't play any more, you know."

"I shan't want to," said Stannard. "But, Mr. Hayn—"

Hayn stopped. "Yes, old man?"

"Would you mind if I asked you for that check? I'll give you an IOU now."

"I'll see that you get it before you leave."

"It's awfully good of you, Mr. Hayn," said Stannard apologetically. "Three thousand pounds it was."

"I hadn't forgotten," said Hayn shortly. He moved off, cursing the damaged waiter out of his path; and Stannard watched him go, thoughtfully. So far, it had all been too easy, but how long was it going to last?

He was watching the early dancers assembling when a waiter, whose face was obscured by a large piece of sticking-plaster, came through with a sealed envelope. Stannard ripped it open, inspected the check it contained, and scribbled his signature to the promissory note that came with it. He sent this back to Hayn by the same waiter.

Although he had disposed of several cocktails before dinner, and during the meal had partaken freely of wine, and afterwards had done his full share in the consumption of liqueurs, his subsequent abstemiousness was remarkable. He sat with an untasted brandy-and-soda in front of him while the coloured orchestra broke into its first frenzies of syncopation, and watched the gyrating couples with a jaundiced eye for an hour. Then he drained his glass, rose, and made his way to the stairs.

Through the window of the office he saw Hayn and Braddon still engaged in earnest conversation. He tapped on the pane, and Hayn looked up and nodded. The hidden door swung open as Stannard reached it, and closed after him as he passed through.

He strolled through the gaming rooms, greeted a few acquaintances, and watched the play for a while without enthusiasm. He left the club early, as soon as he conveniently could.

The next morning, he hired a car and drove rapidly out of London. He met the Saint on the Newmarket road at a prearranged milestone.

"There was a man following me," said the Saint happily. "When I got out of my bus, he took a taxi. I wonder if he gave it up, or he's still toiling optimistically along, bursting the meter somewhere in the wilds of Edmonton." He gave Stannard a cigarette, and received a check in return.

"A thousand pounds," said Stannard. "As I promised." The Saint put it carefully away in his wallet. "And why I should give it to you, I don't know," said Stannard.

"It is the beginning of wisdom," said the Saint. "The two thousand that's left will pay off your debts and give you a fresh start, and I'll get your IOU's back for you in a day or two. A thousand pounds isn't much to pay for that."

"Except that I might have kept the money and gone on working for Hayn."

"But you have reformed," said the Saint gently. "And I'm sure the demonstration you saw last night will help to keep you on the straight and narrow path. If you kept in with Hayn, you'd have me to deal with." He climbed back into his car and pressed the self-starter, but Stannard was still curious.

"What are you going to do with the money?" he asked. "I thought you were against crooks."

"I am," said the Saint virtuously. "It goes to charity. Less my ten per cent commission charged for collecting. You'll hear from me again when I want you. *Au revoir*—or, in the Spanish, *hasta la vista*—or, you prefer it in the German, *auf Wiedersehen!*"

8

ABOUT A WEEK after the Saint's mercurial irruption into Danny's, Gwen Chandler met Mr. Edgar Hayn in Regent Street, one morning by accident. At exactly the same time, Mr. Edgar Hayn met Gwen Chandler on purpose, for he had been at some pains to bring about that accidental meeting.

"We see far too little of you these days, my dear," he said, taking her hand.

She was looking cool and demure in a summer frock of printed chiffon, and her fair hair peeped out under the brim of her picture hat to set off the cornflower blue of her eyes. "Why, it seems no time since Jerry and I were having supper with you," she said.

"No time is far too long for me," said Mr. Hayn cleverly. "One could hardly have too much of anyone as charming as yourself, my dear lady."

At the supper-party which she had unwillingly been induced to join, he had set himself out to be an irreproachable host, and his suave geniality had gone a long way towards undoing the first instinctive dislike which she had felt for him, but she did not know how to take him in this reversion to his earlier pose of exaggerated heartiness. It reminded her of the playful romping advances of an elephant, but she did not find it funny.

Mr. Hayn, however, was for the moment as pachydermatous as the animal on whose pleasantries he appeared to have modelled his own, and her slightly chilling embarrassment was lost on him. He waved his umbrella towards the window of the shop outside which they were standing. "Do you know that name, Miss Chandler?" he asked.

She looked in the direction indicated.

"Laserre? Yes, of course I've heard of it."

"I am Laserre," said Hayn largely. "This is the opportunity I've been waiting for to introduce you to our humble premises—and how convenient that we should meet on the very doorstep."

She was not eager to agree, but before she could frame a suitable reply he had propelled her into the glittering red-carpeted room where the preparations of the firm were purveyed in a hushed and reverent atmosphere reminiscent of a cathedral.

A girl assistant came forward, but in a moment she was displaced by

Braddon himself—frock-coated, smooth oleaginous, hands at washing position.

"This is my manager," said Hayn, and the frock-coated man bowed. "Mr. Braddon, be so good as to show Miss Chandler some samples of the best of our products—the very best."

Thereupon, to the girl's bewilderment, were displayed velvet-lined mahogany trays, serried ranks of them, brought from the shelves that surrounded the room, and set out with loving care on a counter, one after another, till she felt completely dazed. There were rows upon rows of flashing crystal bottles of scent, golden cohorts of lipsticks, platoons of little alabaster pots of rouge, orderly regiments of enamelled boxes of powder. Her brain reeled before the contemplation of such a massed quantity of luxurious panderings to vanity.

"I want you to choose anything you like," said Hayn. "Absolutely anything that takes your fancy, my dear Miss Chandler."

"But—I—I couldn't possibly," she stammered.

Hayn waved her objections aside. "I insist," he said. "What is the use of being master of a place like this if you cannot let your friends enjoy it? Surely I can make you such a small present without any fear of being misunderstood? Accept the trifling gift graciously, my dear lady. I shall feel most hurt if you refuse."

In spite of the grotesqueness of his approach, the circumstances made it impossible to snub him. But she was unable to fathom his purpose in making her the object of such an outbreak. It was a hot day, and he was perspiring, freely, as a man of his build is unhappily liable to do, and she wondered hysterically if perhaps the heat had temporarily unhinged his brain. There was something subtly disquieting about his exuberance. She modestly chose a small vanity-case and a little flask of perfume, and he seemed disappointed by her reluctance. He pressed other things upon her, and she found herself forced to accept two large boxes of powder.

"Make a nice parcel of those things for Miss Chandler, Mr. Braddon," said Hayn, and the manager carried the goods away to the back of the shop.

"It's really absurdly kind of you, Mr. Hayn," said the girl confusedly. "I don't know what I've done to deserve it."

"Your face is your fortune, my dear young lady," answered Hayn, who was obviously in a brilliant mood.

She had a terrified suspicion that in a moment he would utter an invitation to lunch, and she hastily begged to be excused on the grounds of an entirely fictitious engagement. "Please don't think me rude, hurrying away like this,'' she pleaded. "As a matter of fact, I'm already shockingly late.''

He was plainly crestfallen. "No one can help forgiving you anything,'' he said sententiously. "But the loss to myself is irreparable.''

She never knew afterwards how she managed to keep her end up in the exchange of platitudes that followed, until the return of Braddon with a neat package enabled her to make her escape.

Hayn accompanied her out into the street, hat in hand. "At least,'' he said, "promise me that the invitation will not be unwelcome, if I ring you up soon and ask you to suggest a day. I could not bear to think that my company was distasteful to you.''

"Of course not—I should love to—and thank you ever so much for the powder and things,'' she said desperately. "But I must fly now.'' She fled as best she might.

Hayn watched her out of sight, standing stock still in the middle of the pavement where she had left him, with a queer gleam in his pale eyes. Then he put his hat on, and marched off without reëntering the shop. He made his way to the club in Soho, where he was informed that Snake Ganning and some of the Boys were waiting to see him. Hayn let them wait while he wrote a letter, which was addressed to M. Henri Chastel, Poste Restante, Athens; and he was about to ring for the Snake to be admitted when there was a tap on the door and Danny entered.

"There are five of them,'' said Danny helpfully.

"Five of whom?'' said Hayn patiently.

"Five,'' said Danny, "including the man who pulled Mr. Braddon's hat down over his eyes. They said they must see you at once.''

Mr. Hayn felt in the pit of his stomach the dull sinking qualm which had come to be inseparable from the memory of the Saint's electric personality. Every morning without fail since the first warning he had received, there had been the now familiar envelope, beside his plate at breakfast, containing the inevitable card; and every afternoon, when he reached Danny's he found a similar reminder among the letters on his desk. He had not had a chance to forget Simon Templar, even if he had wished to do so—as a matter of fact, the Snake and his Boys were at that moment waiting to receive their instructions in connection with a plot which Hayn had formed for disposing of the menace.

But the Saint's policy was rapidly wearing out Hayn's nerves. Knowing what he did, the Saint could only be refraining from passing his knowledge along to Scotland Yard because he hoped to gain more by silence, yet there had been no attempt to blackmail—only those daily melodramatic reminders of his continued interest.

Hayn was starting to feel like a mouse that has been tormented to the verge of madness by an exceptionally sportive cat. He had not a doubt that the Saint was scheming and working against him still, but his most frenzied efforts of concentration had failed to deduce the most emaciated shred of an idea of the direction from which the next assault would be launched, and seven days and nights of baffled inaction had brought Edgar Hayn to the borders of a breakdown.

Now the Saint—and the rest of his gang also from all appearances—was paying a second visit. The next round was about to begin, and Hayn was fighting in a profounder obscurity than ever. "Show them in," he said in a voice that he hardly recognized as his own.

He bent over some writing, struggling to control his nerves for the bluff that was all he had to rely on, and with an effort of will he succeeded in not looking up when he heard the door opening and the soft footsteps of men filing into the room.

"Walk right in, souls," said the Saint's unmistakable cheery accents. "That's right. Park yourselves along that wall in single rank and stand easy."

Then Hayn raised his eyes, and saw the Saint standing over the desk regarding him affectionately.

"Good morning, Edgar," said the Saint affably. "How's Swan?"

"Good morning, Mr. Templar," said Hayn.

He shifted a gaze to the four men ranged beside the door. They were a nondescript quartet, in his opinion—not at all the sort of men he had pictured in his hazy attempts to visualize Templar's partners. Only one of them could have been under thirty, and the clothes of all of them had seen better days.

"These are the rest of the gang," said the Saint. "I noticed that I was followed home from here last time I called, so I thought it'd save you a lot of sleuthing if I brought the other lads right along and introduced them." He turned. "Squad—shun! Souls, this is dear Edgar, whom you've heard so much about. As I call your names, reading from left to right, you will each take one pace smartly to your front, bow snappily from the hips, keeping the eyebrows level and the thumb in line with seam of the trousers, and fall in again. . . . First, Edgar, meet Saint Winston Churchill. Raise your hat, Winny. . . . On his left, Saint George Robey. Eyebrows level, George. . . . Next, Saint Herbert Hoover, President of the United States, and no relation to the vacuum cleaner. Wave your handkerchief to the pretty gentleman, Herb! Last, but not least, Saint Hannen Swaffer. Keep smiling, Hannen—I won't let anyone slap your face here. . . . That's the lot, Edgar, except for myself. Meet me!''

Hayn nodded. ''That's very considerate of you, Mr. Templar,'' he said, and his voice was a little shaky, for an idea was being born inside him. ''Is that all you came to do?''

''Not quite, Precious,'' said the Saint, settling down on the edge of the desk. ''I came to talk business.''

''Then you won't want to be hurried,'' said Hayn. ''There are some other people waiting to see me. Will you excuse me while I go and tell them to call again later?''

The Saint smiled. ''By all manner of means, sonny,'' said he. ''But I warn you it won't be any use telling the Snake and his Boys to be ready to beat us up when we leave here, because a friend of ours is waiting a block away with a letter to our friend Inspector Teal—and that letter will be delivered if we don't report safe and sound in ten minutes from now!''

''You needn't worry,'' said Hayn. ''I haven't underrated your intelligence!''

He went out. It was a mistake he was to regret later—never before had he left even his allies alone in that office, much less a confessed enemy. But the urgency of his inspiration had, for the moment, driven every other thought out of his head. The cleverest criminal must make a slip sooner or later, and it usually proves to be such a childish one that the onlooker is amazed that it should have been made at all. Hayn made his slip then, but it must be remembered that he was a very rattled man.

He found Snake Ganning, sitting at the bar with three picked Boys, and beckoned them out of earshot of the bartender. ''The Saint and the rest of his band are in the office,'' he said, and Ganning let out a virulent exclamation. ''No—there won't be any rough business now. I want to have a chance to find out what his game is. But when the other four go, I want you to tail them and find out all you can about them. Report here at midnight, and I'll give you your instructions about Templar himself.''

''When I get hold of that swine,'' Ganning ground out vitriolically, ''he's going to—''

Hayn cut him short with an impatient sweep of his hand. ''You'll wait till I've finished with him,'' he said. ''You don't want to charge in like a bull at a gate, before you know what's on the other side of the gate. I'll tell you when to start—you can bet your life on that!''

And in that short space of time the Saint, having shamelessly seized the opportunity provided by Hayn's absence, had comprehensively ransacked the desk. There were four or five IOU's with Stannard's signature in an unlocked drawer, and these he pocketed. Hayn had been incredibly careless. And then the Saint's eye was caught by an envelope on which the ink was still damp. The name "Chastel" stood out as if it had been spelt in letters of fire, so that Simon stiffened like a pointer. . . . His immobility lasted only an instant. Then, in a flash, he scribbled something on a blank sheet of notepaper and folded it into a blank envelope. With the original before him for a guide, he copied the address in a staggeringly lifelike imitation of Hayn's handwriting. . . .

"I shall now be able to give you an hour, if you want it," said Hayn, returning, and the Saint turned with a bland smile.

"I shan't take nearly as long as that, my cabbage," he replied. "But I don't think the proceedings will interest the others, and they've got work to do. Now you've met them, do you mind if I dismiss the parade?"

"Not at all, Mr. Templar."

There was a glitter of satisfaction in Hayn's eyes; but if the Saint noticed it, he gave no sign. "Move to the right in column o'route— etcetera," he ordered briskly. "In English, hop it!"

The parade, after a second's hesitation, shuffled out with expressionless faces. They had not spoken a word from the time of their entrance to the time of their exit. It may conveniently be recorded at this juncture that Snake Ganning and the Boys spent eleven laboriously profitless hours following a kerbstone vendor of bootlaces, a pavement artist, and a barrel-organ team of two ex-servicemen, whom the Saint had hired for ten shillings apiece for the occasion; and it may also be mentioned that the quartet, assembling at a near-by dairy to celebrate the windfall, were no less mystified than were the four painstaking bloodhounds who dogged their footsteps for the rest of the day.

It was the Saint's idea of a joke—but then, the Saint's sense of humour was remarkably good.

9

"AND NOW LET'S get down to business—as the bishop said to the actress," murmured Simon, fishing out his cigarette-case, and tapping a gasper on his thumbnail. "I want to ask you a very important question."

Hayn sat down. "Well, Mr. Templar?"

"What would you say," asked the Saint tentatively, "if I told you I wanted ten thousand pounds?"

Hayn smiled. "I should sympathize with you," he answered. "You're not the only man who'd like to make ten thousand pounds as easily as that."

"But just suppose," said Simon persuasively—"just suppose I told you that if I didn't get ten thousand pounds at once, a little dossier about you would travel right along to Inspector Teal to tell him the story of the upstairs rooms here and the inner secrets of the Maison Laserre? I could tell him enough to send you to penal servitude for five years."

Hayn's eye fell on the calendar hung on the wall, with a sliding red ring round the date. His brain was working very rapidly then. Suddenly, he felt unwontedly confident. He looked from the calendar to his watch, and smiled.

"I should write you a check at once," he said.

"And your current account would stand it?"

"All my money is in a current account," said Hayn. "As you will understand, it is essential for a man in my position to be able to realize his estate without notice."

"Then please write," murmured the Saint.

Without a word, Hayn opened a drawer, took out his check book, and wrote. He passed the check to Templar, and the Saint's eyes danced as he read it.

"You're a good little boy, son," said the Saint. "I'm so glad we haven't had any sordid argument and haggling about this. It makes the whole thing so crude, I always think."

Hayn shrugged. "You have your methods," he said. "I have mine. I ask you to observe the time." He showed his watch, tapping the dial with a stubby forefinger. "Half-past twelve of a Saturday afternoon. You cannot cash that check until ten o'clock Monday morning. Who knows what may have happened by then? I say you will never pay that check into your bank. I'm not afraid to tell you that. I know you won't set the police on to me until Monday morning, because you think you're going to win—because you think that at ten o'clock on Monday morning you'll be sitting on the bank's doorstep waiting for it to open. I know you won't. Do you honestly believe I would let you blackmail me for a sum like that—nearly as much money as I have saved in five years?"

The crisis that he had been expecting for so long had come. The cards were on the table, and the only thing left for Edgar Hayn to wonder was why the Saint had waited so many days before making his demand. Now the storm which had seemed to be hanging fire interminably had broken, and it found Edgar Hayn curiously unmoved.

Templar looked at Hayn sidelong, and the Saint also knew that the gloves were off. "You're an odd cove," he said. "Your trouble is that you're too serious. You'll lose this fight because you've no sense of humour—like all second-rate crooks. You can't laugh."

"I may enjoy the last laugh, Templar," said Hayn.

The Saint turned away with a smile and picked up his hat. "You kid yourself," he said gently. "You won't, dear one." He took up his stick and swung it delicately in his fingers. The light of battle glinted in his blue eyes. "I presume I may send your kind donation to the London Hospital anonymously, son?"

"We will decide that on Monday," said Hayn.

The Saint nodded. "I wonder if you know what my game is?" he said soberly. "Perhaps you think I'm a kind of hijacker—a crook picking crooks' pockets? Bad guess, dearie. I'm losing money over this. But I'm just a born-an'-bred fighting machine, and a quiet life on the moss-gathering lay is plain hell for this child. I'm not a dick, because I can't be bothered with red tape, but I'm on the same side. I'm out to see that unpleasant insects like you are stamped on, which I grant you the dicks could do; but to justify my existence I'm going to see that the said insects contribute a large share of their ill-gotten gains to charity, which you've got to grant me the dicks can't do. It's always seemed a bit tough to me that microbes of your breed should be able to make a pile swindling, and then be free to enjoy it after they've done a month or two in stir—and I'm here to put that right. Out of the money I lifted off the Snake I paid Tommy Mitre back his rightful property, plus a bonus for damages; but the Snake's a small bug, anyway. You're big, and I'm going to see that your contribution is in proportion."

"We shall see," said Hayn.

The Saint looked at him steadily. "On Monday night you will sleep at Marlborough Street Police Station," he said dispassionately. The next moment he was gone. Simon Templar had a knack of making his abrupt exits so smoothly that it was generally some minutes before the other party fully realized that he was no longer with him.

Hayn sat looking at the closed door without moving. Then he glanced down, and saw the envelope that lay on the blotter before him, addressed in his own to M. Henri Chastel. And Hayn sat fascinated, staring, for although the imitation of his hand might have deceived a dozen people who knew it, he had looked at it for just long enough to see that it was not the envelope he had addressed.

It was some time before he came out of his trance, and forced himself to slit open the envelope with fingers that trembled. He spread out the sheet of paper on the desk in front of him, and his brain went numb. As a man might have grasped a concrete fact through a murky haze of dope, Hayn realized that his back was to the last wall. Underneath the superficial veneer of flippancy, the Saint had shown for a few seconds the seriousness of his real quality and the intentness of his purpose, and Hayn had been allowed to appreciate the true mettle of the man who was fighting him.

He could remember the Saint's last words. "On Monday night you will sleep at Marlborough Street Police Station." He could hear the Saint saying it. The voice had been the voice of a judge pronouncing sentence, and the memory of it made Edgar Hayn's face go grey with fear.

10

THE SAINT READ Edgar Hayn's letter in the cocktail bar of the Piccadilly, over a timely Martini, but his glass stood for a long time untasted before him, for he had not to read far before he learned that Edgar Hayn was bigger game than he had ever dreamed.

Then he smoked two cigarettes, very thoughtfully, and made certain plans with a meticulous attention to detail. In half an hour he had formulated his strategy, but he spent another quarter of an hour and another cigarette going over it again and again in search of anything that he might have overlooked.

He did not touch his drink until he had decided that his plans were as fool-proof as he could make them at such short notice.

The first move took him to Piccadilly Post Office, where he wrote out and despatched a lengthy telegram in code to one Norman Kent, who was at that time in Athens on the Saint's business; and the Saint thanked his little gods of chance for the happy coincidence that had given him an agent on the spot. It augured well for the future.

Next, he shifted across from the counter to a telephone-box, and called a number. For ten minutes he spoke earnestly to a certain Roger Conway, and gave minute directions. He had these orders repeated over to him to make sure that they were perfectly memorized and understood, and presently he was satisfied.

"Hayn will have found out by now that I know about his connections with Chastel," he concluded, "that is, unless he's posted that letter without looking at it. We've got to act on the assumption that he *has* found out, and therefore the rule about having nothing to do with me except through the safest of safe channels is doubly in force. I estimate that within the next forty-four hours a number of very strenuous efforts will be made to bump me off, and it won't be any good shutting your eyes to it. It won't be dear Edgar's fault if I haven't qualified for Kensal Green by Monday morning."

Conway protested, but the Saint dealt shortly with that. "You're a heap more useful to me working unknown," he said. "I can't help it if your natural vanity makes you kick at having to hide your light under a bushel. There's only need for one of us to prance about in the line of fire, and since they know me all round and upside down as it is I've bagged the job. You don't have to worry, I've never played the corpse yet, and I don't feel like starting now!"

He was in the highest of spirits. The imminent prospect of the violent and decisive action always got him that way. It made his blood tingle thrillingly through his veins, and set his eyes dancing recklessly, and made him bless the perfect training in which he had always kept his nerves and sinews. The fact that his life would be charged a five hundred per cent premium by any cautious insurance company failed to disturb his cheerfulness one iota. The Saint was made that way.

The "needle" was a sensation that had never troubled his young life. For the next few hours there was nothing that he could do for the cause that he had made his own, and he therefore proposed to enjoy those hours on his own to the best of his ability. He was completely unperturbed by the thought of the hectic and perilous hours which were to follow the interlude of enjoyment—rather, the interlude gathered an added zest from the approach of zero hour.

He could not, of course, be sure that Hayn had discovered the abstraction of the letter; but that remained a distinct probability in spite of the Saint's excellent experiment in forgery. And even without that discovery, the check he had obtained, and Hayn's confidence in giving it, argued that there were going to be some very tense moments before the Monday morning. Simon Templar's guiding principle, which had brought him miraculously unscathed through innumerable desperate adventures in the past, was to assume the worst and take no chances; and in this instance subsequent events were to prove that pessimistic principle the greatest and most triumphant motto that had ever been invented.

The Saint lunched at his leisure, and then relaxed amusingly in a convenient cinema until half-past six. Then he returned home to dress, and was somewhat disappointed to find no reply to his cable waiting for him at his flat.

He dined and spent the night dancing at the Kit-Cat with the lovely and utterly delightful Patricia Holm, for the Saint was as human as the next man, if not more so, and Patricia Holm was his weakness then.

It was a warm evening, and they walked up Regent Street together, enjoying the fresh air. They were in Hanover Square, just by the corner of Brook Street, when the Saint saw the first thundercloud, and unceremoniously caught Patricia Holm by the shoulders and jerked her back round the corner and out of sight. An opportune taxi came prowling by at that moment, and the Saint had hailed it and bundled the girl in before she could say a word.

"I'm telling him to take you to the Savoy," he said. "You'll book a room there, and you'll stay there without putting even the tip of your pretty nose outside the door until I come and fetch you. You can assume that any message or messenger you receive is a fake. I don't think they saw you, but I'm not risking anything. Refuse to pay any attention to anything or anybody but myself in person. I'll be round Monday lunchtime, and if I'm not you can get hold of Inspector Teal and the lads and start raising Cain—but not before."

The girl frowned suspiciously. "Saint," she said, in the dangerous tone that he knew and loved, "you're trying to elbow me out again."

"Old darling," said the Saint quietly, "I've stopped trying to elbow you out and make you live a safe and respectable life. I know it can't be done. You can come in on any game I take up, and I don't care if we have to fight the massed gangs of bad hats in New York, Chicago, Berlin and London. But there's just one kind of dirty work I'm not going to have you mixed up, and this is it. Get me, old Pat? . . . Then s'long!"

He closed the door of the taxi, directed the driver, and watched it drive away. The Saint felt particularly anxious to keep on living at that moment. . . . And then the taxi's tail-light vanished round the corner, and Patricia Holm went with it; and the Saint turned with a sigh and an involuntary squaring of the shoulders, and swung into Brook Street.

He had observed the speedy-looking closed car that stood by the kerb directly outside the entrance to his flat, and he had seen the four men who stood in a little group on the pavement beside it conversing with all apparent innocence, and he had guessed the worst. The sum total of those deceptively innocuous fixtures and fittings seemed to him to bear the unmistakable hall-mark of the Hayn confederacy; for the Saint had what he called a nasty suspicious mind.

He strolled on at a leisurely pace. His left hand, in his trouser pocket, was sorting out the key of his front door; in his right hand he twirled the stick that in those days he never travelled without. His black felt hat was tilted over to the back of his head. In everything outward and visible he wore the mildest and most Saintly air of fashionable and elegant harmlessness, for the Saint was never so cool as when everything about him was flaming with red danger-signals. And as he drew near the little group he noticed that they fell suddenly silent, all turning in his direction.

The Saint was humming a little tune. It all looked too easy—nothing but a welcome and entertaining limbering-up for the big stuff that was to follow. He had slipped the front door key off the ring and transferred it to a side pocket of his jacket, where it would be more easily found in a hurry.

"Excuse me," said the tallest of the four, taking a step forward to meet him.

"I'm afraid I can't excuse you, Snake," said the Saint, regretfully, and swayed back from his toes as Ganning struck at him with a loaded cane.

The Saint felt the wind of the blow caress his face, and then a lightning left uppercut came rocketing up from his knees to impact on the point of Snake's jaw, and Ganning was catapulted back into the arms of his attendant Boys.

Before any of them could recover from their surprise, Templar had leapt lightly up the steps to the portico, and had slipped the key into the lock. But as he turned and withdrew it, the other three came after him, leaving their chief to roll away into the gutter, and the Saint wheeled round to face them with the door swinging open behind him. He held his stick in both hands, gave it a half-turn, and pulled. Part of the stick stripped away, and in the Saint's right hand a long slim blade of steel glinted in the dim light. His first thrust took the leading Boy through the shoulder, and the other two checked.

The Saint's white teeth flashed in an unpleasant smile. "You're three very naughty children," said the Saint, "and I'm afraid I shall have to report you to your Sunday-School teacher. Go a long way away, and don't come near me again for years and years!"

The rapier in his hand gleamed and whistled, and the two Boys recoiled with gasps of agony as the supple blade lashed across their faces. And then, as they sprang blindly to attack, the Saint streaked through the door and slammed it on them. He turned the sword back into a tick, and went unhurriedly up the stairs to his flat, which was the first floor.

Looking down from the window, he saw the four men gathered together engaged in furious deliberation. One of them was mopping about inside his coat with an insanitary handkerchief, and the Snake was sagging weakly back against the side of the car holding his jaw. There were frequent gesticulations in the direction of the Saint's windows. After a time, the four men climbed into the car and drove away.

The brief affray had left the Saint completely unruffled. If you had taken his pulse then, you would have found it ticking at one beat above or below its normal 75. He sauntered across the room, switched on the lights, and put away his hat and stick, still humming gently to himself.

Propped up on the table, in a prominent position, was a cable envelope. Without any hurry, the Saint poured himself out a modest whisky, lighted a cigarette, and then fetched a small black notebook from its hiding-place behind a picture. Provided with these essentials, the Saint settled down on the edge of the table, ripped up the envelope, and extracted the flimsy.

"Elephant revoke," the message began. A little further on was the name Chandler. And near the end of the closely written sheet were the words: "Caterpillar diamonds ten spades four chicane hearts knave overcall."

"Elephant" was the code word for Hayn; Chastel was "Caterpillar." "Revoke" meant "has changed his mind." And the Saint could almost decode the sentence which included the words "chicane" and "overcall" at sight.

In his little black book, against the names of every card in the pack, and every bridge and poker term, were short sentences broadly applicable to almost any purpose about which his fellowship of freebooters might wish to communicate; and with the aid of this book, and a pencil, the Saint translated the message and wrote the interpretation between the lines. The information thus gleaned was in confirmation of what he had already deduced since purloining and reading Hayn's letter to Chastel, and the Saint was satisfied.

He opened his portable typewriter, and wrote a letter. It was the Saint's first official communiqué.

To Chief Inspector Teal,
Criminal Investigation Department,
New Scotland Yard,
S.W.1.

Sir,

I recommend to your notice Edgar Hayn, formerly Hein, of 27 Portugal Mansions, Hampstead. He is the man behind Danny's Club in Soho, and a well-timed raid on that establishment, with particular attention to a secret door in the panelling of the ground floor lounge (which is opened by an electric control in Hayn's office in the basement) will give you an interesting insight into the methods of cardsharping de luxe.

More important than this, Hayn is also the man behind Laserre, the Regent Street parfumeurs, the difference being that George Edward Braddon, the manager, is not a figurehead, but an active partner. A careful watch kept on future consignments received from the Continent by Laserre will provide adequate proof that the main reason for the existence of Laserre is cocaine. The drug is smuggled into England in cases of beauty preparations shipped by Hayn's foreign agents and quite openly declared—as dutiable products, that is. In every case, there will be found a number of boxes purporting to contain face powder, but actually containing cocaine.

Hayn's European agent is a French national of Levantine extraction named Henri Chastel. The enclosed letter, in Hayn's own handwriting, will be sufficient to prove that Hayn and Chastel were up to their necks in the whole European dope traffic.

Chastel, who is at present in Athens, will be dealt with by my agent there. I regret that I cannot hand him over to the regular processes of justice; but the complications of nationality and extradition treaties would, I fear, defeat this purpose.

By the time you receive this, I shall have obtained from Hayn the donation to charity which it is my intention to exact before passing him on to you for punishment, and you may at once take steps to secure his arrest. He had a private Moth aëroplane at Stag Lane Aërodrome, Edgware, which has for some time been kept in readiness against the necessity for either himself or one of his valued agents to make a hasty

*getaway. A watch kept on the aërodome, therefore, should
ensure the frustration of this scheme.*

*In the future, you may expect to hear from me at frequent
intervals.*

Assuring you of my best services at all times,

I remain, etc.,

THE SAINT.

With this epistle, besides Hayn's letter, Templar enclosed his artistic
trade-mark. So that there should be no possibility of tracing him, he had
had the paper on which it was drawn specially obtained by Stannard from
the gaming rooms at Danny's for the purpose. He addressed the letter,
and, after a preliminary survey of the street to make sure that the Snake
had not returned or sent deputies, he walked to a near-by pillar-box and
posted it. It would not be delivered until Monday morning, and the Saint
reckoned that that would give him all the time he needed.

Back in his flat, the Saint called up the third of his lieutenants, who
was one Dicky Tremayne, and gave him instructions concerning the
protection of Gwen Chandler. Finally he telephoned another number and
called Jerry Stannard out of bed to receive orders. At last he was satisfied
that everything had been done that he had to do.

He went to the window, drew the curtains aside a cautious half-inch,
and looked down again. A little further up Brook Street, on the other
side of the road, a blue Furillac sports saloon had drawn up by the kerb.
The Saint smiled approvingly.

He turned out the lights in the sitting-room, went through to his bedroom, and began to undress. When he rolled up his left sleeve, there was
visible a little leather sheath strapped to his forearm, and in this sheath
he carried a beautifully balanced knife—a mere six inches of razor-keen,
leaf-shaped blade and three inches of carved ivory hilt. This was Anna,
the Saint's favourite throwing-knife. The Saint could impale a flying
champagne cork with Anna at twenty paces. He considered her present
place of concealment a shade too risky, and transferred the sheath to the
calf of his right leg. Finally, he made sure that his cigarette-case contained
a supply of a peculiar kind of cigarette.

Outside, in the street, an ordinary bulb motor-horn hooted with a
peculiar rhythm. It was a prearranged signal, and the Saint did not have
to look out again to know that Ganning had returned. And then, almost

immediately, a bell rang, and the indicator in the kitchen showed him that it was the bell of the front door. "They must think I'm a mug!" murmured the Saint. But he was wrong—he had forgotten the fire-escape across the landing outside of his flat.

A moment later he heard, down the tiny hall, a dull crash and a sound of splintering wood. It connected up in his mind with the ringing of the front door bell, and he realized that he had no monopoly of prearranged signals. That ringing had been to tell the men who had entered at the back that their companions were ready at the front of the building. The Saint acknowledged that he had been trapped into underrating the organizing ability of Edgar Hayn.

Unthinkingly, he had left his automatic in his bedroom. He went quickly out of the kitchen into the hall, and at the sound of his coming the men who had entered with the aid of a jemmy swung round. Hayn was one of them, and his pistol carried a silencer. "Well, well, *well!*" drawled the Saint, whose mildness in times of crisis was phenomenal, and prudently raised his hands high above his head.

"You are going on a journey with me, Templar," said Hayn. "We are leaving at once, and I can give no date for return. Kindly turn round and put your hands behind you." Templar obeyed. His wrists were bound, and the knots tightened by ungentle hands. "Are you still as optimistic, Saint?" Hayn taunted him, testing the bonds.

"More than ever," answered the Saint cheerfully. "This is my idea of a night out—as the bishop said to the actress."

Then they turned him round again. "Take him downstairs," said Hayn. They went down in a silent procession, the Saint walking without resistance between two men. The front door was opened and a husky voice outside muttered: "All clear. The flattie passed ten minutes ago, and his beat takes him half an hour."

The Saint was passed on to the men outside and hustled across the pavement into the waiting car. Hayn and two other men followed him in; a third climbed up beside the driver. They moved off at once, heading west.

At the same time, a man rose from his cramped position on the floor of the Furillac that waited twenty yards away. He had been crouched down there for three-quarters of an hour, without a word of complaint for his discomfort, to make it appear that the car was empty, and the owner inside the house opposite which the car stood. The self-starter whirred under his foot as he sidled round behind the wheel, and the powerful engine woke to a throaty whisper. The car in which the Saint rode with Hayn flashed up the street, gathering speed rapidly; and as it went by, the blue sports Furillac pulled out from the kerb and purred westwards at a discreet distance in its wake.

Roger Conway drove. The set of his coat was spoiled by the solid bulge of the automatic in one pocket, and there was a stern set to his face which would have amazed those who only knew that amiable young man in his more flippant moods.

From his place in the leading car Simon Templar caught in the driving mirror a glimpse of the following Furillac, and smiled deep within himself.

11

GWEN CHANDLER LIVED in a microscopic flat in Bayswater, the rent of which was paid by the money left by her father. She did the housekeeping herself, and, with this saving on a servant, there was enough left over from her income to feed her and give her a reasonably good time. None of the few relations she had ever paid much attention to her. She should have been happy with her friends, and she had been, but all that had stopped abruptly when she had met and fallen in love, head over heels, with Jerry Stannard.

He was about twenty-three. She knew that, for the past two years, he had been leading a reckless life, spending most of his time and money in night clubs and usually going to bed at dawn. She also knew that his extravagant tastes had plunged him into debt, and that since the death of his father he had been accumulating bigger and bigger creditors; and she attributed these excesses to his friends, for the few people of his acquaintance she had met were of a type she detested. But her advice and inquiries had been answered with such a surliness, that at last she had given up the contest and nursed her anxiety alone.

But a few days ago her fiancé's grumpiness had strangely vanished. Though he still seemed to keep the same Bohemian hours, he had been smiling and cheerful whenever she met him; and once, in a burst of good spirits, he had told her that his debts were paid off and he was making a fresh start. She could get no more out of him than this, however—her eager questions had made him abruptly taciturn, though his refusal to be cross-examined had been kindly enough. He would be able to tell her all about it one day, he said, and that day would not be long coming.

She knew that it was his practice to lie in bed late on Sunday mornings— but then, it was his practice to lie in bed late on all the other six days of the week. On this particular Sunday morning, therefore, when a ring on the front door bell had disturbed her from the task of preparing breakfast, she was surprised to find that he was her visitor.

He was trying to hide agitation, but she discerned that the agitation was not of the harassed kind. "Got any breakfast for me?" he asked. "I had to come along at this unearthly hour, because I don't know that I'll have another chance to see you all day. Make it snappy, because I've got an important appointment."

"It'll be ready in a minute," she told him.

He loafed about the kitchen, whistling, while she fried eggs and bacon, and sniffed the fragrant aroma appreciatively. "It smells good," he said, "and I've got the appetite of a lifetime!"

She would have expected him to breakfast in a somewhat headachy silence, but he talked cheerfully.

"It must be years since you had a decent holiday," he said. "I think you deserve one, Gwen. What do you say if we get married by special licence and run over to Deauville next week?"

He laughed at her bewildered protests.

"I can afford it," he assured her. "I've paid off everyone I owe money to, and in a fortnight I'm getting a terribly sober job, starting at five pounds a week."

"How did you get it?"

"A man called Simon Templar found it for me. Have you ever met him, by chance?"

She shook her head, trying to find her voice.

"I'd do anything in the world for that man," said Jerry.

"Tell me about it," she stammered.

He told her—of his miraculous rescue by the Saint and the interview that followed it, of the Saint's persuasiveness, of the compact they had made. He also told her about Hayn; but although the recital was fairly inclusive, it did not include the machinations of the Maison Laserre. The Saint never believed in telling anybody everything, and even Hayn had secrets of his own.

The girl was amazed and shocked by the relevation of what Stannard's life had been and might still have been. But all other emotions were rapidly submerged in the great wave of relief swept over her when she learned that Stannard had given his word to break away, and was even then working on the side of the man who had brought him back to a sense of honour—even if that honour worked in an illegal method.

"I suppose it's crooked, in one way," Stannard admitted. "They're out to get Hayn and his crowd into prison, but first they're swindling them on behalf of charity. I don't know how they propose to do it. On the other hand, though, the money they've got back for me from Hayn is no more than I lost in cash at his beastly club."

"But why did Hayn let you keep on when he knew you'd got no money left?"

Stannard made a wry grimace. "He wanted to be able to force me into his gang. I came in, too—but that was because Templar told me to agree to anything that would make Hayn pay me that three thousand pound check."

She digested the information in a daze. The revelation of the enterprise in which Jerry Stannard was accompliced to the Saint did not shock her. Woman-like, she could see only the guilt of Hayn and the undoubted justice of his punishment. Only one thing made her afraid. "If you were caught—"

"There'll be no fuss," said Jerry. "Templar promised me that, and he's the kind of man you'd trust with anything. I haven't had to do anything criminal. And it'll all be over in a day of two. Templar rang me up last night."

"What was it about?"

"That's what he wouldn't tell me. He told me to go to the Splendide at eleven and wait there for a man called Tremayne, who may arrive any time up to one o'clock, and he'll tell me the rest. Tremayne's one of Templar's gang."

Then she remembered Hayn's peculiar behavior of the previous morning. The parcel she had brought away from Laserre still lay unopened on her dressing-table.

Jerry was interested in the account. Hayn's association with Laserre, as has been mentioned, was news to him. But he could make nothing of the story. "I expect he's got some foolish crush on you," he suggested. "It's only the way you'd expect a man like that to behave. I'll speak to Templar about it when I see him."

He left the dining-room as soon as he had finished breakfast, and was back in a moment with his hat.

"I must be going now," he said, and took her in his arms. "Gwen, dear, with any luck it'll all be over very soon, and we'll be able to forget it. I'll be back as soon as ever I can.''

She kissed him. "God bless you. And be careful, my darling!"

He kissed her again, and went out singing blithely. The world was very bright for Jerry Stannard that morning.

But the girl listened to the cheerful slamming of the door with a little frown, for she was troubled with misgivings. It had all seemed so easy at the time, in the optimistic way in which he had told her the story, but reviewed in cold blood it presented dangers and difficulties in legion. She wished, for both their sakes, that he had been able to stay with her that day, and her fears were soon to be justified.

Half an hour after he had gone, when the breakfast things had been cleared away, and she was tidying herself to go out for a walk, there was a ring on the front door bell. She answered it; and when she saw that it was Edgar Hayn, after what Jerry had been able to tell her, she would have closed the door in his face. But he had pushed through before she could collect her wits. He led the way into the sitting-room, and she followed in mingled fear and anger. Then she saw that there were dark rings round his eyes, and his face was haggard. "What is it?" she asked coldly.

"The police," he said. "They're after me—and they're after you, too. I came to warn you."

"But why should they be after me?" she demanded blankly.

He was in a terrible state of nerves. His hands fidgeted with his umbrella all the time he was talking, and he did not meet her eyes. "Drugs!" he said gruffly. "Illicit drugs. Cocaine. You know what I mean! There's no harm in your knowing now—we're both in the same boat. They've been watching me, and they saw me with you yesterday and followed you."

"But how do you know?"

"I've got friends at Scotland Yard," he snapped. "It's necessary. Policemen aren't incorruptible. But my man let me down—he never gave me the tip till the last moment. They're going to raid this flat and search it this morning."

Her brain was like a maelstrom, but there was one solid fact to hold on to. "There's nothing for them to find."

"That's where you're wrong! Those things I gave you—one of our other boxes got mixed up in them. I've just found that out. That's why I'm here. There's six ounces of cocaine in this flat!"

She recoiled, wide-eyed. Her heart was thumping madly. It all seemed too impossible, too fantastic. . . . And yet it only bore out and amplified what Jerry had been able to tell her. She wondered frantically if the excuse of innocence would convince a jury. Hayn saw the thought cross her mind, and shattered it.

"You know how Jerry's lived," he said. "No one would believe that you weren't both in it!" He looked out of the window. She was impelled to follow his example, and she was in time to see two broad-shouldered men in bowler hats entering the house. "They're here!" said Hayn breathlessly. "But there may be a chance. I recognized one of the men—he's a friend of mine. I may be able to square him."

Outside, a bell rang.

Hayn was scribbling something on a card. "Take this," he muttered. "My car's outside. If I can get them away from you for a moment, slip out and show the card to the chauffeur. I've got a house at Hurley. He'll take you there, and I'll come down later and discuss how we're going to get you and Jerry out of the country."

The bell rang again, more urgently. Hayn thrust the pasteboard into the girl's hand. "What're you hesitating for?" he snarled. "Do you want to stand in the dock at the Old Bailey beside your lover?"

Hardly knowing what she did, she put the card in her bag.

"Go and open the door," Hayn commanded. "They'll break in if you don't." As he spoke, there came yet a more insistent ringing, and the flat echoed with the thunder of a knocker impatiently plied.

The girl obeyed, and at the same time she was thinking furiously. Jerry—or his chief, this man Templar—would know how to deal with the crisis; but for the moment there was no doubt that Hayn's plan was the only practicable one. Her one idea was to stay out of the hands of the police long enough to make sure that Jerry was safe, and to give them time to think out an escape from the trap in which Hayn had involved them.

The two broad-shouldered men entered without ceremony as she opened the door. "I am Inspector Baker, of Scotland Yard," said one of them formally, "and I have a warrant to search your flat. You are suspected of being in illegal possession of a quantity of cocaine."

The other man took her arm and led her into the sitting-room. Hayn came forward, frowning. "I must protest about this," he said. "Miss Chandler is a friend of mine."

"That's unlucky for you," was the curt reply.

"I'll speak to Baker about this," threatened Hayn hotly, and at that moment Baker came in.

He was carrying a small cardboard box with the label of Laserre.

"Poudre Laserre," the label said; but the powder was white and crystalline. "I think this is all we need," said Baker, and stepped up to Gwen. "I shall take you into custody on a charge—"

Hayn came between them. "I should like a word with you first," he said quietly.

Baker shrugged. "If you must waste your time—"

I'll take the risk," said Hayn. "In private, please."

Baker jerked his thumb.

"Take Chandler into another room, Jones."

"Jones had better stay," interrupted Hayn. "What I have to say concerns him also. If you let Miss Chandler leave us for a minute, I will guarantee that she will not attempt to escape."

There was some argument, but eventually Baker agreed. Hayn opened the door for the girl, and as she went out gave her an almost imperceptible nod. She went into her bedroom and picked up the telephone. It seemed an eternity before the paging system of the Splendide found Jerry. When he answered, she told him what had happened. "I'm going to Hayn's house at Hurley," she said. "It's the only way to get out at the moment. But tell Tremayne when he comes, and get hold of Templar, and do something quickly!"

He was beginning to object, to ask questions, but there was no time for that, and she hung up the receiver. She had no means of knowing what Hayn's methods of "squaring" were, or how long the negotiations might be expected to keep the detectives occupied.

She tiptoed down the hall, and opened the door.

From the window, Hayn, Baker and Jones watched her cross the pavement and enter the car.

"She's a peach, boss," said Baker enviously.

"You've said all I wanted you to say," Hayn returned shortly. "But it's worked perfectly. If I'd simply tried to kidnap her, she'd have been twice as much nuisance. As it is, she'll be only too glad to do everything I say."

Dicky Tremayne arrived two minutes after Hayn's car had driven off. He should have been there over an hour ago, but the cussedness of Fate had intervened to baulk one of the Saint's best-laid plans. A bus had skidded into Tremayne's car in Park Lane, the consequent policeman had delayed him interminably, the arrangements for the removal of his wrecked car had delayed him longer, and when at last he had got away in a taxi a series of traffic blocks had held him up at every crossing. Now he had to act on his own initiative. After a second's indecision, Tremayne realized that there was only one thing to do. If Hayn and his men were already in the flat, he must just blind in and hope for the best; if they had not yet arrived, no harm would be done.

He went straight into the building, and on the way up the stairs he met Hayn and two other men coming down. There was no time for deliberation or planning a move in advance. "You're the birds I'm looking for," Tremayne rapped, barring the way. "I'm Inspector Hancock, of Scotland Yard, and I shall arrest you—"

So far he got before Hayn lashed out at him. Tremayne ducked, and the next instant there was an automatic in his hand.

"Back up those stairs to the flat you've just left," he ordered, and the three men retreated before the menace of his gun.

They stopped at the door of the flat, and he told Hayn to ring. They waited. "There seems no reply," said Hayn sardonically.

"Ring again," Tremayne directed grimly.

Another minute passed. "There can't really be anyone at home," Hayn remarked.

Tremayne's eyes narrowed. It was something about the tone of Hayn's sneering voice. . . .

"You swine!" said Tremayne through his teeth. "What have you done with her?"

"With whom?" inquired Hayn blandly.

"With Gwen Chandler!"

Tremayne could have bitten his tongue off as soon as the words were out of his mouth. That fatal, thoughtless impetuousity which was always letting him down! He saw Hayn suddenly go tense, and knew that it was useless to try and bluff further.

"So you're a Saint?" said Hayn softly.

"Yes, I am!" Tremayne let out recklessly. "And if you scabs don't want me to plug you full of holes—"

He had been concentrating on Hayn, the leader, and so he had not noticed the other men edging nearer. A hand snatched at his gun, and wrenched. . . . As Dicky Tremayne swung his fist to the man's jaw, Hayn dodged behind him and struck at the back of his head with a little rubber truncheon. . . .

12

JERRY STANNARD NEVER understood how he managed to contain himself until one o'clock. Much less did he understand how he waited the further half-hour which he gave Dicky Tremayne for grace. Perhaps no other man in the world but Simon Templar could have inspired such a blind loyalty. The Saint was working some secret stratagem of his own, Stannard argued, and he had to meet Tremayne for reasons appertaining to the Saint's tactics. In any case, if Gwen had left when she telephoned, he could not have reached the flat before she had gone—and then he might only have blundered into the police trap that she had tried to save him from. But it all connected up now—Gwen's Laserre story, and what Stannard himself knew of Hayn, and more that he suspected—and the visions that it took only a little imagination to conjure up were dreadful.

When half-past one came, and there was still no sign of Tremayne, the suspense became intolerable. Stannard went to the telephone, and fruitlessly searched London over the wire for Simon Templar. He could learn nothing from any of the clubs or hotels or restaurants which he might have frequented, nor was he any more successful with his flat. As for Dicky Tremayne, Stannard did not even know him by sight—he had simply been told to leave his card with a page, and Tremayne would ask for him.

It was after two o'clock by that time, and Tremayne had not arrived. He tried to ring up Gwen Chandler's flat, but after an interminable period of ringing, the exchange reported "No reply."

Jerry Stannard took a grip on himself. Perhaps that emergency was the making of him, the final consolidation of the process that had been started by the Saint, for Stannard had never been a fighting man. He had spoken the truth when he told Templar that his weakness was lack of "guts." But now he'd got to act. He didn't know nearly everything about Hayn, but he knew enough not to want to leave Gwen Chandler with that versatile gentleman for a moment longer than was absolutely necessary. But if anything was going to be done, Stannard had got to do it himself.

With a savage resolution, he telephoned to a garage where he was known. While he waited, he scribbled a note for Tremayne in which he described the whole series of events and stated his intentions. It was time wasted, but he was not to know that.

When the car arrived, he dismissed the mechanic who had brought it round, and drove to Hurley.

He knew how to handle cars—it was one of his few really useful accomplishments. And he sent the Buick blazing west with his foot flat down on the accelerator for practically every yard of the way.

Even so it was nearly five o'clock when he arrived there and then he realized a difficulty. There were a lot of houses at Hurley, and he had no idea where Hayn's house might be. Nor had the post office, nor the nearest police.

Stannard, in the circumstances, dared not press his enquiries too closely. The only hope left to him was that he might be able to glean some information from a villager, for he was forced to conclude that Hayn tenanted his county seat under another name. With this forlorn hope in view, he made his way to the Bell Inn, and it was there that he met a surprising piece of good fortune.

As he pulled up outside, a man came out, and the man hailed him. "Thank the Lord you're here," said Roger Conway without preface. "Come inside and have a drink."

"Who are you?" asked a mystified Jerry Stannard.

"You don't know me, but I know you," answered the man. "I'm one of the Saint's haloes."

He listened with a grave face to Stannard's story.

"There's been a hitch somewhere," he said, when Jerry had finished. "The Saint kept you in the dark because he was afraid your natural indignation might run away with you. Hayn had designs on your girl friend—you might have guessed that. The Saint pinched a letter of Hayn's to Chastel—Hayn's man abroad—in which, among other things, Edgar described his plot for getting hold of Gwen. I suppose he wanted to be congratulated on his ingenuity. The rough idea was to plant some cocaine on Gwen in a present of powder and things from Laserre, fake a police raid, and pretend to square the police for her. Then, if she believed the police were after you and her—Hayn was banking on making her afraid that you were also involved—he thought it would be easy to get her away with him."

"And the Saint wasn't doing anything to stop that?" demanded Jerry, white-lipped.

"Half-a-minute! The Saint couldn't attend to it himself, having other things to deal with, but he put the man Tremayne, you were supposed to have met at the Splendide, on the job. Tremayne was to get hold of Gwen before Hayn arrived, and tell her the story—we were assuming that you hadn't told her anything—and then bring her along to the Splendide and join up with you. The two of you were then to take Gwen down by car to the Saint's bungalow at Maidenhead and stay down there till the trouble had blown over.''

The boy was gnawing his finger-nails. He had more time to think over the situation on the drive down, and Conway's story had only confirmed his own deductions. The vista of consequences that it opened up was appalling.

''What's the Saint been doing all this time?''

''That's another longish story,'' Conway answered. ''He'd got Hayn's check for five figures and that made the risk bigger. There was only one way to settle it.'' Roger Conway briefly described the Saint's employing of the four spoof Cherubs. ''After that was found out, Simon reckoned Hayn would think the gang business was all bluff, and he'd calculate there was only the Saint against himself. Therefore he wouldn't be afraid to try on his scheme about Gwen, even though he knew the Saint knew it, because the Saint was going to be out of the way. Anyhow, Hayn's choice was between getting rid of the Saint and going to prison, and we could guess which he'd try first. The Saint had figured out that Hayn wouldn't simply try a quick assassination, because it wouldn't help him to be wanted for murder. There had got to be a murder, of course, but it would have to be well planned. So the Saint guessed he'd be kidnapped first and taken away to some quiet spot to be done in, and he decided to play stalking horse. He did that because if Hayn were arrested, his checks would be stopped automatically, so Hayn had got to be kept busy till tomorrow morning. I was watching outside the Saint's flat in a fast car last night, as I'd been detailed to do, in case of accidents. The Saint was going to make a fight of it. But they got him somehow—I saw him taken out to a car they had waiting—and I followed down here. Tremayne was to be waiting at the Splendide for a phone call from me at two o'clock. I've been trying to get him ever since, and you as well, touring London over the toll line, and it's cost a small fortune. And I didn't dare to go back to London, because of leaving the Saint here. That's why I'm damned glad you've turned up.''

''But why haven't you told the police?''

''Simon'd never forgive me. He's out to make the Saint the terror of the underworld, and he won't do that by simply giving information to Scotland Yard. The idea of the gang is to punish people suitably before

handing them over to the law, and our success over Hayn depends on
sending five figures of his money to charity. I know it's a terrible risk.
The Saint may have been killed already. But he knew what he was doing.
We were ordered not to interfere and the Saint's the head man in this
show." Stannard sprang up. "But Hayn's got Gwen!" he half sobbed.
"Roger, we can't hang about, not for anything, while Gwen's—"

"We aren't hanging about any longer," said Roger quietly.

His hand fell with a firm grip on Jerry Stannard's arm, and the youngster
steadied up. Conway led him to the window of the smoke-room, and
pointed.

"You can just see the roof of the house, over there," he said. "Since
last night, Hayn's gone back to London, and his car came by again about
two hours ago. I couldn't see who was in it, but it must have been Gwen.
Now—"

He broke off suddenly. In the silence, the drone of a powerful car
could be heard approaching. Then the car itself whirled by at speed, but
it did not pass too quickly for Roger Conway to glimpse at the men who
rode in it. "Hayn and Braddon in the back with Dicky Tremayne between
them!" he said tensely. He was in time to catch Stannard by the arm as
the boy broke away wildly.

"What the blazes are you stampeding for?" he snapped. "Do you
want to go charging madly in and let Hayn rope you in, too?"

"We can't wait!" Stannard panted, struggling.

Conway thrust him roughly into a chair and stood over him. The boy
was as helpless as a child in Conway's hands. "You keep your head and
listen to me!" Roger commanded sharply. "We'll have another drink
and tackle this sensibly. And I'm going to see that you wolf a couple of
sandwiches before you do anything. You've been in a panic for hours,
with no lunch, and you look about all in. I want you to be useful."

"If we 'phone the police—"

"Nothing doing!"

Roger Conway's contradiction ripped out almost automatically, for he
was not the Saint's right-hand man for nothing. He had learnt the secret
of the perfect lieutenant, which is the secret of, in any emergency, divining
at once what your superior officer would want you to do. It was no use
simply skinning out any old how—the emergency had got to be dealt
with in a way that would dovetail in with the Saint's general plan of
campaign. "The police are our last resort," he said. "We'll see if the
two of us can't fix this alone. Leave this to me."

He ordered a brace of stiff whiskies and a pile of sandwiches, and while these were being brought he wrote a letter which he sealed. Then he went in search of the proprietor, whom he knew of old, and gave him the letter. "If I'm not here to claim that in two hours," he said, "I want you to open it and telephone what's inside to Scotland Yard. Will you do that for me, as a great favour, and ask no questions?"

The landlord agreed, somewhat perplexedly. "Is it a joke?" he asked good-humouredly.

"It may grow into one," Roger Conway replied. "But I give you my word of honour that if I'm not back at eight o'clock, and that message isn't opened and phoned punctually, the consequences may include some of the most un-funny things that ever happened!"

13

THE SAINT HAD slept. As soon as they had arrived at the house at Hurley (he knew it was Hurley, for he had traveled that road many times over the course of several summers) he had been pushed into a bare-furnished bedroom and left to his own devices. These were not numerous, for the ropes had not been taken off his wrists.

A short tour of inspection of the room had shown that, in the circumstances, it formed an effective prison. The window, besides being shuttered, was closely barred; the door was of three-inch oak, and the key had been taken away after it had been locked. For weapons with which to attack either window or door there was the choice of a light table, a wooden chair, or a bedpost. The Saint might have employed any of these, after cutting himself free—for they had quite overlooked, in the search to which he had been subjected, the little knife strapped to his calf under his sock—but he judged that the time was not yet ripe for any such drastic action. Besides, he was tired; he saw strenuous times ahead of him, and he believed in husbanding his energies. Therefore, he had settled down on the bed for a good night's rest, making himself as comfortable as a man can when his hands are tied behind his back, and it had not been long before he had fallen into an untroubled sleep. It had struck him, drowsily, as being the most natural thing to do.

Glints of sunlight were stabbing through the interstices of the shutters when he was awakened by the sound of his door opening. He rolled over, opening one eye, and saw two men enter. One carried a tray of food, and the other carried a club. This concession to the respect in which the gang held him, even bound and helpless, afforded the Saint infinite amusement.

"This is sweet of you," he said; and indeed he thought it was, for he had not expected such a consideration, and he was feeling hungry. "But, my angels of mercy," he said, "I can't eat like this."

They sat him down in a chair and tied his ankles to the legs of it, and then the cords were taken off his wrists and he was able to stretch his cramped arms. They watched him eat, standing by the door, and the cheerful comments with which he sought to enliven the meal went unanswered. But a request for the time evoked the surly information that it was past one o'clock. When he had finished, one of the men fastened his hands again, while the other stood by with his bludgeon at the ready. Then they untied his ankles and left him, taking the tray with them.

The searchers had also left him his cigarette-case and matches, and with some agility and a system of extraordinary contortions the Saint managed to get a cigarette into his mouth and light it. This feat of double-jointed juggling kept him entertained for about twenty minutes, but as the afternoon wore on he developed, in practice, a positively brilliant dexterity. He had nothing else to do.

His chief feeling was one of boredom, and he soon ceased to find any enjoyment in wondering how Dick Tremayne had fared in Bayswater. By five o'clock he was yawning almost continuously, having thought out seventeen original and fool-proof methods of swindling swindlers without coming within reach of the law, and this and similar exercises of ingenuity were giving him no more kick at all. He would have been a lot more comfortable if his hands had not been bound, but he decided not to release himself until there was good cause for it. The Saint knew the tactical advantage of keeping a card up his sleeve.

The room, without any noticeable means of ventilation, was growing hotter and stuffier, and the cigarettes he was smoking were not improving matters. Regretfully, the Saint resigned himself to giving up that pleasure, and composed himself on the bed again. Some time before he had heard a car humming up the short drive, and he was hazily looking forward to Hayn's return and the renewed interest that that would bring. But the heaviness of the atmosphere did not conduce to mental alertness. The Saint found himself dozing. . . . For the second time, it was the sound of his door opening that roused him, and he blinked his eyes open with a sigh.

It was Edgar Hayn who came in. Physically he was in much worse case than the Saint, for he had had no sleep at all since the Friday night, and his mind had been much less carefree. His tiredness showed in the pallor of his face and the bruise-like puffiness of his eyes, but he had the air of one who feels himself the master of a situation.

"Evening," murmured Simon politely.

Hayn came over to the bedside, his lips drawn back in an unlovely smile.

"Still feeling bumptious, Templar?" he asked.

"Ain't misbehavin'," answered the Saint winningly. "I'm savin' my love for you."

The man who had held the bludgeon at lunch stood in the doorway. Hayn stood aside and beckoned him in. "There are some friends of yours downstairs," said Hayn. "I should like to have you all together."

"I should be charmed to oblige you—as the actress said to the bishop," replied the Saint. And he wondered whom Hayn could be referring to, but he showed nothing of the chill of uneasiness that had leaped at him for an instant like an Arctic wind.

He was not left long in doubt.

The bludgeon merchant jerked him to his feet and marched him down the corridor and down the stairs, Hayn bringing up the rear. The door of a room opening off the hall stood ajar, and from within came a murmur of voices which faded into stillness as their footsteps were heard approaching. Then the door was kicked wide, and the Saint was thrust into the room.

Gwen Chandler was there—he saw her at once. There were also three men whom he knew, and one of them was a dishevelled Dicky Tremayne.

Hayn closed the door and came into the centre of the room. "Now, what about it, Templar?" he said.

"What, indeed?" echoed the Saint. His lazy eyes shifted over the assembled company. "Greetings, Herr Braddon," he murmured. "Hullo, Snake. . . . Great heavens, Snake!—what's the matter with your face?"

"What's the matter with my face?" Ganning snarled.

"Everything, honeybunch," drawled the Saint. "I was forgetting. You were born like that."

Ganning came close, his eyes puckered with fury.

"I owe you something," he grunted, and let fly with both fists.

The Saint slipped the blows, and landed a shattering kick to the Snake's

shins. Then Braddon interposed a foot between the Saint's legs, and as
Simon went down Ganning loosed off with both feet. . . .

"That'll do for the present," Hayn cut in at last.

He took Templar by the collar and yanked him into a sitting position
on a chair.

"You filthy blots!" Tremayne was raving, with the veins standing out
purply on his forehead. "You warts—you flaming, verminous . . ."

It was Braddon who silenced him, with a couple of vicious, backhand
blows across the mouth. And Dick Tremayne, bound hand and foot,
wrestled impotently with ropes that he could not shift.

"We'll hear the Haynski speech," Simon interrupted. "Shut up,
Dicky! We don't mind, but it isn't nice for Gwen to have to watch!" He
looked across at the girl, fighting sobbingly in Hayn's hold. "It's all
right, Gwen, old thing," he said. "Keep smiling, for Jerry's sake. We
don't worry about anything that these dregs can do. Don't let them see
they can hurt you!"

Hayn passed the girl over to Braddon and Ganning and went over to
the Saint's chair. "I'm going to ask you one or two questions, Templar,"
he said. "If you don't want to let the Snake have another go at you,
you'll answer them truthfully."

"Pleasure," said the Saint briefly. "George Washington was the idol
of my childhood." Everything he had planned had suffered a sudden
reversal. Gwen Chandler had been caught, and so had Dicky. Their only
hope was in Roger Conway—and how long would it be before he discovered the disaster and got busy? . . . The Saint made up his mind.

"How many of you are there?"

"Seventy-six," said the Saint. "Two from five—just like when you
were at Borstal." There was no one behind him. He had got his legs
well back under the chair. His arms were also reaching back, and he was
edging his little knife out of its sheath. "You can save the rest of your
questions," he said, "I'll tell you something. You'll never get away with
this. You think you're going to find out all about my organization, the
plans I've made, whether I've arranged for a squeal to the police. Then
you'll countermove accordingly. Hold the line while I laugh!"

"I don't think so," said Hayn.

"Then you don't think as much as a weevil with sleepy sickness,"
said the Saint equably. "You must think I was born yesterday! Listen,
sweetheart! Last night I posted a little story to Inspector Teal, which he'll
get Monday morning. That letter's in the post now—and nothing will
stop it—and the letter to friend Henri I enclosed with it will make sure

the dicks pay a lot of attention to the rest of the things I had to say. You haven't an earthly, Edgarvitch!''

Hayn stepped back as if he had received a blow, and his face was horribly ashen. The Saint had never imagined that he would cause such a sensation.

"I told you he'd squeak!" Braddon was raging. "You fool—I told you!"

"I told him, too," said the Saint. "Oh, Edgar—why didn't you believe your Uncle Simon?"

Hayn came erect, his eyes blazing. He swung round on Braddon. "Be quiet, you puppy!" he commanded harshly. "We've all come to this— that's why we've got those aëroplanes. We leave to-night, and Teal can look for us tomorrow as long as he likes.''

He turned on the Saint.

"You'll come with us—you and your friend. You will not be strapped in. Somewhere in mid-Channel we shall loop the loop. You understand? . . . Templar, you've undone years of work, and I'm going to make you pay for it! I shall escape, and after a time I shall be able to come back and start again. But you—"

"I shall be flitting through Paradise, with a halo round my hat," murmured the Saint. "What a pleasant thought!" And as he spoke he felt his little knife biting into the cords on his wrists.

"We lose everything we've got," Braddon babbled.

"Including your liberty," said the Saint softly, and the knife was going through his ropes like a wire through cheese. They all looked at him. Something in the way he had spoken those three words, something in the taut purposefulness of his body, some strange power of personality, held them spellbound. Bound and at their mercy, for all they knew, an unarmed man, he was yet able to dominate them. There was hatred and murder flaring in their eyes, and yet for a space he was able to hold them on a curb and compel them to listen.

"I will tell you why you have lost, Hayn," said the Saint, speaking in the same gentle, leisured tones that nevertheless quelled them as definitely as if he had backed them up with a gun. "You made the mistake of kidding yourself that when I told you I was going to put you in prison, I was bluffing. You were sure that I'd never throw away such an opening for unlimited blackmail. Your miserable warped temperament couldn't conceive the idea of a man doing and risking all that I did and risked for nothing but an ideal. You judged me by your own crooked standards. That's where you crashed, because I'm not a crook. But I'm going to make crooks go in fear of me. You and your kind aren't scared enough of the police. You've got used to them—you call them by their first names and swap cigarettes with them when they arrest you—it's become a game to you, with prison as a forfeit for a mistake, and bull-baiting's just the same as tiddlywinks, in your lives. But I'm going to give you something new to fear—the Unknown. You'll rave about us in the dock, and all the world will hear. And when we have finished with you, you will go to prison, and you will be an example to make others afraid. But you will tell the police that you cannot describe us, because there are still three left whom you do not know; and if we two came to any harm through you, the other three would deal with you and they would not deal gently. You understand? You will never dare to speak. . . ."

"And do you think you will ever be able to speak, Templar?" asked Hayn in a quivering voice, and his right hand was leaping to his hip pocket.

And the Saint chuckled, a low triumphant murmur of a laugh. "I'm sure of it!" he said, and stood up with the cords falling from his wrists.

The little throwing-knife flashed across the room like a chip of flying quicksilver, and Hayn, with his automatic half out of his pocket, felt a pain like the searing of a hot iron across his knuckles, and all the strength went out of his fingers.

Braddon was drawing at that moment, but the Saint was swift. He had Edgar Hayn in a grip of steel, and Hayn's body was between the Saint and Braddon.

"Get behind him, Snake!" Braddon shrilled; but as Ganning moved to obey, the Saint reached a corner.

"Aim at the girl, you fool!" Hayn gasped, with the Saint's hand tightening on his throat.

The Saint held Hayn with one hand only, but the strength of that hold was incredible. With the other hand, he was fumbling with his cigarette-case.

Braddon had turned his gun into Gwen Chandler's face, while Ganning pinioned her arms. And the Saint had a cigarette in his mouth and was striking a match with one hand.

"Now do you surrender?" Braddon menaced.

"Like hell I do!" cried the Saint.

His match touched the end of his cigarette, and in the same movement he threw the cigarette far from him. It made an explosive hiss like a launched rocket, and in a second everything was blotted out in a swirl of impenetrable fog.

Templar pushed Hayn away into the opacity. He knew to a fraction of a square inch where his knife had fallen after it had severed the tendons of Hayn's hand, and he dived for it. He bumped against Tremayne's chair, and cut him free in four quick slashes.

Came, from the direction of the window, the sound of smashing glass. A shadow showed momentarily through the mist.

"Gwen!" It was Jerry Stannard's agonized voice. The girl answered him. They sought each other in the obscurity.

A sudden draught parted the wreathing clouds of the Saint's rapid-action smoke-screen. Stannard, with the girl in his arms, saw that the door was open. The Saint's unmistakable silhouette loomed in the oblong of light. "Very, very efficient, my Roger," said the Saint.

"You can always leave these little things to me," said Mr. Conway modestly, leaning against the front door, with Edgar Hayn, Braddon, and Snake Ganning herded into a corner of the hall at the unfriendly end of his automatic.

14

THEY TOOK THE three men into a room where there was no smoke.

"It was my fiancée," pleaded Jerry Stannard.

"That's so," said the Saintly tolerantly. "Dicky, you'll have to be content with Braddon. After all, he sloshed you when your hands were tied. But nobody's going to come between the Snake and this child!"

It lasted half an hour all told, and then they gathered up the three components of the mess and trussed them very securely into chairs.

"There were two other men," said the Saint hopefully, wrapping his handkerchief round a skinned set of knuckles.

"I stuck them up, and Jerry dotted them with a spanner," said Conway. "We locked them in a room upstairs."

The Saint sighed. "I suppose we'll have to leave them," he said. "Personally, I feel I've been done. These guys are rotten poor fighters when it comes to a straight-down."

Then Conway remembered the message he had left in the landlord's hands at the Bell, and they piled hurriedly into the car in which Conway

and Stannard had driven up. They retrieved the message, tidied themselves, and dined. "I think we can call it a day," said the Saint comfortably, when the coffee was on the table. "The check will be cashed
on Monday morning, and the proceeds will be registered to the London
Hospital, as arranged—less our ten per cent commission, which I don't
mind saying I think we've earned. I think I shall enclose one of my
celebrated self-portraits—a case like this ought to finish in a worthy
dramatic manner, and that opportunity's too good to miss."

He stretched himself luxuriously, and lighted a fresh cigarette which
did not explode. "Before I go to bed tonight," he said, "I'll drop a line
to old Teal and tell him where to look for our friends. I'm afraid they'll
have a hungry and uncomfortable night, but I can't help that. And now,
my infants, I suggest that we adjourn to London."

They exchanged drinks and felicitations with the lord and master of
the Bell, and it should stand to the eternal credit of that amiable gentleman
that not by the twitch of an eyebrow did he signify any surprise at the
somewhat battered appearance of two of the party. Then they went out
to their cars.

"Who's coming back with me?" asked Tremayne.

"I'm going back without you, laddie," said Jerry Stannard. "Gwen's
coming with me!"

They cheered the Buick out of sight; and then the Saint climbed into
the back of the Furillac and settled himself at his ease.

"Mr. Conway will drive," he said. "Deprived of my charming conversation, you will ponder over the fact that our friend is undoubtedly
for it. You may also rehearse the song which I've just composed for us
to sing at his funeral—I mean wedding. It's about a wicked young lover
named Jerry, who had methods decidedly merry. When the party got
very! . . . Oh, very! . . . Take me to the Savoy, Roger. I have a date.
. . . Night-night, dear old bacteria!"

The Lawless Lady

1

FOR A LAW-BREAKER, in the midst of his law-breaking, to be attempting at the same time to carry on a feud with a chief inspector of police, might be called heroically quixotic. It might equally well be called pure blame-foolishness of the most suicidal variety—according to the way you look at these things. Simon Templar found it vastly entertaining.

Chief Inspector Claud Eustace Teal, of the Criminal Investigation Department, New Scotland Yard, the great detective (and he was nearly as great in mere bulk as he was in reputation) found it an interesting novelty. Teal was reputed to have the longest memory of any man at the Yard. It was said, perhaps with some exaggeration, that if the Records Office happened to be totally destroyed by fire, Teal could personally have rewritten the entire dossier of every criminal therein recorded, methods, habits, haunts, and notable idiosyncrasies completely included—and added thereto a rough but reliable sketch of every set of fingerprints therewith connected. Certainly, he had a long memory.

He distinctly remembered a mysterious Policeman, whom an enterprising journalist called the Policeman with Wings, who was strangely reincarnated some time after the originator and (normal) patentee of the idea had departed to heaven—or some other place beginning with the same letter—on top of a pile of dynamite, thereby depriving Teal of the pleasure of handing over to his commissioner fifty thousand pounds' worth of diamonds which had been lost for seven years. Mr. Teal suspected—not without reason—that Simon Templar's fertile brain had given birth to the dénouement of that gentle jest. And Mr. Teal's memory was long. Therefore the secret activities of the Saint came to be somewhat hampered by a number of massive gentlemen in bowler hats, who took to patrolling Brook Street in relays like members of a Scottish clan mounting guard over the spot where their chieftain is sure he had dropped a sixpence.

The day arrived when Simon Templar tired of this gloomy spectacle, and, having nothing else to do, armed himself with a stout stick and sallied forth for a walk, looking as furtive and conspiratorial as he knew how. He was as fit as a fiddle and shouting for exercise. He walked westward through London, and crossed the Thames by Putney Bridge. He left Kingston behind him. Continuing southwest, he took Esher and Cabham in his stride. He walked fast, enjoying himself. Not until he reached Ripley did he pause, and there he swung into a convenient hostel towards six o'clock, after twenty-three brisk miles had been spurned by his walking shoes.

The afternoon had been sunny and warm. Simon knocked back a couple of pints of beer as if he felt he had earned every drop of them, smoked a couple of cigarettes, and then started back to the road with a refreshed spring in his step. On his way out, in another bar, he saw a man with a very red face. The man had a bowler hat on the seat beside him, and he appeared to be melting steadily into a large spotted handkerchief.

Simon approached him like an old friend. "Are you ready to go on?" he asked. "I'm making for Guildford next. From there, I make for Winchester, where I shall have dinner, and I expect to sleep in Southampton to-night. At six-thirty to-morrow morning I start for Liverpool, via Land's End. Near Manchester, I expect to murder a mulatto gasfitter with a false nose. After which, if you care to follow me to John o'Groats—" The rest of the conversation was conducted, on one side at least, in language which might have made a New York stevedore feel slightly shocked.

Simon passed on with a pained expression, and went on his way: A mile farther on, he slowed his pace to a stroll, and was satisfied that Red Face was no longer bringing up the rear. Shortly afterwards, a blue sports saloon swept past him with a rush and stopped a few yards away. As he reached it, a girl leaned out, and Simon greeted her with a smile. "Hullo, Pat, darling," he said. "Let's go and have a cocktail and some dinner."

He climbed in, and Patricia Holm let in the clutch.

"How's the market in bowler hats?" she asked.

"Weakening," murmured the Saint. "Weakening, old dear. The bulls weren't equal to the strain. Let's change the subject. Why are you so beautiful, Pat?"

She flung him a dazzling smile. "Probably," she said, "because I find I'm still in love with you—after a whole year. And you're still in love with me. The combination's enough to make anyone beautiful."

It was late when they got back to London. At the flat in Brook Street, Roger Conway and Dick Tremayne were drinking the Saint's beer.

"There was some for you," said Roger, "only we drank it in case it went flat."

"Thoughtful of you," said the Saint.

He calmly annexed Mr. Conway's tankard, and sank into a chair. "Well, soaks," he remarked, "how was the English countryside looking this afternoon?"

"I took the North Road," said Roger. "My little Mary's lamb petered out at St. Albans, and Dicky picked me up just beyond. Twenty-one miles by the clock—in five hours forty-five minutes Fahrenheit. How's that?"

"Out," said the Saint. "I did twenty-three miles in five and a half hours dead. My sleuth was removed to hospital on an asbestos stretcher, and when they tried to revive him with brandy he burst into flames. We shall hear more of this."

Nevertheless, the following morning, Orace, bringing in his master's early tea, reported that a fresh detachment of bowler hats had arrived in Brook Street, and the Saint had to devote his ingenuity to thinking out other means of evading their vigilance.

In the next fortnight, the Saint sent £9,000 to charity, and Inspector Teal, who knew that to obtain that money the Saint must have "persuaded" someone to write him a check for £10,000, from which had been deducted the 10 per cent commission which the Saint always claimed according to his rules, was annoyed. His squad, interrogated, were unable to make any suggestions as to the source of the gift. No, Simon Templar had done nothing suspicious. No, he had not been seen visiting or associating with any suspicious characters. No, he—"You're as much use as so many sick headaches," said Teal unkindly. "In fact, less use. You can stop watching that house. It's obviously a waste of your time—not," he added sweetly, "that the Department has missed you."

The climax came a few days later, when a cocaine smuggler whom Teal had been watching for months was at last caught with the goods as he stepped ashore at Dover. Teal, "acting on information received," snapped the bracelets on his wrists in the Customs House, and personally accompanied his prisoner on the train to London, sitting alone in a reserved compartment with his captive.

He did not know that Simon Templar was on the train until they were fifteen minutes out of Victoria Station, when the Saint calmly walked in and hailed him joyfully. "Can you read?" asked Teal.

"No," said the Saint.

Teal pointed to the red labels posted on the windows. "R-E-S-E-R-V-E-D," he spelt out. "Do you know the word?"

"No," said the Saint. He sat down, after one curious glance at the man at Teal's side, and produced a gold cigarette-case. "I believe I owe you an apology for walking one of your men off his feet a while ago," he said. "Really, I think you asked for it, but I'm told you're sore. Can't we kiss and be friends?"

"No," said Teal.

"Have a cigarette?"

"I don't smoke cigarettes."

"A cigar, then?"

Teal turned warily. "I've had some of your jokes," he said. "Does this one explode, or is it the kind that blows soot all over your face when you light it?"

Simon handed over the weed. It was unmistakably excellent. Teal wavered, and bit off the end absent-mindedly. "Maybe I was unreasonable," he conceded, puffing. "But *you* asked for something before I ever did. And one day you'll get it. See this bright boy?" He aimed his cigar at the prisoner, and the Saint nodded. "I've been after him for the best part of a year. And he's had plenty of laughs off me before I got him. Now it's my turn. It'll be the same with you. I can wait. One day you'll go too far, you'll make a mistake, and—"

"I know that man," said the Saint. He looked across the compartment with cold eyes. "He is a blackmailer and a dealer in drugs. His name is Cyril Farrast, and he is thirty-two years old. He has one previous conviction."

Teal was surprised, but he concealed it by lowering his eyelids sleepily. He always looked most bored when he was most interested. "I know all that," he said. "But how do you know?"

"I've been looking for him," said the Saint simply, and the man stared. "Even now I still want him. Not for the dope business—I see you're going to take care of that—but for a girl in Yorkshire. There are thousands of stories like it, but this one happened to come to my notice. He'll recognize the name—but does he know who I am?"

"I'll introduce you," said Teal, and turned to his captive. "Cyril, this is Mr. Simon Templar. You've heard of him. He's known as the Saint."

The man shrank away in horror, and Simon grinned gently. "Oh, no," he drawled. "That's only Teal's nasty suspicious mind. . . . But if I *were* the Saint, I should want you, Cyril Farrast, because of Elsa Gordon, who committed suicide eleven days ago. I ought to kill you, but Teal has told me to be good. So, instead—''

Farrast was white to the lips. His mouth moved, but no sound came. Then—''It's a lie!'' he screamed. ''You can't touch me—''

Teal pushed him roughly back, and faced the Saint.

''Templar, if you think you're going to do anything funny—''

''I'm sure of it.'' Simon glanced at his watch. ''That cigar, for instance, is due to function about now. No explosives. No soot. A much better joke than that.'' . . .

Teal was holding the cigar, staring at it. He felt very weak. His head seemed to have been aching for a long time. With a sudden convulsive effort he pitched the cigar through the window, and his hand began to reach round to his pocket. Then he sprawled limply sideways. A porter woke him at Victoria.

That night there were warrants out for the arrest of Simon Templar and all his friends. But the flat in Brook Street was shut up, and the janitor stated that the owners had gone away for a week—destination unknown. The press was not informed. Teal had his pride.

Three days later, a large coffin, labelled FRAGILE—HANDLE CARE-LESSLY—ANY OLD SIDE UP, was delivered at New Scotland Yard, addressed to Chief Inspector Teal. When examined, it was heard to tick loudly, and the explosives experts opened it at dead of night in some trepidation in the middle of Hyde Park. They found a large alarm clock—and Cyril Farrast. He was bound hand and foot, and gagged. And his bare back showed that he had been terribly flogged.

Also in the coffin was a slip of paper bearing the sign of the Saint. And in a box, carefully preserved in tissue paper and corrugated card-board, was a cigar. When Teal arrived home that night he found Simon Templar patiently waiting on his doorstep. ''I got your cigar,'' Teal said grimly.

''Smoke it,'' said the Saint. ''It's a good one. If you fancy the brand, I'll mail you the rest of the box to-morrow.''

''Come in,'' said Teal. He led the way, and the Saint followed. In the tiny sitting-room, Teal unwrapped the cigar, and the Saint lighted a cigarette. ''Also,'' said Teal, ''I've got a warrant for your arrest.''

''And no case to use it on,'' said Simon. ''You've got your man back.''

''You flogged him.''

''He's the only man who can bring that charge against me. You can't.''

''If you steal something and send it back, that doesn't dispose of the charge of theft—if we care to prosecute.''

"But you wouldn't," smiled the Saint, watching Teal light the cigar. "Frankly, now, between ourselves, would it be worth it? I notice the papers haven't said anything about the affair. That was wise of you. But if you charged me, you couldn't keep it out of the papers. And all England would be laughing over the story of how the great Claud Eustace Teal"— the detectice winced—"was caught on the bend with the old, old doped cigar. Honestly—wouldn't it be better to call it a day?"

Teal frowned, looking straight at the smiling young man before him. From the hour of his first meeting with the Saint, Teal had recognized an indefinable superiority. It lay in nothing that the Saint did or said. it was simply there. Simon Templar was not common clay; and Teal, who was of the good red earth earthy, realized the fact without resentment. "Seriously, then, Templar," said Teal, "don't you see the hole you put me in? You took Farrast away and flogged him—that remains. And he saw you talking to me in the train. If he liked, he could say in court that we were secretly aiding and abetting you. The police are in the limelight just now, and a lot of the mud would stick."

"Farrast is dumb," answered Simon. "I promise you that. Because I told him that if he breathed a word of what had happened, I should find him and kill him. And he believes it. You see, I appreciated your difficulty."

Teal could think fast. He nodded. "You win again," he said. "I think the commissioner'll pass it—this once—since you've sent the man back. But another time—"

"I never repeat myself," said the Saint. "That's why you'll never catch me. But thanks, all the same."

He picked up his hat, but he turned back at the door. "By the way— has this affair, on top of the diamonds, put you in bad with the commissioner?"

"I won't deny it."

The Saint looked at the ceiling. "I'd like to put that right," he said. "Now, there's a receiver of stolen goods living in Notting Hill, named Albert Handers. Most of the big stuff passes through his hands, and I know you've been wanting him for a longish while."

Teal started. "How the deuce—"

"Never mind that. If you really want to smooth down the commissioner, you'll wait for Handers at Croydon Aërodrome tomorrow morning, when he proposes to fly to Amsterdam with the proceeds of the Asheton robbery. The diamonds will be sewn into the carrying handle of his valise. I wonder you've never thought of that, the times you've stopped him and searched him. . . . Night-night, sonny boy!'' He was gone before the plump detective could stop him; and that night the Saint slept again in Brook Street.

But the information which the Saint had given came from Dicky Tremayne, another of the gang, and it signalled the beginning of the end of the coup to which Tremayne had devoted a year of patient preparation. This is the story of Dicky Tremayne.

2

DICKY TREMAYNE WALKED into the Saint's flat late one night, and found the Saint, in pajamas and dressing-gown, reading by the open window. Dicky Tremayne was able to walk in at any hour, because, like Roger Conway, he had his own key. Dicky Tremayne said: ''Saint, I feel I'm going to fall in love.''

The Saint slewed round, raising his eyes to heaven.

''What—not again?'' he protested.

''Again,'' snapped Dicky. ''It's an infernal nuisance, but there you are. A man must do something.''

Simon put away his book and reached for a cigarette from the box that stood conveniently open on the table at his elbow. ''Burn it,'' said Simon. ''I always thought Archie Sheridan was bad enough. Till he went and got married, I used to spend my spare time wondering why he never got landed. But since you came out of your hermitage, and we let you go and live unchaperoned in Paris—''

''I know,'' snapped Dicky. ''I can't help it. But it may be serious this time.''

Match in hand, Simon regarded him. Norman Kent was the most darkly attractive of the Saints; Archie Sheridan had been the most delightfully irresponsible; Roger Conway was the most good-looking; but Dicky— Dicky Tremayne was dark and handsome in the clean keen-faced way which is the despairing envy of the Latin, and with it Dicky's elegance had a Continental polish and his eye a wicked Continental gleam. Dicky was what romantic maidens call a sheik—and yet he was unspoiled. Also he had a courage and a cheerfulness which never failed him. The Saint had a very real affection for Dicky. "Who is it this time, son?" he asked.

Tremayne walked to the window and stared out. "Her house in Park Lane was taken in the name of the Countess Anusia Marova," he said. "So was the yacht she's chartered for the season. But she was born in Boston, Mass., twenty-three years ago, and her parents called her Audrey Perowne. She's had a lot of names since then, but the Amsterdam police knew her best as 'Straight' Audrey. You know who I mean."

"And you—"

"You know what I've done. I spent all my time in Paris working in with Hilloran, who was her right-hand man in the States, because we were sure they'd get together sooner or later, and then we'd make one killing of the pair. And they *are* together again, and I'm in London as a fully accredited member of the gang. Everything's ready. And now I want to know why we ever bothered."

Simon shrugged. "Hilloran's name is bad enough, and she's made more money—"

"Why do they call her 'Straight' Audrey?"

"Because she's never touched or dealt in dope, which is considered eccentric in a woman crook. And because it's said to be unhealthy to get fresh with her. Apart from that, she's dabbled in pretty well everything—"

Dicky nodded helplessly. "I know, old man," he said. "I know it all. You're going to say that she and Hilloran, to us, were just a pair of crooks who'd made so much out of the game that we decided to make them contribute. We'd never met her. And it isn't as if she were a man—"

"And yet," said the Saint, "I remember a woman whom you wanted to kill. And I expect you'd have done it, if she hadn't died of her own accord."

"She was a—"

"Quite. But you'd've treated her exactly the same as you'd've treated a man engaged in the same traffic."

"There's nothing like that about Audrey Perowne."

"You're trying to argue that she's really hardly more of a crook than we are. Her crime record's pretty clean, and the man she's robbed could afford to lose."

"Isn't that so?"

Simon studied his cigarette-end. "Once upon a time," he observed, "there was a rich man named John L. Morganheim. He died at Palm Beach—mysteriously. And Audrey Perowne was—er—keeping him company. You understand? It had to be hushed up, of course. His family couldn't have a scandal. Still—''

Tremayne went pale. ''We don't know the whole of that story,'' he said.

''We don't,'' admitted the Saint. ''We only know certain facts. And they mayn't be such thundering good facts, anyhow. But they're there— till we know something better.'' He got to his feet and laid a hand on Dicky's shoulder. ''Let's have some straight talk, Dicky,'' he suggested. ''You're beginning to feel you can't go through with the job. Am I right?''

Tremayne spread out his hands. ''That's about the strength of it. We've got to be sure—''

''Let's be sure, then,'' agreed the Saint. ''But meanwhile, what's the harm in carrying on? You can't object to the thrashing of Farrast. You can't feel cut up about the shopping of Handers. And you can't mind what sort of a rise we take out of Hilloran. What we do about the girl can be decided later—when we're sure. Till then, where's the point in chucking in your hand?''

Tremayne looked at him. ''There's sense in that.''

''Of course there's sense in it!'' cried the Saint. ''There's more in the gang than one girl. We want the rest. We want them like I want the mug of beer you're going to fetch me in a minute. Why shouldn't we have 'em?''

Dicky nodded slowly. ''I knew you'd say that. But I felt you ought to know. . . .''

Simon clapped him on the back. ''You're a great lad,'' he said. ''And now, what about that beer?'' Beer was brought and tasted with a fitting reverence. The discussion was closed.

With the Saint, momentous things could be brought up, argued, and dismissed like that. With Roger Conway, perhaps, the argument would have been pursued all night—but that was only because Roger and the Saint loved arguing. Dicky was reserved. Rarely did he throw off his reserve and talk long and seriously. The Saint understood, and respected his reticence. Dicky understood also. By passing on so light-heartedly to a cry for beer, the Saint did not lose one iota of the effect of sympathy; rather, he showed that his sympathy was complete.

Dicky could have asked for nothing more; and when he put down his tankard and helped himself to a cigarette, the discussion might never have raised its head between them. ''To resume,'' he said, ''we leave on the twenty-ninth.''

Simon glanced at the calendar on the wall. "Three days," he murmured. "And the cargo of billionaires?"

"Complete." Dicky grinned. "Saint, you've got to hand it to that girl. Seven of 'em—with their wives. Of course, she's spent a year dry-nursing them. Sir Esdras Levy—George Y. Ulrig—Matthew Sankin—" He named four others whose names could be conjured with in the world of high finance. "It's a peach of an idea."

"I can't think of anything like it," said the Saint. "Seven bloated perambulating gold-mines with diamond studs, and their wives loaded up with enough jewelry to sink a battleship. She gets them off on the rolling wave—knowing they'll have all their sparklers ready to make a show at the ports they touch—on a motor yacht manned by her own crew—"

"Chief Steward, J. Hilloran—"

"And the first thing the world'll know of it will be when the cargo is found marooned on the Barbary coast, and the *Corsican Maid* has sailed off into the blue with the whichnots. . . . Oh, boy! As a philosophic student, I call that the elephant's tonsils."

Dicky nodded. "The day after to-morrow," he said, "we leave by special train to join the yacht at Marseilles. You've got to say that girl does her jobs in style."

"How do you go?"

"As her secretary. But—how do you go?"

"I haven't quite made up my mind yet. Roger's taking a holiday—I guess he deserves it. Norman and Pat are still cruising the Mediterranean. I'll handle this one from the outside alone. I leave the inside to you—and that's the most important part."

"I mayn't be able to see you again before we leave."

"Then you'll have to take a chance. But I think I shall also be somewhere on the ocean. If you have to communicate, signal in Morse out of a porthole, with an electric torch, either at midnight or four in the morning. I'll be on the look-out at those times. If . . ."

They talked for two hours before Tremayne rose to go. He did so at last. "It's the first real job I've had," he said. "I'd like to make it a good one. Wish me luck, Saint!"

Simon held out his hand. "Sure—you'll pull it off, Dicky. All the best, son. And about that girl—"

"Yes, about that girl," said Dicky shortly. Then he grinned ruefully. "Good-night, old man."

He went, with crisp handshake and a frantic smile. He went as he had come, by way of the fire escape at the back of the building, for the Saint's friends had caution thrust upon them in those days. The Saint watched him go in silence, and remembered that frantic smile after he had gone. Then he lighted another cigarette and smoked it thoughtfully, sitting on the table in the centre of the room. Presently he went to bed. Dicky Tremayne did not go home to bed at once. He walked round to the side street where he had left his car, and drove to Park Lane.

The lights were still on in an upper window of the house outside which he stopped; and Tremayne entered without hesitation, despite the lateness of the hour, using his own key. The room in which he had seen the lights was on the first floor; it was used as a study and communicated with the Countess Anusia Marova's bedroom. Dicky knocked, and walked in. "Hullo, Audrey," he said.

"Make yourself at home," she said, without looking up. She was in a rich blue silk kimono and brocade slippers, writing at a desk. The reading lamp at her elbow struck gold from her hair.

There was a cut-glass decanter on the side table, glasses, a siphon, an inlaid cigarette-box. Dicky helped himself to a drink and a cigarette, and sat down where he could see her. The enthusiastic compilers of the gossip columns in the daily and weekly press had called her the most beautiful hostess of the season. That in itself would have meant little, seeing that fashionable hostesses are always described as "beautiful"—like fashionable brides, bridesmaids and debutantes. What, therefore, can it mean to be the most beautiful of such a galaxy?

But in this case something like the truth might well have been told. Audrey Perowne had grave grey eyes and an enchanting mouth. Her skin was soft and fine without the help of beauty parlours. Her colour was her own. And she was tall, with the healthy grace of her kind; and you saw pearls when she smiled.

Dicky feasted his eyes. She wrote. She stopped writing. She read what she had written, placed the sheet in an envelope, and addressed it. Then she turned. "Well?"

"I just thought I'd drop in," said Dicky. "I saw the lights were on as I came past, so I knew you were up."

"Did you enjoy your golf?"

Golf was Dicky's alibi. From time to time he went out in the afternoon, saying that he was going to play a round at Sunningdale. Nearly always, he came back late, saying that he had stayed late playing cards at the club. Those were the times when he saw the Saint. Dicky said that he had enjoyed his golf.

"Give me a cigarette," she commanded. He obeyed. "And a match.
. . . Thanks. . . . What's the matter with you, Dicky? I shouldn't have
had to ask for that."

He brought her an ashtray and returned to his seat. "I'm hanged if I
know," he said. "Too many late nights, I should think. I feel tired."

"Hilloran's only just left," she said, with deceptive inconsequence.

"Has he?"

She nodded. "I've taken back his key. In future, you'll be the only
man who can stroll in here when and how he likes." Dicky shrugged,
now knowing what to say. She added: "Would you like to live here?"

He was surprised. "Why? We leave in a couple of days. Even then,
it hadn't occurred to me—"

"It's still occurring to Hilloran," she said, "even if we are leaving
in a couple of days. But you live in a poky little flat in Bayswater, while
there are a dozen rooms going to waste here. And it's never occurred to
you to suggest moving in?"

"It never entered my head."

She smiled. "That's why I like you, Dicky," she said. "And it's why
I let you keep your key. I'm glad you came to-night."

"Apart from your natural pleasure at seeing me again—why?"

The girl studied a slim ankle. "It's my turn to ask questions," she
said. "And I ask you—why are you a crook, Dicky Tremayne?"

She looked up at him quickly as she spoke, and he met her eyes with
an effort. The blow had fallen. He had seen it coming for months—the
day when he would have to account for himself. And he had dreaded it,
though he had his story perfectly prepared. Hilloran had tried to deliver
the blow; but Hilloran, shrewd as he was, had been easy. The girl was
not easy. She had never broached the subject before, and Dicky had
begun to think that Hilloran's introduction had sufficiently disposed of
questions. He had begun to think that the girl was satisfied, without
making inquiries of her own. And that delusion was now rudely shattered.

He made a vague gesture. "I thought you knew," he said. "A little
trouble in the Guards, followed by the O.B.E. You know. Order of the
Boot—Everywhere. I could either accept the licking, or fight back, I
chose to fight back. On the whole, it's paid me."

"What's your name?" she asked suddenly.

He raised his eyebrows. "Dicky Tremayne."

"I meant—your real name."

"Dicky is real enough."

"And the other?"

"Need we go into that?"

She was still looking at him. Tremayne felt that the grim way in which he was returning her stare was becoming as open to suspicion as shiftiness would have been. He glanced away, but she called him back peremptorily. "Look at me—I want to see you."

Brown eyes met grey steadily for an intolerable minute. Dicky felt his pulse throbbing faster, but the thin straight line of smoke that went up from his cigarette never wavered. Then, to his amazement, she smiled.

"Is this a joke?" he asked evenly.

She shook her head. "I'm sorry," she said. "I wanted to make sure if you were straight—straight as far as I'm concerned, I mean. You see, Dicky, I'm worried."

"You don't trust me?"

She returned his gaze. "I had my doubts. That's why I had to make sure—in my own way. I feel sure now. It's only a feeling, but I go by feelings. I feel that you wouldn't let me down—now. But I'm still worried."

"What about?"

"There's a squeaker in the camp," she said. "Somebody's selling us. Until this moment, I was prepared to believe it was you."

3

TREMAYNE SAT LIKE an image, mechanically flicking the ash from his cigarette. Every word had gone through him like a knife, but never by a twitch of a muscle had he shown it. He said calmly enough: "I don't think anyone could blame you."

"Listen," she said. "You ask for it—from anyone like me. Hilloran's easy to fool. He's cleverer than most, but you could bamboozle him any day. I'm more inquisitive—and you're too secretive. You don't say anything about your respectable past. Perhaps that's natural. But you don't say anything about your disreputable past, either—and that's extraordinary. If it comes to the point, we've only got your word for it that you're a crook at all."

He shook his head. "Not good enough," he replied. "If I were a dick, sneaking into your gang in order to shop you—first, I'd have been smart enough to get Headquarters to fix me up with a convincing list of previous convictions, with the cooperation of the press, and second, we'd have pulled in the lot of you weeks ago.''

She had taken a chair beside him. With an utterly natural gesture, that nevertheless came strangely and unexpectedly from her, she laid a hand on his arm. "I know, Dicky," she said. "I told you I trusted you—now. Not for any logical reasons, but because my hunch says you're not that sort. But I'll let you know that if I hadn't decided I could trust you—I'd be afraid of you.''

"Am I so frightening?"

"You were."

He stirred uncomfortably, frowning. "This is queer talk from you, Audrey," he said, rather brusquely. "Somehow, one doesn't expect any sign of weakness—or fear—from you. Let's be practical. What makes you so sure there's a squeaker?"

"Handers. You saw he was taken yesterday?" Dicky nodded. "It wasn't a fluke. I'll swear Teal would never have tumbled to that valise-handle trick. Besides, the papers said he was 'acting on information received.' You know what that means?''

"It sounds like a squeal, but—''

"The loss doesn't matter so much—ten thousand pounds and three weeks' work—when we're set to pull down twenty times that amount in a few days. But it makes me rather wonder what's going to happen to the big job.''

Tremayne looked at her straightly. "If you don't think I'm the squeaker," he said, "who do you think it is?''

"There's only one other man, as far as I know, who was in a position to shop Handers.''

"Namely?"

"Hilloran."

Dicky stared. The situation was grotesque. If it had been less grotesque, it would have been laughable; but it was too grotesque even for laughter. And Dicky didn't feel like laughing.

The second cut was overwhelming. First she had half accused him of being a traitor; and then, somehow, he had convinced her of a lie without speaking a word, and she had declared that she trusted him. And now, making him her confidant, she was turning the eyes of her suspicion upon the man who had been her chief lieutenant on the other side of the Atlantic. "Hilloran," objected Dicky lamely, "worked for you—''

"Certainly. And then I fired him—with some home truths in lieu of notice. I patched it up and took him back for this job because he's a darned useful man. But that doesn't say he's forgiven and forgotten.''

"You think he's out to double-cross you and get his own back and salve his vanity?''

"It's not impossible.''

"But—''

She interrupted with an impatient movement. "You don't get the point. I thought I'd made it plain. Apart from anything else, Hilloran seems to think I'd made a handsome ornament for his home. He's been out for that lay ever since I first met him. He was particularly pressing to-night, and I sent him away with several large fleas in each ear. I'll admit he was well oiled, and I had to show him a gun—''

Dicky's face darkened. "As bad as that?''

She laughed shortly. "You needn't be heroic about it, Dicky. The ordinary conventions aren't expected to apply in our world. Being outside the pale, we're reckoned to be frankly ruddy, and we usually are. However, I just happen to be funny that way—Heaven knows why. The point is that Hilloran's as sore and spiteful as a coyote on hot tiles, and if he didn't know it was worth a quarter of a million dollars to keep in with me—''

"He might try to sell you?''

"Even now,'' said the girl, "when the time comes, he mightn't be content with his quarter share.''

Dicky's brain was seething with this new spate of ideas. On top of everything else, then, Hilloran was playing a game of his own. That game might lead him to laying information before the police on his own account, or, far more probably, to the conception of a scheme for turning the entire proceeds of the "big job'' into his own pocket. It was a factor which Tremayne had never considered. He hadn't yet absorbed it properly. And he had to get the main lines of it hard and clear, get the map of the situation nailed out in his mind in a strong light, before—Zzzzzzzz . . . zzzzzzzz . . . "What's that?''

"The front door,'' said the girl, and pointed. "There's a buzzer in my bedroom. See who it is.''

Dicky went to a window and peered out from behind the curtains. He came back soberly. "Hilloran's back again,'' he said. "Whatever he's come about, he must have seen my car standing outside. And it's nearly four o'clock in the morning.'' She met his eyes. "Shall we say it's—difficult.''

She understood. It was obvious, anyway. "What would you like me to do?" asked Dicky.

The buzzer sounded again—a long, insistent summons. Then the smaller of the two telephones on the desk tinkled. The girl picked up the receiver. "Hullo. . . . Yes. He can come up." She put down the instrument and returned to her armchair. "Another cigarette, Dicky."

He passed her the box and struck a match. "What would you like me to do?" he repeated.

"Anything you like," she said coolly. "If I didn't think your gentlemanly instincts would be offended, I'd suggest that you took off your coat and tried to look abandoned, draping yourself artistically on the arm of this chair. In any case you can be as objectionable as Hilloran will be. If you can help him to lose his temper, he may show some of his hand."

Dicky came thoughtfully to his feet, his glass in his hand. Then the girl raised her voice, clearly and sweetly. "Dicky—darling—"

Hilloran stood in the doorway, a red-faced giant of a man, swaying perceptibly. His dinner jacket was crumpled, his tie askew, his hair tousled. It was plain that he had had more to drink since he left the house. "Audrey—"

"It is usual," said the girl coldly, "to knock."

Hilloran lurched forward. In his hand he held something which he flung down into her lap. "Look at that!"

The girl picked up the cards languidly. "I didn't know you were a proud father," she remarked. "Or have you been taking up art yourself?"

"Two of 'em!" blurted Hilloran thickly. "I found one pinned to my door when I got home. The other I found here—pinned to your front door—since I left! Don't you recognize it—the warning. It means that the Saint has been here to-night!"

The girl's face had changed colour. She held the cards out to Dicky. Hilloran snatched them viciously away. "No, you don't!" he snarled. "I want to know what you're doing here at all, in this room, at this hour of the morning."

Audrey Perowne rose. "Hilloran," she said icily, "I'll thank you not to insult my friend in my own house."

The man leered at her. "You will, will you? You'd like to be left alone with him, when you know the Saint's sitting round waiting to smash us. If you don't value your own skin, I value mine. You're supposed to be the leader—"

"I am the leader."

"Are you? . . . Yes, you lead. You've led me on enough. Now you're leading him on. You little—"

Tremayne's fist smashed the word back into Hilloran's teeth. As the man crashed to the floor, Dicky whipped off his coat. Hilloran put a hand to his mouth, and the same came away wet and red. Then he shot out a shaky forefinger. "You—you skunk—I know you! You're here making love to Audrey, crawling in like a snake—and all the time you're planning to squeal on us. Ask him, Audrey!" The pointing finger stiffened, and the light of drunken hate in the man's eyes was bestial. *"Ask him what he knows about the Saint!"*

Dicky Tremayne stood perfectly still. He knew that the girl was looking at him. He knew that Hilloran could have no possible means of substantiating his accusation. He knew also how a seed sown in a bed of panic could grow, and realized that he was very near death. And he never moved. "Get up, Hilloran," he said quietly. "Get up and have the rest of your teeth knocked out."

Hilloran was scrambling to his feet. "Yes, I'll get up!" he rasped, and his hand was making for his pocket. "But I've my own way of dealing with rats—" And there was an automatic in his hand. His finger was trembling over the trigger. Dicky saw it distinctly.

Then, in a flash, the girl was between them. "If you want the police here," she said, "you'll shoot. But I shan't be here to be arrested with you."

Hilloran raved. "Out of the way, you—"

"Leave him to me," said Dicky. He put her aside, and the muzzle of the automatic touched his chest. He smiled into the flaming eyes. "May I smoke a cigarette?" he asked politely.

His right hand reached to his breast pocket in the most natural way in the world. Hilloran's scream of agony shattered the silence. Like lightning, Dicky's right hand had dropped and gripped Hilloran's right hand, at the same instant as Dicky's left hand fastened paralyzingly on Hilloran's right arm just above the elbow. The wrench that almost broke Hilloran's wrist was made almost in the same movement.

The gun thudded into the carpet at their feet, but Tremayne took no notice. Retaining and strengthening his grip, he turned Hilloran round and forced him irresistibly to his knees. Tremayne held him there with one hand. "We can talk more comfortably now," he remarked. He looked at the girl, and saw that she had picked up the fallen automatic. "Before we go any further, Audrey," he said, "I should like to know what you think of the suggestion—that I might be a friend of the Saint's. I needn't remind you that this object is jealous as well as drunk. I won't deny the charge, because that wouldn't cut any ice. I'd just like your opinion.''

"Let him go, first."

"Certainly."

With a twist of his hand, Dicky released the man and sent him toppling over onto his face. "Hilloran, get up!"

"If you—"

"Get up!"

Hilloran stumbled to his feet. There was murder in his eyes, but he obeyed. No man of his calibre could have challenged that command. Dicky thought. "A crook—and she can wear power like a queen. . . ."

"I want to know, Hilloran," observed the girl frostily, "why you said what you said just now."

The man glared. "He can't account for himself, and he doesn't look or behave like one of us. We know there's a squeaker somewhere—someone who squealed on Handers—and he's the only one—"

"I see." The contempt in the girl's voice had the quality of concentrated acid. "What I see most is that because I prefer his company to yours, you're ready to trump up any wild charge against him that comes into your head—in the hope of putting him out of favour."

"And *I* see," sneered Hilloran, "that *I'm* the one who's out of favour—because he's taken my place. He's—"

"Either," said the girl, "you can walk out on your own flat feet, or you can be thrown out. Take your choice. And whichever way you go, don't come back here till you're sober and ready to apologize."

Hilloran's fists clenched. "You're supposed to be bossing this gang—"

"I am," said Audrey Perowne. "And if you don't like it, you can cut out as soon as you like."

Hillorn swallowed. "All right—"

"Yes?" prompted Audrey silkily.

"One day," said Hilloran, staring from under black brows, "you're going to be sorry for this. We know where we are. You don't want to fire me before the big job, because I'm useful. And I'll take everything lying down for the present time, because there's a heap of money in it for me. Yes, I'm drunk, but I'm not too drunk to be able to see that."

"That," said the girl sweetly, "is good news. Have you finished?"

Hilloran's mouth opened, and closed again deliberately. The knuckles showed whitely in his hands. He looked at the girl for a long time. Then, for a long time in exactly the same way, he looked at Tremayne, without speaking. At last. "Good-night," he said, and left the room without another word.

From the window, Tremayne watched him walk slowly up the street, his handkerchief to his mouth. Then Dicky turned and found Audrey Perowne beside him. There was something in her eyes which he could not interpret. He said: "You've proved that you trust me—"

"He's crazy," she said.

"He's mad," said Dicky. "Like a mad dog. We haven't heard the last of this evening. From the moment you step on board the yacht, you'll have to watch him night and day. You understand that, don't you?"

"And what about you?"

"A knowledge of ju-jitsu is invaluable."

"Even against a knife in the back?"

Dicky laughed. "Why worry?" he asked. "It doesn't help us."

The grey eyes were still holding his. "Before you go," she said, "I'd like your own answer—from your own mouth."

"To what question?"

"To what Hilloran said."

He was picking up his coat. He put it down and came towards her. A madness was upon him. He knew it, felt everything in him rebelling against it; yet he was swept before it out of reason, like a leaf before the wind. He held out his hand. "Audrey," he said, "I give you my word of honour that I'd be burnt alive sooner than let you down."

The words were spoken quite simply and calmly. The madness in him could only prompt them. He could still keep his face impassive and school the intensest meaning out of his voice. Her cool fingers touched his, and he put them to his lips with a smile that might have meant anything—or nothing. A few minutes later he was driving home with the first streaks of dawn in the sky, and his mouth felt as if it had been seared with a hot iron. He did not see the Saint again before they left for Marseilles.

4

THREE DAYS LATER, Dicky Tremayne, in white trousers, blue reefer and peaked cap, stood at the starboard rail of the *Corsican Maid* and stared moodily over the water. The sun shone high overhead, turning the water to a sea of quicksilver, and making of the Château d'If a fairy castle. The *Corsican Maid* lay in the open roadstead, two miles from Marseilles Harbour; for the Countess Anusia Marova, ever thoughtful for her guests, had decided that the docks, with their grime and noise and bustle, were no place for holiday-making millionaires and their wives to loiter, even for a few hours. But over the water, from the direction of the harbour, approached a fussy little tender. Dicky recognized it as the tender that had been engaged to bring the millionaires, with their wives and other baggage, to the countess's yacht, and watched it morosely.

That is to say that his eyes followed it intently; but his mind was in a dozen different places. The situation was rapidly becoming intolerable—far too rapidly. That, in fact, was the only reflection which was seriously concerned with the approach of the tender. For every yard of that approach seemed, in a way, to entangle him ten times more firmly in the web that he had woven for himself.

The last time he had seen the Saint, Dicky hadn't told him the half of it. One very cogent reason was that Dicky himself, at the time, hadn't even known the half well enough to call it Dear Sir or Madam. Now, he knew it much too well. He called it by its first name now—and others—and it sat back and grinned all over its ugly face at him. Curse it. . . .

When he said that he *might* fall in love with Audrey Perowne, he was underestimating the case by a mile. He *had* fallen in love with her, and there it was. He'd done his level best not to; and when it was done, he'd fought for all he was worth against admitting it even to himself. By this time, he was beginning to see that the struggle was hopeless.

And if you want to ask why the pink parakeets he should put up a fight at all, the answer is that that's the sort of thing men of Dicky Tremayne's stamp do. If everything had been different—if the Saint had never been heard of—or, at least, if Tremayne had only known him through his morning newspaper—the problem would never have arisen. Say that the problem, having arisen, remains a simple one—and you're wrong. Wrong by the first principles of psychological arithmetic.

The Saint might have been a joke. The press, at first, had suggested that he must be a joke—that he couldn't, reasonably, be anything else. Later, with grim demonstrations thrust under their bleary eyes, the press admitted that it was no joke. In spite of which, the jest might have stood, had the men carrying it out been less under the Saint's spell.

There exists a loyalty among men of a certain type which defies instinct, and which on occasion can rise about the limitations of mere logic. Dicky

Tremayne was of that breed. And he didn't find the problem simple at all. He figured it out in his own way.

"She's a crook. On the other hand, as far as that goes, so am I— though not the way she thinks of it. She's robbing people who can afford to stand the racket. Their records, if you came to examine them closely, probably wouldn't show up any too clean. In fact, she's on much the same ground as we are ourselves. Except that she doesn't pass on ninety per cent of the profits to charity. But that's only a private sentimentality of our own. It doesn't affect the main issue. Hilloran isn't the same proposition. He's a real bad *hombre*. I'd be glad to see him go down.

"The snag with the girl is the late John L. Morganheim. She probably murdered him. But then, there's not one of our crowd that hasn't got blood on his hands. What matters is why the blood was shed. We don't know anything about Morganheim, and action's going to be forced on me before I've time to find out. In a story, the girl's always innocent. Or, if she's guilty, she's always got a cast-iron reason to be. But I'm not going to be led away. I've seen enough to know that that kind of story is mostly based on vintage boloney, according to the recipe. I'm going to look at it coldly and sanely, till I find an answer or my brain busts. Because—

"Because, in fact, things being as they are, I've as good as sworn to the Saint that I'd bring home the bacon. Not in so many words, but that's what he assumes. And he's got every right to assume it. He gave the me the chance to cry off if I wanted to—and I turned it down. I refused to quit. I dug this perishing pitfall, and it's up to me to fight my own way out—and no whining. . . ."

Thus Dicky Tremayne had balanced the ledger, over and over again, without satisfying himself. The days since the discomfiture of Hilloran had not made the account any simpler.

Hilloran had come round the next morning and apologized. Tremayne had been there—of course. Hilloran had shaken his hand heartily, boisterously disclaimed the least animosity, declared that it had been his own silly fault for getting canned, and taken Dicky and Audrey out to lunch. Dicky would have had every excuse for being deceived—but he wasn't. That he pretended to be was nobody's business.

But he watched Hilloran when he was not being watched himself; and from time to time he surprised in Hilloran's eyes a curiously abstracted intentness that confirmed his misgivings. It lasted only for a rare second here and there; and it was swallowed up again in a fresh flood of open-handed good humour so quickly that a less prejudiced observer might have put it down to imagination. But Dicky understood, and knew that there was going to be trouble with Hilloran.

Over the lunch, the intrusion of the Saint had been discussed, and a decision had been reached—by Audrey Perowne. "Whoever he is, and whatever he's done," she said, "I'm not going to be scared off by any comic-opera threats. We've spent six thousand pounds on ground bait, and we'd be a cheap lot pikers to leave the pitch without a fight. Besides, sooner or later, this Saint's going to bite off more than he can chew, and this may very well be the time. We're going to be on the broad Mediterrean, with a picked crew, and not more than twenty per cent of them can be double-crossing us. That gives us an advantage of four to one. Short of pulling out a ship of their own and making a pitched battle of it, I don't see what the Saint can do. I say we go on—with our eyes twice skinned." The argument was incontestable.

Tremayne, Hilloran and Audrey had left London quietly so as to arrive twelve hours before their guests were due. Dicky had spent another evening alone with the girl before the departure. "Do you believe in Hilloran's apology?" he had asked.

She had answered, at once: "I don't."

"Then why are you keeping him on?"

"Because I'm a woman. Sometimes, I think, you boys are liable to forget that. I've got the brain, but it takes a man to run a show like this, with a crew like mine to handle. You're the only other man I'd trust it to, but you—well, Dicky, honestly, you haven't the experience, have you?"

It had amazed him that she could discuss a crime so calmly. Lovely to look upon, exquisitely dressed, lounging at her ease in a deep chair, with a cigarette between white fingers that would have served the most fastidious sculptor for a model, she looked as if she should have been discussing, delightfully—anything but that. Of his own feelings he had said nothing. He kept them out of his face, out of his eyes, out of his voice and manner. His dispassionate calm rivalled her own. He dared hold no other pose. The reeling tumult of his thoughts could only be masked by the most stony solidness. Some of the turmoil could inevitably have broken through any less sphinx-like disguise.

He was trying to get her in her right place—and, in the attempt, he was floundering deeper and deeper in the mire of mystification. There was about her none of the hard flashiness traditionally supposed to brand the woman criminal. For all her command, she remained completely feminine, gentle of voice, perfectly gracious. The part of the Countess

Anusia Marova, created by herself, she played without effort; and, when she was alone, there was no travesty to take off. The charmingly broken English disappeared—that was all. But the same woman moved and spoke.

If he had not known, he would not have believed. But he knew—and it had rocked his creed to its foundations. There had only been one moment, that evening, when he had been in danger of stumbling. "If we bring this off," she had said, "you'll get your quarter share, of course. Two hundred and fifty thousand dollars. Fifty thousand pounds of your money. You need never do another job as long as you live. What will you do?"

"What will you do with yours?" he countered.

She hesitated, gazed dreamily into a shadowy corner as though she saw something there. Then: "Probably," she said lightly, "I'll buy a husband."

"I might buy a few wives," said Dicky, and the moment was past. Now he looked down into the blue Mediterranean and mediated that specimen of repartee with unspeakable contempt. But it had been the only thing that had come into his head, and he'd had to say something promptly. "Blast it all," thought Dicky, and straightened up with a sigh.

The tender had nosed up to the gangway, and Sir Esdras Levy, in the lead, was helping Lady Levy to the grating. Mr. George Y. Ulrig stood close behind. Dicky caught their eye. He smiled with his mouth, and saluted cheerily.

He ought to know them, for he himself had been the means of introducing them to the house in Park Lane. That had been his job, on the Continent, under Hilloran, for the past three months—to travel about the fashionable resorts, armed with plenty of money, an unimpeachable wardrobe and his natural charm of manner, and approach the Unapproachables when they were to be found in holiday moods with their armour laid aside.

It had been almost boringly simple. A man who would blow up high in the air if addressed by a perfect stranger in the lounge of the Savoy Hotel, London, may be addressed by the same stranger with perfect impunity in the lounge of the Helipolis Hotel, Biarritz. After which, to a man of Dicky Tremayne's polished worldliness, the improvement of the shining hour came automatically. Jerking himself back to the realities of immediate importance, he went down to help to shepherd his own selected sheep to the slaughter.

Audrey Perowne stood at the head of the gangway, superbly gowned in a simple white skirt and coloured jumper—superbly gowned because she wore them. She was welcoming her guest inimitably, with an intimate word for each, while Hilloran, in uniform, stood respectfully ready to conduct them to their cabins.

"Ah, Sir Esdras, ve 'ardly dare expec' you. I say, ' 'E vill not com' to my seely leetle boat.' But 'e is nize, and 'e com' to be oncomfortable to pleasse me. . . . And Lady Levy. My dear, each day you are more beautiful." Lady Levy, who was a fat fifty, glowed audibly. "And Mrs. Ulrig. Beefore I let you off my boat, you shall tell me 'ow eet iss you keep zo sleem." The scrawny and faded Mrs. George Y. Ulrig squirmed with pleasure. "George Y.," said the Countess, "I see you are vhat zey call a sheek. Ozairvize you could not 'ave marry 'er. And Mrs. Sankin . . ."

Dicky's task was comparatively childish. He had only to detach Sir Esdras Levy, Mr. George Y. Ulrig, and Matthew Sankin from their respective spouses, taking them confidentially by the arm, and murmur that there were cocktails set out in the saloon.

Luncheon, with Audrey Perowne for hostess, could not have been anything but a success. The afternoon passed quickly. It seemed no time before the bell rung by the obsequious Hilloran indicated that it was time to dress for dinner.

Tremayne went below with the rest to dress. It was done quickly; but the girl was already in the saloon when he arrived. Hilloran also was there, pretending to inspect the table. "When?" Hilloran was asking.

"To-morrow night. I've told them we're due at Monaco about half-past six. We shan't be near the place, but that doesn't matter. We'll take them in their cabins when they go below to change."

"And afterwards?" questioned Dicky.

"We make straight across to Corsica during the night, and land them near Calvi the next morning. Then we make round the south of Sicily, and lose ourselves in the Greek Archipelago. We should arrive eventually at Constantinople—repainted, rechristened, and generally altered. There we separate. I'll give the immediate orders to-morrow afternoon. Come to my cabin about three."

Hilloran turned to Dicky. "By the way," he said, "this letter came with the tender. I'm afraid I forgot to give it to you before."

Dicky held the man's eyes for a moment, and then took the envelope. It was postmarked in London. With a glance at the flap, he slit it open. The letter was written in a round feminine hand.

Darling:
This is just a line to wish you a jolly good time on your cruise.

You know I'll miss you terribly. Six weeks seems such a long time for you to be away. Never mind. I'm going to drown my sorrows in barley-water.

I refuse to be lonely. Simple Simon, the man I told you about, says he'll console me. He wants me to go with a party he's taking to the Aegean Islands. I don't know yet if I shall accept, but it sounds awfully thrilling. He's got a big aëroplane, and wants us to fly all the way.

If I go, I shall have to leave on Saturday. Won't you be jealous?

Darling, I mustn't pull your leg any more. You know I'm always thinking of you, and I shan't be really happy till I get you back again.

Here come all my best wishes, then. Be good, and take care of yourself.

It's eleven o'clock, and I'm tired. I'm going to bed to dream of you. It'll be twelve by the time I'm there. My eyes are red from weeping for you.

You have all my love. I trust you.

Patricia.

Tremayne folded the letter, replaced it in its envelope, and put it in his pocket.

"Does she still love you?" mocked Audrey Perowne, and Dicky shrugged.

"So she says," he replied carelessly. "So she says."

5

MUCH LATER THAT night, in the privacy of his cabin, Dicky read the letter again. The meaning to him was perfectly obvious. The Saint had decided to work his end of the business by aëroplane. The reference to the Aegean Islands, Tremayne decided, had no bearing on the matter—the Saint could have had no notion that the *Corsican Maid's* flight would take her to that quarter. But Saturday—the next day—was mentioned, and Dicky took that to mean that the Saint would be on the lookout for signals from Saturday onwards. "Take care of yourself," was plain enough.

The references to "eleven o'clock" and "twelve" were ambiguous. "It'll be twelve the the time I'm there" might mean that, since the aëroplane would have to watch for signals from a considerable distance, to avoid being betrayed by the noise of the engines, it would be an hour from the time of the giving of the signal before the Saint could arrive on the scene. But why "eleven o'clock" and "twelve" instead of "twelve o'clock" and "one"—since they had previously arranged that signals were to be made either at midnight or four o'clock in the morning? Dicky pondered for an hour; and decided that either he was trying to read too much between the lines, or that a signal given an hour before the appointed time, at eleven o'clock instead of twelve, would not be missed.

"My eyes are red from weeping for you." He interpreted that to mean that he was to signal with a red light if there seemed to be any likelihood of their having cause to weep for him. He had a pocket flash-lamp fitted with colour screens, and that code would be easy to adopt.

It was the last sentence that hit him fairly between the eyes. "I trust you." A shrewd blow—very shrewd. Just an outside reminder of what he'd been telling himself for the past three days. Simon couldn't possibly understand. He'd never met Audrey Perowne. And, naturally, he'd do his level best to keep Dicky on the lines.

Dicky crumpled the paper slowly into a ball, rolling it thoughtfully between his two palms. He picked up the envelope and rolled that into the ball also. Hilloran had steamed open the envelope and sealed it again before delivering the letter—Dicky was sure of that. He went to the porthole and pitched the ball far out into the dark waters.

He undressed and lay down in his bunk, but he could not compose his mind to sleep. The night was close and sultry. The air that came through the open porthole seemed to strike warm on his face, and to circulate that torrid atmosphere with the electric fan was pointless. He tried it, but it brought no relief. For an hour and a half he lay stifling; and then he rose, pulled on his slippers and a thin silk dressing-gown, and made his way to the deck.

He sprawled in a long cane chair and lighted a cigarette. Up there it was cooler. The ghost of a breeze whispered in the rigging and fanned his face. The soft hiss and wash of the sea cleft by the passage of their bows was very soothing. After a time, he dozed. He awoke with a curious sensation forcing itself through his drowsiness. It seemed as if the sea were rising, for the chair in which he lay was lurching and creaking under him. Yet the wind had not risen, and he could hear none of the thrash of curling waves which he should have been able to hear.

All this he appreciated hazily, roused but still half asleep. Then he opened one eye, and saw no rail before him, but only the steely glint of waters under the moon. Looking upwards and behind him he saw the foremast light riding serenely among the stars of a cloudness sky.

The convulsive leap he made actually spread-eagled him across the rail; and he heard his chair splash into the sea below as he tumbled over onto the deck.

Rolling on his shoulder, he glimpsed a sea-boot lashing at his head. He ducked wildly, grabbed, and kept his hold. All the strength he could muster went into the wrench that followed, and he heard the owner of the boot fall heavily with a strangled oath. An instant later he was on his feet—to find Hilloran's face two inches from his own. "Would you!" snapped Dicky.

He slipped the answering punch over his left shoulder, changed his feet, and crammed every ounce of his weight into a retaliatory jolt that smacked over Hilloran's heart and dropped the man as if his legs had been cut away from beneath him.

Dicky turned like a whirlwind as the man he had tripped up rose from the ground and leaped at him with flailing fists.

Scientific boxing, in that light, was hopeless. Dicky tried it, and stopped a right swing with the side of his head. Three inches lower, and it would probably have put an end to the fight. As it was, it sent him staggering back against the rail, momentarily dazed, and it was more by luck than judgment that his shoulder hunched in the way of the next blow. He hit back blindly, felt his knuckles make contact, and heard the man grunt with pain.

Then his sight cleared. He saw the seaman recover his balance and gather himself for a renewed onslaught. He saw Hilloran coming unsteadily off the deck, with the moonlight striking a silvery gleam from something in his right hand. And he understood the issue quite plainly.

They had tried to dump him overboard, chair and all, while he slept. A quiet and gentle method of disposing of a nuisance—and no fuss or mess. That having failed, however, the execution of the project had boiled down to a free fight for the same end. Dicky had a temporary advantage, but the odds were sticky. With the cold grim clarity of vision that comes to a man at such moments, Dicky Tremayne realized that the odds were very sticky indeed.

But not for a second could he consider raising his voice for help. Apart from the fact that the battle was more or less a duel of honour between Hilloran and himself—even if Hilloran didn't choose to fight his side single-handed—it remained to be assumed that, if Hilloran had one ally among the crew, he was just as likely to have half a dozen. The whole crew, finally, were just as likely to be on Hilloran's side as one. The agreement had been that Audrey, Hilloran and Dicky were to divide equally three-quarters of the spoil, and the crew were to divide the last quarter. Knowing exactly the type of men of which the crew was composed, Tremayne could easily reckon the chance of their falling for the bait of a half share to divide instead of a quarter, when the difference would amount to a matter of about four thousand pounds per man.

And that, Tremayne realized, would be a pretty accurate guess at the position. He himself was to be eliminated as Audrey Perowne's one loyal supporter and a thorn in Hilloran's side. The quarter share thus saved would go to bribe the crew. As for Hilloran's own benefit, Audrey Perowne's quarter share . . .

Dicky saw the whole stark idea staring him in the face, and wondered dimly why he'd never thought of it before. Audrey Perowne's only use, for Hilloran, had been to get the millionaires on board the yacht and out to sea. After that, he could take his own peculiar revenge on her for the way she had treated him, revenge himself also on Tremayne for similar things, and make himself master of the situation and a half a million dollars instead of a quarter. A charming inspiration. . . . But Dicky didn't have to think it all out like that. He saw it in a flash, more by intuition than by logic, in the instant of rest that he had while he saw also the seaman returning to the attack and Hilloran rising rockily from the ground with a knife in his hand. And therefore he fought in silence.

The darkness was against him. Dicky Tremayne was a strong and clever boxer, quicker than most men, and he knew more than a little about ju-jitsu; but those are arts for which one needs the speed of vision that can only come with clear light. The light he had was meagre and deceptive—a light that was all on the side of sheer strength and bulk, and all against mere speed and skill.

He was pretty well cornered. His back was against the rail. Hilloran was on his left front, the huge seaman on his right. There was no room to pass between them, no room to escape past either of them along the rail. There was only one way to fight: their own way. The seaman was nearest, and Dicky braced himself. It had to be a matter of give and take, the only question being that of who was to take the most. As the seaman closed in, Tremayne judged his distance, dropped his chin, and drove with a long left.

The sailor's fist connected with Dicky's forehead, knocking back his head with a jar that wricked is neck. Dicky's left met something hard that seemed to snap under the impact. Teeth. But Dicky reeled, hazed by the sickening power of the two tremendous blows he had taken; and he could hardly see for the red and black clouds that swam before his eyes.

But he saw Hilloran and dropped instinctively to one knee. He rose again immediately under Hilloran's knife arm, taking the man about the waist. Summoning all his strength, he heaved upwards, with some mad idea of treating Hilloran to some of his own pleasant medicine—or hurling the man over the rail into the glimmering black sea. And almost at once he realized that he could not do it—Hilloran was too heavy, and Dicky was already weakened. Nor was there time to struggle, for in another moment Hilloran would lift his right arm again and drive the knife into Dicky's back. But Tremayne, in this desperate effort, had Hilloran off his feet for a second. He smashed him bodily against the rail, hoping to slam the breath out of him for a momentary respite, and broke away.

As he turned, the seaman's hands fastened on his throat, and Dicky felt a sudden surge of joy. Against a man who knows his ju-jitsu, that grip is more than futile: it is more than likely to prove fatal to the man who employs it. Particularly was this fact proven then. For most of the holds in ju-jitsu depend on getting a grip on a wrist or hand—which, of course, are the hardest parts of the body to get a grip on, being the smallest and most swiftmoving. Dicky had been hampered all along by being unable to trust himself to get his hold in that light, when the faintest error of judgment would have been fatal. But now there could be no mistake.

Dicky's hands went up on each side of his head, and closed on the seaman's little fingers. He pulled and twisted at the same time, and the man screamed as one finger at least was dislocated. But Dicky went on and the man was forced sobbing to his knees. The surge of joy in Dicky's heart rose to something like a shout of triumph—and died. Out of the tail of his eye, he saw Hilloran coming in again.

Tremayne felt that he must be living a nightmare. There were two of them, both far above his weight, and they were wearing him down gradually, relentlessly. As fast as he gained an advantage over one, the other came to nullify it. As fast as he was able to temporarily to disable one, the other came back refreshed to renew the struggle. It was his own stamina against their combined consecutive staminas—and either of them individually was superior in brute strength to himself, even if one left the knife out of the audit. Dicky knew the beginning of despair.

He threw the seaman from him, sideways, across Hilloran's very knees, and leapt away. Hilloran stumbled, and Dicky's hands shot out for the man's knife wrist, found its mark, twisted savagely. The knife tinkled into the scuppers.

If Dicky could have made a grip with both hands, he would have had the mastery, but he could only make it with one. His other hand, following the right, missed. A moment later he was forced to release his hold. He swung back only just in time to avoid the left cross that Hilloran lashed out at his jaw. Then both Hilloran and the sailor came at him simultaneously, almost shoulder to shoulder.

Dicky's strength was spent. He was going groggy at the knees, his arms felt like lead, his chest heaved terribly to every panting breath he took, his head swirled and throbbed dizzily. He was taking his licking. He could not counter the blows they both hurled at him at once. Somehow, he managed to duck under their arms, with some hazy notion of driving between them and brekaing away into the open, but he could not do it. They had him cold.

He felt himself flung against the rail. The sailor's arms pinioned his own arms to his sides; Hilloran's hands were locked about his throat, strangling him to silence, crushing out life. His back was bent over the rail like a bow. His feet were off the ground.

The stars had gone out, and the moon had fallen from the sky. His chest was bound with ever-tightening iron bands. He seemed to be suspended in a vast void of utter blackness, and, though he could feel no wind, there was the roaring of a mighty wind in his ears.

And then, through the infinite distances of the dark gulf in which he hung, above even the great howling of that breathless wind, a voice spoke as a silver bell, saying: "What's this, Hilloran?"

6

DICKY SEEMED TO awake from a hideous dream.

The fingers loosened from his throat, the iron cage that tortured his chest relaxed, the rushing wind in his ears died down to a murmur. He saw a star in the sky; and, as he saw it, a moon that had not been there before seemed to swim out of the infinite dark, back to its place in the heavens. And he breathed.

Also, he suddenly felt very sick. These things happened almost immediately. He knew that they must have been almost immediate, though they seemd to follow one another with the maddening slowness of the minute hand's pursuit of the hour hand round the face of a clock. He tried to whip them to a greater speed. He could not pause to savour the sensations of this return to life. His brain had never lost consciousness. Only his body was dead, and that had to be forced back to activity without a pause.

One idea stood out distinctly from the clearing fog that blurred his vision. Audrey Perowne was there, and she had caused an interruption that was saving him, but he was not safe yet. Neither was she.

She slept, he remembered, in a cabin whose porthole looked out onto the very stretch of deck where they had been fighting, and the noise must have roused her. But, in that light, she could have seen little but a struggling group of men, unless she had watched for a time before deciding to intervene—and that was unlikely. *And she must not be allowed to know the true reason for the disturbance.*

Tremayne now understood exactly how things were. If Hilloran was prepared to dispose of him, he was prepared to dispose of the girl as well—Dicky had no doubt of that. But that would require some determination. The habit of obedience would remain, and to break it would require a conscious effort. And that effort, at all costs, must not be stimulated by an provocation while Hilloran was able to feel that he had things mostly his own way.

All this Dick Tremayne understood, and acted upon it in an instant, before his senses had fully returned. His feet touched the deck; and he twisted and held the seaman in his arms as he himself had been held a moment earlier. Then he looked across and saw Audrey Perowne.

She stood by a bulkhead light, where they could see her clearly, and the light glinted on an automatic in her hand. She said again: "Hilloran—" And by the impatient way she said it, Dicky knew that she could not have been waiting long for her first question to be answered.

"It's all right," said Dicky swiftly. "One of the men's gone rather off his rocker, and he was trying to chuck himself overboard. Hilloran and I stopped him, and he fought. That's all."

The girl came closer, and neither Hilloran nor the seaman spoke. Now it was all a gamble. Would they take the lead he had offered them, and attest the lie? Or, rather, would Hilloran?—for the other man would take the cue from him.

It ws a pure toss-up—with Audrey's automatic on Dicky's side. If Hilloran had a weapon—which he probably had—he would not dare to try and reach it when he was already covered, unless he had a supreme contempt for the girl's intelligence and straight shooting. And Dicky had surmised that the man was not yet prepared for open defiance. . . .

But there was a perceptible pause before Hilloran said; "That's so, Audrey."

She turned to the sailor. "Why did you want to throw yourself overboard?"

Sullenly, the man said, "I don't know, miss."

She looked closely at him. "They seem to have been handling you pretty roughly."

"You should have seen the way he struggled," said Dicky. "I've never seen anyone so anxious to die. I'm afraid I did most of the damage. Here—"

He took the man's hand. 'I'm going to put your finger back," he said. "It'll hurt. Are you ready?" He performed the operation with a sure touch; and then he actually managed a smile. "I should take him below and lock him up, Hilloran," he remarked. "He'll feel better in the morning. It must have been the heat. . . ."

Leaning against the rail, he watched Hilloran, without a word, take the man by the arm and lead him away. He felt curiously weak, now that the crisis was past and he hadn't got to fight any more. The blessing was that the girl couldn't see the bruises that must have been rising on his forehead and the side of his head. But something must have shown in his face that he didn't know was showing, or the way he leaned against the rail must have been rather limp, for suddenly he found her hand on his shoulder.

"It strikes me," she said softly, "that that man wasn't the only one who was roughly handled."

Dicky grinned. "I got some of the knocks, of course," he said.

"Did Hilloran?" she asked quietly.

He met her eyes, and knew then that she was not deceived. But he glanced quickly up and down the deck before he answered. "Hilloran took some knocks, too," he answered, "but it was a near thing."

"They tried to bump you off."

"That, I believe, was the general idea."

"I see." She was thoughtful. "Then—"

"I was trying to sleep on deck," said Dicky suddenly. "Hilloran was here when I arrived. We saw the man come along and try to climb over the rail—"

He broke up as Hilloran's shadow fell between them. "I've locked him up, said Hilloran, "but he seems quite sensible now."

"Good," said the girl casually. "I suppose you'd got the better of him by the time I came out. We'll discuss what's to be done with him in the morning. Dicky, you might take a turn round the deck with me before we go back to bed." She carried off the situation with such an utter naturalness that Hilloran was left with no answer. Her arm slipped through Dicky's, and they strolled away.

They went forward, rounded the deck-house, and continued aft, saying nothing; but when they came to the stern she stopped and leaned over the taffrail, gazing absorbedly down into the creaming wake.

Dicky stopped beside her. Where they stood, no one could approach within hearing distance without being seen. He took cigarettes and matches from his dressing-gown pocket. They smoked. He saw her face by the light of the match as he held it to her cigarette, and she seemed rather pale. But that might have been the light.

"Go on telling me about it," she ordered.

He shrugged. "You've heard most of it. I woke up when they were about to tip me over the side. There was some trouble. I did my best, but I'd have been done if you hadn't turned up when you did."

"Why did you lie to save them?"

He explained the instinctive reasoning which had guided him. "Not that I had time to figure it out as elaborately as that," he said, "but I'm still certain that it was a darned good guess."

"It's easily settled," she said. "We'll put Hilloran in irons—and you'll have to do the best you can in his place."

"You're an optimist," said Dicky sardonically. "Haven't I shown you every necessary reason why he should have the crew behind him to a man? They aren't the kind that started the story about honour among thieves."

She turned her head. "Are you suggesting that I should quit?"

He seemed to see his way clearly. "I am. We haven't an earthly— short of outbribing Hilloran, which 'ud mean sacrificing most of our own shares. We aren't strong enough to fight. And we needn't bank on Hilloran's coming back into the fold like a repentant sheep, because we'd lose our bets. He's got nothing to lose and everything to gain. We've served our purpose. He can handle the hold-up just as well without us, and earn another quarter of a million dollars for the shade of extra work. I don't say I wouldn't fight it out if I were alone. I would. But I'm not alone, and I suspect that Hilloran's got a nasty mind. If he's only thinking of taking your *money*—I'll be surprised."

She said coolly: "In that case, it doesn't look as if we'd gain anything by quitting."

"I could guarantee to get you away."

"How?"

"Don't ask me, Audrey. But I know how."

She appeared to contemplate the glowing end of her cigarette as though it were a crystal in which she could see the solution of all problems. Then she faced him. She said: "I don't quit."

"I suppose," said Dicky roughly, "you think that's clever. Let me tell you that it isn't. If you know that the decison's been framed against you right from the first gong, you don't lose caste by saving yourself the trouble of fighting."

"The decision on points may have been framed against you," she said, "but you can get round that one. You can win on a knockout."

"Possibly—if that were the whole of it. But you're forgetting something else, aren't you?"

"What's that?"

"The Saint."

He saw the exaggerated shrug of kimono'd shoulders. "I should worry about him. I'll stake anything he isn't among the passengers. I've had the ship searched from end to end, so he isn't here as a stowaway. And I haven't taken many chances with the crew. What is he going to do?"

"I don't know. But if the people he's beaten before now had known what the Saint was going to do—they wouldn't have been beaten. We aren't the first people who've been perfectly certain they were safe. We aren't the only clever crooks in the world."

Then she said again: "I've told you—I don't quit."

"All right—"

"This is the biggest game I've ever played!" she said, with a kind of savage enthusiasm. "It's more—it's one of the biggest games that ever *has* been played. I've spent months preparing the ground. I've sat up night after night planning everything out to the smallest detail, down to the last item of our getaways. It's a perfect machine. I've only got to press the button, and it'll run from to-morrow night to safety—as smoothly as any human machine ever ran. And you ask me to give that up!"

A kind of madness came over Dicky Tremayne. He turned, and his hands fell on her shoulders, and he forced her round with unnecessary violence. "All right!" he snapped. "You insist on keeping up this pose that you think's so brave and clever. You're damned pleased with yourself about it. Now listen to what I think. You're just a spoilt, silly fool—"

"Take your hands off me!"

"When I've finished. You're just a spoilt, silly little fool that I've a good mind to spank here and now, as I'd spank any other child—"

The moonlight gleamed on something blue-black and metallic between them. "Will you let me go?" she asked dangerously.

"No. Go ahead and shoot. I say you ought to be slapped, and, by the Lord . . . Audrey, Audrey, why are you crying?"

"Damn you," she said, "I'm not crying."

"I can see your eyes."

"Some smoke—"

"You dropped your cigarette minutes ago."

His fierce grip had slackened. She moved swiftly, and flung off his hands. "I don't want to get sentimental," she said shakily. "If I'm crying, it's my own business, and I've got my good reasons for it. You're quite right. I *am* a fool. I want that quarter of a million dollars, and I'm going to have it—in spite of Hilloran—in spite of you, too, if you want to take Hilloran's side—"

"I'm not taking Hilloran's side, I'm—"

"Whose side are you taking, then?" There's only two sides to this."

The moment had passed. He had chanced his arm on a show of strength—and failed. He wasn't used to bullying a girl. And through the dispersal of that shell-burst madness he ws aware again of the weakness of his position. A barefaced bluffer like the Saint might still have carried it off, but Dicky Tremayne couldn't. He dared not go too far. He was tied hand and foot. It had been on the tip of his tongue to throw up the game then—to tell the truth, present his ultimatum, and damn the consequences. Prudence—perhaps too great a prudence had stopped him. In that, in a way, he was like Hilloran. Hilloran was in the habit of obedience; Tremayne was in the habit of loyalty; neither of them could break his habit on the spur of the moment. "I'm taking your side," said Dicky. And he wondered, at the same time, whether he oughtn't to have given way to the impulse of that moment's loss of temper.

"Then what's the point of all this?" she demanded.

"I'm taking your side," said Dicky, "better than you know. But we won't go into that any more—not just now, anyway. Let it pass. Since you're so clever—what's your idea for dealing with the situation?"

"Another cigarette."

He gave her one, lighted it, and turned to stare moodily over the sea. It was a hopeless dilemma. "I wonder," he thought bitterly, "why a man should cling so fanatically to his word of honour? It's sheer unnatural lunacy, that's what it is." He knew that was what it was. But he was on parole, and he would have no chance to take back his parole until the following night at the earliest.

"What do you think Hilloran'll do now?" she asked. "Will he try again to-night, or will he wait till to-morrow?"

The moment was very much past. It might never have been. Dicky tried to concentrate, but his brain seemed to have gone flabby. "I don't know," he said vaguely. "In his place, I'd probably try again tonight. Whether Hilloran has that type of mind is another matter. You know him better than I do."

"I don't think he has. He's had one chance to-night to make the stand against me, and he funked it. That's a setback, psychologically, that'll take him some time to get over. I'll bet he doesn't try again till to-morrow. He'll be glad to be able to do some thinking, and there's nothing to make him rush it."

"Will you have any better answer to-morrow than you have now?"

She smiled. "I shall have slept on it," she said carelessly. "That always helps. . . . Good-night, Dicky. I'm tired."

He stopped her. "Will you promise me one thing?"

"What is it?"

"Lock your door to-night. Don't open to anyone—on any excuse."

"Yes," she said. "I should do that, in any case. You'd better do the same."

He walked back with her to the cabin. Her hair stirred in the breeze, and the moon silvered it. She was beautiful. As they passed by a bulkhead light, he was observing the serenity of her proud lovely face. He found that he had not lost all his madness.

They reached the door. "Good-night, Dicky," she said again.

"Good-night," he said. And then he said, in a strange strained voice: "I love you, Audrey. Good-night, my dear." He was gone before she could answer.

7

DICKY DREAMED THAT he was sitting on Hilloran's chest, with his fingers round Hilloran's throat, banging Hilloran's head on the deck. Every time Hilloran's head hit the deck, it made a lot of noise. Dicky knew that this was absurd. He woke up lazily, and traced the noise to his cabin door. Opening one eye, he saw the morning sunlight streaming in through his porthole.

Yawning, he rolled out of the bunk, slipped his automatic from under the pillow, and went to open the door. It was a white-coated steward, bearing a cup of tea. Dicky thanked the man, took the cup, closed the door on him, locking it again.

He sat on the edge of the bunk, stirring the tea thoughtfully. He looked at it thoughtfully, smelt it thoughtfully, got up thoughtfully, and poured it thoughtfully out of the porthole. Then he lighted a cigarette. He went to his bath with the automatic in his dressing-gown pocket and his hand on the automatic. He finished off with a cold shower, and returned to his cabin to dress, with similar caution, but feeling better.

The night before, he had fallen asleep almost at once. Dicky Tremayne had an almost Saintly faculty for carrying into practice the ancient adage that the evil of the day is sufficient thereto; and, since he reckoned that he would need all his wits about him on the morrow, he had slept. But now the morrow had arrived, he was thoughtful.

Not that the proposition in front of him appeared any more hopeful in the clear light of day. Such things have a useful knack of losing many of their terrors overnight, in the ordinary way—but this particular specimen didn't follow the rules.

It was true that Dicky had slept peacefully, and, apart from the perils that might have lurked in the cup of tea which he had not drunk, no attempt had been made to follow up the previous night's effort. That fact might have been used to argue that Hilloran hadn't yet found his confidence. In a determined counter-attack, such trifles as locked doors would not for long have stemmed his march; but the counter-attack had not been made. Yet this argument gave Dicky little reassurance.

An estimated value of one million dollars' worth of jewelry was jay-walking over the Mediterranean in that yacht, and every single dollar of that value was an argument for Hilloran—and others. Audrey Perowne had described her scheme as a fool-proof machine. So it was—granted the trustworthiness of the various cogs and bearings. And that was the very snag upon which it was liable to take it into its head to seize.

The plot would have been excellent if its object had been money-nuts or hot dogs—things of no irresistible interest to anyone but an incorrigible collector. Jewels that were readily convertible into real live dollars were another matter. Even then, they might have been dealt with in comparative safety on dry land. But when they and their owners were more or less marooned in the open sea, far beyond the interference of the policeman at the street corner, with a crew like that of the *Corsican Maid,* each of these dollars became not only an argument but also a very unstable charge of high explosive.

Thus mused Dicky Tremayne while he dressed, while he breakfasted and while he strolled round the deck afterwards with Sir Esdras Levy and Mr. Matthew Sankin. And the question that was uppermost in his mind was how he could possibly stall off the impending explosion until eleven or twelve o'clock that night.

He avoided Audrey Perowne. He saw her at breakfast, greeted her curtly, and plunged immediately into a discussion with Mr. George Y. Ulrig on the future of the American South—a point of abstract speculation which interested Dicky Tremayne rather less than the future of the Patagonian paluka. Walking round the deck, he had to pass and repass the girl, who was holding court in a shady space under an awning. He did not meet her eye, and was glad that she did not challenge him. If she had, she could have made him feel intolerably foolish.

The madness of the night before was over, and he wondered what had weakened him into betraying himself. He watched her out of the tail of his eye each time he passed. She chattered volubly, joked, laughed delightfully at each of her guests' clumsy sallies. It was amazing—her impudent nerve, her unshakable self-possession. Who would have imagined, he asked himself, that before the next dawn she was proposing that those same guests that she was then entertaining so charmingly should see her cold and masterful behind a loaded gun?

And so to lunch. Afterwards—It was hot. The sun, a globe of eye-aching fire, swung naked over the yard-arm in a burnished sky. It made the tar bubble between the planks of the open deck, and turned the scarcely rippling waters to a sheet of steel. With one consent, guests and their wives, replete, sought long chairs and the shade. Conversation suffocated—died.

At three o'clock, Dicky went grimly to the rendezvous. He saw Hilloran entering as he arrived, and was glad that he had not to face the girl alone.

They sat down on either side of the table, with one measured exchange of inscrutable glances. Hilloran was smoking a cigar. Dicky lighted a cigarette.

"What have you done about that sailor?" asked Audrey.

"I let him out," said Hilloran. "He's quite all right now."

She took an armchair between them. "Then we'll get to business," she said. "I've got it all down to a time-table. We want as little fuss as possible, and there's going to be no need for any shooting. While we're at dinner, Hilloran, you'll go through all the cabins and clean them out. Do it thoroughly. No one will interrupt you. Then you'll go down to the galley and serve out—this."

She held up a tiny flash of a yellowish liquid. "Butyl," she said, "and it's strong. Don't overdo it. Two drops in each cup of coffee, with the last two good ones for Dicky and me. And there you are. It's too easy— and far less trouble than a gun holdup. By the time they come to, they'll be tied hand and foot. We drop anchor off the Corsican coast near Calvi at eleven, and put them ashore. That's all."

Dicky rose. "Very neat," he murmured. "You don't waste time."

"We haven't to do anything. It all rests with Hilloran, and his job's easy enough."

Hilloran took the flask and slipped it into his pocket.

"You can leave it to me," he asked; and that reminder of the favorite expression of Dicky's friend, Roger Conway, would have made Dicky wince if his face hadn't been set so sternly.

"If that's everything," Dicky, "I'll go. There's no point in anyone having a chance to notice that we're both absent together." It was a ridiculous excuse, but it was an excuse. She didn't try to stop him.

Hilloran watched the door close without making any move to follow. He was carefully framing a speech in his mind, but the opportunity to use it was taken from him.

"Do you trust Dicky?" asked the girl.

It was so exactly the point he had himself been hoping to lead up to that Hilloran could have gasped. As it was, some seconds passed before he could trust himself to answer. "It's funny you should say that now," he remarked. "Because I remember that when I suggested it, you gave me the air."

"I've changed my mind since last night. As I saw it—mind you, I couldn't see very well because it was so dark—but it seemed to me that the situation was quite different from the way you both described it. It seemed," said the girl bluntly, "as if Dicky were trying to throw *you* overboard, and the sailor was trying to stop him."

"That's the truth," said Hilloran blindly.

"Then why did you lie to save him?"

"Because I didn't think you'd believe me if I told the truth."

"Why did the sailor lie?"

"He'd take his tip from me. If I chose to say nothing, it wasn't worth his while to contradict me."

The girl's slender fingers drummed on the table.

"Why do you think Dicky should try to kill you?"

Hilloran had an inspiration. He couldn't stop to give thanks for the marvellous coincidence that had made the girl play straight into his hands. The thanksgiving could come later. The immediate thing was to leap for the heaven-sent opening. He took a sheet of paper from his pocket and leaned forward. "You remember me giving Dicky a letter yesterday evening before dinner?" he asked. "I opened it first and took a copy. Here it is. It looks innocent enough, but—"

"Did you test it for invisible ink?"

"I made every test I knew. Nothing showed up. But just read the letter. Almost every sentence in it might be a hint to anyone who knew how to take it."

The girl read, with a furrow deepening between her brows. When she looked up, she was frowning. "What's your idea?"

"What I told you before. I think Dicky Tremayne is one of the Saint's gang. An arrangement."

"That can't be right. I don't know much about the Saint, but I don't imagine he'd be the sort to send a man off on a job like this and leave his instructions to a letter delivered at the last minute. The least delay in the post, and he mightn't have received the letter at all."

"That's all very well, but—"

"Besides, whoever sent this letter, if it's what you think it is, must have guessed that it might be opened and read. Otherwise the instructions would have been written in plain language. Now, these people are clever. The hints may be good ones. They may just as probably be phoney. I wouldn't put it above them to use some kind of code that anyone might tumble to—and hide another code behind it. You think you've found the solution—in the hints, if you can interpret them—but I say that's too easy. It's probably a trap.''

"Can you find any other code?"

"I'm not a code expert. But that doesn't say there isn't one."

Hilloran scowled. "I don't see that that makes any difference," he said. "I say that that letter's suspicious. If you agree with me, there's only one thing to be done."

"Certainly."

"He can go over the side, where he might have put me last night."

She shook her head. "I don't like killing, Hilloran. You know that. And it isn't necessary." She pointed to his pocket. "You have the stuff. Suppose there was only *one* coffee without it after dinner to-night?"

Hilloran's face lighted up with a brutal eagerness. He had a struggle to conceal his delight. It was too simple—too utterly, utterly simple. Verily, his enemies were delivered into his hands. . . . But he tried to make acknowledgment of the idea restraining and calculating. "It'd be safer," he conceded. "I must say I'm relieved to find you're coming round to my way of thinking, Audrey."

She shrugged, with a crooked smile. "The more I know you," she said, "the more I realize that you're usually right."

Hilloran stood up. His face was like the think crust of a volcano, under which fires and horrible forces boil and batter for release. "Audrey—"

"Not now, Hilloran—"

"I've got a first name," he said slowly. "It's John. Why don't you ever use it?"

"All right—John. But please . . . I want to rest this afternoon. When all the work's done. I'll—I'll talk to you."

He came closer. "You wouldn't try to double-cross John Hilloran, would you?"

"You know I wouldn't!"

"I want you!" he burst out incoherently. "I've wanted you for years. You've always put me off. When I found you were getting on too well with that twister Tremayne, I went mad. But he's not taking you in any more, is he?"

"No—"

"And there's no one else?"

"How could there be?"

"You little beauty!"

"Afterwards, Hilloran. I'm so tired. I want to rest. Go away now—"

He sprang at her and caught her in his arms, and his mouth found her lips. For a moment she stood passively in his embrace. Then she pushed him back, and dragged herself away. "I'll go now," he said unsteadily.

She stood like a statue, with her eyes riveted on the closing door, till the click of the latch snapping home seemed to snap also the taut cord that held her rigid and erect. Then she sank limply back into her chair. For a second she sat still. Then she fell forward across the table, and buried her face in her arms.

8

"VE VERE SUPPOSE'," said the Countess Anusia Marova, "to come to Monaco at nine o'clock. But ve are delay', and ze captayne tell me ve do nod zere arrive teel ten o'clock. So ve do nod af to urry past dinair to see ourselves come in ze port."

Dicky Tremayne heard the soft accents across the saloon, above the bull-voice drawl of Mr. George Y. Ulrig, who was holding him down with a discourse on the future of the Japanese colony in California. Dicky was rather less interested in this than he would have been in a discourse on the future of the Walloon colony in Cincinnati. A scrap of paper crumpled in the pocket of his dinner-jacket seemed to be burning his side.

The paper had come under his cabin door while he dressed. He had been at the mirror, fidgeting with his tie, and he had seen the scrap sliding on to the carpet. He had watched it, half-hypnotized, and it had been some time before he moved to pick it up. When he had read it, and jerked open the door, the alleyway outside was deserted. Only, at the end, he had seen Hilloran, in his uniform, pass across by the alley athwartships without looking to right or left.

The paper had carried one line of writing, in block letters:

DON'T DRINK YOUR COFFEE.

Nothing else. No signature, or even an initial. Not a word of explanation. Just that. But he knew that there was only one person on board
who could have written it. He had hurried over the rest of his toilet in
the hope of finding Audrey Perowne in the saloon before the other guests
arrived, but she had been the last to appear. He had not been able to
summon up the courage to knock on the door of her cabin. His desire
to see her and speak to her again alone, on any pretext, was tempered
by an equal desire to avoid giving her any chance to refer to his last
words of the previous night.

"The Jap is a good citizen," George Y. Ulrig droned on, holding up
his cocktail-glass like a sceptre. "He has few vices, he's clean, and he
doesn't make trouble. On the other hand, he's too clever to trust. He
. . . Say, boy, what's eatin' you?"

"Nothing," denied Dicky hastily. "What makes you think the Jap's
too clever to trust?"

"Now, the Chinaman's the honestest man in the world, whatever they
say about him," resumed the drone. "I'll tell you a story to illustrate
that. . . ."

He told his story at leisure, and Dicky forced himself to look interested.
It wasn't easy. He was glad when they sat down to dinner. His partner
was the less eagle-eyed Mrs. George Y. Ulrig, who was incapable of
noticing the absent-minded way in which he listened to her detailed
description of her last illness. But halfway through the meal he was
recalled to attention by a challenge, and for some reason he was glad of
it.

"Deeky," said the girl at the end of the table. Dicky looked up. "Ve
are in ze middle of an argument," she said.

"Id iss this," interrupted Sir Esdras Levy. "Der Gountess asks, if for
insdance you vos a friendt off mine, ant bromised to tell nobody nothing,
ant I see you vill be ruined if you don't know off der teal, and I know
der teal vill ruined be if you know off it—vot shoot I to?"

This lucid exposition was greeted with a suppressed titter which made
Sir Esdras whiffle impatiently through his beard. He waved his hands
excitedly. "I say," he proclaimed magisterially, "dot a man's vort iss
his pond. I am sorry for you, bud I must my vort keep."

" 'Owever," shipped in Mr. Matthew Sankin, and, catching his wife's
basilisk eye upon him, choked redly. "*However,*" said Mr. Matthew
Sankin, "I 'old by the British principle that a man oughter stick by his

mates—friends—an' he ain't—'asn't—*hasn't* got no right to let 'em down. None of 'em. That's wot."

"Matthew, deah," said Mrs. Sankin silkily, "the Countess was esking Mr. Tremayne the question, ay believe. Kaindly give us a chance to heah his opinion."

"What about a show of hands?" suggested Dicky. "How many of you say that a man should stand by his word—whatever it costs him?" Six hands went up. Sankin and Ulrig were alone among the male dissenters. "Lost by one," said Dicky.

"No," said the Countess. "I do not vote. I make you ze chairman, Deeky, and you 'ave ze last vord. 'Ow do you say?"

"In this problem, there's no chance of a compromise? The man couldn't find a way to tell his friend so that it wouldn't spoil the deal for his other friends?"

"Ve hof no gompromises," said Sir Esdras sternly.

Dicky looked down the table and met the girl's eyes steadily. "Then," he remarked, "I should first see my partners and warn them that I was going to break my word, and then I should go and do it. But the first condition is essential."

"A gompromise," protested Sir Esdras. "Subbose you hof nod der dime or der obbortunity?"

"How great is this friend?"

"Der greatest friendt you hof," insisted the honourable man vehemently. "Id mags no tifference."

"Come orf it," urged Mr. Sankin. "A Britisher doesn't let 'is best pal dahn."

"Well," drawled George Y. Ulrig, "does an American?"

"You say I am nod Briddish?" fumed Sir Esdras Levy, whiffling. "You hof der imberdinence—"

"Deeky," said the girl sweetly, "you should make up your mind more queekly. Ozairvise ve shall 'ave a quarrel. Now, 'ow do you vote?" Dicky looked round the table. He wondered who had started that fatuous argument. He could have believed that the girl had done it deliberately, judging by the way she was thrusting the casting vote upon him so insistently. But, if that were so, it could only mean . . .

But it didn't matter. With zero hour only a few minutes away, a strange mood of recklessness was upon him. It had started as simple impatience— impatience with the theories of George Y. Ulrig, impatience with the ailments of Mrs. Ulrig. And now it had grown suddenly to a hell-for-leather desperation.

Audrey Perowne had said it. "You should make up your mind more quickly." And Dicky knew that it was true. He realized that he had squandered all his hours of grace on fruitless shilly-shallying which had taken him nowhere. Now he answered in a kind of panic. "No," he said. "I'm against the motion. I'd let down any partners, and smash the most colossal deal under the sun, rather than hurt anyone I loved. Now you know—and I hope you're satisfied."

And he knew, as the last plates were removed, that he was fairly and squarely in the cart. He was certain then that Audrey Perowne had engineered the discussion, with intent to trap him into a statement. Well, she'd got what she wanted.

He was suspect. Hilloran and Audrey must have decided *that* after he'd left her cabin that afternoon. Then why the message before dinner? They'd decided to eliminate him along with the rest. That message must have been a weakness on her part. She must have been banking on his humanity—and she'd inaugurated the argument, and brought him into it, simply to satisfy herself on a stone-cold certainty. All right. . . .

That was just where she'd wrecked her own bet. A grim, vindictive resentment was freezing his heart. She chose to trade on the love he'd confessed—and thereby she lost it. He hated her now, with an increasing hatred. She'd almost taken him in. Almost she'd made him ready to sacrifice his honour and the respect of his friends to save her. And now she was laughing at him.

When he'd answered, she'd smiled. He'd seen it—too late—and even then the meaning of that smile hadn't dawned on him immediately. But he understood it all now. *Fool! Fool! Fool!* he cursed himself savagely and the knowledge that he's so nearly been seduced from his self-respect by such a waster was like a worm in his heart.

"But she doesn't get away with it," he swore savagely to himself. "By God, she doesn't get away with it!"

And savagely that vindictive determination lashed down his first fury to an intensely simmering malevolence. Savagely he cursed the moment's panic that had made him betray himself—speaking from his heart without having fully reckoned all that might be behind the question. And then suddenly he was very cold and watchful. The steward was bringing in the tray of coffee.

As if from a great distance, Dicky Tremayne watched the cups being set before the guests. As each guest accepted his cup, Dicky shifted his eyes to the face above it. He hated nearly all of them. Of the women, Mrs. Ulrig was the only one he could tolerate—for all her preoccupation with the diseases which she imagined afflicted her. Of the men, there were only two whom he found human: Matthew Sankin, the henpecked Cockney who had, somehow, come to be cursed rather than blessed with more money than he knew how to spend, and George Y. Ulrig, the didactic millionaire from the Middle West. The others he would have been delighted to rob at any convenient opportunity—particularly Sir Esdras Levy, an ill-chosen advertisement for a noble race.

Dicky received his cup disinterestedly. His right hand was returning from his hip pocket. Of the two things which it brought with it, he had one under his napkin: the cigarette-case he produced, and offered. The girl caught his eye, but his face was expressionless. An eternity seemed to pass before the first cup was lifted. The others followed. Dicky counted them, stirring his own coffee mechanically. Three more to go . . . two more . . .

Matthew Sankin drank last. He alone dared to comment. "Funny taste in this cawfy," he said.

"It tastes good to me," said Audrey Perowne, having tasted.

And Dicky Tremayne, watching her, saw something in her eyes which he could not interpret. It seemed to be meant for him, but he hadn't the least idea what it was meant to be. A veiled mockery? A challenge? A gleam of triumph? Or what? It was a curious look. Blind. . . .

Then he saw Lady Levy half rise from her chair, clutch at her head, and fall sprawling across the table.

"Fainted," said Matthew Sankin, on his feet. "It's a bit stuffy in here—I've just noticed. . . ."

Dicky sat still, and watched the man's eyes glaze open, and saw him fall before he could speak again. They fell one by one, while Dicky sat motionless, watching, with the sensation of being a spectator at a play. Dimly he appreciated the strangeness of the scene; dimly he heard the voices, and the smash of crockery swept from the table; but he himself was aloof, alone with his thoughts, and his right hand held his automatic pistol hidden under his napkin. He was aware that Ulrig was shaking him by the shoulder, babbling again and again: "Doped—that coffee was doped—some goldurned son of a coot!"—until the American in his turn crumpled to the floor. And then Dicky and the girl were alone, she standing at her end of the table and Dicky sitting at his end with the gun on his knee.

That queer blind look was still in her eyes. She said, in a hushed voice: "Dicky—"

"I should laugh now," said Dicky. "You needn't bother to try and keep a straight face any longer. And in a few minutes you'll have nothing to laugh about—so I should laugh now.''

"I only took a sip," she said.

"I see the rest was split," said Dicky. "Have some of mine."

She was working round the table towards him, holding on the backs of the swivel chairs. He never moved. "Dicky, did you mean what you answered—just now?''

"I *did*. I suppose I might mean it still, if the conditions were fulfilled. You'll remember that I said—*anyone I loved*. That doesn't apply here. Last night, I said I loved you. I apologize for the lie. I don't love you. I never could. But I thought—'' He paused, and then drove home the taunt with all the stony contempt that was in him: "I thought it would amuse me to make a fool of you.''

He might have struck her across the face. But he was without remorse. He still sat and watched her, with the impassivity of a graven image, till she spoke again. "I sent you that note—''

"Because you thought you had a sufficient weapon in my love. Exactly. I understand that.''

She seemed to be keeping her feet by an effort of will. Her eyelids were drooping, and he saw tears under them. "Who are you?'' she asked.

"Dicky Tremayne is my real name," he said, "and I am one of the Saint's friends.''

She nodded so that her chin touched her chest.

"And—I—suppose—you—doped—my coffee,'' she said, foolishly, childishly, in that small hushed voice that he had to strain to hear; and she slid down beside the chair she was holding and fell on her face without another word.

Dicky Tremayne looked down at her in a kind of numb perplexity, with the ice of a merciless vengefulness holding him chilled and unnaturally calm. He looked down at her, at her crumpled dress, at her bare white arms, at the tousled crop of golden hair tumbled disorderly over her head by the fall, and he was like a figure of stone.

But within him something stirred and grew and fought with the foundations of his calm. He fought back at it, hating it, but it brought him slowly up from his chair at last, till he stood erect, still looking down at her, with his napkin fallen to his feet and the gun naked in his right hand. "Audrey!" he cried suddenly.

His back was to the door. He heard the step behind him, but he could not move quicker than Hilloran's tongue. "Stand still!" rapped Hilloran.

Dicky moved only his eyes.

These he raised to the clock in front of him, and saw that it was twenty minutes past nine.

9

"DROP THAT GUN," said Hilloran. Dicky dropped the gun.

"Kick it away." Dicky kicked it away.

"Now you can turn round," Dicky turned slowly.

Hilloran, with his own gun in one hand and Dicky's gun in the other, was leaning back against the bulkhead by the door with a sneer of triumph on his face. Outside the door waited a file of seamen. Hilloran motioned them in.

"Of course, I was expecting this," said Dicky.

"Mother's Bright Boy, you are," said Hilloran.

He turned to the seamen, pointing with his gun.

"Frisk him and tie him up."

"I'm not fighting," said Dicky. He submitted to the search imperturbably. The scrap of paper in his pocket was found and taken to Hilloran, who waived it aside after one glance at it.

"I guessed it was something like that," he said. "Dicky, you'll be glad to hear that I saw her slip it under your door. Lucky for me!"

"Very," agreed Dicky dispassionately. "She must have come as near fooling you as she was to fooling me. We ought to get on well after this."

"Fooling *you!*"

Dicky raised his eyebrows.

"How much did you hear outside that door?"

"Everything."

"Then you must have understood—unless you're a born fool."

"I understand that she double-crossed me, and warned you about the coffee."

"Why d'you think she did that? Because she thought she'd got me under her thumb. Because she thought I was so crazy about her that I was as soundly doped that way as I could have been doped by a gallon of knock-out.' And she was right—then."

The men were moving about with lengths of rope, binding wrists and ankles with methodical efficiency. Already pinioned himself, Dicky witnessed the guests being treated one by one in similar fashion, and remained outwardly unmoved. But his brain was working like lightning.

"When they're all safe," said Hilloran, with a jerk of one gun, "I'm going to ask you some questions—Mr. Dicky Tremayne! You'd better get ready to answer right now, because I shan't be kind to you if you give trouble."

Dicky stood in listless submission. He seemed to be in a kind of stupor. He had been like that ever since Hilloran had disarmed him. Except for the movements of his mouth, and the fact that he remained standing, there might have been no life in him. Everything about him pointed to a paralyzed and fatalistic resignation. "I shan't give any trouble," he said tonelessly. "Can't you understand that I've no further interest in anything—after what I've found out about her?"

Hilloran looked at him narrowly, but the words, and Dicky's slack pose, carried complete conviction. Tremayne might have been half-chloroformed. His apathetic, benumbed indifference was beyond dispute. It hung on him like a cloak of lead. "Have you any friends on board?" asked Hilloran.

"No," said Dicky flatly. "I'm quite alone."

"Is that the truth?"

For a moment Tremayne seemed stung to life.

"Don't be so damned dumb!" he snapped. "I say I'm telling you the truth. Whether you believe me or not, you're getting just as good results this way as you would by torture. You've no way of proving my statements—however you obtain them."

"Are you expecting any help from outside?"

"It was all in the letter you read."

"By aëroplane?"

"Seaplane."

"How many of your gang?"

"Possibly two. Possibly only one."

"At what time?"

"Between eleven and twelve, any night from tonight on. Or at four o'clock any morning. I should have called them by flashing—a red light."

"Any particular signal?"

"No. Just a regular intermittent flash," said Dicky inertly. "There's no catch in it."

Hilloran studied his face curiously. "I'd believe you—if the way you're surrendering wasn't the very opposite of everything that's ever been said about the Saint's gang.''

Tremayne's mouth twitched. "For heaven's sake!'' he burst out seethingly. "Haven't I told you, you poor blamed boob? I'm fed up with the Saint. I'm fed up with everything. I don't give another lonely damn for anything anyone does. I tell you, I was mad about that double-crossing little slut. And now I see what she's really worth, I don't care what happens to her or to me. You can do what you like. Get on with it!''

Hilloran looked round the saloon. By then, everyone had been securely bound except the girl, and the seamen were standing about uncertainly, waiting for further instructions. Hilloran jerked his head in the direction of the door. "Get out,'' he ordered. "There's two people here I want to interview—alone.''

Nevertheless, when the last man had left the room, closing the door behind him, Hilloran did not immediately proceed with the interview. Instead, he pocketed one gun, and produced a large bag of soft leather. With this he went round the room, collecting necklaces, earrings, brooches, rings, studs, bracelets, wallets—till the bag bulged and weighed heavy. Then he added to it the contents of his pockets. More and more jewels slipped into the bag like a stream of glittering hailstones. When he had finished, he had some difficulty in tightening the cords that closed the mouth of the bag.

He balanced it appreciatively on the palm of his hand. "One million dollars,'' he said.

"You're welcome,'' said Dicky.

"Now I'll talk,'' said Hilloran.

He talked unemotionally, and Dicky listened without the least sign of feeling. At the end, he shrugged. "You might shoot me first,'' he suggested.

"I'll consider it.''

No sentence of death could ever have been given or received more calmly. It was a revelation to Dicky, in its way, for he would have expected Hilloran to bluster and threaten luridly. Hilloran, after all, had a good deal to be vindictive about. But the man's restraint was inhuman.

Tremayne's stoicism matched it. Hilloran promised death as he might have promised a drink: Dicky accepted the promise as he might have accepted a drink. Yet he never doubted that it was meant. The very unreality of Hilloran's command of temper made his sincerity more real than any theatrical elaboration could have done. "I should like to ask a last favour,'' said Dicky calmly.

"A cigarette?"

"I shouldn't refuse that. But what I should appreciate most would be the chance to finish telling—her—what I was telling her when you came in."

Hilloran hesitated.

"If you agree," added Dicky callously, "I'd advise you to have her tied up first. Otherwise, she might try to untie me in the hope of saving her own skin. Seriously—we haven't been melodramatic about this to-night, so you might go on in the same way."

"You're plucky," said Hilloran.

Tremayne shrugged. "When you've no further interest in life, death loses its terror."

Hilloran went and picked up a length of rope that had been left over. He tied the girl's wrists behind her back; then he went to the door and called, and two men appeared. "Take those two to my cabin," he said. "You'll remain on guard outside the door." He turned back to Dicky. "I shall signal at eleven. At any time after that, you may expect me to call you out on deck."

"Thank you," said Dicky quietly. The first seaman had picked up Audrey Perowne, and Dicky followed him out of the saloon. The second brought up the rear. The girl was laid down on the bunk in Hilloran's cabin. Dicky kicked down the folding seat and made himself as comfortable as he could. The men withdrew, closing the door.

Dicky looked out of the porthold and waited placidly. It was getting dark. The cabin was in twilight; and, beyond the porthold, a faintly luminous blue-grey dusk was deepening over the sea. Sometimes he could hear the tramp of footsteps passing over the deck above. Apart from that, there was no sound but the murmuring undertone of slithering waters slipping past the hull, and the vibration, felt rather than heard, of the auxiliary engines. It was all strangely peaceful. And Dicky waited. After a long time, the girl sighed and moved. Then she lay still again. It was getting so dark that he could hardly see her face as anything but a pale blur in the shadow. But presently she said softly: "So it worked."

"What worked?"

"The coffee."

He said. "I had nothing to do with that."

"Almost neat butyl, it was," she said. "That was clever. I guessed my own coffee would be doped of course. I put the idea into Hilloran's head, because it's always helpful to know how you're going to be attacked. But I didn't think it'd be as strong as that. I thought it'd be safe to sip it.''

"Won't you believe that I didn't do it, Audrey?"

"I don't care. It was somebody clever who thought of catching me out with my own idea."

He said: "I didn't do it, Audrey."

Then for a time there was silence.

Then she said: "My hands are tied."

"So are mine."

"He got you as well?"

"Easily. Audrey, how awake are you?"

"I'm quite awake now," she said. "Just very tired. And my head's splitting. But that doesn't matter. Have you got anything else to say?"

"Audrey, do you know who I am?"

"I know. You're one of the Saint's gang. You told me. But I knew it before."

"You knew it before?"

"I've known it for a long time. As soon as I noticed that you weren't quite an ordinary crook, I made inquiries—on my own, without anyone knowing. It took a long time, but I did it. Didn't you meet at a flat in Brook Street?"

Dicky paused. "Yes," he said slowly. "That's true. Then why did you keep it quiet?"

"That," she said, "is my very own business."

"All the time I was with you, you were in danger—yet you deliberately kept me with you."

"I chose to take the chance. That was because I loved you."

"You what?"

"I loved you," she said wearily. "Oh, I can say it quite safely now. And I will, for my own private satisfaction. You hear me, Dicky Tremayne? I loved you. I suppose you never thought I could have the feelings of an ordinary woman. But I did. I had it worse than an ordinary woman has it. I've always lived recklessly, and I loved recklessly. The risk was worth it—as long as you were with me. But I never thought you cared for me, till last night. . . ."

"Audrey, you tell me that!"

"Why not? It makes no difference now. We can say what we like—and there are no consequences. What exactly is going to happen to us?"

"My friends are coming in a seaplane. I told Hilloran, and he proposes to double-cross the crew. He's got all the jewels. He's going to give my signal. When the seaplane arrives, he's going to row out with me in a boat. My friends will be told that I'll be shot if they don't obey. Naturally, they'll obey—they'll put themselves in his hands, because they're that sort of fool. And Hilloran will board the seaplane and fly away—with you. He knows how to handle an aëroplane.''

"Couldn't you have told the crew that?"

"What for? One devil's better than twenty."

"And what happens to you?"

"I go over this side with a lump of lead tied to each foot. Hilloran's got a grudge to settle—and he's going to settle it. He was so calm about it when he told me that I knew he meant every word. He's a curious type," said Dicky meditatively. "I wish I'd studied him more. Your ordinary crook would have been noisy and nasty about it, but there's nothing like that about Hilloran. You'd have thought it was the same thing to him as squashing a fly."

There was another silence, while the cabin grew darker still. Then she said: "What are you thinking, Dicky?"

"I'm thinking," he said, "how suddenly things can change. I loved you. Then, when I thought you were trading on my love, and laughing at me up your sleeve all the time, I hated you. And then, when you fell down in the saloon, and you lay so still, I knew nothing but that I loved you whatever you did, and that all the hell you could give me was nothing, because I had touched your hand and heard your blessed voice and seen you smile." She did not speak. "But I lied to Hilloran," he said. "I told him nothing more than that my love had turned to hate, and not that my hate had turned back to love again. He believed me. I asked to be left alone with you before the end, to hurl my dying contempt on you— and he consented. That again makes him a curious type—but I knew he'd do it. That's why we're here now."

"Why did you do that?"

"So that I could tell you the truth, and try to make you tell me the truth—and, perhaps, find some way out with you."

The darkness had become almost the darkness of night. She said, far away: "I couldn't make up my mind. I kept on putting myself off and putting myself off, and in order to do that I *had* to trade on your love. But I forced you into that argument at dinner to find out how great your love could be. That was a woman's vanity—and I've paid for it. And I told Hilloran to dope your coffee, and told you not to drink it, so that you'd be ready to surprise him and hold him up when he thought you were doped. I was going to double-cross him, and then leave the rest in your hands, because I couldn't make up my mind.''

''It's a queer story, isn't it?'' said Dicky Tremayne.

''But I've told you the truth now,'' she said. ''And I tell you that if I can find the chance to throw myself out of the boat, or out of the seaplane, I'm going to take it. Because I love you.'' He was silent. ''I killed Morganheim,'' she said, ''because I had a sister—once.'' He was very quiet. ''Dicky Tremayne,'' she said, ''didn't you say you loved me—once?''

He was on his feet. She could see him.

''That was the truth.''

''Is it—still—true?''

''It will always be true,'' he answered; and he was close beside her, on his knees beside the bunk. He was so close beside her that he could kiss her on the lips.

10

SIMON TEMPLAR SAT at the controls of the tiny seaplane and stared thoughtfully across the water. The moon had not yet risen, and the parachute flares he had thrown out to land had been swallowed up into extinction by the sea. But he could see, a cable's length away, the lights of the yacht riding sulkily on a slight swell; and the lamp in the stern of the boat that was stealing darkly across the intervening stretch of water was reflected a thousand times by a thousand ripples, making a smear of dancing luminance across the deep.

He was alone. And he was glad to be alone, for undoubtedly something funny was going to happen. He had himself, after much thought, written Patricia's letter to Dicky Tremayne, and he was satisfied that it had been explicit enough. ''My eyes are red from weeping for you.'' It couldn't have been plainer. Red light—danger. A babe in arms couldn't have missed it.

And yet, when he had flown nearer, he had seen the yacht was not moving; and his floats had hardly licked the first flurry of spray from the sea before the boat he was watching had put off from the ship's side. He could not know that Dicky had given away that red signal deliberately, hoping that it would keep him on his guard and that the inspiration of the moment might provide for the rest. All the same, the Saint was a good guesser, and he was certainly on his guard. He knew that something very fishy was coming towards him across that piece of fish-pond, and the only question was—what?

Thoughtfully the Saint fingered the butt of the Lewis gun that was mounted on the fuselage behind him. It had not been mounted there when he left San Remo that evening; for the sight of private seaplanes equipped with Lewis guns is admittedly unusual, and may legitimately cause comment. But it was there now. The Saint had locked it onto its special mounting as soon as his machine had come to rest. The tail of the seaplane was turned towards the yacht; and, twisting round in the roomy cockpit, the Saint could comfortably swivel the gun round and keep the sights on the approaching boat.

The boat, by that time, was only twenty yards away.

"Is that you, sonny boy?" called the Saint sharply.

The answering hail came clearly over the water.

"That's me, Saint."

In the dark, the cigarette between the Saint's lips glowed with the steady redness of intense concentration. Then he took his cigarette from his mouth and sighted carefully. "In that case," he said, "you can tell your pals to heave to, Dicky Tremayne. Because, if they come much nearer, they're going to get a lead shower-bath."

The sentence ended in a stuttering burst from the gun; and five tracer bullets hissed through the night like fireflies and cut the water in a straight line directly across the boat's course. The Saint heard a barked command, and the boat lost way; but a laugh followed at once, and another voice spoke.

"It that the Saint?"

The Saint only hesitated an instant. "Present and correct," he said, "complete with halo. What do your friends call you, honeybunch?"

"This is John Hilloran speaking."

"Good evening, John," said the Saint politely.

The boat was close enough for him to be able to make out the figure standing up in the stern, and he drew a very thoughtful bead upon it. A Lewis gun is not the easiest weapon in the world to handle with a microscopic accuracy, but his sights had been picked out with luminous paint, and the standing figure was silhouetted clearly against the reflection in the water of one of the lights along the yacht's deck.

"I'll tell you," said Hilloran, "that I've got your friend at the end of my gun—so don't shoot any more."

"Shoot, and be damned to him!" snapped in Dicky's voice. "I don't care. But Audrey Perowne's here as well, and I'd like her to get away."

"My future wife," said Hilloran, and again his throaty chuckle drifed through the gloom.

Simon Templar took a long pull at his cigarette, and tapped some ash fastidiously into the water. "Well—what's the idea, big boy?"

"I'm coming alongside. When I'm there, you're going to step quietly down into this boat. If you resist, or try any funny business, your friend will pass in his checks."

"Is—that—so?" drawled Simon.

"That's so. I want to meet you—Mr. Saint!"

"Well, well, *well!*" mocked the Saint alertly.

And there and then he had thrust upon him one of the most desperate decisions of a career that continued to exist only by the cool swift making of desperate decisions.

Dicky Tremayne was in that boat, and Dicky Tremayne had somehow or other been stung. That had been fairly obvious ever since the flashing of that red signal. Only the actual details of the stinging had been waiting to be disclosed. Now the Saint knew. And, although the Saint would willingly have stepped into a burning fiery furnace if he thought that by so doing he could help Dicky's getaway, he couldn't see how the principle applied at that moment. Once the Saint stepped down into that that, there would be two of them in the *consommé* instead of one—and what would have been gained?

What, more important, would Hilloran have gained? Why should J. Hilloran be so anxious to increase his collection of Saints? The Saint thoughtfully rolled his cigarette-end between his finger and thumb, and dropped it into the water.

"Why," ruminated the Saint—"because the dear soul wants this blinkin' bus what I'm sitting in. He wants to take it and fly away into the wide world. Now, again—why? Well, there was supposed to be a million dollars' worth of jools in that there hooker. It's quite certain that their original owners haven't got them any longer—it's equally apparent that Audrey Perowne hasn't got them, or Dicky wouldn't have said that he wanted her to get away—and, clearly, Dicky hasn't got them. Therefore, Hilloran's got them. And the crew will want some of them. We don't imagine Hilloran proposes to load up the whole crew on this airy-plane for their getaway: therefore, he only wants to load up himself and

Audrey Perowne—leaving the ancient mariners behind to whistle for their share. Ha! Joke. . . .''

And there seemed to be just one solitary way of circumventing the opposition. Now, Hilloran wasn't expecting any fight at all. He'd had several drinks, for one thing, since the hold-up, and he was very sure of himself. He'd got everyone cold—Tremayne, Audrey, the crew, the Saint, and the jewels. He didn't see how anyone could get out of it.

He wasn't shaking with the anticipation of triumph, because he wasn't that sort of crook. He simply felt rather satisfied with his own ingenuity. Not that he was preening himself. He found it as natural to win that game as he would have found it natural to win a game of stud poker from a deaf, dumb, and blind imbecile child. That was all.

Of course, he didn't know the Saint except by reputation, and mere word-of-mouth reputations never cut much ice with Hilloran. He wasn't figuring on the Saint's uncanny intuition of the psychology of the crook, nor on the Saint's power of lightning logic and lightning decision. Nor had he reckoned on that quality of reckless audacity which lifted the Saint as far above the rut of ordinary adventurers as Walter Hagen is above the man who has taken up golf to amuse himself in his old age—a quality which infected and inspired also the men whom the Saint led.

There was one desperate solution to the problem, and Hilloran ought to have seen it. But he hadn't seen it—or, if he had, he'd called it too desperate to be seriously considered. Which was where he was wrong to all eternity.

He stood up in the stern of the boat, a broad dominant figure in black relief against the shimmering waters, and called out again: "I'm coming alongside now, Saint, if you're ready."

"I'm ready," said the Saint; and the butt of the Lewis gun was cuddled into his shoulder as steadily as if it had lain on a rock.

Hilloran gave an order, and the sweeps dipped again. Hilloran remained standing. If he knew what happened next, he had no time to coordinate his impressions. For the harsh stammer of the Lewis gun must have merged and mazed his brain with the sharp tearing agony that ripped through his chest, and the numbing darkness that blinded his eyes must have been confused with the numbing weakness that sapped all the strength from his body, and he could not have heard the choking of the breath of his throat, and the cold clutch of the waters that closed over him and dragged him down could have meant nothing to him at all. . . .

But Dicky Tremayne, staring stupidly at the widening ripples that marked the spot where Hilloran had been swallowed up by the sea, heard the Saint's hail. "Stand by for the mermaids!"

And at once there was a splash such as a seal makes in plunging from a high rock, and there followed the churning sounds of a strong swimmer racing through the water.

The two men, who were the boat's crew, seemed for a moment to sit in a trance; then, with a curse, one of them bent to his oars. The other followed suit.

Dicky knew that it was his turn. He came to his feet and hurled himself forward, throwing himself anyhow across the back of the man nearest to him. The man was flung sideways and over onto his knees, so that the boat lurched periously. Then Dicky had scrambled up again, somehow, with bruised shins, and feet that seemed to weigh a ton, and launched himself at the back of the next man in the same way.

The first man whom he had knocked over struck at him, with an oath, but Dicky didn't care. His hands were tied behind his back, but he kicked out, swung his shoulders, butted with his head—fought like a madman. His only object was to keep the men from any effective rowing until the Saint could reach them.

And then, hardly a foot from Dicky's eyes, a hand came over the gunwale, and he lay still, panting. A moment later the Saint had hauled himself over the side, almost overturning the boat as he did so. "O.K., sonny boy!" said the Saint, in that inimitably cheerful way that was like new life to those who heard it on their side, and drove his fist into the face of the nearest man.

The other man felt the point of a knife prick his throat. "You heard your boss telling you to row over to the seaplane," remarked the Saint gently, "and I'm very hot on carrying out the wishes of the dead. Put your back into it!"

He held the knife in place with one hand, with the other hand he reached for the second little knife which he carried strapped to his calf. "This way, Dicky boy, and we'll have you loose in no time." It was so. And then the boat was alongside the seaplane, and Dicky had freed the girl.

The Saint helped them up, and then went down to the stern of the boat and picked up the bag which lay fallen there. He tossed it into the cockpit, and followed it himself. From that point of vantage he leaned over to address the crew of the boat.

"You've heard all you need to know," he said. "I am the Saint. Remember me in your prayers. And when you've got the yacht to a port, and you're faced with the problem of accounting for all that's happened to your passengers—remember me again. Because to-morrow morning every port in the Mediterranean will be watching for you, and on every quay there'll be detectives waiting to take you away to the place where you belong. So remember the Saint!'' And Simon Templar roused the engine of the seaplane and began to taxi over the water as the first shot spat out from the yacht's deck and went whining over the sea.

A week later, Chief Inspector Teal paid another visit to Brook Street. ''I'm very much obliged to you, Mr. Templar,'' he said. ''You'll be interested to hear that *Indomitable* picked up the *Corsican Maid* as she was trying to slip through the Straits last night. They didn't put up much of a scrap.''

''You don't say!'' murmured the Saint mockingly. ''But have some beer.''

Mr. Teal sank ponderously into his chair. ''Fat man,'' he declined, ''didn't ought to drink—if you won't be offended. But listen, sir—what happened to the girl who was the leader of the gang? And what happened to the jewels?''

''You'll hear to-day,'' said the Saint happily, ''that the jewels have been received by a certain London hospital. The owners will be able to get them back from there, and I leave the reward they'll contribute to the hospital to their own consciences. But I don't think public opinion will let them be stingy. As for the money that was collected in cash, some twenty-five thousand dollars. I—er—well, that's difficult to trace, isn't it?''

Mr. Teal nodded sleepily. ''And Audrey Perowne, *alias* the Countess Anusia Marova?''

''Were you wanting to arrest her?''

''There's a warrant—''

The Saint shook his head sadly. ''What a waste of time, energy, paper, and ink! You ought to have told me that before. As it is, I'm afraid I—er—that is, she was packed off three days ago to a country where extradition doesn't work—I'm afraid I shouldn't know how to intercept her. Isn't that a shame?''

Teal grimaced. ''However,'' said the Saint, ''I understand that she's going to reform and marry and settle down, so you needn't worry about what she'll do next.''

''How do you know that?'' asked Teal suspiciously.

The Saint's smile was wholly angelic. He flung out his hand.

''A little Dicky bird,'' he said musically, ''a little Dicky bird told me so this morning.''

The Saint Closes the Case

To
JEAN and JEANNINE
from whom I have learned so much

Contents

Prelude

IT IS SAID that in these hectic days no item of news is capable of holding the interest of the public for more than a week; wherefore journalists and news editors age swiftly, and become prematurely bald and bad-tempered, Tatcho and Kruschen availing them naught. A new sensation must be provided from day to day, and each sensation must eclipse its predecessor, till the dictionary is bled dry of superlatives, and the imagination pales before the task of finding or inventing for to-morrow a story fantastic and colossal enough to succeed the masterpiece of yesterday.

That the notorious adventurer known as the Saint should have contrived to keep in the public eye for more than three months from the date of his first manifestation, thereby smithereening all records of that kind, was due entirely to his own energy and initiative. The harassed sensationalists of Fleet Street welcomed him with open arms. For a time the fevered hunt for novelty could take a rest. The Saint himself did everything in that line that the most exacting editor could have asked for—except, of course, that he failed to provide the culminating sensation of his own arrest and trial. But each of his adventures was more audacious than the last, and he never gave the interest aroused by his latest activity time to die down before he burst again upon a startled public with a yet more daring coup.

And the same enterprising lawlessness continued for over three months, in the course of which time he brought to a triumphant conclusion some twenty raids upon the persons and property of evildoers.

Thus it came to pass that in those three months the name of the Saint gathered about itself an aura of almost supernatural awe and terror, so that men who had for years boasted that the law could not touch them began to walk in fear; and the warning of the Saint—a ridiculous picture of a little man with one-dimensional body and limbs, such as children draw, but wearing above his blank round head an absurd halo such as it rarely occurs to children to add to their drawings—delivered to a man's door in a plain envelope, was found to be as fatal as any sentence ever signed by a Judge of the High Court. Which was exactly what the Saint himself had desired should happen. It amused him very much.

For the most part, he worked secretly and unseen, and his victims could give the police nothing tangible in the way of clues by which he might have been traced. Yet sometimes it was inevitable that he should be known to the man whose downfall he was engineering; and, when that happened, the grim silence of the injured party was one of the most surprising features of the mystery. Chief Inspector Teal, after a number of fruitless attempts, had resigned himself to giving up as a bad job the task of trying to make the victims of the Saint give evidence.

"You might as well try to get a squeak out of a deaf-and-dumb oyster in a tank of chloroform," he told the Commissioner. "Either the Saint never tackles a man on one count unless he's got a second count against him by which he can blackmail him to silence, or else he's found the secret of threatening a man so convincingly that he still believes it the next day—and all the days after that."

His theory was shrewd and sound enough, but it would have been shrewder and sounder and more elaborate if he had been a more imaginative man; but Mr. Teal had little confidence in things he could not see and take hold of, and he had never had a chance of watching the Saint in action.

There were, however, other occasions when the Saint had no need to fall back upon blackmail or threats to insure the silence of those with whose careers he interfered.

There was, for instance, the case of a man named Golter, an anarchist and incorrigible firebrand, whose boast it was that he had known the inside of every prison in Europe. He belonged to no political faction, and apparently had no gospel to forward except his own mania for destruction; but he was anything but a harmless lunatic.

He was the leader of a society known as the Black Wolves, nearly every member of which had at some time or another served a heavy sentence for some kind of political offence—which, more often than not, consisted of an attempted assassination, usually by bomb.

The reason for such societies, and the mentality of their adherents, will always provide an interesting field of speculation for the psychiatrist; but occasions will arise when the interest ceases to be the abstract diversion of the scientist, and becomes the practical problem of those whose business it is to keep peace under the law.

The law awoke to this fact, and simultaneously to a rather alarmed recognition of the existence of the Black Wolves, after a week in which two factories in the North of England were the scenes of explosions which resulted in no little loss of life, and the bullet of an undiscovered sniper actually grazed across the back of the Home Secretary as he stepped into his car outside the House of Commons.

The law found Golter; but the man who had been detailed to follow him and report on his movements somehow contrived to lose him on the afternoon in which a Crown Prince drove in state through the streets of London on his way to a luncheon given by the Lord Mayor.

The procession was arranged to pass by way of the Strand and Fleet Street to the City. From a tiny office which he had rented for the purpose in Southampton Row, of which the police knew nothing, Golter had found an easy way to the roofs of the houses on the north side of Fleet Street. He sat there, in a more or less comfortable position, among the chimney-stacks, from which he could look down and see the street below, while armed men scoured London for a trace of him, and a worried Commissioner ordered a doubling of the plain-clothes detectives stationed along the route.

Golter was a careful and a thoughtful man, and he had a fair grounding in the principles of dynamics. He knew to an inch how high he was from the ground, and he had calculated exactly how many seconds a bomb would take to fall to the street; the fuses of the Mills bombs in his pockets were adjusted accordingly. Again, in Fleet Street, a little farther down towards the Strand, he had measured the distance between two lamp-posts. With the aid of a stop-watch he would discover how long the leading car took to pass between them; then, by consulting an elaborate chart which he had prepared, he would be able to learn at once, without further calculation, exactly at what instant he had to launch his bombs so that they would fall directly into the back of the Crown Prince's car as it passed. Golter was proud of the scientific precision with which he had worked out every detail.

He smoked a cigarette, drumming his heels gently against the leads. It was fifteen minutes before the procession was due to arrive at that point, according to the official time-table, and already the street below was packed with a dense crowd which overflowed the pavements and wound hampering tentacles into the stream of traffic. The mass of people below looked like ants, Golter thought. Bourgeois insects. He amused himself by picturing the ant-like confusion that would follow the detonation of his three bombs. . . .

"Yes, it should be an interesting spectacle."

Golter's head snapped round as though it had been jerked by an invisible wire.

He had heard nothing of the arrival of the man who now stood over him, whose gentle, drawling voice had broken into his meditations far more shatteringly than any explosion could have done. He saw a tall, trim, lean figure in a grey fresco suit of incredible perfection, with a soft grey felt hat whose wide brim shaded pleasant blue eyes. This man might have posed for any illustration of the latest and smartest effort of Savile Row in the way of gents' natty outfitting—that is, if he could have been persuaded to discard the automatic pistol, which is not generally considered to form an indispensable adjunct to What the Well-Dressed Man will Wear this Season.

"Extraordinarily interesting," repeated the unknown, with his blue eyes gazing down in a rather dreamy way at the throng a hundred feet below. "From a purely artistic point of view, it's a pity we shan't be able to watch it."

Golter's right hand was sidling towards a bulging pocket. The stranger, with his automatic swinging in a lazy arc that centred over Golter's stomach, encouraged the movement.

"But leave the pins in, Beautiful," he murmured, "and pass 'em to me one by one. . . . That's a good boy!"

He took the bombs in his left hand as Golter passed them over, and handed them to someone whom Golter could not see—a second man who stood behind a chimney-stack.

A minute passed, in which Golter stood with his hands hanging loosely at his sides, waiting for a chance to make a grab at the gun which the stranger held with such an affectation of negligence. But the chance never came.

Instead, came a hand from behind the chimney-stack—a hand holding a bomb. The stranger took the bomb and handed it back to Golter.

"Put it in your pocket," he directed.

The second and third followed, and Golter, with his coat once again dragged out of shape by the weight, stood staring at the stranger, who, he thought, must be a detective, and who yet behaved in such an incomprehensible manner.

"What did you do that for?" he demanded suspiciously.

"My own reasons," answered the other calmly. "I am now leaving you. Do you mind?"

Suspicion—fear—perplexity—all these emotions chased and mingled with one another over Golter's unshaven face. Then inspiration dawned in his pale eyes.

"So you aren't a busy!"

The stranger smiled.

"Unfortunately for you—no. You may have heard of me. I am called the Saint. . . ."

His left hand flashed in and out of his coat pocket in a swift movement, and Golter, in the grip of a sudden paralysis of terror, stared as if hypnotised while the Saint chalked his grotesque trade-mark on the chimney-stack.

Then the Saint spoke again.

"You are not human. You are a destroyer—an insane killer without any justification but your own lust for blood. If you had had any motive, I might have handed you over to the police, who are at this moment combing London for you. I am not here to judge any man's creed. But for you there can be no excuse. . . ."

He had vanished when Golter looked round for him, wondering why the condemnation did not continue, and the roof was deserted. The Saint had a knack of disappearing like that.

The procession was approaching. Golter could hear the cheering growing rapidly louder, like the roar of many waters suddenly released from burst flood-gates. He peered down. A hundred yards away he could see the leading car crawling through the lane of human ants.

His brain was still reeling to encompass the understanding of what the Saint had come to do. The Saint had been there, accusing—and then he had gone, giving Golter back his bombs. Golter could have believed himself to have been the victim of an hallucination. But the fantastic sketch on the chimney-stack remained to prove that he had not been dreaming.

With an hysterical sweep of his arm, he smeared his sleeve over the drawing, and took from his pocket his stop-watch and the time-chart he had made. The leading car had just reached the first of the two lamp-posts on which he had based his calculations. He watched it in a kind of daze.

The Crown Prince drove in the third car. Golter recognised the uniform. The Prince was saluting the crowd.

Golter found himself trembling as he took the first bomb from his pocket and drew the pin; but he threw it on the very instant that his stop-watch and chart indicated.

"The true details of the case," wrote the *Daily Record*, some days later, "are likely to remain a mystery for ever, unless the Saint should one day elect to come out into the open and elucidate them. Until then the curiosity of the public must be satisfied with the findings of the committee of Scotland Yard experts who have been investigating the affair—'that in some way the Saint succeeded in so tampering with the fuses of the Mills bombs with which Golter intended to attempt the life of the Crown Prince, that they exploded the moment he released the spring handle, thereby blowing him to pieces. . . .'

"Whatever the opinions which may be expressed concerning the arrogance of this gentleman who presumes to take the law into his own lawless hands, it cannot be denied that in this case his intervention undoubtedly saved the life of our royal guest; and few will be found to deny that justice was done—though perhaps it was justice of too poetic a character to be generally accepted as a precedent. . . ."

With this sensational climax, which put the name of the Saint on the lips of every man and woman in the civilised world, came the end of a clearly defined chapter in his history.

The sensation died down, as the most amazing sensations will die down for lack of re-stimulation. In an open letter which was published in every newspaper throughout Europe, the Crown Prince offered his thanks to the unknown, and promised that the debt should not be forgotten if at any time the Saint should stand in need of help from high places. The British Government followed almost immediately with the offer of a free pardon for all past offences on condition that the Saint revealed himself and took an oath to turn his energy and ingenuity into more legitimate channels. The only answer was a considered letter of acknowledgement and regretful refusal, posted simultaneously to all the leading news-agencies.

"Unfortunately," wrote the Saint, "I am convinced, and my friends with me, that for us to disband at the very moment when our campaign is beginning to justify itself in the crime statistics of London—and (which is even more important) in those more subtle offences against the moral code about which there can be no statistics—would be an act of indefensible cowardice on my part. We cannot be tempted by the mere promise of safety for ourselves to betray the motive which brought us together. The game is more than the player of the game. . . . Also, speaking for myself, I should find a respectable life intolerably dull. It isn't easy to get out of the rut these days: you have to be a rebel, and you're more likely to end up in Wormwood Scrubs than Westminster Abbey. But I believe, as I have never believed anything before, that I am on the right road. The things of value are the common, primitive things. Justice is good—when it's done fanatically. Fighting is good—when the thing you fight for is simple and sane and you love it. And danger is good—it wakes you up, and makes you live ten times more keenly. And vulgar swashbuckling may easily be the best of all—because it stands for a magnificent belief in all those things, a superb faith in the glamour that civilisation is trying to sneer at as a delusion and a snare. . . . As long as the ludicrous laws of this country refuse me these, I shall continue to set those laws at defiance. The pleasure of applying my own treatment to the human sores whose persistent festering offends me is one which I will not be denied. . . ."

And yet, strangely enough, an eagerly expectant public waited in vain for the Saint to follow up this astonishing manifesto. But day after day went by, and still he held his hand; so that those who had walked softly, wondering when the uncanny omniscience of the Unknown would find them out, began to lift up their heads again and boast themselves with increasing assurance, saying that the Saint was afraid.

A fortnight grew into a month, and the Saint was rapidly passing into something like a dim legend of bygone ages.

And then, one afternoon in June, yelling newsboys spread a special edition of the *Evening Record* through the streets of London, and men and women stood in impatient and excited groups on the pavements and read the most astounding story of the Saint that had ever been given to the Press.

It was the story that is told again here, as it has already been retold, by now, half a hundred times. But now it is taken from a different and more intimate angle, and some details are shown which have not been told before.

It is the story of how Simon Templar, known to many as the Saint (plausibly from his initials, but more probably from his saintly way of doing the most unsaintly things), came by chance upon a thread which led him to the most amazing adventure of his career. And it is also the story of Norman Kent, who was his friend, and how at one moment in that adventure he held the fate of two nations, if not of all Europe, in his hands; how he accounted for that stewardship; and how, one quiet summer evening, in a house by the Thames, with no melodrama and no heroics, he fought and died for an idea.

1

How Simon Templar Went for a Drive and Saw a Strange Sight

SIMON TEMPLAR READ newspapers rarely, and when he did read them he skimmed through the pages as quickly as possible and gleaned information with a hurried eye. Most of the matter offered in return for his penny was wasted on him. He was not in the least interested in politics; the announcement that the wife of a Walthamstow printer had given birth to quadruplets found him unmoved; articles such as "A Man's Place is in the Home" (by Anastasia Gowk, the brilliant authoress of *Passion in Pimlico*) left him completely cold. But a quarter-column, with photograph, in a paper he bought one evening for the racing results chanced to catch his roving gaze, and roused a very faint flicker of attention.

Two coincidences led him from that idly assimilated item of news to a red-hot scent, the fascination of which for him was anything but casual.

The first came the next day, when, finding himself at Ludgate Circus towards one o'clock, it occurred to him to call in at the Press Club in the hope of finding someone he knew. He found Barney Malone, of the *Clarion,* and was promptly invited to lunch, which was exactly what he had been looking for. The Saint had an ingrained prejudice against lunching alone.

Conversation remained general throughout the meal, except for one bright interlude.

"I suppose there's nothing new about the Saint?" asked Simon innocently, and Barney Malone shook his head.

"He seems to have gone out of business."

"I'm only taking a rest," Simon assured him. "After the calm, the storm. You wait for the next scoop."

Simon Templar always insisted on speaking of the Saint as "I"—as if he himself was that disreputable outlaw. Barney Malone, for all his familiarity with Simon's eccentric sense of humour, was inclined to regard this affectation as a particularly aimless pleasantry.

It was half an hour later, over coffee, that the Saint recalled the quarter-column which had attracted his attention, and asked a question about it.

"You may be quite frank with your Uncle Simon," he said. "He knows all the tricks of the trade, and you won't disappoint him a bit if you tell him that the chief sub-editor made it up himself to fill the space at the last moment."

Malone grinned.

"Funnily enough, you're wrong. These scientific discoveries you read about under scare headlines are usually stunt stuff; but if you weren't so uneducated you'd have heard of K. B. Vargan. He's quite mad, but as a scientist his class is A 1 at the Royal Society."

"So there may be something in it?" suggested the Saint.

"There may, or there may not. These inventions have a trick of springing a leak as soon as you take them out of the laboratory and try using them on a large scale. For instance, they had a death-ray years ago that would kill mice at twenty yards, but I never heard of them testing it on an ox at five hundred."

Barney Malone was able to give some supplementary details of Vargan's invention which the sub-editor's blue pencil had cut out as unintelligible to lay public. They were hardly less unintelligible to Simon Templar, whose scientific knowledge stopped a long way short of Einstein, but he listened attentively.

"It's curious that you should refer to it," Malone said, a little later, "because I was only interviewing the man this morning. He burst into the office about eleven o'clock, storming and raving like a lunatic because he hadn't been given the front page."

He gave a graphic description of the encounter.

"But what's the use?" asked the Saint. "There won't be another war for hundreds of years."

"You think so?"

"I'm told so."

Malone's eyebrows lifted in that tolerantly supercilious way in which a journalist's eyebrows will sometimes lift when an ignorant outsider ventures an opinion on world affairs.

"If you live for another six months," he said, "I shall expect to see you in uniform. Or will you conscientiously object?"

Simon tapped a cigarette deliberately on his thumbnail.

"You mean that?"

"I'm desperately serious. We're nearer to these things than the rest of the public, and we see them coming first. In another few months the rest of England will see it coming. A lot of funny things have been happening lately.''

Simon waited, suddenly keyed up to interest; and Barney Malone sucked thoughtfully at his pipe, and presently went on:

''In the last month, three foreigners have been arrested, tried, and imprisoned for offences against the Official Secrets Act. In other words, espionage. During the same period, four Englishmen have been similarly dealt with in different parts of Europe. The foreign governments concerned have disowned the men we've pinched; but since a government always disowns its spies as soon as they get into trouble, on principle, no one ever believes it. Similarly, we have disclaimed the four Englishmen, and, naturally, nobody believes us, either—and yet I happen to know that it's true. If you appreciate really subtle jokes, you might think that one over, and laugh next time I see you.''

The Saint went home in a thoughtful mood.

He had a genius that was all his own—an imaginative genius that would take a number of ordinary facts, all of which seemed to be totally unconnected, and none of which, to the eye of anyone but himself, would have seemed very remarkable, and read them into a sign-post pointing to a mystery. Adventure came to him not so much because he sought it as because he brazenly expected it. He believed that life was full of adventure, and he went forward in the full blaze and surge of that belief. It has been said of a man very much like Simon Templar that he was ''a man born with the sound of trumpets in his ears''; that saying might almost equally well have been said of the Saint, for he also, like Michael Paladin, had heard the sound of the trumpet, and had moved ever afterwards in the echoes of the sound of the trumpet, in such a mighty clamour of romance that at least one of his friends had been moved to call him the last hero, in desperately earnest jest.

'' 'From battle, murder, and sudden death, Good Lord, deliver us!' '' he quoted once. ''How can any live man ask for that? Why, they're meat and drink—they're the things that make life worth living! *Into* battle, murder, and sudden death, Good Lord, deliver me up to the neck! That's what I say. . . .''

Thus spoke the Saint, that man of superb recklessness and strange heroisms and impossible ideals; and went on to show, as few others of his age have shown, that a man inspired can swashbuckle as well with cloak and stick as any cavalier of history with cloak and sword, that there can be as much chivalry in the setting of a modern laugh as there can ever have been in the setting of a medieval lance, that a true valour and venture finds its way to fulfilment, not so much through the kind of world into which it happens to be born, as through the heart with which it lives.

But even he could never have guessed into what a strange story this genius and this faith of his were to bring him.

On what he had chanced to read, and what Barney Malone had told him, the Saint built in his mind a tower of possibilities whose magnitude, when it was completed, awed even himself. And then, because he had the priceless gift of taking the products of his vivid imagination at their practical worth, he filed the fancy away in his mind as an interesting curiosity, and thought no more about it.

Too much sanity is sometimes dangerous.

Simon Templar was self-conscious about his imagination. It was the one kind of self-consciousness he had, and certainly he kept it a secret which no one would have suspected. Those who knew him said that he was reckless to the point of vain bravado; but they were never more mistaken. If he had chosen to argue the point, he would have said that his style was, if anything, cramped by too much caution.

But in this case caution was swept away, and imagination triumphantly vindicated, by the second coincidence.

This came three days later, when the Saint awoke one morning to find that the showery weather which had hung over England for a week had given place to cloudless blue skies and brilliant sunshine. He hung out of his bedroom window and sniffed the air suspiciously, but he could smell no rain. Forthwith he decided that the business of annoying criminals could be pardonably neglected while he took out his car and relaxed in the country.

"Darling Pat," said the Saint, "it'd be a crime to waste a day like this!"

"Darling Simon," wailed Patricia Holm, "you know we'd promised to have dinner with the Hannassays."

"Very darling Pat," said the Saint, "won't they be disappointed to hear that we've both been suddenly taken ill after last night's binge?"

So they went, and the Saint enjoyed his holiday with the comfortable conviction that he had earned it.

They eventually dined at Cobham, and afterwards sat for a long time over cigarettes and coffee and matters of intimate moment which have no place here. It was eleven o'clock when the Saint set the long nose of his Furillac on the homeward road.

Patricia was happily tired; but the Saint drove very well with one hand.

It was when they were still rather more than a mile from Esher that the Saint saw the light, and thoughtfully braked the car to a standstill.

Simon Templar was cursed, or blessed, with an insatiable inquisitiveness. If ever he saw anything that trespassed by half an inch over the boundaries of the purely normal and commonplace, he was immediately fired with the desire to find out the reason for such erratic behaviour. And it must be admitted that the light had been no ordinary light.

The average man would undoubtedly have driven on somewhat puzzledly, would have been haunted for a few days by a vague and irritating perplexity, and would eventually have forgotten the incident altogether. Simon Templar has since considered, in all sober earnestness, what might have been the consequences of his being an average man at that moment, and has stopped appalled at the vista of horrors opened up by the thought.

But Simon Templar was not an average man, and the gift of minding his own business had been left out of his make-up. He slipped into reverse and sent the car gently back a matter of thirty yards to the end of a lane which opened off the main road.

A little way down this lane, between the trees, the silhouette of a gabled house loomed blackly against the star-powdered sky, and it was in an upper window of this house that the Saint had seen the light as he passed. Now he skilfully lighted a cigarette with one hand, and stared down the lane. The light was still there. The Saint contemplated it in silence, immobile as a watching Indian, till a fair, sleepy head roused on his shoulder.

"What is it?" asked Patricia.

"That's what I'd like to know," answered the Saint, and pointed with the glowing end of his cigarette.

The blinds were drawn over that upper window, but the light could be clearly seen behind them—a light of astounding brilliance, a blindingly white light that came and went in regular, rhythmic flashes like intermittent flickers of lightning.

The night was as still as a dream, and at that moment there was no other traffic on that stretch of road. The Saint reached forward and switched off the engine of the Furillac. Then he listened—and the Saint had ears of abnormal sensitiveness—in a quiet so unbroken that he could hear the rustle of the girl's sleeve as she moved her arm.

But the quiet was not silence—it was simply the absence of any isolated noise. There was sound—a sound so faint and soothing that it was no more than a neutral background to a silence. It might have been a soft humming, but it was so soft that it might have been no more than a dim vibration carried on the air.

"A dynamo," said the Saint; and as he spoke he opened the door of the car and stepped out into the road.

Patricia caught his hand.

"Where are you going, Saint?"

Simon's teeth showed white in the Saintly smile.

"I'm going to investigate. A perfectly ordinary citizen might be running a dynamo to manufacture his own electric light—although this dynamo sounds a lot heavier than the breed you usually find in home power plants. But I'm sure no perfectly ordinary citizen uses his dynamo to make electric sparks that size to amuse the children. Life has been rather tame lately, and one never knows. . . ."

"I'll come with you."

The Saint grimaced.

Patricia Holm, he used to say, had given him two white hairs for every day he had known her. Ever since a memorable day in Devonshire, when he had first met her, and the hectic days which followed, when she had joined him in the hunting of the man who was called the Tiger, the Saint had been forcing himself to realise that to try and keep the girl out of trouble was a hopeless task. By this time he was getting resigned to her. She was a law unto herself. She was of a mettle so utterly different to that of any girl he had ever dreamed of, a mettle so much finer and fiercer, that if she had not been so paradoxically feminine with it he would have sworn that she ought to have been a man. She was—well, she was Patricia Holm, and that was that. . . .

"O.K., kid," said the Saint helplessly.

But already she was standing beside him. With a shrug, the Saint climbed back into his seat and moved the car on half a dozen yards so that the lights could not be seen from the house. Then he rejoined her at the corner of the lane.

They went down the lane together.

The house stood in a hedged garden thickly grown with trees. The Saint, searching warily, found the alarm on the gate, and disconnected it with an expert hand before he lifted the latch and let Patricia through to the lawn. From there, looking upwards, they could see that queer, bleak light still glimmering behind the blinds of the upper window.

The front of the house was in darkness, and the ground-floor windows closed and apparently secured. The Saint wasted no time on those, for he was without the necessary instrument to force the catch of a window, and he knew that front doors are invariably solid. Back doors, on the other hand, he knew equally well, are often vulnerable, for the intelligent foresight of the honest householder frequently stops short of grasping the fact that the best-class burglar may on occasion stoop to using the servants' entrance. The Saint accordingly edged round the side of the house, Patricia following him.

They walked over grass, still damp and spongy from the rain that had deluged the country for the past six days. The humming of the dynamo was now unmistakable, and with it could be heard the thrum and whir of the motor that drove it. The noise seemed, at one point, to come from beneath their feet.

Then they rounded the second corner, and the Saint halted so abruptly that Patricia found herself two paces ahead of him.

"This is fun!" whispered the Saint.

And yet by daylight it would have been a perfectly ordinary sight. Many country houses possess greenhouses, and it is even conceivable that an enthusiastic horticulturist might have attached to his house a greenhouse some twenty five yards long, and high enough to give a tall man some four feet of head-room.

But such a greenhouse brightly lighted up at half-past eleven at night is no ordinary spectacle. And the phenomenon becomes even more extraordinary—to an inquisitive mind like the Saint's—when the species of vegetable matter for which such an excellent illumination is provided is screened from the eyes of the outside world by dark curtains closely drawn under the glass.

Simon Templar needed no encouragement to probe further into the mystery, and the girl was beside him when he stepped stealthily to a two-inch gap in the curtains.

A moment later he found Patricia Holm gripping his arm with hands that trembled ever so slightly.

The interior of the greenhouse was bare of pots and plants; for four-fifths of its length it was bare of anything at all. There was a rough concrete floor, and the concrete extended up the sides of the greenhouse for about three feet, thus forming a kind of trough. And at one end of the trough there was tethered a goat.

At the other end of the building, on a kind of staging set on short concrete pillars, stood four men.

The Saint took them in at a glance. Three of them stood in a little group—a fat little man with a bald head and horn-rimmed spectacles, a tall, thin man of about forty-five with a high, narrow forehead and iron-grey hair, and a youngish man with pince-nez and a notebook. The fourth man stood a little apart from them, in front of a complicated switchboard, on which glowed here and there little bulbs like the valves used in wireless telegraphy. He was of middle height, and his age might have been anything from sixty to eighty. His hair was snow-white, and his clothes were shapeless and stained and shabby.

But it was on nothing human or animal in the place that the Saint's gaze concentrated after that first swift survey.

There was something else there, on the concrete floor, between the four men and the goat at the other end. It curled and wreathed sluggishly, lying low on the ground and not rising at all; and yet, though the outside of it was fleecily inert, it seemed as if the interior of the thing whirled and throbbed as with the struggling of a tremendous force pent up in ineffectual turmoil. This thing was like a cloud; but it was like no cloud that ever rode the sky. It was a cloud such as no sane and shining sky had ever seen, a pale violet cloud, a cloud out of hell. And here and there, in the misty violet of its colour, it seemed as if strange little sparks and streaks of fire shot through it like tiny cornets, gleamed momentarily, and were gone, so that the cloud moved and burned as with an inner phosphorescence.

It had been still when the Saint first set eyes on it, but now it moved. It did not spread aimlessly over the floor; it was creeping along purposefully, as though imbued with life. The Saint, afterwards, described it as like a great, ghostly, luminous worm travelling sideways. Stretched out in a long line that reached from side to side of the greenhouse, it humped itself forward in little whirling rushes, and the living power within it seemed to burn more and more fiercely, until the cloud was framed in a faint halo of luminance from the whirl of eye-searing violet at its core.

It had seemed to be creeping at first, but then the Saint saw that that impression had been deceptive. The creeping of the cloud was now the speed of a man running, and it was plain that it could have only one objective. The goat at the end of the trough was cringing against the farthest wall, frozen with terror, staring wild-eyed at the cloud that rolled towards it with the relentlessness of an inrushing tide.

The Saint flashed a lightning glance back at the staging, and divined, without comprehending, why the cloud moved so decisively. The white-haired man was holding in one hand a thing of shining metal rather like a small electric radiator, which he trained on the cloud, moving it from side to side. From this thing seemed to come the propulsive force which drove the cloud along as a controlled wind might have done.

Then the Saint looked back at the cloud; and at that instant the foremost fringe of it touched the petrified goat.

There was no sound that the Saint could hear from outside. But at once the imprisoned power within the cloud seemed to boil up into a terrible effervescence of fire; and where there had been a goat was nothing but the shape of a goat starkly outlined in shuddering orange-hued flame. For an instant, only the fraction of a second, it lasted, that vision of a dazzling glare in the shape of a goat; and then, as if the power that had produced it was spent, the shape became black. It stood of itself for a second; then it toppled slowly and fell upon the concrete. A little black dust hung in the air, and a little wreath of bluish smoke drifted up towards the roof. The violet cloud uncoiled slothfully, and smeared fluffily over the floor in a widening pool of mist.

Its force was by no means spent—that was an illusion belied by the flickering lights that still glinted through it like a host of tiny fireflies. It was only that the controlling rays had been diverted. Looking round again, Simon saw that the white-haired man had put down the thing of shining metal with which he had directed the cloud, and was turning to speak to the three men who had watched the demonstration.

The Saint stood like a man in a dream.

Then he drew Patricia away, with a soft and almost frantic laugh.

"We'll get out of here," he said. "We've seen enough for one night."

And yet he was wrong, for something else was to be added to the adventure with amazing rapidity.

As he turned, the Saint nearly cannoned into the giant who stood over them; and, in the circumstances, Simon Templar did not feel inclined to argue. He acted instantaneously, which the giant was not expecting. When one man points a revolver at another, there is, by convention, a certain amount of back-chat about the situation before anything is done; but the Saint held convention beneath contempt.

Moreover, when confronted by an armed man twice his own size, the Saint felt that he needed no excuse for employing any damaging foul known to the fighting game, or even a specialty of his own invention. His left hand struck the giant's gun arm aside, and at the same time the Saint kicked with one well-shod foot and a clear conscience.

A second later he was sprinting, with Patricia's hand in his.

There was a car drawn up in front of the house. Simon had not noticed it under the trees as he passed on his way round to the back; but now he saw it, because he was looking for it; and it accounted for the stock figure in breeches and a peaked cap which bulked out of the shadows round the gate and tried to bar the way.

"Sorry, son," said the Saint sincerely, and handed him off with some vim.

Then he was flying up the lane at the girl's side, and the sounds of the injured chauffeur's pursuit were too far behind to be alarming.

The Saint vaulted into the Furillac, and came down with one foot on the self-starter and the other on the clutch pedal.

As Patricia gained her place beside him he unleashed the full ninety-eight horse-power that the speedster could put forth when pressed.

His foot stayed flat down on the accelerator until they were running into Putney, and he was sure that any attempt to give chase had been left far astern; but even during the more sedate drive through London he was still unwontedly taciturn, and Patricia knew better than to try to make him talk when he was in such a mood. But she studied, as if she had never seen it before, the keen, vivid intentness of his profile as he steered the hurtling car through the night, and realised that she had never felt him so sheathed and at the same time shaken with such a dynamic savagery of purpose. Yet even she, who knew him better than anyone in the world, could not have explained what she sensed about him. She had seen, often before, the inspired wild leaps of his genius; but she could not know that this time that genius had rocketed into a more frantic flight than it had ever taken in all his life. And she was silent.

It was not until they were turning into Brook Street that she voiced a thought that had been racking her brain for the past hour.

"I can't help feeling I've seen one of those men before—or a picture of him—"

"Which one?" asked the Saint, a trifle grimly. "The young secretary bird—or Professor K. B. Vargan—or Sir Roland Hale—or Mr. Lester Hume Smith, His Majesty's Secretary of State for War?"

He marked her puzzlement, turning to meet her eyes. Now Patricia Holm was very lovely; and the Saint loved her. At that moment, for some reason, her loveliness took him by the throat.

He slipped an arm around her shoulders, and drew her close to him.

"Saint," she said, "you're on the trail of more trouble. I know the signs."

"It's even more than that, dear," said the Saint softly. "To-night I've seen a vision. And if it's a true vision it means that I'm going to fight something more horrible than I've ever fought before; and the name of it may very well be the same as the name of the devil himself.''

2

How Simon Templar Read Newspapers, and Understood What Was Not Written

HERE MAY CONVENIENTLY be quoted an item from one of the stop press columns of the following morning.

> The *Clarion* is officially informed that at a late hour last night Mr. Lester Hume Smith, the Secretary for War, and Sir Roland Hale, Director of Chemical Research to the War Office, attended a demonstration of Professor K. B. Vargan's ''electroncloud.'' The demonstration was held secretly, and no details will be disclosed. It is stated further that a special meeting of the Cabinet will be held this morning to receive Mr. Hume Smith's report, and, if necessary, to consider the Government's attitude towards the invention.

Simon Templar took the paragraph in his stride, for it was no more than a confirmation and amplification of what he already knew.

This was at ten o'clock—an extraordinary hour for the Saint to be up and dressed. But on this occasion he had risen early to break the habits of a lifetime and read every page of every newspaper that his man could buy.

He had suddenly become inordinately interested in politics; the news that an English tourist hailing from Manchester and rejoicing in the name of Pinheedle had been arrested for punching the nose of a policeman in Wiesbaden fascinated him; only such articles as ''Why Grandmothers Leave Home'' (by Ethelred Sapling, the brilliant author of *Lovers in Leeds*) continued to leave him entirely icebound.

But he had to wait for an early edition of the *Evening Record* for the account of his own exploit.

> . . . From footprints found this morning in the soft soil, it appears that three persons were involved—one of them a woman. One of the men, who must have been of exceptional stature, appears to have tripped and fallen in his flight, and then to have made off in a different direction from that taken by his companions, who finally escaped by car.
>
> Mr. Hume Smith's chauffeur, who attempted to arrest these two, and was knocked down by the man, recovered too late to reach the road in time to take the number of their car. From the sound of the exhaust, he judges it to have been some kind of high-powered sports model. He had not heard its approach or the entrance of the three intruders, and he admits that when he first saw the man and the woman he had just woken from a doze.
>
> The second man, who has been tracked across two fields at the back of Professor Vargan's house, is believed to have been picked up by his confederates further along the road. The fact of his presence was not discovered until the arrival of the detectives from London this morning.
>
> Chief Inspector Teal, who is in charge of the case, told an *Evening Record* representative that the police have as yet formed no theory as to what was the alarm which caused the hurried and clumsy departure of the spies. It is believed, however, that they were in a position to observe the conclusion of the experiment. . . .

There was much more, stunted across the two middle columns of the front page.

This blew in with Roger Conway, of the Saint's very dear acquaintance, who had been rung up in the small hours of that morning to be summoned to a conference; and he put the sheet before Simon Templar at once.

"Were you loose in England last night?" he demanded accusingly.

"There are rumours," murmured the Saint, "to that effect."

Mr. Conway sat down in his usual chair, and produced cigarettes and matches.

"Who was your pal—the cross-country expert?" he inquired calmly.

The Saint was looking out of the window.

"No one I know," he answered. "He kind of horned in on the party. You'll have the whole yarn in a moment. I phoned Norman directly after I phoned you; he came staggering under the castle walls a few seconds ago."

A peal on the bell announced that Norman Kent had reached the door of the apartment, and the Saint went out to admit him. Mr. Kent carried a copy of the *Evening Record,* and his very first words showed how perfectly he understood the Saint's eccentricities.

"If I thought you'd been anywhere near Esher last night——"

"You've been sent for to hear a speech on the subject," said the Saint.

He waved Norman to a chair, and seated himself on the edge of a littered table which Patricia Holm was trying to reduce to some sort of order. She came up and stood beside him, and he slid an arm round her waist.

"It was like this," he said.

And he plunged into the story without preface, for the time when prefaces had been necessary now lay far behind those four. Nor did he need to explain the motives for any of his actions. In clipped, slangy, quiet, and yet vivid sentences he told what he had seen in the greenhouse of the house near Esher; and the two men listened without interruption.

Then he stopped, and there was a short silence.

"It's certainly a marvellous invention," said Roger Conway at length, smoothing his fair hair. "But what is it?"

"The devil."

Conway blinked.

"Explain yourself."

"It's what the *Clarion* called it," said the Saint; "something we haven't got simple words to describe. A scientist will pretend to understand it, but whether he will or not is another matter. The best he can tell us is that it's a trick of so modifying the structure of a gas that it can be made to carry a tremendous charge of electricity, like a thunder-cloud does—only it isn't a bit like a thunder-cloud. It's also something to do with a ray—only it isn't a ray. If you like, it's something entirely impossible—only it happens to exist. And the point is that this gas just provides the flimsiest sort of sponge in the atmosphere, and Vargan knows how to saturate the pores in the sponge with millions of volts and amperes of compressed lightning."

"And when the goat got into the cloud——"

"It was exactly the same as if it had butted into a web of live wires.

For the fraction of a second that goat burnt like a scrap of coal in a blast furnace. And then it was ashes. Sweet idea, isn't it?''

Norman Kent, the dark and saturnine, took his eyes off the ceiling. He was a most unsmiling man, and he spoke little and always to the point.

"Lester Hume Smith has seen it," said Norman Kent. "And Sir Roland Hale. Who else?"

"Angel Face," said the Saint; "Angel Face saw it. The man our friend Mr. Teal assumes to have been one of us—not having seen him wagging a Colt at me. An adorable pet, built on the lines of something between Primo Carnera and an overgrown gorilla, but not too agile with the trigger finger—otherwise I mightn't be here. But which country he's working for is yet to be discovered."

Roger Conway frowned.

"You think——"

"Frequently," said the Saint. "But that was one think I didn't need a cold towel round my head for. Vargan may have thought he got a raw deal when they missed him off the front page, but he got enough publicity to make any wideawake foreign agent curious."

He tapped a cigarette gently on his thumb-nail and lighted it with slow and exaggerated deliberation. In such pregnant silences of irrelevant pantomime he always waited for the seeds he had sown to germinate spontaneously in the brains of his audience.

Conway spoke first.

"If there should be another war——"

"Who is waiting for a chance to make war?" asked Norman Kent.

The Saint picked up a selection of the papers he had been reading before they came, and passed them over. Page after page was scarred with blue pencillings. He had marked many strangely separated things— a proclamation of Mussolini, the speech of a French delegate before the League of Nations, the story of a break in the Oil Trust involving the rearrangement of two hundred million pounds of capital, the announcement of a colossal merger of chemical interests, the latest movements of warships, the story of an outbreak of rioting in India, the story of an inspired bull raid on the steel market, and much else that he had found of amazing significance, even down to the arrest of an English tourist hailing from Manchester and rejoicing in the name of Pinheedle, for punching the nose of a policeman in Wiesbaden. Roger Conway and Norman Kent read, and were incredulous.

"But people would never stand for another war so soon," said Conway. "Every country is disarming——"

"Bluffing with everything they know, and hoping that one day somebody'll be taken in," said the Saint. "And every nation scared stiff of the rest, and ready to arm again at any notice. The people never make or want a war—it's sprung on them by the statesmen with the business interests behind them, and somebody writes a 'We-Don't-Want-to-Lose-You-but-We-Think-You-Ought-to-Go' song for the brass bands to play, and millions of poor fools go out and die like heroes without ever being quite sure what it's all about. It's happened before. Why shouldn't it happen again?"

"People," said Norman Kent, "may have learnt their lesson."

Simon swept an impatient gesture.

"Do people learn lessons like that so easily? The men who could teach them are a past generation now. How many are left who are young enough to convince our generation? And even if we are on the crest of a wave of literature about the horrors of war, do you think that cuts any ice? I tell you, I've listened till I'm tired to people of our own age discussing those books and plays—and I know they cut no ice at all. It'd be a miracle if they did. The mind of a healthy young man is too optimistic. It leaps to the faintest hint of glory, and finds it so easy to forget whole seas of ghastliness. And I'll tell you more. . . ."

And he told them of what he had heard from Barney Malone.

"I've given you the facts," he said. "Now, suppose you saw a man rushing down the street with a contorted face, screaming his head off, foaming at the mouth, and brandishing a large knife dripping with blood. If you like to be a fool, you can tell yourself that it's conceivable that his face is contorted because he's trying to swallow a bad egg, he's screaming because someone had trodden on his pet corn, he's foaming at the mouth because he's just eaten a cake of soap, and he's just killed a chicken for dinner and is tearing off to tell his aunt all about it. On the other hand, it's simpler and safer to assume that he's a homicidal maniac. In the same way, if you like to be fools, and refuse to see a complete story in what spells a complete story to me, you can go home."

Roger Conway swung one leg over the arm of his chair and rubbed his chin reflectively.

"I suppose," he said, "our job is to find Tiny Tim and see that he doesn't pinch the invention while the Cabinet are still deciding what they're going to do about it?"

The Saint shook his head.

For once, Roger Conway, who had always been nearest to the Saint in all things, had failed to divine his leader's train of thought; and it was Norman Kent, that aloof and silent man, who voiced the inspiration of breath-taking genius—or madness—that had been born in Simon Templar's brain eight hours before.

"The Cabinet," said Norman Kent, from behind a screen of cigarette smoke, "might find the decision taken out of their hands . . . without the intervention of Tiny Tim. . . ."

Simon Templar looked from face to face.

For a moment he had an odd feeling that it was like meeting the other three again for the first time, as strangers. Patricia Holm was gazing through the window at the blue sky above the roofs of Brook Street, and who is to say what vision she saw there? Roger Conway, the cheerful and breezy, waited in silence, the smoke of his neglected cigarette staining his fingers. Norman Kent waited also, serious and absorbed.

The Saint turned his eyes to the painting over the mantelpiece, and did not see it.

"If we do nothing but suppress Tiny Tim," he said, "England will possess a weapon of war immeasurably more powerful than all the armaments of any other nation. If we stole that away, you may argue that sooner or later some other nation will probably discover something just as deadly, and then England will be at a disadvantage."

He hesitated, and then continued in the same quiet tone.

"But there are hundreds of Tiny Tims, and we can't suppress them all. No secret like that has ever been kept for long; and when the war came we might very well find the enemy prepared to use our own weapon against us."

Once again he paused.

"I'm thinking of all the men who'll fight in that next war, and the women who love them. If you saw a man drowning, would you refuse to rescue him because, for all you know, you might only be saving him for a more terrible death years later?"

There was another silence; and in it the Saint seemed to straighten and strengthen and grow, imperceptibly and yet tremendously, as if something gathered about him which actually filled every corner of the room and made him bulk like a preposterously normal giant. And, when he resumed, his voice was as soft and even as ever; but it seemed to ring like a blast of trumpets.

"There are gathered here," he said, "three somewhat shop-soiled musketeers—and a blessed angel. Barring the blessed angel, we have all of us, in the course of our young lives, broken half the Commandments and most of the private laws of several countries. And yet, somehow, we've contrived to keep intact certain ridiculous ideals, which to our perverted minds are a justification for our sins. And fighting is one of those ideals. Battle and sudden death. In fact, we must be about the last three men in the wide world who ought to be interfering with the makings of a perfectly good war. Personally, I suppose we should welcome it— for our own private amusement. But there aren't many like us. There are too many—far too many—who are utterly different. Men and boys who don't want war. Who don't live for battle, murder, and sudden death. Who wouldn't be happy warriors, going shouting and singing and swaggering into the battle. Who'd just be herded into it like dumb cattle to the slaughter, drunk with a miserable and futile heroism, to struggle blindly through a few days of squalid agony and die in the dirt. Fine young lives that don't belong to our own barbarous god of battles. . . . And we've tripped over the plans for the next sacrifice, partly by luck and partly by our own brilliance. And here we are. We don't give a damn for any odds or any laws. Will you think me quite mad if I put it to you that three shabby, hell-busting outlaws might, by the grace of God . . ."

He left the sentence unfinished; and for a few seconds no one spoke. Then Roger Conway stirred intently.

"What do you say?" he asked.

The Saint looked at him.

"I say," he answered, "that this is our picnic. We've always known— haven't we?—at the back of our minds, dimly, that one day we were bound to get our big show. I say that this is the cue. It might have come in any one of a dozen different ways; but it just happens to have chosen this one. I'll summarise. . . ."

He lighted a fresh cigarette and hitched himself further on to the table, leaning forward with his forearms on his knees and the fine, rake-hell, fighting face that they all knew and loved made almost supernaturally beautiful with such a light of debonair daredevilry as they had never seen before.

"You've read the story," he said. "I grant you it reads like a dime novelette; but there it is, staring you in the face, just the same. All at once, in both England and America, there's some funny business going on in the oil and steel and chemical trades. The amount of money locked up in those three combines must be nearly enough to swamp the capitals of any other bunch of industries you could name. We don't know exactly what's happening, but we do know that the big men, the secret moguls of Wall Street and the London Stock Exchange, the birds with the fat cigars and the names in *-heim* and *-stein,* who juggle the finances of this cockeyed world, are moving on some definite plan. And then look at the goods they're on the road with. Iron and oil and chemicals. If you know any other three interests that'd scoop a bigger pool out of a really first-class war, I'd like to hear of them. . . . Add on Barney Malone's spy story. Haven't you realised how touchy nations are, and how easy it really would be to stir up distrust? And distrust, sooner or later, means war. The most benevolent and peaceful nation, if it's continually finding someone else's spies snooping round its preserves, is going to make a certain song and dance about it. Nobody before this has thought of doing that sort of thing on a large scale—trying to set two European Powers at each other's throats with a carefully wangled quarrel—and yet the whole idea is so gloriously simple. And now it's happened—or happening. . . . And behind it all is the one man in the world with the necessary brain to conceive a plot like that, and the influence and qualifications to carry it through. You know who I mean. The man they call the Mystery Millionaire. The man who's supposed to have arranged half a dozen wars before, on a minor scale, in the interests of high finance. You've seen his name marked in red in those newspapers every time it crops up. It fits into the scheme in a darn sight too many ways—you can't laugh that off. Dr. Rayt Marius. . . ."

Norman Kent suddenly spun his cigarette into the fireplace.

"Then Golter might fit in——"

Conway said: "But the Crown Prince is Marius's own Crown Prince!"

"Would that mean anything to a man like Marius?" asked the Saint gently. "Wouldn't that just make things easier for him? Suppose . . ."

The Saint caught his breath; and then he took up his words again in a queerly soft and dreamy voice.

"Suppose Marius tempted the Crown Prince's vanity? The King is old; and there have been rumours that a young nation is calling for a young leader. And the Prince is ambitious. Suppose Marius were able to say: 'I can give you a weapon with which you can conquer the world. The only price I make is that you should use it. . . .' "

They sat spellbound, bewildered, fascinated. They wanted to laugh that vision away, to crush and pulverise and annihilate it with great flailing sledgehammers of rational incredulity. And they could find nothing to say at all.

The clock ticked leaden seconds away into eternity.

Patricia said breathlessly: "But he couldn't——"

"But he could!"

Simon Templar had leapt to his feet, his right arm flung out in a wild gesture.

"It's the key!" he cried. "It's the answer to the riddle! It mayn't be difficult to nurse up an international distrust by artificial means, but a tension like that can't be as fierce as a genuine international hatred. It'd want a much bigger final spark to make it blaze up. And the Crown Prince and his ambitions—and Vargan's invention—they'd make the spark! They're Marius's trump card. If he didn't bring them off his whole scheme might be shipwrecked. I know that's right!"

"That man in the garden," whispered Patricia. "If he was one of Marius's men——"

"It was Marius!"

The Saint snatched a paper from the table, and wrung and smashed it out so that she could see the photograph.

Bad as had been the light when they had found themselves face to face with the original, that face could never have been mistaken anywhere—that hideous, rough-hewn, nightmare expressionlessness, like the carved stone face of a heathen idol.

"It was Marius. . . ."

Roger Conway came out of his chair.

"If you're right, Saint—I'll believe that you didn't dream last night——"

"It's true!"

"And we haven't all suddenly got softening of the brain—to be listening to these howling, daft deductions of yours——"

"God knows I was never so sure of anything in my life."

"Then——"

The Saint nodded.

"We have claimed to execute some sort of justice," he said. "What is the just thing for us to do here?"

Conway did not answer, and the Saint turned to meet Norman Kent's thoughtful eyes; and then he knew that they were both waiting for him to speak their own judgment.

They had never seen the Saint so stern.

"The invention must cease to be," said Simon Templar. "And the brain that conceived it, which could recreate it—that also must cease to be. It is expedient that one man should die for many people. . . ."

3

How Simon Templar Returned to Esher, and Decided to Go There Again

THIS WAS ON the 24th of June—about three weeks after the Saint's reply to the offer of a free pardon.

On the 25th, not a single morning paper gave more than an inconspicuous paragraph to the news which had filled the afternoon editions of the day before; and thereafter nothing more at all was said by the Press about the uninvited guests at Vargan's demonstration. Nor was there more than a passing reference to the special Cabinet meeting which followed.

The Saint, who now had only one thought day and night, saw in this unexpected reticence the hand of something dangerously like an official censorship, and Barney Malone, appealed to, was so uncommunicative as to confirm the Saint in his forebodings.

To the Saint it seemed as if a strange tension had crept into the atmosphere of the season in London. This feeling was purely subjective, he knew; and yet he was unable to laugh it away. On one day he had walked through the streets in careless enjoyment of an air fresh and mild with the promise of summer, among people quickened and happy and alert; on the next day the clear skies had become heavy with the fear of an awful thunder, and a doomed generation went its way furtively and afraid.

"You ought to see Esher," he told Roger Conway. "A day away from your favourite bar would do you good."

They drove down in a hired car; and there the Saint found further omens.

They lunched at the Bear, and afterwards walked over the Portsmouth Road. There were two men standing at the end of the lane in which Professor Vargan lived, and two men broke off their conversation abruptly as Conway and the Saint turned off the main road and strolled past them under the trees. Further down, a third man hung over the garden gate sucking a pipe.

Simon Templar led the way past the house without glancing at it, and continued his discourse on the morrow's probable runners; but a sixth sense told him that the eyes of the man at the gate followed them down the lane, as the eyes of the two men at the corner had done.

"Observe," he murmured, "how careful they are not to make any fuss. The last thing they want to do is to attract attention. Just quietly on the premises, that's what they are. But if we did anything suspicious we should find ourselves being very quietly and carefully bounced towards the nearest clink. That's what we call Efficiency."

A couple of hundred yards further on, on the blind side of a convenient corner, the Saint stopped.

"Walk on for as long as it takes you to compose a limerick suitable for the kind of drawing-room to which you would never be admitted," he ordered. "And then walk back. I'll be here."

Conway obediently passed on, carrying in the tail of his eye a glimpse of the Saint sidling through a gap in the hedge into the fields on the right. Mr. Conway was no poet, but he accepted the Saint's suggestion, and toyed lazily with the lyrical possibilities of a young lady of Kent who whistled wherever she went. After wrestling for some minutes with the problem of bringing this masterpiece to a satisfactory conclusion, he gave it up and turned back; and the Saint returned through the hedge, a startlingly immaculate sight to be seen coming through a hedge, with a punctuality that suggested that his estimate of Mr. Conway's poetical talent was dreadfully accurate.

"For the first five holes I couldn't put down a single putt," said the Saint sadly, and he continued to describe an entirely imaginary round of golf until they were back on the main road and the watchers at the end of the lane were out of sight.

Then he came back to the point.

"I wanted to do some scouting round at the back of the house to see how sound the defences were. There was a sixteen-stone seraph in his shirtsleeves pretending to garden, and another little bit of fluff sitting in a deck chair under a tree reading a newspaper. Dear old Teal himself is probably sitting in the bathroom disguised as a clue. They aren't taking any more chances!"

"Meaning," said Conway, "that we shall either have to be very cunning or very violent."

"Something like that," said the Saint.

He was preoccupied and silent for the rest of the walk back to the Bear, turning over the proposition he had set himself to tackle.

He had cause to be—and yet the tackling of tough propositions was

nothing new to him. The fact of the ton or so of official majesty which
lay between him and his immediate objective was not what bothered him;
the Saint, had he chosen to turn his professional attention to the job,
might easily have been middle-weight champion of the world, and he had
a poor opinion both of the speed and fighting science of policemen. In
any case, as far as that obstacle went, he had a vast confidence in his
own craft and ingenuity for circumventing mere massive force. Nor did
the fact that he was meddling with the destiny of nations give him pause:
he had once, in his quixotic adventuring, run a highly successful one-
man revolution in South America, and could have been a fully accredited
Excellency in a comic-opera uniform if he had chosen. But this problem,
the immensity of it, the colossal forces that were involved, the millions
of tragedies that might follow one slip in his enterprise . . . Something
in the thought tightened tiny muscles around the Saint's jaw.

Fate was busy with him in those days.

They were running into Kingston at the modest pace which was all the
hired car permitted, when a yellow sedan purred effortlessly past them.
Before it cut into the line of traffic ahead, Conway had had indelibly
imprinted upon his memory the bestial, ape-like face that stared back at
them through the rear window with the fixity of a carved image.

"Ain't he sweet?" murmured the Saint.

"A sheik," agreed Conway.

A smile twitched at Simon Templar's lips.

"Known to us," he said, "as Angel Face or Tiny Tim—at the option
of the orator. The world knows him as Rayt Marius. He recognised me,
and he's got the number of the car. He'll trace us through the garage we
hired it from, and in twenty-four hours he'll have our names and addresses
and Y.M.C.A. records. I can't help thinking that life's going to be very
crowded for us in the near future."

And the next day the Saint was walking back to Brook Street towards
midnight, in the company of Roger Conway, when he stopped suddenly
and gazed up into the sky with a reflective air, as if he had thought of
something that had eluded his concentration for some time.

"Argue with me, Beautiful," he pleaded. "Argue violently, and wave
your hands about, and look as fierce as your angelic dial will let you.
But don't raise your voice."

They walked the few remaining yards to the door of the Saint's apartment with every appearance of angry dissension. Mr. Conway, keeping
his voice low as directed, expatiated on the failing of the Ford car with
impassioned eloquence. The Saint answered, with aggressive gesticulations:

"A small disease in a pot hat has been following me half the day. He's a dozen yards behind us now. I want to get hold of him, but if we chase him he'll run away. He's certain to be coming up now to try and overhear the quarrel and find out what it's about. If we start a fight we should draw him within range. Then you'll grab him while I get the front door open."

"The back axle——" snarled Mr. Conway.

They were now opposite the Saint's house; and the Saint halted and turned abruptly, placed his hand in the middle of Conway's chest, and pushed.

Conway recovered his balance and let fly. The Saint took the blow on his shoulder, and reeled back convincingly. Then he came whaling in and hit Mr. Conway on the jaw with great gentleness. Mr. Conway retaliated by banging the air two inches from the Saint's nose.

In the uncertain light it looked a most furious battle; and the Saint was satisfied to see Pot Hat sneaking up along the area railings only a few paces away, an interested spectator.

"Right behind you," said the Saint softly. "Stagger back four steps when I slosh you."

He applied his fist caressingly to Conway's solar plexus, and broke away without waiting to see the result, but he knew that his lieutenant was well trained. Simon had just time to find his key and open the front door. A second later he was closing the door again behind Conway and his burden.

"Neat work," drawled the Saint approvingly. "Up the stairs with the little darling, Roger."

As the Saint led the way into the sitting-room, Conway put Pot Hat down and removed his hand from the little man's mouth.

"Hush!" said Conway in a shocked voice, and covered his ears.

The Saint was peering down through the curtains.

"I don't think anyone saw us," he said. "We're in luck. If we'd planned it we might have had to wait years before we found Brook Street bare of souls."

He came back from the window and stood over their prisoner, who was still shaking his fist under Conway's nose and burbling blasphemously.

"That'll be all for you, sweetheart," remarked the Saint frostily. "Run through his pockets, Roger."

"When I find a pleeceman," began Pot Hat quiveringly.

"Or when a policeman finds what's left of you," murmured Simon pleasantly. "Yes?"

But the search revealed nothing more interesting than three new five-pound notes—a fortune which such a seedy-looking little man would never had been suspected of possessing.

"So it will have to be third degree," said the Saint mildly, and carefully closed both windows.

He came back with his hands in his pockets and a very Saintly look in his eyes.

"Do you talk, Rat Face?" he asked.

"Wotcher mean—talk? Yer big bullies——"

"Talk," repeated the Saint patiently. "Open your mouth, and emit sounds which you fondly believe to be English. You've been tailing me all day, and I don't like it."

"Wotcher mean?" demanded the little man again, indignantly. "Tailing yer?"

The Saint sighed, and took the lapels of the little man's coat in his two hands. For half a hectic minute he bounced and shook the little man like a terrier shaking a rat.

"Talk," said the Saint monotonously.

But Pot Hat opened his mouth for something that could only have been either a swear or a scream; and the Saint disapproved of both. He tapped the little man briskly in the stomach, and he never knew which of the two possibilities had been the little man's intention, for whichever it was died in a choking gurgle. Then the Saint took hold of him again.

It was certainly very like bullying, but Simon Templar was not feeling sentimental. He had to do it, and he did it with cold efficiency. It lasted five minutes.

"Talk," said the Saint again, at the end of the five minutes; and the blubbering sleuth said he would talk.

Simon took him by the scruff of his neck and dropped him into a chair like a sack of peanuts.

The story, however, was not very helpful.

"I dunno wot 'is name is. I met 'im six months ago in a pub off Oxford Street, an' 'e gave me a job to do. I've worked for 'im on an' off ever since—followin' people an' findin' out things about 'em. 'E allus paid well, an' there wasn't no risk——"

"Not till you met me," said the Saint. "How do you keep in touch with him if he hasn't told you his name?"

"When 'e wants me, 'e writes to me, an' I meet 'im in a pub somewhere, an' 'e tells me wot I've got to do. Then I let 'im know wot's 'appening by telephone. I got 'is number."

"Which is?"

"Westminster double-nine double-nine."

"Thanks," said the Saint. "Good-looking man, isn't he?"

"Not 'arf! Fair gives me the creeps, 'e does. Fust time I sore 'im——"

The Saint shouldered himself off the mantelpiece and reached for the cigarette-box.

"Go home while the goin's good, Rat Face," he said. "You don't interest us any more. Door, Roger."

" 'Ere," whined Pot Hat, "I got a wife an' four children——"

"That," said the Saint gently, "must be frightfully bad luck on them. Give them my love, won't you?"

"I bin assaulted. Supposin' I went to a pleeceman——"

The Saint fixed him with a clear blue stare.

"You can either walk down the stairs," he remarked dispassionately, "or you can be kicked down by the gentleman who carried you up. Take your choice. But if you want any compensation for the grilling you've had, you'd better apply to your handsome friend for it. Tell him we tortured you with hot irons and couldn't make you open your mouth. He might believe you—though I shouldn't bet on it. And if you feel like calling a policeman, you'll find one just up the road. I know him quite well, and I'm sure he'd be interested to hear what you've got to say. Good-night."

"Callin' yerselves gentlemen!" sneered the sleuth viciously. "You——"

"Get out," said the Saint quietly.

He was lighting his cigarette, and he did not even look up, but the next thing he heard was the closing of the door.

From the window he watched the man slouching up the street. He was at the telephone when Conway returned from supervising the departure, and he smiled lazily at his favourite lieutenant's question.

"Yes, I'm just going to give Tiny Tim my love. . . . Hullo—are you Westminster double-nine double-nine? . . . Splendid. How's life, Angel Face?"

"Who is that?" demanded the other end of the line.

"Simon Templar," said the Saint. "You may have heard of me. I believe we—er—ran into each other recently." He grinned at the stifled exclamation that came faintly over the wire. "Yes, I suppose it *is* a pleasant surprise. Quite overwhelming. . . . The fact is, I've just had to give one of your amateur detectives a rough five minutes. He's walking home. The next friend of yours I find walking on my shadow will be removed in an ambulance. That's a tip from the stable. Pleasant dreams, old dear!''

He hung up the receiver without waiting for a reply.

Then he was speaking to Inquiry.

"Can you give me the name and address of Westminster double-nine double nine? . . . What's that? . . . Well, is there no way of finding out? . . . Yes, I know that; but there are reasons why I can't ring up and ask. Fact is, my wife eloped yesterday with the plumber, and she said if I really wanted her back I could ring her up at that number; but one of the bath-taps is dripping, and . . . Oh, all right. Thanks very much. Love to the supervisors.''

He put down the instrument and turned to shrug at Conway's interrogatively raised eyebrows.

'' 'I'm sorry—we are not permitted to give subscribers' names and addresses,' '' he mimicked. "I knew it, but it was worth trying. Not that it matters much.''

"You might," suggested Conway, "have tried the directory.''

"Of course. Knowing that Marius doesn't live in England, and that therefore Westminster double-nine double-nine is unlikely to be in his name—— Oh, of course.''

Conway grimaced.

"Right. Then we sit down and try to think out what Tiny Tim'll do next.''

"Nope," contradicted the Saint cheerfully. "We know that one. It'll either be prussic acid in the milk to-morrow morning, or a snap shot from a passing car next time I walk out of the front door. We can put our shirts on that, and sit tight and wait for the dividends. But suppose we didn't wait. . . .''

The emphatic briskness of his first words had trailed away while he was speaking into the gentle dreamy intonation that Conway knew of old. It was the sign that the Saint's thoughts had raced miles ahead of his tongue, and he was only mechanically completing a speech that had long since become unimportant.

Then for a little while he was silent, with his cigarette slanting up between his lips, and a kind of crouching immobility about his lean body, and a dancing blue light of recklessness kindling in his eyes. For a moment he was as still and taut as a leopard gathering itself for a spring. Then he relaxed, straightening, and smiled; and his right arm went out in one

of those magnificently romantic gestures that only the Saint could make
with such a superb lack of affectation.

"But why should we wait?" he challenged.

"Why, indeed?" echoed Conway vaguely. "But——"

Simon Templar was not listening. He was already back at the telephone,
calling up Norman Kent.

"Get out your car, fill her up with gas, and come right round to Brook
Street. And pack a gun. This is going to be a wild night!"

A few minutes later he was through to his bungalow at Maidenhead—
to which, by the grace of all the Saint's gods, he had sent his man down
only that very day to prepare the place for a summer tenancy that was
never to materialise as Simon Templar had planned it.

"That you, Orace? . . . Good. I just phoned up to let you know that
Mr. Kent will be arriving in the small hours with a visitor. I want you
to get the cellar ready for him—for the visitor, I mean. Got me?"

"Yessir," said Orace unemotionally, and the Saint rang off.

There was only one Orace—late sergeant of Marines, and Simon Templar's most devoted servant. If Simon had said that the visitor would be
a kidnapped President of the United States, Orace would still have answered no more than that gruff, unemotional "Yessir!"—and carried on
according to his orders.

Said Roger Conway, climbing out of his chair and squashing his cigarette end into an ash-try: "The idea being——"

"If we leave it any longer one of two things will happen. Either (*a*)
Vargan will give his secret away to the Government experts, or (*b*) Marius
will pinch it—or Vargan—or both. And then we'd be dished for ever.
We've only got a chance for so long as Vargan is the one man in the
wide world who carries that invention of the devil under his hat. And
every hour we wait gives Tiny Tim a chance to get in before us!"

Conway frowned at a photograph of Patricia Holm on the mantelpiece.
Then he nodded at it.

"Where is she?"

"Spending a couple of days in Devonshire with the Mannerings. The
coast's dead clear. I'm glad to have her out of it. She's due back to-
morrow evening, which is just right for us. We take Vargan to Maidenhead
to-night, sleep off our honest weariness to-morrow, and toddle back in
time to meet her. Then we all go down to the bungalow—and we're
sitting pretty. How's that?"

Conway nodded again slowly. He was still frowning, as if there was
something troubling the back of his mind.

Presently it came out.

"I never was the bright boy of the class," he said, "but I'd like one thing plain. We agree that Vargan, on behalf of certain financial interests, is out to start a war. If he brings it off we shall be in the thick of it. We always are. The poor blessed Britisher gets roped into everybody else's squabbles. . . . Well, we certainly don't want Vargan's bit of frightfulness used against us, but mightn't it save a lot of trouble if we could use it ourselves?"

The Saint shook his head.

"If Marius doesn't get Vargan," he said, "I don't think the war will come off. At least, we'll have said check to it—and a whole heap may happen before he can get the show started again. And as for using it ourselves—— No, Roger, I don't think so. We've argued that already. It wouldn't be kept to ourselves. And even if it could be—do you know, Roger?—I still think the world would be a little better and cleaner without it. There are foul things enough in the armoury without that. And I say that it shall not be. . . ."

Conway looked at him steadily for some seconds.

Then he said: "So Vargan will take a trip to Maidenhead. You won't kill him to-night?"

"Not unless it's forced on me," said the Saint quietly. "I've thought it out. I don't know how much hope there is of appealing to his humanity, but as long as that hope exists, he's got a right to live. What the hope is, is what we've got to find out. But if I find that he won't listen——"

"Quite."

The Saint gave the same explanation to the third musketeer when Norman Kent arrived ten minutes later, and Norman's reply was only a little less terse than Roger Conway's had been.

"We may have to do it," he said.

His dark face was even graver than usual, and he spoke very quietly, for although Norman Kent had once sent a bad man to his death, he was the only one of the three who had never seen a man die.

4

How Simon Templar Lost an Automobile, and Won an Argument

"THE ANCIENT ART of generalship," said the Saint, "is to put yourself in the enemy's place. Now, how should I guard Vargan if I were as fat as Chief Inspector Teal?"

They stood in a little group on the Portsmouth Road about a mile from Esher, where they had stopped the cars in which they had driven down from London. They had been separated for the journey, because the Saint had insisted on taking his own Furillac as well as Norman Kent's Hirondel, in case of accidents. And he had refused to admit that there was time to make plans before they started. That, he had said, he would attend to on the way, and thereby save half an hour.

"There were five men when we came down yesterday," said Conway. "If Teal hasn't got many more than that on the night shift I should say they'd be arranged much as we saw them—outposts in the lane, the front garden, and the back garden, and a garrison in the greenhouse and the house itself. Numbers uncertain, but probably only couples."

The Saint's inevitable cigarette glowed like a fallen star in the darkness.

"That's the way I figured it out myself. I've roughed out a plan of attack on that basis."

He outlined it briefly. That was not difficult, for it was hardly a plan at all—it was little more than an idea for desperate and rapid action, a gamble on the element of surprise. The Saint had a pleasant habit of tackling some things in that mood, and getting away with it. And yet, on this occasion, as it happened, even that much planning was destined to be unnecessary.

A few minutes later they were on their way again.

The Saint led, with Conway beside him, in the Furillac. The Hirondel, with Norman Kent, followed about fifty yards behind. Norman, much to his disgust, was not considered as an active performer in the early stages of the enterprise. He was to stop his car a little way from the end of the lane, turn round, and wait with the engine ticking over until either

Conway or the Saint arrived with Vargan. The simplicity of this arrangement was its great charm, but they were not able to make Norman see their point—which, they said, was the fault of his low and brawlsome mind.

And yet, if this reduction of their mobile forces had not been an incidental part of the Saint's sketchy plan of campaign, the outcome of the adventure might have been very different.

As Simon pulled up at the very mouth of the lane, he flung a lightning glance over his shoulder, and saw the Hirondel already swerving across the road for the turn.

Then he heard the shot.

"For the love of Pete!"

The invocation dropped from the Saint's lips in a breathless undertone. He was getting out of the car at that moment, and he completed the operation of placing his second foot on the road with a terrifically careful intentness. As he straightened up with the same frozen deliberation, he found Conway at his elbow.

"You heard it?" Conway's curt, half-incredulous query.

"And *how*. . . ."

"Angel Face——"

"Himself!"

Simon Templar was standing like a rock. He seemed, to Conway's impatience, to have been standing like that for an eternity, as though his mind had suddenly left him. And yet it had only been a matter of a few seconds, and in that time the Saint's brain had been whirling and wheeling with a wild precision into the necessary readjustments.

So Angel Face had beaten them to the jump—it could have been by no more than a fraction. And, as they had asked for trouble, they were well and truly in the thick of it. They had come prepared for the law; now they had to deal with both law and lawlessness, and both parties united in at least one common cause—to keep K. B. Vargan to themselves. Even if both parties were at war on every other issue. . . .

"So we win this hands down," said the Saint softly, amazingly. "We're in luck!"

"If you call this luck!"

"But I do! Could we have arrived at a better time? When both gangs have rattled each other—and probably damaged each other—and Tiny Tim's boy friends have done the dirty work for us——"

He was cut short by another shot . . . then another . . . then a muddled splutter of three or four. . . .

"Our cue!" snapped the Saint, and Roger Conway was at his side as he leapt down the lane.

There was no sign of the sentries, but a man came rushing towards them out of the gloom, heavy-footed and panting. The Saint pushed Conway aside and flung out a well-timed foot. As the man sprawled head-long, Simon pounced on him and banged his head with stunning force against the road. Then he yanked the dazed man to his feet and looked closely at him.

"If he's not a policeman, I'm a Patagonian Indian," said the Saint. "A slight error, Roger."

The man answered with a wildly swinging fist, and the Saint hit him regretfully on the point of the jaw and saw him go down in a limp heap.

"What next?" asked Conway; and a second fusillade clattered out of the night to answer him.

"This is a very rowdy party," said the Saint mournfully. "Let's make it worse, shall we?"

He jerked an automatic from his pocket and fired a couple of shots into the air. The response was far more prompt than he had expected— two little tongues of flame that spat at them out of the further blackness, and two bullets that sang past their heads.

"Somebody loves us," remarked Simon calmly. "This way——"
He started to lead down the lane.

And then, out of the darkness, the headlights of a car came to life dazzlingly, like two monstrous eyes. For a second Conway and the Saint stood struck to stillness in the glare that had carved a great trough of luminance out of the obscurity as if by the scoop of some gigantic dredge. So sudden and blinding was that unexpected light that an instant of time was almost fatally lost before either of them could see that it was not standing still but moving towards them and picking up speed like an express train.

"Glory!" spoke the Saint, and his voice overlapped the venomous *rat-tat-tat!* of another unseen automatic.

In the same instant he was whirling and stooping with the pace of a striking snake. He collared Conway at the knees and literally hurled him bodily over the low hedge at the side of the lane with an accuracy and expedition that the toughest and most seasoned footballer could hardly have bettered.

The startled Conway, getting shakily to his feet, found the Saint landing from a leap beside him, and was in time to see the dark shape of a closed car flash past in the wake of that eye-searing blaze of headlights—so close that its wings and running-board tore a flurry of crackling twigs from the hedge. And he realised that, but for the Saint's speed of reaction, they would have stood no chance at all in that narrow space.

He might have said something about it. By ordinary procedure he should have given thanks to his saviour in a breaking voice; they should have wrung each other's hands and wept gently on each other's shoulders for a while; but something told Conway that it was no time for such trimmings. Besides, the Saint had taken the incident in his stride: by that time it had probably slithered through his memory into the dim limbo of distant reminiscence, and he would probably have been quite astonished to be reminded of it at that juncture. By some peaceful and lazy fireside, in his doddering old age, possibly . . . But in the immediate present he was concerned only with the immediate future.

He was looking back towards the house. There were lights showing still in some of the windows—it might altogether have been a most serene and tranquil scene, but for the jarring background of intermittent firing, which might have been nothing worse than a childish celebration of Guy Fawkes' day if it had been Guy Fawkes' day. But the Saint wasn't concerned with those reflections, either. He was searching the shadows by the gate, and presently he made out a deeper and more solid-looking shadow among the other shadows, a bulky shadow. . . .

Crack!

A tiny jet of flame licked out of the bulky shadow, and they heard the tinkle of shattered glass; but the escaping car was now only a few yards from the main road.

Conway was shaking Simon by the shoulder, babbling: "They're getting away! Saint, why don't you shoot?"

Mechanically the Saint raised his automatic, though he knew that the chance of putting in an effective shot, in that light, was about a hundred to one against anybody—and the Saint, as a pistol shot, had never been in the championship class.

Then he lowered the gun again, with something like a gasp, and his left hand closed on Conway's arm in a vice-like grip.

"They'll never do it!" he cried. *"I left the car slap opposite the lane, and they haven't got room to turn!"*

And Roger Conway, watching, fascinated, saw the lean blue shape of the Furillac revealed in the blaze of the flying headlights, and heard, before the crash, the scream of tortured tyres tearing ineffectually at the road.

Then the lights vanished in a splintering smash, and there was darkness and a moment's silence.

"We've got 'em!" rapped the Saint exultantly.

The bulky shadow had left the gate and was lumbering towards them up the lane. The Saint was over the hedge like a cat, landing lightly on his toes directly in Teal's path, and the detective saw him too late.

"Sorry!" murmured the Saint, and really meant it; but he crowded every ounce of his one hundred and sixty pounds of dynamic fighting weight into the blow he jerked at the pit of Teal's stomach.

Ordinarily, the Saint entertained a sincere regard for the police force in general and Chief Inspector Teal in particular, but he had no time that night for more than the most laconic courtesies. Moreover, Inspector Teal had a gun, and, in the circumstances, would be liable to shoot first and ask questions afterwards. Finally, the Saint had his own ideas and plans on the subject of the rescue of Vargan from the raiding party, and they did not include either the co-operation or interference of the law. These three cogent arguments he summed up in that one pile-driving jolt to Teal's third waistcoat button; and the detective dropped with a grunt of agony.

Then the Saint turned and went flying up the lane after Roger Conway.

He heard a shout behind him, and again a gun barked savagely in the night. The Saint felt the wind of the bullet actually stroke his cheek. Clearly, then, there was at least one more police survivor of Marius's raid; but Simon judged that further disputes with the law could be momentarily postponed. He swerved like a hare and raced on, knowing that only the luckiest—or unluckiest—of blind shots could have come so near him in such a light, and having no fear that a second would have the same fortune.

As it happened, the detective who had come out of the garden behind Teal must have realised the same feeling, for he held his fire. But as the Saint stopped by the yellow sedan, now locked inextricably with the wreckage of the battered Furillac, he heard the man pounding on through the darkness towards him.

Conway was opening the near-side door; and it was a miracle that his career was not cut short then and there by the shot from the interior of the car that went snarling past his ear. But there was no report—just the throaty *plop!* of an efficient silencer—and he understood that the only shooting they had heard had been done by the police guards. The raiders had not been so rowdy as the Saint had accused them of being.

The next moment Simon Templar had opened a door on the other side of the sedan.

"Naughty boy!" said Simon Templar reproachfully.

His long arm shot over the gun artist's shoulder, and his sinewy hand closed and twisted on the automatic in time to send the next shot through the roof of the car instead of through Conway's brain.

Then the Saint had the gun screwed round till it rammed into the man's own ribs.

"Now shoot, honeybunch," encouraged the Saint; but the man sat quite still.

He was in the back of the car, beside Vargan. There was no one in the driver's seat, and the door on that side was open. The Saint wondered who the chauffeur had been, and where he got to, and whether it had been Angel Face himself; but he had little time to give to that speculation, and any possibility of danger from the missing driver's quarter would have to be faced if and when it materialized.

Conway yanked Vargan out into the road on one side; and the Saint, taking a grip on the gun artist's neck with his free hand, yanked him out into the road on the other side. One wrench disarmed the man, and then the Saint spun him smartly round by the neck.

"Sleep, my pretty one," said the Saint, and uppercut him with a masterly blend of science and brute strength.

He turned, to look down the muzzle of an automatic, and put up his hands at once. He had slipped his own gun into his pocket in order to deal more comfortably with the man from the car, and he knew it would be dangerous to try to reach it.

"Lovely weather we've been having, haven't we?" drawled the Saint genially.

This, he decided, must be the guard who had fired at him down the lane; the build, though hefty, was nothing like Angel Face's gigantic proportions. Besides, Angel Face, or any of his men, would have touched off the trigger ten seconds ago.

The automatic nosed into the Saint's chest, and he felt his pocket deftly lightened of its gun. The man exhaled his satisfaction in a long breath.

"That's one of you, anyway," he remarked grimly.

"Pleased to meet you," said the Saint.

And there it was.

The Saint's voice was as unperturbed as if he had been conducting some trivial conversation in a smoke-room, instead of talking with his hands in the air and an unfriendly detective focussing a Smith-Wesson aphragm. And the corner was undoubtedly tight. If the circumstances had been slightly different, the Saint might have dealt with this obstacle in the same way as he had dealt with Marius on their first encounter. Marius had had the drop on him just as effectively as this. But Marius had been expecting a walk-over, and had therefore been just the necessary fraction below concert pitch; whereas this man was obviously expecting trouble. In view of what he must have been through already that night, he would have been a born fool if he hadn't. And something told Simon that the man wasn't quite a born fool. Something in the businesslike steadiness of that automatic . . .

But the obstacle had to be surmounted, all the same.

"Get Vargan away, Roger," sang the Saint cheerfully, coolly. "See you again some time. . . ."

He took two paces sideways, keeping his hands well up.

"Stop that!" cracked the detective, and the Saint promptly stopped it; but now he was in a position to see round the back of the sedan.

The red tail-light of the Hirondel was moving—Norman Kent was backing the car up closer to save time.

Conway bent and heaved the Professor up on to his shoulder like a bag of potatoes; then he looked back hesitantly at Simon.

"Get him away while you've got the chance, you fool!" called the Saint impatiently.

And even then he really believed that he was destined to sacrifice himself to cover the retreat. Not that he was going quietly. But . . .

He saw Conway turn and break into a trot, and sighed his relief.

Then, in a flash, he saw how a chance might be given, and tensed his muscles warily. And the chance was given him.

It wasn't the detective's fault. He merely attempted the impossible. He was torn between the desire to retain his prisoner and the impulse to find out what was happening to the man it was his duty to guard. He knew that that man was being taken away, and he knew that he ought to be trying to do something to prevent it; and yet his respect for the desperation of his captive stuck him up as effectively as if it had been the captive who held the gun. And, of course, the detective ought to have shot the captive and gone on with the rest of the job; but he tried, in a kind of panic, to find a less bloodthirsty solution, and the solution he found wasn't a solution at all. He tried to divide his mind and apply it to two things at once; and that, he ought to have known, was a fatal thing to do with a man like the Saint. But at that moment he didn't know the Saint very well.

Simon Templar, in those two sideways steps that the detective had allowed him to take, had shifted into such a position that the detective's lines of vision, if he had been able to look two ways at once, at Conway with one eye and at the Saint with the other, would have formed an obtuse angle. Therefore, since the detective's optic orbits were not capable of this feat, he could not see what Conway was doing without taking his eyes off Simon Templar.

And the detective was foolish.

For an instant his gaze left the Saint. How he imagined he would get away with it will remain a mystery. Certainly Simon did not inquire the answer then, nor discover it afterwards. For in that instant's grace, ignoring the menace of the automatic, the Saint shot out a long, raking left that gathered strength from every muscle in his body from the toes to the wrist.

And the Saint was on his way to the Hirondel before the man reached the ground.

Conway had only just dumped his struggling burden into the back seat when the Saint sprang to the running-board and clapped Norman Kent on the shoulder.

"Right away, sonny boy!" cried the Saint; and the Hirondel was sliding away as he and Conway climbed into the back.

He collected Vargan's flailing legs in an octopus embrace, and held the writhing scientist while Conway pinioned his ankles with the rope they had brought for the purpose. The expert hands of the first set of kidnappers had already dealt with the rest of him—his wrists were lashed together with a length of stout cord, and a professional gag stifled the screams which otherwise he would undoubtedly have been loosing.

"What happened?" asked Norman Kent, over his shoulder; and the Saint leaned over the front seat and explained.

"In fact," he said, "we couldn't have done better if we'd thought it out. Angel Face certainly brought off that raid like no amateur. But can you beat it? No stealth or subtlety, as far as we know. Just banging in like a Chicago bandit, and hell to the consequences. That shows how much he means business."

"How many men on the job?"

"Don't know. We only met one, and that wasn't Angel Face. Angel Face himself may have been in the car with Vargan, but he'd certainly taken to the tall timber when Roger and I arrived. A man like that wouldn't tackle the job with one solitary car and a couple of pals. There must have been a spare bus, with load, somewhere—probably up the lane. There should be another way in, though I don't know where it is. . . . You'd better switch on the lights—we're out of sight now."

He settled back and lighted a cigarette.

In its way, it had been a most satisfactory effort, even if its success had been largely accidental; but the Saint was frowning rather thoughtfully. He wasn't worrying about the loss of his car—that was a minor detail. But that night he had lost something far more important.

"This looks like my good-bye to England," he said; and Conway, whose brain moved a little less quickly, was surprised.

"Why—are you going abroad after this?"

The Saint laughed rather sadly.

"Shall I have any choice?" he answered. "We couldn't have got the Furillac away, and Teal will trace me through that. He doesn't know I'm the Saint, but I guess they could make the Official Secrets Act heavy enough on me without that. Not to mention that any damage Angel Face's gang may have done to the police will be blamed on us as well. There's nothing in the world to show that we weren't part of the original raid, except the evidence of the gang themselves—and I shouldn't bet on their telling. . . . No, my Roger. We are indubitably swimming in a large pail of soup. By morning every policeman in London will be looking for me, and by to-morrow night my photograph will be hanging up in every police station in England. Isn't it going to be fun?—as the bishop said to the actress."

But the Saint wasn't thinking it as funny as it might have been.

"Is it safe to go to Maidenhead?" asked Conway.

"That's our consolation. The deeds of the bungalow are in the name of Mrs. Patricia Windermere, who spends her spare time being Miss Patricia Holm. I've had that joke up my sleeve for the past year in case of accidents."

"And Brook Street?"

The Saint chuckled.

"Brook Street," he said, "is held in your name, my sweet and respectable Roger. I thought that'd be safer. I merely installed myself as your tenant. No—we're temporarily covered there, though I don't expect that to last long. A few days, perhaps. . . . And the address registered with my car is one I invented for the purpose. . . . But there's one snag. . . . Finding it's a dud address, they'll get on to the agents I bought it from. And I sent it back to them for decarbonising only a month ago, and gave Brook Street as my address. That was careless! . . . What's to-day?"

"It's now Sunday morning."

Simon sat up.

"Saved again! They won't be able to find out much before Monday. That's all the time we want. I must get hold of Pat. . . ."

He sank back again in the seat and fell silent, and remained very quiet for the rest of the journey; but there was little quietude in his mind. He was planning vaguely, scheming wildly, daydreaming, letting his imagination play as it would with this new state of affairs, hoping that something would emerge from the chaos; but all he found was a certain rueful resignation.

"At least, one could do worse for a last adventure," he said.

It was four o'clock when they drew up outside the bungalow, and found a tireless Orace opening the front door before the car had stopped. The Saint saw Vargan carried into the house, and found beer and sandwiches set out in the dining-room against their arrival.

"So far, so good," said Roger Conway, when the three of them reassembled over the refreshment.

"So far," agreed the Saint—so significantly that the other two both looked sharply at him.

"Do you mean more than that?" asked Norman Kent.

Simon smiled.

"I mean—what I mean. I've a feeling that something's hanging over us. It's not the police—as far as they're concerned I should say the odds are two to one on us. I don't know if it's Angel Face. I just don't know at all. It's a premonition, my cherubs."

"Forget it," advised Roger Conway sanely.

But the Saint looked out of the window at the bleak pallor that had bleached the eastern rim of the sky, and wondered.

5

How Simon Templar Went Back to Brook Street, and What Happened There

BREAKFAST WAS SERVED in the bungalow at an hour when all ordinary people, even on a Sunday, are finishing their midday meal. Conway and Kent sat down to it in their shirtsleeves and a stubby tousledness; but the

Saint had been for a swim in the river, shaved with Orace's razor, and dressed himself with as much care as if he had been preparing to pose for a magazine cover, and the proverbial morning daisy would have looked positively haggard beside him.

"No man," complained Roger, after inspecting the apparition, "has a right to look like this at this hour of the morning."

The Saint helped himself to three fried eggs and bacon to match, and sat down in his place.

"If," he said, "you could open your bleary eyes enough to see the face of that clock, you'd see that it's after half-past two of the afternoon."

"It's the principle of the thing," protested Conway feebly. "We didn't get to bed till nearly six. And three eggs . . ."

The Saint grinned.

"Appetite of the healthy open-air man. I was splashing merrily down the Thames while you two were snoring."

Norman opened a newspaper.

"Roger was snoring," he corrected. "His mouth stays open twenty-four hours a day. And now he's talking with his mouth full," he added offensively.

"I wasn't eating," objected Conway.

"You were," said the Saint crushingly. "I heard you."

He reached for the coffee-pot and filled a cup for himself with a flourish.

The premonition of danger that he had had earlier that morning was forgotten—so completely that it was as if a part of his memory had been blacked out. Indeed, he had rarely felt fitter and better primed to take on any amount of odds.

Outside, over the garden and the lawn running down to the river, the sun was shining; and through the open French windows of the morning-room came a breath of sweet, cool air fragrant with the scent of flowers.

The fevered violence of the night before had vanished as utterly as its darkness, and with the vanishing of darkness and violence vanished also all moods of dark foreboding. Those things belonged to the night; in the clear of daylight they seemed unreal, fantastic, incredible. There had been a battle—that was all. There would be more battles. And it was very good that it should be so—that a man should have such a cause to fight for, and such a heart and a body with which to fight it. . . . As he walked back from his bathe an hour ago, the Saint had seemed to hear again the sound of the trumpet. . . .

At the end of the meal he pushed back his chair and lighted a cigarette, and Conway looked at him expectantly.

"When do we go?"

"We?"

"I'll come with you."

"O.K.," said the Saint. "We'll leave when you're ready. We've got a lot to do. On Monday, Brook Street and all it contains will probably be in the hands of the police, but that can't be helped. I'd like to salvage my clothes, and one or two other trifles. The rest will have to go. Then there'll be bags to pack for you two, to last you out our stay here, and there'll be Pat's stuff as well. Finally, I must get some money. I think that's everything—and it'll keep us busy."

"What train is Pat travelling on?" asked Norman.

"That might be worth knowing," conceded the Saint. "I'll get through on the phone and find out while Roger's dressing."

He got his connection in ten minutes, and then he was speaking to her.

"Hullo, Pat, old darling. How's life?"

She did not have to ask who was the owner of that lazy, laughing voice.

"Hullo, Simon, boy!"

"I rang up," said the Saint, "because it's two days since I told you that you're the loveliest and most adorable thing that ever happened, and I love you. And further to ours of even date, old girl, when are you coming home? . . . No, no particular engagement. . . . Well, that doesn't matter. To tell you the truth, we don't want you back too late, but also, to tell you the truth, we don't want you back too early, either. . . . I'll tell you when I see you. Telephones have been known to have ears. . . . Well, if you insist, the fact is that Roger and I are entertaining a brace of Birds, and if you came back too early you might find out. . . . Yes, they are very Game. . . . That's easily settled—I'll look you out a train now if you like. Hold on."

He turned.

"Heave over the time-table, Norman—it's in that corner, under the back numbers of *La Vie Parisienne*. . . ."

He caught the volume dexterously.

"What time can you get away from this fête effect? . . . Sevenish? . . . No, that'll do fine. Terry can drive you over to Exeter, and if you get there alive you'll have heaps of time to catch a very jolly-looking train at—— Damn! I'm looking at the week-day trains. . . . And the Sunday trains are as slow as a Scotchman saying good-bye to a bawbee.

. . . Look here, the only one you'll have time to catch now is the 4:58. Gets in at 9:20. The only one after that doesn't get to London till nearly four o'clock to-morrow morning. I suppose you were thinking of staying over till to-morrow. . . . I'm afraid you mustn't, really. That *is* important. . . . Good enough, darling. Expect you at Brook Street about half-past nine. . . . So long, lass. God bless . . .''

He hung up the reciever with a smile as Roger Conway returned after a commendably quick toilet.

"And now, Roger, me bhoy, we make our dash!"

"All set, skipper."

"Then let's go."

And the Saint laughed softly, hands on hips. His dark hair was at its sleekest perfection, his blue eyes danced, his brown face was alight with an absurdly boyish enthusiasm. He slipped an arm through Conway's, and they went out together.

Roger approached the car with slower and slower steps. An idea seemed to have struck him.

"Are you going to drive?" he asked suspiciously.

"I am," said the Saint.

Conway climbed in with an unhappy sigh. He knew, from bitter past experience, that the Saint had original and hair-rising notions of his own about the handling of high-powered automobiles.

They reached Brook Street at half-past four.

"Are you going to drive back as well?" asked Roger.

"I am," said the Saint.

Mr. Conway covered his eyes.

"Put me on a nice slow train first, will you?" he said. "Oh, and make a will leaving everything to me. Then you can die with my blessing."

Simon laughed, and took him by the arm.

"Upstairs," he said, "there is beer. And then—work. Come on, sonny boy!"

For three hours they worked. Part of that time Conway gave to helping the Saint; then he went on to attend to his own packing and Norman Kent's. He returned towards eight o'clock, and dumped the luggage he brought with him directly out of his taxi into the Hirondel. The Saint's completed contribution—two steamer trunks on the carrier, and a heavy valise inside—was already there. The Hirondel certainly had the air of assisting in a wholesale removal.

Conway found the Saint sinking a tankard of ale with phenomenal rapidity.

"Oi!" said Conway, in alarm.

"Get yours down quickly," advised the Saint, indicating a second mug, which stood, full and ready, on the table. "We're off."

"Off?" repeated Roger puzzledly.

Simon jerked his empty can in the direction of the window.

"Outside," he said, "are a pair of prize beauties energetically doing nothing. I don't suppose you noticed them as you came in. I didn't myself, until a moment ago. I'll swear they've only just come on duty— I couldn't have missed them when I was loading up the car. But they've seen too much. Much too much."

Conway went to the window and looked out.

Presently:

"I don't see anyone suspicious."

"That's your innocent and guileless mind, my pet," said the Saint, coming over to join him. "If you were as old in sin as I am, you'd . . . Well, I'll be b-b-blowed!"

Conway regarded him gravely.

"It's the beer," he said. "Never mind. You'll feel better in a minute."

"Damned if I will!" crisped the Saint.

He slammed his tankard down on the window-sill, and caught Roger by both shoulders.

"Don't be an old idiot, Roger!" he cried. "You know me. I tell you this place was being watched. Police or Angel Face. We can't say which, but almost certainly Angel Face. Teal couldn't possibly have got as far as this in the time, I'll bet anything you like. But Angel Face could. And the two sleuths have beetled off with the news about us. So, to save trouble, we'll beetle off ourselves. Because, if I know anything about Angel Face yet, Brook Street is going to be rather less healthy than a hot spot in hell—inside an hour!"

"But Pat——"

The Saint looked at his watch.

"We've got two hours to fill up somehow. The Hirondel'll do it easy. down to Maidenhead, park the luggage, and back to Paddington Station in time to meet the train."

"And suppose we have a breakdown?"

"Breakdown hell! . . . But you're right. . . . Correction, then: I'll drop you at the station, and make the return trip to Maidenhead alone. You can amuse yourself in the bar, and I'll meet you there. . . . It's a good idea to get rid of the luggage, too. We don't know that the world won't have become rather sticky by half-past nine, and it'd be on the safe side to make the heavy journey while the going's good. If I leave now they won't have had time to make any preparations to follow me; and later we'd be able to slip them much more easily, if they happened to get after us, without all the impediments to pull our speed down.''

Conway found himself being rushed down the stairs as he listened to the Saint's last speech. The speech seemed to begin in Brook Street and finish at Paddington. Much of this impression, of course, was solely the product of Conway's overwrought imagination; but there was a certain foundation of fact in it, and the impression built thereon was truly symptomatic of Simon Templar's appalling velocity of transforming decision into action.

Roger Conway recovered coherent consciousness in the station buffet in a kind of daze; and by that time Simon Templar was hustling the Hirondel westwards.

The Saint's brain was in a ferment of questions. Would Marius arrange a raid on the flat in Brook Street? Or would he, finding that the loaded car which his spies had reported had gone, assume that the birds had flown? Either way, that didn't seem to matter; but the point it raised was what Marius would do next, after he had either discovered or decided that his birds had flown. . . . And, anyway, since Marius must have known that the Saint had attended the rough party at Esher, why hadn't Brook Street been raided before? . . . Answer: Because (*a*) a show like that must take a bit of organising, and (*b*) it would be easier, anyhow, to wait until dark. Which, at that time of year, was fairly late at night. Thereby making it possible to do the return journey to and from Maidenhead on good time. . . . But Marious would certainly be doing something. Put yourself in the enemy's place. . . .

So the Saint reached Maidenhead in under an hour, and was on the road again five minutes later.

It was not his fault that he was stopped halfway back by a choked carburettor jet which it took him fifteen minutes to locate and remedy.

Even so, the time he made on the rest of the trip amazed even himself.

In the station entrance he actually cannoned into Roger Conway.

''Hullo,'' said the Saint. ''Where are you off to? The train's just about due in.''

Conway stared at him.

Then he pointed dumbly at the clock in the booking-hall.

Simon looked at it, and went white.

''But my watch,'' he began stupidly, ''my watch——''

''You must have forgotten to wind it up last night.''

"You met the train?"

Conway nodded.

"It's just possible that I may have missed her, but I'd swear she wasn't on it. Probably she didn't catch it——"

"Then there's a telegram at Brook Street to say so. We'll go there—if all the armies of Europe are in the way!"

They went. Conway, afterwards, preferred not to remember that drive.

And yet peace seemed to reign in Brook Street. The lamps were alight, and it was getting dark rapidly, for the sky had clouded over in the evening. As was to be expected on a Sunday, there were few people about, and hardly any traffic. There was nothing at all like a crowd—no sign that there had been any disturbance at all. There was a man leaning negligently against a lamp-post, smoking a pipe as though he had nothing else to do in the world. It happened that, as the Hirondel stopped, another man came up and spoke to him. The Saint saw the incident, and ignored it.

He went through the front door and up the stairs like a whirlwind. Conway followed him.

Conway really believed that the Saint would have gone through a police garrison or a whole battalion of Angel Faces; but there were none there to go through. Nor had the flat been entered, as far as they could see. It was exactly as they had left it.

But there was no telegram.

"I might have missed her," said Conway helplessly. "She may be on her way now. The taxi may have broken down—or had a slight accident——"

He stopped abruptly at the blaze in the Saint's eyes.

"Look at the clock," said the Saint, with a kind of curbed savagery.

Roger looked at the clock. The clock said that it was a quarter of ten.

And he saw the terrible look on the Saint's face, and it hypnotised him. The whole thing had come more suddenly than anything that had ever happened to Roger Conway before, and it had swirled him to the loss of his bearings in the same way that a man in a small boat in tropical seas may be lost in a squall. The blow had fallen too fiercely for him. He could feel the shock, and yet he was unable to determine what manner of blow had been struck, or even if a blow had been struck at all, in any comprehensible sense.

He could only look at the clock and say helplessly: "It's a quarter to ten."

The Saint was saying: "She'd have let me know if she'd missed the train——"

"Or waited for the next one."

"Oh, for the love of Mike!" snarled the Saint. "Didn't you hear me ring her up from Maidenhead? I looked out all the trains then, and the only next one gets in at three fifty-one to-morrow morning. D'you think she'd have waited for that one without sending me a wire?"

"But if I didn't see her at Paddington, and anything had happened to her taxi——"

But the Saint had taken a cigarette, and was lighting it with a hand that could never have been steadier; and the Saint's face was a frozen mask.

"More beer," said the Saint.

Roger moved to obey.

"And talk to me," said the Saint, "talk to me quietly and sanely, will you? Because fool suggestions won't help me. I don't have to ring up Terry and ask if Pat caught that train, because I know she did. I don't have to ask if you're quite sure you couldn't have missed her at the station, because I know you didn't. . . ."

The Saint was deliberately breaking a match-stick into tiny fragments and dropping them one by one into the ash-tray.

"And don't tell me I'm getting excited about nothing," said the Saint, "because I tell you I know. I know that Pat was coming on a slow train, which stops at other places before it gets to London. I know that Marius has got Pat, and I know that he's going to try to use her to force me to give up Vargan, and I know that I'm going to find Dr. Rayt Marius and kill him. So talk to me very quietly and sanely, Roger, because if you don't I think I shall go quite mad."

6

How Roger Conway Drove the Hirondel, and the Saint Took a Knife in His Hand

CONWAY HAD A full tankard of beer in each hand. He looked at the tankards as a man might look at a couple of dragons that have strayed into his drawing-room. It seemed to Roger, for some reason, that it was unaccountably ridiculous for him to be standing in the middle of the Saint's room with a tankard of beer in each hand. He cleared his throat.

He said: "Are you sure you aren't—making too much of it?"

And he knew, as he said it, that it was the fatuously useless kind of remark for which he would cheerfully have ordered anyone else's execution. He put down the tankards on the table and lighted a cigarette as if he hated it.

"That's not quiet and sane," said the Saint. "That's wasting time. Damn it, old boy, you know how it was between Pat and me! I always knew that if anything happened to her I'd know it at once—if she were a thousand miles away. *I know.*"

The Saint's icy control broke for a moment. Only for a moment. Roger's arm was taken in a crushing grip. The Saint didn't know his strength. Roger could have cried out with pain; but he said nothing at all. He was in the presence of something that he could only understand dimly.

"I've seen the whole thing," said the Saint, with a cold devil in his voice. "I saw it while you were gaping at that clock. You'll see it, too, when you've got your brain on to it. But I don't have to think."

"But how could Marius——"

"Easy! He'd already tracked us here. He'd been watching the place. The man's thorough. He'd naturally have put other agents on to the people he saw visiting me. And how could he have missed Pat? . . . One of his men probably followed her down to Devonshire. Then, after the Esher show, Marius got in touch with that man. She could easily be got at on the train. They could take her off, say, at Reading—doped. . . . She wasn't on her guard. She didn't know there was any danger. That one man could have done it. . . . With a car to meet him at Reading. . . . And Marius is going to hold Pat in the scales against me—against everything we've set out to do. Binding me hand and foot. Putting my dear one in the forefront of the battle, and daring me to fire. And laying the powder-train for his foul slaughter under the shield of her blessed body. *And laughing at us.* . . ."

Then Roger begin to understand less dimly, and he stared at the Saint as he would have stared at a ghost.

He said, like a man waking from a dream: "If you're right, our show's finished."

"I am right," said the Saint. "Ask yourself the question."

He released Roger's arm as if he had only just become aware that he was holding it.

Then, in three strides, the Saint was at the window; and Conway had just started to realise his intention when the Saint justified, and at the same time smithereened, that realisation with one single word.

"Gone."

"You mean the——"

"Both of 'em. Of course, Marius kept up the watch on the house in case we were being tricky. The man who arrived at the same time as we did was the relief. Or a messenger to say that Marius had lifted the trump card, and the watch could pack up. Then they saw us arrive."

"But they can't have gone a moment——"

The Saint was back by the table.

"Just that," snapped the Saint. "They've gone—but they can't have been gone a moment. The car's outside. Could you recognize either of them again?"

"I could recognise one."

"I could recognise the other. Foreign-looking birds, with ugly mugs. Easy again. Let's go!"

It was more than Roger could cope with. His brain hadn't settled down yet. He couldn't get away from a sane, reasonable, conventional conviction that the Saint was hurling up a solid mountain from the ghost of a molehill. He couldn't quite get away from it even while the clock on the mantel-piece was giving him the lie with every tick. But he got between the Saint and the door, somehow—he wasn't sure how.

"Hadn't you better sit down and think it out before you do anything rash?"

"Hadn't you better go and hang yourself?" rapped the Saint impatiently.

Then his bitterness softened. His hands fell on Roger's shoulders.

"Don't you remember another time when we were in this room, you and I?" he said. "We were trying to get hold of Marius then—for other reasons. We could only find out his telephone number. And that's all we know to this day—unless we can make one of those birds who were outside tell us more than the man who gave us the telephone number. They're likely to know more than that—we're big enough now to have the bigger men after us. They're the one chance of a clue we've got, and I'm taking it. This way!"

He swept Conway aside, and burst out of the flat. Conway followed. When the Saint stopped in Brook Street, and turned to look Roger was beside him.

"You drive."

He was opening the door of the car as he cracked the order. As Roger touched the self-starter, the Saint climbed in beside him.

Roger said hopelessly: "We've no idea which way they've gone."

"Get going! There aren't so many streets round here. Make this the centre of a circle. First into Regent Street, cut back through Conduit Street to New Bond Street—Oxford Street—back through Hanover Square. Burn it, son, haven't you any imagination?"

Now, in that district the inhabited streets are slashed across the map in a crazy tangle, and the two men might have taken almost any of them, according to the unknown destination for which they were making. The task of combing through that tangle, with so little qualification, struck Roger as being rather more hopeless than looking for one particular grain of sand in the Arizona Desert; but he couldn't tell the Saint that. The Saint wouldn't have admitted it, anyway, and Roger wouldn't have had the heart to try to convince him.

And yet Roger was wrong, for the Saint sat beside him and drove with Roger's hands. And the Saint knew that people in cities tend to move in the best-beaten tracks, particularly in a strange city, for fear of losing their way—exactly as a man lost in the bush will follow a tortuous trail rather than strike across open country in the direction which he feels he should take. And the men looked foreign and probably were foreign, and the foreigner is afraid of losing himself in any but the long, straight, bright roads, though they may take him to his objective by the most roundabout route.

Unless, of course, the foreigners had taken a native guide in the shape of a taxi. But Conway could not suggest that to the Saint, either.

"Keep on down here," Simon Templar was saying. "Never mind what I told you before. Now I should cut away to the right—down Vigo Street."

Roger spun the wheel, and the Hirondel skidded and swooped across the very nose of an omnibus. For one fleeting second, in the bottleneck of Vigo Street, a taxi-driver appeared to meditate, disputing their right of way; fortunately for all concerned, he abandoned that idea hurriedly.

Then Simon was speaking again.

"Right up Bond Street. That's the spirit."

Roger said: "You'll collect half a dozen summonses before you've finished with this. . . ."

"Damn that," said the Saint; and they swept recklessly past a constable who had endeavoured to hold them up, and drowned his outraged shout in the stutter of their departing exhaust.

By Roger Conway that day's driving was afterwards to be remembered in nightmares, and that last drive more than any other journey.

He obeyed the Saint blindly. It wasn't Roger's car, anyway. But he would never have believed that such feats of murderous road-hogging could have been performed in a London street—if he had not been made to perform them himself.

And yet it seemed to be to no purpose; for although he was scanning, in every second of that drive in which he was able to take his eyes off the road, the faces of the pedestrians they passed, he did not see the face he sought. And suppose, after all, they did find the men they were after? What could be done about it in an open London street—except call for the police, whom they dared not appeal to?

But Roger Conway was alone in discouragement.

"We'll try some side streets now," said the Saint steadily. "Down there——"

And Roger, an automaton, lashed round the corner on two wheels.

And then, towards the bottom of George Street, Roger pointed, and the Saint saw two men walking side by side.

"Those two!"

"For Heaven's sake!" said the Saint softly, meaninglessly, desperately; and the car sprang forward like a spurred horse as Roger opened the throttle wide.

The Saint was looking about him and rising from his seat at the same moment. In Conduit Street there had been traffic; but in George Street, at that moment, there was nothing but a stray car parked empty by the kerb, and three pedestrians going the other way, and—the two.

Said the Saint: "I think so. . . ."

"I'm sure," said Roger; and, indeed, he was quite sure, because they had passed the two men by that time, and the Hirondel was swinging in to the kerb with a scream of brakes a dozen feet in front of them.

"Watch me!" said the Saint, and was out of the car before it had rocked to a standstill.

He walked straight into the path of the two men, and they glanced at him with curious but unsuspecting eyes.

He took the nearest man by the lapels of his coat with one hand, and the man was surprised. A moment later the man was not feeling surprise or any other emotion, for the Saint looked one way and saw Roger Conway following him, and then he looked the other way and hit the man under the jaw.

The man's head whipped back as if it had been struck by a cannon-ball; and, in fact, there was very little difference between the speed and force of the Saint's fist and the speed and force of a cannon-ball.

But the man never reached the ground. As his knees gave limply under him, and his companion sprang forward with a shout awakening on his lips, the Saint caught him about the waist and lifted him from his feet, and heaved him bodily across the pavement, so that he actually fell into Conway's arms.

"Home, James," said the Saint, and turned again on his heel.

On the lips of the second man there was that awakening of a shout, and in his eyes was the awakening of something that might have been taken for fear, or suspicion, or a kind of vague and startled perplexity; but these expressions were nebulous and half-formed, and they never came to maturity, for the Saint spun the man round by one shoulder and locked an arm about his neck in such a way that it was impossible for him to shout or register any other expression than that of a man about to suffocate.

And in the same hold the Saint lifted him off the ground, mostly by the neck, so that the man might well have thought that his neck was about to be broken; but the only thing that was broken was the spring of one of the cushions at the back of the car when the Saint heaved him on to it.

The Saint followed him into the back seat; and, when the man seemed ready to try another shout, Simon seized his wrists in a grip that might have changed the shout to a scream if the Saint had not uttered a warning.

"Don't scream, sweetheart," said the Saint coldly. "It might break both your arms."

The man did not scream. Nor did he shout. And on the floor of the car, at the Saint's feet, his companion lay like one dead.

In the cold light of sanity that came long afterwards, Simon Templar was to wonder how on earth they got away with it. Roger Conway, who was even then far too coldly sane for his own comfort, was wondering all the time how on earth they were getting away with it. But for the moment Simon Templar was mad—and the fact remained that they had got away with it.

The Saint's resourceful speed, and the entirely fortuitous desertedness of the street, had made it possible to carry out the abduction without a sound being made that might have attracted attention. And the few people there were whose attention might have been attracted had passed on, undisturbed, unconscious of the swift seconds of hectic melodrama that had whirled through George Street, Hanover Square, behind their peaceful backs.

That the Saint would have acted in exactly the same way if the street had been crowded with an equal mixture of panicky population, plain-clothes men, and uniformed policemen, was nothing whatever to do with anything at all. Once again the Saint had proved, to his own sufficient satisfaction, as he had proved many times in his life before, that desperate dilemmas are usually best solved by desperate measures, and that intelligent foolhardiness will often get by where too much discretion betrays valour into the mulligatawny. And the thought of the notice that must have been take of the Hirondel during the first part of that wild chase (it was not an inconspicuous car at the best of times, even when sedately driven, that long, lean, silver-grey King of the Road) detracted nothing from the Saint's estimate of his success. One could not have one's cake and eat it. And certainly he had obtained the cake to eat. Two cakes. Ugly ones. . . .

Even then there might have been trouble in Brook Street when they returned with the cargo, but the Saint did not allow any trouble.

There were two men to be taken across the strip of pavement to the door of the flat. One man was long and lean, and the other man was short and fat; and the lean man slept. The Saint kept his grip on one wrist of the fat man, and half supported the lean man with his other arm. Roger placed himself on the other side of the lean man.

"Sing," commanded the Saint; and they crossed the pavement discordantly and drunkenly.

A man in evening dress passed them with a supercilious nose. A man in rags passed them with an envious nose. A patrolling policeman peered at them with an officious nose; but the Saint had opened the door, and they were reeling cacophonously into the house. So the officious nose went stolidly upon its way, after taking the number of the car from which they had disembarked, for the law has as yet no power to prevent men being as drunk and disorderly as they choose in their own homes. And, certainly, the performance, extempore as it was, had been most convincing. The lean man had clearly failed to last the course; the two tall and well-dressed young men who supported him between them were giving most circumstantial evidence of the thoroughness with which they had lubricated their withins; and if the sounds emitted by the fat man were too wild and shrill to be easily classified as song, and if he seemed somewhat unwilling to proceed with his companions into further dissipations, and if there was a strange, strained look in his eye—well, the state which he had apparently reached was regrettable, but nobody's business. . . .

And before the suspicious nose had reached the next corner, the men who had passed beneath it were in the first-floor apartment above it, and the lean one was being carelessly dropped spread-eagle on the sitting-room carpet.

"Fasten the door, Roger," said the Saint shortly.

Then he released his agonising hold on the fat man's wrist, and the fat man stopped yelping and began to talk.

"Son of a pig," began the fat man, rubbing his wrist tenderly; and then he stopped, appalled at what he saw.

There was a little knife in the Saint's hand—a toy with a six-inch leaf-shaped blade and a delicately chased ivory hilt. It appeared to have come from nowhere, but actually it had come from the neat leather sheath strapped to the Saint's forearm under the sleeve, where it always lived; and the name of the knife was Anna. There was a story to Anna, a savage and flamboyant story of the godless lands, which may be told one day: she had taken many lives. To the Saint she was almost human, that beautifully fashioned, beautifully balanced little creature of death; he could do tricks with her that would have made most circus knife-throwers look like amateurs. But at that moment he was not thinking of tricks.

As Roger switched on the light, the light glinted on the blade; but the light in the Saint's eyes was no less cold and inclement than the light on the steel.

7

How Simon Templar Was Saintly, and Received Another Visitor

SIMON TEMPLAR, IN all his years of wandering and adventure, had only fallen for one woman, and that was Patricia Holm. Therefore, as might have been expected, he fell heavily. And yet—he was realising it dimly, as one might realise an unthinkable heresy—in the eighteen months that they had been together he had started to get used to her. He had, he realised, been growing out of the first ecstatic wonder; and the thing that had taken its place had been so quiet and insidious that it had enchanted him while he was still unaware of it. It had had to await this shock to be revealed.

And the relevation, when it came, carried with it a wonder that infinitely eclipsed the more blatant brilliance of the wonder that had slipped away. This was the kind of wild and awful wonder that might overtake a man who, having walked in the sunshine all the days of his life, sees the sun itself for the first time, with a dreadful and tremendous understanding, and sees at once a vision of the darkness that would lie over the world if the sun ceased from shining.

The Saint said, very softly, to the fat man: "Son of a pig to you, sweetheart. And now listen. I'm going to ask you some questions. You can either answer them, or die slowly and painfully, just as you like—but you'll do one or the other before you leave this room."

The fat man was in a different class from that of the wretched little weed in the pot hat from whom Simon Templar had extracted information before. There was a certain brute resolution in the fat man's beady eyes, a certain snarling defiance in the twist of the thin lips, like the desperate determination of a beast at bay. Simon took no count of that.

"Do you understand, you septic excrescence?" said the Saint gently.

And there was hatred in the Saint's heart, a hatred that was his very own, that no one else could have understood; but there was another kind of devilry in the Saint's eyes and in the purring gentleness of his voice, a kind of devilry that no one could have helped understanding, that the man in front of him understood with terror, an outward and visible and malignant hatred; and it was plainly centred upon the fat man; and the fat man recoiled slowly, step by step, as the Saint advanced, until he came up against the table and could not move backwards any farther.

"I hope you don't think I'm bluffing, dear little fat one," the Saint went on, in the same velvety voice. "Because that would be foolish of you. You've done, or had a hand in doing, something which I object to very much. I object to it in a general way, and always have; but this time I object to it even more, in a personal way, because this time it involves someone who means more to me than your gross mind will ever understand. Do you follow the argument, you miserable wart?"

The man was trying to edge away backwards round the table, but he could not break away, for the Saint moved sideways simultaneously. And he could not break away from the Saint's eyes—those clear blue eyes that were ordinarily so full of laughter and bubbling mischief that were then so bleak and pitiless.

And the Saint went on speaking.

"I'm not concerned with the fact that you're merely the agent of Dr. Rayt Marius—ah, that makes you jump! I know a little more than you thought I did, don't I? . . . But we're not concerned with that, either. . . . If you insist on mixing with people like that, you must be prepared to take the consequences. And if you think the game's worth the candle, you must also be prepared for an accident with the candle. That's fair, isn't it? . . . So that the point we're going to disagree about is that you've had a share in annoying me—and I object very much to being annoyed. . . . No, you don't, sonny boy!"

There was a gun in the fat man's hand, and then there was not a gun in the fat man's hand; for the Saint moved forwards and to one side with a swift, stealthy, cat-like movement, and this time the fat man could not help screaming as he dropped the gun.

"*Ach!* You would my wrist break——"

"Cheerfully, beloved," said Simon. "And your neck later on. But first . . ."

Tightening instead of slackening that grip on the fat man's wrist, the Saint bent him backwards over the table, holding him easily with fingers of incredible strength; and the man saw the blade of the knife flash before his eyes.

"Once upon a time, when I was in Papua," said the Saint, in that dispassionately conversational way which was indescribably more terrifying than any loud-voiced anger, "a man came out of the jungle into the town where I was. He was a prospector, and a pig-headed prospector, and he had insisted on prospecting a piece of country that all the old hands had warned him against. And the natives had caught him at the time of the full moon. They're always very pleased to catch white men at that time, because they can be used in the scheme of festivities and entertainment. They have primitive forms of amusement—very. And one of their ways of amusing themselves with this man had been to cut off his eyelids. Before I start doing the same thing to you, will you consider for a moment the effect that operation will probably have on your beauty sleep?"

"God!" babbled the man shrilly. "You cannot——"

The man tried to struggle, but he was held with a hand of iron. For a little while he could move his head, but then the Saint swung on to the table on top of him and clamped the head between his knees.

"Don't talk so loud," said the Saint, and his fingers left the wrist and sidled round the throat. "There are other people in this building, and I should hate you to alarm them. With regard to this other matter, now—did I hear you say I couldn't do it? I beg to differ. I could do it very well. I shall be very gentle, and you should not feel very much pain—just at the moment. It's the after-effects that will be so unpleasant. So think. If you talk, and generally behave like a good boy, I might be persuaded to let you off. I won't promise you anything, but it's possible."

"I will not——"

"Really not? . . . Are you going to be difficult, little one? Are you going to sacrifice your beautiful eyelids and go slowly blind? Are you going to force me to toast the soles of your feet at the gas-fire, and drive chips of wood under your finger-nails, and do other crude things like that—before you come to your senses? Really, you'll be giving yourself a lot of unnecessary pain. . . ."

And the Saint held the knife quite close to the man's eyes and brought it downwards very slowly. The point gleamed like a lonely star, and the man stared at it, hypnotised, mute with horror. And Roger Conway was also hypnotised, and stood like a man carved in ice.

"Do you talk?" asked the Saint caressingly.

Again the man tried to scream, and again the Saint's fingers choked the scream back into his windpipe. The Saint brought the knife down farther, and the point of it actually pricked the skin.

Roger Conway felt cold beads of perspiration breaking out on his forehead, but he could not find his voice. He knew that the Saint would do exactly what he had threatened to do, if he were forced to do it. He knew the Saint. He had seen the Saint in a hundred strange situations and a hundred moods, but he had never seen the Saint's face chiselled into such an inexorable grimness as it wore then. It was like granite.

And Roger Conway knew then, in the blazing light of experience, what before he had only understood mistily, in the twilight of theory—that the wrath of saints can be a far more dreadful thing than the wrath of sinners.

The man on the table must have understood it also—the fantastic fact that a man of Simon Templar's calibre, in such an icy rage, even in civilised England, would stop for nothing. And the breath that the Saint let him take came in a kind of shuddering groan.

"Do you talk, beautiful?" asked the Saint again, ever so gently.

"I talk."

It was not a voice—it was a whimper.

"I talk," whimpered the man. "I will do anything. Only take away that knife——"

For a moment the Saint did not move.

Then, very slowly, like a man in a trance, he took the knife away and looked at it as if he had never seen it before. And a queer little laugh trickled through his lips.

"Very dramatic," he remarked. "And almost horrible. I didn't know I had it in me."

And he gazed at the man curiously, as he might have gazed at a fly on a window-pane in an idle moment and remembered stories of school-boys who were amused to pull off their wings.

Then he climbed slowly down from the table and took out his cigarette-case.

The man he had left did not so much raise himself off the table as roll off it; and, when his feet touched the floor, it was seen that he could scarcely stand.

Roger pushed him roughly into a chair, from which, fingering his throat, he could see the man who still lay where he had fallen.

"Don't look so surprised," said Roger. "the last man the Saint hit like that was out for half an hour, and your pal's only been out twenty minutes."

Simon flicked a match into the fireplace and returned to face the prisoner.

"Let's hear your little song, honeybunch," he said briefly.

"What do you want to know?"

"First thing of all, I want to know what's been done with the girl who was taken to-night."

"That I do not know."

The Saint's cigarette tilted up to a dangerous angle between his lips, and his hands went deep into his trousers pockets.

"You don't seem to have got the idea, beautiful," he remarked sweetly. "This isn't a game—as you'll find out if you don't wake yourself up in rather less time than it takes me to get my hands on you again. I'm quite ready to resume the surgical operation as soon as you like. So go on talking, because I just love your voice, and it helps me to forget all the unpleasant things I ought to be doing to your perfectly appalling face."

The man shuddered and cowered back into the depths of the chair. His hands flew to his eyes; it may have been to shut out a ghastly vision, or it may have been to try to escape from Saint's merciless blue stare.

"I do not know!" he almost screamed. "I swear it——"

"Then tell me what you do know, you rat," said Simon, "and then I'll make you remember some more."

Words came to the fat man in an incoherent, pelting stream, lashed on by fear.

He was acting on the instructions of Dr. Marius. That was true. The house in Brook Street had been closely watched for the last twenty-four hours, he himself being one of the watchers. He had seen the departure the previous night, but they had not had the means to follow a car. Two other men had been sent to inspect the premises that afternoon, had seen the loaded car outside, and had rushed away together to report.

"Both of them?" interrupted the Saint.

"Both of them. It was a criminal mistake. But they will be punished."

"How will you be rewarded, I wonder?" murmured Simon.

The fat man shivered, and went on.

"One was sent back immediately, but the car had gone. The Doctor then said that he had made other plans, and one man would be enough to keep watch, in case you return. I was that man. Hermann"—he pointed to the inert figure on the floor—"had just come to relieve me when you came back. We were going to report it."

"Both of you?"

"Both of us."

"A criminal mistake," drawled the Saint sardonically. "But I expect you will be punished. Yes?"

The man winced.

Another of his comrades, he said, had been told off to follow the girl. It had been impressed upon the sleuths that no movement should be missed, and no habit overlooked, however trifling. Marius had not divulged the reason for this vigilance, but he had left them in no doubt of its importance. In that spirit Patricia had been followed to Devonshire.

"Your boss seems very unwilling to meet me again personally," observed the Saint grimly. "How wise of him!"

"We could afford to take no risks——"

" 'We'?"

Simon swooped on the pronoun like a hawk.

"I mean——"

"I know what you mean, sweetness," said the Saint silkily. "You mean that you didn't mean to let on that you knew more about this than you said. You're not just a hired crook, like the last specimen of your kind I had to tread on. You're a secret agent. We understand that. We understand also that, however much respect you may have for the continued wholeness of your own verminous hide, a most commendable patriotism for your misbegotten country will make you keep on fighting and lying as long as you can. Very good. I applaud. But I'm afraid my appreciation of your one solitary virtue will have to stop there—at just that one theoretical pat on the back. After which, we go back to our own private, practical quarrel. And what you've got to get jammed well into the misshapen lump of bone that keeps your unwashed ears apart, is that I'm a bit of a fighter myself, and I think—somehow, somehow, I think, dear one—I think I'm a better fighter than you are.''

"I did not mean——"

"Don't lie," said the Saint, in a tone of mock reproach that held behind its superficial flippance a kind of glacial menace. "Don't lie to me. I don't like it."

Roger moved off the wall which he had been propping up.

"Put him back on the table, old boy," he suggested.

"I'm going to," said the Saint, "unless he spills the beans in less than two flaps of a duck's rudder."

He came a little closer to the fat man.

"Now, you loathsome monstrosity—listen to me. The game's up. You've put both feet in it with that little word 'we.' And I'm curious. Very, very curious and inquisitive. I want to know everything about you—the story of your life, and your favourite movie star, and your golf handicap, and whether you sleep with your pyjama trousers inside or outside the jacket. I want you to tell me about yourself. For instance, when Marius told you that you could let up on the watch here, as he'd made 'other plans'—didn't he say that there was a girl concerned in those plans?''

"No."

"That's two lies," said the Saint. "Next time you lie, you will be badly hurt. Second question: I know that Marius arranged for the girl to be drugged on the train, and taken off it before it reached London—but where was she to be taken to?''

"I do not—— *A-a-a-a-ah!*"

"I warned you," said the Saint.

"Are you a devil?" sobbed the man, and the Saint showed his teeth.

"Not really. Just an ordinary man who objects to being molested. I thought I'd made that quite plain. Of course, I'm in a hurry this evening, so that may make me seem a little hasty. Now are you going to remember things—truthful things—or shall we have some more unpleasantness?''

The man shrank back from him, quivering.

"I do not know any more," he blubbered. "I swear——"

"Where is Marius now?"

But the man did not answer immediately, for the sudden ringing of a bell sounded clearly through the apartment.

For a second the Saint was immobile.

Then he stepped round behind the prisoner's chair, and the little knife slid out of its sheath again. The prisoner saw the flash of it, and his eyes dilated with terror. A cry rose to his lips, and the Saint stifled it with a hand over his mouth. Then the point stung the man over the heart.

"Just one word," said the Saint—"just one word, and you'll say the rest of the sentence to the Recording Angel. Who d'you think it is, Roger?"

"Teal?"

"Having traced that motor agent to his Sunday lair, and got on our trail?"

"If we don't answer——"

"They'll break in. There's the car outside to tell them we're here. No, they'll have to come in——"

"Just when we're finding out things?"

Simon Templar's eyes glittered.

"Give me that gun!"

Conway picked up the automatic that the fat man had dropped, which had lain neglected on the floor ever since, and handed it over obediently.

"I'll tell you," said the Saint, "that no man born of woman is going to interfere with me. I'm going to finish getting everything I want out of this lump of refuse, and then I'm going to act on it—to find Pat—and I'll shoot my way through the whole of Scotland Yard to do it, if I have to. Now go and open that door."

Conway nodded.

"I'm with you," he said, and went out.

The Saint waited calmly.

His left hand still held the slim blade of Anna over the fat man's heart, ready to drive it home, and his ears were alert for the faintest sound of a deeply drawn breath that might be the prelude to a shout. His right hand held the automatic, concealed behind the back of the chair.

But when Roger came back, and the Saint saw the man who came with him, he remained exactly as he was; and no one could have remarked the slightest change in the desolate impassivity of his face. Only his heart leapt sickeningly, and slithered back anyhow into its place, leaving a strange feeling of throbbing emptiness spreading across the track of that thudding somersault.

"Pleased to meet you again, Marius," said the Saint.

8

How Simon Templar Entertained His Guest and Broke Up the Party

THEN, SLOWLY, THE Saint straightened up.

No one would ever know what an effort his calm and smiling imperturbability cost him; and yet, as a matter of fact, it was easier than the calm he had previously maintained before Roger Conway when there was really nothing to be calm about.

For this was something that the Saint understood. He had not the temperament to remain patient in periods of enforced inaction; he could never bring his best to bear against an enemy whom he could not see; subtleties were either above or beneath him, whichever way you like to look at it.

In Simon Templar there was much of his celebrated namesake, the Simple One. He himself was always ready to confess it, saying that, in spite of his instinctive understanding of the criminal mind, he would never have made a successful detective. His brain was capable of it, but his character wasn't. He preferred the more gaudy colours, the broader and more clean-cut line, the simple and straight-forward and startling things. He was a fighting man. His genius and inspiration led him into battles and showed him how to win them; but he rarely thought about them. He had ideals, and he rarely thought about those: they were laid down for him by an authority greater than himself, and remained apart and unquestionable. He disliked any sort of thought that was not as concrete as a weapon. To him, any other sort of thought was a heresy and a curse, and insidious sickness, sapping honesty and action. He asked for different things—the high heart of the happy warrior, the swagger and the flourish, the sound of the trumpet. He had said it himself; and it should go down

as one of the few statements the Saint ever made about himself with no
suggestion of pose. "Battle, murder, and sudden death," he had said.

And now, at last, he was on ground that he knew, desperate and
dangerous as it might be.

"Take over the pop-gun, Roger."

Cool, smooth, mocking, with a hint of laughter—the voice of the old
Saint. He turned again to Marius, smiling and debonair.

"It's nice of you," he said genially, "to give us a call. Have a drink,
Tiny Tim?"

Marius advanced a little further into the room.

He was robed in conventional morning coat and striped trousers. The
stiff perfection of the garb contrasted grotesquely with his neolithic stature
and the hideously ugly expressionlessness of a face that might have been
fashioned after the model of some savage devil-god.

He glanced round without emotion at Roger Conway, who leaned
against the door with his commandeered automatic comfortably concentrating on an easy target; and then he turned again to the Saint, who was
swinging his little knife like a pendulum between his finger and thumb.

Thoughtful was the Saint, calm with a vivid and violent calm, like a
leopard gathering for a spring; but Marius was as calm as a gigantic
Buddha.

"I see you have some servants of mine here," said Marius.

His voice, for such a man, was extraordinary soft and high-pitched;
his English would have been perfect but for its exaggerated precision.

"I have," said the Saint blandly. "You may think it odd of me, but
I've given up standing on my dignity, and I'm now a practising Socialist.
I go out into the highways and byways every Sunday evening and collect
bits and pieces. These are to-night's bag. How did you know?"

"I did not know. One of them should have reported to me a long time
ago, and my servants know better than to be late. I came to see what had
happened to him. You will please let him go—and his friend."

The Saint raised one eyebrow.

"I'm not sure that they want to," he remarked. "One of them, at
least, is temporarily incapable of expressing his views on the subject. As
for the other—well, we were just starting to get on so nicely together.
I'm sure he'd hate to have to leave me."

The man thus indirectly appealed to spat out some words in a language
which the Saint did not understand. Simon smothered him with a cushion.

"Don't interrupt," he drawled. "It's rude. First I have my say, then you have yours. That's fair. And I'm sure Dr. Marius would like to share our little joke, particularly as it's about himself."

The giant's mouth formed into something like a ghastly smile.

"Hadn't you better hear my joke first?" he suggested.

"Second," said the Saint. "Quite definitely second. Because your joke is sure to be so much funnier than mine, and I'd hate mine to fall flat after it. This joke is in the form of a little song, and it's about a man whom we call Tiny Tim, whom I once had to kick with some vim. He recovered, I fear, but fox-hunting this year will have little attraction for him. You haven't given us time to rehearse it, or I'd ask the boys to sing it to you. Never mind. Sit right down and tell me the story of your life."

The giant was not impressed.

"You appear to know my name," he said.

"Very well," beamed the Saint. "Any relation to the celebrated Dr. Marius?"

"I am not unknown."

"I mean," said the Saint, "the celebrated Dr. Marius whose living was somewhat precarious, for his bedside technique was decidedly weak, though his ideas were many and various. Does that ring the bell and return the penny?"

Marius moved his huge right hand in an inpatient gesture.

"I am not here to listen to your humour, Mr.——"

"Templar," supplied the Saint. "So pleased to be met."

"I do not wish to waste any time——"

Simon lowered his eyes, which had been fixed on the ceiling during the labour of poetical composition, and allowed them to rest upon Marius. There was something very steely and savage about those eyes. The laughter had gone out of them utterly. Roger had seen it go.

"Naturally, we don't want to waste any time," said the Saint quietly. "Thank you for reminding me. It's a thing I should hate very much to forget while you're here. I may tell you that I'm going to murder you, Marius. But before we talk any more about that, let me save you the trouble of saying what you were going to say."

Marius shrugged.

"You appear to be an intelligent man, Mr. Templar."

"Thanks very much. But let's keep the bouquets on ice till we want them, will you? Then they might come in handy for the wreath. . . . The business of the moment interests me more. One: you're going to tell me that a certain lady named Patricia Holm is now your prisoner."

The giant bowed.

"I'm sorry to have had to make such a conventional move," he said. "On the other hand, it is often said that the most conventional principles have the deepest foundations. I have always found that saying to be true when applied to the time-honoured expedient of taking a woman whom a man loves as a hostage for his good behaviour—particularly with a man of what I judge to be your type, Mr. Templar."

"Very interesting," said the Saint shortly. "And I suppose Miss Holm's safety is to be the price of the safety of your—er—servants? I believe that's also in the convention."

Marius spread out his enormous hands.

"Oh, no," he said, in that thin, soft voice. "Oh, dear me, no! That convention is not by any means as trivial as that. Is not the fair lady's safety always the price of something more than mere pawns in the game?"

"Meaning?" inquired the Saint innocently.

"Meaning a certain gentleman in whom I am interested, whom you were successful in removing from the protection of my servants last night."

"Was I?"

"I have reason to believe that you were. Much as I respect your integrity, Mr. Templar, I fear that in this case your contradiction will not be sufficient to convince me against the evidence of my own eyes."

The Saint swayed gently on his heels.

"Let me suggest," he said, "that you're very sure I got him."

"Let me suggest," said Marius suavely, "that you're very sure I've got Miss Holm."

"I haven't got him."

"Then I have not got Miss Holm."

Simon nodded.

"Very ingenious," he murmured. "Very ingenious. Not quite the way I expected it—but very ingenious, all the same. And quite unanswerable. Therefore——"

"Therefore, Mr. Templar, why not put the cards on the table? We have agreed not to waste time. I frankly admit that Miss Holm is my prisoner. Why don't you admit that Professor Vargan is yours?"

"Not so fast," said the Saint. "You've just admitted, before witnesses, that you are a party to an abduction. Now, suppose that became known to the police? Wouldn't that be awkward?"

Marius shook his head.

"Not particularly," he said. "I have a very good witness to deny any such admission——''

''A crook!''

''Oh no. A most respectable countryman of mine. I assure you, it would be quite impossible to discredit him.''

Simon lounged back against the table.

''I see,'' he drawled. ''And that's your complete song-and-dance act, is it?''

''I believe I have stated all the important points.''

''Then,'' said the Saint, ''I will now state mine.''

Carefully he replaced the little knife in its sheath and adjusted his sleeve. A glance at the man on the floor told him that that unlucky servant of the Cause was recovering; but Simon was not interested. He addressed himself to the man in the chair.

''Tell your master about the game we were playing,'' he invited. ''Confess everything, loveliness. He has a nice kind face, and perhaps he won't be too hard on you.''

The man spoke again in his own language. Marius listened woodenly. The Saint could not understand a word of what was being said; but he knew, when the giant interrupted the discourse with a movement of his hand and a sharp, harsh syllable of impatience, that the recital had passed through the stage of being a useful statement of facts, and had degenerated into a string of excuses.

Then Marius was looking curiously at Simon Templar. There seemed to be a kind of grim humour in that gaze.

''And yet you do not look a ferocious man, Mr. Templar.''

''I shouldn't rely too much on that.''

Again that jerky gesture of impatience.

''I am not relying on it. With a perspicacity which I should have expected, and which I can only commend, you have saved me many words, many tedious explanations. You have summed up the situation with admirable briefness. May I ask you to be as brief with your decision? I may say that the fortunate accident of finding you at home, which I did not expect, has saved me the considerable trouble of getting in touch with you through the agony columns of the daily papers, and has enabled me to put my proposition before you with the minimum of delay. Would it not be a pity, now, to mar such an excellent start with unnecessary paltering?''

''It would,'' said the Saint.

And he knew at once what he was going to do. It had come to him

in a flash—an inspiration, a summarising and deduction and realisation
that were instantaneous, and more clear and sure than anything of their
kind which could have been produced by any mental effort:

That he was on toast, and that there was no ordinary way off the toast.
That the situation was locked and double-locked into exactly the tangle
of dithering subtleties and cross-causes and cross-menaces that he hated
more than anything else in the world, as has been explained—the kind
of chess-problem tangle that was probably the one thing in the world
capable of reeling him off his active mental balance and sending him
raving mad. . . . That to think about it and try to scheme about it would
be the one certain way of losing the game. That, obviously, he could
never hope to stand up in the same class as Rayt Marius in a complicated
intrigue—to try to enter into an even contest with such a past professional
master of the art would be the act of a suicidal fool. That, therefore, his
only chance to win out was to break the very rules of the game that
Marius would least expect an opponent to break. That it was the moment
when all the prejudices and convictions that made the Saint what he was
must be put to the test. That all his fundamental faith in the superiority
of reckless action over laborious ratiocination must now justify itself, or
topple down to destruction and take him with it into hell. . . . That, in
fact, when all the pieces on the chessboard were so inweaved and
dove-tailed and counter-blockaded, his only chance was to smash up the
whole stagnant structure and sweep the board clean—with the slash of
a sword. . . .

"Certainly," said the Saint, "I'll give you my decision at once. Roger,
give me back that gun, and go and fetch some rope. You'll find some
in the kitchen."

As Conway went out, the Saint turned again to Marius.

"You have already observed, dear one," he remarked gently, "that
I have a genius for summarising situations. But this one can be stated
quite simply. The fact is, Angel Face, I propose to apply to you exactly
the same methods of persuasion that I was about to employ on your
servant. You observe that I have a gun. I can't shoot the pips out of a
playing-card at thirty paces, or do any other Wild West stuff like that;
but still, I don't think I'm such a bad shot that I could miss anything
your size at this range. Therefore, you can either submit quietly to being
tied up by my friend, or you can be killed at once. Have it whichever
way you like."

A flicker of something showed in the giant's eyes, and was gone as
soon as it had come.

"You seem to have lost your grip on the situation, Mr. Templar," he said urbanely. "To anyone as expert in these matters as you appear to be, it should be unnecessary to explain that I did not come here unprepared for such an obvious riposte. Must I bore you with the details of what will happen to Miss Holm if I fail to return to the place where she is being kept? Must I be compelled to make my conventional move still more conventional with a melodramatic exposition of her peril?"

"It's an odd thing," said the Saint, in mild reminiscence, "that more than half the crooks I've dealt with have been frantically anxious to avoid melodrama. Now, personally, I just love it. And we're going to have lots of it now—lots and lots and lots, Marius, my little ray of sunshine. . . ."

Marius shrugged.

"I thought better of your intelligence, Mr. Templar."

The Saint smiled, a very Saintly smile.

His hands on his hips, teetering gently on his toes, he answered with the most reckless defiance of his life.

"You're wrong," he said. "You didn't think well enough of my intelligence. You thought it'd be feeble enough to let me be bluffed into meeting you on your own ground. And that's just what it isn't quite feeble enough to do."

"I do not follow you," said Marius.

"Then I'm not the one with softening of the brain," said Simon sweetly, "but you are. I invite you to apply your own admirable system of logic to the situation. I could tell the police things about you, but you could tell the police things about me. Deadlock. You could harm Miss Holm, but I could deprive you of Vargan. Deadlock again—with a shade of odds in your favour on each count."

"We can rule out the police for the present. If we did so, an exchange of prisoners——"

"But you don't get the point," said Simon, with a terrible simplicity. "That would be a surrender on my part. And I never surrender."

Marius moved his hands.

"I also surrender Miss Holm."

"And there's still a difference, loveliness," said the Saint. "You see, you don't really want Miss Holm, except as a hostage. And I do want Vargan very much indeed. I want to wash him and comb him and buy him a little velvet suit and adopt him. I want him to yadder childishly to me about the binomial theorem after breakfast. I want to be able to bring him into the drawing-room after dinner to amuse my guests with recitations from the differential calculus. But most of all I want one of his little toys. . . . And so, you see, if I let you go, Miss Holm would be in exactly the same danger as if I kept you here, since I couldn't agree to your terms of ransom. But the difference is that if I let you go I lose my one chance of finding her, and I should have to trust to luck to come on the scent again. While I keep you here, though, I hold a very good card—and I'm not letting it go.''

"You gain nothing——"

"On the contrary, I gain everything," said the Saint, in that dreamy sing-song. "I gain everything, or lose more than everything. But I'm tired of haggling. I'm tired of playing your safety game. You're going to play my game now, Marius, my cherub. Wait a second while I rearrange the scene. . . .''

As Conway came back with a length of cord, the Saint took from his pocket a little shining cylinder and screwed it swiftly on to the muzzle of the gun he held.

"This will now make no noise worth mentioning," he said. "You know the gadget, don't you? So let me have *your* decision quickly, Marius, before I remember what I want to do more than anything else in the world."

"It will not help you to kill me."

"It will not help me to let you go. But we've had all that before. Besides, I mightn't kill you. I might just shoot you through the kidneys, and long before you died of the wound you'd be ready to give me anything to put you out of your agony. I grant you it wouldn't improve my chance of finding Miss Holm, but, on the other hand, it wouldn't make it any worse—and you'd be so dead that it wouldn't worry you, anyway. Think it over. I give you two minutes. Roger, time him by that clock!''

Marius put his hands behind him at once.

"Suppose I save you the time. I will be tied now—if you think that will help you."

"Carry on, Roger," said the Saint.

He knew that Marius still did not believe him—that the fat man's description of his ordeal had not made the impression it should have made. He knew that Marius's acquiescence was nothing but a bland calling of what the giant estimated to be a hopeless bluff. And he stood by, watching with a face of stone, while Conway tied the man's hands behind his back and thrust him into a chair.

"Take over the peashooter again, Roger."

Then an idea struck the Saint.

He said: "Before we begin, Roger, you might search him."

A glimmer of fear, which nothing else in that interview had aroused, contorted the giant's face like a spasm, and the Saint could have shouted for joy. Marius struggled like a fiend, but he had been well bound, and his effort was wasted.

The weak spot in the armour. . . .

Simon waited, almost trembling. Torture he had been grimly prepared to apply; but he recognised, at the same time, how futile it was likely to prove against a man like Marius. He might have resumed the torture of the fat man; but that also would have been less efficacious now that the moral support—or threat—of Marius was there to counteract it. He would obtain some sort of information, certainly—the limits of human endurance would inevitably see to that—but he would have no means of proving its truth. Something in writing, though . . .

And the colossal facility of the success made the Saint's heart pound like a trip-hammer, in a devastating terror lest the success should turn out to be no success at all. For, if success it was, the rightness of his riposte could not have been more shatteringly demonstrated. If it were true—if Marius had plunged so heavily on the rules of the game as he knew them—if Marius had been so blindly certain that, under the menace which he knew he could hold over them, neither of the men in Brook Street would dare to lay a hand on him—if . . .

"English swine!"

"Naughty temper," said Roger equably.

"Thank you," said the Saint, taking the letter which Roger handed to him. "Careless of you, Marius, to come here with that on you. Personally, I never commit anything to writing. It's dangerous. But perhaps you meant to post it on your way, and forgot it."

He glanced at the address.

"Our old friend the Crown Prince," he murmured. "This should be interesting."

He slit open the envelope with one swift flick of his thumb, and drew out the typewritten sheet.

It was in Marius's own language, but that was a small difficulty. The Saint took it with him to the telephone; and in a few minutes he was through to a friend who held down a soft job at the Foreign Office by virtue of an almost incredible familiarity with every language on the map of Europe.

"Glad to find you in," said the Saint rapidly. "Listen—I've got a

letter here which I want translated. I don't know how to pronounce any
of it, but I'll spell it out word by word. Ready?''

It took time; but the Saint had found an unwonted patience. He wrote
between the lines as the receiver dictated; and presently it was finished.

He came back smiling.

Roger prompted him: "Which, being interpreted, means———''

"I'm leaving now."

"Where for?"

"The house on the hill, Bures, Suffolk."

"She's there?"

"According to the letter."

The Saint passed it over, and Conway read the scribbled notes between
the lines: ". . . *the girl, and she is being taken to a quiet part of Suffolk.*
. . . *Bures* . . . *house on the hill, far enough from the village to be safe*
. . . *cannot fail this time*. . . .''

Conway handed it back.

"I'll come with you."

The Saint shook his head.

"Sorry, son, but you've got to stay here and look after the menagerie.
They're my hostages."

"But suppose anything goes wrong, Simon?"

The Saint consulted his watch. It was still stopped. He wound it up
and set it by the mantelpiece clock.

"I'll be back," he said, "before four o'clock tomorrow morning. That
allows for punctures, breakdowns, and everything else. If I'm not here
on the stroke, shoot these birds and come after me."

Marius's voice rasped in on Conway's hesitation.

"You insist on being foolish, Templar? You realise that my men at
Bures have orders to use Miss Holm as a hostage in an attack or any
other emergency?"

Simon Templar went over and looked down at him.

"I could have guessed it," he said. "And it makes me weep for your
bad generalship, Marius. I suppose *you* realise that if they sacrifice her,
your first and last hold over me is gone? But that's only half the fundamental weakness in your bright scheme. The other half is that you've
got to pray against yourself. Pray that I win to-night, Marius—pray as
you've never prayed before in your filthy life! Because, if I fail, I'm
coming straight back here to kill you in the most hideous way I can
invent. I mean that."

He swung round, cool, cold, deliberate, and went to the door as if he were merely going for a stroll round the block before turning in. But at the door he turned to cast a slow, straight glance over Marius, and then to smile at Roger.

"All the best, old boy," said Roger.

" 'Battle, murder, and sudden death,' " quoted the Saint softly, with a gay, reckless gesture; and the Saintly smile could never have shone more superbly. "Watch me," said the Saint, and was gone.

9

How Roger Conway Was Careless, and Hermann Also Made a Mistake

ROGER CONWAY SHIFTED vaguely across the room as the hum of Norman Kent's Hirondel faded and was lost in the noises of Regent Street. He came upon the side table where the decanter lived, helped himself to a drink, and remembered the last cavalier wave of the Saint's hand and the pitiful torment in the Saint's eyes. Then he put down the drink and took a cigarette instead, suddenly aware that he might have to remain wide awake and alert all night.

He looked at Marius. The giant had sunk into an inscrutable apathy; but he spoke.

"If you would allow it, I should like to smoke a cigar."

Roger deliberated.

"It might be arranged—if you don't need your hands free."

"I can try. The case is in my breast pocket."

Conway found it, bit the end, and put it in Marius's mouth and lighted it. Marius thanked him.

"Will you join me?"

Roger smiled.

"Try something newer," he advised. "I never take smokes from strangers these days, on principle. Oh, and by the way, if I catch you trying to burn through your ropes with the end, I shall have much pleasure in grinding it into your face till it goes out."

Marius shrugged and made no reply; and Roger resumed his cigarette.

Coming upon the telephone, he hesitated, and then called a number. He was through in a few minutes.

"Can I speak to Mr. Kent, Orace? . . . Oh, hullo, Norman!"

"Who's that? Roger?"

"Yes. I rang up in case you were getting worried about us. Heaven knows what time we shall get down. . . . No, the car's all right—as far as I know. Simon's gone off in it. . . . Brook Street. . . . Well—Marius has got Pat. . . . Yes, I'm afraid so. Got her on the train. But we've got Marius. . . . Yes, he's here. I'm standing guard. We've found out where Pat's been taken, and Simon's gone after her. . . . Somewhere in Suffolk."

"Shall I come up?"

"How? It's too late for a train, and you won't be able to hire anything worth calling a car at this hour. I don't see what you could do, anyway. . . . Look here, I can't talk any more now. I've got to keep both eyes on Marius and Co. . . . I'll leave it to you. . . . Right. So long, old boy."

He hooked up the receiver.

It occurred to him afterwards that there was something that Norman could have done. He could have tied up the fat man and the lean man, both of whom were now conscious and free to move as much as they dared. That ought to have been done before Simon left. They ought to have thought of it—or Simon ought to have thought of it. But the Saint couldn't, reasonably, have been expected to think of it, or anything else like it, at such a time. Roger knew both the Saint and Pat too well to be able to blame Simon for the omission. Simon had been mad when he left. The madness had been there all the time, since half-past nine, boiling up in fiercer and fiercer waves behind all the masks of calmness and flippancy and patience that the Saint had assumed at intervals, and it had been at its whitest heat behind that last gay smile and gesture from the door.

Half an hour passed.

Roger was beginning to feel hungry. He had had a snack in the station buffet while he was waiting, but the satisfaction of that was starting to wear off. If he had gone to the kitchen to forage, that would have meant compelling his three prisoners to precede him at the point of his gun. And the kitchen was small. . . . Ruefully Roger resigned himself to a hungry vigil. He looked unhappily at the clock. Four and a half hours before he could shoot the prisoners and dash to the pantry, if he obeyed the Saint's orders. But it would have to be endured. The Saint might have managed the cure, and got away with it; but then, the Saint was a fully qualified adventurer, and what he didn't know about the game was not knowledge. Conway was infinitely less experienced, and knew it. In the cramped space of the kitchen, while he was trying to locate food with one eye and one hand, he might easily be taken off his guard and overpowered. And, in the circumstances, the risk was too great to take.

If only Norman decided to come. . . .

Roger Conway sat on the edge of the table, swinging the gun idly in his hand. Marius remained silent. His cigar had gone out, and he had not asked for it to be relighted. The fat man slouched in another chair, watching Roger with venomous eyes. The lean man stood awkwardly in one corner. He had not spoken since he recovered consciousness; but he also watched. The clock ticked monotonously. . . .

Roger started to whistle to himself. It was extraordinary how quickly the strain began to tell. He wished he were like the Saint. The Saint wouldn't have gone hungry, for one thing. The Saint would have made the prisoners cook him a four-course dinner, lay the table, and wait on him. The Saint would have kept them busy putting on the gramophone and generally running his errands. The Saint would probably have written a letter and composed a few limericks into the bargain. He certainly wouldn't have been oppressed by the silence and the concentrated malevolence of three pairs of eyes. He would have dismissed the silence and whiled away the time by indulging in airy persiflage at their expense.

But it was the silence and the watchfulness of the eyes. Roger began to understand why he had never felt an irresistible urge to become a liontamer. The feeling of being alone in a cage of wild beasts, he decided, must be very much like what he was experiencing at that moment. The same fragile dominance of the man, the same unresting watchfulness of the beasts, the same tension, the same snarling submission of the beasts, the same certainty that the beasts were only waiting, waiting, waiting. These human beasts were sizing him up, searching his soul, stripping him naked of all bluff, finding out all his weaknesses in silence, planning, scheming, considering, alert to pounce. It was getting on Roger's nerves. Presently, sooner or later, somehow, he knew, there would be a bid for liberty. But how would it happen?

And that uncertainty must go on for hours and hours, perhaps. Move and counter-move, threat and counter-threat, the snarl and the lash, the silence and the watchfulness and the eyes. How long? . . .

Then from the fat man's lips broke the first rattle of words, in his own language.

"Stop that!" rapped Conway, with his nerves all on edge. "If you've anything to say, say it in English. Any more of that, and you'll get a clip over the ear with the soft end of this gun."

And the man deliberately and defiantly spoke again, still in his own language.

Roger came off the table as though it had been red-hot. He stood over the man with his hand raised, and the man stared back with sullen insolence.

Then it happened.

The plan was beautifully simple.

Roger had forgotten for the moment that only Marius's hands were tied. The giant's feet were free. And, standing over the fat man's chair, where he had been so easily lured by the bait that was also an explanation of the trap to the others, Roger's back was half turned to Marius.

Conway heard the movement behind him, but he had no time to spin round to meet it. The giant's foot crashed into the small of his back with a savage force that might well have broken the spine—if it had struck the spine. But it struck to one side of the spine, in a place almost as vulnerable, and Roger went to the floor with a gasp of agony.

Then both the fat man and the lean man leapt on him together.

The gun was wrenched out of Roger's hand. He could not have seen to shoot, anyway, for the pain had blinded him. He could not cry out—his throat was constricted with a horrible numbing nausea, and his lungs seemed to be paralysed. The lean man's fist smacked again and again into his defenceless jaw.

"Untie me quickly, fool!" hissed Marius, and the fat man obeyed, to the accompaniment of a babbling flood of excuses.

Marius cut him short.

"I will consider your punishment later, Otto. Perhaps this will atone for a little of your imbecility. Tie him up now with this rope——"

Roger lay still. Somehow—he did not know how—he retained his consciousness. There was no strength in any of his limbs; he could see nothing; his battered head sang and ached and throbbed horribly; the whole of his body was in the grip of a crushing, cramping agony that centered on the point in his back where he had taken the kick, and from that point spread iron tentacles of helplessness into every muscle; yet his mind hung aloof, high and clear above the roaring blackness, and he heard and remembered every word that was said.

"Look for more rope, Hermann," Marius was ordering.

The lean man went out and returned. Roger's feet were bound as his wrists had been.

Then Marius was at the telephone.

"A trunk call. . . . Bures. . . ."

An impatient pause. Then Marius cursed gutturally.

"The line is out of order? Tell me when it will be working again. It is a matter of life and death. . . . To-morrow? . . . God in heaven! A telegram—would a telegram be delivered in Bures to-night?"

"I'll put you through to——"

Pause again.

"Yes. I wish to ask if a telegram would be delivered in Bures to-night. . . . Bures, Suffolk. . . . You think not? . . . You are almost sure not? . . . Very well. Thank you. No, I will not send it now."

He replaced the receiver, and lifted it again immediately.

This time he spoke to Westminster 9999, and gave staccato instructions which Roger could not understand. They appeared to be detailed instructions, and they took some time. But at last Marius was satisfied.

He rang off, and turned and kicked Roger contemptuously.

"You stay here, pig. You are a security for your friend's behavior."

Then again he spoke to the lean man in the language which was double-Dutch to Roger: "Hermann, you remain to guard him. I will leave you the gun. Wait—I find out the telephone number. . . ." He read it off the instrument. "If I have orders to give, I will telephone. You will not leave here without my permission. . . . Otto, you come with me. We go after Templar in my car. I have agents on the road, and I have ordered them to be instructed. If they are not all as incapable as you, he will never reach Bures alive. But we follow to make sure. . . . Wait again! That pig on the floor spoke to a friend at Maidenhead who may be coming to join him. You will capture him and tie him up also. Let there be no mistake, Hermann."

"There shall be no mistake."

"Good! Come, Otto."

Roger heard them go; and then the roaring blackness that lay all about him welled up and engulfed that lonely glitter of clarity in his mind.

He might have been unconscious for five minutes or five days; he had lost all idea of time. But the first thing he saw when he opened his eyes was the clock, and he knew that it must have been about twenty minutes.

The man Hermann sat in a chair opposite him, turning the pages of a magazine. Presently he looked up and saw that Roger was awake; and he put down the magazine and came over and spat in his face.

"Soon, English swine, you will be dead. And your country——"

Roger controlled his tongue with a tremendous effort.

He found that he could breathe. The iron bands about his chest had slackened, and the bodily anguish had lessened. There was still the throbbing pain in his back and the throbbing pain in his head; but he was better. And he wasn't asking for any unnecessary aggravation of his troubles—not just then, anyway.

The man went on: "The Doctor is a great man. He is the greatest man in the world. You should have seen how he arranged everything in two minutes. It was magnificent. He is Napoleon born again. He is going to make our country the greatest country in the world. And you fools try to fight him——"

The speech merged into an unintelligible outburst in the man's native tongue; but Roger understood enough. He understood that a man who could delude his servants into such a fanatical loyalty was no small man. And he wondered what chance the Saint would ever have had of convincing anyone that Marius was concerned with no patriotism and no nationalities, but only with his own gods of money and power.

The first flush of futile anger ebbed from Conway's face, and he lay in stolid silence as he was tied, revolving plot and counter-plot in his mind. Hermann, failing to rouse him with taunts, struck him twice across the face. Roger never moved. And the man spat at him again.

"It is as I thought. You have no courage, you dogs of Englishmen. It is only when you are many against one little one—then you are brave."

"Oh, quite," said Roger wearily.

Hermann glowered at him.

"Now, if you had been the one who hit me——"

Zzzzzzzzzzzing!

The shrill scream of a bell wailed through the apartment with a suddenness that made the conventional sound electrifying. Hermann stopped, stiffening, in the middle of his sentence. And a sour leer came into his face.

"Now I welcome your friend, pig."

Roger drew a deep breath.

He must have been careless, obvious about it, for Roger Conway's was not a mind much given to cunning. Or possibly Hermann had been expecting some such move, subconsciously, and had his ears pricked for the sound. But he stopped on his way to the door and turned.

"You would try to give warning, Englishman?" he purred.

His gun was in his hand. He reached Roger in three strides.

Roger knew he was up against it. If he didn't shout, his one chance of rescue, so far as he could see, was dished—and Norman Kent with it. If he looked like shouting, he'd be laid out again. And, if it came to that, since his intention of shouting had already been divined, he'd probably be laid out anyway. Hermann wasn't the sort of man to waste time gagging his prisoner. So——

"Go to blazes," said Roger recklessly.

Then he yelled.

An instant later Hermann's gun-butt crashed into the side of his head.

Again he should have been stunned; but he wasn't. He decided afterwards that he must have a skull a couple of inches thick, and the constitution of an ox with it, to have stood up to as much as he had. But the fact remained that he was laid out without being stunned; and he lay still, trying to collect himself in time to loose a second yell as Hermann opened the door.

Hermann straightened up, turning his gun round again. He put it in his coat pocket, keeping his finger on the trigger; and then, with something like a panicking terror that the warning might have been heard and accepted by the person outside the front door, he scrambled rather than ran out of the room, cursing under his breath.

But the ring was repeated as he reached the front door, and the sound reassured him. He could not believe that anyone who had heard and understood that one yell would have rung again so promptly after it. Whereby Hermann showed himself a less ingenious psychologist than the man outside. . . .

He opened the door, keeping himself hidden behind it.

No one entered.

He waited, with a kind of superstitious fear trickling down his back like a tiny cascade of ice-cold water. Nothing happened—and yet the second ring had sounded only a moment before he opened the door, and no one who had rung a second time would go away at once, without waiting to see if the renewed summons would be answered.

Then Conway yelled again: "Look out, Norman!"

Hermann swore in a whisper.

But now he had no choice. He had been given his orders. The man who came was to be taken. And certainly the man who had come, who must have heard Conway's second cry even if he had not heard the first, could not be allowed to escape and raise an alarm.

Incautiously, Hermann stepped to the door.

His feet were scarcely clear of the threshold, outside on the landing, when a hand like a ham caught his throat from behind, over his shoulder, and another enormous hand gripped his gun-wrist like a vice. He was as helpless as a child.

The hand at his throat twisted his face round to the light. He saw a ponderous red face with sleepy eyes, connected by a pillar of neck with shoulders worthy of a buffalo.

"Come along," said Chief Inspector Claud Eustace Teal drowsily. "Come along back to where you sprang from, and open your heart to Uncle!"

10

How Simon Templar Drove to Bures, and Two Policemen Jumped in Time

THE ROAD OUT of London on the north-east is one of the less pleasant ways of finding the open country. For one thing, it is infested with miles of tramway, crawling, interminable, blocking the traffic, maddening to the man at the wheel of a fast car—especially maddening to the man in a hurry at the wheel of a fast car.

Late as it was, there was enough traffic on the road to balk the Saint of clear runs of more than a few hundred yards at a time. And every time he was forced to apply the brakes, pause, and reaccelerate, was pulling his average down.

There was a quicker route than the one he was taking, he knew. He had been taken over it once—a route that wound intricately through deserted side streets, occasionally crossing the more populous thoroughfares, and then hurriedly breaking away into the empty roads again. It was longer, but it was quicker to traverse. But the Saint had only been over it that once, and that by daylight; now, in the dark, he could not have trusted himself to find it again. The landmarks that a driver automatically picks out by day are of little use to him in the changed aspect of lamplight. And to get lost would be more maddening than the obstruction of the traffic. To waste minutes, and perhaps miles, travelling in the wrong direction, to be muddled by the vague and contradictory directions of accosted pedestrians and police, to be plagued and pestered with the continual uncertainty—that would have driven him to the verge of delirium. The advantage that might be gained wasn't worth all that might be lost. He had decided as much when he swung into the car in Brook Street. And he kept to the main roads.

He smashed through the traffic grimly, seizing every opportunity that offered, creating other opportunities of his own in defiance of every law and principle and point of etiquette governing the use of His Majesty's highway, winning priceless seconds where and how he could.

Other drivers cursed him; two policemen called on him to stop, were ignored, and took his number; he scraped a wing in a desperate rush through a gap that no one else would ever have considered a gap at all; three times he missed death by a miracle while overtaking on a blind corner; and the pugnacious driver of a baby car who ventured to insist on his rightful share of the road went white as the Hirondel forced him on to the kerb to escape annihilation.

It was an incomparable exhibition of pure hogging, and it made everything of that kind that Roger Conway had been told to do earlier in the evening look like a child's game with a push-cart; but the Saint didn't care. He was on his way; and if the rest of the population objected to the manner of his going, they could do one of two things with their objections.

Some who saw the passage of the Saint that night will remember it to the end of their lives; for the Hirondel, as though recognising the hand of a master at its wheel, became almost a living thing. King of the Road its makers called it, but that night the Hirondel was more than a king: it was the incarnation and apotheosis of all cars. For the Saint drove with the devil at his shoulder, and the Hirondel took its mood from his. If this had been a superstitious age, those who saw it would have crossed themselves and sworn that it was no car at all they saw that night, but a snarling silver fiend that roared through London on the wings of an unearthly wind.

For half an hour . . . with the Saint's thumb restless on the button of the klaxon, and the strident voice of the silver fiend howling for avenue in a tone that brooked no contention . . . and then the houses thinned away and gave place to the first fields, and the Saint settled down to the job—coaxing, with hands as sure and gentle as any horseman's, the last possible ounce of effort out of the hundred horses under his control. . . .

There was darkness on either side: the only light in the world lay along the tunnel which the powerful headlights slashed out of the stubborn blackness. From time to time, out of the dark, a great beast with eyes of fire leapt at him, clamouring, was slipped as a charging bull is slipped by a toreador, went by with a baffled grunt and a skimming slither of wind. And again and again, in the dark, the Hirondel swooped up behind ridiculous, creeping glow-worms, sniffed at their red tails, snorted derisively, swept past with a deep-throated blare. No car in England could have held the lead of the Hirondel that night.

The drone of the great engine went on as a background of gigantic song; it sang in tune with the soft swish of the tyres and the rush of the cool night air; and the song it sang was: *"Patricia Holm. . . . Patricia. . . . Patricia. . . . Patricia Holm!"*

And the Saint had no idea what he was going to do. Nor was he thinking about it. He knew nothing of the geography of the "house on the hill"—nothing of the lie of the surrounding land—nothing of the obstacles that might bar his way, nor of the resistance that would be offered to his attack. And so he was not jading himself with thinking of these things. They were beyond the reach of idle speculation. He had no clue: therefore it would have been a waste of time to speculate. He could only live for the moment, and the task of the moment—to hurl himself eastwards across England like a thunderbolt into the battle that lay ahead.

"Patricia. . . . Patricia! . . ."

Softly the Saint took up the song; but his own voice could not be heard from the voice of the Hirondel. The song of the car bayed over wide spaces of country, was bruised and battered between the walls of startled village streets, was flung back in rolling echoes from the walls of hills.

That he was going to an almost blindfold assault took nothing from his rapture. Rather, he savoured the adventure the more; for this was the fashion of forlorn sally that his heart cried for—the end of inaction, the end of perplexity and helplessness, the end of a damnation of doubt and dithering. And in the Saint's heart was a shout of rejoicing, because at last the God of all good battles and desperate endeavour had remembered him again.

No, it wasn't selfish. It wasn't a mere lust for adventure that cared nothing for the peril of those who made the adventure worth while. It was the irresistible resurgence of the most fundamental of all the inspirations of man. A wild stirring in its ancient sleep of the spirit that sent the knights of Arthur out upon their quests, of Tristan crying for Isolde, of the flame in a man's heart that brought fire and sword upon Troy, of Roland's shout and the singing blade of Durendal amid the carnage of Roncesvalles. "The sound of the trumpet. . . ."

Thus the miles were eaten up, until more than half the journey must have been set behind him.

If only there was no engine failure. . . . He had no fear for fuel and oil, for he had filled up on the way back from Maidenhead.

Simon touched a switch, and all the instruments on the dashboard before him were illuminated from behind with a queer ghostly luminance. His eye flickered from the road and found one of them.

Seventy-two.

Seventy-four.

Seventy-five . . . six. . . .

"Patricia! . . ."

"Battle, murder, and sudden death. . . ."

"You know, Pat, we don't have a chance these days. There's no chance for magnificent loving. A man ought to fight for his lady. Preferably with dragons. . . ."

Seventy-eight.

Seventy-nine.

A corner loomed out of the dark, flung itself at him, menacing, murderous. The tyres, curbed with a cruel hand, tore at the road, shrieking. The car swung round the corner, on its haunches, as it were . . . gathered itself, and found its stride again. . . .

Ping!

Something like the crisp twang of the snapping of an over-strained wire. The Saint, looking straight ahead, blinking, saw that the windscreen in front of him had given birth to a star—a star of long slender points radiating from a neat round hole drilled through the glass. And a half-smile came to his lips.

Ping!

Bang!

Bang!

The first sound repeated; then, in quick succession, two other sounds, sharp and high, like the smack of two pieces of metal. In front of him they were. In the gleaming aluminum bonnet.

"Smoke!" breathed the Saint. "This is a wild party!"

He hadn't time to adjust himself to the interruption, to parse and analyse it and extract its philosophy. How he came to be under fire at that stage of the journey—that could wait. Something had gone wrong. Someone had blundered. Roger must have been tricked, and Marius must have escaped—or something. But, meanwhile . . .

Fortunately the first shot had made him slow up. Otherwise he would have been killed.

The next sound he heard was neither the impact of a bullet nor the thin, distant rattle of the rifle that fired it. It was loud and close and explosive, under his feet it seemed; and the steering wheel was wrenched out of his hand—nearly.

He never knew how he kept his grip on it. An instinct swifter than thought must have made him tighten his hold at the sound of that explosion, and he was driving with both hands on the wheel. He tore the wheel round in the way it did not want to go, bracing his feet on clutch and brake pedals, calling up the last reserve of every sinew in his splendid body.

Death, sudden as anything he could have asked, stared him in the face. The strain was terrific. The Hirondel had ceased to be his creature. It was mad, runaway, the bit between its tremendous teeth, caracoling towards a demoniac plunge to destruction. No normal human power should have been able to hold it. The Saint, strong as he was, could never have done it—normally. He must have found some supernatural strength.

Somehow he kept the car out of the ditch for as long as it took to bring it to a standstill.

Then, almost without thinking, he switched out the lights.

Dimly he wondered why, under that fearful gruelling, the front axle hadn't snapped like a dry stick, or why the steering hadn't come to pieces under his hands.

"If I come out of this alive," thought the Saint, "the Hirondel Motor Company will get an unsolicited testimonial from me."

But that thought merely crossed his mind like a swallow swimming a quiet pool—and was lost. Then, in the same dim way, he was wondering why he hadn't brought a gun. Now he was likely to pay for the reckless haste with which he had set out. His little knife was all very well—he could use it as accurately as any man could use a gun, and as swiftly— but it was only good for one shot. He'd never been able to train it to function as a boomerang.

It was unlikely that he was being sniped by one man alone. And that one solitary knife, however expertly he used it, would be no use at all against a number of armed men besieging him in a lamed car.

"Obviously, therefore," thought Simon, "get out of the car."

And he was out of it instantly, crouching in the ditch beside it. In the open, and the darkness, he would have a better chance.

He wasn't thinking for a moment of a getaway. That would have been fairly easy. But the Hirondel was the only car he had on him, and it had to be saved—or else he had to throw in his hand. Joke. The obvious object of the ambuscade was to make him do just that—to stop him, anyhow—and he wasn't being stopped. . . .

Now, with the switching off of the lights, the darkness had become less dark, and the road ran through it, beside the black bulk of the flanking trees, like a ribbon of dull steel. And, looking back, the Saint could see shadows that moved. He counted four of them.

He went to meet them, creeping like a snake in the dry ditch. They were separated. Avoiding the dull gleam of that strip of road, as if afraid that a shot from the car in front might greet their approach, they slunk along in the gloom at the sides of the road, two on one side and two on the other.

It was no time for soft fighting. There was that punctured front wheel to be changed, and those four men in the way. So the four men had to be eliminated—as quickly and definitely as possible. The Saint was having no fooling about.

The leader of the two men on Simon's side of the road almost stepped on the dark figure that seemed to rise suddenly out of the ground in front of him. He stopped, and tried to draw back so that he could use the rifle he carried, and his companion trod on his heels and cursed.

Then the first man screamed; and the scream died in a choking gurgle.

The man behind him saw his leader sink to the ground, but there was another man beyond his leader—a man who had not been there before, who laughed with a soft whisper of desperate merriment. The second man tried to raise the automatic he carried; but two steely hands grasped his wrists, and he felt himself flying helplessly through the air. He seemed to fly a long way—and then he slept.

The Saint crossed the road.

A gun spoke from the hand of one of the two men on the other side, who had paused, irresolute, at the sound of the first scream. But the Saint was lost again in the shadows.

They crouched down, waiting, watching, intent for his next move. But they were looking down along the ditch and the grass beside the road, where the Saint had vanished like a ghost; but the Saint was above them then, crouched like a leopard under the hedge at the top of the embankment beside them, gathering himself stealthily.

He dropped on them out of the sky; and the heels of both his shoes impacted upon the back of the neck of one of them with all the Saint's hurtling weight behind, so the man lay very still where he was and did not stir again.

The other man, rising and bringing up his rifle, saw a spinning silver of bright steel whisking towards him like a flying fish over a dark sea, and struck to guard. By a miracle he succeeded, and the knife glanced from his gun-barrel and tinkled away over the road.

Then he fought with the Saint for the rifle.

He was probably the strongest of the four, and he did not know fear; but there is a trick by which a man who knows it can always take a rifle or a stick from a man who does not know it, and the Saint had known that trick from his childhood. He made the man drop the rifle; but he had no chance to pick it up for himself, for the man was on him again in a moment. Simon could only kick the gun away into the ditch, where it was lost.

An even break, then.

They fought hand to hand, two men on that dark road, lion and leopard.

This man had the advantage of strength and weight, but the Saint had the speed and fighting savagery. No man who was not a Colossus, or mad, would have attempted to stand in the Saint's way that night: but this man, who may have been something of both, attempted it. He fought like a beast. But Simon Templar was berserk. The man was not only standing in the way: he was the servant and the symbol of all the powers that the Saint hated. He stood for Marius, and the men behind Marius, and all the conspiracy that the Saint had sworn to break, and that had caused it to come to pass that at that moment the Saint should have been riding recklessly to the rescue of his lady. Therefore the man had to go, as his three companions had already gone. And perhaps the man recognised his doom, for he let out one sobbing cry before the Saint's fingers found an unshakable grip on his throat.

It was to the death. Simon had no choice, even if he would have taken it, for the man fought to the end; and even when unconsciousness stilled his struggles Simon dared not let him go, for he might be only playing 'possum, and the Saint could not afford to take any chances. There was only one way to make sure. . . .

So presently the Saint rose slowly to his feet, breathing deeply like a man who has been under water for a long time, and went to find Anna. And no one else moved on the road.

As an afterthought, he commandeered a loaded automatic from one of the men who had no further use for it.

Then he went to change the wheel.

It should only have taken him five minutes; but he could not have foreseen that the spare tyre would settle down to a futile flatness as he slipped the jack from under the dumb-iron and lowered the wheel to the road.

There was only the one spare.

It was a very slight consolation to remember that Norman Kent, the ever-thoughtful, always carried an outfit of tools about twice as efficient as anything the ordinary motorist thinks necessary. And the wherewithal to mend punctures was included.

Even so, with only the spotlight to work by, and no bucket of water with which to find the site of the puncture, it would not be an easy job.

Simon stripped off his coat with a groan.

It was more than half an hour before the Hirondel was ready to take the road again. Nearly three-quarters of an hour wasted altogether. Precious minutes squandered, that he had gambled life and limb to win. . . .

But it seemed like forty-five years, instead of forty-five minutes, before he was able to light a cigarette and climb back into the driver's seat.

He started the engine and moved his hand to switch on the headlights; but even as his hand touched the switch the road about him was flooded by lights that were not his.

As he engaged the gears, he looked back over his shoulder, and saw that the car behind was not overtaking. It had stopped.

Breathless with the reaction from the first foretaste of battle, he was not expecting another attack so soon. As he moved off, he was for an instant more surprised than hurt by the feel of something stabbing through his left shoulder like a hot spear-point.

Then he understood, and turned in his seat with the borrowed automatic in his hand.

He was not, as he had admitted, the greatest pistol shot in the world; but on that night some divine genius guided his hand. Coolly he sighted, as if he had been practising on a range, and shot out both the headlights of the car behind. Then, undazzled, he could see to puncture one of its front wheels before he swept round the next corner with a veritable storm of pursuing bullets humming about his ears and multiplying the stars in the windscreen.

He was not hit again. The same power must have guarded him as with a shield.

As he straightened the car up he felt his injured shoulder tenderly. As far as he could discover, no bone had been touched: it was simply a flesh wound through the trapezius muscle, not in itself fatally disabling, but liable to numb the arm and weaken him from loss of blood. He folded his handkerchief into a pad, and thrust it under his shirt to cover the wound.

It was all he could do whilst driving along; and he could not stop to examine the wound more carefully or improvise a better dressing. In ten minutes, at most, the chase would be resumed. Unless the pursuers were as unlucky with their spare as he had been. And that was too much to bank on.

But how had that car come upon the scene? Had it been waiting up a side turning in support of the four men, and had it started on the warning of the first man's scream or the fourth man's cry? Impossible. He had been delayed too long with the mending of the puncture. The car would have arrived long before he had finished. Or had it been on its way to lay another ambush further along the road, in case the first one failed?

Simon turned the questions in his mind as a man might flick over the pages of a book he already knew by heart, and passed over them all, seeking another page more easily read.

None was right. He recognised each of them, grimly, as a subconscious attempt to evade the facing of the unpleasant truth; and grimly he choked them down. The solution he had found when that first shot pinged through the window-screen still fitted in. If Marius had somehow escaped, or been rescued, or contrived somehow to convey a warning to his gang, the obvious thing to do would be to get in touch with agents along the road. And warn the men in the house on the hill itself, at Bures. Then Marius would follow in person. Yes, it must have been Marius. . . .

Then the Saint remembered that the fat man and the lean man had not been tied up when he left Roger. And Roger Conway, incomparable lieutenant as he was, was a mere tyro at this game without the hand of his chief to guide him.

"Poor old Roger," thought the Saint; and it was typical of him that he thought only of Roger in that spirit.

And he drove on.

He drove with death in his heart and murder in the clear, cold blue eyes that followed the road like twin hawks swerving in the wake of their prey. And a mere wraith of the Saintly smile rested unawares on his lips.

For, figured out that way, it meant that he was on a foredoomed errand.

The thought gave him no pause.

Rather, he drove on faster, with the throbbing of his wounded shoulder submerged and lost beneath the more savage and positive throbbing of every pulse in his body.

Under the relentless pressure of his foot on the accelerator, the figures on the speedometer cylinder, trembling past the hairline in the little window where they were visible, showed crazier and crazier speeds.

Seventy-eight.

Seventy-nine.

Eighty.

Eighty-one . . . two . . . three . . . four . . .

Eighty-five.

"Not good enough for a race-track," thought the Saint, "but on an ordinary road—and at night . . ."

The wind of the Hirondel's torrential passage buffeted him with almost animal blows, bellowing in his ears above the thunderous fanfare of the exhaust.

For a nerve-shattering minute he held the car at ninety.

"Patricia! . . ."

And he seemed to hear her voice calling him: *"Simon!"*

"Oh, my darling, my darling, I'm on my way!" cried the Saint, as if she could have heard him.

As he clamoured through Braintree, with thirteen miles still to go by the last signpost, two policemen stepped out from the side of the road and barred his way.

Their intention was plain, though he had no idea why they should wish to stop him. Surely his mere defiance of a London constable's order to stop would not have merited such a drastic and far-flung effort to bring him promptly to book! Or had Marius, to make the assurance of his own ambushes doubly sure, informed Scotland Yard against him with some ingenious and convincing story about his activities as the Saint? But how could Marius have known of those? And Teal, he was certain, couldn't. . . . Or had Teal traced him from the Furillac more quickly than he had expected? And, if so, how could Teal have known that the Saint was on that road?

Whatever the answers to those questions might be, the Saint was not stopping for anyone on earth that night. He set his teeth, and kept his foot flat down on the accelerator.

The two policemen must have divined the ruthlessness of his defiance, for they jumped to safety in the nick of time.

And then the Saint was gone again, breaking out into the open country with a challenging blast of klaxon and a snarling stammer of unsilenced exhaust, blazing through the night like the shouting vanguard of a charge of forgotten valiants.

11

How Roger Conway Told the Truth, and Inspector Teal Believed a Lie

INSPECTOR TEAL SET Hermann down in the sitting-room, and adroitly snapped a pair of handcuffs on his wrists. Then he turned his slumbrous eyes on Roger.

"Hullo, unconscious!" he sighed.

"Not quite," retorted Roger shortly. "But darn near it. I got a good crack on the head giving you that shout."

Teal shook his head. He was perpetually tired, and even that slight movement seemed to cost him a gargantuan effort.

"Not me," he said heavily. "My name isn't Norman. What are you doing there?"

"Pretending to be a sea-lion," said Roger sarcastically. "It's a jolly game. Wouldn't you like to join in? Hermann will throw us the fish to catch in our mouths."

Mr. Teal sighed again, slumbrously.

"What's your name?" he demanded.

Roger did not answer for a few seconds.

In that time he had to make a decision that might alter the course of the Saint's whole life, and Roger's own with it—if not the course of all European history. It was a tough decision to take.

Should he give his name as Simon Templar? That was the desperate question that leapt into his head immediately. . . . It so happened that he never carried much in his pockets, and so far as he could remember

there was nothing in his wallet that would give him away when he was
searched. The fraud would certainly be discovered before very long, but
he might be able to bluff it out for twenty-four hours. And in all that
time the Saint would be free—free to save Pat, return to Maidenhead,
deal with Vargan, complete the mission to which he had pledged himself.

To the possible, and even probable, consequences to himself of such
a course, Roger never gave a thought. The sacrifice would be a small
one compared with what it might achieve.

"I am Simon Templar," said Roger. "I believe you're looking for
me."

Hermann's eyes widened.

"It is a lie!" he burst out. "*He* is not Templar!"

Teal turned his somnambulistic gaze upon the man.

"Who asked you to speak?" he demanded.

"Don't take any notice of him," said Roger. "He doesn't know anything about it. I'm Templar, all right. And I'll go quietly."

"But he is not Templar!" persisted Hermann excitedly. "Templar has
been gone an hour! That man——"

"You shut your disgusting mouth!" snarled Roger. "And if you don't,
I'll shut it for you. You——"

Teal blinked.

"*Somebody's* telling a naughty fib," he remarked sapiently. "Now
will you both shut up a minute?"

He locomoted fatly across the room, and stooped over Roger. But he
based his decision on the tailor's tab inside Roger's coat pocket, and
Roger had not thought of that.

"I'm afraid you're the story-teller, whoever you are," he sighed.

"That's my real name," said Roger bitterly. "Conway—Roger
Conway."

"It sounds more likely."

"Though what that fatherless streak of misery——"

"A squeal," explained Teal patiently. "A time-honoured device
among crooks to get off lightly themselves by helping the police to jump
more heavily on their pals. I suppose he *is* your pal?" added the detective
sardonically. "You seem to know each other's names."

Roger was silent.

So that was that. Very quickly settled. And what next?

Hermann, then, had patently decided to squeal. Which seemed odd,
considering the type of man he had made Hermann out to be.
But. . . .

Roger looked at the man, and suddenly saw the truth. It wasn't a squeal. The protest had been thoughtless, instinctive, made in a momentary access of panic lest his master should be proved to have made a mistake. Even at that moment Hermann was regretting it, and racking his brains for a lie to cover it up. Racking his brains, also, for his own defence. . . .

The situation remained just about as complicated as it had been before the incident. Now Hermann would be racking his brains for lies, and Conway would be racking his brains for lies, and both of them would have the single purpose of covering their leaders at all costs, and they'd both inevitably be contradicting each other right and left, and both inevitably ploughing deeper and deeper into the mire. And neither of them could tell the truth. . . .

But could neither of them tell the truth?

The idea shattered the groping darkness of Roger's dilemma like the sudden kindling of a battery of Kleig arcs. The boldness of it took his breath away.

Could neither of them tell the truth?

As Roger would have prayed for the guidance of his leader at that moment, his leader was there to help him.

Wasn't the dilemma the same in principle as the one which the Saint had solved an hour ago? The same deadlock, the same cross-purposes, the same cataleptic standstill? The same old story of the irresistible force and the immovable object? . . . And the Saint had solved it. By sweeping the board clear with the one wild move that wasn't allowed for in the rules.

Mightn't it work again—at least, to clear the air—and, in the resultant reshuffling, perhaps disclose a loophole that had not been there before— if Roger did much the same thing—did the one thing that he couldn't possibly do—*and told the truth?*

The truth should convince Teal. Roger could tell the truth so much more convincingly and circumstantially than he could tell a lie, and it would be so easy to substantiate. Even Hermann would find it hard to discredit. And——

"Anyway," said Teal, "I'll be taking you boys along to the Yard, and we can talk there."

And the departure to the Yard might be postponed. The truth might be made sufficiently interesting to keep Teal in Brook Street. And then Norman Kent might arrive—and Norman was a much more accomplished conspirator than Roger. . . .

"Before we go," said Roger, "there's something you might like to hear."

Teal raised his eyebrows one millimetre.

"What is it?" he asked. "Going to tell me you're the King of the Cannibal Islands?"

Roger shook his head. How easy it was! Teal might have been the one man in the C.I.D. who would have fallen for it, but he at least was a certainty. Such a lethargic man could not by any stretch of imagination be in a hurry over anything—least of all over the prosaic task of taking his prisoners away to the station.

"I'll do a squeal of my own," said Roger.

Teal nodded.

As if he had nothing to do for the rest of the night, he settled himself in a chair and took a packet of chewing-gum from his pocket.

With his jaws moving rhythmically, he prompted: "Well?"

"If it's all the same to you," said Roger, to waste time, "I'd like to sit in a chair. This floor isn't as soft as it might be. And if I could smoke a cigarette——"

Teal rose again and lifted him into an armchair; provided him also with a cigarette. Then the detective resumed his own seat with mountainous patience.

He made no objection to the delay on the grounds that there were men waiting for him outside the building. Which meant, almost certainly, that there weren't. Roger recalled that Teal had the reputation of playing a lone hand. It was a symptom of the man's languid confidence in his own experienced ability—a confidence, to give him his due, that had its justification in his record. But in this case. . . .

"I'm telling you the truth this time," said Roger. "We're in the cart—Simon Templar included—thanks to some pals of Hermann there—only Templar doesn't know it. I don't want him to be pinched; but if you don't pinch him quickly something worse is going to happen to him. You see, we've got Vargan. But we weren't the first raiders. They were Hermann's pals——"

"Another lie!" interposed Hermann venomously. "Do you have to waste any more time with him, Inspector? You have already caught him in one lie——"

"And caught you sneaking about with a gun," snapped Roger. "What about that? And why the hell am I tied up here? Go on—tell him you're a private detective, and you were just going out to fetch a policeman and give me in charge!"

Teal closed his eyes.

"I can't listen to two people at once," he said. "Which of you is supposed to be telling this story?"

"I am," said Roger.

"You sound more interesting," admitted Teal, "even if Hermann does prove it to be a fairy-tale afterwards. Go on, Conway. Hermann—you wait for your turn, and don't butt in again."

Hermann relapsed into a sullen silence; and Roger inhaled deeply from his cigarette and blew out with the smoke a brief prayer of thanksgiving.

"We went down to Esher to take Vargan," he said. "But when we got there, we found Vargan was already being taken. He seemed very popular all round, that night. However, we were the party that won the raffle and got him away."

"Where did you take him?"

"You follow your own advice, and don't butt in," said Roger shortly. "I'll tell this story in my own way, or not at all."

"Go on, then."

"We took Vargan—somewhere out of London. Then Templar and I came back here to collect a few things. . . . How did you find this place, by the way?"

"I went to Brighton, and found your motor agent," said Teal comfortably. "All motor agents spend Sunday in Brighton and the most expensive cars out of their showrooms. That was easy."

Roger nodded.

He went on, slowly, with one eye on the clock:

"Hermann's pals knew we were interested in Vargan before the fun started. Never mind how—that's another story. . . . No, it isn't—now I come to think of it. You remember the first stunt at Esher?"

"I do."

"Two people escaped past Hume Smith's chauffeur—a man and a woman. They were Templar and a friend of his. They stumbled on the place by accident. They were driving past, and they saw a light and went to investigate. The alarm that scared them off was the second man—the giant whose footprints you found. I'll tell you his name, because he's the leader of Hermann's gang——"

Hermann cut in: "Inspector, this will be another lie!"

Teal lifted one eyelid.

"How do you know?" he inquired mildly.

"He knows I'm telling the truth!" cried Roger triumphantly. "He's given himself away. Now I'll tell you—the man's name was Dr. Rayt

Marius. And if you don't believe me, get hold of one of his shoes and
see how it matches the plaster casts you've got of the footprints!''

Both Mr. Teal's chins were sunk on his chest. He might have been
asleep. His voice sounded as if he was.

"And these people traced you here?"

"They did," said Roger. "And on the way they got hold of the girl
who was with Templar that first night—the girl he's in love with—and
Marius came to say that he would exchange her with Templar for Vargan.
But Templar wasn't swapping. He wanted 'em both. We were able to
find out where the girl was being taken, and Templar went off to rescue
her. I was left to guard the prisoners—Marius and Hermann and another
man called Otto. They tricked me and got away—Marius and Otto—and
Hermann was left to guard me. I was to be an additional hostage against
Templar. Marius and Otto went off in pursuit—they'd already arranged
for an ambush to stop Templar on the road. Marius did that by telephone,
from here—you can ring up the exchange and verify that, if you don't
believe me. And Templar doesn't know what he's in for. He thinks he'll
take the men in the house on the hill off their guard. And he's gone
blinding off to certain death——"

"Half a minute," said Teal. "What house on the hill is this you're
talking about?"

The tone of the question indicated that the authentic ring of truth in
the story had not been lost on Teal's ears; and Roger drew a deep breath.

Now—what? He'd told as much as he'd meant to tell—and that was
a long and interesting preface of no real importance. Now how much
could he afford to add to it? How great was the Saint's danger?

Roger knew the Saint's fighting qualities. Would those qualities be
great enough to pull off a victory against all the odds? And would the
arrival of the police just after that victory serve for nothing but to give
the Saint another battle to fight? . . . Or was the Saint likely to be really
up against it? Might it be a kind treachery to spill the rest of the beans—
if only to save Pat? How could a man weigh a girl's safety against the
peace of the world? For, even if the betrayal meant the sacrifice of the
Saint and himself, it would leave Vargan with Norman Kent. And, in
case of accidents, Norman had definite instructions. . . .

But where was Norman?

Roger looked into the small bright eyes of Chief Inspector Teal. Then
he looked away, to meet the glittering, veiled eyes of Hermann. And,
in the shifting of his gaze, he managed to steal another glimpse of the
clock—without letting Teal see that he did so.

"What house on what hill?" demanded Teal again.

"Does that matter?" temporised Roger desperately.

"Just a little," said Teal, with frightful self-restraint. "If you don't tell me where Templar's gone, how am I going to rescue him from this trap you say he's going into?"

Roger bent his head.

Unless Norman Kent came quickly, now, and outwitted Teal, so that Roger and Norman could go together to the relief of the Saint, there would be nothing for it but to tell some more of the truth. It would be the only way to save the Saint—whatever that salvation might cost. Roger saw that now.

"Get through on the phone to the police at Braintree first," he said. "Templar will pass through there. Driving an open Hirondel. I'll go on when you've done that. There's no time to lose. . . ."

All at once, Teal's weary eyes had become very wide awake. He was studying Roger's face unblinkingly.

"That story's the truth?"

"On my word of honour!"

Teal nodded very deliberately.

"I believe you," he said, and went to the telephone with surprising speed.

Roger flicked his cigarette-end into the fireplace, and sat with his eyes on the carpet and his brain reeling to encompass the tumult unleashed within it.

If Norman was coming, he should have arrived by then. So Norman had decided not to come. And that was that.

The detective's voice came to Roger through a dull haze of despair.

"An open Hirondel . . . probably driving hell-for-leather. . . . Stop every car that comes through to-night, anyway. . . . Yes, better be armed. . . . When you've got him, put a guard in the car and send him back to London—New Scotland Yard—at once. . . . Ring me up and tell me when he's on his way. . . ."

Then the receiver went back on its hook.

"Well, Conway—what about this house?"

Something choked Roger's throat for a moment.

Then:

"We only know it as 'the house on the hill.' That was what it was called in the letter we found on Marius. But it's at———"

Zzzzzzing . . . zzzzzing!

Teal looked at the door. Then he turned sharply.

"Do you know who that is?"

"I haven't the faintest idea."

Zzzzzzzzing!

Again the strident summons; and Roger's heart leapt crazily. He never knew how he kept the mask of puzzlement on his face, but he knew that he did it: the fading suspicion in Teal's stare told him that. And he had put everything he knew into his lie. *"I haven't the faintest idea. . . ."*

But he knew that it could only be one man out of all the world.

Hermann also knew.

But Roger gave no sign, and never looked at the man. It remained a gamble. With Roger telling the truth—and intending, for all Hermann knew, to go on telling the truth—the man was in a quandary. The story that Roger was building up against himself was also giving Hermann a lot to answer. . . . Would Hermann be wise and swift enough to see that he would have a better chance with his unofficial enemies than with the police? . . .

Hermann never spoke.

Then Teal went out into the hall; and Roger could have cried his relief aloud.

But he could not cry out—not even to warn Norman. That would be no use against Teal, as it would have been of use against Hermann. Norman had got to walk into the snare—and might all the Saint's strange gods inspire him as they would have inspired the Saint himself. . . .

Teal opened the front door. And he kept his right hand in his coat pocket.

Norman hesitated only the fraction of a second.

Afterwards, Norman said that the words came to his lips without any conscious thought, as if a guardian angel had put them unbidden into his mouth.

"Are you Mr. Templar?" asked Norman Kent.

And, as he heard the words that he had not known he was going to speak, he stood appalled at the colossal simplicity and colossal daring of the ruse.

"No, I'm not," said Teal curtly.

"Is Mr. Templar in?"

"Not at the moment."

"Well, is there anything you could do? I've never met Mr. Templar; but I've just had an extraordinary message, and I thought, before I went to the police——"

The word pricked Teal's ears.

"Maybe I can do something for you," he said, more cordially. "Will you come in?"

"Certainly," said Norman.

Teal stood aside to let him pass, and turned to fasten the door again.

Hanging on the walls of the hall were a number of curious weapons, relics of the Saint's young lifetime of wandering in queer corners of the globe. There were Spanish knives, and a matador's sword; muskets and old-fashioned pistols; South Sea Island spears, Malay krises and krambits and parangs; a scimitar, a boomerang from New Zealand, an Iroquois bow, an assegai, a bamboo blow-pipe from Papua; and other things of the same kind.

Norman Kent's eye fell on a knobkerry. It hung very conveniently to his hand.

He took it down.

12

How Simon Templar Parted with Anna, and Took Patricia in His Arms

To ATTEMPT TO locate, in a strange part of the country and on a dark night, a house distinguished by nothing but the fact of being situated on "the" hill—particularly in a district where hills are no more than slight undulations—might well have been considered a hopeless task even by the most optimistic man. As he began to judge himself near the village, the Saint realised that.

But even before he could feel despair, if he would have felt despair, his hurtling headlights picked up the figure of a belated rustic plodding down the road ahead. The Saint, no stranger to country life, and familiar with its habit of retiring to bed as soon as the village pub has ejected it at ten o'clock, knew that this gift could only have been an angel in corduroys, sent direct from heaven. The Saint's gods were surely with him that night.

"Do you know the house on the hill?" demanded Simon brazenly.

"Ay, that Oi doo!"

Then the Saint understood that in the English country districts all things are possible, and the natives may easily consider "the house on the hill" a full and sufficient address, just as a townsman may be satisfied with "the pub round the corner."

"Throo the village, tourrn round boi the church an' keep straight as ever you can goo for 'arf a moile. You can't miss ut." So the hayseed declared; and the Saint sped on. But he ran the car into a side turning near the crest of the hill, parked it with lights out, and continued on foot. He might be expected, but he wasn't advertising his arrival unnecessarily.

He had been prepared to break into and shoot up every single house in the district to which the description "on the hill" might possibly have applied, until he came to the right one. But he had been saved that; and it remained to capitalise the godsend.

The gun in his pocket bumped his hip as he walked; and in the little sheath on his forearm he could feel the slight but reassuring weight of Anna, queen of knives, earned with blood and christened with blood. She was no halfling's toy. In blood she came, and in blood that night she was to go.

But this the Saint could not know, whatever presentiments he may have had, as he stealthily skirted the impenetrable blackthorn hedge that walled in the grounds of the house he had come to raid. The hedge came higher than his head; and impenetrable it was, except for the one gap where the gate was set, as he learned by making a complete circuit. But, standing back, he could see the upper part of the house looming over it, a black bulk against the dark sky; and in the upper story a single window was lighted up. He could see nothing of the ground floor from behind the hedge, so that he had no way of knowing what there might be on three sides of it; but in the front he could see at least one room alight. Standing still, listening with all the keyed acuteness of his ears, he could pick up no sound from the house.

Then that lighted upper window gave him an idea.

On the face of it, one single lighted upper window could only mean one thing—unless it were a trap. But if it were a trap, it was such a subtle one that the Saint couldn't see it.

What he did see, with a crushing force of logic, was that the garrison of a fortified house, expecting an attempt to rescue their prisoner, would be likely to put her as far away from the attacker's reach as possible. Prisoners are usually treated like that, almost instinctively, being ordinarily confined in attics or cellars even when no attempt at rescue is expected. And a country house of that type would be unlikely to have a cellar large enough to confine a prisoner whose value would drop to zero if asphyxiated. Patricia could surely be in but one place—and that lighted window seemed to indicate it as plainly as if the fact had been labelled on the walls outside in two-foot Mazda letters.

The Saint could not know that this was the simple truth—that the same fortune that had watched over him all through the adventure had engineered that breakdown on the long-distance wire to prevent Marius communicating with the house on the hill. But he guessed and accepted it (except for the breakdown) with a force of conviction that nothing could have strengthened. And he knew, quite definitely, without any recourse to deduction or guesswork, that Marius by that time must be less than ten minutes behind him. His purpose must be achieved quickly if it were to be achieved at all.

For a moment the Saint hesitated, standing in a field on the wrong side of the blackthorn hedge. Then he bent and searched the ground for some small stones. He wanted very small stones, for they must not make too much noise. He found three that satisfied his requirements.

Then he wrote, by the light of a match cupped cautiously in one hand, on a scrap of paper he found in his pocket:

> I'm here, Pat darling. Throw Anna back over the hedge and
> then start a disturbance to divide their attention. I'll be right
> in.—SIMON.

He tied the scrap to the handle of Anna with a strip of silk ripped from his shirt, and straightened up.

Gently and accurately he lobbed up two stones, and heard each of them tap the lighted pane. Then he waited.

Now, if there were no response—suppose Pat had been tied up, or was doped, or anything like that. . . . The thought made his muscles tighten up so that he felt them quivering all over his body like a mass of braced steel hawsers. . . . He'd have to wade in without the help of distracting disturbance, of course. . . . But that wasn't the thought that made his pulse beat quicker and his mouth narrow down into a line that hardly smiled at all. It was the thought of Patricia herself—the thought of all that might have happened to her, that might be happening. . . .

"By God!" thought the Saint, with an ache in his heart, "if any of their filthy hands . . ."

But he wanted to see her once more before he went into the fight that

he was sure was jeopardised against him. In case of accidents. Just to
see her blessed face once more, to take the memory of it as a banner
with him in to the battle. . . .

Then he held his breath.

Slowly the sash of the window was being raised, with infinite precautions against noise. And the Saint saw, at the same time, that what he
had taken, in silhouette, to be leaded panes, were, in fact, the shadows
of a network of closely set bars.

Then he saw her.

She looked out, down into the garden below, and along the side of the
house, puzzledly. He saw the faltered parting of the red lips, the disor-
dered gold of her hair, the brave light in the blue eyes. . . .

Then he balanced Anna in his hand and sent her flickering through the
dark. The knife fell point home, quivering in the wooden sill beside the
girl's hand.

He saw Patricia start, and stare at it with a wild surmise. Then she
snatched it out of the wood and disappeared into the room.

Half a minute ticked away whilst the Saint waited with a tingling
impatience, fearing at any moment to hear a car, which could only belong
to one man, come purring up the hill. But, fearfully as he strained his
ears, he found the stillness of the night unbroken.

And at last he saw the girl again. Saw her hand come through the bars,
and watched Anna swooping back towards him like a scrap stripped from
a moonbeam. . . .

He found the little knife, after some difficulty, in a clump of long
grass. His slip of paper was still tied to the handle, but when he unrolled
it he found fresh words pencilled on the other side.

Eight men here. God bless you, darling.—PAT.

The Saint stuffed the paper into his pocket and slid Anna back into her
sheath.

"God bless us both, Pat, you wonderful, wonderful child!" he whispered to the stillness of the night; and, looking up again, he saw her still
at the window, straining her eyes to find him.

He waved his handkerchief for her to see, and she waved back. Then
the window closed again. But she had smiled. He had seen her. And the
ache in his heart became a song. . . .

He was wasting no more time looking for a way through the hedge.

His first survey had already shown that it was planted and trained as an effective palisade. But there was always the gate.

On the road. A perfectly ordinary gate.

That, of course, was the way they would expect him to come.

Pity to disappoint them!

He hardly spared the gate a glance. It was probably electrified. It was almost certainly wired with alarms. And it was covered by a rifleman somewhere, for a fiver. But it remained the only visible way in.

The Saint took a short run and leapt it cleanly.

Beyond was the gravel of the drive, but he only touched that with one foot. As he landed on that one foot, he squirmed aside and leapt again— to the silent footing of the lawn and the covering shadow of a convenient shrub. He stooped there, thumbing back the safety-catch of the automatic he had drawn, and wondering why no one had fired at him.

Then wondering went by the board; for he heard, through the silence, faintly, very far off, but unmistakable, the rising and falling drone of a powerful car. And he had barely attuned his hearing to that sound when another sound slashed through it like a sabre-cut—the scream of a girl in terror.

He knew it wasn't the real thing. Hadn't he directed it himself? Didn't he know that Patricia Holm wasn't the kind that screamed? Of course. . . . But that made no difference to the effect that the sound had upon him. It struck deep-rooted chords of fierce protectiveness, violently re-minding him that the cause for the scream might still be there, even if Pat would never have released it without his prompting. It froze something in him as a drench of icy water might have done; and, again as a drench of icy water might have done, it braced and stung and savaged something else into a fury of reaction, something primitive and homicidal and ruth-less, something out of an age that had nothing to do with such clothes as he wore, or such weapons as he carried, or such a fortress as lay before his storming.

The Saint went mad.

There was neither sanity nor laughter in the way he covered the stretch of lawn that separated him from the house and the lighted ground-floor window which he had marked down as his objective directly he had cleared the gate. He was even unable to feel astonished that no shots spat at him out of the darkness, or to feel that the silence might forebode a trap. For Simon Templar had seen red.

Eight men, Patricia's note had told him, were waiting to oppose his entrance. . . . Well, let 'em all come. The more the bloodier. . . .

He who had always been the laughing cavalier, the man who would always exchange a joke as he exchanged a blow, who never fought but he smiled, nor greeted peril without a song in his heart, was certainly not laughing at all.

He went through that window as surely no man ever went through a window before, except in a film studio. He went through it in one flying leap, with his right shoulder braced to smash through the flimsy obstacle of the glass, and his left arm raised to shield his face from the splinters.

That mad rush took him into the room without a pause, to land on the floor inside with a jolt, stumbling for an instant, which gave the six men who were playing cards around the table time to scramble to their feet.

Six of them—meaning that the other two were probably dealing with the scream. It ought to have been possible to distract more of their attention than that; but since it had so fallen out. . . .

And where, anyway, were the defences that he should have to break through? As far as that window, he had an easy course to cover. And these men had none of the air of men prepared to be attacked.

These thoughts flashed through the Saint's mind in the split second it took him to recover his balance; and then he was concerned with further questions.

The gun was ready in his hand; and two who were swift to draw against him were not swift enough, and died in their tracks before the captured automatic jammed and gave the other four their chance.

Never before had the Saint attacked with such a fire of murderous hatred; for the cry from the upper room had not been repeated, and that could only mean that it had been forcibly stifled—somehow. And the thought of Patricia fighting her fight alone upstairs, as she would have to go on fighting alone unless Simon Templar won his own fight against all the odds. . . . The first hint of a smile came to his lips when the first man fell; and when the gun froze useless in his hand he looked at it and heard someone laugh, and recognised the voice as his own.

Then Anna flicked from her sheath and whistled across half the room like a streak of living light, to bite deep of the third man's throat.

If the Saint had thought, perhaps he would never have let Anna go, since she could only have been thrown once against the many times she could have stabbed. But he had not thought. He had only one idea, clear and bright above the swirl of red, murderous mist that rimmed his vision, and that was to work the most deadly havoc he could in the shortest possible space of time.

And the first man he met with his bare hands was catapulted back against the wall by a straight left that packed all the fiendish power of a sledge-hammer gone mad, a blow that shattered teeth in their sockets and smithereened a jawbone as if it had been made of glass.

And then the Saint laughed again—but this time he knew that he did it. The first outlet of his blind fury, the first taste of blood, that first primevally ferocious satisfaction in the battering contract of flesh and bone, had cleared his eyes and steadied down his nerves to their old fighting coolness.

"Come again, my beautifuls," he drawled breathlessly, and there was something more Saintly in the laugh in his voice, but his eyes were still as cold and bleak as two chips of blue ice. . . . "Come again!"

The remaining two came at him together.

Simon Templar would not have cared if they had been twenty-two. He was warmed up now, and through the glacial implacability of his purpose was creeping back some of the heroic mirth and magnificence that rarely forsook him for long.

"Come again!"

They came abreast; but Simon, with one lightning spring sideways, made the formation tandem. The man who was left nearest swung round and lashed out a mule-kick of a punch at the Saint's mocking smile; but the Saint swerved a matter of a mere three inches, and the blow whipped harmlessly past his ear. Then, with another low laugh of triumph, Simon pivoted on his toes, his whole body seeming to uncoil in one smooth spasm of effort, and flashed in an uppercut that snapped the man's head back as if it had been struck by a pneumatic riveter, and dropped him like a poleaxed steer.

Then the Saint turned to meet the second man's attack; and at the same moment the door burst open and flopped the odds back again from evens to two to one against.

In theory. But actually this new arrival was fresh life to the Saint. For this man must have been one of those who had been busy suppressing the scream, who had laid his hands on Patricia. . . . And against him and his fellow the Saint had a personal feud. . . .

As Simon saw him come, the chips of blue ice under Simon's straight-lined brows glinted with an unholy light.

"Where have you been all my life, sonny boy?" breathed the Saint's caressing undertone. "Why haven't you come down before—so that I could knock your miscarriage of a face through the back of your monstrosity of a neck?"

He wove in towards the two in a slight crouch, on his toes, his fists stirring gently. And from the limit of his reach he snaked in a long, swerving left that only a champion could have guarded; and it split the man's nose neatly, for the Saint was only aiming to hurt—sufficiently— before he finished off the job.

And he should have won the fight on his head, according to plan, from that point onwards. Lithe, strong as a horse, swift as a rapier, schooled in the toughest schools of the fighting game ever since the day when he first learned to put up his hands, and always in perfect training, the Saint would never have hesitated to take on any two ordinary men. And in the mood in which they found him that night he was superman.

But he had forgotten his wound.

The nearest man was swinging a wild right at him—the kind of blow for which any trained, cool-headed boxer has a supreme contempt. And contemptuously, almost lazily, and certainly without thinking at all about a guard which approximated to a habit, Simon put up his shoulder.

The impact should have been nothing to a bunched pad of healthy muscle; but the Saint had forgotten. And it shot a tearing twinge of agony through him which seemed to find out every nerve in his system.

Suddenly he felt very sick; and for a second he could see nothing through the haze which whirled over his eyes.

In that second's blindness he took a high-explosive left cross to the side of the jaw from the man with the split nose.

Simon reeled, crumpling, against the wall.

For some reason, perhaps because they could not both conveniently reach him at once, the two men held back for a moment instead of charging in at once to finish him off. And for that moment's grace the Saint sagged where he leaned, titanically scourging numbed and tortured muscles to obey his will, wrestling with a brain that seemed to have gone to sleep.

And through the singing of a thousand thrumming dynamos in his head, he heard again the song of the Hirondel: *"Patricia! . . . Patricia! . . ."*

Suddenly he realised how much he had been exhausted by loss of blood. The first excitement, the first thrill and rapture of the fight, had masked his own weakness from him; but now he felt it all at once, in the dreadful slowness of his recovery from a punch on the jaw. And the blow he had taken on the shoulder had re-opened his wound. He could feel the blood coursing down his back in a warm stream. Only his will seemed left to him, bright and clear and aloof in the paralysing darkness, a thing with the terrible power of a cornered giant, fighting as it had never fought before.

And then, through the mists that doped his senses, he heard what all the time he had dreaded to hear—the sound of a car slowing up outside.

Marius.

Through the Saint's mind flashed again, like a long, shining spear, the brave, reckless, vain-glorious words that he had spoken, oh, infinite ages ago: "Let 'em all come. . . ."   •

And perhaps that recollection, perhaps anything else, perhaps the indomitable struggle of his fighting will, snapped the slender fetters of weary dizziness that bound him, so that he felt a little life stealing back into his limbs.

As the two men stepped in to end it, the Saint held up one hand in a gesture that could not be denied.

"Your master is here," he said. "Perhaps you'd better wait till he's seen me."

They stopped, listening, for their hearing would have had to be keen indeed to match the Saint's; and for Simon that extra second's breather was the difference between life and death.

He gathered himself, with a silent prayer, for the mad gamble. Then he launched himself off the wall like a stone from a sling, and in one desperate rush he had passed between them.

They awoke too late; and he was at the door.

On the stairs he doubled his lead.

At the top of the stairs a corridor faced him, with doors on either side; but he would have had no excuse for hesitation, for as he set foot in the corridor, the eighth man looked out of a door halfway along it.

The eighth man, seeing the Saint, tried to close the door again in his face; but he was too slow, or the Saint was too fast. The Saint fell on the door like a tiger, and it was the man inside who had it slammed in his face—literally slammed in his face, so that he was flung back across the room as helplessly as a scrap of thistledown might have been flung before a cyclone. And the Saint followed him in and turned the key in the lock.

One glance round the room the Saint took, and it showed him the eighth man coming off the floor with a mixture of rage and fear in his eyes, and Patricia bound to the bed by wrists and ankles.

Then, as the leader of the pursuit crashed against the door, the Saint whipped round again like a whirlwind, and, with one terrific heave, hurled a huge chest of drawers across the room from its place on the wall.

It stopped short of the door by a couple of feet; and, as Simon sprang to send it the rest of the way, the eighth man intercepted him with a knife.

The Saint caught his wrist, wrenched . . . and the man cried out with pain and dropped the knife.

He was strong above the average, but he could not stand for a moment against the Saint's desperation. Simon took him about the waist and threw him bodily against the door, knocking most of the breath out of him. And before the man could move again, the Saint had pinned him where he stood with the whole unwieldy bulk of the chest of drawers. A moment later the massive wardrobe followed, toppled over to reinforce the barricade, and the man was held there, fluttering feebly, like an insect nailed to a board.

The Saint heard the cursing and thundering beyond the door, and laughed softly, blessing the age of the house. That door was of solid oak, four inches thick, and set like a rock; and the furniture matched it. It would be a long time before the men outside would be able to force the barrier. Though that might only be postponing the inevitable end. . . .

But the Saint wasn't thinking of that. He could still laugh, in that soft and Saintly way, for all his pain and weariness. For he was beside Patricia again, and no harm could come to her while he still lived with strength in his right arm. And he wanted her to hear him laugh.

With that laugh, and a flourish with it, he swept up the fallen knife from the floor. It was not Anna, but for one purpose, at least, it would serve him every whit as well. And with it, in swift, clean strokes, he slashed away the ropes that held Patricia.

"Oh, Simon, my darling. . . ."

Her voice again, and the faith and unfaltering courage in it that he loved! . . . And the last rope fell away before the last slash of the knife, and she was free, and he gathered her up into his arms as if she had been a child.

"Oh, Pat, my sweet, they haven't hurt you, have they?"

She shook her head.

"But if you hadn't come . . ."

"If I'd come too late," he said, "there'd have been more dead men downstairs than there are even now. And they wouldn't have cleared a penny off the score. But I'm here!"

"But you're hurt, Simon!"

He knew it. He knew that in that hour of need he was a sorry champion. But she must not know it—not while there remained the least glimmer of hope—not while he could still keep on keeping on. . . . And he laughed again, as gay and as devil-may-care a laugh as had ever passed his lips.

"It's nothing," he said cheerfully. "Considering the damage I've done to them, I should say it works out at about two thousand per cent. clear profit. And it's going to be two hundred thousand per cent. before I go to bed to-night!"

13

How Simon Templar Was Besieged, and Patricia Holm Cried for Help

SIMON HELD HER very close to him for a moment that was worth an eternity of battle; and then, very gently, he released her.

"Stand by for a sec., old dear," he murmured, "while I improve the fortifications."

The room was a narrow one, fortunately, and it held a large mass of furniture for its size. By dragging up the bed, the washstand, and another chest, it was just possible to extend the barricade in a tight jam across the room from the door to the opposite wall, so that nothing short of a battering-ram could ever have forced the door open. On the other hand, it was impossible to extend the barricade upwards in the same way to the height of the door. The Saint had been able to topple the wardrobe over; but even his strength, even if he had been fresh and uninjured, could not have shifted the thing to cover the doorway in an upright position. And if axes were brought . . .

But that again was a gloomy probability, which it wouldn't help anyone to worry about.

"They've got something to think about, anyway," said the Saint, standing back to view the result of his labours.

He had the air of listening while he talked; and when the sentence was finished he still listened.

The tumult outside had died down, and one voice rose clearly and stood alone out of the fading confusion.

Simon could not understand what it said, but he had no doubt who it was that spoke. No one could have mistaken that high-pitched, arrogant tone of command.

"Hullo, Marius, my little lamb!" he sang out breezily. "How's life?"

Then Marius spoke in English.

"I should stand well away from the door, Templar," he remarked suavely. "I am about to shoot out the lock."

The Saint chuckled.

"It's all the same to me, honeybunch," he answered, "but I think you ought to know that one of your bright boys is stuck against the door, right over the lock, and I'm afraid he can't move—and I can't get him away without busting the works."

"That will be unlucky for him," said Marius callously; and the man pinned against the door shrieked once, horribly.

The Saint had Patricia away in a corner, covering her with his own body, when Marius fired. But looking over his shoulder, he saw the man at the door bare his teeth dreadfully before he slopped limply forwards over the chest of drawers and lay still. The Saint's nerves were of pure tungsten, but the inhuman deliberateness of that murder made his blood run cold for an instant.

"Poor devil," he muttered.

But outside, Marius had barked an order, and the assault was being renewed.

Simon went to the window; but one look at the bars told him that they had been too well laid for any unaided human effort to dislodge them. And there was nothing in the room that might have been used as a lever, except, perhaps, one of the bedposts—to obtain which would have meant disorganising the whole of the barricade.

The trap was complete.

And no help could be expected from outside, unless Roger . . . But the mere fact that Marius was there ruled Roger Conway out.

"How did you get here?" the girl was asking.

Simon told her the whole story, with his mind on other things. Perhaps because his attention was so divided, he forgot that her quick intelligence would not take long to seize upon the salient deduction; and he was almost startled when she interrupted him.

"But if you left Roger with Marius——"

The Saint looked at her and nodded ruefully.

"Let's face it," he said. "Old Roger's dropped a stitch. But he may still be knitting away somewhere. Roger isn't our star pupil, but he has a useful knack of tumbling out of trouble. Unless Teal's chipped in——"

"Why Teal?"

Simon came back to earth. So much had happened since he last saw her that he had overlooked her ignorance of it.

He told her what she had missed of the story—the adventure at Esher and the flight to Maidenhead. For the first time she fully understood all that was involved, and understood also why she had been taken to the house on the hill.

Quietly and casually, with flippancy and jest, in his own vivid way, he told the story as if it were nothing but a trivial incident. And a trivial incident it had become for him, in fact: he could no longer see the trees for the wood.

"So," he said, "you'll see that Angel Face means business, and you'll see why there's so much excitement in Bures to-night."

And, as he spoke, he glanced involuntarily at the lifeless figure sprawled over the chest of drawers, a silent testimony to the truth of his words; and the girl followed his gaze.

Then Simon met her eyes, and shrugged.

He made her sit down on the bed, and sat down himself beside her; he took a cigarette from his case and made her take one also.

"It won't help us to get worked up about it," he said lightly. "It's unfortunate about Sam Stick-my-gizzard over there; but the cheerful way to look at it is to think that he makes one less of the ungodly. Let's be cheerful. . . . And while we're being cheerful, tell me how you came into this mess from which I'm rescuing you at such great peril."

"That was easy. I wasn't expecting anything of the sort, you see. If you'd said more when you rang me up. . . . But I fell for it like a child. There was hardly anyone on the train, and I had a compartment to myself. We must have been near Reading when a man came along the corridor and asked if I had a match. I gave him one, and he gave me a cigarette. . . . I know I was a fool to take it; but he looked a perfectly ordinary man, and I had no reason to be suspicious——"

Simon nodded.

"Until you woke up in a motor-car somewhere?"

"Yes. . . . Tied hand and foot, with a bag over my head. . . . We drove for a long time, and then I was brought in here. That was only about an hour before you threw the stones at my window. . . . Oh, Simon, I'm so glad you came!''

''So am I,'' he said.

He was looking at the door. Clearly, the efficiency of his barricade had been proved, for the attack had paused. Then Marius gave another order.

For a while there was only the murmur of conversation; and then that stopped with the sound of someone coming heavily down the corridor. And Simon Templar caught his breath, guessing that his worst forebodings were to be realised.

An instant later he was justified by a rendering crash on the door that was different from all the other thundering that had smashed upon it before.

''What is it?'' asked Patricia.

''They've brought up the meat-axe,'' said the Saint carelessly; but he did not feel careless at heart, for the noise on the door and the crack that had appeared in one panel told him that an axe was being employed that would not take very long to damage even four inches of seasoned oak.

The blow was repeated.

And again.

The edge of a blade showed through the door like a shin strip of silver at the fourth blow.

A matter of minutes, now, before a hole was cut large enough for the besiegers to fire into the room—with an aim. And when that was done . . .

The Saint knew that the girl's eyes were upon him, and tried desperately to postpone the question he knew she was framing.

''Marius, little pal!''

There was a lull; and then Marius answered.

''Are you going to say,'' sneered the giant, ''that you will save us the trouble of breaking in the door?''

''Oh no. I just wanted to know how you were.''

''I have nothing to complain of, Templar. And you?''

''When there are grey skies,'' said the Saint, after the manner of Al Jolson, ''I don't mind the grey skies. You make them blue, sonny boy. . . . By the way, how did you leave my friend?''

Marius's sneering chuckle curdled through the door.

''He is still at Brook Street, in charge of Hermann. You remember Hermann, the man you knocked out? . . . But I am sure Hermann will be very kind to him. . . . Is there anything else you wish to know?''

"Nothing at the moment," said the Saint.

Marius spoke in his own language, and the axe struck again.

Then Patricia would no longer be denied. The Saint met her eyes, and saw that she understood. But she showed no fear.

Quite quietly they looked at each other; and their hands came together quite gently and steadily.

"I'm sorry," said Simon in a low voice. "I can never tell you how sorry I am."

"But I understand, Simon," she said; and her voice was still the firm, clear, unfaltering voice that he loved. "The gods haven't forgotten you, after all. Isn't this the sort of end you've always prayed for?"

"It is the end of the world," he said quietly. "Roger was my only reinforcement. If I didn't get back to Brook Street by a certain time, he was to come after me. But, obviously, Roger can't come now. . . ."

"I know."

"I won't let you be taken alive, Pat."

"And you?"

He laughed.

"I shall try to take Marius with me. But—oh, Pat, I'd sell my soul for you not to be in it! This is my way out but it isn't yours——"

"Why not? Shouldn't I want to see the last fight through with you?"

Her hands were on his shoulders then, and he was holding her face between his hands. She was looking up at him.

"Dear," he said, "I'm not complaining. We don't live in a magnificent age, but I've done my best to make life magnificent as I see it—to live my ideal of the happy warrior. But you made that possible. You made me seek and fight for the tremendous things. Battle and sudden death— yes, but battle and sudden death in the name of peace and life and love. You know how I love you, Pat. . . ."

She knew. And if she had never given him the ultimate depths of her heart before, she gave them all to him then, with a gladness in that kiss as vivid as a shout in silence.

"Does anything matter much beside that?" she asked.

"But I've sacrificed you! If I'd been like other men—if I hadn't been so fool crazy for danger—if I'd thought more about *you,* and what I might be letting *you* in for——"

She smiled.

"I wouldn't have had you different. You've never apologised for your-self before: why do it now?"

He did not answer. Who could have answered such a generosity?

So they sat together; and the battering on the door went on. The great door shook and resounded to each blow, and the sound was like the booming of a muffled knell.

Presently the Saint looked up, and saw that in the door was a hole the size of a man's hand. And suddenly a strange strength came upon him, weak and weary as he was.

"But, by Heaven, this isn't going to be the end!" cried the Saint. "We've still so much to do, you and I!"

He was on his feet.

He couldn't believe that it was the end. He wasn't ready, yet, to pass out—even in a blaze of some sort of glory. He wouldn't believe that that was his hour at last. It was true that they still had so much to do. There was Roger Conway, and Vargan, and Marius, and the peace of the world wrapped up in these two. And adventure and adventure beyond. Other things. . . . For in that one adventure, and in that one hour, he had seen a new and wider vision of life, wider even than the ideal of the happy warrior, wider even than the fierce delight of battle and sudden death, but rather a fulfilment and a consummation of all these things—and how should he die before he had followed that vision farther?

And he looked at the door, and saw the eyes of Marius.

"I should advise you to surrender, Templar," said the giant coldly. "If you are obstinate, you will have to be shot."

"That'd help you, wouldn't it, Angel Face? And then how would you find Vargan?"

"Your friend Conway might be made to speak."

"You've got a hope!"

I have my own methods of persuasion, Templar, and some of them are almost as ingenious as yours. Besides, have you thought that your death would leave Miss Holm without a protector?"

"I have," said the Saint. "I've also thought that my surrender would leave her in exactly the same position. But she has a knife, and I don't think you'll find her helpful. Think again!"

"Besides," said Marius, in the same dispassionate tone, "you need not be killed at once. It would be possible to wound you again."

The Saint threw back his head.

"I never surrender," he said.

"Very well," said Marius calmly.

He snapped out another order, and again the axe crashed on the door. The Saint knew that the hole was being enlarged so that a man could

shoot through it and know what he was shooting at, and he knew that
the end could not now be long in coming.

There was no cover in the room. They might have flattened themselves
against the wall in which the door was, so that they could not be seen
from outside, but that would make little difference. A few well-grouped
shots aimed along the wall by an automatic would be certain of scoring.

And the Saint had no weapon but the captured knife; and that, as he
had said, he had given to Patricia.

The odds were impossible.

As he watched the chips flying from the gap which the axe had already
made—and it was now nearly as big as a man's head—the wild thought
crossed his mind that he might challenge Marius to meet him in single
combat. But immediately he discarded the thought. Dozens of men might
have accepted, considering the difference in their sizes: the taunt of
cowardice, the need to maintain their prestige among their followers, at
least, might have forced their hand and stung them to take the challenge
seriously. But Marius was above all that. He had one object in view, and
it was already proved that he viewed it with a singleness of aim that was
above all ordinary motives. The man who had cold-bloodedly shot a way
through the body of one of his own gang—and got away with it—would
not be likely to be moved by any argument the Saint could use.

Then—what?

The Saint held Patricia in his arms, and his brain seemed to reel like
the spinning of a great crazy fly-wheel. He knew that he was rapidly
weakening now. The heroic effort which had taken him to that room and
barricaded it had cost him much, and the sudden access of supernatural
strength and energy which had just come upon him could not last for
long. It was like a transparent mask of glittering crystal, hard but brittle,
and behind it and through it he could see the foundations on which it
based its tenacity crumbling away.

It was a question, as it had been in other tight corners, of playing for
time. And it was also the reverse. Whatever was to be done to win the
time must be done quickly—before that forced blaze of vitality fizzled
out and left him powerless.

The Saint passed a hand across his eyes, and felt strangely futile. If
only he were whole and strong, gifted again with the blood that he had
lost, with a shoulder that wasn't spreading a numbing pain all over him,
and a brain cleared of the muzzy aftermath of that all-but-knock-out swipe
on the jaw, to be of some use to Patricia in her need!

"Oh, God!" he groaned. "God help me!"

But still he could see nothing useful to do—nothing but the forlorn thing that he did. He put Patricia from him and leapt to the door on to part of the barricade, covering with his body the hole that was being cut. Marius saw him.

"What is it now, Templar?" asked the giant grimly.

"Nothing, honey," croaked the Saint, with a breathless little laugh. "Just that I'm here, and I'm carefully arranging myself so that if anyone shoots at me it will be fatal. And I know you don't want me to die yet. So it'll keep you busy a bit longer—won't it?—making that hold big enough for it to be safe to shoot through. . . ."

"You are merely being foolishly troublesome," said Marius unemotionally, and added an order.

The man with the axe continued his work.

But it would take longer—that was all the Saint cared about. There was hope as long as there was life. The miracle might happen . . . might happen. . . .

He found Patricia beside him.

"Simon—what's the use?"

"We'll see, darling. We're still kicking, anyway—that's the main thing."

She tried to move him by force, but he held her hands away. And then she tore herself out of his grasp; and with dazed and uncomprehending eyes he watched her at the window—watched her raise the sash and look out into the night.

"Help!"

"You fool!" snarled the Saint bitterly. "Do you want them to have the last satisfaction of hearing us whine?"

He forgot everything but that—that stern point of pride—and left his place at the door. He reached her in a few lurching strides, and his hands fell roughly on her shoulders to drag her away.

She shouted again: *"Help!"*

"Be quiet!" snarled the Saint bitterly.

But when he turned her round he saw that her face was calm and serene, and not at all the face that should have gone with those cries.

"You asked God to help you, old boy," she said. "Why shouldn't I ask the men who have come?"

And she pointed out of the window.

He looked; and he saw that the gate at the end of the garden, and the drive within, were lighted up as with the light of day by the headlights of a car that had stopped in the road beyond. But for the din of the axe at the door he would have heard its approach.

And then into that pathway of light stepped a man, tall and dark and trim; and the man cupped his hands about his mouth and shouted:

"Coming, Pat! . . . Hullo, Simon!"

"Norman!" yelled the Saint. "Norman—my seraph—my sweet angel!"

Then he remembered the odds and called again:

"Look out for yourself! They're armed——"

"So are we," said Norman Kent happily. "Inspector Teal and his merry men are all round the house. We've got 'em cold."

For a moment the Saint could not speak.

Then:

"Did you say Inspector Teal?"

"Yes," shouted Norman. And he added something. He added it brilliantly. He knew that the men in the house were foreigners—that even Marius, with his too-perfect English, was a foreigner—and that no one but the Saint and Patricia could be expected to be familiar with the more abstruse perversions and defilements possible to the well of native English. And he made the addition without a change of tone that might have hinted at his meaning. He added: *"All breadcrumbs and breambait. Don't bite!"*

Then Simon understood the bluff.

It must have been years since the sedate and sober Norman Kent had played such irreverent slapstick with the tongue that Shakespeare spake, but the Saint could forgive the lapse.

Simon's arm was round Patricia's shoulders, and he had seen a light in the darkness. The miracle had happened, and the adventure went on.

And he found his voice.

"Oh, *boy!*" he cried; and dragged Patricia down into the temporary shelter of the barricade as the first shot from outside the smashed door smacked over their heads and sang away into the blackness beyond the open window.

14

How Roger Conway Drove the Hirondel, and Norman Kent Looked Back

A SECOND BULLET snarled past the Saint's ear and flattened itself in a silvery scar on the wall behind him; but no more shots followed. From outside the house came the rattle of other guns. Simon heard Marius speaking crisply, and then he was listening to the sound of footsteps hurrying away down the corridor. He raised his head out of cover, and saw nothing through the hole in the door.

"They're going to try and make a dash through the cordon that isn't there," he divined; and so it was to prove.

He stood up, and began to tear away the barricade, the girl helping him.

They raced down the corridor together, and paused at the top of the stairs. But there was no one to be seen in the hall below.

Simon led the way downwards. Without considering where he went, he burst into the nearest room, and found that it was the room in which he had fought the opening skirmish. The window through which he had hurled himself was now open, and through it drifted the sounds of a scattered fusillade.

He caught up a gun from the floor without halting in his rush to the window.

Outside, on the lawn, with the light behind him, he could see a little knot of men piling into a car. The engine started up a second later.

A smile touched the Saint's lips—the first entirely carefree smile that had been there that night. There was something irresistibly entertaining about the spectacle of that death-or-glory sortie whose reckless daring was nothing but the saying of a loud "Boo" to a tame goose—if the men who made the sortie had only known. But they could not have known, and Marius was doing the only possible thing. He could not have hoped to survive a siege, but a sortie was a chance. Flimsy, but a chance. And certainly the effect of a posse shooting all round the house had been very convincingly obtained. Simon guessed that the rescue party had spared neither ammunition nor breath. They must have run themselves off their legs to maintain that impression of revolver fire coming from every quarter of the garden at once.

The car, with its frantic load, was sweeping down the drive in a moment. Simon levelled his gun and spat lead after it, but he could not tell whether he did any damage.

Then another gun poked into his ribs, and he turned.

"Put it up," said the Saint. "Put it up, Roger, old lad!"

"Well, you old horse-thief!"

"Well, you low-down stiff!"

They shook hands.

Then Norman Kent loomed up out of the darkness.

"Where's Pat?"

But Patricia was beside the Saint.

Norman swung her off her feet and kissed her shamelessly. Then he clapped Simon on the shoulder.

"Do we go after them?" he asked.

The Saint shook his head.

"Not now. Is Orace with you?"

"No. Just Roger and I—the old firm."

"Even then—we've got to get back to Vargan. We can't risk throwing away the advantage, and getting the whole bunch of us tied up again. And in about ten seconds more this place is going to be infested with stampeding villagers thinking the next war's started already. We'll beat it while the tall timber looks easy!"

"What's that on your coat—blood?"

"Nothing."

He led the way to the Hirondel, walking rather slowly for him. Roger went beside him. At one step, the Saint swayed, and caught at Roger's arm.

"Sorry, son," he murmured. "Just came all over queer, I did. . . ."

"Hadn't you better let us have a look——"

"We'll leave now," said the Saint, with more quietly incontestable iciness than he had ever used to Roger Conway in his life before.

The strength, the unnatural vigour which had carried him through until then, was leaving him as it ceased to be necessary. But he felt a deep and absurd contentment.

Roger Conway drove, for Norman had curtly surrendered the wheel of his recovered car. Thus Roger could explain to the Saint, who sat beside him in the front.

"Norman brought us here. I always swore you were the last word in drivers, but there isn't much you could teach Norman."

"What was the car?"

"A Lancia. He was stuck at Maidenhead without anything, so the only thing to do was to pinch something. He walked up to Skindle's, and took his pick."

"Let's have this from the beginning," said the Saint patiently. "What happened to you?"

"That was a bad show," said Roger. "Fatty distracted my attention, and Angel Face laid me out with a kick. Then Skinny finished the job, near enough. Marius got on the phone, but couldn't get Bures. He arranged other things with Westminster double-nine double-nine——"

"I met 'em. Four of 'em."

"Then Marius went off with Fatty, leaving Hermann in charge. Before that, I'd been ringing up Norman, and Norman had said he might come up. When the bell rang, I shouted to warn him, and got laid out again. But it wasn't Norman—it was Teal. Teal collared Hermann. I told Teal part of the story. It was the only thing I could think of to do—partly to keep us in Brook Street for a bit in case Norman turned up, and partly to help you. I told Teal to get through to the police at Braintree. Did they miss you?"

"They tried to stop me, but I ran through."

"Then Norman turned up. Took Teal in beautifully—and laid him out with a battle-axe or something off your wall. We left Teal and Hermann trussed up like chickens——"

The Saint interrupted.

"Half minute," he said quietly. "Did you say you rang up Norman?"

Conway nodded.

"Yes. I thought——"

"While Marius was there?"

"Yes."

"He heard you give the number?"

"Couldn't have helped hearing, I suppose. But——"

Simon leaned back.

"Don't tell me," he said, "don't tell me that we already know that the exchange is not allowed to give subscriber's names and addresses. Don't tell me that Hermann, who's with Teal, mayn't have remembered the number. *But what fool wouldn't remember the one word 'Maidenhead'?*"

Roger clapped a hand to his mouth.

The murder was out—and he hadn't seen the murder until that moment. The sudden understanding of what he had done appalled him.

"Won't you kick me, Saint? Won't you——?"

Simon put a hand on his arm, and laughed.

"Never mind, old Roger," he said. "I know you didn't think. You weren't bred to this sort of game, and it isn't your fault if you trip up. Besides, you couldn't have known that it was going to make any difference. You couldn't have known Angel Face was going to get away, or Teal was going to arrive——"

"You're making excuses for me," said Roger bitterly. "And there aren't any. I know it. But it's just the sort of thing you would do."

The hand on Roger's arm tightened.

"Ass," said the Saint softly, "why cry over spilt milk? We're safe for hours yet, and that's all that matters."

Conway was silent; and the Hirondel sped on through the night without a check.

Simon leaned back and lighted a cigarette. He seemed to sleep, but he did not sleep. He just relaxed and stayed quiet, taking the rest which he so sorely needed. No one would ever know what a gigantic effort of will it had cost him to carry on as he had done. But he would say nothing of that to anyone but Roger, who had found him out. He would not have Patricia know. She would have insisted on delaying the journey, and that he dared not allow.

He explored his wound cautiously, taking care that his movements should not be observed from the back. Fortunately, the bullet had passed cleanly through his shoulder, and there were not likely to be any complications. To-morrow, with his matchless powers of recuperation and the splendid health he had always enjoyed, he should be left with nothing more seriously disabling than a stiff and sore shoulder. The only real danger was the weakness after losing so much blood. But even that he felt he would be able to cope with now.

So he sat back with eyes closed and the cigarette smouldering, almost forgotten, between his fingers, and thought over the brick that Roger had dropped.

And he saw one certain result of it staring him in the face, and that was that Maidenhead would not be safe for his democracy for very long.

Marius, still at large, wouldn't be likely to lose much time in returning to the attack. And Maidenhead was not a large place, and the number of houses which could seriously be considered was strictly limited. By morning, Marius would be on the job, working with a desperation that would be doubled by the belief that in some way the police had been enleagued against him. In the morning, also, Teal would be rescued, and would start trying to obtain information from Hermann: and how long would Hermann hold out? Not indefinitely—that was certain. In the circumstances, the Powers Higher Up might turn a conveniently blind eye to methods of persuasion which the easy-going officialdom of England would never tolerate in ordinary times: for the affair might be called a national emergency. And once Teal had the telephone number . . .

Exactly. Say to-morrow evening. By which time Marius, with a good start to make up for his lack of official facilities, would also be getting hot on the trail.

The Saint was no fool. He knew that the Criminal Investigation Department, except in the kind of detective story in which some dude amateur with a violin and a taste for exotic philosophies made rings round their hardened highnesses, was not composed entirely of nit-wits. Here and there, Simon did not hesitate to admit, among the men at New Scotland Yard, there was a brain not utterly cretinous. Claud Eustace Teal's, for instance. And Teal, though he might be something of a dim bulb at the spectacular stuff, was a hound for action when he had anything definite to act upon. And there might be more concrete things to act upon than a name and address in a chase of that sort; but, if there were, the Saint couldn't think of them.

Marius also. Well, Marius spoke for himself.

Taken by and large, it seemed as if Maidenhead was likely to become the centre of some considerable activity before the next nightfall.

"But we won't cry over spilt milk, my lads, we won't cry over spilt milk," went Simon's thoughts in a kind of refrain that harmonised with the rush of the big car. "We ought to have the best part of a day to play with, and that's the hell of a lot to me. So we won't cry over spilt milk, my lads—and so say all of us!"

But Roger Conway wasn't saying it.

He was saying: "We shall have to clear out of Maidenhead to-morrow—with or without Vargan. Have you any ideas about that?"

"Dozens," said the Saint cheerfully. "As for Vargan, by to-morrow evening there'll either be no more need to keep him a prisoner, or—well, there'll still be no need to keep him a prisoner. . . . As for ourselves, there's my Desoutter at Hanworth. Teal won't have had time to find out about that, and I don't think he'll allow anything to be published about us in the papers so long as he's got a chance of clearing up the trouble without any publicity. To the ordinary outside world we're still perfectly respectable citizens. No one at Hanworth will say anything if I announce that we're pushing off to Paris by air. I've done it before. And once we're off the deck we've got a big cruising range to choose our next landing out of.''

And he was silent again, revolving schemes further ahead.

In the back of the car, Patricia's head had sunk on to Norman's shoulder. She was asleep.

The first pale streaks of dawn were lightening the sky when they ran into the east of London. Roger put the Hirondel through the City as quickly as the almost deserted streets would allow.

He turned off on to the Embankment by New Bridge Street, and so they came to pass by Parliament Square on their way westwards. And it was there that Norman Kent had a strange experience.

For some while past, words had been running through his head, so softly that he had not consciously been aware of them—words with which he was as familiar as he was with his own name, and which, nevertheless, he knew he had not heard for many years. Words to a kind of chanting tune that was not a tune. . . . And at that moment, as the Hirondel was murmuring past the Houses of Parliament, he became consciously aware of the words that were running through his head, and they seemed to swell and become louder and clearer, as if a great choir took them up; and the illusion was so perfect that he had looked curiously round towards the spires of Westminster Abbey before he realised that no service could be proceeding there at that hour.

"To give light to them that sit in darkness, and in the shadow of death: and to guide our feet into the way of peace. . . ."

And, as Norman Kent turned his eyes, they fell upon the great statue of Richard Cœur-de-Lion, which stands outside the House. And all at once the voices died away. But Norman still looked back, and saw Richard Cœur-de-Lion riding there, the last of his breed, huge and heroic against the pale dawn sky, with his right hand and arm hurling up his great sword in a gesture. And for some reason Norman Kent suddenly felt himself utterly alone and aloof, and very cold. But that might have been the chill of the dawn.

15

How Vargan Gave His Answer, and Simon Templar Wrote a Letter

IT WAS FULL daylight when they came to Maidenhead.

Orace was not in bed. Orace was never in bed when he could be useful, no matter at what unearthly hour that might be. But whether it was because he never went to bed at all, or whether it was because some strange clairvoyance always roused him in time to be ready for all emergencies, was his own mysterious secret.

He produced a great dish of sizzling bacon and eggs and a steaming pot of coffee as if by the waving of a magic wand.

Then the Saint gave orders.

"We will sleep till lunch-time," he said. "The difference it'll make to our strength will be worth the waste of time."

He himself was feeling ready to drop.

He took Orace with him to his room, and swore him to silence before he allowed him to see the wound. But Orace, seeing it, said: "Wot the thunderinell——"

Simon fluttered a tired hand.

"Don't swear, Orace," he rambled vaguely. "I didn't swear when it happened. And Miss Patricia doesn't know yet. . . . You'll look after Miss Patricia and the boys, Orace, if I conk out. Keep them out of mischief and so forth. . . . And if you see Angel Face, you'll shoot him through the middle of his ugly mug, with my compliments, Orace. . . ."

He slid sideways off the chair suddenly, but Orace's strong arms caught him as he fell.

Orace put him to bed as tenderly as if he had been a child.

And yet, next morning, the Saint was up and dressed before any of the others. He was rather pale under his tan, and his lean face seemed leaner than ever; but there was still a spring in his step. He had slept like a healthy schoolboy. His head was as clear as his eyes, and a cold shower had sent fresh life tingling through his veins.

"Learn a lesson from me," he said over his third egg. "If you had constitutions like mine, invigorated by my spiritual purity, and unimpaired, like mine, by the dissipation and riotous living that has brought you to the wrecks you are——"

And in this he was joking less than they thought. Sheer ruthless willpower had forced his splendid physique on to the road of an almost miraculously swift recovery. Simon Templar had no time to waste on picturesque convalescences.

He sent Orace out for newspapers, and read them all. Far too much that should have been said was still left unsaid. But he could glean a hint here, a warning there, a confirmation everywhere; until at the end of it he seemed to see Europe lying under the shadow of a dreadful darkness. But nothing was said in so many words. There were only the infuriating inadequate clues for a suspicious man to interpret according to his suspicions. It seemed as if the face of the shadow was waiting for something to happen, before which it would not unveil itself. The Saint knew what that something was, and doubted himself for the first time since he had gathered his friends together under him to serve the ends of a quixotic ideal.

But still nothing whatever was said in the newspapers about the affair at Esher; and the Saint knew that this silence could only mean one thing.

It was not until three o'clock that he had a chance to discuss Vargan again with Roger and Norman; for it had been agreed that, although Patricia had to know that Vargan was a prisoner, and why he was a prisoner, and although his possible fate had once been mentioned before her, the question should not be raised again in her presence.

"We can't keep him for ever," said Simon, when the chance came. "For one thing, we look like spending a large part of the rest of our lives on the run, and you can't run well with a load of unwilling luggage. Of course, we might get away with it if we found some lonely place and decided to live like hermits for the rest of our days. But, either way, there'd still always be the risk that he might escape. And that doesn't amuse me in the least."

"I spoke to Vargan last night," said Norman Kent soberly. "I think he's mad. A megalomaniac. His one idea is that his invention will bring him worldwide fame. His grievance against us is that we're holding up his negotiations with the Government, and thereby postponing the frontpage headlines. I remember he told he was naming a peerage as part of the price of his secret."

The Saint recalled his lunch with Barney Malone, of the *Clarion,* and the conversation which had reinforced his interest in Vargan, and found Norman's analysis easy to accept.

"I'll speak to him myself," he said.

He did so shortly afterwards.

The afternoon had grown hot and sunny, and it was easy to arrange that Patricia should spend it on the lawn with a book.

"Give your celebrated impersonation of innocent English girlhood, old dear," said the Saint. "At this time of year, and in this weather, anyone searching Maidenhead for a suspicious-looking house, and seeing one not being used in the way that houses at Maidenhead are usually used, will be after it like a cat after kippers. And now you're the only one of us who's in balk—bar Orace. So you'll just have to give the local colour all by yourself. And keep your eyes skinned. Look out for a fat man chewing gum. We're shooting all fat men who chew gum on sight, just to make sure we don't miss Claud Eustace. . . ."

When she had gone, he sent Roger and Norman away also. To have had the other two present would have made the affair too much like a kangaroo court for his mood.

There was only one witness of that interview: Orace, a stolid and expressionless sentinel, who stood woodenly beside the prisoner like a sergeant-major presenting a defaulter to his orderly officer.

"Have a cigarette?" said the Saint.

He knew what his personality could do; and, left alone to use it, he still held to a straw of hope that he might succeed where Norman had failed.

But Vargan refused the cigarette. He was sullenly defiant.

"May I ask how much longer you propose to continue this farce?" he inquired. "You have now kept me here three days. Why?"

"I think my friend has explained that to you," said Simon.

"He's talked a lot of nonsense——"

Simon cut the speech short with a curt movement of his hand.

He was standing up, and the professor looked small and frail beside him. Tall and straight and lean was the Saint.

"I want to talk to you seriously," he said. "My friend has appealed to you once. I'm appealing to you now. And I'm afraid this is the last appeal we can make. I appeal to you in the name of whatever you hold most sacred. I appeal to you in the name of humanity. In the name of the peace of the world."

Vargan glared at him short-sightedly.

"An impertinence," he replied. "I've already heard your proposition, and I may say that I've never heard anything so ridiculous in my life. And that's my answer."

"Then," said Simon quietly, "I may say that I've never in my life heard anything so damnable as your attitude. Or can it be that you're merely a fool—an overgrown child playing with fire?"

"Sir——"

The Saint seemed to grow even taller. There was an arrogance of command in his poise, in an instant, that brooked no denial. He stood there, in that homely room, like a king of men. And yet, when he continued, his voice was even milder and more reasonable than ever.

"Professor Vargan," he said, "I haven't brought you here to insult you for my amusement. I ask you to try for the moment to forget the circumstances and listen to me as an ordinary man speaking to an ordinary man. You have perfected the most horrible invention with which science has yet hoped to torture a world already sickened with the beastliness of scientific warfare. You intend to make that invention over to hands that would not hesitate to use it. Can you justify that?"

"Science needs no justification."

"In France, to-day, there are millions of men buried who might have been alive now. They were killed in a war. If that war had been fought before science applied itself to the perfection of slaughter, they would have been only thousands instead of millions. And, at least, they would have died like men. Does science need no justification for the squandering of those lives?"

"Do you think you can stop war?"

"No. I know I can't. That's not the argument. Listen again. In England to-day there are thousands of men blind, maimed, crippled for ife, who might have been whole now. There are as many again in France, Belgium, Germany, Austria. The bodies that God gave, and made wonderful and intricate and beautiful—torn and wrecked by your science, often made so hideous that men shudder to see them. . . . Does science need no justification for that?"

"That is not my business."

"You're making it your business."

The Saint paused for a moment; and then he went on in a voice that no one could have interrupted, the passionate voice of a prophet crying in the wilderness.

"There is science that is good and science that is evil. Yours is the evil science, and all the blessings that good science has given to mankind are no justification for your evil. If we must have science, let it be good science. Let it be a science in which men can still be men, even when they kill and are killed. If there must be war, let it be holy war. Let men fight with the weapons of men, and not with the weapons of fiends. Let us have men to fight and die as champions and heroes, as men used to die, and not as the beasts that perish, as men have to die in our wars now."

"You are an absurd idealist———"

"I am an absurd idealist. But I believe that all that must come true. For, unless it comes true, the world will be laid desolate. And I believe that it can come true. I believe that, by the grace of God, men will awake presently and be men again, and colour and laughter and splendid living will return to a grey civilisation. But that will only come true because a few men will believe in it, and fight for it, and fight in its name against everything that sneers and snarls at that ideal. You are such a thing."

"And you are the last hero—fighting against me?"

Simon shook his head.

"Not the last hero," he said simply. "Perhaps not a hero at all. I call myself a soldier of life. I have sinned as much as any man, and more than most. I have been a hunted criminal. I am that now. But everything I've done has been done for the glory of an invisible ideal. I never understood it very clearly before, but I understand it now. But you. . . . Why haven't you even told me that you want to do what you want to do for the glory of your own ideal—for the glory, if you like, of England?"

A fantastic obstinacy flared in Vargan's eyes.

"Because it wouldn't be true," he said. "Science is international. Honour among scientists is international. I've offered my invention first to England—that's all. If they're fools enough to refuse to reward me for it, I shall find a country that will."

He came closer to the Saint, with his head sideways, his faded lips curiously twisted. And the Saint saw that he had wasted all his words.

"For years I've worked and slaved," babbled Vargan. "Years! And what have I got for it? A few paltry letters to put after my name. No honour for everybody to see. No money. I'm poor! I've starved myself, lived like a pauper, to save money to carry on my work! Now you ask me to give up everything that I've sacrificed the best years of my life to win—to gratify your Sunday-school sentimentality! I say you're a fool, sir—an imbecile!"

The Saint stood quite still, with Vargan's bony hands clawing the air

a few inches from his face. His impassivity seemed to infuriate the
professor.

"You're in league with them!" screamed Vargan. "I knew it. You're
in league with the devils who've tried to keep me down! But I don't care!
I'm not afraid of you. You can do your worst. I don't care if millions
of people die. I hope you die with them! If I could kill you——"

Suddenly he flung himself at the Saint like a mad beast, blubbering
incoherently, tearing, kicking. . . ."

Orace caught him about the middle and swung him off his feet in arms
of iron; and the Saint leaned against the table, rubbing a shin that he had
not been quick enough to get out of the way of that maniacal onslaught.

"Lock him up again," said Simon heavily, and saw Orace depart with
his raving burden.

He had just finished with the telephone when Orace returned.

"Get everybody's things together," he ordered. "Your own included.
I've phoned for a van to take them to the station. They'll go as luggage
in advance to Mr. Tremayne, in Paris. I'll write out the labels. The van
will be here at four, so you'll have to move."

"Yessir," said Orace obediently.

The Saint grinned.

"We've been a good partnership, haven't we?" he said. "And now
I'm clearing out of England with a price on my head. I'm sorry we've
got to . . . break up the alliance. . . ."

Orace snorted.

"Ya bin arskin forrit, aintcha?" he demanded unsympathetically.
"Ain't I tolja so arfadozen times? . . . Where ya goin' ta?" he added,
in the same ferocious tone.

"Lord knows," said the Saint.

"Never bin there," said Orace. "Allus wanted ta, but never adno
invitashun. I'll be ready ta leave when you are, sir."

He turned smartly on his heel and marched to the door. Simon had to
call him back.

"Shake, you darned old fool," said the Saint, and held out his hand.
"If you think it's worth it——"

" 'Tain't," said Orace sourly. "But I'll avta look arfter ya."

Then Orace was gone; and the Saint lighted a cigarette and sat down
by the open window, gazing dreamily out over the lawn and the sunlit
river.

And it seemed to him that he saw a cloud like a violet mist unrolled
over the lawn and the river and the white houses and the fields behind,

a gigantic cloud that crept over the country like a living thing; and the cloud scintillated as with the whirling and flashing of a thousand thousand sparks of violet fire. And the grass shrivelled in the searing breath of the cloud; and the trees turned black and crumpled in hot cinders as the cloud engulfed them. And men ran before the cloud, men agonised for breath, men with white, haggard faces and eyes glazed and staring, men . . . But the creeping of the cloud was faster than the swiftest man could run. . . .

And Simon remembered the frenzy of Vargan.

For the space of two cigarettes he sat there with his own thoughts; and then he sat down and wrote a letter.

To Chief Inspector Teal,
  Criminal Investigation Department,
   New Scotland Yard,
    London, S.W.1.

Dear old Claud Eustace,
  Before anything else, I want to apologise for assaulting you and one of your men at Esher on Saturday, and also to apologise for the way a friend of mine treated you yesterday. Unfortunately, on both occasions, the circumstances did not permit us to dispose of you by more peaceful means.
  The story that Roger Conway told you last night was nothing but the truth. We rescued Professor Vargan from the men who first took him—who were led, as Conway told you, by the celebrated Dr. Rayt Marius—and removed him to a place of safety. By the time you receive this, you will know our reason; and, since I have not the time to circularise the Press myself, I hope this explanation will be safe in your hands.
  Little remains for me to add to what you already know.
  We have tried to appeal to Vargan to suppress his invention on humanitarian grounds. He will not listen. His sole thought is the recognition which he thinks his scientific genius deserves. One cannot argue with monomaniacs: therefore, we find ourselves with only one course open to us.
  We believe that for this diabolical discovery to take its place in the armament of the nations of Europe, at a time when jealousies and fears and the rumours of wars are again lifting

their heads, would be a refinement of "civilisation" which the world could well be spared. You may say that the exclusive possession of this invention would confirm Great Britain in an unassailable supremacy, and perhaps thereby secure the peace of Europe. We answer that no secret can be kept for ever. The sword is two-edged. And, as Vargan answered me by saying, "Science is international!"—so I answer you by saying that humanity is also international.

We are content to be judged by the verdict of history, when all the facts are made known.

But in accomplishing what we have accomplished, we have put you in the way of learning our identities; and that, as you will see, must be an almost fatal blow to such an organisation as mine.

Nevertheless, I believe that in time I shall find a way for us to continue the work that we have set ourselves to do.

We regret nothing that we have already done. Our only regret is that we should be scattered before we have time to do more. Yet we believe that we have done much good, and that this last crime of ours is the best of all.

Au revoir!

Simon Templar
("The Saint").

He had heard, while he wrote, the sounds of Orace despatching luggage; and, as he signed his name, Orace entered with a tray of tea and the report that the van had departed.

Patricia came in through the French windows a moment later. He thought she could never have looked so slim and cool and lovely. And, as she came to him, he swung her up in one arm as if she had been a feather.

"You see," he smiled, as he set her down, "I'm not quite a back number yet."

She stayed close to him, with cool golden-brown arms linked round his neck, and he was surprised that she smiled so slowly.

"Oh, Simon," she said, "I do love you so much!"

"Darling," said the Saint, "this is so sudden! If I'd only known. . . ."

But something told him that it was not a time for jesting, and he stopped.

But of course she loved him. Hadn't he known it for a whole heavenly year, ever since she confessed it on the tor above Baycombe—that peaceful Devonshire village—only a week after he'd breezed into the district as a smiling swashbuckler in search of trouble, without the least notion that he was waltzing into a kind of trouble to which he had always been singularly immune? Hadn't she proved it, since, in a hundred ways? Hadn't the very night before, at Bures, been enough in itself to prove the fact beyond question for all time?

And now, in the name of fortune and all the mysteries of women, she had to blurt it out of the blue like that, almost as if . . . "Burn it!" thought the Saint. "Almost as if she thought I was going to leave her!"

"Darling old idiot," said the Saint, "what's the matter?"

Roger Conway answered, from the Saint's shoulder, having entered the room unnoticed. He answered with a question.

"You've seen Vargan?"

"I have."

Roger nodded.

"We heard some of the noise. What did he say?"

"He went mad, and gibbered. Orace rescued me, and carried him away—fighting like a wild cat. Vargan's a lunatic, as Norman said. And a lunatic said . . . 'No.' "

Conway went to the window and looked up the river, shading his eyes against the sun. Then he turned back.

"Teal's on his way," he said, in a matter-of-fact voice. "For the last half-hour the same energetic bird has been scuttling up and down the river in a motorboat. We spotted him through the kitchen window, while we were drinking beer and waiting for you."

"Well, well, *well!*" drawled the Saint, very gently and thoughtfully.

"He was snooping all round with a pair of binoculars. Pat being out on the lawn may have put him off for a bit. I left Norman on the lookout, and sent Orace out for Pat as soon as we heard you were through."

Norman Kent came in at that moment, and Simon took his arm and drew him into the group.

"Our agile brain," said the Saint, "deduces that Hermann has squealed, but has forgotten the actual number of our telephone. So Teal has to investigate Maidenhead generally. That may yet give us another hour or two; but it doesn't alter the fact that we have our marching orders. They're easy. Your luggage has already gone. So, if you beetle off to your rooms and have a final wash and brush-up, we'll be ready to slide. Push on, souls!''

He left them to it, and went to the kitchen in search of Orace.

"Got your bag packed, Orace?"

"Yessir."

"Passport in order?"

"Yessir."

"Fine. I'd like to take you in the Desoutter, but I'm afraid there isn't room. However, the police aren't after you, so you won't have any trouble."

"Nossir."

The Saint took five ten-pound notes from a bulging wallet.

"There's a train to London at 4:48," he said. "Paddington, 5:40. That'll give you time to say good-bye to all your aunts, and catch a train from Victoria at 8:20, which will take you via Newhaven and Dieppe to Paris, where you arrive at 5:23 to-morrow morning at the Gare St. Lazare. While you're waiting in London, you'd better tear yourself away from your aunts for as long as it takes you to send a wire to Mr. Tremayne and ask him to meet you at the station and protect you from those wild French ladies you've read about. We'll meet you at Mr. Tremayne's. . . . Oh, and you might post this letter for me.''

"Yessir."

"O.K., Orace. You've just got time to get to the station without bursting a bloodvessel. S'long!''

He went on to his room, and there he found Patricia.

Simon took her in his arms at once.

"You're coming on this getaway?" he asked.

She held tightly to him.

"That's what I was wondering when I came in from the garden," she said. "You've always been such a dear old quixotic ass, Simon. You know how it was at Baycombe."

"And you thought I'd want to send you away."

"Do you?"

"I should have wanted to once," said the Saint. "In the bad old days. . . . But now—oh, Pat, dear lass, I love you too much to be unselfish! I love your eyes and your lips and your voice and the way your hair shines like gold in the sun. I love your wisdom and your understanding and your kindliness and your courage and your laughter. I love you with every thought of my mind and every minute of my life. I love you so much that it hurts. I couldn't face losing you. Without you, I just shouldn't have anything to live for. . . . And I don't know where we shall go or what we shall do or what we shall find in the days that are coming. But I do know that if I never find more than I've got already—just you, lass!—I shall have had more than my life. . . .''

"I shall have had more than mine, Simon. . . . God bless you!"

He laughed.

"He has," said the Saint. "You see how it is. . . . And I know a gentleman would be strong and silent, and send you out into the night for your own sake. But I don't care. I'm not a gentleman. And if you think it's worth it, to be hunted out of England with me——"

But her lips silenced his, and there was no need to say more. And in Simon Templar's heart was a marvel of thanksgiving that was also a prayer.

16

How Simon Templar Pronounced Sentence, and Norman Kent Went to Fetch His Cigarette-case

A FEW MINUTES later, the Saint joined Roger Conway and Norman Kent in the sitting-room. He had already started up the Hirondel, tested its smooth running as well as he could, and examined the tyres. The sump showed no need of oil, and there was gasoline enough in the tank to make a journey twice as long as the one they had to take. He had left the car ticking over on the drive outside, and returned to face the decision that had to be taken.

"Ready?" asked Norman quietly.

Simon nodded.

In silence he took a brief survey through the French windows; and then he came back and stood before them.

"I've only one preliminary remark to make," he said. "That is— where is Tiny Tim?"

They waited.

"Put yourselves in his place," said the Saint. "He hasn't got the facilities for trailing us that Teal has had. But Teal is here; and wherever old Teal is, Angel Face won't be far behind. Angel Face, being presumably anything but a bonehead, would naturally figure that the smartest thing to do, knowing Teal was trailing us, would be to trail Teal. That's the way I'd do it myself, and you can bet that Angel Face is nearly as rapid on the bounce, in the matter of brainwaves, as we are ourselves. I just mention that as a factor to be remembered during this fade-away act—and because it's another reason for us to solve a certain problem quickly.''

They knew what he meant, and met his eyes steadily—Roger Conway grim, Norman Kent grave and inscrutable.

"Vargan will not listen to reason," said the Saint simply. "You heard him. . . . And there's no way out for us. We've only one thing to do. I've tried to think of other solutions, but there just aren't any. . . . You may say it's cold-blooded. So is any execution. But a man is cold-bloodedly executed by the law for one murder that is a matter of ancient history. We execute Vargan to save a million murders. There is no doubt in any of our minds that he will be instrumental in those murders if we let him go. And we can't take him with us. . . . So I say that he must die.''

"One question," said Norman. "I believe it's been asked before. If we remove Vargan, how much of the menace of war do we remove with him?''

"The question has been answered before. I think Vargan is a keystone. But even if he isn't—even if the machinery that Marius has set in motion is able to run on without wanting more fuel—even if there is to be war— I say that the weapon that Vargan has created must not be used. We may be accused of betraying our country, but we must face that. Perhaps there are some things even more important than winning a war. . . . Do you understand, I wonder?''

Norman looked through the window; and some whimsical fancy, unbidden alien at such a conference, touched his lips with the ghost of a smile.

"Yes," he said, "there are so many important things to think of.''

The Saint turned to Roger Conway.

"And you, Roger—what do you say?''

Conway fingered an unlighted cigarette.

"Which of us shall do it?" he asked simply.

Simon Templar looked from Roger to Norman; and he said what he had always meant to say.

"If we are caught," he said, "the man who does it will be hanged. The others may save themselves. I shall do it."

Norman Kent rose.

"Do you mind?" he said. "I've just remembered I left my cigarette-case in my bedroom. I'll be back in a moment."

He went out, and passed slowly and thoughtfully down the little hall to a door that was not his own.

He knocked, and entered; and Patricia Holm looked round from the dressing-table to see him.

"I'm ready, Norman. Is Simon getting impatient?"

"Not yet," said Norman.

He came forward and set his hands on her shoulders. She turned, with a smile awakening on her lips; but the smile died at the sight of a queer light burning deep in his dark eyes.

"Dear Pat," said Norman Kent, "I've always longed for a chance to serve you. And now it's come. You knew I loved you, didn't you?"

She touched his hand.

"Don't, Norman dear . . . please! . . . Of course I knew. I couldn't help knowing. I'm so sorry. . . ."

He smiled.

"Why be sorry?" he answered gently. "I shall never bother you. I wouldn't, even if you'd let me. Simon's the whitest man in the world, and he's my dearest friend. It will be my happiest thought, to know that you love him. And I know how he loves you. You two will go on together until the stars fall from the sky. See that you never lose the splendour of life."

"What do you mean?" she pleaded.

The light in Norman Kent's eyes had in it something like a magnificent laughter.

"We're all fanatics," he said. "And perhaps I'm the most fanatical of us all. . . . Do you remember, Pat, how it was I who first said that Simon was a man born with the sound of trumpets in his ears? . . . That was the truest thing I ever said. And he'll go on in the sound of the trumpet. I know, because to-day I heard the trumpet myself. . . . God bless you, Pat."

Before she knew what was happening, he had bent and kissed her lightly on the lips. Then he walked quickly to the door, and it was closing behind him when she found her voice. She had been left with no idea of what he meant by half the things he had said, and she could not let him go so mysteriously.

She called him—an imperative Patricia.

"Norman!"

He was back in a moment, almost before she had spoken his name. Something had changed in his face.

His finger signed her to silence.

"What is it?" she whispered.

"The last battle," said Norman Kent quietly. "Only a little sooner than we expected. Take this!"

He jerked back the jacket of a small automatic, and thrust it into her hands. An instant later he was rapidly loading a larger gun which he took from his hip pocket.

Then he opened the window noiselessly, and looked out. He beckoned her over. The Hirondel stood waiting on the drive, less than a dozen yards away. He pointed.

"Hide behind the curtains," he ordered. "When you hear three shots in quick succession, it's your cue to run for the car. Shoot down anyone who tries to stop you."

"But where are you going?"

"To collect the troops." He laughed soundlessly. "Good-bye, dear!"

He put his hand to his lips, and was gone, closing the door softly behind him.

It was when he had left the room for the first time that he heard, through the open door of the sitting-room, the terse command, *"Put up your hands!"* in a voice that was certainly neither Roger's nor Simon's. Now he stood still for a moment outside Patricia's door, listening, and heard the inimitably cheerful accents of Simon Templar in a tight corner.

"You're welcome—as the actress said to the bishop on a particularly auspicious occasion. But why haven't you brought Angel Face with you, sweetheart?"

Norman Kent heard the last sentence as he was opening the door of the kitchen.

He passed through the kitchen and opened another door. A flight of steps showed before him in the light which he switched on. He went down, and a third door faced him—a ponderous door of three-inch oak, secured by two heavy bars of iron. He lifted the bars and went in, closing that third door behind him as carefully as he had closed the first two. The three doors between them should be enough to deaden any sound. . . .

Vargan was sitting huddled up in a chair, scribbling with a stump pencil in a tattered notebook.

He raised his head at the sound of Norman's entrance. His white hair was dishevelled, and his stained and shabby clothes hung loosely on his bones. The eyes seemed the only vital things in a lined face like a creased old parchment, eyes with the dull fire of his madness stirring in them like the pale flickering flame that simmers over the crust of an awakening volcano.

Norman felt a stab of absurd pity for this pitifully crazy figure. And yet he knew that his business was not with that man, but the madness of the man—the madness that could, and would, let loose upon the world a greater horror than anything that the murderous madness of other men had yet conceived.

And the face of Norman Kent was like a face graven in dark stone.

"I have come for your answer, Professor Vargan," he said.

The scientist sat deep in his chair, peering aslant at the stern dark figure framed against the door. His face twitched spasmodically, and his yellow hands clutched his notebook clumsily into his coat; he made no other movement. And he did not speak.

"I am waiting," said Norman Kent presently.

Vargan passed a shaky hand through his hair.

"I've given you my answer." he said harshly.

"Think," said Norman.

Vargan looked down the muzzle of the automatic, and his lips curled back from his teeth in an animal snarl.

"You are a friend of my persecutors," he croaked, and his voice rose to a shrill sobbing scream as he saw Norman Kent's knuckle whiten over the trigger.

17

How Simon Templar Exchanged Back-chat, and Gerald Harding Shook Hands

"WE WERE EXPECTING Angel Face," remarked the Saint. "But not quite so soon. The brass band's ordered, the Movietone cameramen are streaming down, the reporters are sharpening their pencils as they run, and we were just going to unroll the red carpet. In fact, if you hadn't been so sudden, there'd have been a full civic reception waiting for you. All except the mayor. The mayor was going to present you with an illuminated address, but he got lit up himself while he was preparing it, so I'm afraid he's out of the frolic, anyway. However . . .''

He stood beside Roger Conway, his hands prudently held high in the air.

He'd been caught on the bend—as neatly as he'd ever been caught in the whole of his perilous career. Well and truly bending, he'd been. Bending in a bend which, if he could have repeated it regularly and with the necessary adornments of showmanship, would undoubtedly have made his fortune in a Coney Island booth as The Man with the Plasticene Spine. In fact, when he reviewed that bend with a skinned eye, he could see that nothing short of the miracle which is traditionally supposed to save fools from the consequences of their folly could have saved him from hearing that imponderable inward *ping!* which informs a man supple on the uptake that one of his psychological suspender-buttons has come unstuck.

It struck the Saint that this last adventure wasn't altogether his most brilliant effort. It didn't occur to him to blame anyone else for the various leaks it had sprung. He might, if he had been that sort of man, have put the blame on Roger Conway, for Roger's two brilliant contributions, in the shape of dropping the brick about Maidenhead and then letting Marius escape, could certainly be made out to have something to do with the present trouble; but the Saint just wasn't that sort of man. He could only visualise the adventure, and those taking part in it, as one coherent whole, including himself; and, since he was the leader, he had to take an equal share of the blame for the mistakes of his lieutenants, like any other general. Except that, unlike any other general, he kept the blame to himself, and declined to pass on the kick to those under him. Any bricks that were dropped must, in the nature of things, flop on everybody's toes simultaneously and with the same sickening thud: therefore the only intelligent and helpful thing to do was to consider the bricks as bricks, and deal with the bricks as bricks simple and absolute, without wasting time over the irrelevant question of who dropped the brick and why.

And here, truly, was an admirable example of the species brick, a brick colossal and catastrophic, a very apotheosis of Brick, in the shape of this fresh-faced youngster in plus eights, who'd coolly walked in through the French window half a minute after Norman Kent had walked out of the door.

It had been done so calmly and impudently that neither Simon nor Roger had had a chance to do anything about it. That was when they had been so blithely on the bend. At one moment they had been looking through the window at a garden; at the next moment they had been looking through the window at a gun. They hadn't been given a break.

And what had happened to Norman Kent? By rights, he should have been back by that time. He should have been cantering blindfolded into the hold-up—and Patricia with him, as like as not. Unless one of them had heard the conversation. Simon had noticed that Norman hadn't closed the door behind him, and for that reason deliberately raised his voice. Now, if Norman and Patricia received their cue before the hold-up merchant heard them coming . . .

"You wouldn't believe me," Simon went on affably, "if I told you how much I've been looking forward to renewing my acquaintance with Angel Face. He's so beautiful, and I love beautiful boys. Besides, I feel that a few more informal chats will make us friends for life. I feel that there's a kind of soul affinity between us. It's true that there was some unpleasantness at our first few meetings; but that's only natural between men of such strong and individual personalities as ours, at a first acquaintance. It ought not to last. Deep will call to deep. I feel that we shall not separate again before he's wept on my shoulder and vowed again eternal friendship and lent me half a dollar. . . . But perhaps he's just waiting to come in when you give him the All Clear?"

A slight frown appeared on the face of the young man with the gun.

"Who is this friend of yours—Angel Face—anyway?"

The Saint's eyebrows went up.

"Don't you know Angel Face, honeybunch?" he murmured. "I had an idea you'd turn out to be bosom friends. My mistake. Let's change the subject. How's dear old Teal? Still living on spearment and struggling with the overflow of that boyish figure? You know, I can't help thinking he must have thought it very inhospitable of us to leave him lying about Brook Street all last night with only Hermann for company. Did he think it was very rude of us?"

"I suppose you're Templar?"

Simon bowed.

"Right in one, loveliness. What's your name—Ramon Novarro? Or are you After Taking Wuggo? Or are you just one of the strong silent men from the musical comedy chorus? You know: Gentlemen's clothes by Morris Angel and the brothers Moss. Hair by Marcel. Faces by accident. What?"

"As a low comedian you'd be a sensation," said the youngster calmly. "As a clairvoyant, you'd probably make a most successful coal-heaver. Since you're interested, I'm Captain Gerald Harding, British Secret Service, Agent 2238."

"Pleased to meet you," drawled the Saint.

"And this is Conway?"

Simon nodded.

"Right again, son. You really are God's little gift to the General Knowledge Class, aren't you? . . . Speak your piece, Roger, and keep nothing back. You can't bamboozle Bertie. I shouldn't be surprised if he even knew where you hired your evening clothes."

"Same place where he had the pattern tattooed on those pants," said Roger. "Very dashing, isn't it? D'you think it reads from left to right, or up and down?"

Harding leaned one shoulder against the wall, and regarded his captures with a certain reluctant admiration.

"You're a tough pair of wags," he conceded.

"Professionally," said the Saint, "we play twice nightly to crowded houses, and never fail to bring them down. Which reminds me. May we do the same thing with our hands? I don't want you to feel nervous, but this position is rather tiring and so bad for the circulation. You can relieve us of our artillery first, if you like, in the approved style."

"If you behave," said Harding. "Turn round."

"With pleasure," murmured the Saint. "And thanks."

Harding came up behind them and removed their guns. Then he backed away again.

"All right—but no funny business, mind!"

"We never indulge in funny business," said Simon with dignity.

He reached for a cigarette from the box on the table and prepared to light it unhurriedly.

To all outward appearances he was completely unruffled, and had been so ever since Harding's arrival. But that was merely the pose which he habitually adopted when the storm was gathering most thickly; the Saint reserved his excitements for his spare time. He could always maintain that air of leisured nonchalance in any emergency, and other men before Harding had been perplexed and disconcerted by it. It was always the same—that languid affectation of indifference, and that genial flow of idle persiflage that smoked effortlessly off the mere surface of his mind without disturbing the concentrated thought which it concealed.

The more serious anything was, the more extravagantly the Saint refused to treat it seriously. And thereby he was never without some subtle advantage over the man who had the drop on him; for Simon's bantering assurance was so perfectly assumed that only an almost suicidally self-confident opponent could have been left untroubled by a lurking uneasiness. Only a fool or a genius would have failed to jump to the conclusion that such a tranquil unconcern must base itself on a high card somewhere up its frivolous sleeve. And very often the man who was neither a fool nor a genius was right.

But on this occasion the card up the sleeve was very ordinary. The Saint, inwardly revolving every aspect of the interruption with a furious attention, could still find nothing new to add to his first estimate of the deal. Norman Kent remained the only hidden card.

By now, Norman Kent must know what had happened. Otherwise he would have been in the boat with them long ago, reaching down the ceiling while a youngster in plus eights whizzed his Webley. And if Norman Kent knew, Patricia would know. The question was—what would they be most likely to do? And how could Simon Templar, out of touch with them and practically powerless under the menace of Harding's automatic, divine their most probable plan of action and do something in collaboration?

That was the Saint's problem—to reverse the normal process of strategy and put himself in the place of the friend instead of in the place of the enemy. And, meanwhile, to keep Harding amused. . . .

"You're a clever child," said the Saint. "May one inquire how you come to be doing Teal's job?"

"We work in with the police on a case like this," said Harding grimly, "but we don't mind stealing a march on them if we can. Teal and I set out on an independent tour. He took the high road and I took the low road, and I seem to have got there before him. I saw your car outside on the drive, and came right in."

"You should have a medal," said Simon composedly. "I'm afraid I can't give you anything but love, baby, but I'll write to the War Office about you, if you think that might help."

Harding grinned and smoothed his crisp hair.

"I like your nerve," he said.

"I like yours," reciprocated the Saint. "I can see you're a good man gone wrong. You ought to have been of Us. There's a place in the gang vacant for you, if you care to join. Perhaps you'd like to be my halo?"

"So you *are* the Saint!" crisped Harding alertly.

Simon lowered his eyelids, and his lips twitched.

"*Touché!* . . . Of course, you didn't know that definitely, did you? But you tumbled to the allusion pretty smartly. You're a bright spark, sonny boy—I'll tell the cockeyed world."

"It wasn't so difficult. Teal's told everyone that he'd eat his hat if Vargan didn't turn out to be your show. He said he knew your work too well to make any mistake about it, even if it wasn't signed as usual."

Simon nodded.

"I wonder which hat Teal would have eaten?" he murmured. "The silk one he wears when he goes to night-clubs disguised as a gentleman or the bowler with the beer-stain? Or has he got a third hat? If he has, I've never seen it. It's a fascinating thought. . . ."

And the Saint turned his eyes to the ceiling as if he really were fascinated by the thought.

But the Saint thought: "If Bertie and Teal have been putting their heads together, Bertie must know that there's likely to be a third man on the premises. A man already proved handy with the battleaxe, moreover. . . . Now, why hasn't Bertie said anything about him? Can it be that Bertie, our bright and bouncing Bertie, is having a moment of mental aberration and overlooking Norman?"

Then the Saint said aloud: "However—about that halo job. How does it appeal to you?"

"Sorry, old man."

"Oh, not at all," sighed the Saint. "Don't apologise. . . . What else can we do for you? You seem to have everything your own way, so we'll try to oblige. Name your horse."

"Yes, I seem to have rounded you up fairly easily."

So the cunningly hidden question was answered. It was true. Norman Kent, being for the moment out of sight, had fallen for the moment out of mind.

For a fleeting second the Saint met Roger Conway's eyes.

Then:

"What do we do?" asked the Saint amiably. "Stand and deliver?"

The youngster retired to the window and glanced out. Simon took one step towards him, stealthily, but there was an awkward distance between them, and Harding's eyes were only turned away for an instant. Then Harding turned round again, and the Saint was serenely selecting another cigarette.

"Have you got Vargan here?"

The Saint looked up.

"Ah!" said the Saint cautiously.

Harding set his lips.

In the few minutes of their encounter Simon Templar had had time to appreciate in the younger man a quiet efficiency that belied the first impression of youthfulness, combined with a pleasant sense of humour that was after the Saint's own heart. And at that moment the sense of humour was not so evident; but all the efficiency was there, and with it went a certain grimness of resolution.

"I don't know why you took Vargan," he said. "In spite of what we know about your ideas generally, that's still a mystery we haven't solved. Who are you working for?"

"Our own sweet selves," answered the Saint. "You see, our lawn's been going all to hell, and none of the weed-killers we've tried seem to do it any good, so we thought perhaps Vargan's electric exterminator might——"

"Seriously!"

Simon looked at him.

"Seriously, if you want to know," said the Saint, and he said it very seriously, "we took Vargan so that his invention should not be used in the war. And that decision of ours still stands."

"That was Teal's theory."

"Dear old Teal! The man's a marvel, isn't he? Just like a blinkin' detective in a story-book. . . . Yes, that's why we took Vargan. Teal will get a letter from me in the morning explaining ourselves at length."

"Something about the good of humanity, I suppose?"

"Correct," said the Saint. "Thereby snookering Angel Face, who certainly isn't thinking about the good of humanity."

Harding looked puzzled.

"This man you keep talking about—Angel Face——"

"Tiny Tim," explained Simon.

A light of understanding dawned upon the other.

"A man like an overgrown gorilla—with a face according——"

"How beautifully you put it, old dear! Almost the very words I used myself. You know——"

"Marius!" snapped Harding.

The Saint nodded.

"It rings the bell," he said, "and your penny will be returned in due course. But you don't surprise us. We knew."

"We guessed Marius was in this——"

"We could have told you."

Harding's eyes narrowed.

"How much more do you know?" he asked.

"Oh, lots of things," said the Saint blandly. "In my more brilliant moments I can run Teal a close race on some tracks. For instance, I wouldn't mind betting my second-best pair of elastic-sided boots that you were followed to-day—by one of Marius's men. But you mightn't have noticed that."

"But I did!"

Harding's automatic was still coolly and steadily aimed at the Saint's stomach, as it had been throughout the interview—when the aim was not temporarily diverted to Roger Conway. But now there was just a little more steadiness and rigidity in the hand that held it. The change was almost imperceptible, but Simon Templar never missed anything like that. He translated the inflection in his own way; and when he shifted his gaze back to Harding's eyes he found the interpretation confirmed there.

"I shook off my shadow a mile back," said Harding. "But I don't mind telling you that I shouldn't have come in here alone without waiting for reinforcements if I hadn't seen that somebody was a darned sight too interested in what I was doing. And the same reason is the reason why I want Vargan at once!"

The Saint rested gracefully against the table and blew two smoke-rings of surpassing perfection.

"Is—that—so!"

"That is so," said Harding curtly. "I'll give you two minutes to decide."

"The alternative being?"

"I shall start shooting holes in you. Arms, legs. . . . I think you'll tell me what I want to know before that's gone on very long."

Simon shook his head.

"You mayn't have noticed it," he said, "but I have an impediment in my speech. I'm very sensitive, and if anyone treats me unkindly it makes my impediment worse. If you started shooting at me it'd make me stammer so frightfully that I'd take half an hour to get out the first d-d-d-d-damn—let alone answering any questions."

"And," said Harding relentlessly, "I'll treat your friend in the same way."

The Saint flashed Roger Conway a smile.

"You wouldn't breathe a word, would you, old Roger?"

"Let him try to make me!" Conway scoffed.

Simon turned again.

"Honestly, Algernon," he said quietly, "you'll get nothing that way. And you know it."

"We shall see," said Harding.

The telephone stood on a small table beside the window. Still keeping the Saint and Conway covered, he took up the receiver.

"Hullo. . . . Hullo. . . . Hullo. . . ."

Harding looked at his watch, fidgeting with the receiver-hook.

"Fifteen seconds gone. . . . Blast this exchange! Hullo. . . . Hullo!"

Then he listened for a moment in silence, and after that he replaced the receiver carefully. He straightened up again, and the Saint read his face.

"There was another man in your gang," said Harding. "I remember now. Is he here?"

"Is the line dead?"

"As pork."

"No one in this house would have cut the line," said Simon. "I'll give you my word for that."

Harding looked at him straightly.

"If that's true——"

"It can only be Marius," said the Saint slowly. "Perhaps the man who followed you wasn't so easy to shake off."

Roger Conway was looking out of another window, from which he could see the lawn and the river at the end of the garden. Beyond the Saint's motor-boat another motor-boat rode in mid-stream, but it was not the motor-boat in which he had seen Teal. It seemed to Roger that the two men in the second motor-boat were looking intently towards the bungalow; but he could not be sure.

"Naturally," he agreed, "it might be Marius."

It was then that Simon had his inspiration, and it made him leap suddenly to his feet.

"Harding!"

Simon cried the name in a tone that would have startled anyone. Harding would not have been human if he had not turned completely round.

He had been looking through a window, with the table between himself and the Saint for safety, trying to discover what Conway was looking at. But all the time he had been there he had kept the windows in the corner of his eye. Simon had realised the fact in the moment of his inspiration, and had understood it. Norman had not been overlooked. But Harding admitted that he had come alone, and he had to make the best of a bad job. He had to keep covering the two prisoners he had already taken, and wait and hope that the third man would blunder unsuspectingly into the hold-up. And as long as part of Harding's alertness was devoted to that waiting and hoping, Norman's hands were tied. But now . . .

"What is it?" asked Harding.

He was staring at the Saint, and his back was squarely turned to the window behind him. Roger Conway, from the other side of the room, was also looking at the Saint in perplexed surprise. Only the Saint saw Norman Kent step through the window behind Harding.

But Harding felt and understood the iron grip that fell upon his gun wrist, and the hard bluntness that nosed into the small of his back.

"Don't be foolish," urged Norman Kent.

"All right."

The words dropped bitterly from the youngster's lips after a second's desperate hesitation. His fingers opened grudgingly to release his gun, and the Saint caught it neatly off the carpet.

"And our own peashooters," said Simon.

He took the other two automatics from Harding's pocket, restored one to Roger, and stepped back to the table with a gun in each of his own hands.

"Just like the good old story-book again," he remarked. "And here we are—all armed to the teeth. Place looks like an arsenal, and we all feel at home. Come over and be sociable, Archibald. There's no ill-feeling. . . . Norman, will you have a dud cheque or a bag of nuts for that effort?"

"I was wondering how much longer it'd be before you had the sense to create a disturbance?"

"I'm as slow as a freight car to-day," said the Saint. "Don't know what's the matter with me. But all's well that ends well, as the actress used to say, and——"

"It is?" asked Norman soberly.

Simon lifted an eyebrow.

"Why?"

"I heard you talking about the telephone. You were right. I didn't cut the line. Didn't think of it. And if the line *is* dead——"

The sentence was not finished.

No one heard the sound that interrupted it. There must have been a faint sound, but it would have been lost in the open air outside. But they all saw Norman Kent's face suddenly twist and go white, and saw him stagger and fall on one knee.

"Keep away from that window!"

Norman had understood as quickly as anyone, and he got the warning out in an agonised gasp. But the Saint ignored it. He sprang forward, and caught Norman Kent under the arms; and dragged him into shelter as a second bullet splintered the window-frame a few inches from their heads.

"They're here!"

Harding was standing recklessly in the open, careless of what his captors might be doing. The Saint rapped out a command to take cover, but Harding took no notice. Roger Conway had to haul him out of the danger zone almost by the scruff of the neck.

Simon had jerked a settee from its place by the wall and run it across three-quarters of the width of the window opening; and he lay behind it, looking towards the road, with his guns in his hands. He saw something move behind the hedge, and fired twice at a venture, but he could not tell how much damage he had done.

There was the old Saint smile back on the Saint's lips, and the old Saintly light back in his eyes. Against Harding, he hadn't really enjoyed himself. Against Teal, if it had been Teal outside, he wouldn't really have enjoyed himself. But it definitely wasn't Teal outside. Neither Chief Inspector Teal nor any of his men would have started blazing away like that with silenced guns and no preliminary parley. There was only one man in the cast who could conceivably behave like that; and against that man the Saint could enjoy himself thoroughly. He couldn't put his whole heart into the job of fighting men like Harding and Teal, men whom in any other circumstances he would have liked to have for his friends. But Marius was quite another matter. The feud with Marius was over something more than an outlook and a technical point of law. It was a personal and vital thing, like a blow in the face and a glove thrown down. . . .

So Simon watched, and presently fired again. This time a cry answered him. And one bullet in reply zipped past his ear, and another clipped into the upholstery of the settee an inch from his head; and the Saintly smile became positively beatific.

"This is like war," said the Saint happily.

"It *is* war!" Harding shot back. "Don't you realise that?"

Roger Conway was kneeling beside Norman Kent, cutting away a trouser-leg stained with a spreading dark stain.

"What do you mean?" he demanded.

Harding stepped back.

"Didn't you understand? You seemed to know so much. . . . But you hadn't a chance to know that. Still, it would have been announced in the lunch editions, and plenty of people knew about it last night. Our ultimatum was delivered at noon to-day, and they've got till noon to-morrow to answer.''

"What country? And what's the ultimatum about?''

Harding answered. The Saint was not very surprised. He had not read between the lines of his newspapers so assiduously for nothing.

"Of course, it's all nonsense, like anything else that any country ever sent an ultimatum to another about,'' said Harding. "We've put it off as long as we can, but they've left us no choice. They're asking for trouble, and they're determined to have it. Half the Government still can't understand it—they think our friends ought to know better. Just swollen head, they say. That's why everything's been kept so dark. The Government thought the swelling was bound to pass off naturally. Instead of which, it's been getting worse.''

The Saint remembered a phrase from the letter which he had taken from Marius: *"Cannot fail this time. . . ."*

And he understood that the simple word of a man like Marius, with all the power that he represented standing in support behind the word, might well be enough to sway the decisions of kings and councils.

He said, with his eyes still watching the road: "How many people have a theory to account for the swelling?''

"My chief, and a handful of others,'' said Harding. "We knew that Marius was in it, and Marius spells big money. But what's the use of telling ordinary people that? They couldn't see it. Besides, there was still a flaw in our theory, and we couldn't fill it up—until the show at Esher on Saturday. Then we knew.''

"I figured it out the same way,'' said the Saint.

"Everything hangs on this,'' said Harding quietly. "If Marius gets Vargan for them, it means war.''

Simon raised one gun, and then lowered it again as his target ducked.

"Why have you told me all this?'' he asked.

"Because you ought to be on our side,'' Harding said steadily. "I don't care what you are. I don't care what you've done. I don't care what you're working for. But Marius is here now, and I know you can't be with Marius. So——''

"Somebody's waving a white flag,'' said the Saint.

He got to his feet, and Harding came up beside him. Behind the hedge, a man stood up and signalled with a handkerchief.

Then Simon saw that the road beyond the hedge was alive with men.

"What would you do here?" he asked.

"See them!" rapped Harding. "Hear what they've got to say. We can still fight afterwards. They *will* fight! Templar——"

The Saint beckoned, and saw a man rise from his crouched position under the hedge and walk alone up the drive. A giant of a man. . . .

"Angel Face himself!" murmured Simon.

He swung round, hands on hips.

"I've heard your argument, Harding," he said. "It's a good one. But I prefer my own. In the circumstances, I'm afraid you'll have to accept it. And I want your answer quickly. The offer I made you is still open. Do you join us for the duration, or have I got to send you out there to shift for yourself? I'd hate to do it, but if you're not for us——"

"That's not the point," said Harding steadfastly. "I was sent here to find Vargan, and I think I've found him. As far as that's concerned, there can't be peace between us. You'll understand that. But for the rest of it . . . Beggars can't be choosers. We agree that Marius must not have Vargan, whatever else we disagree about. So, while we have to fight Marius——"

"A truce?"

The youngster shrugged. Then he put out his hand.

"And let's give 'em hell!" he said.

18

How Simon Templar Received Marius, and the Crown Prince Remembered a Debt

A MOMENT LATER the Saint was on his knees beside Norman Kent, examining Norman's wound expertly. Norman tried to delay him.

"Pat," whispered Norman; "I left her hiding in your room."

Simon nodded.

"All right. She'll be safe there for a bit. And I'd just as soon have her out of the way while Tiny Tim's beetling around. Let's see what we can do for you first."

He went on with the examination. The entrance was three inches above the knee, and it was much larger than the entrance of even a large-calibre automatic bullet should have been. There was no exit hole, and Norman let out an involuntary cry of agony at the Saint's probing.

"That's all, sonny boy," said the Saint; and Norman loosened his teeth from his lips.

"Smashed the bone, hasn't it?"

Simon stripped off his coat, and tore off the sleeve of his shirt to improvise a bandage.

"Smashed to bits, Norman, old boy," he said. "The swine are using dum-dums. . . . A large whisky, Roger. . . . That'll be a consolation for you, Norman, old warrior."

"It's something," said Norman huskily.

He said nothing else about it, but he understood one thing very clearly.

No man can run very far or very fast with a thigh-bone splintered by an expanding bullet.

Strangely enough, Norman did not care. He drink the whisky they gave him gratefully, and submitted indifferently to the Saint's ministrations. In the pallor of Norman Kent's face was a strange calm.

Simon Templar also understood what that wound meant; but he did not think of it as Norman did.

He knew that Marius was standing in the window, but he did not look up until he had completed the rough dressing with practised hands that were as gentle as a woman's. He wanted to start some hard thinking before he began to bait Marius. Once well under way, the thinking process could continue by itself underneath the inevitable froth of banter and back-chat; but the Saint certainly wanted to get a stranglehold on the outstanding features of the situation first. And they were a pretty slim set of features to have to pin down. What with Patricia on the premises to cramp his style, and Norman Kent crippled, and the the British Secret Service, as represented by Captain Gerald Harding, a prisoner inside the fort on a very vague parole, and Chief Inspector Teal combing the district and liable to roll up on the scene at any moment, and Rayt Marius surrounding the bungalow with a young army corps that had already given proof enough that it wasn't accumulated in Maidenhead for a Sunday afternoon bun-fight—well, even such an optimistic man as the Saint had to admit that the affair had begun to look distinctly sticky. There had been a time when the Saint was amused to call himself a professional trouble-hunter. He remember that pleasant bravado now, and wondered if he had ever guessed that his prayers would be so abundantly answered.

Verily, he had cast his bread upon the waters and hauled up a chain of steam bakeries. . . .

He rose at last to his feet with these meditations simmering down into the impenetrable depths of his mind; and his face had never been milder.

"Good-afternoon, little one," he said softly. "I've been looking forward to meeting you again. Life, for the last odd eighteen hours, has seemed very empty without you. But don't let's talk about that."

The giant inclined his head.

"You know me," he said.

"Yes," said the Saint. "I think we've met before. I seem to know your face. Weren't you the stern of the elephant in the circus my dear old grandmother took me to just before I went down with measles? Or were you the whatsit that stuck in the how's-your-father and upset all our drains a couple of years ago?"

Marius shrugged. He was again wearing full morning dress, as he had been when the Saint first met him in Brook Street, but the combination of that costume with this new setting, together with the man's colossal build and hideously rugged face, would have been laughably grotesque if it had not been subtly horrible.

He said: "I have already had some samples of your humour, Templar——"

"On a certain occasion which we all remember," said the Saint gently. "Quite. But we don't charge extra for an encore, so you might as well have your money's worth."

Marius's little eyes took in the others—Roger Conway lounging against the bookcase swinging an automatic by the trigger-guard, Norman Kent propped up against the sofa with a glass in his hand, Gerald Harding on the other side of the window with his hands in his pockets and a faint flush on his boyish face.

"I have only just learnt that you are the gentleman who calls himself the Saint," said Marius. "Inspector Teal was indiscreet enough to use a public telephone in the hearing of one of my men. The boxes provided are not very sound-proof. I presume this is your gang?"

"Not 'gang,' " protested the Saint—"not 'gang.' I'm sure saints never go in gangs. But, yes—these are other wearers of the halo. . . . But I'm forgetting. You've never been formally introduced, have you? . . . Meet the boys. . . . On your left, for instance, Captain Acting Saint Gerald Harding, sometime Fellow of Clark's College, canonised for many charitable works, including obtaining a miserly millionaire's signature to a five-figure cheque for charity. The millionaire was quite annoyed when

he heard about it. . . . Over there, Saint Roger Conway, winner of the
Men's Open Beauty Competition at Noahsville, Ark., in '25, canonised
for glorifying the American girl. At least, she told the judge it glorified
her. . . . On the floor, Saint Norman Kent, champion beer-swiller at the
last Licensed Victuallers' and Allied Trades Centennial Jamboree, canonised for standing free drinks to a number of blind beggars on the Feast
of Stephen. The beggars, by the way, were not blind until after they'd
had the drinks. . . . Oh, and myself. I'm the Simple Simon who met a
pieman coming through the rye. Or words to that effect. I can't help
feeling that if I'd been christened Sootlegger I should have met a boot-
legger, which would have been much more exciting; but I suppose it's
too late to alter that now.''

Marius heard out this cataract of nonsense without a flicker of expression. At the end of it he said, patiently: ''And Miss Holm?''

''Absent, I'm afraid,'' said the Saint. ''It's my birthday, and she's
gone to Woolworth's to buy me a present.''

Marius nodded.

''It is not of importance,'' he said. ''You know what I have come
for?''

Simon appeared to ponder.

''Let's see. . . . You might have come to tune the piano, only we
haven't got a piano. And if we had a mangle you might have come to
mend the mangle. No—the only think I can think of is that you're travelling a line of straw hats and natty neckwear. Sorry, but we're stocked
for the season.''

Marius dusted his silk hat with a tenderly wielded handkerchief. His
face, as always, was a mask.

Simon had to admire the nerve of the man. He still had a long score
to settle with Marius, and Marius knew it; but here was Marius dispassionately dusting a silk hat in the very presence of a man who had
promised to kill him. It was true that Marius came under a flag of truce,
which he would justly expect a man like the Saint to respect; but still
Marius gave no sign of recognising that he was in the delicate position
of having to convey an ultimatum to a man who, given the flimsiest rag
of excuse, would cheerfully shoot him through the stomach.

''You gain nothing by wasting time,'' said Marius. ''I have come in
the hope of saving the lives of some of my men, for some will certainly
be killed if we are forced to fight.''

''How touching!—as the actress said to the bishop. Is it possible that your conscience is haunted by the memory of the man you killed at Bures, ducky? Or is it just because funerals are so expensive these days?''

Marius shrugged.

"That is my business," he said. "Instead of considering that, you would do better to consider your own position. Every telephone line for ten miles has been cut—that was done as soon as we had definitely located you. Therefore there can be no quicker communication with London than by car. And the local police are not dangerous. Even Inspector Teal is now out of touch with his headquarters, and there is an ambush prepared for him into which he cannot help falling. In addition to that, at the nearest cross-roads on either side of this house, I have posted men in police uniforms, who will turn back any car which attempts to come this way, and who will explain away the noise of shooting to any inquisitive persons. It must be over an hour before any help can come to you—and then it can only end in your own arrest. That is, if you are still alive. And you cannot possibly hope to deceive me a second time with the bluff which you employed so successfully last night.''

"You're sure it was a bluff?"

"If it had not been a bluff I should not have found you here. Do you really think me so ignorant of official methods as to believe that you could possibly have been released so quickly?''

"And yet," said the Saint thoughtfully, "we might have been put here to bait a police trap—for you!''

Marius smiled. The Saint would never have believed that such a face could smile if he had not seen it smile once before. And it smiled with ghastly urbanity.

"Since Inspector Teal left London," said Marius, "he has never been out of the sight of my agents. Therefore I have good reason to be convinced that he still does not know where you are. Shall we say, Templar, that this time you will have to think of something more tangible than—er—what was the phrase your friends used?—than breadcrumbs and breambait?''

Simon nodded.

"A charming phrase," he murmured.

"So," said Marius, "you may choose between surrendering Vargan or having him taken from you by force.''

The Saint smiled.

"Heads you win, tails I lose—what? . . . But suppose the coin falls on its blinkin' edge? Suppose, sweet pea, you got pinched yourself? This isn't Chicago, you know. You can't run little wars of your own all over the English countryside. The farmers might get annoyed and start throwing broccoli at you. I'm not sure what broccoli is, but they might throw it.''

Again that ghastly grin flitted across the giant's face.

"You have not understood me. My country requires Vargan and his invention. In order to obtain that, I will sacrifice as many lives as I may be forced to sacrifice; and my men will die here for their country as readily as they would die on any other battlefield.''

"Your country!"

The Saint had been lighting a cigarette with a cool and steady hand; and for all that might have been read in the scene by an observer who could not hear the words, they might have been discussing nothing more than the terms of a not-too-friendly golf match—instead of a situation in which the fates of nations were involved. . . . At one moment. . . . And then the Saint split the thin crust of calm with those two electric words. The voice that spoke them was no longer the Saint's gently mocking drawl. It was a voice of pure steel and rock and acid. It took those three simple syllables, ground and honed a hundred knife-edges around them, fenced them about with a thousand stinging needle-points, and spoke them in a breath that might have whipped off the North Pole.

"Your country!"

"That is what I said.''

"Has a man like you a country? Is there one acre of God's earth that a man like you loves for no other reason than that it's his home? Have you a loyalty to anything—except the bloated golden spiders whose webs you weave? Are there any people you can call your people—people you wouldn't sacrifice without a qualm to put thirty pieces of silver into your pocket? Do you care for anything in the world but your own greasy god of money, Rayt Marius?''

For the first time Marius's face changed.

"It is my country,'' he said.

The Saint laughed shortly.

"Tell us any lie but that, Marius,'' he said. "Because that one won't get by.''

"But it is still my country. And the men outside lent to me by my country for this work——''

"Has it occurred to you,'' said the Saint, "that we also might be prepared to die for our country—and that the certainty of being imprisoned if we were rescued might not influence us at all?''

"I have thought of that.''

"And don't you place too great a reliance on our honesty? Is there anything to stop us forgetting the armistice and holding you as a hostage?"

Marius shook his head.

"What, then," he said silkily, "was there to stop my coming here under a white flag to distract your attention while my men occupied the rest of the house from the other side? When the fortune of one's country is at stake one has little time for conventional honesty. A white flag may be honoured on a battlefield, but this is more than a mere battlefield. It is all the battlefields of the war."

Simon was teetering watchfully on his heels, his cigarette canted up between his lips. His hands hung loosely at his sides, but in each of them he held sudden death.

"You'd still be our hostage, loveliness," he said. "And if there's going to be any treachery——"

"My life is nothing," said Marius. "There is a leader out there"—he gestured towards the road—"who would not hesitate to sacrifice me and many others."

"Namely?"

"His Highness——"

Simon Templar drew a deep breath.

"His Highness the Crown Prince Rudolf of——"

"Hell!" said the Saint.

"A short time ago you saved his life," said Marius. "It is for that reason that His Highness has directed me to give you this chance. He also wished me to apologise for wounding you yesterday, although it happened before we knew that you were the Saint."

"Sweetest lamb," said the Saint, "I'll bet you wouldn't have obeyed His Highness if you hadn't needed his men to do your dirty work!"

Marius spread his huge hands.

"That is immaterial. I have obeyed. And I await your decision. You may have one minute to consider it."

Simon sent his cigarette spinning through the window with a reckless flourish.

"You have our decision now," he said.

Marius bowed.

"If you will answer one question," said the Saint.

"What do you want to know?"

"When you kidnapped Vargan, you couldn't take his apparatus with you——"

"I follow your thoughts," said the giant. "You are thinking that even if you surrender Vargan the British experts will still possess the apparatus, which they can copy even if they do not understand it. Let me disillusion you. While some of my men were taking Vargan, others were destroying his apparatus—very effectively. You may be sure that nothing was left which even Sir Roland Hale could make workable. I'm sorry to disappoint you——''

"But you don't disappoint me, Angel Face," said the Saint. "On the contrary, you bring me the best news I've had for a long time. If you weren't so unspeakably repulsive, I believe I'd—I'd fling my arms round your bull neck, Angel Face, dear dewdrop! . . . I'd guessed I could rely on your efficiency, but it's nice to know for certain. . . .''

Roger Conway interposed from the other side of the room.

He said: "Look here, Saint, if the Crown Prince is outside, we've only got to tell him the truth about Marius——''

Marius turned.

"What truth?" he inquired suavely.

"Why—the truth about your septic patriotism! Tell him what we know. Tell him how you're just leading him up the garden for your own poisonous ends——''

"And you think he would believe you?" sneered Marius. "You are too childish, Conway! Even you cannot deny that I am doing my best to place Vargan's invention in His Highness's hands.''

The Saint shook his head.

"Angel Face is right, Roger," he said. "The Crown Prince is getting his caviar, and he isn't going to worry why the sturgeon died. No—I've got a much finer bead on the problem than that.''

And he faced Marius again.

"It's really truly true, dear one, that Vargan is the key to the whole situation?" he asked softly, persuasively.

"Exactly.''

"Vargan is the really true cream in your coffee?''

The giant twitched his shoulders.

"I do not understand all your idioms. But I think I have made myself plain.''

"I was wondering who did it," said Roger sympathetically.

But a new smile was coming to Simon Templar's lips—a mocking, devil-may-care, swashbuckling, Saintly smile. He sat his hands on his hips and smiled.

"Then this is our answer," smiled the Saint. "If you want Vargan, you can either come and fetch him or go home and suck jujubes. Take your choice, Angel Face!''

Marius stood still.

"Then His Highness wishes to say that he disclaims all responsibility for the consequences of your foolishness——''

"One minute!''

It was Norman Kent, trying painfully to struggle up on to his sound leg. The Saint was beside him in a moment, with an arm about his shoulders.

"Easy, old Norman!''

Norman smiled faintly.

"I want to stand up, Simon.''

And he stood up, leaning on the Saint, and looked across at Marius. Very dark and stern and aloof he was.

And—

"Suppose,'' said Norman Kent—"suppose we said that we hadn't got Vargan?''

"I should not believe you.''

Roger Conway cut in: "Why should we keep him? If we'd only wanted to take him away from you, he'd have been returned to the Government before now. You must know that he hasn't been sent back. What use could we have for him?''

"You may have your own reasons. Ransom, perhaps. Your Government should be prepared to pay well for his safety——''

Norman Kent broke in with a clear, short laugh that shattered Marius's theory more fatally than any of the words that followed could have done.

"Think again, Marius! You don't understand us yet! . . . We took Vargan away for the sake of the peace of the world and the sparing of millions of good lives. We hoped to persuade him to turn back from the thing he proposed to do. But he was mad, and he would not listen. So this evening, for the peace of the world . . .''

He paused, and passed a hand across his eyes.

Then he drew himself erect, and his dark eyes gazed without fear into a great distance, and there was no flinching in the light of his eyes.

His voice came again, clear and strong.

"I shot him like a mad dog,'' he said.

"You——''

Harding started forward, but Roger Conway was barring his way in an instant.

"For the peace of the world,'' Norman Kent repeated. "And—for the peace of my two dearest friends. You'll understand, Saint. I knew at once that you'd never let Roger or me risk what that shot meant. So I took the law into my own hands. Because Pat loves you, Simon, as I do. I couldn't let her spend the rest of her life with you under the shadow of the gallows. I love her, too, you see. I'm sorry. . . ."

"You killed Vargan?" said Marius incredulously.

Norman nodded. He was quite calm.

And, outside the window, the shadows of the trees were lengthening over the quiet garden.

"I found him writing in a notebook. He'd covered sheets and sheets. I don't know what it was about, or whether there's enough for an expert to work on. I'm not a scientist. But I brought them away to make sure. I'd have burnt them before, but I couldn't find any matches. But I'll burn them now before your eyes; and that'll be the end of it all. Your lighter, Saint——"

He was fumbling in his pocket.

Roger Conway saw Marius's right hand leap to his hip, and whirled round with his automatic levelled at the centre of the giant's chest.

"Not just yet, Marius!" said Roger, through his teeth.

The Saint, when he went to support Norman, had dropped one gun into his coat pocket. Now, with one arm holding Norman, he had had to put his other gun down on the arm of the sofa while he searched for his petrol-lighter.

He had not realised that the grouping of the others had so fallen that Conway could not now cover both Harding and Marius. Just two simple movements had been enough to bring about that cataclysmic rearrangement—when Norman Kent stood up and Marius tried to draw. And Simon hadn't noticed it. He'd confessed that he was as slow as a freight car that day, which may or may not have been true; but the fact remained that for a fraction of a second he'd allowed the razor-edge of his vigilance to be taken off. And he saw his mistake that fraction of a second too late.

Harding reached the gun on the arm of the sofa in two steps and a lightning dive; and then he had his back to the wall.

"Drop that gun, you! I give you three seconds. *One*——"

Conway, moving only his head to look round, knew that the youngster could drop him in his tracks before he had time to more than begin to move his automatic. And he had no need to wonder whether the other would carry out his threat. Harding's grim and desperate determination was sufficiently attested by the mere fact that he had dared to make the gamble that gave him the gun and the strategic advantage at the same time. And Harding's eyes were as set and stern as the eyes of a young man can be.

"*Two*——"

Suppose Roger chanced his arm? He'd be pipped, for a million. But would it give Simon time to draw? But Marius was ready to draw, also. . . .

"*Three!*"

Roger Conway released the gun, even as Harding had had to do not many minutes before; and he had all the sense of bitter humiliation that Harding must have had.

"Kick it over to me."

Conway obeyed; and Harding picked up the gun, and swung two automatics in arcs that included everyone in the room.

"The honour of the British Secret Service!" drawled the Saint, with a mildness that only emphasised the biting sting of his contempt.

"The truce is over," said Harding, dourly. "You'd do the same in my place. Bring me those papers!"

The Saint lowered Norman Kent gently; and Norman rested, half-standing, half-sitting, on the high arm of the settee. And Simon tensed himself to dice the last foolhardy throw.

Then a shadow fell on him; and he looked round and saw that the number of the congregation had been increased by one.

A tall, soldierly figure in grey stood in the opening of the window. A figure utterly immaculate and utterly at ease. . . . And it is, of course, absurd to say that any accident of breeding makes a man stand out among his fellows; but this man could have been nothing but the man he was.

"Marius," spoke the man in grey, and Marius turned.

"Back, Highness! For God's sake——"

The warning was rapped out in another language, but the man in grey answered in English.

"There is no danger," he said. "I came to see why you had overstayed your time limit."

He walked calmly into the room, with no more than a careless glance and lift of his fine eyebrows for Gerald Harding and Gerald Harding's two circling guns.

And then the Saint heard a sound in the hall, beyond the door, which still stood ajar.

He reached the door in a reckless leap, and slammed it. Then he laid hold of the heavy bookcase that stood by the wall, and with a single titanic heave toppled it crashing over to fall like a great bolt across the doorway. An instant later the table from the centre of the room had followed to reinforce the bookcase.

And Simon Templar stood with his back to the pile, breathing deeply, with his head thrown back defiantly. He spoke.

"So you're another man of honour—Highness!"

The Prince stroked his moustache with a beautifully manicured finger.

"I gave Marius a certain time in which to make my offer," he said. "When that time was exceeded, I could only presume that you had broken the truce and detained him, and I ordered my men to enter the house. They were fortunate enough to capture a lady——"

The Saint went white.

"I say 'fortunate' because she was armed, and might have killed some of them, or at least raised an alarm, if they had not taken her by surprise. However, she has not been harmed. I mention the fact merely to let you see that my intrusion is not so improvident as you might otherwise think. Are you Simon Templar?"

"I am."

The Prince held out his hand.

"I believe I owe you my life. I had hoped for an opportunity of making your acquaintance, but I did not expect that our meeting would be in such unpropitious circumstances. Nevertheless, Marius should have told you that I am not insensitive to the debt I owe you."

Simon stood where he was.

"I saved your life, Prince Rudolf," he answered, in a voice like a whip-lash, "because I had nothing against you. But now I have something against you, and I may take your life before the end of the day."

The Prince shrugged delicately.

"At least," he remarked, "while we are discussing that point, you might ask your friend to put away his weapons. They distress me."

Captain Gerald Harding leaned comfortably against the wall, and devoted one of his distressing weapons entirely to the Prince.

"I'm not Templar's friend," he said. "I'm a humble member of the British Secret Service, and I was sent here to get Vargan. I didn't arrive in time to save Vargan, but I seem to have got here in time to save something nearly as valuable. You're late, Your Highness!"

19

How Simon Templar Went to His Lady, and Norman Kent Answered the Trumpet

FOR A MOMENT there was an utter silence; and then Marius began to speak rapidly in his own language.

The Prince listened, his eyes narrowing. Apart from that attentive narrowing of the eyes, neither his attitude nor his expression changed at all. The man had an unhumanly sleek superiority to all ordinary emotion.

Simon made no attempt to interrupt Marius's recital. Someone had to explain the situation; and, since Marius had assumed the job, Marius might as well go on with it. The interval would give the Saint another welcome breather. And the Saint relaxed against his barricade and took out his cigarette-case, and began to tap a cigarette thoughtfully against his teeth.

Then the Prince turned to him, and spoke in his sleek, velvety voice.

"So! I begin to understand. This man caught you, but you came to an agreement when you found that you were at least united against me. Is that right?"

"But what a brain Your Highness has!" murmured the Saint.

"And he has ended the armistice in his own way without giving you notice?"

"I'm afraid so. I think he got some sort of stag fever when he saw the papers. Anyway, he forgot the spirit of the Eton Boating Song."

"And you have no influence with him?"

"None."

"But your friend"—the Prince indicated Norman Kent—"has the papers?"

"And I've got the friend," said Harding cheerfully. "So what do you all do about it?"

In that instant he stood absolutely alone, dominating the situation; and they all looked at him. He was young, but he had the spirit, that boy. And the Saint understood that Harding could not have helped breaking his parole, even where an older man might have hesitated.

And then Harding no longer stood alone; for in the next instant Norman Kent had usurped the limelight with a compelling movement of his hand that drew every eye.

"I should like to have something to say about this," said Norman Kent.

His voice was always low and measured. Now it was quieter than ever, but every syllable was as sure as a clarion.

"I have the papers," he said, "and Captain Harding has me. Perfectly true. But there is one thing you've all overlooked."

"What is that?"

It was the Prince who spoke; but Norman Kent answered to them all. He took one glance out of the window, at the sunlight and the trees and the green grass and a clump of crimson dahlias splashed against the hedge like a wound, and they saw him smile. And then he answered.

"Nothing is won without sacrifice," he said simply.

He looked across at the Saint.

"Simon," he said, "I want you to trust me. Ever since we came together I've done everything you ordered without question. We've all followed you, naturally, because you were always our natural leader. But we couldn't help learning something from your leadership. I've heard how you beat Marius in Brook Street last night—by doing the one thing you couldn't possibly do. And I've heard how Roger used the same principle, and helped us to beat Teal with it—by doing the one thing he couldn't possibly do. It's my turn now. I think I must be very clever to-day. I've seen how to apply the principle to this. In my own way. Because now—here—there is something that no one could do. And I can do it. Will you follow me?"

And Norman's dark eyes, with a queer fanatical light burning in them, met the Saint's clear sea-blue eyes. For a second's tense stillness. . . .

Then:

"Carry on," said the Saint.

Norman Kent smiled.

"It's easy," he said. "You've all appreciated the situation, haven't you? . . . We have you, Prince, and you, Marius, as hostages; but you have as a counter-hostage a lady who is very dear to all but one of us. That in itself would be a deadlock, even if it were not for Captain Harding and his guns."

"You express it admirably," said the Prince.

"On the other hand, Captain Harding, who for the moment is in command, is in a very awkward situation. He is by far the weakest party in a three-cornered fight. Whether the fact that you hold a friend of ours as a hostage would weigh with him is open to doubt. Personally, I doubt it very much. He's never met the lady—she's nothing more than a name to him—and he has to do what he believes to be his duty. Moreover, he has already given us an example of the way in which his sense of duty is able to override all other considerations. So that we are in a very difficult predicament. As Englishmen, we are bound to take his part against you. As mere men, we would rather die than do anything to endanger the lady whom you have in your power. These two motives alone would be complication enough. But there's a third. As the Saint's friends, who hold to his ideals, we have set ourselves to accomplish something that both you and Captain Harding would do anything to prevent.''

''You could not have made a more concise summary,'' said the Prince.

Again Norman Kent smiled.

''So you will agree that the deadlock only exists because we are all trying to win without a sacrifice,'' he said. ''And the answer is—that the situation doesn't admit of a victory without sacrifice, though there are plenty of means of surrender without the sacrifice of more than honour. But we dislike surrenders.''

He took from his pocket three sheets of paper closely written in a small, neat hand, folded them carefully, and held them out.

''Captain Harding—you may take these.''

''Norman! Damn you——''

The Saint was crossing the room. His mouth was set in a hard line, and his eyes were as bleak as an arctic sky. But Norman Kent faced him without fear.

''You agreed to let me handle this, Saint.''

''I never agreed to let you surrender. Sooner than that——''

''But this isn't surrender,'' said Norman Kent. ''This is victory. Look!''

Harding was beside him. Norman turned, the papers loosely held in his finger. And Norman looked straight at Roger Conway.

''Roger,'' he said slowly, ''I think you'll understand. Take the papers, Harding!''

Harding dropped one gun into his pocket, and snatched. . . .

And then the Saint understood.

Harding was, as Norman had said, alone among many enemies. And for a moment he had only one automatic with which to hold them all. The gun was aimed at Roger Conway, who was nearest; but in order to take the papers Harding had to glance away at right angles to his line of aim, towards Norman Kent and the Saint. Just for a sufficient moment.

And Norman let go the papers as Harding touched them; but then, instead of going back, his hand went forward. It had closed upon Harding's wrist in a flash, fastened there like a vice. And it jerked—one sudden heave into which Norman put all the strength at his command.

The gun in Harding's hand exploded once; but the shot smacked harmlessly up into the ceiling. For Roger Conway had understood in time. He had pounced on Harding's left hand and wrenched away the automatic in the instant of time that was given him; and he had the Prince safely covered with it even as Gerald Harding, yanked off his balance by Norman Kent's superhuman effort, stumbled slap into the Saint's left.

It was all over in a split second, before either the Prince or Marius could have realised what was happening and taken advantage of it.

And then Roger's gun was discouraging the movement of the hand towards the hip that Marius had started too late; and Norman Kent, white to the lips with the agony his supreme attempt had cost him, was leaning weakly against the arm of the sofa. And Gerald Harding was stretched out on the floor like a log, with the Saint stooping over him and collecting the second automatic with one hand and the fallen papers with the other.

"That looks better," said Roger Conway contentedly.

But Norman Kent had not finished.

He was saying, through clenched teeth: "Give me back those papers, Simon!"

The Saint hesitated, with the sheets crumpled in his hand.

"But——"

"At once!" rang Norman's voice imperatively. "You've trusted me so far, and I haven't let you down. Trust me a little more."

He took the papers almost by force, and stuffed them into his pocket. Then he held out his hand again.

"And that gun!"

Simon obeyed. It would have been impossible to refuse. For once, the Saint was not the leader. Perhaps the greatest thing he ever did in all his leadership was to surrender it then, as he surrendered it, without jealousy and without condescension.

But Norman Kent was a man inspired. His personality, which had always been so gentle and reserved, flamed in the room then like a dark fire.

"That's the first thing," said Norman. "And there are only two things more."

The Prince had not moved. Nothing in those few momentous and eventful seconds had provoked the faintest ripple on the tranquil surface of his self-control. He still stood in the position he had taken up when he first entered the room—perfectly at his ease, perfectly calm, perfectly impassive, smoothing his wisp of moustache. Suave and imperturbable, he waited without any visible exertion of patience for the ferment to subside and the embroiled items of it to settle down into their new dispositions. It was not until he appeared satisfied that they had done so that he spoke, with the tiniest of smiles curving his lips.

"Gentlemen," he remarked, "you do not disappoint me. I have heard much about you, and seen a little. The little I have seen tells me that the much I have heard may not be greatly exaggerated. If you should ever wish to forsake your careers of crime, and take service with a foreigner, I should be delighted to engage you."

"Thanks," said Norman curtly. "But this is not a crime. In our eyes, it's a far, far better thing than you will ever do. We'll waste no more time. Prince, do you agree that the situation has been simplified?"

The Prince inclined his head.

"I saw you simplify it."

"And you say that if we give you these papers"—Norman Kent touched his pocket—"we may leave at once, without hindrance?"

"That was my offer."

"Have we any assurance that you'll stand by it?"

The thin eyebrows went up in expostulation.

"I have given my word."

"And apart from that?"

"If the word of a gentleman is not enough for you, may I point out that I have twenty-five men here—some in the garden, some inside the house on the other side of the door which Mr. Templar has so adroitly barricaded, and some on the river. I have but to give the signal—they have but to hear my voice——" The sentence ended in a significant shrug. "You are at my mercy. And, after you have given up the papers, what reason could there be for me to detain you further? And, in any case, why should I trouble to offer terms at all, if I did not remember the service you once did me? It is true that Mr. Templar has refused to shake hands with me, but I bear him no malice for that. I may be able to understand his feelings. I have already said that I regret the circumstances. But it is the fortune of war. I make the most generous compromise I can."

"And yet," said Norman Kent, "I should like to be sure that there can be no mistake. I have the papers. Let my friends go, with the girl, in the car that's waiting outside. I'll undertake that they won't warn the police, or come back to attack you; and I'll stay here myself, as a hostage, to give you the papers half an hour after they've left. For that half-hour, you and Marius must remain here as security for the safe-conduct of my friends—at the end of this gun.''

''Highness!''

Marius spoke, standing stiffly to attention.

''Highness, need we have more of this parleying? A word to the men——''

The Prince raised his hand.

''This is not my way, Marius. I owe these gentlemen a debt. And I accept their terms, strange as they seem.'' He turned back to Norman. ''But I need hardly add, sir, that if I find any cause to suspect you of treachery, I shall consider the debt cancelled.''

''Of course,'' said Norman Kent. ''That is quite fair.''

The Prince stepped to the window.

''Then, if you will permit me——''

He stood in the opening and beckoned, and two men came running. Inside the room, they pocketed their automatics and saluted.

The Prince addressed them briefly, and they saluted again. Then he turned and spoke again in English, with a graceful gesture of his sensitive hands.

''Your car is waiting, gentlemen.''

Both Roger and the Saint looked at Norman Kent puzzledly, doubtfully, almost incredulously; but Norman only smiled.

''Don't forget that you promised to trust me,'' he said. ''I know you think I'm mad. But I was never saner in my life. I have found the only solution—the only way to peace with honour.''

Still Simon Templar looked at him, trying to read what was not to be read.

It tore at his heart to leave Norman Kent there like that. And he couldn't make out what inspiration Norman could be acting on. Norman couldn't possibly mean the surrender. That couldn't possibly be called peace with honour. And how Norman could see any way out for himself, alone, hurt and lame as he was . . . But Norman seemed to be without doubt or fear—that was the only thing that could be read in his face, that super-natural confidence and contentment.

And the Saint himself could see no way out, even for the three of them together. The Prince held all the cards. Even if Patricia had been in no danger, and they had shot the Prince and Marius and stood the siege, they must inevitably have been beaten. Even if they had made up their minds to sell their lives in the achievement of their purpose. . . . But Norman had not the air of a man who was facing death.

And the Prince's men held Patricia, even as Marius had held her the night before. But the same methods could not possibly be applied this time.

Yet the Saint pleaded: "Won't you let me stay, son? I do trust you, but I know you're wounded——"

Norman Kent shook his head.

"It doesn't matter," he said. "I shall be carried out of here in state."

"When do we see you?" asked Roger.

Norman gazed dreamily into the distance, and what he saw there seemed to amuse him.

"I shall be some time," he said.

And he turned to the Prince.

"May I write a short note?"

"I remind you," said the Prince, "that you remain here as a guarantee of the good behaviour of your friends."

"I agreed to that," said Norman. "Give me a pen and paper, Roger."

And once again Marius tried to intervene.

"Highness, you are trusting them too far! This can only be a treachery. If they meant what they said, why should there be any need for all this——"

"It is their way, Marius," said the Prince calmly. "I admit that it is strange. But no matter. You should be a more thorough psychologist, my friend. After what you have seen of them can you believe that two of them would leave the third to face his fate alone while they themselves escaped? It is absurd!"

Norman Kent had scribbled one line. He blotted it carefully, and folded the sheet.

"And an envelope, Roger."

He placed the sheet inside and stuck down the flap.

Then he held out his hand to Roger Conway.

"Good luck, Roger," he said. "Be good."

"All the best, Norman, old man."

They gripped.

And Simon was speaking to the Prince.

"It seems," said Simon, "that this is *au revoir,* Your Highness!"

The Prince made one of his exquisitely courteous gestures.

"I trust," he replied, "that it is not *adieu*. I hope to meet you again in better days."

Then the Saint looked at Marius, and for a long time he held the giant's eyes. And he gave Marius a different good-bye.

"You, also," said the Saint slowly, "I shall meet again."

But, behind the Saint, Norman Kent laughed; and the Saint turned.

Norman stretched out one hand, and the Saint took it in a firm grasp. And Norman's other hand offered the letter.

"Put this in your pocket, Simon, and give me your word not to open it for four hours. When you've read it, you'll know where you'll see me again. I'll be waiting for you. And don't worry. Everything is safe with me. Good hunting, Saint!"

"Very good hunting to you, Norman."

Norman Kent smiled.

"I think it will be a good run," he said.

So Simon Templar went to his lady.

Norman saw Roger and Simon pass through the window and turn to look back at him as they reached the garden; and he smiled again, and waved them a gay good-bye. A moment afterwards he heard the rising drone of the Hirondel and the soft crunching of tyres down the drive.

He caught one last glimpse of them as the car turned into the road— the Saint at the wheel, with one arm about Patricia's shoulders, and Roger Conway in the back, with one of the Prince's men riding on the running-board beside him. That, of course, would be to give them a passage through the guards at the crossroad. . . .

And then they were gone.

Norman sat down on the sofa, feeling curiously weak. His leg was numb with pain. He indicated decanter, siphon, glasses, and cigarette-box with a wave of his automatic.

"Make yourselves at home, gentlemen," he invited. "And pass me something on your way. I'm afraid I can't move. You ought to stop your men using soft-nosed bullets, Marius—they're dirty things."

It was the Prince who officiated with the whisky and lighted Norman a cigarette.

"War is a ruthless thing." said the Prince. "As a man I like and admire you. But as what I am, because you are against my country and myself, if I thought you were attempting to trick me I should kill you without compunction—like that!'' He snapped his fingers. ''Even the fact that you once helped to save my life could not extenuate your offence.''

''Do you think I'm a fool?'' asked Norman, rather tiredly.

He sipped his drink, and the hands of the clock crawled round.

Five minutes.

Ten.

Fifteen.

The Prince sat in an armchair, his legs elegantly crossed with a proper regard for the knife-edge crease in his trousers. In one hand he held a glass; with the other he placidly smoked a cigarette through a long holder.

Marius paced the room like a caged lion. From time to time he glanced at Norman with venom and suspicion in his slitted gaze, and seemed about to say something; but each time he checked himself and resumed his impatient promenade—until the Prince stopped him with a languid wave of his cigarette-holder.

''My dear Marius, your restlessness disturbs me. For Heaven's sake practise some self-control.''

''But, Highness——''

''Marius, you repeat yourself. Repetition is a tedious vice.''

Then Marius sat down.

The Prince delicately stifled a yawn.

Harding, on the floor, groaned, and roused as if from a deep sleep. Norman leaned over and helped him to come to a sitting position. The youngster opened his eyes slowly, rubbing a tender jaw muzzily. He would never know how the Saint had hated having to strike that blow.

Norman allowed him to take in the situation as best he could. And he gave him a good look at the automatic.

''Where are the others?'' asked Harding hazily.

''They've gone,'' said Norman.

In short, compact sentences he explained what had happened.

Then he addressed a question to the Prince.

''What is Captain Harding's position in this affair?''

''If he does not allow his sense of duty to over-ride his discretion,'' answered the Prince carelessly, ''we are no longer interested in him.''

Harding scrambled unsteadily to his feet.

''But I'm damned well interested in you!'' he retorted. And he turned to Norman with a dazed and desperate entreaty. ''Kent—as an Englishman—you're not going to let these swabs——''

''You'll see in seven minutes,'' said Norman calmly.

Harding wavered before the level automatic in Norman's hand. He cursed, raved impotently, almost sobbed.

"You fool! You fool! Oh, *damn* you! . . . Haven't you any decency? Can't you see——"

Norman never moved, but his face was very white. Those few minutes were the worst he had ever spent. His leg was throbbing dreadfully. And Harding swore and implored, argued, pleaded, fumed, begged almost on his knees, lashed Norman Kent with words of searing scorn. . . .

Five minutes to go.

Four . . . three . . . two . . .

One minute to go.

The Prince glanced at the gold watch on his wrist, and extracted the stub of a cigarette from his long holder with fastidious fingers.

"The time is nearly up," he murmured gently.

"Oh, for God's sake!" groaned Harding. "Think, Kent, you worm! You miserable—abject—crawling—coward! Give me a gun and let me fight——"

"There's no need to fight," said Norman Kent.

He put one hand to his pocket, and for a second he thought that Harding would chance the automatic and leap at his throat. He held up the crumpled sheets, and both the Prince and Marius rose—the Prince with polished and unhurried elegance, and Marius like an unleashed fiend.

Somehow Norman Kent was struggling to his feet again. He was very pale, and the fire in his eyes burned with a feverish fierceness. His wounded leg was simply the deadened source of a thousand twinges of torment that shot up the whole of his side at the least movement, like long, jagged needles. But he had a detached determination to face the end on his feet.

"The papers I promised you!"

He pushed them towards Marius, and the giant grabbed them with enormous, greedy hands.

And then Norman was holding out his gun, butt foremost, towards Harding. He spoke in tense, swift command.

"Through the window and down the garden, Harding! Take the Saint's motor-boat. It's moored at the end of the lawn. The two men on the river shouldn't stop you——"

"Highness!"

It was Marius's voice, shrill and savage. The giant's face was hideously contorted.

Norman thrust Harding behind him, covering his retreat to the window.

"Get out!" he snarled. "There's nothing for you to wait for now. . . . Well, Marius?"

The Prince's voice slashed in with a deadly smoothness: "Those are not Vargan's papers, Marius?"

"An absurd letter—to this man himself—from one of his friends!"

"So!"

The word fell into the room with the sleek crispness of a drop of white-hot metal. Yet the Prince could never have been posed more gracefully, nor could his face have ever been more serene.

"You tricked me after all!"

"Those are the papers I promised you," said Norman coolly.

"He must have the real papers still, Highness!" babbled Marius. "I was watching him—he had no chance to give them to his friends——"

"That's where you're wrong!"

Norman spoke very, very quietly, almost in a whisper, but the whisper held a ring of triumph like a trumpet call. The blaze in his dark eyes was not of this world.

"When Harding grabbed Templar's gun—you remember, Marius?— I had the papers in my hands. I put them in Templar's pocket. He never knew what I did. I hardly knew myself. I did it almost without thinking. It was a sheer blind inspiration—the only way to spoof the lot of you and get my friends away. And it worked! I beat you. . . ."

He heard a sound behind him, and looked round. Harding had started— he was racing down the lawn, bent low to the ground like a greyhound. Perhaps there were silenced guns plopping at him from all round the house, but they could not be heard, and he must have been untouched, for he ran on without a false step, swerving and zigzagging like a snipe.

A smile touched Norman's lips. He didn't mind being left alone now that his work was done. And he knew that Harding could not have stayed. Harding also had work to do. He had to find help—to deal with Marius and intercept Simon Templar and the precious papers. But Norman smiled, because he was sure the Saint wouldn't be intercepted. Still, he liked the mettle of that fair-haired youngster. . . .

His leg hurt like blazes.

But the Saint had never guessed the impossible thing. That had been Norman Kent's one fear, that the Saint would suspect and refuse to leave him. But Norman's first success, when he had tricked Harding with the offer of the papers, had won the Saint's faith, as it had to win it. And Simon had gone, and Patricia with him. It was enough.

And in the fulness of time Simon would find the papers; and he would open the letter and read the one line that was written there. And that line Norman had already spoken, but no one had understood.

"Nothing is won without sacrifice."

Norman turned again, and saw the automatic in Marius's hand. There was something in the way the gun was held, something in the face behind it, that told him that this man did not miss. And the gun was not aimed at Norman, but beyond him, at the flying figure that was nearing the motor-boat at the end of the lawn.

That gentle far-away smile was still on Norman Kent's lips as he took two quick hops backwards and to one side, so that his body was between Marius and the window.

He knew that Marius, blind, raging mad with fury, would not relax his pressure on the trigger because Norman Kent was standing directly in his line of fire; but Norman didn't care. It made no difference to him. Marius, or the Prince, would certainly have shot him sooner or later. Probably he deserved it. He had deliberately cheated, knowing the price of the revoke. He thought no more of himself. But an extra second or two ought to give Harding time to reach comparative safety in the motor-boat.

Norman Kent wasn't afraid. He was smiling.

It was a strange way to come to the end of everything, like that, in that quiet bungalow by the peaceful Thames, with the first mists of the evening coming up from the river like tired clouds drifted down from heaven, and the light softening over the cool, quiet garden. That place had seen so much of their enjoyment, so much comradeship and careless laughter. They had been lovely and pleasant in their lives. . . . He wished his leg wasn't giving him such hell. But that would be over soon. And there must be many worse ways of saying farewell to so full a life. It was something to have heard the sound of the trumpet. And the game would go on. It seemed as if the shadows of the peaceful evening outside were the foreshadowings of a great peace over all the world.

The Avenging Saint

To
RAYMOND SAVAGE
London, May, 1930

Contents

1

How Simon Templar Sang a Song, and Found Some of It True

The Saint sang:

> *"Strange adventure! Maiden wedded*
> *To a groom she'd never seen—*
> *Never, never, never seen!*
> *Groom about to be beheaded,*
> *In an hour on Tower Green!*
> *Tower, Tower, Tower Green!*
> *Groom in dreary dungeon lying—"*

" 'Ere," said an arm of the Law. "Not so much noise!"

The Saint stopped, facing round, tall and smiling and debonair.

"Good-evening—or morning—as the case may be," said the Saint politely.

"And what d'you think *you're* doing?" demanded the Law.

"Riding on a camel in the desert," said the Saint happily.

The Law peered at him suspiciously. But the Saint looked very respectable. The Saint always looked so respectable that he could at any time have walked into an ecclesiastical conference without even being asked for his ticket. Dressed in rags, he could have made a bishop look like two cents at a bad rate of exchange. And in the costume that he had donned for the night's occasion his air of virtue was overpowering. His shirtfront was of a pure and beautiful soul. His tuxedo, even under the poor illumination of a street lamp, was cut with such a dazzling perfection, and worn moreover with such a staggering elegance, that no tailor with a pride in his profession could have gazed unmoved upon such a stupendous apotheosis of his art. The Saint, as he stood there, might have

321

been taken for an unemployed archangel—if he had remembered to wear his soft black felt a little less rakishly, and to lean a little less rakishly on his gold-mounted stick. As it was, he looked like a modern pugilist, the heir to a dukedom, a successful confidence man, or an advertisement for Wuggo. And the odour of sanctity about him could have been scented a hundred yards up-wind by a man with a severe cold in the head and no sense of smell.

The Law, slightly dazed by its scrutiny, pulled itself together with a visible effort.

"You can't," said the Law, "go bawling about the streets like that at two o'clock in the morning."

"I wasn't bawling," said the Saint aggrievedly. "I was singing."

"Bawling, I call it," said the Law obstinately.

The Saint took out his cigarette case. It was a very special case; and the Saint was very proud of it, and would as soon have thought of travelling without it as he would have thought of walking down Piccadilly in his pajamas. Into that cigarette case had been concentrated an enthusiastic ingenuity that was typical of the Saint's flair for detail—a flair that had already enabled him to live about twenty-nine years longer than a good many people thought he ought to have. There was much more in that case than met the eye. Much more. But it wasn't in action at that particular moment. The cigarette which the Law was prevailed upon to accept was innocent of deception, as also was the one which the Saint selected for himself.

"Anyway," said the Saint, "wouldn't *you* bawl, as you call it, if you knew that a man with a name like Heinrich Dussel had recently received into his house an invalid who wasn't ill?"

The Law blinked, bovinely meditative.

"Sounds fishy to me," conceded the Law.

"And to me," said the Saint. "And queer fish are my hobby. I'd travel a thousand miles any day to investigate a kipper that was the least bit queer on the kip—and it wouldn't be for the first time. There was a smear of bloater paste, once, that fetched me from the Malay Peninsula *via* Chicago to a very wild bit of Devonshire. . . . But this is more than bloater paste. This is real red herring."

"Are you drunk?" inquired the Law, kindly.

"No," said the Saint. "British Constitution. Truly rural. The Leith police dismisseth us. . . . No, I'm not drunk. But I'm thinking of possible accidents. So would you just note that I'm going into that house up there—number 90—perfectly sound and sane? And I shan't stay more than half an hour at the outside—voluntarily. So if I'm not out here again at two-thirty, you can walk right in and demand the body. *Au revoir, sweetheart.* . . .''

And the Saint smiled beatifically, hitched himself off his gold-mounted stick, adjusted the rakish tilt of his hat, and calmly resumed his stroll and his song, while the Law stared blankly after him.

> *"Groom in dreary dungeon lying,*
> *Groom as good as dead, or dying,*
> *For a pretty maiden sighing—*
> *Pretty maid of seventeen!*
> *Seven-seven-seventeen!''*

"Blimey," said the Law, blankly.

But the Saint neither heard nor cared what the Law said. He passed on, swinging his stick, into his adventure.

II

MEET THE SAINT.

His godfathers and his godmothers, at his baptism, had bestowed upon him the name of Simon Templar; but that coincidence of initials was not the only reason for the nickname by which he was far more widely known. One day, the story of how he came by that nickname may be told: it is a good story, in its way, though it goes back to the days when the Saint was nineteen, and almost as respectable as he looked. But the name had stuck. It was inevitable that it should stick, for obviously it had been destined to him from the beginning. And in the ten years that had followed his second and less godly baptism, he had done his very best to live up to that second name—according to his lights. But you may have heard the story of the very big man whose friends called him Tiny.

He looked very Saintly indeed as he sauntered up Park Lane that night.

Saintly . . . you understand . . . with the capital S. That was how Roger Conway always liked to spell the adjective, and that pleasant conceit may very well be carried on here. There was something about the way Simon wore the name, as there was about the way he wore his clothes, that naturally suggested capital letters in every context.

Of course, he was all wrong. He ought never to have been let loose upon this twentieth century. He was upsetting. Far too often, when he spoke, his voice struck disturbing chords in the mind. When you saw him, you looked, instinctively and exasperatedly, for a sword at his side, a feather in his hat, and spurs at his heels. There was a queer keenness in the chiselling of his tanned face, seen in profile—something that can only be described as a *swiftness* of line about the nose and lips and chin, a swiftness as well set off by the slick sweep of patent-leather hair as by the brim of a filibustering felt hat—a laughing dancing devil of mischief that was never far from the very clear blue eyes, a magnificently medieval flamboyance of manner, an extraordinary vividness and vital challenge about every movement he made, that too clearly had no place in the organization of the century that was afflicted with him. If he had been anyone else, you would have felt that the organization was likely to make life very difficult for him. But he was Simon Templar, the Saint, and so you could only feel that he was likely to make life very difficult for the organization. Wherefore, as a respectable member of the organization, you were liable to object. . . .

And, in fact, objections had been made in due season—to such effect that, if anything were needed to complete the Saint's own private entertainment at that moment, it could have been provided by the reflection that he had no business to be in England at all that night. Or any other night. For the name of the Saint was not known only to his personal friends and enemies. It was something like a legend, a public institution; not many months ago, it had been headlined over every newspaper in Europe, and the Saint's trademark—a childish sketch of a little man with straight-line body and limbs, and a round blank head under an absurd halo—had been held in almost superstitious awe throughout the length and breadth of England. And there still reposed, in the desk of Chief Inspector Teal, at New Scotland Yard, warrants for the arrest of Simon Templar and the other two who had been with him in all his misdeeds—Roger Conway and Patricia Holm. Why the Saint had come back to England was nobody's business. He hadn't yet advertised his return; and, if he had advertised it, nothing is more certain than that Chief Inspector Claud Eustace Teal would have been combing London for him within the hour—with a gun behind each ear, and an official address of welcome according to the Indictable Offences Act, 1848, in his pocket. . . .

Wherefore it was very good and amusing to be back in London, and very good and amusing to be on the trail of an invalid who was not ill, though sheltering in the house of a man with a name like Heinrich Dussel. . . .

The Saint knew that the invalid was still there, because it was two o'clock on Sunday morning, and near the policeman a melancholy-looking individual was selling very early editions of the Sunday papers, apparently hoping to catch returning Saturday-night revellers on the rebound, and the melancholy-looking individual hadn't batted an eyelid as the Saint passed. If anything interesting had happened since the melancholy-looking individual had made his last report, Roger Conway would have batted one eyelid, and Simon would have bought a paper and found a note therein. And if the invalid who was not ill had left the house, Roger wouldn't have been there at all. Nor would the low-bodied long-nosed Hirondel parked close by. On the face of it, there was no connection between Roger Conway and the Hirondel; but that was part of the deception. . . .

> *"Strange adventure that we're trolling:*
> *Modest maid and gallant groom—*
> *Gallant, gallant, gallant groom!*
> *While the funeral bell is tolling,*
> *Tolling, tolling—"*

Gently the Saint embarked upon the second verse of his song. And through his manifest cheerfulness he felt a faint electric tingle of expectation. . . .

For he knew that it was true. He, of all men living, should have known that the age of strange adventures was not past. There were adventures all around, then, as there had been since the beginning of the world; it was a matter for the adventurer to go out and challenge them. And adventure had never yet failed Simon Templar—perhaps because he had never doubted it. It might have been luck, or it might have been his own uncanny genius; but at least he knew, whatever it was he had to thank, that whenever and wherever anything was happening, he was there. He had been born to it, the spoiled child of a wild tempestuous destiny— born for nothing else, it seemed, but to find all the fun in the world.

And he was on the old trail again.

But this time it was no fluke. His worst enemy couldn't have said that Simon Templar hadn't worked for all the trouble he was going to find that night. For weeks past he had been hunting two men across Europe— a slim and very elegant man, and a huge and very ugly man—and one

of them at least he had sworn to kill. Neither of them went by the name
of Heinrich Dussel, even in his spare time; but Heinrich Dussel had
conferred with them the night before in the slim and very elegant man's
suite at the Ritz, and accordingly the Saint had become interested in
Heinrich Dussel. And then, less than two hours before the Saint's brief
conversation with the Law, had commenced the Incident of the Invalid
who was not ill.

> *"Modest maiden will not tarry;*
> *Though but sixteen year she carry,*
> *She must marry, she must marry,*
> *Though the altar be a tomb—*
> *Tower, Tower, Tower tomb!"*

Thus the Saint brought both his psalm and his promenade to a triumphant conclusion; for the song stopped as the Saint stopped, which was
at the foot of a short flight of steps leading up to a door—the door of the
house of Heinrich Dussel.

And then, as Simon Templar paused there, a window was smashed
directly above his head, so that chips of splintered glass showered onto
the pavement all around him. And there followed a man's sudden sharp
yelp of agony, clear and shrill in the silence of the street.

" 'Ere," said a familiar voice, "is this the 'ouse you said you were
going into?"

The Saint turned.

The Law stood beside him, its hands in its belt, having followed him
all the way on noiseless rubber soles.

And Simon beamed beatifically upon the Law.

"That's so, Algernon," he murmured, and mounted the steps.

The door opened almost as soon as he had touched the bell. And the
Law was still beside him.

"What's wrong 'ere?" demanded the Law.

"It is nothing."

Dussel himself had answered the bell, suave and self-possessed—exactly as the Saint would have expected him to be.

"We have a patient here who is—not right in the head. Sometimes he
is violent. But he is being attended to."

"That's right," said the Saint calmly. "I got your telephone message,
and came right around."

He turned to the Law with a smile.

"I am the doctor in charge of the case," he said, "so you may quite safely leave things in my hands."

His manner would have disarmed the chief commissioner himself. And before either of the other two could say a word, the Saint had stepped over the threshold as if he owned the house.

"Good-night, officer," he said sweetly, and closed the door.

III

Now THE UNKIND critic may say that the Saint had opened his break with something like the most fantastic fluke that ever fell out of the blue; but the unkind critic would be wrong, and his judgment would merely indicate his abysmal ignorance of the Saint and all Saintly methods. It cannot be too clearly understood that, having determined to enter the house of Heinrich Dussel and dissect the mystery of the Invalid who was not Ill, Simon Templar had walked up Park Lane with the firm intention of ringing the bell, walking in while the butler was still asking him his business, closing the door firmly behind him, and leaving the rest to Providence. The broken window, and the cry that came through it, had not been allowed for in such nebulous calculations as he had made—admitted; but in fact they made hardly any difference to the general plan of campaign. It would be far more true to say that the Saint refused to put off his stroke by the circumstances, than to say that the circumstances helped him. All that happened was that an unforeseen accident intervened in the smooth course of the Saint's progress; and the Saint, with the inspired audacity that lifted him so high above all ordinary adventurers, had flicked the accident into the accommodating machinery of his stratagem, and passed on. . . .

And the final result was unaltered; for the Saint simply arrived where he had meant to arrive, anyway—with his back to the inside of the door of Heinrich Dussel's house, and all the fun before him. . . .

And Simon Templar smiled at Heinrich Dussel, a rather thoughtful and reckless smile; for Heinrich Dussel was the kind of man for whom the Saint would always have a rather thoughtful and reckless smile. He was short, heavily built, tremendously broad of shoulder, thin-lipped, with a high bald dome of a forehead, and greenish eyes that gleamed like glazed pebbles behind thick gold-rimmed spectacles.

"May I ask what you mean by this?" Dussel was blustering furiously.
The Saint threw out his hands in a wide gesture.

"I wanted to talk to you, dear heart."

"And what do you imagine I can do for you?"

"On the contrary," said the Saint genially, "the point is—what can
I do for you? Ask, and you shall receive. I'm ready. If you say 'Go and
get the moon,' I'll go right out and get the moon—that's how I feel about
you, sweetheart."

Dussell took a step forward.

"Will you stand away from that door?"

"No," said the Saint, courteous but definite.

"Then you will have to be removed by force."

"If you could spare me a moment—" began the Saint warily.

But Heinrich Dussel had half turned, drawing breath, his mouth opening for one obvious purpose.

He could hardly have posed himself better.

And before that deep purposeful breath had reached Dussel's vocal
cords on the return journey, his mouth closed again abruptly, with a crisp
smack, under the persuasive influence of a pile-driving uppercut.

"Come into my study," invited the Saint, in a very fair imitation of
Heinrich Dussel's guttural accent.

"Thank you," said the Saint in his own voice.

And his arms were already around Heinrich Dussel, holding up the
unconscious man; and, as he accepted his own invitation, the Saint
stooped swiftly, levered Dussel onto his shoulder, moved up the hall,
and passed through the nearest door.

He did not stay.

He dropped his burden unceremoniously on the floor, and passed out
again, locking the door behind him and putting the key in his pocket.
Then, certainly, luck was with him, for, in spite of the slight disturbance,
none of the household staff was in view. The Saint went up the stairs as
lightly as a ghost.

The broken window had been on the first floor, and the room to which
it belonged was easy to locate. The Saint listened for a couple of seconds
at the door, and then opened it and stepped briskly inside.

The room was empty.

"Bother," said the Saint softly.

Then he understood.

"If the cop had insisted on coming in, he'd have wanted to see this
room. So they'd have shifted the invalid. One of the gang would have

played the part. And the real cripple—further up the stairs, I should think. . . ."

And Simon was out of the empty room in an instant, and flashing up the next flight.

As he reached the upper landing, a man—a villainous foreign-looking man, in some sort of livery—emerged from a door.

The Saint never hesitated.

"All right?" he queried briefly.

"Yes," came the automatic answer.

No greater bluff could ever have been put up in two words and a stride. It was such a perfect little cameo of the art that the liveried man did not realize how he had been bluffed until three seconds after the Saint had spoken. And that was about four seconds too late. For by that time the Saint was only a yard away.

"That's fine," said the Saint crisply. "Keep your face shut, and everything will still be all right. Back into that room. . . ."

There was a little knife in the Saint's hand. The Saint could do things with that knife that would have made a circus performer blink. But at that moment the Saint wasn't throwing the knife—he was just pricking the liveried man's throat with the point. And the liveried man recoiled instinctively.

The Saint pushed him on, into the room, and kicked the door shut behind him. Then he dropped the knife, and took the man by the throat. . . .

He made very little noise. And presently the man slept. . . .

Then the Saint got to his feet and looked about him.

The invalid lay on the bed—an old man, it seemed, judging by the thick gray beard. A shabby tweed cap was pulled down over eyes shielded by dark glasses, and his clothes were shapeless and ill-fitting. He wore black gloves, and above these there were ropes, binding his wrists together; and there were ropes also about his ankles.

The Saint picked him up in his arms. He seemed to weigh hardly anything at all.

As swiftly and silently as he had come, the Saint went down the stairs again with his light load.

Even then, it was not all perfectly plain sailing. A hubbub began to arise from below as Simon reached the first floor; and as he turned the corner onto the last flight, he saw a man unlocking the door of the room in which Heinrich Dussel had been locked. And Simon continued calmly downwards.

He reached the hall level in time to meet two automatics—one in the hand of the man who had unlocked the door, and one in the hand of Heinrich Dussel.

"Your move, Heinrich," said the Saint calmly. "May I smoke while you're thinking it over?"

He put the shabby old man carefully down on a convenient chair, and took out his cigarette case.

"Going to hand me over to the police?" he murmured. "If you are, you'll have to figure out a lot of explanations pretty quickly. The cop outside heard me say I was your doctor, and he'll naturally want to know why you've waited such a long time before denying it. Besides, there's Convalescent Cuthbert here. . . ." The Saint indicated the old man in the chair, who was trying ineffectually to say something through a very efficient gag. "Even mental cases aren't trussed up quite like that."

"No," said Dussel deliberately—"you will not be handed over to the police, my friend."

"Well, you can't keep me here," said the Saint, puffing. "You see, I had some words with the cop before I came to your door, and I told him I shouldn't be staying more than half an hour—voluntarily. And after the excitement just before I walked in, I should think he'll still be waiting around to see what happens."

Dussel turned to his servant.

"Go to a window, Luigi, and see if the policeman is still outside."

"It *is* a bit awkward for you, Heinrich, old dear, isn't it?" murmured Simon, smoking tranquilly, as the servant disappeared. "I'm so well known to the police. I'd probably turn out to be well known to you, too, if I told you my name. I'm known as the Saint. . . ." He grinned at Dussel's sudden start. "Anyway, your pals know me. Ask the Crown Prince—or Dr. Marius. And remember to give them my love. . . ."

The Saint laughed shortly; and Heinrich Dussel was still staring at him, white-lipped, when the servant returned to report that the constable was watching the house from the opposite pavement, talking to a newspaperman.

"You seem annoyed, Heinrich," remarked the Saint, gently bantering, though the glitter behind Dussel's thick glasses should have told him that he was as near sudden death at that moment as it is healthy for any man to be. "Now, the Crown Prince never looks annoyed. He's much more strong and silent than you are, is Rudolf. . . ."

Simon spoke dreamily, almost in a whisper, and his gaze was intent upon his cigarette end. And, all the while, he smiled. . . . Then—

"I'll show you a conjuring trick," he said suddenly. "Look!"

He threw the cigarette end on the carpet at their feet, and closed his eyes. But the other two looked.

They heard a faint hiss; and then the cigarette burst into a flare of white-hot eye-aching light that seemed to scorch through their eyeballs and sear their very brains. It only lasted a moment, but that was long enough. Then a dense white smoke filled the hall like a fog. And the Saint, with the old man in his arms again, was at the front door. They heard his mocking voice through their dazed blindness.

"Creates roars of laughter," said the Saint. "Try one at your next party—and invite me. . . . So long, souls!"

The *plop* of a silenced automatic came through the smoke, and a bullet smacked into the door beside the Saint's head. Then he had the door open, and the smoke followed him out.

"Fire!" yelled the Saint wildly. "Help!" He rushed down the steps, and the policeman met him on the pavement. "For heaven's sake try to save the others, officer! I've got this old chap all right, but there are more in there—"

He stood by the curb, shaking with silent laughter, and watched the Law brace itself and plunge valiantly into the smoke. Then the Hirondel purred up beside him, with the melancholy-looking vendor of newspapers at the wheel, and the Saint stepped into the back seat.

"O.K., big boy," he drawled; and Roger Conway let in the clutch.

IV

"ALTOGETHER A MOST satisfactory beginning to the Sabbath," the Saint remarked, as the big car switched into a side street. "I won't say it was dead easy, but you can't have everything. The only real trouble came at the very end, and then the old magnesium cigarette was just what the doctor ordered. . . . Have a nice chat with the police?"

"Mostly about you," said Roger. "The ideas that man had about the Saint were too weird and wonderful for words. I steered him onto the subject, and spent the rest of the time wishing I hadn't—it hurt so much trying not to laugh."

Simon chuckled.

"And now," he said, "I'm wondering what story dear Heinrich is trying to put over. That man won't get any beauty sleep tonight. Oh, it's a glorious thought! Dear Heinrich. . . .''

He subsided into a corner, weak with merriment, and felt for his cigarette case. Then he observed the ancient invalid, writhing helplessly on the cushions beside him, and grinned.

"Sorry, Beautiful," he murmured, "but I'm afraid you'll have to stay like that till we get home. We can't have you making a fuss now. But as soon as we arrive we'll untie you and give you a large glass of milk, and you shall tell us the story of your life."

The patriarch shook his head violently; then, finding that his protest was ignored, he relapsed into apathetic resignation.

A few minutes later the Hirondel turned into the mews where Simon Templar had established his headquarters in a pair of luxuriously converted garages. As the car stopped, Simon picked up the old man again and stepped out. Roger Conway opened the front door for him, and the Saint passed through the tiny hall into the sitting room, while Roger went to put the car away. Simon deposited the he-ancient in a chair and drew the blinds; not until after he had assured himself that no one could look in from outside did he switch on the lights and turn to regard his souvenir of the night's entertainment.

"Now you shall say your piece, Uncle," he remarked, and went to untie the gag. "Roger will make your Glaxo hot for you in a minute, and—Holy Moses!"

The Saint drew a deep breath.

For, as he removed the gag, the long gray beard had come away with it. For a moment he was too amazed to move. Then he snatched off the dark glasses and the shabby tweed cap, and a mass of rich brown hair tumbled about the face of one of the loveliest girls he had ever seen.

2

How Simon Templar Entertained a Guest, and Spoke of Two Old Friends

"THAT HAND-BRAKE'S still a bit feeble, old boy." Roger Conway came in, unfastening the gaudy choker which he had donned for his character part. "You ought to get—"

His voice trailed away, and he stood staring.

The Saint was on his knees, his little throwing knife in his hand, swiftly cutting ropes away from wrists and ankles.

"I'll have it seen to on Monday," said the Saint coolly.

Roger swallowed.

"Damn it, Saint—"

Simon looked round with a grin.

"Yes, I know, sonny boy," he said. "It *is* our evening, isn't it?"

He stood up and looked down at the girl.

"How are you feeling, old thing?"

She had her hands clasped to her forehead.

"I'll be all right in a minute," she said. "My head—hurts. . . ."

"That dope they gave you," murmured the Saint. "And the crack you got afterwards. Rotten, isn't it? But we'll put that right in a brace of shakes. Roger, you beetle off to the kitchen and start some tea, and I'll officiate with the dispensary."

Roger departed obediently; and Simon went over to a cupboard, and took therefrom a bottle and a glass. From the bottle he shook two pink tablets into the glass. Then he fizzed soda-water onto them from the siphon, and thoughtfully watched them dissolve.

"Here you are, old dear." He touched the girl lightly on the shoulder, with the foaming drink in his other hand. "Just shoot this down, and in about five minutes, when you've lowered a cup of tea on top of it, you'll be prancing about like a canary on a hot pancake."

She looked up at him a little doubtfully, as if she were wondering whether her present headache might not be so bad as the one she might get from the glass he was offering. But the Saint's smile was reassuring.

"Good girl. . . . And it wasn't so very foul, was it?"

Simon smiled approval as she handed him back the empty glass.

"Thank you—so much. . . ."

"Not at all," said the Saint. "Any little thing like that. . . . Now, all you've got to do, lass, is just to lie back and rest and wait for that cup of tea."

He lighted a cigarette and leaned against the table, surveying her in silence.

Under her tousled hair he saw a face that must have been modelled by happy angels. Her eyes were closed then, but he had already seen them open—deep pools of hazel, shaded by soft lashes. Her mouth was proud and imperious, yet with laughter lurking in the curves of the red lips. And a little colour was starting to ebb back into the faultless cheeks. If

he had ever seen real beauty in a woman, it was there. There was a serene
dignity in the forehead, a fineness of line about the small, straight nose,
a wealth of character in the moulding of the chin that would have singled
her out in any company. And the Saint was not surprised; for it was
dawning upon him that he knew who she was.

The latest *Bystander* was on the table beside him. He picked it up and
turned the pages. . . . She was there. He knew he could not have been
mistaken, for he had been studying the picture only the previous afternoon. He had thought she was lovely then; but now he knew that the
photograph did her no justice.

He was still gazing at her when Roger entered with a tray.

"Good man." Simon removed his gaze from the girl for one second,
with an effort, and then allowed it to return. He shifted off the table.
"Come along, lass."

She opened her eyes, smiling.

"I feel ever so much better now," she said.

"Nothing to what you'll feel like when you've inhaled this Château
Lipton," said the Saint cheerfully. "One or two lumps? Or three?"

"Only two."

She spoke with the slightest of American accents, soft and utterly
fascinating.

Simon handed her the cup.

"Thank you," she said; and then, suddenly: "Oh, tell me how you
found me. . . ."

"Well, that's part of a long story," said the Saint. "The short part of
it is that we were interested in Heinrich Dussel—the owner of the house
where I found you—and Roger here was watching him. About midnight
Roger saw an old man arrive in a car—drugged—"

"How did you know I was drugged?"

"They brought a wheel chair out of the house for you," Roger explained. "They seemed to be in rather a hurry, and as they lifted you out
of the car they caught your head a frightful crack on the door. Now, even
a paralyzed old man doesn't take a bang on the head like that without
making some movement or saying something; but you took it like a
corpse, and no one even apologized."

The Saint laughed.

"It was a really bright scheme," he said. "A perfect disguise, perfectly
thought out—right down to those gloves they put on you in case anyone
noticed your hands. And they'd have brought it off if it hadn't been for

that one slip—and Roger's eagle eye. But after that, the only thing for us to do was to interview Heinrich. . . ."

He grinned reminiscently, and retailed the entire episode for Roger Conway's benefit. The latter half of it the girl already knew, but they laughed again together over the thought of the curtain to the scene—the Law ploughing heroically in to rescue other gray-beards from the flames, and finding Mr. Dussel. . . .

"The only thing I haven't figured out," said the Saint, "is how it was a man I heard cry out, when the window was smashed in the frolic before I came in."

"I bit him in the hand," said the girl simply.

Simon held up his hands in admiring horror.

"I get you. . . . You came to, and tried to make a fight of it—and you—*you*—bit a man in the hand?"

She nodded.

"Do you know who I am?"

"I do," said the Saint helplessly. "That's what makes it so perfect."

II

SIMON TEMPLAR PICKED up the *Bystander*.

"I recognized you from your picture in here," he said, and handed the paper to Roger. "See if you can find it, sonny boy."

The girl passed him her cup, and he took and replenished it.

"I was at a ball at the Embassy," she said. "We're staying there. . . . It was very dull. About half-past eleven I slipped away to my room to rest—it was so hot in the ballroom. I'm very fond of chocolates"— she smiled whimsically—"and there was a lovely new box on my dressing table. I didn't stop to think how they came there—I supposed the Ambassador's wife must have put them in my room, because she knows my weakness—and I just naturally took one. I remember it had a funny bitter taste, and I didn't like it; and then I don't remember anything until I woke up in that house. . . ."

She shuddered; then she laughed a little.

"And then you came in," she said.

The Saint smiled, and glanced across at Roger Conway, who had put down the *Bystander* and was staring at the girl. And she laughed again, merrily, at Roger's consternation.

"I may be a millionaire's daughter," she said, "but I enjoyed your tea like anyone else."

Simon offered his cigarette case.

"Those are the ones that don't explode," he said, pointing, and helped himself after her. Then he said: "Have you started wondering who was responsible?"

"I haven't had much time."

"But now—can you think of anyone? Anyone who could do a thing like that in an Embassy, and smuggle you out in those clothes?"

She shook her head.

"It seems so fantastic."

"And yet I could name the man who could have done it—and did it."

"But who?"

"You probably danced with him during the evening."

"I danced with so many."

"But he would be one of the first to be presented."

"I can't think—"

"But you can!" said the Saint. "A man of medium height—slim—small moustache—very elegant." He watched the awakening comprehension in her eyes, and forestalled it. "The Crown Prince Rudolf of—"

"But that's impossible!"

"It is—but it's true. I can give you proof. . . . And it's just his mark. It's worthy of him. It's one of the biggest things that has ever been done!"

The Saint was striding up and down the room in his excitement, with a light kindling in his face and a fire in his eyes that Roger Conway knew of old. Simon Templar's thoughts, inspired, had leaped on leagues beyond his spoken words, as they often did when those queer flashes of genius broke upon him. Roger knew that the Saint would come back to earth in a few moments and condescend to make his argument plain to less vivid minds; Roger was used to these moods, and had learned to wait patiently upon them, but bewildered puzzlement showed on the girl's face.

"I knew it!" Simon stopped pacing the room suddenly, and met the girl's smiling perplexity with a laugh. "Why, it's as plain as the nose on your—on—on Roger's face! Listen. . . ."

He swung onto the table, discarded a half-smoked cigarette, and lighted a fresh one.

"You heard me tell Dussel that I was—the Saint?"

"Yes."

"Hadn't you heard that name before?"

"Of course, I'd seen it in the newspapers. You were the leader of a gang."

"And yet," said the Saint, "you haven't looked really frightened since you've been here."

"You weren't criminals."

"But we committed crimes."

"Just ones—against men who deserved it."

"We have killed men."

She was silent.

"Three months ago," said the Saint, "we killed a man. It was our last crime, and the best of all. His name was Professor K. B. Vargan. He had invented a weapon of war which we decided that the world would be better without. He was given every chance—we risked everything to offer him his life if he would forget his diabolical invention. But he was mad. He wouldn't listen. And he had to die. Did you read that story?"

"I remember it very well."

"Other men—agents of another country—were also after Vargan, for their own ends," said the Saint. "That part of the story never came out in the papers. It was hushed up. Since they failed, it was better to hush up the story than to create an international situation. There was a plot to make war in Europe, for the benefit of a group of financiers. At the head of this group was a man who's called the Mystery Millionaire and the Millionaire Without a Country—one of the richest men in the world— Dr. Rayt Marius. Do you know that name?"

She nodded.

"Everyone knows it."

"The name of the greatest private war-maker in modern history," said Simon grimly. "But this plot was his biggest up to date. And he was using, for his purpose, Prince Rudolf. It was one of those two men who killed one of my dearest friends, in my bungalow up the river, where we had taken Vargan. You may remember reading that one of our little band was found there. Norman Kent—one of the whitest men that ever walked this earth. . . ."

"I remember."

The Saint was gazing into the fireplace, and there was something in his face that forbade anyone to break the short silence which followed.

Then he pulled himself together.

"The rest of us got away, out of England," he went on quietly. "You see, Norman had stayed behind to cover our retreat. We didn't know then that he'd done it deliberately, knowing he hadn't a hope of getting away himself. And when we found out, it was too late to do anything. It was then that I swore to—pay my debt to those two men. . . ."

"I understand," said the girl softly.

"I've been after them ever since, and Roger with me. It hasn't been easy, with a price on our heads; but we've had a lot of luck. And we've found out—many things. One of them is that the work that Norman died to accomplish isn't finished yet. When we put Vargan out of Marius's reach we thought we'd knocked the foundations from under his plot. I believe Marius himself thought so, too. But now he seems to have discovered another line of attack. We haven't been able to find out anything definite, but we've felt—reactions. And Marius and Prince Rudolf are hand in glove again. Marius is still hoping to make his war. That is why Marius must die very soon—but not before we're sure that his intrigue will fall to pieces with his death."

The Saint looked at the girl.

"Now do you see where you come in?" he asked.

She passed a hand across her eyes.

"You're terribly convincing." Her eyes had not left his face all the time he had been talking. "You don't seem like a man who'd make things like that up . . . or dream them. . . . But—"

"Your left hand," said the Saint.

She glanced down. The ring on the third finger caught the light and flung it back in a blaze of brilliance. And was he mistaken, or did he see the faintest shadow of fear touch a proud face that should never have looked afraid?

But her voice, when she spoke, told him nothing.

"What has that to do with it?"

"Everything," answered Simon. "It came to me when I first mentioned Prince Rudolf's name to you. But I'd already got the key to the whole works in the song I was singing just before I barged into Heinrich Dussel's house—and I didn't know it. . . ."

The girl wrinkled her brow.

"What do you mean?"

"I told you that Marius was working for a group of financiers—men who hoped to make millions out of the war he was engineering for them," said the Saint. "Now, what kind of financier do you think would make the most out of another great war?"

She did not answer; and Simon took another cigarette. But he did not light it at once. He turned it between his fingers with a savage gentleness, as if the immensity of his inspiration cried aloud for some physical expression.

He went on, in the same dispassionate tone:

"In the story I've just told you, Vargan wasn't the whole of the plot. He was the key piece—but the general idea went deeper and wider. Before he came into the story, there'd been an organized attempt to create distrust between this country and others in Europe. You must see how easy that would be to wealthy and unscrupulous men. A man alleged to be, say, a French spy, is arrested—here. A man alleged to be a spy of ours is arrested—in France. And it goes on. Spies aren't shot in time of peace. They merely go to prison. If I can afford to send for a number of English crooks, say, and tell them: 'I want you to go to such and such a place, with certain things which I will give you. You will behave in such and such a manner, you will be arrested and convicted as a spy, and you will be imprisoned for five years. If you take your sentence and keep your mouth shut, I will pay you ten thousand pounds'—aren't there dozens of old lags in England who'd tumble over each other for the chance? And it would be the same with men from other countries. Of course, their respective governments would disown them; but governments always disown their spies. That wouldn't cut any ice. And as it went on, the distrust would grow. . . . That isn't romance. It's been done before, on a smaller scale. Marius was doing it before we intervened, in June last. What they call 'situations' were coming to dangerous heads. When Marius fell down over Vargan, the snake was scotched. We thought we'd killed it; but we were wrong. Do you remember the German who was caught trying to set fire to our newest airship, the R103?"

"Yes."

"Marius employed him—for fifteen thousand pounds. I happened to know that. In fact, it was intended that the R103 should actually be destroyed. The plot only failed because I sent information to Scotland Yard. But even that couldn't avert the public outcry that followed. . . . Then, perhaps, you remember the Englishman who was caught trying to photograph a French naval base from the air?"

"The man there was so much fuss about a month ago?"

The Saint nodded.

"Another of Marius's men. I know, because I was hiding in Marius's wardrobe at the Hotel Edouard VII, in Paris, when that man received his instructions. . . . And the secret treaty that was stolen from our Foreign Office messenger between Folkestone and Boulogne—"

"I know."

"Marius again."

The Saint stood up; and again he began to pace the room.

"The world's full of Peace Pacts and Disarmament Conferences," he said, "but where do those things go to when there's distrust between nations? No one may want war—those who saw the last war through would do anything to prevent another—but if a man steals your chickens, and throws mud at your wife when she goes for a walk, and calls you names over the garden wall, you just naturally have to push his teeth through the back of his neck. You can be as long-suffering as you like; but presently he carefully lays on the last straw just where he knows it'll hurt most, and then you either have to turn round and refashion his face or earn the just contempt of all your neighbours. Do you begin to understand?"

"I do. . . . But I still don't see what I've got to do with it."

"But I told you!"

She shook her head, blankly.

"When?"

"Didn't you see? When I was talking about financiers—after I'd recognized you? Isn't your father Hiram Delmar, the Steel King? And aren't you engaged to marry Sir Isaac Lessing, the man who controls a quarter of the world's oil? And isn't Lessing, with his Balkan concessions, practically the unofficial dictator of southeastern Europe? And hasn't he been trying for years to smash R.O.P.? . . . Suppose, almost on the eve of your wedding, you disappear—and then you're found—on the other side—*in Russia.* . . ."

The Saint's eyes were blazing.

"Why, it's an open book!" he cried. "It's easy enough to stir up distrust among the big nations; but it's not so easy to get them moving—there's a hell of a big coefficient of inertia to overcome when you're dealing with solid old nations like England and France and Germany. But the Balkans are the booster charge—they've been that dozens of times before—and you and Lessing make up the detonator. . . . It's worthy of Marius's brain! He's got Lessing's psychology weighed up to the last lonely milligram. He knows that Lessing's notorious for being the worst man to cross in all the world of high finance. Lessing's gone out of his way to break men for nothing more than an argument over the bridge table, before now. . . . And with you for a lever, Marius could engineer Lessing into the scheme—Lessing could set fire to the Balkans—and there might be war in Europe within the week!"

III

ONCE, MONTHS BEFORE, when Simon Templar had expounded a similar theory, Roger Conway had looked at him incredulously, as if he thought the Saint must have taken leave of his senses. But now there was no incredulity in Roger's face. The girl looked at him, and saw that he was as grave as his leader.

She shook her head helplessly.

"It's like a story-book," she said, "and yet you make it sound so convincing. You *do*. . . ."

She put her hand to her sweet head; and then, only then, Simon struck a match for his mauled cigarette, and laughed gently.

"Poor kid! It *has* been a thick night, hasn't it? . . . But you'll feel heaps better in the morning; and I guess our council of war won't grow mould if it stands over till breakfast. I'll show you your room now; and Roger shall wade out into the wide world first thing to-morrow, and borrow some reasonable clothes for you off a married friend of mine."

She stood up, staring at him.

"Do you mean that—you're going to keep me here?"

The Saint nodded.

"For to-night, anyway."

"But the Embassy—"

"They'll certainly be excited, won't they?"

She took a step backwards.

"Then—after all—you're—"

"No, we aren't. And you know it."

Simon put his hands on her shoulders, smiling down at her. And the Saint's smile, when he wished, could be a thing no mortal woman could resist.

"We're playing a big game, Roger and I," he said. "I've told you a little of it to-night. One day I may be able to tell you more. But already I've told you enough to show you that we're out after something more than pure soft roe and elephant's eggs. You've said it yourself."

Again he smiled.

"There'll be no war if you don't go back to the Embassy to-night," he said. "Not even if you disappear for twenty-four hours—or even forty-eight. I admit it's a ticklish game. It's rather more ticklish than trying to walk a tight-rope over the crater of Vesuvius with two sprained ankles and a quart of bootleg hooch inside you. But, at the moment, it's the only thing I can see for us—for Roger and me—to make Marius's own especial battle-axe and hang it over his own ugly head. I can't tell you yet how the game will be played. I don't know myself. But I shall think something out overnight. . . . And meanwhile—I'm sorry—but you can't go home.''

"You want to keep me a prisoner?"

"No. That's the last thing I want. I just want your parole—for twelve hours.''

In its way the half-minute's silence that followed was perhaps as tense a thirty seconds as Simon Templar had ever endured.

Since he started talking he had been giving out every volt of personality he could command. He knew his power to a fraction—every inflection of voice and gesture, every flicker of expression, every perfectly timed pause. On the stage or the screen he could have made a fortune. When he chose he could play upon men and women with a sure and unfaltering touch. And in the last half-hour he had thrown all his genius into the scale.

If it failed . . . He wondered what the penalty was for holding a millionaire's daughter prisoner by force. Whatever it was, he had every intention of risking it. The game, as he had told her, was very big. Far too big for any half-hearted player. . . .

But none of this showed on his face. Poised, quiet, magnificently confident, with that ghost of a swashbuckling smile on his lips, he bore her calm and steady scrutiny. And, looking deep into her eyes, he thought his own thoughts; so that a faint strange tremor moved him inwardly, in a way that he would not have thought possible.

But the girl could see none of this; and the hands that rested on her shoulders were as cool and firm as a surgeon's. She saw only the Saint's smile, the fineness of the clear blue eyes, the swift swaggering lines of the lean brown face. And perhaps because she was what she was, she recognized the quality of the man. . . .

"I'll give you my parole," she said.

"Thank you," said the Saint.

Then Simon showed her to his own room.

"You'll find a very good selection of silk pajamas in the wardrobe," he remarked lightly. "If they aren't big enough for you, wear two suits. That door leads into the bathroom. . . ." Then he touched her hand. "One day," he said, "I'll try to apologize for all this."

She smiled.

"One day," she said, "I'll try to forgive you."

"Good-night, Sonia."

He kissed her hand quickly and turned and went down the stairs again.

"Just one swift one, Roger, my lad," he murmured, picking up a tankard and steering towards the barrel in the corner, "and then we also will retire. Something accomplished, something done, 'as earned a knight's repose. . . . Bung-ho!"

Roger Conway reached morosely for the decanter.

"You have all the luck, you big stiff," he complained. "She only spoke to me once, and I couldn't get a word in edgeways. And then I heard you call her Sonia."

"Why not?" drawled the Saint. "It's her name."

"You don't call a Steel Princess by her first name—when you haven't even been introduced."

"Don't I!"

Simon raised his tankard with a flourish, and quaffed. Then he set it down on the table, and clapped Roger on the shoulder.

"Cheer up," he said. "It's a great life."

"It may be for you," said Roger dolefully. "But what about me? If you'd taken the girl straight back to the Embassy I might have taken a few easy grands off papa for my share in the rescue."

"Whereas all you're likely to get now is fifteen years—or a bullet in the stomach from Marius." Simon grinned; then his face sobered again. "By this time both Marius and Rudolf know that we're back. And how much the police know will depend on how much Heinrich has told them. I don't think he'll say much about us without consulting the Prince and Marius."

"Well, you can bet Marius will spread the alarm."

"I'm not so sure. As long as he knows that we've got Sonia, I think he'll prefer to come after us with his own gang. And he'll find out to-morrow that she hasn't been sent back to the loving arms of the Embassy."

Roger Conway flicked some ash from his cigarette. Those who had known him in the old days, before his name, after the death of K. B. Vargan, became almost as notorious as the Saint's, would have been surprised at his stern seriousness. Fair-haired and handsome (though less beautiful now on account of the make-up that went with his costume) and as true to a type as the Saint was true to none, he had led a flippant and singularly useless life until the Saint enlisted him and trained him on into the perfect lieutenant. And in the strenuous perils of his new

life, strange to say, Roger Conway was happier than he had ever been
before. . . .

Roger said: "How much foundation had you got for that theory you
put up to Sonia?"

"Sweet damn all," confessed the Saint. "It was just the only one I
could see that fitted. There may be a dozen others; but if there are, I've
missed them. And that's why we've got to find out a heap more before
we restore that girl to the bosom of the Ambassador's wife. But it was
a good theory—a damned good theory—and I have hunches about theories. That one rang a distinct bell. And I can't see any reason why it
shouldn't be the right one."

"Nor do I. But what beats me is how you're going to use Sonia."

"And that same question beats me, too, Roger, at the moment. I know
that for us to hold her is rather less cautious than standing pat on a bob-
tailed straight when the man opposite has drawn two. And yet I can't get
away from the hunch that she's heavy artillery, Roger, if we can only
find a way to fire the guns. . . ."

And the Saint relapsed into a reverie.

Certainly, it was difficult. It would have been difficult enough at the
best of times—in the old days, for instance, when only a few select
people knew that Simon Templar, gentleman of leisure, and the Saint,
of doubtful fame, were one and the same person, and he had four able
lieutenants at his call. Now his identity was known, and he had only
Roger—though Roger was worth a dozen. The Saint was not the kind
of man to have any half-witted Watson gaping at his Sherlock—any futile
Bunny balling up his Raffles. But, even so, with the stakes as high as
they were, he would have given anything to be able to put back the clock
of publicity by some fourteen weeks.

An unprofitable daydream . . . of a kind in which the Saint rarely
indulged. And with a short laugh he got to his feet, drained his tankard,
and stretched himself.

"Bed, my Roger," he murmured decisively. "That's where I solve
all my problems."

And it was so.

3

How Sonia Delmar Ate Bacon and Eggs, and Simon Templar Spoke on the Telephone

A SILVER COFFEE machine was chortling cheerfully to itself when Sonia Delmar came down to the sitting room at about ten o'clock; and the fragrance of grilling bacon, to the accompaniment of a sizzling noise off, was distilling into the atmosphere. The room had been newly swept and garnished; and bright September sunshine was pouring through the open windows. Almost immediately Roger Conway entered by another door bearing a frying pan in one hand and a chafing dish in the other.

"Excuse the primitive arrangements," he remarked. "I'm afraid we don't employ a staff of servants—they're liable to see too much."

She seemed surprised to see him; and it was not until then that he realized that she had had some excuse for ignoring him earlier in the day, when his face and hands had been villainously grimed for his role of unsuccessful street news-agent.

She was wearing one of the Saint's multifarious dressing gowns—a jade-green one—with the sleeves turned up and the skirt of the gown trailing the floor; but Roger wondered if any woman could have looked more superbly robed. In the circumstances, she could have used no artifical aids to beauty, yet she had lost none of her fresh loveliness. And if Roger's enslavement had not already been complete, it would have been completed by the smile with which she rewarded his efforts in the kitchen.

"Bacon and eggs!" she said. "My favourite breakfast!"

"They're my favourite, too," said Roger; and thus a friendship was sealed.

But it was not without a certain rueful humility that he noticed that she seemed to be looking for someone else. He supplied the information unasked.

"The Saint went off to get you some clothes himself. He shouldn't be long now."

" 'Saint.' . . . Hasn't he any other name?"

"Most people call him the Saint," said Roger. "His real name is Simon Templar."

" 'Simon'?" She made enchantment of the name, so that Roger wished she would change the subject. And, in a way, she did. She said: "I remembered a lot more after I left you last night. There were three of you who escaped, weren't there? There was a girl—"

"Patricia Holm?"

"That's right."

Roger nodded, impaling another rasher of bacon.

"She isn't here," he said. "As a matter of fact, she's somewhere in the Mediterranean. The Saint wouldn't let her come back with us. She's been with him in most things, but he put his foot down when it came to running the risk of a long term in prison—if not worse. He roped in an old friend who has a private yacht, and sent her off on a long cruise. And just we two came back."

"Had she been with him a long time?"

"About three years. He picked her up in another adventure, and they've stuck together ever since."

"Were they—married?"

"No."

Even then, when Roger was reflecting miserably within him upon the ease with which conquests came to some men who didn't deserve them, he couldn't be guilty of even an implied disloyalty to his leader.

He added, with simple sincerity: "You see, the question never really arose. We're outlaws. We've put ourselves outside the pale—and ordinary standards don't apply. One day, perhaps—"

"You'll win back your place inside the pale?"

"If we could, everything would be different."

"Would you like to go back?"

"For myself? I don't know."

She smiled.

"Somehow," she said, "I can't picture your friend handing round cakes at tea parties, and giving his duty dances to gushing hostesses."

"The Saint?" Roger laughed. "He'd probably start throwing knives at the orchestra, just to wake things up. . . . And here he is."

A car hummed down the mews and stopped outside. A moment later a bent old man, with gray beard, smoked glasses, a shabby hat, entered the sitting room. He leaned on a stick, with an untidy brown-paper parcel in his other hand.

"Such a lovely morning," he wheezed, in a quavering voice. "And two such lovely young people having breakfast together. Well, well, *well!*" He straightened up. "Roger, have you left anything for me, you four-flushing son of a wall-eyed horse thief?"

He heaved parcel and stick into a corner—sent beard, glasses, and hat to join them—and smoothed his coat. By some magic he shed all the illusion of shabbiness from his clothes without further movement; and it was the Saint himself who stood there, adjusting his tie with the aid of the mirror over the mantelpiece—trim, immaculate, debonair.

"Getting younger and more beautiful every day," he murmured complacently; then he turned with a laugh. "Forgive the amateur theatricals, Sonia. I had an idea there might be several policemen out looking for me this morning—and I was right. I recognized three in Piccadilly alone, and I stopped to ask one of them the time. Anyway, I raised you an outfit. You needn't be shy about wearing it, because it belongs to a lady who married a real live lord—though I did my best to save him."

He sank into a chair with a sigh, and surveyed the plate which Roger set before him.

"What—only one egg? Have the hens gone on strike, or something?"

"If you want another," said Roger offensively, "you'll have to lay it yourself. There were only four in the house and our guest had two."

Simon turned to the girl with a smile.

"Well," he said, "it's something to hear you were fit enough to cope with them."

"I feel perfectly all right this morning," she said. "It must have been that drink you gave me last night."

"Wonderful stuff," said the Saint. "I'll give you the prescription before you go, so that you can have some ready for the next time you're doped. It's also an infallible preventive of the morning after—if that's any use to you."

He picked up his knife and fork.

"Did I hear you say you saw some detectives?" asked Roger.

"I saw several. All in very plain clothes, and all flat-footed. A most distressing sight for an old man on his way home from church. And they weren't just out for constitutionals—sniffing the balmy breezes and thinking about their dinners. They weren't keeping holy the Sabbath Day. They were doing all manner of work. Rarely have I run such a gauntlet of frosty stares. It was quite upsetting." The Saint grinned gently. "But what it most certainly means is that the cat has leaped from the portmanteau with some agility. Enough beans have been spilt to keep Heinz busy for a year. The gaff has been blown from here to Honolulu. You know, I had an idea Heinrich would rise to the occasion.''

II

IT WAS THE girl who spoke first.

''The police are after you?''

''They've been after me for years,'' said the Saint cheerfully, ''in a general sort of way. But just recently the hunt's been getting a bit fierce. Yes, I think I can claim that this morning I'm at the height of my unpopularity, so far as Scotland Yard's concerned.''

''After all,'' said Roger, ''you can't go round kidnapping Steel Princesses without *something* happening.''

Simon helped himself to marmalade.

''True, O King,'' he murmured. ''Though that's hardly likely to be the charge. If Heinrich had sung a song about a stolen Steel Princess they'd have wanted to know what she was doing in his house. . . . Curse Sunday! On any other day I could have bought an evening paper and found out exactly what psalm he warbled. As it is, I shall have to go round and inquire in person.''

''You'll have to *what?*'' spluttered Roger.

''Make personal inquiries,'' said the Saint. ''Disguised as a gentleman, I shall interview Prince Rudolf at the Ritz Hotel, and hear all the news.''

He pushed back his chair and reached for the cigarette box.

''It may not have occurred to your mildewed intellect,'' he remarked pleasantly, ''that the problems of international intrigue can usually be reduced to quite simple terms. Let's reduce Rudolf. A, wishing to look important, desires to smite B on the nose. But B, unfortunately, is a bigger man than A. C comes along and offers A a gun, wherewith B can be potted from a safe distance. But we destroyed that gun. C then suggests a means of wangling an alliance between A and D, whereby the disgusting superiority of B may be overcome. C, of course, is sitting on the fence, waiting to take them into his very expensive nursing-home when they've all half killed each other. Is that clear?''

''Like mud,'' said Roger.

''Well,'' said the Saint, unmoved, ''if you wanted to find out exactly how the alliance was to be wangled, mightn't it be helpful to ask A?''

"And, naturally, he'd tell you at once."

Simon shook his head sadly.

"There are subtleties in this game," he said, "which are lost upon you, Roger. But they may be explained to you later. Meanwhile . . ."

The Saint leaned back, with a glance at his watch, and looked across the table at the girl. The bantering manner which he wore with such an ease slipped from his shoulders like a cloak; and he studied her face soberly, reading what he could in the deep brown eyes. She had been watching him ever since he came into the room; and he knew that the fate of his plan was already sealed—one way or the other.

"Your parole has still more than four hours to run," he said, "but I give it back to you now."

She could thank him coldly, and go. She could thank him nicely, rather puzzledly—and go. And if she had made the least move to do either of those things, he would not have said another word. It would be no use, unless she delayed of her own free will. And only one thing could so bend her will—a thing that he hardly dared to contemplate. . . .

"Why do you do that?" she asked simply.

III

"Why do you do that?" . . . *"I'll give you my parole."* . . . He turned over those forthright sentences in his mind. And the way in which they had been spoken. The way in which everything he had heard her say had been spoken. Her superb simplicity . . .

"America's Loveliest Lady," the *Bystander* caption had called her; and the Saint reflected how little meaning was left in that last word. And yet it was the only word for her. There was something about her that one had to meet to understand. If he had had to describe it he could only have done so in flowery phrases—and a flowery phrase would have robbed the thing of all its fresh naturalness, would have tarnished it, might even have made it seem pretentious. And it was the most unpretending thing he had ever known. It was so innocent that it awed him; and yet it made his heart leap with a fantastic hope.

"I did my thinking last night, as I said I would," he answered her quietly.

Still she did not move.

She prompted him: "And you made your plan?"

"Yes."

"I wonder if it was the same as mine?"

Simon raised his eyebrows.

"The same as yours?"

She smiled.

"I can think, too, Mr.—Saint," she said. "I've been taught to. And last night I thought a lot. I thought of everything you'd said, and everything I'd heard about you. And I believed what you'd told me. So—I knew there was only one thing to do."

"Namely?"

"Didn't you call me—Marius's battle-axe? I think you were right. And that's something for us to know. But there's so much else that we don't know—how the axe is to be used, and what other weapons there are to reinforce it. You've taken the axe away, but that's all. Marius still means to bring down the tree. Once before you've thought he was beaten; but you were wrong. This time, if you just take away his ace, you'll know he isn't beaten. He's already undermined the tree. Even now it may fall before the next natural storm. It may be hard enough to prop it up now, until the roots grow down again—without leaving Marius free to strike at it again. And to make sure that he won't strike again, you've got to break his arm."

"Or his neck," said the Saint grimly.

Again she smiled.

"Haven't I read your thoughts?"

"Perfectly."

"And what was your plan?"

Simon met her eyes.

"I meant," he said deliberately, "to ask you to go back—to Heinrich Dussel."

"That was what I meant to suggest."

In that moment Roger Conway felt utterly off the map. The Saint had told him nothing. The Saint had merely sung continuously in his bath—which, with the Saint, was a sure sign of peace of mind. And, in the circumstances, Roger Conway had wondered. . . . But Simon had donned his disguise and departed in the car without a word in explanation of his high spirits; and Roger had been left to wonder. . . . And then—this. He saw the long, deliberate glance which the other two exchanged, and felt that they were moving and speaking in another world—a world to which he could never aspire. And like a man in a dream he heard them discussing the impossible thing.

He knew the Saint, and the thunderbolts of dazzling audacity which the Saint could launch, as no other man could have claimed to know them; and yet this detonation alone would have reeled him momentarily off his balance. But it didn't stand alone. It was matched—without a second's pause. They were of the same breed, those two. Though their feet were set on different roads, they walked in the same country—a country that ordinary people could never reach. And it was then that Roger Conway, who had always believed that no one in all the world could walk shoulder to shoulder with the Saint in that country, began to understand many things.

He heard them, in his dream—level question and answer, the quiet, crisp words. He would have been less at sea if either of them had said any of the things that he might have expected, in any way that he might have expected; but there was none of that. Those things did not exist in their language. Their calm, staccato utterances plunged into his brain like clear-cut gems falling through an infinite darkness.

"You've considered the dangers?"

"To myself?"

"Yes."

"I'm never safe—at any time."

"The destinies we're playing with, then. I might fail you. That would mean we'd given Marius the game."

"You might not fail."

"Have we the right?" asked the Saint.

And then Roger saw him again—the new Saint to whom he had still to grow accustomed. Simon Templar, with the old careless swashbuckling days behind him, more stern and sober, playing bigger games than he had ever touched before—yet with the light of all the old ideals in blue eyes that would never grow old, and all the old laughing hell-for-leather recklessness waiting for his need.

"Have we the right to risk failure?" Simon asked.

"Have you the right to turn back?" the girl answered him. "Have you the right to turn back and start all over again—when you might go forward?"

The Saint nodded.

"I just meant to ask you, Sonia. And you've given your answer. More—you've taken the words out of my mouth, and the objections I'm making are the ones you ought to have made."

"I've thought of them all."

"Then—we go forward."

The Saint spoke evenly, quite softly; yet Roger seemed to hear a blast of bugles. And the Saint went on:

"We've had enough of war. Fighting is for the strong—for those who know what they're fighting for, and love the fight for its own sake. We were like that, my friends and I—and yet we swore that it should not happen again. Not this new fighting—not this cold-blooded scientific maiming and slaughter of school-boys and poor grown-up fools herded to squalid death to make money for a bunch of slimy financiers. We saw it coming again. The flags flying, and the bands playing, and the politicians yaddering about a land fit for heroes to live in, and the poor fools cheering and being cheered, and another madness, worse than the last. Just another war to end war. . . . But we know that you can't end war by war. You can't end war by any means at all, thank God, while men believe in right and wrong, and some of them have the courage to fight for their belief. It has always been so. And it's my own creed. I hope I never live to see the day when the miserable quibbling hair-splitters have won the earth, and there's no more black and white, but everything's just a dreary relative gray, and everyone has a right to his own damned heresies, and it's more noble to be broadminded about your disgusting neighbours than to push their faces in as a preliminary to yanking them back into the straight and narrow way. . . . But this is different. There's no crusading about it. It's just mass murder—for the benefit of the men with the big bank balances. That's what we saw—and we were three blistered outlaws who'd made scrap-iron of every law in Europe, on one quixotic excuse or another, just to make life tolerable for ourselves in this half-hearted civilization. And when we saw that, we knew that we'd come to the end of our quest. We'd found the thing worth fighting for—really worth fighting for—so much more worth fighting for than any of the little things we'd fought for before. One of us has already died for it. But the work will go on. . . ."

And suddenly the Saint stood up.

And all at once, in that swift movement, with the old gay devil-may-care smile awakening again on his lips, Simon Templar seemed to sweep the room clear of all doubts and shadows, leaving only the sunlight and the smile and the far cry of impossible fanfares.

"Let's go!"

"Where?" demanded Roger helplessly; and the Saint laughed.

"On the job, sweetheart," he said—"on the job! Here—shunt yourself and let me get at that telephone."

Roger shunted dazedly, and watched the Saint dial a number. The Saint's face was alight with a new laughter; and, as he waited, he began to hum a little tune. For the wondering and wavering was over, the speculating and the scheming, the space for physical inaction and sober counsel—those negative things at which the Saint's flaming vitality would always fret impatiently. And once again he was on the move—swift, smiling, cavalier, with a laugh and a flourish for battle and sudden death and all good things, playing the old game with all the magnificent zest that only he could bring to it.

"Hullo. Can I speak to Dr. Marius, please? . . . Templar—Simon Templar. . . . Thank you."

Roger Conway said, suddenly, sharply: "Saint—you're crazy! You can't do it! The game's too big—"

"Who wants to play for brickdust and birdseed?" Simon required to know.

And then, before Roger could think of an adequate retort to such an arrogance, he had lost any audience he might have had. For the Saint was speaking to the man he hated more than anyone else in the world.

"Is that you, Marius, my little lamb?" Genially, almost caressingly, the Saint spoke. "And how's Heinrich? . . . Yes, I thought you'd have heard I was back. I'd have rung you up before, only I've been so busy. As a medical man, I can't call my time my own. Only last night I had an extraordinary case. Did Heinrich tell you? . . . Yes, I expected he would. I think he was very struck with my methods. Quite—er—dazzled, in fact. . . . No, nothing in particular. It just occurred to me to soothe my ears with the sound of your sweet voice. It's such a long time since we had our last heart-to-heart talk. . . . The invalid? . . . Oh, getting on as well as can be expected. She ought to be fit to go back to the Embassy to-morrow. . . . No, not to-day. That dope you used on her seems to have a pretty potent follow-through, and I never send my patients home till they've got a bounce on them that's a free advertisement for the cure. . . . Well, you can remember me to Rudolf. I may drop in at the Ritz and have a cocktail with him before lunch. Bye-bye, Angel Face. . . ."

He hung up the receiver.

"Beautiful," he murmured ecstatically. "Too, too beautiful! When it comes to low cunning, I guess that little cameo makes Machiavelli look like Little Red Riding Hood. Angel Face was great—he kept his end up right through the round—but I heard him take the bait. Distinctly. It fairly whistled through his epiglottis. . . . D'you get the idea, my Roger?''

"I don't," Conway admitted.

Simon looked at the girl.

"Do you, Sonia?"

She also shook her head; and the Saint laughed and helped himself to another cigarette.

"Marius knows I've got you," he said. "He thinks he knows that you're still laid out by his dope. And he knows that I wouldn't tell the world I've got you—things being as they are. On that reckoning, then, he's got a new lease of life. He's got a day in which to find me and take you away. And he thinks I haven't realized that—and he's wrong!''

"Very lucid," observed Roger sarcastically. "But I gather he's supposed to find out where we are."

"I've told him."

"How?"

"At this moment, he's finding out my telephone number from the exchange."

"What good will that do him? The exchange won't give him your address."

The Saint grinned.

"Roger," he remarked dispassionately, "you have fully half as much brain as a small boll-weevil. A very small boll-weevil. Your genius for intrigue would probably make you one of the most successful glue-boilers that ever lived.''

"Possibly. But if you'd condescend to explain—"

"But it's so easy!" cried the Saint. "I had to do it tactfully, of course. I couldn't say anything that would let him smell the hook. Thanks to our recent encounter, he knows we're not solid bone from the gargle upwards; and if I'd dropped a truckload of bricks on his Waukeezis, he'd've stopped and thought for a long time before he picked one up. But I didn't. I only dropped that one little bricklet—just big enough for him to feel the impact, and just small enough for him to be able to believe I hadn't seen it go. And Angel Face is so clever. . . . What d'you think he's doing now?''

"Boiling glue," suggested Roger.

"He's got his whole general staff skidding through the telephone directory like so many hungry stockbrokers humming down the latest Wall Street prices during a slump. The exchange will have told him that the call didn't come from a public call box, and that alone will have made him shift his ears back two inches. The only other thing that could put salt horse in his *soufflé* would be if the call turned out to have been put through from a hotel or a restaurant; but he'd have to take his chance on that. And he'd know there was a shade of odds in his favour. No, Roger— you can bet your last set of Aertex that the entire personnel of the ungodly is at this moment engaged in whiffling through every telephone number in the book as they've never whiffled before; and in anything from one to thirty minutes from now, according to how they split up the comic *annuaire* between them, one of them will be letting out a shrill squawk of triumph and starting to improvise a carol about 7, Upper Berkeley Mews.''

"And how does that help us?" asked Roger.

"Like this," said the Saint, and proceeded to explain thus and thus.

4

How Simon Templar Dozed in the Green Park, and Discovered a New Use for Toothpaste

TO WALK FROM Upper Berkeley Mews to the Ritz Hotel should ordinarily have taken a man with the Saint's stride and the Saint's energy about four minutes. Simon Templar in motion, his friends used to say, was the most violent man that ever fumed through London; all his physical movements wre made as if they were tremendously important. Buccaneer he was in fact, and buccaneer of life he always looked—most of all when he strode through London on his strange errands, with his incredibly vivid stride, and a piratical anachronism of a hat canted cavalierly aslant over the face of a fighting troubadour.

But there was nothing of that about the aged graybeard who emerged inconspicuously from a converted garage in Upper Berkeley Mews at half-past eleven that Sunday morning. He did not look as if he had ever been anything in the least like a buccaneer, even fifty years ago; and, if in those decorously wild young days he had once cherished lawless aspirations, he must long since have decently buried all such disturbing thoughts. He walked very slowly, almost apologetically, as if he doubted his own right to be at large; and when he came to Piccadilly he stopped at the edge of the sidewalk and blinked miserably through his dark glasses at the scanty traffic, looking so forlorn and helpless that a plain-clothes man who had been searching for him for hours was moved to offer to help him across the road—an offer which was accepted with plaintive gratitude, and acknowledged with pathetic effusiveness. So an officer of the Criminal Investigation Department did his day's good deed; and the pottering patriarch shuffled into the Green Park by the gate at the side of the Ritz Hotel, found a seat in the shade, sat there, folded his arms, and presently appeared to sleep. . . .

He slept for an hour; and then he climbed stiffly to his feet and shambled out of the park by the way he had entered it, turning under the shadow of the Ritz. He pushed through the revolving doors without hesistation; and it says much for the utter respectablity of his antique appearance that the flunkey who met him within made no attempt to eject him, but greeted him deferentially, hoping that he would prove to be a millionaire, and certain that he could turn out to be less than an earl.

"I wish to see Prince Rudolf," said the Saint; and he said it in such a way that the lackey almost grovelled.

"What name, sir?"

"You may send up my card."

The Saint fumbled in his waistcoat pocket; he had a very fine selection of visiting cards, and the ones he had brought with him on this expedition bore the name of Lord Craithness. On the back of one, he wrote: "Maidenhead, June 28."

It was the day on which he had last seen the prince—the day on which Norman Kent had died.

"Will you take a seat, your lordship?"

His lordship would take a seat. And he waited there only five minutes, a grave and patient old aristocrat, before the man returned to say that the prince would see him—as Simon had known he would say.

It was a perfect little character study, that performance—the Saint's slow and sober progress down the first-floor corridor, his entrance into the prince's suite, the austere dignity of his poise in the moment that he waited for the servant to announce him.

"Lord Craithness."

The Saint heard the door close behind him, and smiled in his beard. And yet he could not have told why he smiled; for at that moment there came back to him all that he had to remember of his first and last meeting with the man who now faced him—and those were not pleasant memories.

Once again he saw the friendly house by the Thames, the garden cool and fresh beyond the open French windows, the sunlit waters at the end of the lawn, and Norman Kent with a strange peace in his dark eyes, and the nightmare face of Rayt Marius, and the prince . . . Prince Rudolf, calmest of them all, with a sleek and inhuman calm, like a man of steel and velvet, impeccably groomed, exquisite, impassive—exactly as he stood at that moment, gazing at his visitor with his fine eyebrows raised in faint interrogation . . . not betraying by so much as the flicker of an eyelid the things that must have been in his mind. He would not possibly have forgotten the date that had been written on that card, it could not by any stretch of imagination have omened good news for him: and yet he was utterly master of himself, utterly at his ease. . . .

"You're a wonderful man," said the Saint; and the prince shrugged delicately.

"You have the advantage of me."

"Have you forgotten so quickly?"

"I meet so many people."

The Saint put up his hand and removed his gray wig, his glasses, his beard . . . straightened up.

"You should remember me," he said.

"My dear Mr. Templar!" The prince was smiling. "But why such precautions? Or did you wish to make your call an even greater surprise?"

The Saint laughed.

"The precautions were necessary," he said—"as you know. But I'll say you took it well—Highness. I never expected you to bat an eye-lash, though—I remember so well that your self-control was your greatest charm."

"But I am delighted to see you."

"Are you?" asked Simon Templar, gently.

II

THE PRINCE PROFFERED a slim gold case.

"At least," he said, "you will smoke."

"One of my own," said the Saint affably. "I find that these are the only brand I can indulge in with safety—my heart isn't what it was."

The prince shrugged.

"You have missed your vocation, Mr. Templar," he said regretfully. "You should have been a diplomat."

"I could have made a job of it," said Simon modestly.

"I believe I once made you an offer to enter my own service."

"You did."

"And you refused."

"I did."

"Perhaps you have reconsidered your decision."

The Saint smiled.

"Listen," he said. "Suppose I said I had. Suppose I told you I'd forgotten the death of my dearest friend. Suppose I said that all the things I once believed in and fought for—the things that he died for—meant nothing more to me. Would you welcome me?"

"Candidly," said the prince, "I should not. I admire you. I know your qualities, and I would give much to have them in my service. But that is an ideal—a daydream. If you turned your coat, you would cease to be what you are, and so you would cease to be desirable. But it is a pity. . . ."

Simon strolled to a chair. He sat there, watching the prince through a curling feather of cigarette smoke. And the prince, sinking onto the arm of another chair, with a long thin cigarette holder between his perfect teeth, returned the gaze with a glimmer of amusement on his lips.

Presently the prince made one of his indescribably elegant gestures.

"As you have not come to enlist with me," he remarked, "I presume you have some other reason. Shall we deal with it?"

"I thought we might have a chat," said the Saint calmly. "I've discovered a number of obscure odours in the wind during the last twenty-four hours, and I had an idea you might have something to say which would clear the air. Of course, for one thing, I was hoping our dear friend Marius would be with you."

The prince glanced at his watch.

"I am expecting him at any moment. He was responsible for your friend's unfortunate—er—accident, by the way. I fear that Marius has never been of a very even temper."

"That is one thing I've been wanting to know for many weeks," said the Saint quietly; and for a moment something blazed in his eyes like a sear of blue flame.

And then, once again, he was smiling.

"It'll be quite a rally, won't it?" he murmured. "And we shall have such a lot to tell each other. . . . But perhaps you'd like to open the palaver yourself—Highness? For instance, how's Heinrich?''

"I believe him to be in good health.''

"And what did he tell the police?''

"Ah! I thought you would ask that question.''

"I'm certainly curious.''

The prince tapped his cigarette fastidiously against the edge of an ashtray.

"If you wish to know, he said that his uncle—an invalid, and unhappily subject to violent fits—had arrived only yesterday from Munich. You entered the house, pretending to be a doctor, before he could disclaim you; and you immediately threatened him with an automatic. You then informed him that you were the Saint, and abducted his uncle. Dussel, naturally, had no idea why you should have done so—but, just as naturally, he considered that that was a problem for the police to solve.''

Simon nodded admiringly.

"I'm taking a distinct shine to Heinrich,'' he drawled.

"You will admit that it was an ingenious explanation.''

"I'll tell the world.''

"But your own strategy, my dear Mr. Templar—that was superb! Even if I had not been told that it was your work, I would have recognized the artist at once.''

"We professionals!'' sighed the Saint.

"And where did you take the lady?''

The question was thrown off so carelessly, and yet with such a perfect touch, that for an instant the Saint checked his breath. And then he laughed.

"Oh, Rudolf, that wasn't worthy of you!''

"I am merely being natural,'' said the prince, without annoyance. "There was something you wanted to know—you asked me—I answered. And then I followed your example.''

Simon shook his head, smiling, and sank deeper into his chair, his eyes intent upon an extraordinarily uninteresting ceiling. And he wondered, with a certain reckless inward merriment, what thoughts were sizzling through the brain of the imperturbable hidalgo opposite him.

He wondered . . . but he knew that it would be a waste of time to attempt to read anything in the prince's face. The prince was his match, if not more than his match, at any game like that. If Simon had come there to fence—that would have been a duel! Already, in the few words they had exchanged, each had tested afresh the other's mettle, and each had tacitly recognized that time had fostered no illusions about the other: neither had changed. Weave and feint, thrust, parry, and riposte—each movement was perfect, smooth, cool, effortless—and futile. . . . And neither would yield an inch of ground. . . . And now, where cruder and clumsier exponents would still be ineffectually lunging and blundering, they had admitted the impasse. The pause was of mutual consent.

Their eyes met and there was a momentary twist of humour in each gaze.

"We appear," observed the prince politely, "to be in the position of two men who are fighting with invisible weapons. We are both equally at a disadvantage."

"Not quite," said the Saint.

The prince fluttered a graceful hand.

"It is agreed that you are an obstacle in my path which I should be glad to remove. I might hand you over to the police—"

"But then you might have some embarrassing questions to answer."

"Exactly. And as for any private action—"

"Difficult—in the Ritz Hotel."

"Exceedingly difficult. Then there is reason to believe that you are— or were—temporarily in possession of a property which it is necessary for me to recover."

"Dear old Heinrich's uncle."

"Whereas my property is the knowledge of why it is necessary for me to recover—your property."

"Perhaps."

"And an exchange is out of the question."

"Right out."

"So that the deadlock is complete."

"Not quite," said the Saint again.

The prince's eyes narrowed a fraction.

"Have I forgotten something?"

"I wonder!"

There was another moment of silence; and, in the stillness, the Saint's amazingly sensitive ears caught the ghost of a sound from the corridor outside the room. And, at that instant, with the breaking of the silence by the perfunctory knock that followed on the door, the grim mirth that had been simmering inside the Saint for minutes past danced mockingly into his eyes.

"Highness—"

It was Marius, looming gigantically in the doorway, with a flare of triumph in the face that might have served as a model for some hideous heathen idol, and triumph in his thin rasping voice.

And then he saw the Saint and stopped dead.

"You see that our enterprising young friend is with us once more, my dear Marius," said the prince suavely; and Simon Templar rose to his feet with his most serpahic smile.

III

"MARIUS—MY OLD college chum!"

The Saint stood there in the centre of the room, lean and swift and devil-may-care, his hands swinging back his coat and resting on his hips; and all the old challenging hints of lazy laughter that both the other men remembered were glinting back through the tones of his voice. The reckless eyes swept Marius from head to foot, with the cold steel masked down into their depths by a shimmer of gay disdain.

"Oh, precious!" spoke on that lazy half-laughing voice. "And where have you been all these months? Why haven't you come round to hold my hand and reminisce with me about the good old days, and the fun we had together? And the songs we used to sing. . . . And do you remember how you pointed a gun at me one night, in one of our first little games, and I kicked you in the—er—heretofore?"

"Marius has a good memory," said the prince dryly.

"And so have I," beamed the Saint, and his smile tightened a little. "Oh, Angel Face, I'm glad to meet you again!"

The giant turned and spoke harshly in his own language; but the prince interrupted him.

"Let us speak English," he said. "It will be more interesting for Mr. Templar."

"How did he come here?"

"He walked up."

"But the police—"

"Mr. Templar and I have already discussed that question, my dear Marius. It is true that Dussel had to make certain charges in order to cover himself, but it might still be inconvenient for us if Mr. Templar were arrested."

"It *is* awkward for you, you know," murmured Simon sympathetically.

The prince selected a fresh cigarette.

"But your own news, my dear Marius? You seemed pleased with yourself when you arrived—"

"I have been successful."

"Our friend will be interested."

Marius looked across at the Saint, and his lips twisted malevolently. And the Saint remembered what lay between them. . . .

"Miss Delmar is now in safe hands," said the giant slowly.

Simon stood quite still.

"When you rang me up—do you remember?—to boast—I asked the exchange for your number. Then the directory was searched, and we learned your address. Miss Delmar was alone. We had no difficulty, though I was hoping to find you and some of your friends there as well—"

"Bluff," said the Saint unemotionally.

"I think not, my dear Mr. Templar," said the prince urbanely. "Dr. Marius is really a most reliable man. I recollect that the only mistake we have made was my own, and he advised me against it."

Marius came closer.

"Once—when you beat me," he said vindictively. "When your friend paid the penalty. You also—"

"I also—pay," said the Saint, with bleak eyes.

"You—"

"My dear Marius!" Once again the prince interrupted. "Let us be practical. You have succeeded. Good. Now, our young friend has elected to interfere in our affairs again, and since he has so kindly delivered himself into our hands—"

Suddenly the Saint laughed.

"What shall we do with the body?" he murmured. "Well, souls, I'll have to give you time to think that out. Meanwhile, I shouldn't like you to think I was getting any gray hairs over Marius's slab of ripe baloney about Miss Delmar. My dear Marius, that line of hooey's got wheels!"

"You still call it a bluff?" sneered the giant. "You will find out—"

"I shall," drawled Simon. "Angel Face, don't you think this is a peach of a beard? Makes me look like Abraham in a high wind. . . ."

Absent-mindedly the Saint had picked up his disguise and affixed the beard to his chin and the dark glasses to his nose. The hat had fallen to the floor. Moving to pick it up, he kicked it a yard away. The second attempt had a similar result. And it was all done with such a puerile innocence that both Marius and the prince must have been no more than vaguely wondering what motive the Saint could have in descending to such infantile depths of clowning—when the manoeuvre was completed with a breath-taking casualness.

The pursuit of his hat had brought the Saint within easy reach of the door. Quite calmly and unhurriedly he picked up the hat and clapped it on his head.

"Strong silent man goes out into the night," he said. "But we must get together again some time. *Au revoir,* sweet cherubs!"

And the Saint passed through the sitting-room door in a flash; and a second later the outer door of the suite banged.

Simon had certainly visited the prince with intent to obtain information; but he had done so, as he did all such things, practially without a plan in his head. The Saint was an opportunist; he held that the development of complicated plans was generally nothing but a squandering of so much energy, for the best of palavers was liable to rocket onto unexpected rails—and these surprises, Simon maintained, could only be turned to their fullest advantage by a mind untrammelled by any preconceived plan of campaign. And if the Saint had anticipated anything, he had anticipated that the arrival of Rayt Marius in the rôle of an angel-faced harbinger of glad tidings would result in a certain amount of more or less informative backchat before the conversation became centered on prospective funerals. And, indeed, the *conversazione* had worn a very up-and-coming air before the prince had switched it back into such a very practical channel. But Prince Rudolf had that sort of mind; wherefore the Saint had chased his hat. . . .

IV

IT HAD BEEN a slick job, that departure; and it was all over before Marius had started to move. Even then, the prince had to stop him.

"My dear Marius, it would be useless to cause a disturbance now."

"He could be arrested—"

"But you must see that he could say things about us, if he chose, which might prove even more annoying than his own interference. At large, he can be dealt with by ourselves."

"He has fooled us once, Highness—"

"He will not do so again. . . . Sit down, sit down, Marius! You have something to tell me."

Impatiently, the giant suffered himself to be soothed into a chair. But the prince was perfectly unruffled—the cigarette glowed evenly in his long holder, and his sensitive features showed no sign of emotion.

"I took the girl," said Marius curtly. "She has been sent to Saltham. The ship will call there again to-night, and Vassiloff will be on board. They can be married as soon as they are at sea—the captain is my slave."

"You think the provocation will be sufficient?"

"I am more sure of it than ever. I know Lessing. I will see him myself—discreetly—and I guarantee that he will accept my proposition. Within a week you should be able to enter Ukraine."

In the bathroom the Saint heard every word. He had certainly banged the outer door of the suite, but the bedroom door had been equally convenient for the purposes of his exit. It has been explained that he came to the Ritz Hotel to gather information.

The communicating door between the sitting room and the bedroom was ajar; so also was that between bedroom and bathroom. And while he listened, the Saint was amusing himself.

He had found a new tube of Prince Rudolf's beautiful pink toothpaste, and the glazed green tiles of the bathroom offered a tempting surface for artistic experiment. Using his material after the style of a chef applying fancy icing to a cake, the Saint had drawn a perfect six-inch circle upon the bathroom wall; from the lowest point of the circle he drew down a vertical line, which presently bifurcated into two downward lines of equal length; and on either side of his first vertical line he caused two further lines to project diagonally upwards. . . .

"And the other arrangements, Marius—they are complete?"

"Absolutely. You have read all the newspapers yourself, Highness—you must see that the strains could not have been more favourably ordered. The mine is ripe for the spark. To-day I received a cable from my most trusted agent, in Vienna—I have decoded it—"

The prince took the form and read it; and then he began to pace the room steadily, in silence.

It was not a restless, fretful pacing—it was a matter of deliberate, leisured strides, as smooth and graceful and eloquent as any of the prince's gestures. His hands were lightly clasped behind his back; the thin cigarette holder projected from between his white teeth; his forehead was serene and unwrinkled.

Marius waited his pleasure, sitting hunched up in the chair to which the prince had led him, like some huge grotesque carving in barbarous stone. He watched the prince with unscrutable glittering eyes.

And Simon Templar was putting the finishing touches to his little drawing.

He understood everything that was said. Once upon a time he had felt himself at a disadvantage because he could not speak a word of the prince's language; but since then he had devoted all his spare time, night and day, to the task of adding that tongue to his already extensive linguistic accomplishments. This fact he had had neither the inclination nor the opportunity to reveal during their brief reunion.

Presently the prince said: "Our friend Mr. Templar—I find it hard to forget that he once saved my life. But when he cheated me, at Maidenhead, I think he cancelled the debt."

"It is more than cancelled, Highness," said Marius malignantly. "But for that treachery, we should have achieved our purpose long ago."

"It seems a pity—I have admitted as much to him. He is such an active and ingenious young man."

"A meddlesome young swine!"

The prince shook his head.

"One should never allow a personal animosity to colour one's abstract appreciations, my dear Marius," he said dispassionately. "On the other hand one should not allow an abstract admiration to overrule one's discretion. I have a most sincere regard for our friend—but that is all the more reason why I should encourage you to expedite his removal. He will endeavour to trace Miss Delmar, of course, when he finds that you were telling the truth."

"I shall take steps to assist him—up to a point."

"And then you will dispose of him in your own way."

"There will be no mistake," said the giant venomously; and the prince laughed softly.

In the bathroom, Simon Templar, with a very Saintly smile on his lips, was crowning his shapely self-portrait with a symbolical halo—at a rakish angle, and in scrupulously correct perspective.

5

How Simon Templar Travelled to Saltham, and Roger Conway Put Up His Gun

A BULGE—A distinct Bulge,'' opined the Saint, as he shuffled out of the Ritz Hotel, leaving a young cohort of oleaginous serfs in his wake. There was, he thought, a lot to be said for the principle of riding on the spur of the moment. If he had called upon the crown prince to absorb information, he had indubitably inhaled the mixture as prescribed—a canful. Most of it, of course, he either knew already or could have guessed without risk of bringing on an attack of cerebral staggers; but it was pleasant to have one's deductions confirmed. Besides, one or two precise and irrefutable details of the enemy's plan of attack had emerged in all their naked glory, and that was very much to the good. ''Verily—a Bulge,'' ruminated the Saint. . . .

He found his laborious footsteps automatically leading him down St. James Street, and then eastwards along Pall Mall. With an *eclat* equalled only by that of his recent assault upon the Ritz, he carried the portals of the Royal Automobile Club—of which he was not a member—and required an atlas to be brought to him. With this aid to geographical research, he settled himself in a quiet corner of the smoke room and proceeded to acquire the dope about Saltham. This he discovered to be a village on the Suffolk coast between Southwold and Aldeburgh; a gazetteer which lay on the table conveniently near him added the enlightening news that it boasted of fine sandy beaches, cliffs, pleasure grounds, a 16th cent. ch., a coasting trade, and a population of 3,128— it was, said the gazetteer, a wat.-pl.

''And that must be frightfully jolly for it,'' murmured the Saint, gently depositing the Royal Automobile Club's property in a convenient wastebasket.

He smoked a thoughtful cigarette in his corner; and then, after a glance at his watch, he left the club again, turned down Waterloo Place, and descended the steps that lead down to the Mall. There he stood, blinking at the sunlight, until a grubby infant accosted him.

"Are you Mr. Smith, sir?"

"I am," said the Saint benignly.

"Gen'l'man gimme this letter for you."

The Saint took the envelope, slit it open, and read the pencilled lines:

No message. Heading N.E. Wire you Waldorf on arrival.
—R.

"Thank you, Marmaduke," said the Saint.

He pressed a piece of silver into the urchin's palm and walked slowly back up the steps, tearing the note into small shreds as he went. At the corner of Waterloo Place and Pall Mall he stopped and glanced around for a taxi.

It seemed a pity that Roger Conway would waste a shilling, but that couldn't be helped. The first bulletin had already meant an unprofitable increase in the overhead. But that, on the other hand, was a good sign. In the Saint's car and a chauffeur's livery Roger Conway had been parked a little distance away from the converted garage, in a position to observe all that happened. If Sonia Delmar had been in a position to drop a note after her abduction she would have done so, and the bones of it would have been passed on to the Saint *via* the infant they had employed for the occasion; otherwise Roger was simply detailed to give inconspicuous chase, and he must have shot his human carrier-pigeon overboard as they neared the northeastern outskirts of London. But the note carried by the human telegraph would only have been interesting if anything unforeseen had happened.

So that all things concerned might be assumed to be paddling comfortably along in warm water—unless Roger had subsequently wrapped the automobile round a lamp-post, or taken a tack into the bosom of a tire. And even that could not now prove wholly disastrous, for the Saint himself knew the destination of the convoy without waiting for further news, and he reckoned that a village with a mere 3,128 souls to call it their home town wasn't anything like an impossible convert to draw, even in the lack of more minute data.

Much, of course, depended on how long a time elapsed before the prince took it into his head to have a bath. . . . Thinking over that touch of melodramatic bravado, Simon was momentarily moved to regret it. For the sight of the work of art which the Saint had left behind him as a souvenir of his visit would be quite enough to send the entire congregation of the ungodly yodelling frantically over the road to Saltham like

so many starving rates on the trail of a decrepit camembert. . . . And
then that very prospect wiped every sober regret out of the Saint's mind,
and flicked a smile on his lips as he beckoned a passing cab.

After all, if an adventurer couldn't have a sense of humour about the
palpitations of the ungodly at *his* time of life—then he might as well hock
his artillery forthwith and blow the proceeds on a permanent wave. In
any case, the ungodly would have to see the night through. The ship of
which Marius had spoken would be stealing in under cover of dark; and
the ungodly, unless they were prepared to heave in their hand, would
blinkin' well have to wait for it—dealing with any interference meanwhile
as best they could.

"That little old watering-place is surely going to hum to-night," figured
the Saint.

The taxi pulled in to the curb beside him; and, as he opened the door,
he glimpsed a mountain of sleepy-looking flesh sauntering along the
opposite pavement. The jaws of the perambulating mountain oscillated
rhythmically, to the obvious torment of a portion of the sweetmeat which
has made the sapodilla tree God's especial favour to Mr. Wrigley. Chief
Inspector Teal seemed to be enjoying his walk. . . .

"Liverpool Street Station," directed the Saint, and climbed into his
cab, vividly appreciating another factor in the equation which was liable
to make the algebra of the near future a thing of beauty and a joy for
Einstein.

II

HE HAD PLENTY of time to slaughter a sandwich and smoke a quartet of
meditative cigarettes at the station before he caught Sunday's second and
last train to Saxmundham, which was the nearest effective railhead for
Saltham. He would have had time to call in at the Waldorf for Roger's
wire on his way if he had chosen, but he did not choose. Simon Templar
had a very finely calibrated judgment in the matter of unnecessary risks.
At Liverpool Street he felt pretty safe: in the past he had always worked
by car, and he fully expected that all the roads out of London were well
picketed, but he was anticipating no special vigilance at the railway
stations—except, perhaps, on the Continental departure platform at Vic-

toria. He may have been right or wrong; it is only a matter of history that he made the grade and boarded the 4:35 unchallenged.

It was half-past seven when the train decanted him at Saxmundham; and in the three hours of his journey, having a compartment to himself, he had effected a rejuvenation that would have made Dr. Voronoff's best experiment look like Methuselah before breakfast. He even contrived to brush and batter a genuine jauntiness into his ancient hat; and he swung off the train with his beard and glasses in his pocket, and an absurdly boyish glitter in his eyes.

He had lost nothing by not bothering to collect Roger Conway's telegram, for he knew his man. In the first bar he entered he discovered his lieutenant attached by the mouth to the open end of a large tankard of ale. A moment later, lowering the tankard in order to draw breath, Roger perceived the Saint smiling down at him, and goggled.

"Hold me up, someone," he muttered. "And get ready to shoo the pink elephants away when I start to gibber. . . . And to think I've been complaining that I couldn't see the point of paying seven-pence a pint for brown water with a taste!"

Simon laughed.

"Bear up, old dear," he said cheerfully. "It hasn't come to that yet."

"But how did you get here?"

"Didn't you send for me?" asked the Saint innocently.

"I did not," said Roger. "I looked out the last train, and I knew my message wouldn't reach you in time for you to catch it. I wired you to phone me here, and for the last three hours I've been on the verge of heart failure every time the door opened. I thought Teal must have got after you somehow, and every minute I was expecting the local cop to walk in and invite me outside."

Simon grinned and sank into a chair. A waiter was hovering in the background, and the Saint hailed him and ordered a fresh consignment of ale.

"I suppose you pinched the first car you saw," Roger was saying. "That'll mean another six months on our sentences. But you might have warned me."

The Saint shook his head.

"As a matter of fact, I never went to the Waldorf. Marius himself put me onto Saltham, and I came right along.

"Good lord—how?"

"He talked, and I listened. It was dead easy."

"At the Ritz?"

Simon nodded. Briefly he ran over the story of the reunion, with its sequel in the bathroom, and the conversation he had overheard; and Conway stared.

"You picked up all that?"

"I did so. . . . That man Marius is the three-star brain of this cockeyed age—I'll say. And by the same token, Roger, you and I are going to have to tune up our gray matters to an extra couple of revs. per if we want to keep Angel Face's tail skid in slight over this course. . . . But what's your end of the story?"

"Three of 'em turned up—one in a police-inspector's uniform. When the bell wasn't answered in about thirty seconds they whipped out a jemmy and bust it in. As they marched in, an ambulance pulled into the mews and stopped outside the door. It was a wonderful bit of team work. There were ambulance men in correct uniforms and all. They carried her out on a stretcher, with a sheet over her. All in broad daylight. And slick! It was under five minutes by my watch from the moment they forced the door to the moment when they were all piling into the wagon, and they pulled out before anything like a crowd had collected. They'd doped Sonia, of course . . . the swine . . ."

"Gosh!" said the Saint softly. "She's just great—that girl!"

Roger gazed thoughtfully at the pewter can which the waiter had placed before him.

"She is—just great. . . ."

"Sweet on her, son?"

Conway raised his eyes.

"Are you?"

The Saint fished out his cigarette case and selected a smoke. He tapped it on his thumbnail abstractedly; and there was a silence. . . .

Then he said quietly: "That ambulance gag is big stuff. Note it down, Roger, for our own use one day. . . . And what's the battlefield like at Saltham?

"A sizeable house standing in its own grounds on the cliffs, away from the village. They're not much, as cliffs go—not more than about fifty feet around there. There are big iron gates at the end of the drive. The ambulance turned in; and I went right on past without looking round—I guessed they were there for keeps. Then I had to come back here to send you that wire. By the way, there was a bird we've met before in that ambulance outfit—your little friend Hermann."

Simon stroked his chin.

"I bust his jaw one time, didn't I?"

"Something like that. And he did his best to bust my ribs and stave my head in."

"It will be pleasant," said the Saint gently, "to meet Hermann again."

He took a pull at his ale and frowned at the table.

Roger said: "It seems to me that all we've got to do now is to get on the phone to Claud Eustace and fetch him along. There's Sonia in that house—we couldn't have the gang more red-handed."

"And we troop along to the pen with them, and take our sentences like little heroes?"

"Not necessarily. We could watch the show from a safe distance."

"And Marius?"

"He's stung again."

The Saint sighed.

"Roger, old dear, if you'd got no roof to your mouth, you'd raise your hat every time you hiccoughed," he remarked disparagingly. "Are we going to be content with simply jarring Marius off his trolley and leaving it at that—leaving him to get busy again as soon as he likes? There's no evidence in the wide world to connect him up with Saltham. All that bright scheme of yours would mean would be that his game would be temporarily on the blink. And there's money in it. Big money. We don't know how much, but we'd be safe enough putting it in the seven-figure bracket. D'you think he'd give the gate to all that capital and preliminary carving and prospective gravy just because we'd trodden on his toes?"

"He'd have to start all over again—"

"And so should we, Roger—just as it happened a few months back. And that isn't good enough. Not by a mile. Besides," said the Saint dreamily, "Rayt Marius and I have a personal argument to settle, and I think—I think, honey-bunch—that that's one of the most important points of all, in this game. . . ."

Conway shrugged.

"Then—what?"

"I guess we might tool over to Saltham and get ready to beat up this house party."

Roger fingered an unlighted cigarette.

"I suppose we might," he said.

The Saint laughed and stood up.

"There seems to be an attack of respectability coming over you, my Roger," he murmured. "First you talk about fetching in the police, and then you have the everlasting crust to sit there in a beer-sodden stupor and *suppose* we might waltz into as good a scrap as the Lord is ever likely to stage-manage for us. There's only one cure for that disease, sweetheart—and that's what we're going after now. Long before dark, Marius himself and a reinforcement of lambs are certain to be steaming into Saltham, all stoked up and sizzling at the safety valve, and the resulting ballet ought to be a real contribution to the gaiety of nations. So hurry up and shoot the rest of that ale through your face, sonny boy, and let's go!''

III

THEY WENT. . . .

Not that it was the kind of departure of which Roger Conway approved. In spite of all the training which the Saint had put into him, Roger's remained a cautious and deliberate temperament. He had no peace of mind about haring after trouble with an armoury composed of precious little more than a sublime faith in Providence and a practised agility at socking people under the jaw. He liked to consider. He liked to weigh pro and con. He liked to get his hooks onto a complete detail map of the campaign proposed, with all important landmarks underlined in red ink. He liked all sorts of things that never seemed to come his way when he was in the Saint's company. And he usually seemed to be tottering through the greater part of their divers adventures in a kind of lobster-supper dream, feeling like a man who is compelled to run a race for his life along a delirious precipice on a dark night in a gale of wind and a pea-soup fog. But always in that nightmare the Saint's fantastic optimism led him on, dancing ahead like a will-o'-the-wisp, trailing him dizzily behind into hell-for-leather audacities which Roger, in the more leisured days that followed, would remember in a cold sweat.

And yet he suffered it all. The Saint was just that sort of man. There was a glamour, a magnificent recklessness, a medieval splendor about him that no one with red blood in his veins could have resisted. In him there was nothing small, nothing half-hearted: he gave all that he had to everything that he did, and made his most casual foolishness heroic.

''Who cares?'' drawled the Saint, with his lean brown hands seeming merely to caress the wheels of the Hirondel, and his mad, mocking eyes lazily skimming the road that hurtled towards them at seventy miles an hour. ''Who cares if a whole army corps of the heathen comes woofling into Saltham to-night, even with a detachment of some of our old friends in support—the Black Wolves, for instance, or the Snake's Boys, or the Tiger Cubs, or even a brigade of the crown prince's own household cavalry—old Uncle Rayt Marius an' all? For it seems years since we had what you might call a one hundred per cent rodeo, Roger, and I feel that unless we get moving again pretty soon we shall be growing barnacles behind the ears.''

Roger said nothing. He had nothing to say. And the big car roared out into the east.

The sun had long since set, and now the twilight was closing down with the suddenness of the season. As the dusk became dangerous for their speed, Simon touched a switch, and the tremendous twin headlights slashed a blazing pathway for them through the darkness.

They drove on in silence; and Roger Conway, strangely soothed by the swift rush of wind and the deep-chested drone of the open exhaust, sank into a hazy reverie. And he remembered a brown-eyed slip of a girl, sweet and fresh from her bath, in a jade-green gown, who was called America's loveliest lady, and who had sat in a sunny room with him that morning and eaten bacon and eggs. Also he remembered the way she and the Saint had spoken together, and how far away and unattainable they had seemed in their communion, and how little the Saint would say afterwards. He was quiet. . . .

And then, it seemed only a few minutes later, Simon was rousing him with a hand on his shoulder; and Roger struggled upright and saw that it was now quite dark, and the sky was brilliant with stars.

"Your cue, son," said the Saint. "The last signpost gave us three miles to Saltham. Where do we go from here?"

"Right on over the next crossroads, old boy. . . ." Roger picked up his bearings mechanically. "Carry on . . . and bear left here. . . . Sharp right just beyond that gate, and left again almost immediately. . . . I should watch this corner—it's a brute. . . . Now stand by to fork right in about half a mile, and the house is about another four hundred yards farther on."

The Saint's foot groped across the floor and kicked over the cut-out control, and the thunder of their passage was suddenly hushed to a murmuring whisper that made figures on the speedometer seem grotesque. The Saint had never been prone to hide any of his lights under a bushel, and in the matter of racing automobiles particularly he had cyclonic tastes; but his saving quality was that of knowing precisely when and where to get off.

"We won't tell the world we're on our way till we've given the lie of the land a brisk double-O," he remarked. "Let's see—where does this comic *chemin* trail to after it's gone past the baronial hall?"

"It works round the grounds until it comes out onto the cliffs," Roger answered. "Then it runs along by the sea and dips down into the village nearly a mile away."

"Any idea how big these grounds are?"

"Oh, large. . . . I could give you a better idea of the size if I knew how much space an acre takes up."

"Park land, or what?"

"Trees all around the edge and gardens around the house—as far as I could see. But part of it's park—you could play a couple of cricket matches on it. . . . The gates are just round this bend on your right now."

"O.K., big boy. . . ."

The Saint eased up the accelerator and glanced at the gates as the Hirondel drifted past. They were tall and broad and massive, fashioned in wrought iron in an antique style; far beyond them, at the end of a long straight drive, he could see the silhouette of a gabled roof against the stars, with one tiny square of window alight in the black shadow. . . . Maybe Sonia Delmar was there. . . . And he looked the other way, and saw the grim line of Roger's mouth.

"Feeling a bit more set for the stampede, son?" he asked softly.

"I am." Roger met his eyes steadily. "And it might amuse you to know, Saint, that there isn't another living man I'd have allowed to make it a stampede. Even now, I don't quite see why Sonia had to go back."

Simon touched the throttle again and they swept on.

"D'you think I'd have let Sonia take the risk for nothing myself?" he answered. "I didn't know what I was going to get out of my trip to the Ritz. And even what I did get isn't the whole works. But Sonia—she's right in their camp, *and* they've no fear of her squealing. It would amuse them to boast to her, Roger—I can see them doing it."

"That Russian they're bringing over—"

"Vassiloff?"

"That's it—"

"I rather think he'll boast more than any of them."

"What's he getting out of it?"

"Power," said the Saint quietly. "That's what they're all playing for—or with. And Rayt Marius most of all, for the power of gold—Marius and the men behind him. But he's the mad dog. . . . Did you know that he was once a guttersnipe in the slums of Prague? . . . Wouldn't

it be the greatest thing in his life to sit on the unofficial throne of Europe—
to play with kings and presidents for toys—to juggle with great nations
as in the past he's juggled with little ones? That's his idea. That's why
he's playing Vassiloff with one finger, because Vassiloff hates Lessing,
and Prince Rudolf with another finger, because Rudolf fancies himself
as a modern Napoleon—and, by the lord, Roger, Rudolf could make that
fancy into fact, with Marius behind him! . . . And God knows how many
other people are on his strings, here and there. . . . And Sonia's the pawn
that's right inside their lines—that might become a queen in one move,
and turn the scales of their tangled chessgame to hell or glory."

"While we're—just dancing round the board. . . ."

"Not exactly," said the Saint.

They had swung out onto the cliff road, and Simon was braking the
car to a gentle standstill. As the car stopped he pointed; and Roger,
looking past him, saw two lights, red and green stealing over the sea.

IV

"THERE'S THE BLEARY old *bateau*. . . ."

A ghost of merriment wraithed through the Saint's voice. Thus the
approach of tangible peril always seized him, with a stirring of stupendous
laughter, and a surge of pride in all gay, glamorous things. And he slipped
out of the car and stood with his hands on his hips, looking down at the
lights and the reflection of the lights in the smooth sea, and then away
to his right, where the shreds of other lights were tattered between the
trees. "Battle and death," went a song in his heart; and he smiled in the
starlight, remembering another adventure and an old bravado.

Then Roger was standing beside him.

"How long would you give it, Saint?"

"All the time in the world. Don't forget we're fifty feet above sea
level, by your reckoning, and that alters the horizon. She's a good two
miles out."

Simon's head went back; he seemed to be listening.

"What is it?" queried Roger.

"Nothing. That's the problem. We didn't pass Marius on the road
here, and he didn't pass us. Question: Did he get here first or is he still

coming? Or isn't the prince likely to find my bathroom decoration till next Saturday? What would you say, Roger?"

"I should say they were here. You had to wait for a slow train, and then we wasted an hour in Saxmundham."

"Not 'wasted,' sweetheart," protested the Saint absently. "We assimilated some ale."

He heard an unmistakable metallic snap at his side, and glanced down at the blue-black sheen of an automatic in Roger's hand.

"We'll soon find out what's happened," said Roger grimly.

"Gat all refuelled and straining at the clutch, old lad?"

"It is."

Simon laughed softly, thoughtfully; and his hand fell on Conway's wrist.

"Roger, I want you to go back to London."

There was an instant's utter silence.

Then—

"You want—"

"I want you to go to London. And find Lessing. Get at him somehow— if you have to shoot up the whole West End. And fetch him along here— even at the end of that gun!"

"Saint, what's the big idea?"

"I want him here—our one and only Ike."

"But Sonia—"

"I'm staying, and that's what I'm staying for. You don't have to worry about her. And it's safer for you in London than it is for me. You've got to make record time on this trip."

"You can get ten miles an hour more out of that car than I can."

"And I can fight twice as many men as you can, and move about twice as quietly, and shoot twice as fast. No, Roger, this end of the game is mine, and you must know it. And Sir Isaac Lessing we must have. Don't you see?"

"Damn it, Saint—"

There were depths of bitterness in Roger's voice that the Saint had never heard before; but Simon could understand.

"Listen, sonny boy," he said gently. "Don't we know that the whole idea of this part of the performance has been staged for Lessing's benefit? And mightn't there be one thing just a shade cleverer than keeping Lessing neutral? That's all we'd be doing if you had your way. But suppose we fetched Ikey himself along here—and showed him the whole frame-up from the wings! Lessing isn't a sack of peanuts. If Marius thinks enough of him to go to all this trouble to josh him into the show as an active partner, mightn't it be the slickest thing we ever did to turn Marius's battle-axe against himself with a vengeance—and get Lessing not just neutral, but a fighting man on our side? If Lessing can say 'War!' to the Balkans, and have them all cutting one another's throats in a week, why shouldn't he just as well say 'Nix!'—and send them all toddling home to their carpet slippers? Roger, it's the chance of a lifetime!''

He took Conway by the shoulders.

"You must see it, old Roger!"

"I know, Saint. But—"

"I promise you shall be in at the death. I don't know exactly what I'm going to do now, but I'm putting off anything drastic until the last possible minute. I don't want to make a flat tire of our own private peepshow if I can possibly help it—not till Ike's here to share the fun. And you'll be here with him, bringing up the beer—rear—in the triumphal procession. Roger, is the bet on?''

They stood eye to eye for ten ticked seconds of silence; and Roger's bleak eyes searched the Saint's face as they had never searched it before. In those ten seconds, all that the Saint signified in Roger's life, all that he incarnated and inspired, all that they had been through together, the whole cumulative force of a lifelong loyalty, rose up and gave desperate battle to the seed of ugly suspicion that had been sown in Roger's mind nearly two hours ago, and devilishly fecundated by this last inordinate demand. The stress of the fight showed in Roger's face, the rebellion of unthinkable things; but Simon waited without another word.

And then, slowly, Roger Conway nodded.

"Shake," he said.

"Attaboy. . . ."

Their hands met in a long grip, and then Roger turned away abruptly and swung into the driving seat of the Hirondel. The Saint leaned on the door.

"Touch the ground in spots," he directed rapidly. "I've got my shirt on you, and I know you won't fizzle, but every minute matters. And understand—if you do have to prod Isaac with the snout of that shooting-iron, prod him gently. He's got to arrive here in good running order— but he's got to arrive. What happens after that is your shout. I'd have liked to make a definite date, and I'm sure you would, too, Roger; but that's more than any of us can do on a night like this, and we'd be boobs to try. If I can manage it, I'll be there myself. If I can't, I'll try to leave

a note—let's see—I'll slip something under a rock by that tree there. If
I can't even do that—''

"Then what?"

"Then I'm afraid, Roger, it'll mean that you're the last wicket up; and
you may give my love to all kind friends, and shoot Rayt Marius through
the stomach for me, raise what you can on my *Ulysses* and the photographs
Dicky Tremayne sent me from Paris.''

The self-starter whirred under Roger's foot, and he listened for a moment to the smooth purr of the great engine; and then he turned again to
the Saint.

"I'll be carrying on," he said quietly.

"I know," said the Saint, in the same tone. "And if you don't find
that note, it mayn't really be so bad as all that—it may only mean that
I've had an attack of writer's cramp, or something. But it'll still be your
call. So don't think you're being elbowed out—because you're not.
Whatever else happens, you're more than likely to have to stand up to
the worst of the bowling before we draw stumps, and the fate of the side
may very well be in your hands. And that does not mean maybe." He
clapped Roger on the shoulder. "So here's luck to you, sonny boy!"

"Good luck, Saint!"

"And give 'em hell!"

And Simon stepped back, with a light laugh and a flourish; and the
Hirondel leaped away like an unleashed fiend.

6

How Simon Templar Threw a Stone, and the Italian Delegate Was Unlucky

FOR A MOMENT the Saint stood there, watching the tail light of the
Hirondel skimming away into the darkness. He knew so well—he could
not have helped knowing—the hideous doubts that must have tortured
Roger's brain, the duel between jealousy and friendship, the agony that
the struggle must have cost. For Roger could only have been thinking

of the ultimate destiny of the girl who had been pitchforked into their
lives less than twelve hours ago, who was now a prisoner in the house
beyond the trees, from whom the Saint had already plundered such a
fantastic allegiance. And Simon thought of other girls that Roger had
known, and of other things that had been in their lives since they first
came together, and of his own lady; and he wondered, with a queer
wistfulness in the eyes that followed that tiny red star down the road.

And then the red star swept out of sight round a bend; and the Saint
turned away with a shrug, and glanced down again at the sea, where lay
another red star, with a green one beside it.

In that, at least, he had deliberately lied. . . . The ship, he was sure,
had been within a mile of the shore when he spoke; and now it had ceased
to move. The rattle of a chain came faintly to his ears, and then he heard
the splash of the anchor.

They had run their time-table close enough! And Roger Conway, with
about a hundred and eighty miles to drive, to London and back, and a
job of work to do on the way, had no mean gag to put over—even in the
Hirondel. The Saint, who was a connoisseur of speed, swore by that car;
and he knew that Roger Conway, for all his modesty, could spin a nifty
wheel when he was put to it; but, even so, he reckoned that Roger hadn't
a heap to beef about. Any verbiage about Roger having nothing to do
that night would be so much applesauce. . . .

"And pray Heaven he doesn't pile that bus up on its front bumpers
on the way," murmured Simon piously.

As he slipped into the shadows of a clump of trees, his fingers strayed
instinctively to his left sleeve, feeling for the hilt of Belle, the little
throwing-knife that was his favourite weapon, which he could use with
such a bewildering speed and skill. Once upon a time, Belle had been
merely the twin sister of Anna, who was his darling; but he had lost Anna
three months ago, in the course of his first fight with Marius. And,
touching Belle, in her little leather sheath strapped to his forearm, the
Saintly smile flickered over his lips, without reaching his eyes. . . .

Then, beyond the clump of trees, he stood beside the wooden fence
that walled off the estate. It was as tall as himself; he stretched up cautious
fingers, and felt a thick entanglement of rusty barbed wire along the top.
But a couple of feet over his head one of the trees in the clump through
which he had just passed extended a long bare branch far over the fence.
Simon limbered his muscles swiftly, judged his distance, and jumped for
it. His hands found their hold as smoothly and accurately as if he had
been performing on a horizontal bar in a gymnasium; and he swung

himself back to the fence hand over hand, pulled up with his arms, carried his legs over, and dropped lightly to the ground on the other side.

Fastidiously settling his tie, which had worked a fraction of an inch out of place during the performance, he stepped through the narrow skirting of forestry in which he had landed, and inspected the view.

In front of him, and away round to his right, spread an expanse of park land, broken by occasional trees, and surrounding the house on the two sides that he could see. Also surrounding the house, and farther in, lay the gardens, trellises and terraces, shrubberies and outbuildings, dimly visible in the gloom. On his left, crowning a steady rise of ground, a kind of balustraded walk cut a clean black line against the sky, and he guessed that this marked the edge of the cliffs.

In this direction he moved, keeping in the sheltering obscurity of the border of trees for as long as he could, and then breaking off at right angles, parallel with the balustrade, before he had mounted enough of the gentle slope for his silhouette to be marked against the skyline. He felt certain that entrance upon the estate was not yet public knowledge, and he was inclined to stay cagey about it: the number and personal habits of the household staff were very much of an unknown quantity so far, and the Saint was not tempted to run any risk of provoking them prematurely. Swiftly as he shifted through the faint starlight, his sensitive ears were alert for the slightest sound, his restless eyes scanned every shadow, and the fingers of his right hand were never far from the chased ivory hilt of Belle. He himself made no more sound than a prowling leopard, and that same leopard could not have constituted a more deadly menace to any member of the opposition gang who might have chanced to be roaming about the grounds on Simon Templar's route.

Presently the house was again on his right, and much nearer to him, for he had travelled round two sides of a rough square. He began to move with an even greater caution. Then, in a moment, gravel grated under his feet. He glanced sharply to his left, to see where the path led, and observed a wide gap in the balustrade at the cliff edge. That would be the top of a flight of steps running down the cliff face to the shore, he figured; and beside the gap he saw a tree that would provide friendly cover for another peep at the developments on the water below.

He turned off the path and melted into the blackness beneath the tree. This grew on the very edge of the scarp; and the break in the balustrade meant what he had thought it meant—a rough stairway that vanished downwards into the darkness.

Looking out, Simon saw a thin paring of new moon slithering out of the rim of the sea. It wouldn't be much of a moon even when it was fully risen, he reflected, with a voiceless thanksgiving to the little gods that had made the adventure this much easier. For all felonious purposes, the light was perfect—nothing but the soft luminance of a sky spangled with a thousand stars—light enough for a cat-eyed *shikari* like Simon Templar to work by, without being bright enough to be embarrassing.

He switched his eyes downwards again, and saw, midway between the anchored ship and the thin white ribbon of sand at the foot of the cliff, a tiny black shape stealing over the waters. Motionless, instinctively holding his breath and parting his lips—the Saint's faculties worked involuntarily, whether they were needed or not—he could catch shreds of the sound of grating rowlocks.

And then he heard another sound, behind him, that was much easier to hear—the gritting of heavy boots on the gravel he had just quitted.

II

HE MERGED A little deeper into the blackness of his cover, and looked round. A lantern was bobbing down the path from the house, and three men tramped along by its light. In a moment their voices came to him quite plainly.

"*Himmel!* I shall vant to go to bet. Last night—to-night—it iss never no sleep for der mans."

"Aw—ya big skeezicks! What sorta tony outfit d'ya think ya've horned in on?

"Ah, 'e will-a always be sleeping, da Gerraman. He would-a make-a all his time, sleeping and-a drinking—but I t'ink 'e like-a best-a da drinking."

"Maybe he's gotta toist like I got. Ya can't do nuth'n about dat kinda toist. . . ."

The Saint leaned elegantly against his tree, watching the advancing group, and there was a hint of genuine admiration in his eyes.

"A Boche, a Wop, and a Bowery Boy," he murmured. "Gee—that man Marius ought to be running the League of Nations!"

The three men marched a few more yards in silence; and they were almost opposite the Saint when the Bowery Boy spoke again.

"Who's bringin' down de goil?"

"Hermann"—the Boche answered with guttural brevity.

"She is-a da nice-a girl, no?" The Wop took up the running senti-mentally. "She remind-a me of-a da girl in Sorrento, 'oo I knew—"

"She sure is a classy skoit. But us poor fish ain't gotta break—it's de big cheese fer hers, sure. . . ."

They passed so close by the Saint that he could have reached out and knifed the nearest of them without an effort—and he did actually meditate that manoeuvre for a second, for he had a forthright mind. But he knew that one minor assassination more or less would not make much differ-ence, and he stood to lose more than he could hope to gain. Besides, any disturbance at that juncture would wreck beyond redemption the plan which he had just formed.

The League of Nations was descending the cliff stairway, the mutter of their voices growing fainter as they went. Simon took another look at the sea and saw that the ship's boat had halved its distance from the shore. And then, after one quick glance round to see if anyone was following on immediately behind the three who had passed on, he slipped out of his shelter and flitted down the steps in the wake of voices.

He could have caught them up easily, but he hung well behind. That cliff path was trickier country to negotiate than the smooth turf above; and a single loose stone, at close range, might tell good-night to the story in a most inconvenient and disastrous fashion. Also, one of the three might for some reason take it into his head to return, and the Saint thought he would like warning of that tergiversation. So he saw to it that they kept their lead, and walked with a delicacy that would have made Agag look like a rheumatic rhinoceros.

Then he found himself on the turn of the last zigzag, while the party below were debouching onto the sands. At the same moment, the ship's boat ran alongside a little jetty, which had been screened from his view when he looked down from the top of the cliff.

He paused there, thinking rapidly, and surveying the scenery.

The shore itself was destitute of cover for the twenty yards of sand that lay between the end of the path and the jetty; but the miscellaneous grasses and shrubs which grew thickly over the sloping cliff extended right down to the beginning of the sands, without any bare patches that he could see, and appeared to become even thicker before they stopped altogether. This was certainly helpful, but . . . He looked out towards the ship and stroked his chin thoughtfully. Then he gazed again at the jetty, where a man from the ship's boat was being helped up into the light of the lantern. Near that boat, alongside the wharf, but more inshore, something else rode gently on the water. . . . The Saint stiffened slowly, straining his eyes, with a kind of delirious ecstasy stealing through him. He was not quite sure—not quite—and it seemed too good to be true. . . . But, while he stared, the man who had got out of the boat, and the man with the lantern, and one other of the three who had come down from the house began to walk slowly towards the cliff path; and the man with the lantern walked on the outside by the edge of the jetty, and the light of the lantern turned speculation into certainty in the matter of the second craft which was moored by the wharf. It was, by the beard of the Prophet, an indisputable and incontrovertible outboard motorboat. . . .

The Saint drew a long lung-easing breath. . . . Too good to be true, but—"Oh, *Baby!*" sighed the Saint.

He was even able to ignore, for a short space, the disconcerting fact that this heaven-sent windfall coincided in the moment of its manifestation with a remarkably compensating disadvantage. For the third member of the reception committee was squatting on the wharf, talking to the boat's crew; and the other two were escorting the boat's passenger to the cliff stairway; and, at the same time as he perceived the movement of these events, Simon heard the sounds of a small party descending that same cliff stairway towards him.

Then he looked round and saw the lantern of the descending party bobbing down the second flight above him; he could distinguish two figures, one of them tall and the other one much shorter.

Slightly annoying. But not desperate. . . .

Reviewing the ground, he stepped lightly off the path, rounded a shrub, caught the stem of a young sapling, and drew himself silently up into the shadows. And it so happened that the two parties met directly beneath him; and he saw, as he had guessed, that the two who had descended after him were the man Hermann and Sonia Delmar.

The five checked their progress and gathered naturally into a small group, talking in an undertone. Sonia Delmar was actually outside the group; temporarily ignored. There was no need for her custodian to fear that she might duck out; Simon could see the cords that bound her wrists together behind her back, and the eighteen-inch hobble of rope between her ankles.

He was crouching where he was, with one arm locked about the slender trunk of the sapling that supported him precariously on the steep slope. The finger of his free hand stroked tenderly over the ground, and picked up a tiny pebble; aiming carefully, he lobbed the stone down.

It struck the girl's hands; but she did not move at once. Then the toe of one shoe kicked restlessly at the gravel under her feet—and if any of the men below had heard the stone fall he would have thought the sound was due to her own movements. The Saint raised his eyes momentarily to the stars above. It was classic. That girl, playing his own game for the first time in her life, so far as he knew, after she'd already walked in under the shadow of the axe as coolly as any qualified adventurer—even with the axe in the act of falling she could watch the subtlest refinements of that game. When any other girl would have been shaking at the knees, thinking hysterically of escape and rescue, she was calmly and methodically chalking her cue. . . .

And then, quite naturally and deliberately, she glanced round; and the Saint stood up out of the shadows so that he could be plainly seen.

She saw him. Even in that dim light he could make out the eager question in her face, and he knew that she must have seen his smile. He nodded, waved his hand, and pointed out to the waiting ship. Then he smiled again; and he crowded into that smile all that he could bring to it of reckless confidence. And when she smiled back, and nodded in semi-comprehension and utter trust, he could have thrown everything to the winds and leaped down to take her in his arms. But he did not. His right hand and arm went out and upwards in a gay cavalier gesture that matched his smile; and then he sank down again into the darkness as Hermann curtly urged her on down the slope and the other three resumed their climb.

III

BUT SHE HAD seen him; she knew that he was there, that there had been no mistake yet, that he had not betrayed her faith, that he was waiting, ready. . . . And that was something to have shown her. . . . And, as he dropped on his toes to the empty path, Simon remembered her fine courage, and Roger Conway, and many things. "Oh, glory," thought the Saint, sinking onto a convenient boulder, his hands on his knees. . . .

He saw her marched alone the jetty and lifted down into the boat. Hermann squatted down on his haunches beside the other man who was chatting with the crew; the flare of the match which he struck to light his pipe brought up in sharp relief the lean predatory face that the Saint could recall so easily. And Simon waited.

Clearly the boat's crew were delaying for the return of the man they had brought ashore—one of the ship's officers, probably, if not the captain himself. And much seemed now to depend on what had happened to Marius, which in its turn depended upon the crown prince's ablutionary programme. And to the answer to these dependent questions the Saint had still no clue. When Marius came slavering into Saltham with the tale of the desecrated royal toothpaste, no small excitement might have been expected. Therefore the Saint was sure that this had not happened before his own arrival on the scene; for, if it had, there would have been a seething cordon of the ungodly around the grounds of the house, and his own modest entrance would have been a much livelier affair—unless Marius had banked on what he knew of the Saint's former ignorance of the prince's language. And that was—well, a thin chance. . . . Of course, Marius might have arrived while the Saint was doing his midnight mountaineering act; but even so, Simon would have expected to hear at least the echoes of some commotion. He estimated that, taken by and large, he and his record combined were an ingredient that might without conceit expect to commotate any brew of blowed-in-the-glass ungodliness, and he would have been very distressed to find that the ungodly had failed to commote as per schedule. Therefore he was blushingly inclined to rule out the possibility. . . . But sooner or later the nocturnal tranquillity of that part of the county was bound to be rudely shattered, and there were more votes for sooner than later; and the quintessential part of the plot, so far as Simon Templar was concerned, was how soon—with a very wiggly mark after it to indicate importunate interrogation.

But presently, after an age of grim anxiety, he heard voices above him, and slipped discreetly off the path. Two men came down—one of them, apparently, the Boche whose dulcet tones had a little earlier been complaining about his enforced insomnia, for they spoke in German. The Saint listened interestingly for any reference to himself as they came nearer, but there was none. The Boche complained about the steepness of the path, about the darkness, about the food on which he was fed, and about his lack of sleep, and the ship's officer expressed perfunctory sympathy at intervals; they passed on. They, at all events, were unperturbed by anything they had heard up at the house.

Simon watched them saunter down the jetty and shake hands. The officer reentered the boat. A man in the bows pushed it off with a boat-hook. The crew bent to their oars.

In the light of the lanterns held by the men on the jetty Simon could see the girl looking back towards the cliff; but she could not have seen him even if he had stood out in the open. And then two of the men on the quay began to trudge back towards the cliff path.

Two of them. . . . Simon saw them pass beneath him, and frowned. Then he looked down to the shore again, seeking the third man, and could not find him. The footsteps and voices of the two who climbed grew fainter and fainter, and presently were lost altogether. They had passed over the top of the scarp; and still the third man had not followed.

Simon hesitated, shrugged, and descended again to the path. Whatever the third man was doing, he would have to take his chance. Time was getting short. The ship must have been ready to weigh anchor as soon as its compulsory passenger was on board; and besides—well, how soon . . . ?

And then, as he paused there, a very Saintly smile bared Simon's teeth in the darkness. For, if the third man was still lurking about on the shore—so much the better. His companions were gone, and the boat was some distance away . . . and the Saint was an efficient worker. The sounds of a slight scuffle need not be fatal. And the third man, whoever he was, could be used—very profitably and entertainingly used—in conjunction with that providential motorboat. . . .

Simon sped down the path like a flying shadow. As he rounded the last corner a stone dislodged by his foot went clinking over the side of the path and flurried into a bush. He heard a sharp movement at another point beneath him, and went on carelessly. Then a stocky figure loomed out of the dark directly in front of him.

"Chi va la?" rapped the startled challenge, in the man's own language; and Simon felt that the occasion warranted a demonstration of his own linguistic prowess.

"L'uomo che ha la penna della tua zia," he answered solemnly.

His feet grounded on the sand, a yard from the challenger; and, as the man opened his mouth to make some remark which was destined never to be given to the world, the Saint slashed a terrific uppercut into a jaw that was positively asking for it.

"Exit Signor Boloni, the Italian delegate," murmured the Saint complacently; and, stooping swiftly, he hoisted the unconscious man onto his shoulder and proceeded on his way thus laden.

IV

IN A FEW moments he stood on the jetty beside the motorboat, and there he dumped his burden. Then, like lightning, he stripped himself to the skin.

The Saint possessed a very elegant and extensive wardrobe when he was at home; but, on this occasion, its extensiveness was not at his disposal, and the elegance of the excerpt that he was wearing therefore became an important consideration. He was certainly going to get wet; but he saw no good reason why his clothes should get wet with him. Besides, he felt that it would be an advantage to preserve immaculate the outward adornments of his natural beauty: there was no knowing how much more that Gent's Very Natty was going to have to amble through before the dawn, and to have been forced to exchange any breezy badinage with Rayt Marius or Prince Rudolf while looking like a deep-sea diver whose umbrella had come ungummed at twenty fathoms would have cramped the Saintly style more grievously than any other conceivable circumstance.

Therefore the Saint stripped. His clothes were of the lightest, and he was able to make them all into one compact bundle, which he wrapped in his shirt.

Then he returned his attention to the motorboat. It was moored by two painters; and these he detached. A loose narrow floorboard taken from the bottom of the boat he lashed at right angles across the tiller, using strips of the Italian delegate's trousers, carved out with Belle, for the purpose; then, to the ends of this board, he fixed the ropes he had obtained, leaving them trailing in the water behind the boat. Finally, he deposited the Italian delegate himself in the sternsheets, propping him up as best he could with another couple of duckboards.

The Saint had worked with incredible speed. The boat which carried Sonia Delmar had not reached the side of the ship when Simon took hold of the motorboat's starting handle. With that he was lucky. The engine spluttered into life after a couple of pulls. And so, stark naked, with his bundle of clothes on his head and the sleeves of his shirt knotted under his chin to hold the bundle in place, the Saint slid into the water, holding one of his tiller ropes in each hand; and the motorboat swerved out from the jetty and began to pick up speed as Sonia Delmar was lifted onto the gangway of the waiting ship.

That crazy surf ride remained ever afterward as one of Simon Templar's brightest memories. The motorboat had a turn of speed that he had not anticipated; its creaming wake stung his eyes, half blinding him, and strangled his nostrils when he breathed; if he had not had fingers of steel his hold on the ropes by which it towed him would have been broken in the first two minutes. And with those very ropes he had to steer a course at the same time, an accurate course—with the hull of the boat in front of him blacking out most of his field of vision, and so much play on his crude steering apparatus that it was a work of art to do no more than prevent the tiller locking over on one side or the other and thereafter ceasing to function at all. Whereupon he would, presumably, have travelled round in a small circle till the petrol tank dried up. . . .

He found that the only way he could keep control of his direction was by travelling on a series of progressive diagonal tacks: otherwise it was impossible to keep his objective in view. Even then, the final rush would have to be a straight one. . . . The blinding stammer of the motor was a hellish affair. Long ago the men out on the water must have been asking questions. Probably the din could have been heard up at the house on the cliffs as well; and he wondered what that section of the unrighteous would make of it. . . . As he swung over on another tack—he had to do this very gently, for any vertical banking business would have been liable to upset the Italian delegate to stay put—he glimpsed the ship's boat hanging from the falls, clear of the water, and little knots of black figures clustered along the starboard rail. Surely they must be asking questions. . . .

He realized, suddenly, that it was time to attempt the last straight dash.

He sighted for it as best he could, rolled all his weight onto one rope for a moment, and then flattened out again. Now, if he hit the side of the ship the fishes would do themselves proud on what was left of him. . . . But he didn't hit. Far from it. Through a lashing lather of spray, he saw the anchor-chain flash past him, half a dozen yards away.

Not good enough. . . .

As he went by, he heard the faint shred of a shout from the deck above, and the Saintly smile twitched a trifle grimly at the corners of his mouth. Then the motorboat was speeding out to sea; and again he rolled his weight carefully onto one rope.

The roughness of the ropes was scorching the inside of his hands. The cords were too thin to be gripped comfortably, and his fingers were numbed and aching with the strain. In spite of his strength, he felt as if his arms were being torn from their sockets; and it seemed centuries since he had drawn a full free breath. . . .

The Saint set his teeth. It had got to be done this next time—he doubted whether he could hang on for a third attempt. Ordinary surf-riding was another matter, when you had a good board beneath you to skim the surface of the water; but when you were immersed yourself. . . . Again he sighted, turned the boat, and prayed. . . . And, as he did so, he heard, high and clear above the clamour of the engine, the sharp sound of a shot.

Well, that was inevitable—and that was what the Italian delegate was sitting in the boat for anyway.

"But what about us?" thought the Saint; and, at that moment, he felt the boat quiver against the ropes he held. "Here goes," thought the Saint, and relaxed his tortured hands. The cords whipped out of his grip like live things. Then the anchor-chain seemed to materialize out of space. It leaped murderously at his head; he grabbed desperately, caught, held it. . . .

As he hauled himself wearily out of the water, drawing great gulps of air into his bursting lungs, he saw the Italian delegate flop sideways over the tiller. The boat heeled over dizzily; then the Italian tumbled forward into the bilge, and the boat straightened up somehow, gathered itself, and headed roaring out to sea. A second shot cracked out from the deck.

Simon felt as if he had been stretched on the rack; but he dared not rest for more than a few seconds. This was his chance, while the attention of everyone on deck was focussed on the flying motorboat. Somehow he clambered upwards. If it had been a rope that he had to climb he could not have done it, for there seemed to be no strength left in his arms; but he was able to get his toes into the links of the chain, and only in that way could he manage the ascent. As he went higher, the bows of the ship cut off the motorboat from his view; but he heard a third shot, and a fourth. . . .

Then he was able to reach up and grip a stanchion. With a supreme effort, he drew himself up until he could get one knee over the side.

No one was looking his way; and, for all his weariness, he made no sound.

As he came over the rail, he saw the motorboat again, scudding towards the rising moon. A figure stood up in the boat, swaying perilously, waving frantic arms. Then it gripped the tiller, and the boat reeled over on its beam-ends and headed once more towards the ship.

The man must have been shouting; but whatever he shouted was lost in the snarl of the motor. And then, for the fifth time, a gun barked somewhere on the deck; and the Italian delegate clutched at his chest and went limply into the dark sea.

7

How Sonia Delmar Heard a Story, and Alexis Vassiloff Was Interrupted

SONIA DELMAR HEARD the shooting as she was hustled across the deck and up an outside companion. Before that, she had seen the speeding motorboat and the shape of the man crouched in the stern. The drone of its engine had rattled deafeningly across the waters as she was hurried up the gangway; she had heard the perplexed mutterings of her captors, without being able to understand what they said; and she herself, in a different way, had been as puzzled as they were. She had seen the Saint on the cliff path, and had understood from the signs he made that he was not yet proposing to interfere; after a fashion, she had been relieved, for so far she had gained no useful information. But she appreciated that, if he had meant to interfere, his chance had been then and there, on the cliff path, when he could have taken by surprise a mere handful of men who would have been additionally hampered by the difficulty of distinguishing friend from foe; and she wondered what could have made him elect instead to come so noisily against a whole boatload.

But these questions had no hope of a leisured survey at that moment; they rocketed hazily across the back of her conscience as she stumbled onto the upper deck. The two men in charge of her, at least, placed the mysterious motorboat second in their considerations, whatever their fellows might be doing. There was a quietly efficient discipline about everything that she had seen done that was unlike anything she had expected to find in such a criminal organization as Simon Templar had pictured for her. Nor had anything that she had read of the ways of crime prepared her for such an efficiency: the gangs on her native side of the Atlantic, by all reports, were not to be compared with this. Again came that vicious snap of the rifle on the lower deck; but the men who led her took no notice. She tripped over a cleat in the darkness, and one of the men caught her and pulled her roughly back to her balance; then a door was opened, and she barely had a glimpse of the lighted cabin within before she herself was inside it, and she heard the key turned in the lock behind her.

The howl of the motorboat grew steadily louder, and then died down again to a fading moan.

Crack! . . . Crack! . . .

The clatter of two more shots came to her ears as she reached an open porthole; and then she could see the boat itself and the swaying figure in the stern. She saw the boat turn and make for the ship again; and then came the last shot. . . .

Slowly she sank onto a couch and closed her eyes. She felt no deep emotion—neither grief, nor terror, nor despair. Those would come afterwards. But at the time the sense of unreality was too powerful for feeling. It seemed incredible that she should be there, on that ship, alone, alive, destined for an unknown fate, with her one hope of salvation lost in the smooth waters outside. Quite quietly she sat there. She heard the empty motorboat whine past, close by, for the last time, and hum away towards the shore. Her mind was cold and numb. When she heard a new sound in the night—a noise not unlike that of the motorboat, but more deep-throated and reverberating—she did not move. And when upon that sound was superimposed the thrum and clutter of steam winch forward, she opened her eyes slowly and felt dully surprised that she could see. . . .

Mechanically she took in her prosaic surroundings.

The cabin in which she sat was large and comfortably furnished. There were chairs, a table, a desk littered with papers, and one bulkhead completely covered with well-filled bookcases. One end of the cabin was curtained off; and she guessed that there would be a tiny bedroom beyond the curtain, but she did not move to investigate.

Presently she knelt up on the couch and looked up again. The ship was turning, and the dark coast swung lazily into view. Somewhere on the black line of land a tiny light winked intermittently for a while, and vanished. After a pause, the light flickered again, more briefly. She knew that it must have been a signal from the house on the cliffs, but she could not read the code. It would not have profited her to know that a question had been asked and answered and felicitations returned; for the answer said that the Saint was dead. . . .

She lay down again, and stared at the ceiling with blind eyes. She did not think. Her brain had ceased to function. She would have liked to weep, to fling herself about in a panic of fear; but though there was the impulse to do both, she knew that neither outlet would have been genuine.

That kind of thing was not in her. She could only lie still, in a paralyzing daze of apathy. She lost track of time. It might have been five minutes or fifty before the cabin door opened, and she turned her head to see who had come.

"Good-evening, Miss Delmar."

It was a tall man, weather-beaten of face and trimly bearded, in a smart blue uniform picked out with gold braid. His greeting was perfectly courteous.

"Are you the captain?" she asked; and he nodded.

"But I am not responsible for your present position," he said. "That is the responsibility of my employer."

"And who's he?"

"I am not at liberty to tell you."

He spoke excellent English; she could only guess at his nationality.

"I suppose," she said, "you know that you're also responsible to the American Government?"

"For you, Miss Delmar? I do not think I shall be charged."

"Also to the British Government—for murder."

He shrugged.

"There is no great risk, even of that accusation."

She was silent for a moment. Then she asked, casually: "And what's your racket—ransom?"

"You have not been informed?"

"I have not."

"Good. That was a question I came to ask."

He sat down at the desk and selected a thin cigar from a box which he produced from a drawer. "You have been brought here, frankly, in order that you may be married to a gentleman who is on board—a Mr. Vassiloff. The ceremony will be performed whether you consent or not; and if there should ever be a need to bring forward witnesses, we have those who will swear that you consented. I am told that it is necessary for you to marry Mr. Vassiloff—I do not know why."

II

THE NEWS DID not startle her. It came as a perfect vindication of the Saint's deductions; but now it had a grim significance that had been lacking before. Yet the sense of unreality that lay at the root of her inertia became by that much greater instead of less. She could not imagine that she was dreaming—not in that bright light, that commonplace atmosphere—but still she could not adjust herself to the facts. She had found herself speaking mechanically, as calmly as if she had been sitting in the drawing room of the American Embassy in London, carrying on the game exactly as she had set out to play it, as if nothing had gone amiss. Her conscious mind was stunned and insentient; but some blind, indomitable instinct had emerged from the recesses of her subconscious to take command, so that she amazed whatever logic was left sensible enough within her to be amazed.

"Who is this man Vassiloff?"

"I am not informed. I have hardly spoken to him. He has kept to his cabin ever since he came on board, and he only came out when we were—shooting. He is on the bridge now, waiting to be presented."

"Don't you even know what he looks like?"

"I have scarcely seen him. I can tell you that he is tall, that he wears glasses, that he has a moustache. He may be young or old—perhaps he has a beard—I do not know. When I have seen him he has always had the collar of his coat buttoned over his chin. I assume that he does not wish to be known."

"Do you even know where we're going?"

"We go to Leningrad."

"And then?"

"As far as you are concerned, that is a matter for Vassiloff. My own employment will be finished."

His manner was impeccably restrained and impeccably distant. It made her realize the futility of her next question before she asked it.

"Aren't you at all interested in the meaning of what you're doing?"

"I am well paid not to be interested."

"People have been punished for what you're doing. You're very sure that you're going to escape."

"My employer is powerful as well as rich. I am well protected."

She nodded.

"But do you know who I am?"

"I have not been told."

"My father is one of the richest men in America. It's possible that he might be able to do even more for you than your present employer."

"I am not fond of your country, Miss Delmar." He rose, deferential and yet definite, dismissing her suggestion without further speech, as if he found the discussion entirely pointless. "May I tell Mr. Vassiloff that he may present himself?"

She did not answer; and, with a faintly cynical bow, he passed to the door and went out.

She sat without moving, as he had left her. In those last few moments of conversation her consciousness had begun to creep back to life, but not at all in the way she would have expected. She was aware of the frantic pounding of her heart as the sole sign of a nervous reaction which she felt in no other way. But a queer fascination had gripped her, born, perhaps, of the utter hopelessness of her plight, a fantastic spell that subordinated every rational reflection to its own grotesque seduction. She was a helpless prisoner on that ship, weaponless, without a single human soul to stand by her, and every pulse of the rhythmic vibrations that she could feel beneath her was speeding her farther and farther from all hope of rescue; she was to be married with or without her consent to a man she had never seen, and whose very name she had only just heard for the first time; and yet she could feel nothing but an eerie, nightmare curiosity. The hideous bizarreness of the experience had taken her in a paralyzing hold; the stark certainty that everything that the captain had announced would inexorably follow in fact seemed to sharpen and vivify all her senses, while it stupefied all initiative; so that a part of her seemed to be detached and infinitely aloof, watching with impotent eyes the drama that was being enacted over herself. There was nothing else that she could do; and so, with that strange fatalism wrapping her in an inhuman impassivity she had only that one superbly insane idea—to see the forlorn game through to the bitter end, for what it was worth . . . facing the inevitable finale with frozen eyes. . . .

And, if she thought of anything else, she thought with a whimsical homesickness of a sunny room on a quiet Sunday morning, and the aromatic hiss and crackle of grilling bacon; and she thought she would like a cigarette. . . .

And then the door opened again.

It was not the captain. This man came alone—a man such as the captain had described, with the wide brim of a black velour overshadowing his eyes, and the fur collar of a voluminous coat turned up about his face.

"Good-evening—Sonia."

She answered quietly, with a soft contempt: "You're Vassiloff, I suppose?"

"Alexis."

"Once," she said, "I had a dog called Alexis. It's a nice name—for a dog."

He laughed, sharply.

"And in a few moments," he said, "you will have a husband of the same name. So are you answered."

He pushed a chair across to the couch where she sat, and settled himself, facing her, his hands clasped over his knees. Through his thick spectacles a pair of pale blue eyes regarded her fixedly.

"You are beautiful," he remarked presently. "I am glad. It was promised me that you would be beautiful."

When he spoke it was like some weird Oriental chant; his voice rose and fell monotonously without reference to context, and remained horribly dispassionate. For the first time the girl felt a qualm of panic, that still was not strong enough to shake her bleak inertia.

She cleared her throat.

"And who made this promise?" she inquired calmly.

"Ah, you would like to know!"

"I'm just naturally interested."

"It was an old friend of me." He nodded ruminatively, still staring, like a bearded mandarin. "Yess—I think Sir Isaac Lessing will be sorry to have lost you. . . ."

Then the nodding slowed up and stopped abruptly, and the stare went on.

"You love him—Sir Isaac?"

"Does that matter? I don't see what difference it makes—now."

"It makes a difference."

"The only difference I can see is that Sir Isaac Lessing had a few gentlemanly instincts. For instance, he did take the trouble to ask my permission before he arranged to marry me."

"Ah!" Vassiloff bent forward. "You think Sir Isaac is a gentleman? Yet he is an ememy of me. This"—he spread out one hand and returned it to his knee—"has been done because he is an enemy."

Sonia shrugged, returning the man's stare coldly. Her composed indifference seemed to infuriate Vassiloff. He leaned further forward, so that his face was close to hers, and a pale flame glinted over his eyes.

"You are ice, yess? But listen. I will melt you. And first I tell you why I do it."

He put his hand on her shoulder; and she recoiled from the touch; but he took no notice.

"Once," he said, in that crooning voice, "there was a very poor young man in London. He went to ask for work of a rich man. He was starving. He could not see the rich man at his office, so he went to the rich man's house, and there he see him. The rich man strike in his face, like he was dirt. And then, for fear the young man should strike him back, he call his servants, and say, 'Throw him out in the street.' I was that young man. The rich man is Sir Isaac Lessing.''

"I should call that one of the most commendable things Lessing ever did," said the girl gently.

He ignored her interruption.

"Years go by. I go back to Russia, and there are revolutions. I am with them. I see many rich men die—men like Lessing. Some of them I kill myself. But always I remember Lessing, who strike in my face. I promoted myself—I have power—but always I remember.''

Overhead, on the bridge, could be head the regular pacing of the officer of the watch; but in that brightly lighted cabin Sonia felt as if there was no one but Alexis Vassiloff on the ship. His presence filled her eyes; his sing-song accents filled her ears.

"Lessing makes money with the oil. I, also, make control of the oil. He does not remember me, but still he try to strike in my face—but this time it is in the oil. I, too, try to fight him, but I cannot. There are great ones with him. And then I meet a great one, and he becomes a friend of me, and I tell him my story. And he make the plan. First, he will take you away from Lessing and give you to me. He show me your picture, and I say—yess. That will make Lessing hurt. It is for the strike in the face he once give me. But that is not enough. I must make to ruin Lessing. And my friend make another plan. he say that when he tell Lessing you are with me, Lessing will try to make war. 'Now,' he say, 'I will make Lessing think that when he make war against you he will have all Europe with him; but when the war come he will find all the big countries fight among themselves, and they cannot take notice of the little country Lessing will use to make his war against you.' All this my friend can do, because he is a great one. He is greater than Lessing. He is Rayt Marius. You know him?''

"I've heard of him."

"You have heard of him? Then you know he can do it. Behind him there are other great ones, greater than there are behind Lessing. He show me his plans. He will send out spies, and make the big countries hate each other. Then, when we have take you, he send men to kill someone— the French President, perhaps—and there is the war. It is easy. It is just another Serajevo. But it is enough. And I have my revenge—I, Vassiloff—for the strike in the face. I will have Sir Isaac Lessing crawl to my feet, but I will not be merciful. And our Russia will be great also. The big countries will fight each other, and they will be tired; and when we have finished one little country we will conquer another, and we shall be victorious over all Europe, we of the Revolution. . . .''

The Russian's voice had risen to a higher pitch as he spoke, and the light of madness burned in his eyes.

Sonia watched him, listening, hypnotized. At no time before, even when she had heard and incredulously accepted the Saint's inspired deductions, had she fully grasped the immensity of the plot in which she had been made a pawn. And now she saw it in a blinding flash, and the vision appalled her.

As Vassiloff went on, the hideously solid facts on which his insanity was balanced showed up with greater and greater definition through his raving. It was here—all the machinery of which the Saint had spoken was there, and strains and stresses and counter-actions measured and calculated and balanced, every cog in the whole ghastly engine cut and ground and trued-up ready for Marius to play with as he chose. How the mechanism would be put together did not matter—whether Marius had lied to Vassiloff, or meant to lie to Lessing. The rocks had been drilled in their most vital parts, the charges loaded and tamped in, the fuses laid; the tremendous fact was that the Saint had been right—right in every prophecy, vague only in the merest details. The axe had been laid to the root of the tree. . . .

She saw the conspiracy then as the Saint himself had seen it, months before: intrigue and counter-plot, deception and deception again, and the fiendish forces that had been disentombed for this devil's sleight-of-hand. And she saw in imagination the unleashing of those forces—the tapping drums and the blast of bugles, the steady tramp of marching feet, the sonorous drone of the war birds snarling through the sky. Almost she could hear the earth-shaking reverberations of the guns, the crisp clatter of rifle fire; and she saw the swirling mists of gas, and men reeling and stumbling through hell; she had seen and heard these things for a dollar's worth of evening entertainment, in a comfortably upholstered chair. But the men there had been only actors, fighting again the battles of a generation that was already left behind; the men she saw in her vision were of her own age, men she knew. . . .

She hardly heard Vassiloff any more. She was thinking, instead, of that morning. ''Have we the right?'' Simon Templar had asked. . . . And she saw once again the sickening sway and plunge of the figure in the motorboat. . . . Roger Conway—where had he been? What had happened to him. He should have been somewhere around; but she had not seen him. And if he were not to be counted in it meant that no power on earth could prevent her vision coming true. . . . *"That'd mean we'd given Marius the game. . . ."*

Slowly, grotesquely, the presence of Alexis Vassiloff drifted in again upon her tempestuous thought.

His voice had sunk back to that eerie crooning note to which it had been tuned before.

"But you—you will not be like the others. You will stand beside me, and we will make a new empire together, you and I. You will like that?"

She started up.

"I'll see you damned first!"

"So you are still cold. . . ."

Hie arms went round her, drawing her to him. With her hands still securely bound behind her back she was at his mercy—and she knew what that mercy would be. She kicked at his legs, but he bore her down upon the couch; she felt his hot breath on her face. . . .

"Let me go—you swine——"

"You are cold, but I will melt you. I will teach you how to be warm—soft—loving. So——"

Savagely she butted her head into his face, but he only laughed. His lips stung her neck, and an uncontrollable shudder went through her. His hands clawed at her dress. . . .

"Are you ready, Mr. Vassiloff?"

The captain spoke suavely from the doorway, and Vassiloff rose unsteadily to his feet.

"Yess," he said thickly. "I am ready."

Then he leered down again at the girl.

"I go to prepare myself," he said. "It is perhaps better that we should be married first. Then we shall not be disturbed. . . ."

III

THE DOOR CLOSED behind him.

Without a flicker of expression, the captain crossed the cabin and sat down at his desk. He drew towards him a large book like a ledger, found a place in it, and left it open in front of him; then, from the box in his drawer, he selected another of his thin cigars, lighted it, and leaned back at his ease. He scarcely spared the girl a glance.

Sonia Delmar waited without speaking. She remembered, then, how often she had seen such situations enacted on the stage and on the screen, how often she had read of them! . . .

She found herself trembling; but the physical reaction had no counterpart in her mind. She could not help recalling all the stereotyped jargon that had been splurged upon the subject by a hundred energetic parrots. "A fate too horrible to contemplate"—"a thing worse than death." . . . All the heroines she had encountered faced the horror as if they had never heard of it before. She felt that she ought to have experienced the same emotions as they did; but she could not. She could only think of the game that had been thrown away—the splendid gamble that had failed.

At the desk, the captain uncrossed his legs and inhaled again from his cigar.

It seemed to Sonia Delmar that that little cabin was the centre of the world—and the world did not know it. It was hard to believe that in other rooms, all over the world, men and women were gathered together in careless comradeship, talking perhaps, reading perhaps, confident of a thousand to-morrows as tranquil as their yesterdays. She had felt the same when she had read that a criminal was to be executed the next day—that same shattering realization that the world was going on unmoved, while one lonely individual waited for dawn and the grim end of the world. . . .

And yet she sat upright and still, staring ahead with unfaltering eyes, buoyed with a bleak and bitter courage that was above reason. In that hour she found within herself a strength that she had not dreamed of, something in her breed that forbade any sign of fear—that would face death, or worse than death, with scornful lips.

And the door opened and Vassiloff came in.

Anything that he had done to "prepare" himself was not readily visible. He still wore his hat, and his fur collar was muffled even closer about his chin; only his step seemed to have become more alert.

He gave the girl one cold-blooded glance; and then he turned to the captain.

"Let us waste no more time," he said harshly.

The captain stood up.

"I have the witnesses waiting, Mr. Vassiloff. Permit me. . . ."

He went to the door and called two names curtly. There was a murmured answer; and the owners of the names came in—two men in coarse trousers and blue seamen's jerseys, who stood gazing uncomfortably about the cabin while the captain wrote rapidly in the book in front of him. Then he addressed them in a language that the girl could not understand; and, hesitantly, one of the men came forward and took the pen. The other followed suit. Then the captain turned to Vassiloff.

"If you will sign——"

As the Russian scrawled his name the captain spoke a brusque word of dismissal, and the witnesses filed out.

"Your wife should also sign," added the captain, turning back to the desk. "Perhaps you will arrange that?"

"I will." Vassiloff put down the pen. "I want to be left alone now—for a little while—with my wife. But I shall require to see you again. Where shall I find you?"

"I shall finish my cigar on the bridge."

"Good. I will call you."

Vassiloff waved his hand in a conclusive gesture; and, with a slightly sardonic bow, the captain accepted his discharge.

The door closed, but Vassiloff did not turn round. He still stood by the desk, with his back to the girl. She heard the snap of a cigarette case, the sizzle of a match; and a cloud of blue smoke wreathed up towards the ceiling. He was playing with her—cat and mouse. . . .

"So," he said softly, "we are married—Sonia."

The girl drew a deep breath. She was shivering, in spite of the warmth of the evening; and she did not want to shiver. She did not want to add that relish to his gloating triumph—to see the sneer of sadistic satisfaction that would flame across his face. She wanted to be what he had called her—ice. . . . To save her soul aloof and undefiled, infinitely aloof and terribly cold. . . .

She said swiftly, breathlessly: "Yes—we're married—if that means anything to you. . . . But it means nothing to me. Whatever you do to me, you'll never be able to call me yours—never."

He had unbuttoned his coat and flung it back; it billowed away from his wide shoulders, making him loom gigantically under the light.

"Perhaps," he said, "you think you love someone else."

"I'm sure of it," she said in a low voice.

"Ah! Is it, after all, that you were not being sold to Sir Isaac Lessing for the help he could give your father?"

"Lessing means nothing to me."

"So there is another?"

"Does that matter?"

Another cloud of smoke went up towards the ceiling.

"His name?"

She did not answer.

"Is it Roger Conway?" he asked; and a new fear chilled her heart.

"What do you know about him?" she whispered.

"Nearly everything, old dear," drawled the Saint; and he turned around, without beard, without glasses, smiling at her across the cabin, a mirthful miracle with the inevitable cigarette slanted rakishly between laughing lips.

8

How Simon Templar Borrowed a Gun, and Thought Kindly of Lobsters

"SAINT!"

Sonia Delmar spoke the name incredulously, storming the silence and the dream with that swift husky breath. And the silence was broken; but the dream did not break. . . .

"Well—how's life, honey?" murmured the dream; but no dream could have miraged that gay, inspiring voice, or the fantastic flourish that went with it.

"Oh, *Saint!*"

He laughed softly, a sudden lilt of a laugh; and in three strides he was across the cabin, his hands on her shoulders.

"Weren't you expecting me, Sonia?"

"But I saw them shoot you—"

"Me? I'm bullet-proof, lass, and you ought to have known it. Besides, I wasn't the man in the comic canoe. That was an Italian exhibit—a sentimental skeezicks with tender memories of the girl he left behind him in Sorrento. And I'm afraid his donna is completely mobile now."

She, too, was half laughing, trembling unashamedly now that the tense cord of suspense was snapped.

"Set me loose, Saint!"

"Half a sec. Has Vassiloff sung his song yet?"

"Yes—everything."

"And all done by kindness. . . . Sonia, you wonderful kid!"

"Oh, but I'm glad to see you, boy!"

"Are you?" The Saint's smile must have been the gayest thing in Europe. "But my show was easy! I came aboard off the motorboat several minutes before Antonio stopped the bit of lead that was meant for me. I'd got all my clothes with me, as good as new; but when I say that my own personal corpse was damp I don't mean peradventure, and I just naturally wandered into the nearest cabin in search of towels. I'd just got dried and dressed, and I was busy putting this beautiful shoeshine on my *chevelure* with a pair of gold-mounted hair-brushes that were lying around, when who should beetle in but old Popoffski himself. There followed some small argument about the tenancy of the cabin, but I got half a pillow into our friend's mouth before he could raise real hell. Then I trussed him up with the sash of his own dressing gown; and after that there was nothing for it but to take his place."

Simon's deft fingers were working on the ropes that bound the girl's hands, and she felt the circulation prickling back through her numbed wrists.

"I breezed in pretty much on the off-chance. I'd still got the beard I used this morning, and that was good enough for the moment, with Vassiloff's own coat buttoned round my chin and his glasses on my nose; but I couldn't trust to it indefinitely. The performance had to be speeded up—particularly, I had to find you. If Vassiloff hadn't laid his egg I should have had to go back to the cabin and perform a Caesarean operation with a hot iron, or something—otherwise the accident that I'd chosen his cabin for my dressing room might have mucked things badly. When I came in here and saw you and the skipper, I just said the first thing that came into my head, and after that I had to take my cue from him." Simon twitched the last turn of Manila from her wrists and grinned. "And there's the bitter blow, old dear; behold us landed in the matrimonial casserole. What sort of a husband d'you think I'll make?"

"Terrible."

"So do I. Now, if it had been Roger—"

"Simon—"

"My name," said the Saint cheerfully. "I know—I owe you an apology for that last bit of cross-examination before the unveiling of the monument, but the chance was too good to miss. The prisoner pleaded guilty under great provocation, and threw himself upon the mercy of the court. Now tell me about Marmaduke.''

He sank onto the couch beside her, flicking open his cigarette case. She accepted gratefully; and then, as quietly and composedly as she could, she told him all she had heard.

He was a surprisingly sober listener. She found that the flippant travesty of his real character with which he elected to entertain the world at large was a flimsy thing; and, when he was listening, it fell away altogether. He sat perfectly still, temporarily relaxed but still vivid in repose, alert eyes intent upon her face; the boyish effervescence that was his lighter charm bubbled down into the background, and the tempered metal of the man stood out alone and unmistakable. He only interrupted her at rare intervals—to ask a question that went to the heart of the story like aimed lightning, or to help her to make plain a point that she had worded clumsily. And, as he listened, the flesh and blood of the plot built itself up with a frightful solidity upon the skeleton that was already in his mind. . . .

It must have taken her a quarter of an hour to give him all the information she had gained; and at the end of that time the clear vision in the Saint's brain was as stark and monstrous as the thing he had imagined so few months ago—only a little while before he had thought that the ghost was laid for ever. All that she told him fitted faultlessly upon the bones of previous knowledge and speculation that were already his; and he saw the thing whole and real, the incarnate nightmare of a megalomaniac's delirium, gigantic, bloated, hideous, crawling over the map of Europe in a foul suppuration of greed and jealousy, writhing slimy tentacles into serene and precious places. The ghost was not laid. It was creeping again out of the poisoned shadows where it had grown up, made stronger and more savage yet by its first frustration, preparing now to fashion for itself a fetid physical habitation in the bodies of a holocaust of men. . . .

And the Saint was still silent, absorbed in his vision, for a while after Sonia Delmar had finished speaking; and even she could not see all that was in his mind.

Presently she said: "Didn't I find out enough, Simon? You see, I believed you'd been killed—I thought it was all over."

"Enough?" repeated the Saint softly, and there was a queer light in the steady sea-blue eyes. "Enough? . . . You've done more than enough—more than I ever dreamed you'd do. And as for thinking it was all over—well, lass, I heard you. I've never heard anything like it in my life. It was plain hell keeping up the act. But—I was just fascinated. And I've apologized. . . . But the game goes on, Sonia!''

II

THE SAINT STARED at the carpet, and for a time there was no movement at all in the cabin; even the cigarette that lay forgotten between his fingers was held so still that the trail of smoke from it went up as straight as a pencilled line. The low-pitched thrum of the ship's engines and the chatter of stirred waters about the hull formed no more than an undercurrent of sound that scarcely disturbed the silence.

Much later, it seemed, Sonia Delmar said: ''What happened to Roger?''

''I sent him back to London to find Lessing,'' answered the Saint. ''It came to me when I was on my way out here—I didn't see why Marius should just break even after we'd got you back, and bringing Ike on the scene seemed a first-class way of stirring up the stew. And the more I think of that scheme, after what you've told me, old girl, the sounder it looks to me. . . . Only, it doesn't seem big enough now—not for the kettle of hash we've dipped our ladles into.''

''How long ago was that?''

''Shortly before I heaved that rock at you.'' Simon glanced at his watch. ''By my reckoning, if we turned this ship round about now, we should all fetch up at Saltham around the same time. I guess that's the next move. . . .''

''To hold up the ship?''

The Saint grinned; and in an instant the old mocking mischief was back in his eyes. She knew at once that if the business of holding up the ship single-handed had been thrust upon him, he would have duly set out to hold up the ship single-handed—and enjoyed it. But he shook his head.

''I don't think it'll be necessary. I shall just wander up on to the bridge and make a few suggestions. There'll only be the captain and the helmsman and one officer to deal with; and the watch has just been changed, so no one will be butting in for hours. There's no reason why the rest of the crew should wake up to what's happening until we're home.''

''And when they do wake up?''

"There will probably be a certain amount of bother," said the Saint happily. "Nevertheless, we shall endeavor to retire with dignity."

"And go ashore?"

"Exactly."

"And then?"

"And then—let us pray. I've no more idea than you have what other cards Rayt Marius is wearing up his sleeve, but from what I know of him I'd say he was certain to be carrying a spare deck. We've got to check up on that. Afterwards—"

The girl nodded quietly.

"I remember what you said last night."

"R.I.P." The Saint laughed softly. "I guess that's all there is to it. . . . And then the last chapter, with you marrying Ike, and Roger and I starting a stamp collection. But who says nothing ever happens?"

And the lazy voice, the cool and flippant turning of the words, scarcely masked the sterner challenge of those reckless eyes.

And then the Saint rose to his feet, and the butt of his cigarette went soaring through the open porthole; and, as he turned, she found that the set of the fine fighting lips had changed again completely. But that was just pure Saint. His normal temperament held every mood at once: he could leap from grave to gay with pause or parley, as the fancy moved him, and do it in such a way that neither seemed inconsequent. And now Sonia Delmar looked at him and found in his changed face an answer to the question that she had no need to ask; and he saw that she understood.

"But all that's a long way off yet, isn't it?" he murmured. "So I think we'll go right ahead and stick up this hoary hooker for a start. Shall we?"

"We?"

"I don't see why you shouldn't come along, old dear. It isn't every day of your life that you have the chance to shove your oar into a spot of twenty-five carat piracy. Burn it!—what's the use of being raised respectable if you never go out for the frantic fun of bucking plumb off the rails and stepping off the high springboard into the dizzy depths of turpitude?"

"But what can I do?"

"Sit in a ring seat and root for me, sweetheart. Cheer on the gory brigand." Swiftly the Saint was replacing beard and glasses and settling Vassiloff's hat to a less rakish angle; and two blue devils of desperate delight danced in his eyes. "It seems to me," said the Saint, "that there's a heap more mirth and horseplay on the menu before we settle down to the speechifying. You ain't heard nothin' yet." And the Saint was buttoning the great fur collar about his chin with sinewy fingers that had an air of playing their own independent part in the surge of joyous anticipation that had suddenly swept up through every inch of his splendid frame. "And it seems to me," said the Saint, "that the best and brightest moments of the frolic are still ahead—so why worry about anything?"

He smiled down at her—at least, there was a Saintly glitter behind the thick glasses that he had perched upon his nose, though his mouth was hidden. And as Sonia Delmar stood up she was shaken by a great wave of unreasoning gratefulness—to the circumstances that made it necessary to switch off thus abruptly from the line of thought that he had opened up so lightly, and to the Saint himself, for making it so easy for her to turn away from the perilous path on which she might have stumbled. And she knew quite definitely that it was as deliberate and calculated a move as ever he made in his life, and he let her know it; yet that took none of the inherent gentleness from the gesture. And she accepted the gesture at it's worth.

"You're right," she said. "There's a long way to go yet. First the crew and then Marius. . . . Haven't you any idea of what you're going to do?"

"None. But the Lord will provide. The great thing is that we know we shall find Marius at Saltham, and that's bound to make the entertainment go with a bang."

"But how do you know that?"

"My dear, you must have heard the aëroplane—"

"Just after they shot the man in the motorboat?"

"Sure."

"I didn't realize—"

"And I thought you knew! But I didn't only hear it—I saw its lights and the flares they lit for it to land by. I haven't had time to tell you, but my trip to the Ritz this morning produced some real news—after I was supposed to have lit out for the tall timber. I left my card in Rudy's bathroom, and right up to the time that kite came down I was wondering how long it'd be before the Heavenly Twins found the memento and got busy. Oh, yes—Rayt Marius is at Saltham all right, and the best part of it is that he thinks I'm at the bottom of the deep blue sea with the shrimps nibbling my nose. There was a great orgy of signalling to that effect shortly after we upped anchor. So now you know why this is going to be no ordinary evening. . . . And with Roger and Ike rolling in on their cue, if all goes well—I ask you, is that or is that not entitled to be called a real family reunion?"

"If you think Roger will be able to bring Sir Isaac—"

"Roger has a wonderful knack of getting things done."

She nodded, very slowly.

"It *will* be—a reunion—"

"Yes." Simon took her hands. "But it's also a story—and so few people have stories. Why not live your story, Sonia? I'm living mine. . . ."

And for a moment, through all his fantastic disguise, she saw that his eyes were bright and level again, with a sober intentness in their gaze that she had yet to read aright.

III

BUT THE SAINT was away before she could speak. The Saint was the most elusive man on earth when he chose to be; and he chose it then, with a breath of careless laughter that took him to the door and left the spell half woven and adrift behind him. He was away with a will-o'-the-wisp of sudden mischievous mirth that he had conjured out of that moment's precipitous silence, waking the moment to surer hazards and less strange adventure.

"Strange adventure! Maiden wedded. . . ."

And the words of the song that he had sung so lightly twenty-four hours ago murmured mockingly in the Saint's ears as he paused for a second outside the cabin, under the stars, glancing round for his bearings and giving his eyes a chance to take the measure of the darkness.

"And it's still a great life," thought the Saint, with a tingle of unabated zest in his veins; and then he found Sonia Delmar at his shoulder. Their hands met. "This way," said the Saint softly, serenely, and steered her to the foot of the starboard companion. She went up after him. Looking upwards, she saw him in the foreground of a queer perspective, like an insurgent giant escalading the last topping pinnacle of a preposterous tower; the pinnacle of the tower swayed crazily against the spangled pageant of the sky; the slithering rush of invisible waters filtered up out of an infinite abyss. . . . And then she saw another figure, already bestriding the battlements of the last tower; then the Saint was also there, speaking with a quiet and precise insistence. . . . Then she also stood on the battlements of the swaying tower beside Simon Templar and the captain; and, as her feet found level boards, and the sea breeze sighed clearly to her face, the illusion of the tower fell away, and she saw the whole black bulk of the ship sheering through dark waters that were no longer infinitely far below, and over the dark waters was laid a golden carpet leading to the moon. And the captain's shoulders shrugged against the stars.

"If you insist—"

"It is necessary."

The moonlight glinted on the dull sheen of an automatic changing hands; then she saw the glimmer of a brighter metal, and the captain's start of surprise.

"Quietly!" urged the Saint.

But the captain was foolish. For an instant he stood motionless, then he snatched. . . . The Saint's steely fingers took him by the throat. . . .

Involuntarily the girl closed her eyes. She heard a swift rustle of cloth, a quiver of fierce muscular effort; and then, away from the ship and down towards the sea, a kind of choking sob . . . a splash . . . silence. . . . And she opened her eyes again, and saw the Saint alone. She saw the white flash of his teeth.

"Now his wives are all widows," said the Saint gently; and she shuddered without reason.

Other feet grated on the boards farther along the bridge; a man stood in the strip of light that came from the open door of the wheelhouse, pausing irresolute and half-interrogative. But the Saint was leaning over the side, looking down to the sea.

"Look!"

The Saint beckoned, but he never turned round. And the officer came forward. He also leaned over the side and looked down; but Simon stepped back. The Saint's right hand rose and fell, with a blue-black gleam in it. The sound of the dull impact was vaguely sickening. . . .

"Two," said the Saint calmly. The officer was a silent heap huddled against the rail. "And that only leaves the quartermaster. Who says piracy isn't easy? Hold on while I show you. . . !"

He slipped away like a ghost; but the girl stayed where she was. She saw him enter the wheelhouse, and then his shadow bulked across one lighted window. She held her breath, tensing herself against the inevitable outcry—surely such luck could not hold for a third encounter! . . . But there was no sound. He appeared again, calling her name, and she went to the wheelhouse in a trance. There was a man sprawled on the floor—she tried to keep her eyes from the sight.

"Shelling peas is hard labour compared to this," Simon was murmuring cheerfully; and then he saw how pale she was. "Sonia!" drawled the Saint reproachfully—"don't say it gives you the wiggles in your little tum-tum to see the skids going under the ungodly!"

"But it doesn't, really. Look." She held up her hand—it was as steady as his own. "Only I'm not so used to it as you are."

He chuckled.

"You'll learn," he said. "It's surprising how the game grows on you. You get so's you can't do without it. Why, if I didn't have plenty of this sort of exercise, I should come out all over pimples and take to writing poetry. . . . See here, sweetheart—what you want is something to do. Now, d'you think you could wangle this wheel effect, while I get active on something else?"

He was stripping off beard and glasses; hat and coat followed them into a corner. She was irresistibly reminded of a similar transformation that very morning in Upper Berkeley Mews; and with the memory of the action returned also a vivid memory of the atmosphere in which it had first been performed. And the Saint was smiling in the same way, as gay and debonair as ever; and his careless confidence was like a draught of wine to her doubts.

She smiled, too.

"If it's the same as it is on Daddy's yacht—"

"The identical article. . . . So I'll leave you to it, lass. Make a wide circle round, and hold her a fraction south of south-southeast—I took a peek at the bouncing binnacle before I strafed the nautical gent over there by the cuspidor, and I reckon that course ought to take us back to somewhere pretty near where we came from. Got it?"

"But where are you going?"

"Well, there's the third officer very busy being unconscious outside—at the moment—and Barnacle Bill under the spittoon isn't dead yet, either; and I'd be happier to feel that they wouldn't be dangerous when they woke up. I won't heave them overboard, because I'm rather partial to lobsters, and you know what lobsters are; but I guess I'll fossick around for some rope and do the next best thing."

"And suppose anyone comes—could you spare a gun?"

"I could." And he did. "That belonged to the late lamented. So long as you don't get rattled and shoot me by mistake everything will be quite all right. . . . All set, lass?''

"All set, Saint."

"Good enough. And I'll be right back." He had hitched the sleeping quartermaster onto his shoulder, and he paused on the return journey to touch one of the cool, small hands that had taken over the helm. "Yo-ho-ho," said the Saint smiling, and was gone like a wraith.

IV

HE DUMPED THE quartermaster beside the third officer, and went quickly down the companion to the upper deck. There he found a plentiful supply of rope, and cut off as much as he required. On his way back he reëntered the cabin in which he had found the girl, and borrowed a couple of towels from the bedchamber section beyond the curtains. That much was easy. He flitted silently back to the bridge, and rapidly bound and gagged the two unconscious men with an efficient hand; the task called for hardly any attention, and while he worked his mind was busy with the details of the job that would have to be done next—which was not quite so easy. But when his victims lay at his feet giving two creditable imitations of Abednego before entering the hot room, the Saint went back to the upper deck without seeing the girl again.

On his first trip he had located one of the most important items in the catalogue—the boat in which Sonia Delmar had been taken to the ship. It still hung over the side, obviously left to be properly stowed away the next morning; and, which was even more important, the gangway still trailed low down by the water, as a glance over the side had revealed.

"And a lazy lot of undisciplined sea-cooks that makes them out," murmured the Saint when he had digested all this good news. "But I'm making no complaints to-night!"

But for that providential slackness, the job he had to do would have been trebly difficult. Even so, it was none too easy; but it had come to him, during part of the buccaneering business on the bridge, that there was no real need to look forward to any superfluous unpleasantness on the return to Saltham, and that a resourceful and athletic man might very well be able to rule that ship's crew out of the list of probable runners for the Death-or-Glory Stakes. That was what the Saint was out to do, being well satisfied with the prospect of the main-line mirth and horseplay that lay ahead, without inviting the intrusion of any imported talent en route; and he proceeded to put the first part of this project into execution forthwith, by lowering the boat gingerly, foot by foot, from alternative davits, until it hung within a yard of the water. Then, with a rope from another boat coiled over his shoulder, he slid down the falls. One end of the rope he made fast in the bows of the boat; and then he spent some time adjusting the fenders. The other end of the rope he carried back with him on his return climb, stepping off on the main deck; and then, going down the gangway, he made that end fast to a convenient stanchion near the water level. Then he went back to the upper deck and paid out some more rope, even more gingerly at first, and then with a rush. The tackle creaked and groaned horrifically, and the boat finally hit the water with a smack that seemed loud enough to wake the dead; but the Saint had neither seen nor heard any sign of life on any of the expeditions connected with the job, and the odds were that the crew were all sleeping soundly in their bunks . . . unless an oiler or someone had taken it into his head to come up on deck for a breather about then. . . . But it was neck or nothing at that point, anyhow, and the Saint gave way on the falls recklessly until the ropes went slack. Then he leaned out over the side and looked down, and saw the boat floating free at the length of the rope by which he had moored it to the gangway; and he breathed a sigh of relief.

"Praise the Lord!" breathed the Saint; and meant it.

He belayed again, and made a second trip down the falls to cast off the blocks. The cockleshell bucked and plunged perilously in the ship's wash; but he noted with renewed satisfaction that it had sustained no damage in the launching, and was shipping no water in spite of its present maltreatment. Again he took a rest on the main deck on his way up and listened in silence for several seconds, but he heard no suspicious sound.

Back on the upper deck, it was the work of a moment to haul the falls well up and clear; and then he made his last trip down the gangway and bent his back to the hardest physical labour of the whole performance— the task of taking in the towrope until the boat was near enough to be easily reached from the grating at the bottom of the gangway. He got it done after a struggle that left every muscle aching, and left the boat less than half a fathom away, with all the slack of the towrope secured in a seamanlike sheep-shank. And then he went back to the bridge.

> *"Strange adventure that we're trolling:*
> *Modest maid and gallant groom—"*

The song came again to his lips as he turned into the wheelhouse and looked down the barrel of the girl's automatic.

"Put it away, honey," he laughed. "I have a tender regard for my thorax, and I've seen fingers less wobbly on the trigger!"

"But what have you been doing?"

"Preparing our getaway. Did I make a lot of noise?"

"I don't know—it seemed a frightful din to me—"

Simon grinned, and took out his cigarette case.

"It seemed the same to me, old dear," he remarked. "But I don't think anyone else noticed it."

With a lighted cigarette between his lips, he relieved her of the wheel, and told her briefly what he had done.

"In its way, it should be a little gem of an escape," he said. "We bring the old tub in as near to the shore as we dare, and then we turn her round again and step off. When the next watch comes on duty they find out what's happened; but the old tub is blinding through the North Sea at its own sweet will, and they won't know whether they're coming or going. Gosh, wouldn't you give a couple of years of your life to be able to listen in on the excitement?"

She moved away, and brought up a chair to sit beside him. Now she definitely felt that she was dreaming. Looking back, it seemed incredible that so much could have happened in such a short time—that even the present position should have come to pass.

"When do you think we should get back?" she asked.

"We ought to sight land in about an hour, the way I figure it out," he answered. "And then—more fun!"

The smiling eyes rested on her face, reading there the helpless incredulity that she could not hide from her expression any more than she could dispel it from her mind; and the Saint laughed again, the soft lilting laughter of sheer boyish delight that carried him through all the adventures that his gods were good enough to send.

"I meant to tell you it was a great life," said the Saint, with that lazy laughter dancing like sunshine through his voice. "Here you are, Sonia— have another of these cigarettes and tell me your story. We've got all the time in the world!"

9

How Simon Templar Looked for Land, and Proved Himself a True Prophet

BUT IT WAS the Saint who talked the most on that strange return voyage, standing up to the wheel, with the breeze through the open door fluttering his tie, and his shoulders sweeping wide and square against the light, and his tanned face seeming more handsome and devil-may-care and swaggeringly swift of line than ever.

She came to know him then as otherwise she might never have come to know him. It was not that he talked pointedly of himself—he had too catholic a range of interests to aim any long speech so monotonously— and yet it would be idle to deny that his own personality impregnated every subject on which he touched, were the touch never so fleeting. It was inevitable that it should be so, for he spoke of things that he had known and understood, and nothing that he said came at secondhand. He told her of outlandish places he had seen, of bad men that he had met, of forlorn ventures in which he had played his part; and yet it was nothing like a detailed autobiography that he gave her—it was a kaleidoscope, an irresponsibly shredded panorama of a weird and wonderful life, strewn extravagantly under her eyes as only the Saint himself could have strewn it, seasoned with his own unique spice of racy illusion and flippant phrase; and it was out of this squandered prodigality of inconsequent reminiscence, and the gallant manner of its telling, that she put together her picture of the man.

And, truly, he told her much of his amazing career, and even more of the ideals that had shaped it to the thing it was. And because she was no fool she gleaned from the tale a clear vision of the fantastic essence of the facts—of D'Artagnan born again without his right to a sword. . . .

"You see," he said, "I'm mad enough to believe in romance. And I was sick of this age—tired of the miserable little mildewed things that people racked their brains about, and wrote books about, and called Life. I'm not interested to read about maundering epileptics, and silly nym-

phomaniacs, and anaemic artists with a Message; and I'm not interested
to meet them. If I notice them at all, they make me want to vomit. There's
no message in life but the message of splendid living—which doesn't
mean crawling about on a dunghill yapping about your putrid little repres-
sions. Nor does it mean putting your feet on the mantelpiece and a soapily
beautific expression on your face, and concentrating on God in the image
of a musical-comedy curate of Aimee Semple McPherson. It means the
things that our forefathers were quite contented with, though their children
have got so damned refined that they really believe the said forefathers
would have been much 'naicer' if they'd spent their days picking over
the scabs on their souls instead of going in for the noisy vulgar things
they did go in for—I mean battle, murder, and sudden death, with plenty
of good beer and a complete callousness about blipping the ungodly over
the beezer. The low-down shocker is a decent and clean and honest-to-
God form of literature, because it does deal with things that have a right
to occupy a man's mind—a primitive chivalry, and damsels in distress,
and virtue triumphant, and a wholesale slaughter of villains at the end,
and a real fight running through it all. It mayn't be true to life as we
know it, but it ought to be true, and that's why it's the best stuff for
people to read—if they must read about things instead of doing them.
Only I preferred to do them. . . .''

And he told her other things, so that the vision grew even clearer in
her mind—that vision of a heroic revolt against circumstance, of a huge
and heroic impatience against the tawdry pusillanimity that had tried and
failed to choke his spirit, of a strange creed and a challenge. . . . And
with it all there was a lack of bitterness, a joyous fatalism, that lent
the recital half its glamour; the champion of lost causes fought with a
smile. . . .

"Of course," he said, "it makes you an outlaw—in spirit as well as
in fact. But that again seems worth while to me. Isn't the outlaw one of
the most popular figures in fiction? Isn't Robin Hood every schoolboy's
idol? There's a reason for everything that people love, and there must
be a reason for that—it must be the response of one of the most fundamental impulses of humanity. And why? For the same reason that Adam
fell for the apple—because it's in the nature of man to break laws—
because there's no real difference between the thrill of overthrowing a
legitimate obstacle and the thrill of overthrowing a legitimate thou-shalt-
not. Man was given legs to walk the earth; and therefore, out of divine
cussedness of his inheritance, he chooses his heroes, not from the men
who walk superlatively well, but from the men who trespass into the

element for which they were never intended, and fly superlatively well. In the same way, man was also given moral limitations by his ancestors after God Almighty; and therefore he reserves his deepest and most secret admiration for those who defy those limitations. He would like to do it himself, but he hasn't the courage; and so he enjoys the defiance even more when it's done for him by someone else. But compare that pleasure with the pleasure of the outlaw himself, when he chooses his outlawry because he loves it, and goes forth into the wide world to rob bigger and better orchards than he ever dreamed of when he was a grubby little urchin with a feather in his cap!''

"Yes, but the end of it!''

"The end?'' said the Saint, with far-away eyes and a reckless smile. "Well—

> 'What gifts hath Fate for all his chivalry?
> Even such as hearts heroic oftenest win:
> Honour, a friend, anguish, untimely death.'

And yet—I don't know that that's a bad reward. . . . Do you remember me telling you about Norman Kent? I found his grave when I came back to England, and I had those lines carved over it. And do you know, I've often thought I should be proud to have earned them on my own.''

He could talk like that with fresh blood upon his hands and his heart set upon another killing! For a moment the girl felt that it could not be true—she could not be sitting there listening to him with no feeling of revulsion for such a smug hypocrisy. But it was so. And she knew, at the same time, that that charge would not have been true—his simple sincerity was as natural as the half smile that went with the words.

So they talked. . . . And the Saint opened up for her a world of whose existence she had never known, a world of flamboyant colours and magnificently medieval delights. His magic made her see it as he saw it—a rich romance that depended on no cloaks or ruffles or other laboriously picturesque trappings for its enchantment, a play of fierce passions and grim dangers and quixotic loyalties, a tale that a man had dreamed and gone out to live. It was Gawain before the Grail, it was Bayard on the bridge of Garigliano, it was Roland at the gates of Spain; a faith that she had thought was dead went through it all, a thread of fairy gold with power to transmute all baser metals that it touched. Thus and thus he showed her glimpses of the dream; and he would have shown her more; but all at once she faltered, she who from the first had matched his stride so easily, she saw a step that he had deliberately missed, and she could not be silent. She said: "Oh, yes, but there are other things—in your own life! Even Robin Hood had to admit it!"

"You mean Maid Marian?"

"Roger told me. I asked him."

"About Patricia?"

"Yes."

The Saint gazed across the tiny cabin; but he could not see beyond the windows.

"Patricia—happened. She came in an adventure, and she stayed. She's been more to me than anyone can ever know."

"Do you love her?"

The Saint turned.

"Love?" said the Saint softly. "What is love?"

"You should know," she said.

"I've wondered."

Now they had been talking for a long time.

"Have you never been in love?" she asked.

The Saint drew back his sleeve and looked thoughtfully at his watch.

"We ought to be getting near land," he said. "Would you mind taking over the wheel again, old dear, while I go and snoop round the horizon?"

II

HE WAS GONE for several minutes; and when he came back it was like the return of a different man. And yet, in truth, he had not changed at all; if anything, he was an even more lifelike picture of himself. It was the Saint as she had first met him who came back, with a Saintly smile, and a Saintly story, and a spontaneous Saintly mischief rekindling in his eyes; but that very quintessential Saintliness somehow set him infinitely apart. Suddenly, in a heart-stopping flash of understanding, she knew why. . . .

"Do they keep a lookout on any of your father's yachts?" he drawled. "Or don't they do any night work?"

"A lookout? I don't know."

"Well, they certainly stock one of this blistered *buque*, as they do on any properly conducted ship, but blow me if I hadn't forgotten the swine!"

"Then he must have heard you lowering that boat!"

The Saint shook his head. His smile was ridiculously happy.

"Not he! That's just one more point we can chalk up to ourselves for the slovenliness of this bunch of Port Mahon sodgers. He must have been fast asleep—if he hadn't, we'd have known all about him before now. But he woke up later, by the same token—I saw him lighting a cigarette up in the bows when I went out on the bridge. And it was just as well for us that he did take the idea of smoking a cigarette at that moment, for there was land on the starboard bow as plain as the hump on a camel, and in another few minutes he couldn't have helped noticing it."

"But what shall we do?"

Simon laughed.

"It's done, old darling," he answered cheerfully, and she did not have to ask another question.

He lounged against the binnacle, a fresh white cylinder between his lips, his lighter flaring in his hand. The adventure had swept him up again: she could mark all the signs. The incident of which he had returned to speak so airily was a slight thing in itself, as he would have seen it; but it had turned a subtle scale. Though he lounged there so lazily relaxed, so easy and debonair, it was a dynamic and turbulent repose. There was nothing about it of permanence or even pause: it was the calm of a couched panther. And she saw the mocking curve of the eager fighting lips, the set of the finely chiselled jaw, the glimmer of laughter in the clear eyes half-sheathed by languid lids; and she read his destiny again in that moment's silence.

Then he straightened up; and it was like the uncoiling of tempered steel. His hand fell on her shoulder.

"Come and have a look," he said.

She secured the wheel amidships and followed him outside.

The wind touched her hair, cool and sweet as a sea nymph's breath; it whispered in the rigging, a muted chant to the rustle and throb of the ship's passage. Somewhere astern, between the bridge and the frayed white feather of their wake, the rattle and swish of a donkey engine shifting clinker jarred into the softness of the night. The sky was a translucent veil of purple, spangled with silver dust, a gossamer canopy flung high above the star-spearing topmasts, with a silver moon riding between yardarm and water. And away ahead and to her right, as the Saint had prophesied, a dark line of land was rising half a hand's-breath from the sea. . . .

She heard the Saint speaking, with a faint tremor of reckless rapture in his voice.

"Only a little while now and then the balloon! . . . I wonder if they've all gone to bed, to dream about my obituary notice in the morning papers. . . . You know, that'd make the reunion too perishingly perfect for words—to have Angel Face trying to do his stuff in a suit of violently striped pajamas and pink moccasins. I'm sure Angel Face is the sort of man who *would* wear striped pajamas," said the Saint judicially. . . .

It did not occur to her to ask why the Saint should take the striping of pajamas as such an axiomatic index of villainy; but she remembered, absurdly, that Sir Isaac Lessing had a delirious taste in stripes. They had been members of the same house party at Ascot that summer, and she had met him on his way back from his bath. . . . And Sonia said abruptly: "Aren't you worried about Roger?"

"In a way. . . . But he's a great lad. I trained him myself."

"Did he—think the same as you?"

"About the life?"

"Yes."

Simon leaned on the rail gazing out to the slowly rising land.

"I don't know," he said. "I'm damned if I know. . . . I led him on, of course, but he wasn't too hard to lead. It gave him something to do. Then he got tied up with a girl one time, and that ought to have been the end of him; but she let him down rather badly. After that—maybe you'll understand—he was as keen as knives. And I can't honestly say I was sorry to have him back."

"Do you think he'll stay?"

"I've never asked him, old dear. There's no contract—if that's what you mean. But I do know that nothing short of dynamite would shift him out of this particular party, and that's another reason why I'm not fretting myself too much about him tonight. You see, he and I and Norman were the original Musketeers, and—well, I guess Roger wants to meet Rayt Marius again as much as I do. . . ."

"And you mean to kill Marius?" said the girl quietly.

The Saint's cigarette end glowed brighter to a long, steady inhalation, and she met the wide, bland stare of Saintly eyes.

"But of course," he said simply. "Why not?"

And Sonia Delmar made no answer, turning her face again towards the shore. Words blazed through her brain; they should have come pelting—but her tongue was tied. He had shown her the warning, made it so plain that only a swivel-eyed half-wit could have missed it: "No

ENTRY—ONE WAY STREET," it said. And not once, but twice, he had edged her gently off the forbidding road, before her own unmannered obstinacy had pricked him to the snub direct. Yet he had broken the strain as easily and forthrightly as he had broken the spell; by now the entire circumstance had probably slipped away to the spacious background of his mind. He was as innocent of resentment as he was innocent of restraint; he pointed her retreat for the third time with no whit less of gentle grace; and she could not find the hardihood to breach the peace again.

III

THE SHIP PLOUGHED on through a slow swell of dark shining steel; and the Saint's lighter gritted and flared again in the gloom. His soft chuckle scarcely rose above the sigh of the breeze.

"If you want to powder your nose or anything, Sonia," he murmured, "this is your chance. I guess we'll be decanting ourselves in a few minutes now. We don't want to drive this gondola right up to the front door—I've no idea what the coast is like around here, and it might be infernally awkward to run aground at the critical moment."

"And even then we don't know where we are," she said.

"Well I'm not expecting we'll find ourselves a hundred miles away, and the nearest signpost will give us our bearings. . . . Glory be! Do you know, old dear?—I believe I shall be more interested in Marius's pantry than in his pajamas when we do arrive!"

He had so many other things to think about that he was only just becoming aware that he had gone through a not uneventful day on nothing but breakfast and a railway-station sandwich; and when the Saint developed an idea like that he never needed roller skates to help him catch up with it. After another wary glance at the land he wandered off the bridge in search of the galley; and in a few minutes he was back, with bulging pockets and a large sandwich in each hand. Even so, he had run it rather fine—the shore was looming up more quickly than he had thought.

"Here we are, che-ild—and off you go," he said briskly. "The orchestra's tuned up again, and we're surely going to start our symphony right now." He grinned, thrusting the sandwiches into her hands. "Paddle along down the gangway, beautiful, and begin gnawing bits out of these; and I'll be with you as soon as I've ported the plurry helm."

"O.K., Simon. . . ."

Yet she did not go at once. She stood there facing him in the starlight. He heard her swift breath, and a puzzled question shaped itself in his mind, on the brink of utterance; but then, before he could speak, her lips brushed his mouth, very lightly.

Then he was alone.

"Thank you, Sonia," whispered the Saint.

He knew there was no one to hear.

Then he went quickly into the wheelhouse; and his hands flashed over the spokes as he put the wheel hard over. And once again he remembered his song:

> *"Modest maiden will not tarry;*
> *Though but sixteen year she carry,*
> *She must marry, she must marry,*
> *Though the altar be a tomb—"*

The Saint smiled crookedly.

For a space he held the wheel locked over, judging his time; and then he went out again onto the bridge. The line of land was slipping round to the starboard quarter, dangerously near. He went back and held the wheel for a few moments longer; when he emerged for a second survey the coast was safely astern, and he permitted himself a brief prayer of contented thanksgiving.

The quartermaster and the third officer, at the starboard end of the bridge, had both returned to life. Simon observed them squirming in helpless fury as he made for the companion, and paused to sweep them a mocking bow.

"*Bon soir, mes enfants,*" he murmured. "Remember me to Monsieur Vassiloff."

He sped down to the upper deck to the cabin below. His business there detained him only for a matter of seconds; and then he raced down another companion to the main deck. Every second lost, now that the ship was headed away from the shore, meant so much more tedious rowing; and the Saint, when pruning down an affliction of that kind of toil, was in the habit of moving so fast that a pursuing jack rabbit would have suffocated in his dust.

The girl was waiting at the foot of the gangway.

"Filled the aching void, baby? . . . Well, stand by to make the jump when I give the word. It's a walk-over really—but don't lose your nerve, because I shan't be able to hold the boat for ever.''

He dropped on one knee, locking one arm round the lowest hand-rail stanchion and gripping the towrope with his other hand. Inch by inch he edged the boat up to the grating on which they stood, until it was plunging dizzily through the wash only a foot away.

''Go!'' said the Saint through his teeth; and she went.

He saw her stumble as the boat heaved up on a vicious flurry of water, and held his breath; but she fell inside the boat—though only just—with one hand on the gunwale and the other in the sea. He watched her scramble away towards the stern; and then he let go the slack of the rope, buttoned his coat, and leaped lightly after her.

A loose oar caught him across the knees, almost bringing him down; but he found his balance, and pivoted round with Belle flashing in his hand. Once, twice, he hacked at the straining rope, and it parted with a dull twang. The side of the ship seemed to gather speed, slipping by like a huge moving wall.

''Hallelujah,'' said the Saint piously.

The transhipment had been a merry moment, in its modest way, as he had known all along it would be, though he had characteristically refused to grow any gray hairs over it in anticipation. And in this case his philosophy was justified of the result.

He waved a cheery hand to the girl, and clambered aft. As he flopped onto a thwart and started to unship a pair of oars the black bulge of the steamer's haunches went past him; so close that he could have put out a hand and touched it; and the flimsy cockleshell, slithering into the unabated maelstrom of the ship's wake, lurched up on its tiller and smashed down into a seething trough with a report like a gunshot. An undercarry of fine spray whipped into his eyes. ''Matchless for the complexion,'' drawled the Saint, and dipped the first powerful oar.

The lifeboat yawed round, reeling back into easier water. A few strong pulls, and the merry moment was over altogether.

''Attaboy. . . .!''

He rested on his oars, with the frail craft settling down under him to comparative equilibrium, and carefully mopped the salt spume from his face. Over the girl's shoulder he could watch the shadowy hull of the departing ship sliding monstrously away into the darkness. The steady pulsebeats of its engines came more and more faintly to his ears—fainter, very soon, than the booming and boiling of its wash against the coast. . . .

The Saint reached forward, lifted a battered sandwich from the girl's lap, and took a large contented bite.

"Feelin' good again, lass?"

"All right now, Big Chief."

"That's the spirit." All the Saint's buoyant optimism reached her through his voice. "And now you'd better get gay with those vitamins, old dear, while I do my Charon act. You can't keep your end up on an empty stomach—and this wild party is just getting into its stride!"

And, with his mouth full, Simon bent again to the oars.

IV

IT WAS A stiff twenty minutes' pull to the shore, but the Saint took it in his night's work cheerfully. It gave him a deep and enduring satisfaction to feel his muscles limbering up to the smooth rhythm of the heavy sweeps; and the fact that the boat had never been designed for one-man sculling practice robbed him of none of his pleasure. The complete night's party wasn't everyone's idea of a solo piece, anyway, if it came to that; but the Saint wasn't kicking. He was essentially a solo performer; and, if the circumstances required him to turn himself into a complete brass band—well, he was quite ready to warm himself up for the concert. So he rowed with a real physical enjoyment of the effort, and when the boat grounded at last, with a grating bump, there was a tingle of new strength rollicking joyously through every inch of his body.

"This way, sweetheart!"

He stood up in the bows. Fortunately the beach shelved steeply; watching his chance with the ebb of a wave he was able to jump easily to dry land. The girl followed. As her feet touched the shingle he caught her up and swung her bodily out of reach of the returning water, and stood beside her, his hands on his hips.

"Home is the sailor, home from the spree. . . . And now, what price Everest?"

With a hand on her arm he steered her over the stones. Something like a low wall rose in front of them. He lifted her to the top of it like a feather, and joined her there himself a moment later; and then he laughed.

"Holy Haggari—this is indubitably our evening!"

"Why—do you know where we are?"

"That's more than I could tell you. But I do know that there's going to be no alpine work. Pass down the car, Sonia!"

The land reared up from where they stood—not the scarp that he had expected, but a whale's back, overgrown with stunted bushes. They moved on in a steady climb, the Saint's uncanny instinct picking a way through the straggling obstacles without a fault. For about fifty yards the slope was steep and the foothold precarious; then, gradually, it began to flatten out gently for the summit. Their feet stumbled off the rubble onto grass. . . .

He stopped by a broken-down fence at the top of the climb to give the girl a breather.

Eighty feet below, the sea was like a dark cloth laid over the floor of the world; and over the cloth moved two steady points of luminance— the masthead lights of the ship that they had left. To right and left of them the coast was shrouded in unbroken obscurity. Behind them, the land fell smoothly away in an easy incline, rising again in the distance to the line of another hill, a long slow undulation with one lonely spangle of light on its farthest curve.

"Where there's a house there's a road," opined the Saint. "We may even find a road before that, but we might as well head that way. Ready?"

"Sure."

He picked her up lightly in his arms and set her down on the other side of the fence. In a moment they were pushing on again together.

His zest was infectious. She found that the spirit of the adventure was gathering her up again, even as it had gathered up the Saint. Reason went by the board; the Saint's own fantastic delight took its place. She managed a glance at the luminous dial of her wrist watch, and could have gasped when she saw the time. A truly comprehensive realization of all that she had lived through in a day and two half-nights was only just beginning to percolate into her brain, and the understanding of it dazed her. In four circuits of the clock she had lived through an age, and yet with no sense of incongruity until that moment; her whole life had been speeded up in one galvanic acceleration, mentally and emotionally as well as in event, and somewhere in that fabulous rush she had found something that would have amazed the Sonia Delmar of a few days ago.

Long ragged grasses rustled about their ankles. They dropped into a hollow, rose again momentarily, faced a hedge; but the Saint found a gap for them as if he could see as clearly in the dark as he could have seen by daylight. Then they plodded over a ploughed field. Once she stumbled, but he caught her. He himself had an almost supernatural sense of country; in the next field he checked her abruptly and guided her round a fallen tree that she would have sworn he could not have been told of by his eyes. Came another hedge, a ditch, and a field of corn; he found a straight path through it, and she heard him husking a handful of ears as he walked.

"It's not even Sunday any longer," he remarked, "so we shan't be bawled out."

And once again she was bewildered by a mind that could remember such pleasant far-off things at such a time—Scribes and Pharisees, old family Bibles, fields of Palestine!

Presently they came to a gate; the Saint ran his fingers lightly along the top, feeling for wire; then he stood still.

"What is it?" she asked.

"The road!"

He might have been Cortés at gaze before the Pacific; his ravishment could not have been greater.

He vaulted over; she followed more cautiously, and he lifted her down, with a breath of laughter. They went on. Road he might have called, but it was really no more than a lane; yet it was something—a less nerve-racking surface for her feet, at least. For about half a mile they took its winding course, until she had lost her bearings altogether. With that loss she lost also an iota of the fickle enthusiasm that had helped her over the fields; about a road, or even a lane, there was a brusque reminder of more prosaic atmospheres and more ordinary nights. And it was definitely the threshold of a destination. . . .

But Simon Templar was happy; as he walked he hummed a little tune; she could feel, as by a sixth sense, the quickened spring in his step, though he never set a pace that would have spent her endurance. His presence was even more vital for this restraint. For the destination and the destiny were his own; and she knew that there was a song in his heart as well as on his lips, an exultation that no one could share.

So they were following the lane. And then, of a sudden, he stopped, his song stopping with him; and she saw that the lane had at last brought them out upon an unquestionable road. She saw the telegraph poles reaching away on either side—not very far, for they stood between two bends. But it was a road. . . .

"I don't see a signpost," she remarked dubiously. "Which way shall we—"

"Listen!"

She strained her ears, and presently she was able to pick up the sound he had heard—the purr of a powerful car.

"Who cares about signposts?" drawled the Saint. "Why, this bird might even give us a lift—it might even be Roger!"

They stood by the side of the road, waiting. Slowly the purr grew louder. Simon pointed, and she saw the reflection of the headlights as a pale nimbus in the sky; then, suddenly a clump of trees stood out black and stark against a direct glare.

"Stand by to glom the Saltham Limited!"

The Saint had slipped out into the middle of the road. Beyond him, at the next bend in the road, a hedge and a tree were picked out in a strengthening shaft of light. The voice of the car was rising to a querulous drone. Then, all at once, the light began to sweep along the hedge; then, in another instant, it blazed clear down the road itself, corrugating the tarmac with shadows; and the Saint stood full in the centre of the blinding beam, waving his arms.

She heard the squeal of the brakes as he stepped aside; and the car slid past with an expiring swish of wind, and came to rest a dozen yards beyond.

The Saint sprinted after it, and Sonia Delmar was only just behind him.

"Could you tell me—"

"*Ja!*"

The monosyllable cracked out with a guttural swiftness that sent the Saint's hand flying to his hip, but the man in the car already had him covered. Simon grasped the fact—in time.

But the girl was not a yard away, and she also had a gun. Simon tensed himself for the shot. . . .

"Put up your hands, Herr Saint."

There was a note of leering triumph in the harsh voice, and the Saint, blinking the last of the glare of the headlights out of his eyes, recognized the man. Slowly he raised his hands, and his breath came in a long sigh.

"Bless my soul!" said the Saint, who was never profane on really distressing occasions. "It's dear old Hermann. And he's going to give us our lift!"

10

How Sir Isaac Lessing Took Exercise, and Rayt Marius Lighted a Cigar

ROGER CONWAY'S FOOT shifted off the accelerator and trod urgently upon the brake, and the Hirondel skidded to a protesting standstill.

"We've arrived," said Roger grimly.

The man beside him glanced at the big iron gates a few yards down the road and gained one momentary glimpse of them before the headlights went out under Roger's hand on the switch.

"This is the place?" he asked.

"It is."

"And where is your friend?"

"If I were a clairvoyant, Sir Isaac, I might be able to tell you. But you saw me get out and look for the message where he arranged to leave one if he could—and there was no message. That's all I know, except—— Have you ever seen a man shot through the stomach, Sir Isaac?"

"No."

"You probably will," said Roger; and Lessing was silent.

He had no idea why he should have been silent. He knew that he ought to have said things—angry and outraged and ordinary things. He ought to have been saying things like that all the way from London. But, somehow, he hadn't said them. He'd certainly started to say them, once, two hours ago, when he had been preparing his second after-dinner Corona, and this curt and crazy young man had forced his way past butler and footman and penetrated in one savage rush to the sanctum sanctorum of the Oil Trade; he had nobly gone on trying to say them for a while after that, while the butler and the footman, torn between duty and discretion, had wavered apoplectically before the discouragement of the automatic in the curt and crazy young man's hand; and yet . . . Somehow that had been as far as he'd got. The young man had had facts. The young man, compelling audience at the business end of his Webley, had punched those facts home one on top of the other with the shattering effect of a procession of mule kicks; and the separate pieces of that preposterous jig-saw had fitted together without one single hiatus that Sir Isaac Lessing could discover—and he was a man cynically practised at discovering the flaws in ingenious stories. And the whole completed edifice, fantastic as were its foundations, and delirious as were the lines on which it reared itself, stood firm and unshakable against the cyclone of reasonable incredulity that he loosed upon it when he got his turn. For the young man spoke freely of the Saint; and that name ran through the astounding structure like a web-work of steel girders, poising its most extravagant members, bearing it up steadfast and indefeasible against the storm. And the climax had come when, at the end of narrative and cross-examination, the crazy young man had laid his gun on the table and invited the millionaire to take his choice—Saltham or Scotland Yard. . . .

"Come on," snapped Roger.

He was already out of the car, and Lessing followed blindly. Roger had his finger on the bell beside the gate when Lessing caught up with him—Lessing was not built for speed. He stood beside his guide, breathing heavily, and they watched a window light up in the cottage that served for a lodge. A grumbling figure came through the gloom to the other side of the gates.

"Who is that?"

"A message for the prince."

"He is not here."

"I said *from* the prince. Open quickly, fool!"

A key grated in the massive lock, and, as the gate swung open on creaking hinges, Roger slipped through in a flash. The muzzle of his gun jabbed into the man's ribs.

"Quiet," said Roger persuasively.

The man was very quiet.

"Turn round."

The gatekeeper obeyed. Roger reversed his gun swiftly, and struck accurately with the butt and with intent to do enduring damage. . . .

"Hurry along, please," murmured Roger briskly.

He went padding up the drive, and Sir Isaac Lessing plodded after him short-windedly. It was a long time since the millionaire had taken any exercise of this sort; and his palmiest athletic days were over, anyway; but Roger Conway hustled him along mercilessly. Having hooked his fish, according to the Saint's instructions, he meant to keep it on the line; but he was in no mood to play it with a delicate hand. He had never seen Isaac Lessing in his life before, and his first glimpse of the man had upset all his expectations, but he had a fundamental prejudice against the Petroleum Panjandrum which could not be uprooted merely by discovering that he neither lisped nor oleaginated.

The drive cut straight to the front door of the house, and Roger travelled as straight as the drive, his automatic swinging in his hand. He did not pause until he had reached the top of the steps, and there he waited an impatient moment to give Lessing a chance. Then, as the millionaire set the first toiling foot on the wide stone stair, Roger pressed the bell.

He braced himself, listening to the approach of heavy footsteps down the hall, as Lessing came panting up beside him. There was the sound of two bolts socketing back; then the rattle of the latch; then, as the door opened the first cautious inch, Roger hurled his weight forward. . . .

The man who had opened the door looked down the snout of the gun; and his hands voyaged slowly upwards.

"Turn round," said Roger monotonously . . .

As he brought the gun butt back into his hand he found the millionaire at his elbow, and surprised a certain dazed admiration in Lessing's crag-like face.

"I wish I had you in my office," Lessing was saying helplessly. "You're such a very efficient young man, Mr.—er—Conway——"

"I'm all of that," agreed an unsmiling Roger.

And then he heard a sound in the far corner of the hall, and whipped round to see an open door and a giant blocking the doorway. And Roger laughed.

"Angel Face!" he breathed blissfully. "The very man. . . . We've just dropped in to see you, Angel Face!"

II

MARIUS STOOD PERFECTLY still—the automatic that was focussed on him saw to that. And Roger Conway walked slowly across the hall, Lessing behind him.

"Back into that room, Angel Face!"

The giant turned with a faint shrug, and led the way into a richly furnished library. In the centre of the room he turned again, and it was then that he first saw Lessing in the full light. Yet the wide, hideous face remained utterly impassive—only the giant's hands expressed a puzzled and faintly cynical surprise.

"You, too, Sir Isaac? What have you done to incur our friend's displeasure?"

"Nothing," said Roger sweetly. "He's just come along for a chat with you, as I have. Keep your hands away from that desk, Angel Face—I'll let you know when we want to be shown the door."

Lessing took a step forward. For all his bulk, he was a square-shouldered man, and his clean-shaven jaw was as square as his shoulders.

"I'm told," he said, "that you have, or have had, my fiancée—Miss Delmar—here."

Marius's eyebrows went up.

"And who told you that, Sir Isaac?"

"I did," said Roger comfortably. "And I know it's true, because I saw her brought here—in the ambulance you sent to take her from Upper Berkeley Mews, as we arranged you should."

Marius still looked straight across at Lessing.

"And you believed this story, Sir Isaac?" he inquired suavely; and the thin, soft voice carried the merest shadow of pained reproach.

"I came to investigate it. There were other circumstances——"

"Naturally there are, Sir Isaac. Our friend is a highly competent young man. But surely—even if his present attitude and behavior are not sufficient to demonstrate his eccentric character—surely you know who he is?"

"He was good enough to tell me."

The giant's slitted gaze did not waver by one millimetre.

"And you still believed him, Sir Isaac?"

"His gang has a certain reputation."

"Yes, yes, yes!" Marius fluttered one vast hand. "The sensational newspapers and their romantic nonsense! I have read them myself. But our friend is still wanted by the police. The charge is—murder."

"I know that."

"And yet you came here with him—voluntarily?"

"I did."

"You did not even inform the police?"

"Mr. Conway himself offered to do that. But he also pointed out that that would mean prison for himself and his friend. Since they'd been good enough to find my fiancée for me, I could hardly offer them that reward for their services."

"So you came here absolutely unprotected?"

"Well, not exactly. I told my butler that unless I telephoned him within three hours he was to go to the police."

Marius nodded tolerantly.

"And may I ask what were the circumstances in which our friend was so ready to go to prison if you refused to comply with his wishes?"

"A war—which I was to be tricked into financing."

"My dear Sir Isaac!"

The giant's remonstrance was the most perfect thing of its kind that Roger had ever seen or heard; the gesture that accompanied it would have been expressive enough in itself. And it shook Lessing's confidence. His next words were a shade less assertive; and the answer to them was a foregone conclusion.

"You still haven't denied anything, Marius."

"But I leave it to your own judgment!"

"And still you haven't denied anything, Angel Face," said Roger gently.

Marius spread out eloquent hands.

"If Sir Isaac is still unconvinced," he answered smoothly, "I beg that he will search my house. I will summon a servant——"

"You keep your hands away from that bell!"

"But if you will not allow me to assist you——"

"I'll let you know when I want any help."

The giant's huge shoulders lifted in deprecating acquiescence. He turned again to Lessing.

"In that case, Sir Isaac," he remarked, "I am unfortunately deprived of my proof that Miss Delmar is not in this house."

"So you got her away on that ship, did you?" said Roger very quietly.

"What ship?"

"I see. . . . And did you meet the Saint?"

"I have seen none of your gang."

Slowly Roger sank down to the arm of a chair, and the hand that held the gun was as cold and steady as an Arctic rock. The knuckle of the trigger finger was white and tense; and for a moment Rayt Marius looked at death with expressionless eyes. . . .

And then the giant addressed Lessing again without a change of tone.

"You will observe, Sir Isaac, that our impetuous young friend is preparing to shoot me. After that, he will probably shoot you. So neither of us will ever know his motive. It is a pity—I should have been interested to know it. Why, after his gang has abducted your fiancée for some mysterious reason, they should have elected to make such a crude and desperate attempt to make you believe that I was responsible—unless it was nothing but an elaborate subterfuge to trap us both simultaneously in this house, in which case I cannot understand why he should continue with the accusation now that he has achieved his end. . . . Well, we are never likely to know, my dear Sir Isaac. Let us endeavour to extract some consolation from the reflection that your butler will shortly be informing the police of our fate.''

III

ROGER'S FACE WAS a mask of stone; but behind that frozen calm two thoughts in concentric circles were spinning down through his brain, and nothing but those thoughts sapped from his trigger finger the last essential milligram of pressure that would have sent Rayt Marius to his death.

He had to know definitely what had happened to the Saint; and perhaps Marius was the only man who could tell him.

Nothing else was in doubt. Marius's brilliantly urbane cross-examination of Lessing had been turned to its double purpose with consummate skill. In a few minutes, a few lines of dialogue, innocently and unobtrusively, Marius had gained all the information that he needed—about their numbers, about the police, about everything. . . . And at the same time, in the turning of those same questions, he had attacked the charge against him with the most cunning weapon in his armoury—derision. Inch by inch he had gone over it with a distorting lens, throwing all its enormities into high relief, flooding its garish colours with the cold, merciless light of common, conventional sense; and then, scorning even to deny, he had simply stepped back and sardonically invited Lessing to form his own conclusions. . . .

It was superb—worthy in every way of the strategic genius that Roger remembered so well. And it had had its inevitable effect. The points that Marius had scored, with those subtly mocking rhetorical question marks in their tails, had struck home one after another with deadly aim. And Lessing was wavering. He was looking at Roger steadily, not yet in downright suspicion but with a kind of grim challenge.

And there was the impasse. Roger faced it. For Lessing, there was a charge to be proven: and if Marius was not bluffing, and Sonia Delmar had really left the house, how could there be any proof? For Roger

himself, there was an unconscious man down by the gates who would
not remain permanently unconscious, and another in the hall who might
be discovered even sooner; and before either of them revived Roger had
got to learn things—even as Marius had had to learn things. Only Roger
was not Rayt Marius. . . .

But the tables were turned—precisely. In that last speech, with murder
staring him in the face, the giant had made a counter-attack of dazzling
audacity. And Sir Isaac Lessing waited. . . .

It was Roger's cue.

A queer feeling of impotence slithered into the pit of his stomach. And
he fought it down—fought and lashed his brains to match themselves
against a man beside whom he was a newborn babe.

"Still the same old Angel Face!"

Roger found his voice somehow, and levelled it with all the dispassionate confidence at his command, striving to speak as the Saint would
have spoken—to bluff out his weakness as the Saint would have bluffed.
And he caught a sudden glitter in the giant's eyes at the sound of that
very creditably Saintly drawl, and gathered a new surge of strength.

He turned to Lessing.

"Perhaps," he said, "I didn't make it quite plain enough that in the
matter of slipperiness you could wrap Angel Face in sandpaper and still
have him giving points to an eel. But I'll put it to you in his very own
words. If I only wanted to trap you both here, why should I keep up the
deception?"

"I believe I discarded that theory as soon as I had propounded it,"
said Marius imperturbably.

Roger ignored him.

"On the other hand, Sir Isaac, if I wanted to bring any charge against
Marius—well, he was generous enough to say that I was competent.
Don't you think I might have invented something a little more plausible?
And when I had invented something, wouldn't you have thought I'd have
taken steps to see that I had some evidence—faked, if necessary? But
I haven't any, except my own word. D'you think a really intelligent crook
would try to put over anything like that?"

"I said our young friend was competent," murmured the giant; and
Lessing looked at him.

"What do you mean?"

"Merely that he is even more competent than I thought. Consider it,
Sir Isaac. To—er—fake evidence is not so easy as it sounds. But boldly
to admit that there is no evidence, and then brazenly to adduce that

confession as evidence in itself—that is a masterpiece of competence which can rarely have been equalled."

Roger laughed shortly.

"Very neat, Angel Face," he remarked. "But that line is wearing a little thin. Now, I've just had a brain wave. You know a lot of things which I certainly don't know, and which I very much want to know—where Sonia Delmar has gone, and what's happened to the Saint, for instance. And you won't tell me—yet. But there are ways of making people talk, Angel Face. You may remember that the Saint nearly had to demonstrate one of those ways on you a few months ago. I've always been sorry that something turned up to stop him, but it mayn't be too late to put that right now."

"My dear young friend——"

"I'm talking," said Roger curtly. "As I said, there are ways of making people talk. In the general circumstances I'm not in a position to apply any of those methods single-handed, and Sir Isaac won't help me unless he's convinced. But you're going to talk, Angel Face—in your proper turn—you've got to be made to. And therefore Sir Isaac has got to be convinced, and that's where my brain wave comes in."

Marius shrugged.

"So far," he said, "you have not been conspicuously successful, but I suppose we cannot prevent your making further efforts."

Roger nodded.

"You don't mind, do you?" he said. "You're quite ready to let me go on until somebody comes in to rescue you. But this will be over very quickly. I'm going to give you a chance to prove your innocence—smashingly. Sir Isaac will remember that in my very competent story I mentioned other names besides yours—among them, one Heinrich Dussel and a certain Prince Rudolf."

"Well?"

"Do you deny that you know them?"

"That would be absurd."

"But you say they know absolutely nothing of this affair?"

"The suggestion is ridiculous. They would be as astonished as I am myself."

"Right." Roger drew a deep breath. "Then here's your chance. Over in that corner there's a telephone—with a spare receiver. We'll ring up Heinrich or the Prince—whichever you like—and as soon as they answer you'll give your name, and you'll say: 'The girl has got away again'—*and let Sir Isaac hear them ask you what you're talking about!*"

IV

THERE HAD BEEN silence before; but now for an instant there was a
silence that seemed to Roger's overwrought nerves like the utter dreadful
stillness before the unleashing of a hurricane, that left his throat parched
and his head singing. He could hear the beating of his own heart, and
the creak of the chair as he moved shrieked in his ears. Once before he
had known the same feeling—he had waited in the same electric hush,
his nerves raw and strained with the premonition of peril, quiveringly
alert and yet helpless to guess how the blow would fall. . . .

And yet the tension existed only in himself. The silence was for a mere
five seconds—just such a silence as might reasonably greet the proposition
he had put forward. And not a flicker of expression passed across the
face he watched—that rough-hewn nightmare face like the face of some
abominable heathen idol. Only, for one sheer scintilla of time, a ferine,
fiendish malignance seared into the gaze of those inhuman eyes.

And Lessing was speaking quite naturally.

"That seems a sensible way of settling the matter, Marius."

Marius turned slowly.

"It is an admirable idea," he said. 'If that will satisfy you—although
it is a grotesque hour at which to disturb my friends."

"I shall be perfectly satisfied—if the answer is satisfactory," returning
Lessing bluntly. "If I've been misled I'm ready to apologize. But Mr.
Conway persists with the charge, and I'd be glad to have it answered."

"Then I should be delighted to oblige you."

In another silence, deeper even than the last, Roger watched Marius
cross to the telephone.

He knew—he was certain—that the giant was cornered. Exactly as
Marius had swung the scale over in his own favour during the first innings,
so Roger had swung it back again, with the inspired challenge that had
blazed into his brain at the moment of his need. And Lessing had swung
back with the scale. The millionaire was looking at Roger, curiously
studying the stern young profile; and the grimness was gone again from
the set of his jaw.

"A trunk call to London, please. . . . Hanover eight five six five
. . . Yes . . . Thank you."

Marius's voice was perfectly self-possessed.

He put down the instrument and turned again blandly.

"The call will be through in a few minutes," he said. "Meanwhile, since I am not yet convicted, perhaps you will accept a cigar, Sir Isaac?"

"He might if you kept well away from that desk," said Roger relentlessly. "Let him help himself; and he can pass you one if you want it."

Lessing shook his head.

"I won't smoke," he said briefly.

Marius glanced at Roger.

"Then, with your permission, perhaps Mr.—er—Conway——"

Roger stepped forward, took a cigar from the box on the desk, and tossed it over. Marius caught it, and bowed his thanks.

Roger had to admire the man's self-control. The giant was frankly playing for time, gambling the whole game on the hope of an interruption before the call came through that would inevitably damn him beyond all redemption; his brain, behind that graven mask, must have been a seething ball-race of whirling schemes; yet not by the most infinitesimal twitch of a muscle did he betray one scantling of concern. And before that supernatural impassivity Roger's glacial vigilance keyed up to aching pitch. . . .

Deliberately Marius bit off the tip of the cigar and removed the band; his right hand moved to his pocket in the most natural way in the world, and Roger's voice rang out like the crack of a whip.

"Stop that!"

Marius's eyebrows went up.

"But surely, my dear young friend," he protested mildly, "you will permit me to light my cigar!"

"I'll give you a light."

Roger fished a match out of his pocket, struck it on the sole of his shoe, and crossed the room.

As he held it out, at arm's length, and Marius carefully put his cigar to the flame, their eyes met. . . .

In the stillness, the shout from the hall outside came plainly to their ears. . . .

"Lessing—we'll see this through!" Roger Conway stood taut and still; only his lips moved. "Come over here. . . . ! Marius, get back——"

And then, even as he spoke, the door behind him burst open, and instinctively he looked round. And the explosion of his own gun came to him through a bitter numbness of despair, for the hand that held it was crushed and twisted in such a grip as he had never dreamed of; and he heard the giant's low chuckle of triumph too late.

He was flung reeling back, disarmed—Marius hurled him away as if he had been a wisp of thistledown. And as he lurched against the wall he saw, through a daze of agony, the Saint himself standing within the room, cool and debonair; and behind the Saint was Sonia Delmar, with her right arm twisted up behind her back; and behind Sonia was Hermann, with an automatic in his hand.

"Good-evening, everybody," said the Saint.

11

How Simon Templar Entertained the Congregation, and Hermann Also Had His Fun

"Love, your magic spell is everywhere . . . ."

GAY, MOCKING, cavalier, the old original Saintly voice! And there was nothing but a mischievous laughter in the clear blue eyes that gazed so delightedly at Marius across the room—nothing but the old hell-for-leather Saintly mirth. Yet the Saint stood there unarmed and at bay; and Roger knew then that the loss of his own gun made little difference, for Hermann was safely sheltered behind the girl and his Browning covered the Saint without a tremor.

And Simon Templar cared for none of these things. . . . Lot's wife after the transformation scene would have looked like an agitated eel on a hot plate beside him. By some trick of his own inimitable art, he contrived to make the clothes that had been through so many vicissitudes that night look as if he had just taken them off his tailor's delivery van; his smiling freshness would have made a rosebud in the morning dew appear to wear a positively debauched and scrofulous aspect; and that blithe, buccaneering gaze travelled round the room as if he were reviewing a rally of his dearest friends. For the Saint in a tight corner had ever been the most entrancing and delightful sight in all the world. . . .

"And there's Roger. How's life, sonny boy? Well up on its hind legs—what? . . . Oh, and our one and only Ike! Sonia—your boy friend."

But Lessing's face was gray and drawn.

"So it was true, Marius!" he said huskily.

"Sure it was," drawled the Saint. "D'you mean to say you didn't believe old Roger? Or did Uncle Ugly tell you a naughty story?" And again the Saint beamed radiantly across at the motionless giant. "Your speech, Angel Face: 'Father, I cannot tell a lie. I am the Big Cheese.' . . . Sobs from pit and gallery. But you seem upset, dear heart—and I was looking to you to be the life and soul of the party. 'Hail, smiling morn,' and all that sort of thing."

Then Marius came to life.

For a moment his studied impassivity was gone altogether. His face was the contorted face of a beast; and the words he spat out came with the snarl of a beast; and the gloating leer on the lips of the man Hermann froze where it grimaced, and faded blankly. And then the Saint intervened.

"Hermann meant well, Angel Face," he murmured peaceably; and Marius swung slowly round.

"So you have escaped again, Templar," he said.

"In a manner of speaking," agreed the Saint modestly. "Do you mind if I smoke?"

He took out his cigarette case, and the giant's mouth writhed into a ghastly grin.

"I have heard about your cigarettes," he said. "Give those to me!"

"Anything to oblige," sighed the Saint.

He wandered over, with the case in his hand, and Marius snatched it from him. The Saint sighed again, and settled himself on the edge of the big desk, with a scrupulous regard for the crease in his trousers. His eye fell on the box of cigars, and he helped himself absent-mindedly.

Then Lessing was facing Marius.

"What have you to say now?" he demanded; and the last atom of emotion drained out of Marius's features as he looked down at the millionaire.

"Nothing at all, Sir Isaac." Once again that thin, soft voice was barren of all expression, the accents cold and precise and unimpassioned. "You were, after all, correctly informed—in every particular."

"But—my God, Marius! That war—everything——Do you realize what this means?"

"I am perfectly well aware of all the implications, my dear Sir Isaac."

"You were going to make me your tool in *that*——"

"It was an idea of mine. Perhaps even now——"

"You devil!"

The words bit the air like hot acid; and Marius waved protesting and impatient hands.

"My dear Sir Isaac, this is not a Sunday school. Please sit down and be quiet for a moment, while I attend to this interruption."

"Sit down?" Lessing laughed mirthlessly. The stunned incredulity in his eyes had vanished, to be replaced by something utterly different. "I'll see you damned first! What's more, I'm going to put you in an English prison for a start—and when you come out of that I'll have you hounded out of every capital in Europe. That's my answer!"

He turned on his heel.

Between him and the door Hermann still held the girl. And Roger Conway stood beside her.

"One moment."

Marius's voice—or something else—brought Lessing up with a snap, and the millionaire faced slowly round again. And, as he turned, he met a stare of such pitiless malevolence that the flush of fury petrified in his face, leaving him paler than before.

"I am afraid you cannot be allowed to leave immediately, my dear Sir Isaac," said the giant silkily; and there was no mistaking the meaning of the slight movement of the automatic in his hand. "A series of accidents has placed you in possession of certain information which it would not suit my purpose to permit you to employ in the way which you have just outlined. In fact, I have not yet decided whether you will ever be allowed to leave."

II

THE SAINT CLEARED his throat.

"The time has come," he remarked diffidently, "for me to tell you all the story of my life."

He smiled across at Lessing; and that smile and the voice with it, slashed like a blast of sunshine through the tenuous miasma of evil that had spawned into the room as Marius spoke.

"Just do what Angel face told you, Sir Isaac," said the Saint winningly. "Park yourself in a pew and concentrate on Big Business. Just think what a half-nelson you'll have on the Banana Oil market when Angel Face has unloaded his stock. And he won't hurt you, really. He's a plain, blunt man, and I grant you his face is against him, but he's a simple soul at heart. Why, many's the time we've sat down to a quiet game of dominoes—haven't we, Angel Face?—and all at once, after playing his third double-six, he's said, in just the same dear dreamy way: 'Templar, my friend, have you never thought that there is something *embolismal* about Life?' And I've said, brokenly: 'It's all so—so *umbilical*.' Just like that. 'It's all so *umbilical*. . . .' Doesn't it all come back to you, Angel Face?''

Marius turned to him.

"I have never been amused by your humour, Templar" he said. "But I should be genuinely interested to know how you have spent the evening."

All the giant's composure had come back, save for the vindictive hatred that burned on in his eyes like a lambent fire. He had been secure in the thought that the Saint was dead, and then for a space the shock of seeing the Saint alive had battered and reeled and ravaged his security into a racketing chaos of raging unbelief; and at the uttermost nadir of that havoc had come the cataclysmic apparition of Sonia Delmar herself, entering that very room, to overwhelm his last tattered hope of bluff and smash down the ripening harvest of weeks of brilliant scheming and intrigue into one catastrophic devastation; and he had certainly been annoyed. . . . Yet not for an instant could his mind have contained the shred of an idea of defeat. He stood there by the desk where the Saint sat, a posed and terrible colossus; and behind that unnatural calm the brain of a warped genius was fighting back with brute ferocity to retrieve the irretrievable disaster. And Simon looked at him, and laughed gently.

"To-night's jaunt," said the Saint, "is definitely part of the story of my life."

"And of how many more of your friends?"

Simon shook his head.

"You never seem to be able to get away from the distressing delusion that I am some sort of gang," he murmured. "I believe we've had words about that before. Saint Roger Conway you've met. That in the middle is a new recruit—Saint Isaac Lessing, Regius Professor of Phlebology at the University of Medicine Hat and Consulting Scolecophagist to the Gotherington Gasworks, recently canonized for his article in *The Suffragette* advocating more clubs for women. 'Clubs, tomahawks, flat-irons, anything you like,' he said. . . . And here we all are."

"And how many more?" repeated Marius.

"Isn't that quite clear?" sighed the Saint. "There are no more. Let me put it in words of one syllable. The unadulterated quintessence of nihility——''

Savagely Marius caught his arm in one gigantic hand, and the Saint involuntarily tensed his muscles.

''Not that way, Angel Face,'' he said softly. ''Or there might be a vulgar brawl. . . .''

Yet perhaps it was that involuntary tensing of an arm of leather and iron, rather than the change in the Saint's voice, that made Marius loose his grip. With a tremendous effort the giant controlled himself again, and his lips relaxed from the animal snarl that had distorted them; only the embers of his fury still glittered in his eyes.

''Very good. There are no more of you. And what happened on the ship?''

''Well, we went for a short booze—cruise.''

''And the man who was shot in the motorboat—was he another of your friends?''

Simon surveyed the ash on his cigar approvingly.

''One hates to cast aspersions on the dead,'' he answered, ''but I can't say that we ever became what you might call bosom pals. Not,'' said the Saint conscientiously, ''that I had anything against the man. We just didn't have the chance to get properly acquainted. In fact, I'd hardly given him the first friendly punch on the jaw, and dumped him in that motorboat to draw the fire, when some of the sharpshooting talent pulled the *voix celeste* stop on him for ever. I don't even known his name; but he addressed me in Grand Opera, so if your ice-cream plant is a bit diminuendo——''

Hermann spoke sharply.

''It was Antonio, *mein Herr!* He stayed on the beach after we took the girl down——''

''So!'' Marius turned again. ''It was one of my own men!''

''Er—apparently,'' said the Saint with sorrow.

''And you were already on the ship?''

''Indeed to goodness. But only just.'' The Saint grinned thoughtfully. ''And then I met Comrade Vassiloff—a charming lad, with a beautiful set of hairbrushes. We exchanged a little backchat, and then I tied him up and passed on. Then came the amusing error.''

''What was that?''

''You see, it was a warm evening, so I'd borrowed Comrade Vassiloff's coat to keep the heat out. The next cabin I got into was the captain's and he promptly jumped to the conclusion that Comrade Vassiloff was still inhabiting the coat.''

Marius stiffened.

''Moeller! That man always was a fool! When I meet him again———''

The Saint shook his head.

''What a touching scene it would have been!'' he murmured. ''I almost wish it could come true. . . . But it cannot be. I'm afraid, Angel Face, that Captain Moeller has also been translated.''

''You killed him?''

''That's a crude way of putting it. Let me explain. Overcome with the shock of discovering his mistake, he went slightly bughouse, and seemed to imagine that he was a seagull. Launching himself into the empyrean— oh, very hot, very hot!—he disappeared from view, and I have every reason to believe that he made a forced landing a few yards farther on. As I didn't know how to stop the ship———''

''When was this?''

''Shortly after the ceremony. That was the amusing error. When I rolled into his cabin Sonia was there as well, and there was a generally festive air about the gathering. The next thing I knew was that I was married.'' He saw Marius start, and laughed softly. ''Deuced awkward, wasn't it, Angel Face?''

He gazed at Marius benevolently; but, after that first unpurposed recoil, the giant stood quite still. The only one in the room who moved was Lessing, who came slowly to his feet, his eyes on the girl.

''Sonia—is that true?''

She nodded, without speaking; and the millionaire sank back again, white-faced.

The Saint slewed round on his perch, and it was at Roger that he looked.

''It was quite an unofficial affair,'' said the Saint deliberately. ''I doubt if the Archbishop of Canterbury would have approved. But the net re-sult———''

''Saint!''

Roger Conway took a pace forward, and the name was cried so fiercely that Simon's muscles tensed again. And then the Saint's laugh broke the hush a second time, with a queer blend of sadness and mockery.

''That's all I wanted,'' said the Saint; and Roger fell back, staring at him.

But the Saint said no more. He deposited an inch and a half of ash in an ashtray, flicked a minute flake of the same from his knee, adjusted the crease in his trousers, and returned his gaze again to Marius.

Marius had taken no notice of the interruption. For a while longer he continued to stare fixedly at the Saint; and then, with an abrupt movement, he turned away and began to pace the room with huge, smooth strides. And once again there was silence.

The Saint inhaled meditatively.

An interval of bright and breezy badinage, he realized distinctly, had just been neatly and unobtrusively bedded down in its appointed niche in the ancient history of the world, and the action of the piece was preparing to resume. And the coming action, by all the portents, was likely to be even brighter and breezier than the badinage—in its own way.

Thus far Simon Templar had to admit that he had had all the breaks; but now Rayt Marius was definitely in play. And the Saint understood, quite quietly and dispassionately, as he had always understood these things, that a succulent guinea pig in the jaws of a lion would have been considered a better risk for life insurance than he. For the milk of human kindness had never entered the reckoning—on either side—and now Marius had the edge . . . As the Saint watched the ruthless, deliberate movements of that massive neolithic figure, there came back to him a vivid recollection of the house by the Thames where they had faced each other at the close of the last round, and of the passing of Norman Kent . . . and the Saint's jaw tightened a little grimly. For between them now there was infinitely more than there had been then. Once again the Saint had wrecked a cast-iron hand at the very moment when failure must have seemed impossible; and he had never thought of the giant as a pious martyr to persecution. He knew, in that quiet and dispassionate way, that Marius would kill him—would kill all of them—without a moment's compunction, once it was certain that they could not be more useful to him alive.

Yet the Saint pursued the pleasures of his cigar as if he had nothing else to think about. In his life he had never walked very far from sudden death; and it had been a good life. . . . It was Lessing who broke first under the strain of that silence. The millionaire started up with a kind of gasp.

"I'm damned if I'll stay here like this!" he babbled. "It's an outrage! You can't do things like this in England."

Simon looked at him coldly.

"You're being obvious, Ike," he remarked, "and also futile. Sit down."

"I refuse——"

Lessing swung violently away towards the door; and even the Saint could not repress a smile of entirely unalloyed amusement as the millionaire fetched up dead for the second time of asking before the discourteous ugliness of Hermann's automatic.

"You'll pick up the rules of this game as we go along, Ike," murmured the Saint consolingly; and then Marius, whose measured pacing had not swerved by a hair's breath for Lessing's protest, stopped by the desk with his finger on the bell.

"I have decided," he said; and the Saint turned with a seraphic smile.

"Loud and prolonged applause," drawled the Saint.

He stood up; and Roger Conway, watching the two men as they stood there eye to eye, felt a queer cold shiver trickle down his spine like a drizzle of ghostly icicles.

III

JUST FOR A couple of seconds it lasted, that clash of eyes—as crisp and cold as a clash of steel. Just long enough for Roger Conway to feel, as he had never felt before, the full primitive savagery of the volcanic hatreds that seethed beneath the stillness. He felt that he was a mere spectator at the climax of a duel to the death between two reincarnate paladins of legend; and for once he could not resent this sense of his own unimportance. These was something prodigious and terrifying about the culmination of that epic feud—something that made Roger pray blasphemously to awake and find it all a dream. . . . And the the Saint laughed; the Saint didn't give a damn; and the Saint said: "You're a wonderful asset to the gayety of nations, Angel Face."

With a faint shrug Marius turned away, and he was placidly lighting a fresh cigar when the door opened to admit three men in various stages of undress.

Simon inspected them interestingly. Evidently the household staff was not very large, for he recognized two of the three at once. The bullet-headed specimen in its shirt-sleeves, unashamedly rubbing the sleep out of its eyes with two flabby fists, was obviously the torpescent and bibulous Bavarian who had spoken so yearningly of his bed. Next to him, the blue-chinned exhibit without a tie, propping itself languidly against a bookcase, could be identified without hesitation as the Bowery Boy who was a suffering authority on thirsts. The third argument for a wider application of capital punishment was a broken-nosed and shifty-eyed individual whom the Saint did not know—nor, having surveyed it comprehensively, did Simon feel that his life had been a howling wilderness until the moment of that meeting.

It was to Broken Nose that Marius spoke.

"Fetch some rope, Prosser," he ordered curtly, "and tie up these puppies."

"Spoken like a man, Angel Face," murmured the Saint approvingly as Broken Nose departed. "You think of everything, don't you? . . . And may one ask what you've decided?"

"You shall hear," he said.

The Saint bowed politely and returned to the serene enjoyment of his cigar. Outwardly he remained as unperturbed as he had been throughout the interview, but all his faculties were tightening up again into cool coordination and razor-edged alertness. Quietly and inconspicuously he flexed the muscles of his forearm—just to feel the reassuring pressure of the straps that secured the little sheath of Belle. When Hermann had taken his gun he had not thought of Belle; nor, since then, had the thought seemed to occur to Marius; and with Belle literally up his sleeve the Saint felt confident of being able to escape from any system of roping that might be employed—provided he was left unobserved for a few minutes. But there were others to think of—particularly the girl. Simon stole a glance at her. Hermann still held her with her right arm twisted up behind her back—holding her like that, in the back seat, he had forced the Saint to drive the car back. "And if you do not behave, English swine," he had said, "I will break the arm." It had been the same on the walk up the long drive. "If you escape, and I do not shoot you, English swine, she will scream until you return." Hermann had the most sweet and endearing inspirations, thought the Saint, with his heart beating a little faster; and then his train of thought was interrupted by the return of Mr. Prosser in charge of a coil of rope.

As he placed his hands helpfully behind his back the Saint's thoughts switched off along another line. And that line ranged out in the shape of a series of question marks towards the decision of Marius which he had yet to hear. From the first he had intended to make certain that the giant's machinations should this time be ended for ever, not merely checked, and with this object he had been prepared to take almost any risk in order to discover what other cards Marius might have to play; and now he was surely going to get his wish. . . . Though what the revelation could possibly by was more than Simon Templar could divine. That there could be any revelation at all, other than the obvious one of revenge, Simon would not have believed of anyone but Marius. The game was smashed—smithereened—blown to ten different kinds of Tophet. There couldn't be any way of evading the fact—unless Marius, with Lessing in his power, had conceived some crazy idea of achieving by torture what cunning had failed to achieve. But Marius couldn't be such a fool. . . .

The rope expert finished his task, tested the knots, and passed on to Roger Conway; and the Saint shifted over to the nearest wall and lounged there elegantly. Marius had seated himself at the desk, and nothing about him encouraged the theory that he was merely plotting an empty vengeance. After a brief search through a newspaper which he took from the wastebasket beside him, he had spread out a large-scale map on the desk in front of him and taken some careful measurements; and now, referring at intervals to an open time-table, he was making some rapid calculations on the blotter at his elbow. The Saint watched him thoughtfully; and then Marius looked up, and the sudden sneering glitter in his eyes showed that he had misconstrued the long silence and the furrows of concentration that had corrugated the Saint's forehead.

"So you are beginning to realize your foolishness, Templar?" said the giant sardonically. "Perhaps you are beginning to understand that there are times when your most amusing bluff is wasted? Perhaps you are even beginning to feel a little—shall we say—uneasy?"

The Saint beamed.

"To tell you the truth," he murmured, "I was composing one of my celebrated songs. This was in the form of an ode on the snags of life which Angel Face could overcome with ease and grace. The limpness of asparagus meant nothing to our Marius: not once did he, with hand austere, drip melted butter in his ear. And with what *maestria* did Rayt inhale spaghetti from the plate! Pursuing the elusive pea——"

For a moment the giant's eyes blazed, and he half rose from his chair; and then, with a short laugh, he relaxed again and picked up the pencil that had slipped from his fingers.

"I will deal with you in a moment," he said. "And then we shall see how long your sense of humor will last."

"Just as you like, old dear," murmured the Saint affably. "But you must admit that Ella Wheeler Wilcox has nothing on me."

He leaned back once more against the wall and watched Broken Nose getting busy with the girl. Roger and Lessing had already been attended to. They stood side by side—Lessing with glazed eyes and an unsteady mouth, and Roger Conway pale and expressionless. Just once Roger looked at the girl, and then turned his stony gaze upon the Saint, and the bitter accusation in that glance cut Simon like a knife. But Sonia Delmar had said nothing at all since she entered the room, and even now she showed no fear. She winced, once, momentarily, when the rope expert hurt her; and once, when Roger was not looking at her, she looked at Roger for a long time; she gave no other sign of emotion. She was as calm and queenly in defeat as she had been in hope; and once again the Saint felt a strange stirring of wonder and admiration. . . .

But—that could wait. . . . Or perhaps there would be nothing to wait for. . . . The Saint became quietly aware that the others were waiting for him—that there was more than one reason for their silence. Even as two of them had followed him blindly into the picnic, so they were now looking to him to take them home. . . . The fingers of the Saint's right hand curled tentatively up towards his left sleeve. He could just reach the hilt of his little knife; but he released it again at once. The only chance there was lay in those six inches of slim steel, and if that were lost he might as well ask permission to sit down and make his will: he had to be sure of his time. . . .

At length the rope expert had finished, and at the same moment Marius came to the end of his calculations and leaned back in his chair. He looked across the room.

"Hermann!"

"*Ja, mein Herr?*"

"Give your gun to Lingrove and come here."

Without moving off the bookcase the Bowery Boy reached out a long arm and appropriated the automatic lethargically; and Hermann marched over to the desk and clicked his heels.

And Marius spoke.

He spoke in German; and, apart from Hermann and the somnolent Bavarian, Simon Templar was probably the only one in the room who could follow the scheme that Marius was setting forth in cold staccato detail. And that scheme was one of such a stupendus enormity, such a monstrous inhumanity, that even the Saint felt an icy thrill of horror as he listened.

IV

HE STARED, FASCINATED, at the face of Hermann, taking in the shape of the long narrow jaw, the hollow cheeks, the peculiar slant of the small ears, the brightness of the sunken eyes. The man was a fanatic, of course—the Saint hadn't realized that before. But Marius knew it. The giant's first curt sentences had touched the chords of that fanaticism with an easy mastery; and now Hermann was watching the speaker raptly, with one high spot of colour burning over each cheek-bone, and the fanned flames of his madness flickering in his gaze. And the Saint could only stand there, spellbound, while Marius's gentle, unimpassioned voice repeated his simple instructions so that there could be no mistake. . . .

It could only have taken five minutes altogether; yet in those five minutes had been outlined the bare and sufficient essentials of an abomination that would set a torch to the powder magazine of Europe and kindle such a blaze as could only be quenched in smoking seas of blood. . . . And then Marius had finished, and had risen to unlock a safe that stood in one corner of the room; and the Saint woke up.

Yet there was nothing that he could do—not then. . . . Casually his eyes wandered round the room, weighing up the groupings and the odds; and he knew that he was jammed—jammed all to hell. He might have worked his knife out of its sheath and cut himself loose, and that knife would then have kissed somebody good-night with unerring accuracy; but it wouldn't have helped. There were two guns against him, besides the three other hoodlums who were unarmed; and Belle could only be thrown once. If he had been alone, he might have tried it—might have tried to edge round until he could stick Marius in the back and take a lightning second shot at the Bowery Boy from behind the shelter of that huge body—but he was not alone. . . . And for a moment, with a deathly soberness, the Saint actually considered that idea in despite of the fact that he was not alone. He could have killed Marius, anyway—and that fiendish plot might have died with Marius—even if Lessing and Roger and Sonia Delmar and the Saint himself also died. . . .

And then Simon realized, grimly, that the plot would not have died. To Hermann alone, even without Marius, the plot would always have been a live thing. And again the Saint's fingers fell away from his little knife. . . .

Marius was returning from the safe. He carried two flat metal boxes, each about eight inches long, and Hermann took them from him eagerly.

"You had better leave at once." Marius spoke again in English, after a glance at the clock. "You will have plenty of time—if you do not have an accident."

"There will be no accident, *mein Herr.*"

"And you will return here immediately."

"Jawohl!"

Hermann turned away, slipping the boxes into the side pockets of his coat. And, as he turned, a new light was added to the glimmering madness in his eyes; for his turn brought him face to face with the Saint.

"Once, English swine, you hit me."

"Yeah." Simon regarded the man steadily. "I'm only sorry, now, that it wasn't more than once."

"I have not forgotten, pig," said Hermann purringly; and then, suddenly, with a bestial snarl, he was lashing a rain of vicious blows at the Saint's face. "You also will remember," he screamed, "that I hit you—pig—like that—and that—and that. . . ."

It was Marius who caught and held the man's arms at last.

"Das ist genug, Hermann. I will attend to him myself. And he will not hit you again."

"Das ist gut." Panting, Hermann drew back. He turned slowly, and his eyes rested on the girl with a gloating leer. And then he marched to the door. "I shall return, *werter Herr,*" he said thickly; and then he was gone.

Marius strolled back to the desk and picked up his cigar. He gazed impassively at the Saint.

"And now, Templar," he said, "we can dispose of you." He glanced at Roger and Lessing. "And your friends," he added.

There was the faintest tremor of triumph in his voice, and for an instant the Saint felt a qualm of desperate fear. It was not for himself, or for Roger. But Hermann had been promised a Reward. . . .

And then Simon pulled himself together. His head was clear—Hermann's savage attack had been too unscientific to do more than superficial damage—and his brain had never seemed to function with more ruthless crystalline efficiency in all his life. Over the giant's shoulder he could see the clock; and that clock face, with the precise position of the hands, printed itself upon the forefront of the Saint's mind as if it had been branded there with red-hot irons. It was exactly twenty-eight minutes past two. Four hours clear, and a hundred and fifteen miles to go. Easy enough on a quiet night with a powerful car—easy enough for Hermann. But for the Saint. . . . for the Saint, every lost minute sped the world nearer to a horror that he dared not contemplate. He saw every facet of the situation at once, with a blinding clarity, as he might have seen every facet of a pellucid jewel suspended in the focus of battery upon battery of thousand-kilowatt sun arcs—saw everything that the slightest psychological fluke might mean—heard, in imagination, the dry, sarcastic welcome of his fantastic story. . . . Figures glazed through his brain in an ordered spate—figures on the speedometer of the Hirondel, trembling past the hairline in the little window where they showed—seventy-five—eighty—eighty-five. . . . Driving as only he could drive, with the devil at his shoulder and a guardian angel's blessing on the road and on the tires, he might average a shade over fifty. Give it two hours and a quarter, then—at the forlorn minimum. . . .

And once again the Saint looked Marius in the eyes, while all these things were indelibly graven upon a brain that seemed to have been turned to ice, so clear and smooth and cold it was. And the Saint's smile was very Saintly.

"I hope," he drawled, "that you've invented a really picturesque way for me to die."

12

How Marius Organized an Accident, and Mr. Prosser Passed On

"IT IS CERTAINLY necessary for you to die, Templar," said Marius dispassionately. "There is a score between us which cannot be settled in any other way."

The Saint nodded, and for a moment his eyes were two flakes of blue steel.

"You're right, Angel Face," he said softly. "You're dead right. . . . This planet isn't big enough to hold us both. And you know as surely as you're standing there that if you don't kill me I'm going to kill you, Rayt Marius!''

"I appreciate that," said the giant calmly.

And then the Saint laughed.

"But still we have to face the question of method, old dear," he murmured, with an easy return of all his old mocking banter. "You can't wander round England bumping people off quite so airily. I know you've done it before—on one particular occasion—but I haven't yet discovered how you got away with it. There are bodies to be got rid of, and things like that, you know—it isn't quite such a soft snap as it reads in story books. It's an awful bore, but there you are. Or were you just thinking of running us through the mincing machine and sluicing the pieces down the kitchen sink?''

Marius shook his head.

"I have noticed," he remarked, "that in the stories to which you refer, the method employed for the elimination of an undesirable busybody is usually so elaborate and complicated that the hero's escape is as inevitable as the reader expects it to be. But I have not that melodramatic mind. If you are expecting an underground cellar full of poisonous snakes, or a trap-door leading to a subterranean river, or a man-eating tiger imported for your benefit, or anything else so conventional—pray disillusion yourself. The end I have designed for you is very simple. You will simply meet with an unfortunate accident—that is all.''

He was carefully trimming the end of his cigar as he spoke; and his tremendous hands moved to the operation with a ruthless deliberation that was more terrible than any violence.

The Saint had to twist his bound hands together until the cords bit into his wrists—to make sure he was awake. Vengeful men he had faced often, angry men a thousand times; more than once he had listened to savage, triumphant men luxuriously describing, with a wealth of sadistic detail, the arrangements that they had made for his demise; but never had he heard is death discussed so quietly, with such an utterly pitiless coldbloodedness. Marius might have been engaged in nothing but an abstract philosophical debate on the subject—the ripple of vindictive satisfaction in his voice might have passed unnoticed by an inattentive ear. . . .

And as Marius passed, intent upon his cigar, the measured tick of the clock and Lessing's stertorous breathing seemed to assault the silence deafeningly, mauling and mangling the nerves like the tortured screech of a knife blade dragged across a plate. . . .

And then the sudden scream of the telephone bell jangled into the tenseness and the torture, a sound so abruptly prosaic as to seem weird and unnatural in that atmosphere; and Marius looked round.

"Ah—that will be Herr Dussel."

The Saint turned his head in puzzled surprise, and saw that Roger Conway's face was set and strained.

And then Marius was talking.

Again he spoke in German; and Simon listened, and understood. He understood everything—understood the grim helplessness of Roger's stillness—understood the quick compression of Roger's lips as Marius broke off to glance at the clock. For Roger Conway's German was restricted to such primitive necessities as *Bahnhof, Speisewagen,* and *Bier;* but Roger could have needed no German at all to interpret that renewed interest in the time.

The Saint's fingers stole up his sleeve, and Belle slid gently down from her sheath.

And Simon understood another reason why Roger had been so silent, and had played such an unusually statuesque part in the general exchange of genial persiflage. Roger must have been waiting, hoping, praying, with a paralyzing intentness of concentration, for Marius to overlook just the one desperate detail that Marius had not overlooked. . . .

The Saint leaned very lazily against the wall. He tilted his head back against it, and gazed at the ceiling with dreamy eyes and a look of profound boredom on his face. And very carefully he turned the blade of Belle towards the ropes on his wrists.

"An unfortunate accident," Marius had said. And the Saint believed it. Thinking it over now, he didn't know why he should ever have imagined that a man like Marius would indulge in any of the theatrical trappings of murder. The Saint knew as well as anyone that the bloodcurdling inventions of the sensational novelist had a real foundation in the mentality of a certain type of crook, that there were men constitutionally incapable of putting the straightforward skates under an enemy whom they had in their power—men whose tortuous minds ran to electrically fired revolvers, or tame alligators in a private swimming bath, as inevitably as water runs downhill. The Saint had met that type of man. But to Rayt Marius such devices would not exist. Whatever was to be done would be done quickly. . . .

And the same applied to the Saint—consequently. Whatever he was going to do, by way of prophylaxis, he would have to do instantly. Whatever sort of gamble it might be, odds or no odds, handicaps or no handicaps, Bowery Boys and miscellaneous artillery notwithstanding,

hellfire and pink damnation inasmuch and hereinafter—be b-blowed.
. . . Simon wondered why he hadn't grasped that elementary fact before.

"Gute Nacht, mein Freund. Schlafen Sie wohl. . . ."

Marius had finished. He hung up the receiver; and the Saint smiled at him.

"I trust," said Simon quietly, "that Heinrich will obey that last instruction—for his own sake. But I'm afraid he won't."

The giant smiled satirically.

"Herr Dussel is perfectly at liberty to go to sleep—after he has followed my other instructions." He turned to Roger. "And you, my dear young friend—did you also understand?"

Roger stood up straight.

"I guessed," he said; and again Marius smiled.

"So you realize—do you not—that there is no chance of a mistake? There is still, I should think, half an hour to go before Sir Isaac's servants will be communicating with the police—plenty of time for them also to meet with an unfortunte accident. And there will be no one to repeat your story."

"Quate," said the Saint, with his eyes still on the ceiling. "Oh, quate."

Marius turned again at the sound of his voice.

"And this is the last of you—you scum!" The sentence began as calmly as anything else that the giant had said, but the end of it was shrill and strident. "You have heard. You thought you had beaten me, and now you know that you have failed. Take that with you to your death! You fool! You have dared to make your puny efforts against me—*me*— Rayt Marius!"

The giant stood at his full height, his gargantuan chest thrown out, his colossal fists raised and quivering.

"You! You have dared to do that—you dog!"

"Quate," said the Saint affably.

And even as he spoke he braced himself for the blow that he could not possibly escape this time; and yet the impossible thing happened. With a frightful effort Marius mastered his fury for the last time; his fists unclenched, and his hands fell slowly to his sides.

"Pah! But I should flatter you by losing my temper with you." Again the hideous face was a mask, and the thin, high-pitched voice was as smooth and suave as ever. "I should not like you to think that I was so interested in you, my dear Templar. Once you kicked me; once, when I was in your hands, you threatened me with torture; but I am not annoyed.

I do not lose my temper with the mosquito who bites me. I simply kill the mosquito.''

II

A SEVERED STRAND of rope slipped down the Saint's wrist, and he gathered it in cautiously. Already the cords were loosening. And the Saint smiled.

"Really," he murmured, "that's awfully ruthless of you. But then, you strong silent men are like that. . . . And are we all classified as mosquitos for this event?"

Marius spread out his hands.

"Your friend Conway, personally, is entirely unimportant," he said. "If only he had been wise enough to confine his adventurous instincts to activities which were within the limits of his intelligence——" He broke off with a shrug. "However, he has elected to follow you into meddling with my affairs."

"And Lessing?"

"He also has interfered. Only at your instigation, it is true; but the result is the same."

The Saint continued to smile gently.

"I get you, Tiny Tim. And he also will have an unfortunate accident?"

"It will be most unfortunate." Marius drew leisurely at his cigar before proceeding. "Let me tell you the story as far as it is known. You and your gang kidnapped Sir Isaac—for some reason unknown—and killed his servants when they attempted to resist you. You brought him out to Saltham—again for some reason unknown. You drove past this house on to the cliff road, and there—still for some reason unknown—your car plunged over the precipice. And if you were not killed by the fall, you were certainly burned to death in the fire which follows. . . . Those are the bare facts—but the theories which will be put forward to account for them should make most interesting reading."

"I see," said the Saint very gently. "And now will you give us the low-down on the tragedy, honey-bunch? I mean, I'm the main squeeze in this blinkin' tear——"

"I do not understand all your expressions. If you mean that you would like to know how the accident will be arranged, I shall be delighted to explain the processes as they take place. We are just about to begin."

He put down his cigar regretfully, and turned to the rope expert.

"Prosser, you will find a car at the lodge gates. You will drive it out to the cliff road, and the drive it over the edge of the cliff. Endeavour not to drive yourself over with it. After this, you will return to the garage, take three or four tins of petrol, and carry them down the cliff path. You will go along the shore until you come to the wreckage of the car, and wait for me there."

The Saint leaned even more lazily against the wall. And the cords had fallen away from his wrists. He had just managed to turn his hand and catch them as they fell.

"I may be wrong," he remarked earnestly, as the door closed behind Mr. Prosser, "but I think you're marvellous. How do you do it, Angel Face?"

"We will now have you gagged," said Marius unemotionally. "Ludwig, fetch some cloths."

Stifling a cavernous yawn, the German roused himself from the corner and went out.

And the Saint's smile could never have been more angelic.

The miracle! . . . He could scarcely believe it. And it was a copper-bottomed wow. It was too utterly superfluously superlative for words. . . . But the blowed-in-the-glass, brass-bound, seventy-five-point-three-five-over-proof fact was that the odds had been cut down by half.

Quite casually, the Saint made sure of his angles.

The Bowery Boy was exactly on his right; Marius, by the desk, was half left.

And Marius was still speaking.

"We take you to the top of the cliffs—bound, so that you cannot struggle, and gagged, so that you cannot cry out—and we throw you over. At the bottom we are ready to remove the ropes and the gags. We place you beside the car; the petrol is poured over you; a match. . . . And there is a most unfortunate accident. . . ."

The Saint looked around.

Instinctively Roger Conway had drawn closer to the girl. Ever afterwards the Saint treasured that glimpse of Roger Conway, erect and defiant, with fearless eyes.

"And if the fall doesn't kill us?" said Roger distinctly.

"It will be even more unfortunate," said Marius. "But for any one of you to be found with a bullet wound would spoil the effect of the accident. Naturally, you will see my point. . . ."

There were other memories of that moment that the Saint would never forget. The silence of the girl, for instance, and the way Lessing's breath suddenly came with a choking sob. And the stolid disinterestedness of the Bowery Boy. And Lessing's sudden throaty babble of words. "Good God—Marius—you can't do a thing like that! You can't—you can't—"

And Roger's quiet voice again, cutting through the babble like the slash of a sabre.

"Are we really stuck this time, Saint?"

"We are not," said the Saint.

He said it so gently that for a few seconds no one could have realized that there was a significant stone-cold deliberateness, infinitely too significant and stone-cold for bluff, about that very gentleness. And for those few seconds Lessing's hysterical incoherent babble went on, and the clock whirred to strike the hour. . . .

And then Marius took a step forward.

"Explain!"

There was something akin to fear in the venomous crack of that one word, so that even Lessing's impotent blubbering died in his throat; and the Saint laughed.

"The reason is in my pocket," he said softly. "I'm sorry to disappoint you, Angel Face, my beautiful, but it's too late now——"

In a flash the giant was beside him, fumbling with his coat.

"So! You will still be humorous. But perhaps, after all, you will not be thrown down the cliff *before* your car is set on fire——"

"The inside breast pocket, darlingest," murmured the Saint very softly. And he turned a little.

He could see the bulge in the giant's pocket, where Roger's captured automatic had dragged the coat out of shape. And for a moment the giant's body cut off most of the Saint from the Bowery Boy's field of vision. And Marius was intent upon the Saint's breast pocket. . . .

Simon's left hand leaped to its mark as swiftly and lightly as the hand of any professional pickpocket could have done. . . .

"Don't move an inch, Angel Face!"

The Saint's voice rang out suddenly like the crack of a whip—a voice of murderous menace, with a tang of tempered steel. And the automatic that backed it up was rammed into the giant's ribs with a savagery that made even Rayt Marius wince.

"Not one inch—not half an inch, Angel Face," repeated that voice of tensile tungsten. "That's the idea. . . . And now talk quickly to Lingrove—quickly! He can't get a beat on me, and he's wondering what to do. Tell him! Tell him to drop his gun!"

Marius's lips parted in a dreadful grin.

And the Saint's voice rapped again through the stillness.

"I'll count three. You die on the three. *One!*" The giant was looking into Simon's eyes, and they were eyes emptied of all laughter. Eyes of frozen ultramarine, drained of the last trace of human pity. . . . And Marius answered in a whisper.

"Drop your gun, Lingrove."

The reply came in a muffled thud on the carpet; but not for an instant did those inexorable eyes cease to bore into the giant's brain.

"Is it down, Roger?" crisped the Saint, and Conway spoke the single necessary word.

"Yes."

"Right. Get over in that corner by the telephone, Lingrove." The Saint, with the tail of his eye, could see the Bowery Boy pass behind the giant's shoulder; and the way was clear. "Get over and join him, Angel Face. . . ."

Marius stepped slowly back; and the Saint slid silently along the wall until he was beside the door. And the door opened.

As it opened it hid the Saint; and the German came right into the room. And then Simon closed the door gently, and had his back to it when the man whipped round and saw him.

"Du bist wie eine Blume," murmured the Saint cordially, and a glimmer of the old lazy laughter was trickling back into his voice. "Incidentally, I'll bet you haven't jumped like that for years. Never mind. It's very good for the liver. . . . And now would you mind joining your boss over in the corner, sweet Ludwig? And if you're a very good boy, perhaps I'll let you go to sleep. . . ."

III

"Good old Saint!"

The commendation was wrung spontaneously from Roger Conway's lips; and Simon Templar grinned.

"Hustle along this way, son," he remarked, "and we'll have you loose in two flaps of a crow's pendulum. Then you can be making merry with that spare coil of hawser while I carry on with the good work ——*Jump!*"

The last word detonated in the end of the speech like the fulmination of a charge of high explosive at the tail of a length of fuse. And Roger jumped—no living man could have failed to obey that trumpet-tongued command.

A fraction of a second later he saw—or rather heard—the reason for it.

As he crossed the room he had carelessly come between the Saint and Marius. And, as he jumped, ducking instinctively, something flew past the back of his neck, so close that the wind of it stirred his hair, and crashed into the wall where the Saint had been standing. Where the Saint had been standing; but Simon was a yard away by then. . . .

As Roger straightened up he saw the Saint's automatic swinging round to check the rush that followed. And then he saw the telephone lying at the Saint's feet.

"Naughty," said the Saint reproachfully.

"Why didn't you shoot the swine?" snapped Roger, with reasonable irritation; but Simon only laughed.

"Because I want him, sonny boy. Because it wouldn't amuse me to bounce him like that. It's too easy. I want our Angel Face for a fight. . . . And *how* I want him!"

Roger's hands were free, but he stood staring at the Saint helplessly. He said suddenly, foolishly: "Saint—what do you mean? You couldn't possibly——"

"I'm going to have a damned good try. Shooting is good—for some people. But there are others that you want to get at with your bare hands. . . ."

Very gently Simon spoke—very, very gently. And Roger gazed in silent wonder at the bleak steel in the blue eyes, and the supple poise of the wide limber shoulders, and the splendid lines of that reckless fighting face; and he could not find anything to say.

And then the Saint laughed again.

"But there are other things to attend to first. Grab that rope and do your stuff, old dear—and mind you do it well. And leave that iron on the floor for a moment—we don't want anyone to infringe our patent in that pickpocket trick."

A moment later he was cutting the rope away from Sonia Delmar's wrists. Lessing came next; and Lessing was as silent during the operation as the girl had been, but for an obviously different reason. He was shaking like a leaf; and, after one comprehensive glance at him, Simon turned again to the girl.

"How d'you feel, lass?" he asked; and she smiled.

"All right," she said.

"Just pick up that gun, would you? . . . D'you think you could use it?"

She weighed the Bowery Boy's automatic thoughtfully in her hand.

"I guess I could, Simon."

"That's great!" Belle was back in the Saint's sleeve, and he put out his free hand and drew her towards him. "Now, park yourself right over here, sweetheart, so that they can't rush you. Have you got them covered?"

"Sure."

"Attababy. And don't take your pretty eyes off the beggars till Roger's finished his job. Ike, you flop into that chair and faint in your own time. If you come blithering into the line of fire it'll be your funeral. . . . Sonia, d'you feel really happy?"

"Why?"

"Could you be a real hold-up wizard for five or ten minutes, all on your ownsome?"

She nodded slowly.

"I'd do my best, big boy."

"Then take this other gat as well." He pressed it into her hand. "I'm leaving you to it, old dear—I've got to see a man about a sort of dog, and it's blamed urgent. But I'll be right back. If you have the least sign of trouble let fly. The only think I ask is that you don't kill Angel Face— not fatally, that is. . . . S'long!"

He waved a cheery hand, and was gone—before Roger, who had been late in divining his intention, could ask him why he went.

But Roger had not understood Hermann's mission.

And even the Saint had taken fully a minute to realize the ultimate significance of the way that hurtling telephone had smashed into the wall; but there was nothing about it that he did not realize now, as he raced down the long, dark drive. That had been a two-edged effort—by all the gods! It was a blazing credit to the giant's lightning grasp on situations— a desperate bid for salvation, and simultaneously a vindictive defiance. And the thought of that last motive lent wings to the Saint's feet. . . .

He reached the lodge gates and looked up and down the road; but he could see no car. And then, as he paused there, he heard, quite distinctly, the unmistakable snarl of the Hirondel with an open throttle.

The Saint spun round.

An instant later he was flying up the road as if a thousand devils were baying at his heels.

He tore round a bend, and thought he could recognize a clump of trees in the gloom ahead. If he was right, he must be getting near the cliff. The snarl of the Hirondel was louder. . . .

He must have covered the last hundred yards in a shade under evens. And then, as he rounded the last corner, he heard a splintering crash.

With a shout he flung himself forward. And yet he knew that it was hopeless. For one second he had a glimpse of the great car rearing like a stricken beast on the brink of the precipice, with its wide flaming eyes hurling a long white spear of light into the empty sky; and then the light went out, and down the cliff side went the roar of the beast and a racking, tearing thunder of breaking shrubs and battered rocks and shattering metal. . . . And then another crash. And a silence. . . .

The Saint covered the rest of the distance quite calmly; and the man who stood in the road did not try to turn. Perhaps he knew it would be useless.

"Mr. Prosser, I believe?" said the Saint caressingly.

The man stood mute, with his back to the gap which the Hirondel had torn through the flimsy rails at the side of the road. And Simon Templar faced him.

"You've wrecked my beautiful car," said the Saint, in the same caressing tone.

And suddenly his fist smashed into the man's face; and Mr. Prosser reeled back, and went down without a sound into the silence.

IV

WHICH WAS CERTAINLY very nice and jolly, reflected the Saint, as he walked slowly back to the house. But not noticeably helpful. . . .

He walked slowly because it was his habit to move slowly when he was thinking. And he had a lot to think about. The cold rage that had possessed him a few minutes before had gone altogether: the prime cause of it had been duly dealt with, and the next thing was to weigh up the consequences and face the facts.

For all the threads were now in his hands, all ready to be wormed and parcelled and served and put away—all except one. And that one was now more important than all the others. And it was utterly out of his reach—not even the worst that he could do to Marius could recall it or change its course. . . .

"Did you get your dog, old boy?" Roger Conway's cheerful accents greeted him as he opened the door of the library; but the Saintly smile was unusually slow to respond.

"Yes and no." Simon answered after a short pause. "I got it, but not soon enough."

The smile had gone again; and Roger frowned puzzledly.

"What was the dog?" he asked.

"The late Mr. Prosser," said the Saint carefully, and Roger jumped to one half of the right conclusion.

"You mean he'd crashed the car?"

"He had crashed the car."

The affirmative came flatly, precisely, coldly—in a way that Roger could not understand.

And the Saint's eyes roved round the room without expression, taking in the three bound men in the corner, and Lessing in a chair, and Sonia Delmar beside Roger, and the telephone on the floor. The Saint's cigarette case lay on the desk where Marius had thrown it; and the Saint walked over in silence and picked it up.

"Well?" prompted Roger, and was surprised by the sound of his own voice.

The Saint had lighted a cigarette. He crossed the room again with the cigarette between his lips, and picked up the telephone. He looked once at the frayed ends of the flex; and then he held the instrument close to his ear and shook it gently.

And then he looked at Roger.

"Have you forgotten Hermann?" he asked quietly.

"I had forgotten him for the moment, Saint. But——"

"And those boxes he took with him—had you guessed what they were?"

"I hadn't."

Simon Templar nodded.

"Of course," he said. "You wouldn't know what it was all about. But I'm telling you now, just to break it gently to you, that the Hirondel's been crashed and the telephone's bust, and those two things together may very well mean the end of peace on earth for God knows how many years. But you were just thinking we'd won the game, weren't you?"

"What do you mean, Saint?"

The newspaper that Marius had consulted was in the waste-basket. Simon bent and took it out, and the paragraph that he knew that he would find caught his eye almost at once.

"Come here, Roger," said the Saint, and Roger came beside him wonderingly.

Simon Templar did not explain. His thumb simply indicated the paragraph; and Conway read it through twice—three times—before he looked again at the Saint with a fearful comprehension dawning in his eyes.

13

How Simon Templar Entered a Post Office, and a Boob Was Blistered

"BUT IT COULDN'T be *that!*"

Roger's dry lips framed the same denial mechanically, and yet he knew that sanity made him a fool even as he spoke. And the Saint's answer made him a fool again.

"But it *is* that!"

The Saint's terrible calm snapped suddenly, as a brittle blade snaps at a turn of the hand. Sonia Delmar came over and took the paper out of Roger's hands, but Roger scarcely noticed it—he was gazing, fascinated, at the blaze in the Saint's eyes.

"That's what Hermann's gone to do. I tell you, I heard every word. It's Angel Face's second string. I don't know why it wasn't his first— unless because he figured it was too desperate to rely on except in the last emergency. But he was ready to put it into action if the need arose, and it just happened that there was a chance this very night—by the grace of the devil——"

"But I don't see how it works," Roger said stupidly.

"Oh, for the love of Pete!" The Saint snatched his cigarette from his mouth, and his other hand crushed Roger's shoulder in a vise-like grip. "Does that count? There are a dozen ways he could have worked it. Hermann's a German. Marius could easily have fixed for him to be caught later, with the necessary papers on him—and there the fat would have been in the fire. But what the hell does it matter now, anyway?''

And Roger could see that it didn't matter; but he couldn't see anything else. He could only say: ''What time does it happen?''

''About six-thirty,'' said the Saint; and Roger looked at the clock.

''It was twenty-five minutes past three.

''There must be another telephone somewhere,'' said the girl.

Simon pointed to the desk.

''Look at that one,'' he said. ''The number's on it—and it's a Sax-mundham number. Probably it's the only private phone in the village.''

''But there'll be a post office.''

''I wonder.''

The Saint was looking at Marius. There might have been a sneer somewhere behind the graven inscrutability of that evil face, but Simon could not be sure. Yet he had a premonition. . . .

''We might try,'' Roger Conway was saying logically; and the Saint turned.

''We might. Coming?''

''But these guys—and Sonia——''

''Right. Maybe I'd better go alone. Give me one of those guns!''

Roger obeyed.

And once again the Saint went flying down the drive. The automatic was heavy in his hip pocket, and it gave him a certain comfort to have it there, though he had no love for firearms in the ordinary way. They made so much noise. . . . But it was more than possible that the post office would look cross-eyed at him, and it might boil down to a hold-up. He realized that he wasn't quite such a paralyzingly respectable sight as he had been earlier in the evening, and that might be a solid disadvantage when bursting into a village post office staffed by startled females at that hour of the morning. His clothes were undamaged, it was true; but Hermann's affectionate farewell had left certain traces on his face. Chiefly, there was a long scratch across his forehead, a thin trickle of blood running down one side of his face, as a souvenir of the diamond ring that Hermann affected. Nothing such as wounds went, but it must have been enough to make him look a pretty sanguinary desperado. . . . And if it did come to a holdup, how the hell did telegraph offices work? The Saint had a working knowledge of Morse, but the manipulation of the divers gadgets connected with the sordid mechanism of transmissions of the same was a bit beyond his education. . . .

How far was it to the village? Nearly a mile, Roger had said when they drove out. Well, it was one river of gore of a long mile. . . . It was some time since he had passed the spot where Mr. Prosser's memorial tablet might or might not be added to the scenic decorations. And, like a fool, he'd started off as if he were going for a hundred yards' sprint; and, fit as he was, the pace would kill his speed altogether if he didn't ease up. He did so, filling his bursting lungs with great gulps of the cool sea air. His heart was pounding like a demented triphammer. . . . But at that moment the road started to dip a trifle, and that must mean that it was nearing the village. He put on a shade of acceleration—it was easier going downhill—and presently he passed the first cottage.

A few seconds later he was in some sort of village street, and then he had to slacken off almost to a walk.

What the hairy hippopotamus were the visible distinguishing marks or peculiarities of a village post office? The species didn't usually run to a private building of its own, he knew. Mostly, it seemed to house itself in an absure corner of the grocery store. And what did a grocery store look like in the dark, anyway? . . . His eyes were perfectly attuned to the darkness by this time; but the feebleness of the moon, which had dealt so kindly with him earlier in the evening, was now catching him on the return swing. If only he had a flashlight. . . . As it was, he had to use his petrol lighter at every door. Butcher—baker—candlestick maker —he seemed to strike every imaginable kind of shop but the right one. . . .

An eternity passed before he came to his goal. . . .

There should have been a bell somewhere around the door . . . but there wasn't. So there was only one thing to do. He stepped back and picked up a large stone from the side of the road. Without hesitation he hurled it through an upper window.

Then he waited.

One—two—three minutes passed, and no indignant head was thrust out into the night to demand the reason for the outrage. Only, somewhere behind him in the blackness, the window of another house was thrown up.

The Saint found a second stone. . . .

" 'Oo's that?''

The quavering voice that mingled with the tinkle of broken glass was undoubtedly feminine, but it did not come from the post office. Another window was opened. Suddenly the woman screamed. A man's shout answered her. . . .

"Hell," said the Saint through his teeth.

But through all the uproar the post office remained as silent as a tomb. "Deaf, doped, or dead," diagnosed the Saint without a smile. "And I don't care which. . . .

He stepped into the doorway, jerking the gun from his pocket. The butt of it crashed through the glass door of the shop, and there was a hole the size of a man's head. Savagely the Saint smashed again at the jagged borders of the hole, until there was a gap big enough for him to pass through. The whole village must have been awake by that time, and he heard heavy footsteps running down the road.

As he went in his head struck against a hanging oil lamp, and he lifted it down from its hook and lighted it. He saw the post office counter at once, and had reached it when the first of the chase burst in behind him.

Simon put the lamp down and turned.

"Keep back," he said quietly.

There were two men in the doorway; they saw the ugly steadiness of the weapon in the Saint's hand and pulled up, open-mouthed.

The Saint sidled along the counter, keeping the men covered. There was a telephone box in the corner—that would be easier than tinkering at a telegraph apparatus——

And then came another man, shouldering his way through the crowd that had gathered at the door. He wore a dark blue uniform with silver buttons. There was no mistaking his identity.

" 'Ere, wot's this?" he demanded truculently.

Then he also saw the Saint's gun, and it checked him for a moment—but only for a moment.

"Put that down," he blustered, and took another step forward.

II

SIMON TEMPLAR'S THOUGHTS moved like lightning. The constable was coming on—there wasn't a doubt of that. Perhaps he was a brave man, in his blunt way; or perhaps Chicago was only a fairy tale to him; but certainly he was coming on. And the Saint couldn't shoot him down in cold blood without giving him a chance. Yet the Saint realized at the same time how threadbare a hope he would have of putting his preposterous story over on a turnip-headed village cop. At Scotland Yard, where there was a different type of man, he might have done it; but here . . .

It would have to be a bluff. The truth would have meant murder—and the funeral procession would have been the cop's. Even now the Saint knew, with an icy intensity of decision, that he would shoot the policeman down without a second's hesitation, if it proved to be necessary. But the man should have his chance. . . .

The Saint drew himself up.

"I'm glad you've come, officer," he remarked briskly. "I'm a Secret Service agent, and I shall probably want you."

A silence fell on the crowd. For the Saint's clothes were still undeniably glorious to behold, and he spoke as one having authority. Standing there at his full height, trim and lean and keen-faced, with a cool half smile of greeting on his lips, he looked every inch a man to be obeyed. And the constable peered at him uncertainly.

"Woi did you break them windoos, then?"

"I had to wake the people here. I've got to get on the phone to London—at once. I don't know why the post-office staff haven't shown up yet—everyone else seems to be here—"

A voice spoke up from the outskirts of the crowd.

"Missus Fraser an' 'er daughter doo 'ave goorn to London theirselves, sir, for to see 'er sister. They ain't a-comin' back till morning."

"I see. That explains it." The Saint put his gun down on the counter and took out his cigarette case. "Officer, will you clear these good people out, please? I've no time to waste."

The request was an order—the constable would not have been human if he had not felt an automatic instinct to carry it out. But he still looked at the Saint.

"Oi doo feel oi've seen your face befoor," he said, with less hostility; but Simon laughed.

"I don't expect you have," he murmured. "We don't advertise."

"But 'ave you got anything on you to show you're wot you says you are?"

The Saint's pause was only fractional, for the answer that had come to him was one of pure inspired genius. It was unlikely that a hayseed cop like this would know what evidence of identity a secret agent should properly carry; it was just as unlikely that he would recognize the document that Simon proposed to show him. . . .

"Naturally," said the Saint, without the flicker of any eyelid. "The only difficulty is that I'm not allowed to disclose my name to you. But I think there should be enough to convince you without that."

And he took out his wallet, and from the wallet he took a little book rather like a driving license, while the crowd gaped and craned to see. The constable came closer.

Simon gave him one glimpse of the photograph which adorned the inside, while he covered the opposite page with his fingers; and then he turned quickly to the pages at the end.

For the booklet he had produced was the certificate of the Fédération of Aéronautique Internationale, which every amateur aviator must obtain—and the Saint, in the spare time of less strenuous days, had been wont to aviate amateurly with great skill and dexterity. And the two back pages of the certificate were devoted to an impressive exhortation of all whom it might concern, translated into six diffenent languages, and saying:

The Civil, Naval, and Military authorities, including the Police, are respectfully requested to aid and assist the holder of this certificate.

Just that and nothing more. . . .

But it ought to be enough. It ought to be. . . . And the Saint, with his cigarette lighted, was quietly taking up his gun again while the constable read; but he might have saved himself the trouble for the constable was regarding him with a kind of awe.

"Oi beg your pardon, sir. . . ."

"That," murmured the Saint affably, "is O.K. by me."

He replaced the little book with a silent prayer of thanksgiving, while the policeman squared his shoulders importantly and began to disperse the crowd; and the dispersal was still proceeding when the Saint went into the telephone booth.

He should have been feeling exultant, for everything should have been plain sailing now. . . . And yet he wasn't. As he took up the receiver he remembered the veiled sneer that he had seen—or imagined—in the face of Marius. And it haunted him. He had had a queer intuition that the giant had foreseen something that the Saint had not foreseen; and now that intuition was even stronger. Could it be that Marius was expecting the prince, or some ally, due to arrive about that time, who might take the others by surprise while the Saint was away? Or might the household staff be larger than the Saint had thought, and might there be the means of a rescue still within the building? Or what? . . . "I'm growing nerves," thought the Saint, and cursed all intuitions categorically.

And he had been listening for some time before he realized that the receiver was absolutely silent—there was none of the gentle crackling undertone that ordinarily sounds in a telephone receiver. . . .

"Gettin' on all roight, sir?"

The crowd had gone, and the policeman had returned. Simon thrust the receiver into his hand.

"Will you carry on?" he said. "The line seems to have gone dead. If you get a reply, ask for Victoria six eight two seven. And tell them to make it snappy. I'm going to telegraph."

"There's noo telegraph, sir."

"What's that?"

"There's noo telegraph, sir."

"Then how do they send and receive telegrams? or don't they?"

"They doo coom through on the telephoon, sir, from Saxmundham." The constable jiggered the receiver hook. "And the loine doo seem to be dead, sir," he added helpfully.

Simon took the receiver from him again.

"What about the station?" he snapped. "There must be a telephone there."

The policeman scratched his head.

"I suppose there is, sir. . . . But, now Oi coom to think of it, Oi did 'ear earlier in the day that the telephoon loine was down somewhere. One o' they charrybangs run into a poost on Saturday noight——"

He stopped, appalled, seeing the blaze in the Saint's eyes.

Then, very carefully, Simon put down the receiver. He had gone white to the lips, and the twist of those lips was not pleasant to see.

"My God in heaven!" said the Saint huskily. "Then there's all hell let loose tonight!"

III

"Is it as bad as that, sir?" inquired the constable weakly; and Simon swung round on him like a tiger.

"You blistered boob!" he snarled. "D'you think this is my idea of being comic?"

And then he checked himself. That sort of thing wouldn't do any good.

But he saw it all now. The first dim inkling had come to him when Marius had hurled that telephone at him in the house; and now the proof and vindication was staring him in the face in all its hideous nakedness. The telegraph post had been knocked down on Saturday night; being an unimportant line, nothing would be done to it before Monday; and Marius had known all about it. Marius's own line must have followed a different route, perhaps joining the other at a point beyond the scene of the accident. . . .

Grimly, gratingly, the Saint bedded down the facts in separate compartments of his brain, while he schooled himself to a relentless calm. And presently he turned again to the policeman.

"Where's the station?" he asked. "They must have an independent telegraph there."

"The station, sir? That'll be a little way oover the bridge. But you woon't foind anyone there at this toime, sir——"

"We don't want anyone," said the Saint. "Come on!"

He had mastered himself again completely, and he felt that nothing else that might happen before the dawn could possibly shake him from the glacial discipline that he had locked upon his passion. And, with the same frozen restraint of emotion, he understood that the trip to the station was probably a waste of time; but it had to be tried. . . .

The crowd of villagers was still gathered outside the shop, and the Saint strode through them without looking to the right or left. And he remembered what he had read about the place before he came there—its reputed population of 3,128, its pleasure grounds, its attractions as a watering-place—and at that moment he would cheerfully have murdered the author of that criminal agglomeration of troutspawn and frogbladder. For any glories that Saltham might once have claimed had long since departed from it: it was now nothing but a forgotten seaside village, shorn of the most elementary amenities of civilization. And yet, unless a miracle happened, history would remember it as history remembers Serajevo. . . .

The policeman walked beside him; but Simon did not talk. Beneath that smooth crust of icy calm a raging wrathlike white-hot lava seethed through the Saint's heart. And while he could have raged, he could as well have wept. For he was seeing all that Hermann's mission would mean if it succeeded, and that vision was a vision of the ruin of all that the Saint had sworn to do. And he thought of the waste—of the agony and blood and tears, of the squandered lives, of the world's new hopes crushed down into the mud, and again of the faith in which Norman Kent had died. . . . And something in the thought of that last superb spendthrift sacrifice choked the Saint's throat. For Norman was a link with the old careless days of debonair adventuring, and those days were very far away—the days when nothing had mattered but the fighting and the fun, the comradeship and the glamour and the high risk, the sufficiency of gay swashbuckling, the wine of battle and the fair full days of quiet. Those days had gone as if they had never been.

So the Saint came soberly to the station, and smashed another window for them to enter the station master's office.

There was certainly a telegraph, and for five minutes the Saint tried to get a response. But he was without hope.

And presently he turned away and put his head in his hands.

"It's no use," he said bitterly. "I suppose there isn't anyone listening at the other end."

The policeman made sympathetic noises.

"O' course, if you woon't tell me wot the trouble is——"

"It wouldn't help you. But I can tell you that I've got to get through to Scotland Yard before six-thirty—well before. If I don't, it means—war."

The policeman goggled.

"Did you say war, sir?"

"I did. No more and no less. . . . Are there any fast cars in this blasted village?"

"Noo, sir—noon as Oi can think of. Noon wot you moight call farst."

"How far is it to Saxmundham?"

" 'Bout twelve moile, sir, Oi should say. Oi've got a map 'ere, if you'd loike me to look it up."

Simon did not answer; and the constable groped in a pocket of his tunic and spilled an assortment of grubby papers onto the table.

In the silence Simon heard the ticking of a clock, and he slewed round and located it on the wall behind him. The hour it indicated sank slowly into his brain, and again he calculated. Two hours for twelve miles. Easy enough—he could probably get hold of a lorry, or something else on four wheels with an engine, that would scrape through in an hour, and leave another hour to deal with the trouble he was sure to meet in Saxmundham. For the bluff that could be put over on a village cop wouldn't cut much ice with the bulls of a rising town. And suppose the lorry broke down and left them stranded on the road. . . . Two lorries, then. Roger would have to follow in the second in case of accidents.

The Saint stood up.

"Will you push off and try to find me a couple of cars?" he said. "Anything that'll go. I've got another man with me—I'll have to fetch him. I'll meet you. . . ."

His voice trailed away.

For the constable was staring at him as if he were a ghost; and a moment later he understood why. The constable held a sheet of paper in his hand—it was one of the bundle that he had taken from his pocket, but it was not a map—and he was looking from the paper to the Saint with bulging eyes. And the Saint knew what the paper was, and his right hand moved quietly to his hip pocket.

Yet his face betrayed nothing.

"What's the matter, officer?" he inquired curtly. "Aren't you well?"

Still staring, the policeman inhaled audibly. And then he spoke.

"Oi knew Oi'd seen your face befoor!"

"What the devil do you mean?"

"Oi knoo wot Oi mean." The policeman put the paper back on the table and thumped it triumphantly. "This is your phootograph, an' it says as you're wanted for murder!"

Simon stood like a rock.

"My good man, you're talking through your hat," he said incisively. "I've shown you my identity card——"

"Ay, that you 'ave. But that's just wot it says 'ere." The constable snatched up the paper again. "You tell me wot this means: ' *As frequently represented 'imself to be a police officer.*' An' if callin' yourself a Secret Service agent ain't as good as callin' yourself a police officer, Oi'd loike to knoo wot's wot!"

"I don't know who you're mixing me up with——"

"Oi'm not mixin' you up with anyone. Oi knoo 'oo you are. An' you called me a blistered boob, didn't you? Tellin' me the tale loike that—the worst tale ever I 'eard! Oi'll shoo you if Oi'm a blistered boob. . . ."

The Saint stepped back and his hand came out of his pocket. After all, there was no crowd here to interfere with a straight fight.

"O.K. again, son," he drawled. "I'll promise to recommend you for promotion when I'm caught. You're a smart lad. . . . But you won't catch me. . . ."

The Saint was on his toes, his hands rising with a little smile on his lips and a twinkle of laughter in his eyes. And suddenly the policeman must have realized that perhaps after all he had been a blistered boob— that he ought to have kept his discovery to himself until he could usefully reveal it. For the Saint didn't look an easy man to arrest at that moment. . . .

And, suddenly, the policeman yelled—once.

Then the Saint's fists lashed into his jaw, left and right, with two crisp smacks like a kiss-cannon of magnified billiard balls, and he went down like a log.

"And that's that," murmured the Saint grimly.

He reached the window in three strides, and stood there, listening. And out of the gloom there came to him the sound of hoarse voices and hurrying men.

"Well, well, *well!*" thought the Saint, with characteristic gentleness, and understood that a rapid exit was the next thing for him. If only the cop hadn't managed to uncork that stentorian bellow. . . . But it was too late to think about that—much too late to sit down and indulge in vain lamentations for the bluff that might have been put over the villagers while the cop lay gagged and bound in the station master's office, if only the cop had passed out with his mouth shut. "It's a great little evening," thought the Saint, as he slipped over the sill.

He disappeared into the shadows down the platform like a prowling cat a moment before the leading pair of boots came pelting over the concrete. At the end of the platform he found a board fence, and he was astride it when a fresh outcry arose from behind him. Still smiling abstractedly, he lowered himself onto a patch of grass beside the road. The road itself was deserted—evidently all the men who had followed them to the station had rushed in to discover the reason for the noise—and no one challenged the Saint as he walked swiftly and silently down the dark street. And long before the first feeble apology for a hue and cry arose behind him he was flitting soundlessly up the cliff road, and he had no fear that he would be found.

IV

IT WAS EXACTLY half-past four when he closed the door of Marius's library behind him and faced six very silent people. But one of them found quite an ordinary thing to say.

"Thank the Lord," said Roger Conway.

He pointed to the open window; and the Saint nodded.

"You heard?"

"Quite enough of it."

The Saint lighted a cigarette with a steady hand.

"There was a little excitement," he said quietly.

Sonia Delmar was looking at him steadfastly, and there was a shining pity in her eyes.

"You didn't get through," she said.

It was a plain statement—a statement of what they all knew without being told. And Simon shook his head slowly.

"I didn't. The telephone line's down between here and Saxmundham, and I couldn't get any answer from station telegraph. Angel Face knew about the telephone—that's one reason why he heaved his own at me."

"And they spotted you in the village?"

"Later. I had to break into the post office—the dames in charge were away—but I got away with that. Told the village cop I was a secret agent. He swallowed that at first, and actually helped me break into the station. And then he got out a map to find out how far it was to Saxmundham, and pulled out his *Police News* with my photograph in it at the same time. I laid him, if course, but I wasn't quite quick enough. Otherwise I might still have got something to take us into Saxmundham—I was just fixing that when the cop tried to earn his medal."

"You might have told him the truth," Roger ventured.

He expected a storm, but the Saint's answer was perfectly calm.

"I couldn't risk it, old dear. You see, I'd started off with a lie, and then I'd called him a blistered boob when I was playing the Secret Service gag—and I'd sized up my man. I reckon I'd have had one chance in a thousand of convincing him. He was as keen as knives to get his own back, and his kind of head can only hold one idea at a time. And if I *had* convinced him, it'd have taken hours, and we'd still have had to get through to Saxmundham; and if I'd failed—"

He left the sentence unfinished. There was no need to finish it.

And Roger bit his lip.

"Even now," said Roger, "we might as well be marooned on a desert island."

Sonia Delmar spoke again.

"That ambulance," she said. "The one they brought me here in——"

It was Marius who answered, malevolently from his corner.

"The ambulance has gone, my dear young lady. It returned to London immediately afterwards."

In a dead silence the Saint turned.

"Then I hope you'll go on enjoying your triumph, Angel Face," he said, and there was a ruthless devil in his voice. "Because I swear to you, Rayt Marius, that it's the last you will ever enjoy. Others have killed; but you have sold the bodies and souls of men. The world is poisoned with every breath you breathe. . . . And I've changed my mind about giving you a fighting chance."

The Saint was resting against the door; he had not moved from it since he came in. He rested there quite slackly, quite lazily; but now his gun was in his hand, and he was carefully thumbing down the safety catch. And Roger Conway, who knew what the Saint was going to do, strove to speak casually.

"I suppose," remarked Roger Conway casually, "you could hardly run the distance in the time. You used to be pretty useful——"

The Saint shook his head.

"I'm afraid it's a bit too much," he answered. "It isn't as if I could collapse artistically at the finish. . . . No, old Roger, I can't do it. Unless I could grow a pair of wings——"

"Wings!"

It was Sonia Delmar who repeated the word—who almost shouted it—clutching the Saint's sleeve with hands that trembled.

But Simon Templar had already started up, and a great light was breaking in his eyes.

"God's mercy!" he cried, with a passionate sincerity ringing through the strangeness of his oath. "You've said it, Sonia! And *I* said it. . . . *We'd forgotten Angel Face's aëroplane!"*

14

How Roger Conway Was Left Alone, and Simon Templar Went to His Reward

THE SAINT'S GUN was back in his pocket; there was a splendid laughter in his eyes, and a more splendid laughter in his heart. And it was with the same laughter that he turned again to Marius.

"After all, Angel Face," he said, "we shall have our fight!"

And Marius did not answer.

"But not now, Saint!" Roger protested in an agony; and Simon swung round with another laugh and a flourish to go with it.

"Certainly not now, sweet Roger! That comes afterwards—with the port and cigars. What we're going to do now is jump for that blessed *avion.*"

"But where can we land? It must be a hundred miles to Croydon in a straight line. That'll take over an hour—after we've got going—and there's sure to be trouble at the other end——"

"We don't land, my cherub. At least, not till it's all over. I tell you, I've got this job absolutely taped. I'm there!"

The Saint's cigarette went spinning across the room, and burst in fiery stars against the opposite wall. And he drew Roger and the girl towards him, with a hand on each of their shoulders.

"Now see here. Roger, you'll come with me, and help me locate and start up the kite. Sonia, I want you to scrounge round and find a couple of helmets and a couple of pairs of goggles. Angel Face's outfit is bound to be around the house somewhere, and he's probably got some spares. After that, find me another nice long coil of rope—I'll bet they've got plenty—and your job's done. Lessing"—he looked across at the millionaire, who had risen to his feet at last—"it's about time you did something for your life. You find some stray bits of string, without cutting into the beautiful piece that Sonia's going to find for me, and amuse yourself splicing large and solid chairs onto Freeman, Hardy, and Willis over in the corner. Then they'll be properly settled to wait here till I come back for them. Is that all clear?"

A chorus of affirmatives answered him.

"Then we'll go," said the Saint.

And he went; but he knew that all that he had ordered would be done. The new magnificent vitality that had come to him, the dazzling daredevil delight, was summed up and blazoned to them all in the gay smile with which he left them; it swept them up, inspired them, kindled within them the flame of his own superb rapture; he knew that his spirit stayed with them, to spur them on. Even Lessing. . . .

And Roger. . . .

And Roger said awkwardly as they turned the corner of the house and went swiftly over the dark grassland: "Sonia told me more about that cruise while you were away, Saint."

"Did she now?"

"I'm sorry I behaved like I did, old boy."

Simon chuckled.

"Did you think I'd stolen her from you, Roger?"

"Do you want to?" Roger asked evenly.

They moved a little way in silence.

Then the Saint said: "You see, there's always Pat."

"Yes."

"I'll tell you something. I think, when she first met me, Sonia fell. I know I did—Got help me—in a kind of way. I still think she's—just great. There's no other word for her. But then, there's no other word for Pat."

"No."

"More than once, it did occur to me——But what's the use? There are all kinds of people in this wall-eyed world, and especially all kinds of women. They're just made different ways, and you can't alter it. I suppose you'll call that trite; but I give you my word, Roger, I had to go on that cruise last night before I really understood the saying. And so did Sonia. But I got more out of it than she did, because it was the sequel that was so frightfully funny, and I don't think she'll ever see the joke. I don't think you will, either; and that's another reason why——"

"What was the joke?" Roger asked.

"When we met Hermann," said the Saint, "and Hermann pointed a gun at me, Sonia also had a gun. And Sonia didn't shoot. Pat wouldn't have missed that chance." He stopped, and raised the lantern he carried. "And that's out kite, isn't it?" he said.

A little way ahead of them loomed up the squat black shape of a small hangar. They reached it in a few more strides, and the Saint pulled back the sliding doors. And the aëroplane was there—a Gypsy Moth in silver and gold, with its wings demurely folded. "Isn't this our evening?" drawled the Saint.

Roger said cautiously: "So long as there's enough juice."

"We'll see," said the Saint, and he was already peering at the gauge. His murmur of satisfaction rang hollowly between the corrugated iron walls. "Ten gallons . . . It's good enough!"

They wheeled the machine out together, and the Saint set up the wings. Then he hustled Roger into the cockpit and took hold of the propeller.

"Switch off—suck in!"

The screw went clicking round; then:

"Contact!"

"Contact!"

The engine coughed once, and then the propeller vibrated back to stillness. Again the Saint bent his back, and this time the engine stuttered round a couple of revolutions before it stopped again.

"It's going to be an easy start," said the Saint. "Half a sec. while I see if they've got any blocks."

He vanished into the hangar, and returned in a moment with a couple of large wooden wedges that trailed cords behind them. These he fixed under the wheels, laying out the cords in the line of the wings; then he went back to the propeller.

"We ought to do it this time. Suck in again!"

Half a dozen brisk winds and he was ready.

"Contact!"

"Contact!"

A heaving jerk at the screw. . . . The engine gasped, stammered, hesitated, picked up with a loud roar. . . .

"Hot dog!" said the Saint.

He sprinted round the wing and leaped to the side, with one foot in the stirrup and a long arm reaching over to the throttle.

"Stick well back, Roger. . . . That's the ticket!"

The snarl of the engine swelled furiously; a gale of wind buffeted the Saint's face and twitched his coat half away from his shoulders. For a while he hung on, holding the throttle open, while the bellow of the engine battered his ears, and the machine strained and shivered where it stood; then he throttled back, and put his lips to Roger's ear.

"Hold on, son. I'll send Sonia out to you. Switch off the engine if she tries to run away."

Roger nodded; and the Saint sprang down and disappeared. In a few moments he was back at the house, with the mutter of the engine scattered through the dark behind him; and Sonia Delmar was waiting for him on the doorstep.

"I've got all the things you wanted," she said.

Simon glanced once at her burdens.

"That's splendid." He touched her hand. "Roger's out there, old dear. Would you like to take those effects out to him?"

"Sure."

"Right. Follow the noise and don't run into the prop. Where's Ike?"

"He's nearly finished."

"O.K. I'll bring him along."

With a smile he left her, and went on into the library. Lessing was just rising from his knees; a glance showed Simon that Marius, the German, and the Bowery Boy had been dealt with as per invoice.

"All clear, Ike?" murmured the Saint; and Lessing nodded.

"I don't think they'll get away, though I'm not an expert at this game."

"It looks good to me—for an amateur. Now, will you filter out into the hall? I'll be with you in one moment."

The millionaire went out submissively; and Simon turned to Marius for the last time. Through the open window came a steady distant drone; and Marius must have heard and understood it, but his face was utterly inscrutable.

"So," said the Saint softly, "I have beaten you again, Angel Face."

The giant looked at him with empty eyes.

"I am never beaten, Templar," he said.

But you are beaten this time," said the Saint. "Tomorrow morning I shall come back, and we shall settle our account. And, in case I fail, I shall bring the police with me. They will be very interested to hear all the things I shall have to tell them. The private plotting of wars for gain may not be punishable by any laws, but men are hanged for high treason. Even now, I'm not sure that I wouldn't rather have you hanged. There's something very definite and unromantic about hanging. But I'll decide that before I return. . . . I leave you to meditate on your victory."

And Simon Templar turned on his heel and went out, closing and locking the door behind him.

Sir Isaac Lessing stood in the hall. He was still deathly pale, but there was a strange kind of courage in the set of his lips and the levelling of the eyes with which he faced the Saint—the strangest of all kinds of courage.

"I believe I owe you my life, Mr. Templar," he said steadily; but the Saint's nod was curt.

"You're welcome."

"I'm not used to these things," Lessing said; "and I find I'm not fitted for them. I suppose you can't help despising me. I can only say that I agree with you. And I should like to apologize."

For a long moment the Saint looked at him, but Lessing met the clear blue gaze without flinching. And then Simon gripped the millionaire's arm.

"The others are waiting for us," he said. "I'll talk to you as we go."

They passed out of the door; and the Saint, glancing back, saw a man huddled in one corner of the hall, very still. By the lodge gates, a little while before, he had seen another man, just as still. And later, he told Roger Conway that those two men were dead. "You want to be careful how you bash folks with the blunt end of a gat," said the Saint. "It's so dreadfully easy to stave in their skulls.'' But he never told Roger what he said to Sir Isaac Lessing in the small hours of that morning as they walked across the landing field under the stars.

II

"AND SO WE leave you,'' said the Saint.

He had been busy for a short time performing some obscure operation with the rope that Sonia Delmar had brought; but now he came round the aëroplane into the light of the lantern, buckling the strap of his helmet. Lessing waited a little way apart; but Simon called him, and he came up and joined the group.

"We'll meet you in London,'' said the Saint. "As soon as we're off you'd better take Sonia down to the station and wait there for the first train. I don't think you'll have any trouble; but if you do it shouldn't be difficult to deal with it. There's nothing you can be held for. But for God's sake don't say anything about Angel Face or this house—I'd as soon trust that village cop to look after Angel Face as I'd leave my favourite white mouse under the charge of a hungry cat. When you get to town I expect you'll want some sleep, but you'll find us in Upper Berkeley Mews this evening. Sonia knows the place.''

Lessing nodded.

"Good luck,'' he said, and held out his hand.

Simon crushed it in a clasp of steel.

He moved away, held up his handkerchief for a moment to check the wind, and went to clear the chocks from under the wheels. Then he climbed into the front cockpit and plugged his telephones into the rubber connection. His voice boomed through the speaking tube.

"All set, Roger?''

"All set.''

The Saint looked back.

He saw Roger catch the girl's hand to his lips; and then she tore herself away. And with that last glimpse of her, the Saint settled his goggles over his eyes and pushed the stick forward; and the tumult of the engine rose to a howl as he threw open the throttle and they began to jolt forward over the grass.

Not quite so damned easy, taking off on a dark night, with the Lord knew what at the end of the run. . . . But he kept the tail up grimly until he had got his full flying speed, and then eased the stick back as quickly as he dared. . . . The bumping lessened, ceased altogether; they rushed smoothly through the air. . . . Looking over the side, he saw a black feather of tree-top slip by six feet below, and grinned his relief. Turning steeply to the west, he saw a tiny speck of light in the darkness beyond his wing tip. The lantern. . . . And then the machine came level again, and went racing through the night in a gentle climb.

The stinging swiftness of the upper air was new life to him. A little while ago he had been weary to death, though no one had known: but now he felt shoutingly fit for the adventure of his life. It might have been because of the fresh hope he had found when there had seemed to be no hope. . . . For he had his chance; and, if human daring and skill and sinew counted for anything, he would not fail. And so the work would be done, and life would go on, and there would be other things to see and new songs to sing. Battle, murder, and sudden death, he had had them all—full measure, pressed down, running over. And he had loved them for their own sake. . . . And his follies he had had, temptations, nonsense, fool's paradise and fool's hell; and those also had gone over. And now a vow had been fulfilled, and much good done, and a great task was near its end; but there must be other things.

> *"For the song and the sword and the pipes of Pan*
> *Are birthrights sold to a usurer;*
> *But I am the last lone highwayman,*
> *And I am the last adventurer."*

Not even all that he had done was a destiny; there must always be other things. So long as the earth turned for the marching seasons, and the stars hung in the sky, for so long there would be other things. There was neither climax nor anticlimax: a full life had no place for such trivial theatricalities. A full life was made up of all that life had to offer; it was complete, taking everything without fear and giving everything without favour; and wherever it ended it would always be whole. So it would go on. To fight and kill one day, to rescue the next; to be rich one day, and to be a beggar the next; to sin one day, and to do something heroic the next—so might a man's sins be forgiven. And there was so much that he had not done. He hadn't walked in the gardens of Monte Carlo, immaculate in evening dress, and he hadn't tramped from one end of Europe to the other in the oldest clothes he could find. He hadn't been a beachcomber on a South Sea island, or built a house with his own hands, or read the lessons in a church, or been to Timbuktu, or been married, or cheated at cards, or learned to talk Chinese, or shot a sitting rabbit, or driven a Ford, or . . . Hell! Was there ever an end? And everything that a man could do must enrich him in some way, and for everything that he did not do his life must be for ever poorer. . . .

So, as the aëroplane fled westwards across the sky, and the sky behind it began to pale with the promise of dawn, the Saint found a strange peace of heart; and he laughed. . . .

His course was set unerringly. In the old days there had been hardly an inch of England over which he had not flown; and he had no need of maps. As the silver in the sky spread wanly up the heavens, the country beneath him was slowly lighted for his eyes; and he began to school Roger in a difficult task.

"You have handled the controls before, haven't you, old dear?" he remarked coolly; and an unenthusiastic reply came back to him.

"Only for a little while."

"Then you've got about half an hour to learn to handle them as if you'd been born in the air!"

Roger Conway said things—naughty and irrelevant things, which do not belong here. And the Saint smiled.

"Come on," he said. "Let's see you do a gentle turn."

After a pause, the machine heeled over drunkenly. . . .

"Verminous," said the Saint scathingly. "You're too rough on that rudder. Try to imagine that you're not riding a bicycle. And don't use the stick as if you were stirring porridge. . . . Now we'll do one together." They did. "And now one to the left. . . ."

For ten minutes the instruction went on.

"I guess you ought to be fairly safe on that," said the Saint at the end of that time. "Keep the turns gentle, and you won't hurt yourself. I'm sorry I haven't time to tell you all about spins, so if you get into one I'm afraid you'll just have to die. Now we'll take the glide."

Then Roger was saying, unhappily: "What's the idea of all this, Saint?"

"Sorry," said the Saint, "but I'm afraid you'll be in sole charge before long. I'm going to be busy."

He explained why; and Roger's gasp of horror came clearly through the telephones.

"But how the hell am I going to get down, Saint?"

"Crash in the Thames," answered Simon succinctly. "Glide down to a nice quiet spot, just as you've been taught, undo your safety belt, flatten out gently when you're near the water, and pray. It's not our aëroplane, anyway.''

"It's my life,'' said Roger gloomily.

"You won't hurt yourself, sonny boy. Now, wake up and try your hand at this contour chasing. . . .''

And the nose of the machine went down, with a sudden scream of wires. The ground, luminous now with the cold pallor of the sky before sunrise, heaved up deliriously to meet them. Roger's head sang with a rush of blood, and he seemed to have left his stomach about a thousand feet behind. . . . Then the stick stroked back between his legs, his stomach flopped nauseatingly down towards his seat, and he felt slightly sick. . . .

"Is it always as bad as that?'' he inquired faintly.

"Not if you don't come down so fast,'' said the Saint cheerfully. "That was just to save time. . . . Now, you simply must get used to this low flying. It's only a matter of keeping your head and going light on the controls.'' The aeroplane shot between two trees, with approximately six inches to spare beyond either wing, and a flock of sheep stampeded under their wheels. "You're flying her, Roger! Let's skim this next hedge. . . . No, you're too high. I said skim, not skyrocket.'' The stick went forward a trifle. "That's better. . . . Now miss this fence by about two feet. . . . No, that was nearer ten feet. Try to do better at the next, but don't go to the other extreme and take the undercarriage off. . . . *That's* more like it! You were only about four feet up that time. If you can get that distance fixed in your eye, you'll be absolutely all right. Now do the same thing again. . . . Good! Now up a bit for these trees. Try to miss them by the same distance—it'll be good practice for you. . . .''

And Roger tried. He tried as he had never before tried anything in his life, for he knew how much depended on him. And the Saint urged him on, speaking all the time in the same tone of quiet encouragement, grimly trying to crowd a month's instruction into a few minutes. And somehow he achieved results. Roger was getting the idea; he was getting that most essential thing, the feel of the machine; and he had started off with the greatest of all blessings—a cool head and an instinctive judgment. It was much later when he found a patch of gray hair on each of his temples. . . .

And so, for the rest of that flight, they worked on together, with the

Saint glancing from time to time at his watch, yet never varying the patient steadiness of his voice.

And then the time came when the Saint said that the instruction must be over, hit or miss; and he took over the controls again. They soared up in a swift climb; and, as the fields fell away beneath them, a shaft of light from the shy rim of the sun caught them like a fantastic spotlight, and the aëroplane was turned to a hurtling jewel of silver and gold in the translucent gulf of the sky.

III

"DOWN THERE, ON your right!" cried the Saint; and Roger looked over where the Saint's arm pointed.

He saw the fields laid out underneath them like a huge unrolled map. The trees and little houses were like the toys that children play with, building their villages on a nursery floor. And over that grotesque vision of a puny world seen as an idle god might see it, a criss-cross of roads and lanes sprawled like a sparse muddle of strings, and a railway line was like a knife-cut across the icing of a cake, and down the railway line puffed the tiniest of toy trains.

The aëroplane swung over in a steep bank, and the map seemed to slide up the sky until it stood like a wall at their wing tip; and the Saint spoke again.

"Hermann's about twenty miles away, but that doesn't give us much time at seventy miles an hour. So you've got to get it over quickly, Roger. If you can do your stuff as you were doing it just now, there's simply nothing can go wrong. Don't get excited, and just be a wee bit careful not to stall when my weight comes off. I'm not quite sure what the effect will be."

"And suppose—suppose you don't bring it off?"

They were flying to meet the toy train now.

"If I miss, Roger, the only thing I can ask you to do is to try to land farther up the line. You'll crash, of course, but if you turn your petrol off first you may live to tell the tale. But whether you try it or not is up to you."

"I'll try it, Saint, if I have to."

"Good scout."

They had passed over the train; and then again they turned steeply, and went in pursuit.

And the Saint's calm voice came to Roger's ears with a hint of reckless laughter somewhere in its calm.

"You've got her, old Roger. I'm just going to get out. So long, old dear, and the best of luck."

"Good luck, Simon."

And Roger Conway took over the controls.

And then he saw the thing that he will never forget. He saw the Saint climb out of the cockpit in front of him, and saw him stagger on the wing as the wind caught him and all but tore him from his precarious hold. And then the Saint had hold of a strut with one hand, and the rope that he had fixed with the other, and he was backing towards the leading edge of the wing. Roger saw him smile, the old incomparable Saintly smile. . . . And then the Saint was on his knees; then his legs had disappeared from view; then there was only his head and shoulders and two hands. . . . one hand. . . . And the Saint was gone.

Roger put the stick gently forward.

He looked back over the side as he did so, in a kind of sick terror that he would se a foolish spread-eagle shape dwindling down into the unrolled map four thousand feet below; but he saw nothing. And then he had eyes only for the train.

Hit or miss. . . .

And Simon Templar also watched the train.

He dangled at the end of his rope, like a spider on a thread, ten feet below the silver and gold fuselage. One foot rested in a loop that he had knotted for himself before they started; his hands were locked upon the rope itself. And the train was coming nearer.

The wind lashed him with invisible whips, billowing his coat, fighting him with savage flailing fingers. It was an effort to breathe; to hold on at all was a battle. And he was supposed to be resting there. He had deliberately taught Roger to fly low, much lower than was necessary, because that extreme was far safer than the possibility of being trailed along twenty feet above the carriage roofs. When the time came he would slip down the rope, hang by his arms, and let go as soon as he had the chance.

And that time was not far distant. Roger was diving rather steeply, with his engine full on. . . . But the train was also moving. . . . At two hundred feet the Saint guessed that they were overtaking the train at about twenty miles an hour. He ought to have told Roger about that. . . . But then Roger must have seen the mistake also, for he throttled the engine down a trifle, and they lost speed. And they were drifting lower. . . .

With a brief prayer, the Saint twitched his foot out of the stirrup and went down the rope hand over hand.

"Glory!" thought the Saint. "If the fool stalls—if he tries to cut his speed down by bringing the stick back . . ."

But they weren't stalling. They were keeping their height for a moment; then they dipped straightly, gaining on the train at about fifteen miles an hour . . . no, ten. . . . And the hindmost carriage slipped under the Saint's feet—a dozen feet under them.

There were only three coaches on the train.

But they were dropping quickly now—Roger was contour-chasing like an ace! He wasn't dead centre, though. . . . A shade to one side. . . . "Just a touch of left rudder!" cried the Saint helplessly; for one of his feet had scraped the outside edge of a carriage roof, and they were still going lower. . . . And then, somehow, it happened just as if Roger could have heard him: the Saint was clear over the roof of the leading coach, and his knees and arms were bent to keep his feet off it. . . .

And he let go.

The train seemed to bear away from under him; his left hand crashed into a projection, and went numb; and the roof became red-hot and scorched his legs. He felt himself slithering towards the side, and flung out his sound right hand blindly. . . . He caught something like a handle . . . held on . . . and the slipping stopped with a jar that sent a twinge of agony stabbing through his shoulder.

He lay there gasping, dumbly bewildered that he should still be alive. For a full minute. . . .

And then the meaning of it filtered into his understanding; and he laughed softly, absurdly, a laughter queerly close to tears.

For the work was done.

Slowly, in a breathless wonder, he turned his head. The aëroplane was turning, coming back towards him, alongside the train, low down. And a face looked out, helmeted, with its big round goggles masking all expression and giving it the appearance of some macabre gargoyle; but all that could be seen of the face was as white as the morning sky.

Simon waved his injured hand; and, as the aëroplane swept by in a droning thunder of noise, the snowy flutter of a handkerchief broke out against its silver and gold. And so the aëroplane passed, rising slowly as it went towards the north, with the sunrise striking it like a banner unfurled.

And five minutes later, in a strange and monstrous contrast to the flamboyant plumage of the great metal bird that was swinging smoothly round into the dawn, a strained and tatterdemalion figure came reeling over the tender of the swaying locomotive; and the two men in the cab, who had been watching him from the beginning, were there to catch him as he fell into their arms.

"You come outa that airyplane?" blurted one of them dazedly; and Simon Templar nodded.

He put up a filthy hand and smeared the blood out of his eyes.

"I came to tell you to stop the train," he said. "There are two bombs on the line."

IV

THE SAINT RESTED where they had laid him down. He had never known what it was to be so utterly weary. All his strength seemed to have ebbed out of him, now that it had served for the supreme effort. He felt that he had not slept for a thousand years. . . .

All around him there was noise. He heard the hoarse roar of escaping steam, the whine of brakes, the fading clatter of movement, the jolt and hiss of the stop. In the sudden silence he heard the far, steady drone of the aëroplane filling the sky. Then there were voices, running feet, questions and answers mingling in an indecipherable murmur. Someone shook him by the shoulder, but at that moment he felt too tired to rouse, and the man moved away.

And then, presently, he was shaken again, more insistently. A cool wet cloth wiped his face, and he heard a startled exclamation. The aëroplane seemed to have gone, though he had not heard its humming die away: he must have passed out altogether for a few seconds. Then a glass was pressed to his lips; he gulped, and spluttered as the neat spirit rawed his throat. And he opened his eyes.

"I'm all right," he muttered.

All he saw at first was a pair of boots. Large boots. And his lips twisted with a rueful humour. Then he looked up and saw the square face and the bowler hat of the man whose arm was around his shoulders.

"Bombs, old dear," said the Saint. "They've got the niftiest little electric firing device attached—you lay it over the line, and it blows up the balloon when the front wheels of the train go over it. That's my dying speech. Now it's your turn.''

The man in the bowler hat nodded.

''We've already found them. You only stopped us with about a hundred yards to spare.'' He was looking at the Saint with a kind of wry regret. ''And I know you,'' he said.

Simon smiled crookedly.

''What a thing is fame!'' he sighed. ''I know you, too, Detective-Inspector Carn. How's trade? I shall come quietly this time, anyway— I couldn't run a yard.''

The detective's lips twitched a trifle grimly. He glanced over his shoulder.

''I think the King is waiting to speak to you,'' he said.

15

How Simon Templar Put Down a Book

IT WAS LATE in a fair September afternoon when Roger Conway turned into Upper Berkeley Mews and admitted himself with his own key.

He found the Saint sitting in an armchair by the open window with a book on his knee, and was somehow surprised.

''What are you doing here?'' he demanded; and Simon rose with a smile.

''I have slept,'' he murmured. ''And so have you, from all accounts.''

Roger spun his peaked cap across the room. ''I have,'' he said. ''I believe the order for my release came through about lunchtime, but they thought it would be a shame to wake me.''

The Saint inspected him critically. Roger's livery covered him uncomfortably. It looked as if it had shrunk. It had shrunk.

''Jolly looking clothes, those are,'' Simon remarked. ''Is it the new fashion? I'd be afraid of catching cold in the elbows, you know. Besides, the pants don't look safe to sit down in.''

Roger returned the survey insultingly.

"How much are you expecting to get on that face in part exchange?" he inquired; and suddenly the Saint laughed.

"Well, you knock-kneed bit of moth-eaten gorgonzola!"

"Well, you cross-eyed son of flea-bitten hobo!"

And all at once their hands met in an iron grasp.

"Still," said the Saint presently, "you don't look your best in that outfit, and I guess you'll feel better when you've had a shave. Some kind soul gave me a ring to say you were on your way, and I've turned the bath on for you and laid out your other suit. Push on, old bacillus; and I'll sing to you when you come back."

"I shall not come back for years," said Roger delicately.

The Saint grinned.

He sat down again as Roger departed and took up his book again, and traced a complicated arabesque in the corner of a page thoughtfully. Then he wrote a few more lines, and put away his fountain pen. He lighted a cigarette and gazed at a picture on the other side of the room: he was still there when Roger returned.

And Roger said what he had meant to say before.

"I was thinking," Roger said, "you'd have gone after Angel Face."

Simon turned the pages of his book.

"And so was I," he said. "But the reason why I haven't is recorded here. This is the tome in which I dutifully make notes of our efforts for the benefit of an author bloke I know, who has sworn to make a blood-and-thunder classic of us one day. This entry is very tabloid."

"What is it?"

"It just says—'Hermann.' "

And the Saint, looking up, saw Roger's face, and laughed softly.

"In the general excitement," he said gently, "we forgot dear Hermann. And Hermann was ordered to go straight back as soon as he'd parked his bombs. I expect he has. Anyway, I haven't heard that he's been caught. There's still a chance, of course. . . . Roger, you may wonder what's happened to me, but I rang up our old friend Chief Inspector Teal and told him all about Saltham, and he went off as fast as a police car could take him. It remains to be seen whether he arrived in time. . . . The crown prince left England last night, but they've collected Heinrich. I'm afraid Ike will have to get a new staff of servants, though. His old ones are dead beyond repair. . . . I think that's all the dope,"

"It doesn't seem to worry you," said Roger.

"Why should it?" said the Saint a little tiredly. "We've done our job. Angel Face is smashed, whatever happens. He'll never be a danger to the world again. And if he's caught he'll be hanged, which will do him a lot of good. On the other hand, if he gets away, and we're destined to have another round—that is as the Lord may provide.''

"And Norman?"

The Saint smiled, a quiet little smile.

"There was a letter from Pat this morning," he said. "Posted at Suez. They're going on down the east coast of Africa, and they expect to get around to Madeira in the spring. And I'm going to do something that I think Norman would have wanted far more than vengeance. I'm going adventuring across Europe; and at the end of it I shall find my lady.''

Roger moved away and glanced at the telephone.

"Have you heard from Sonia?" he asked.

"She called up," said the Saint. "I told her to come right round and bring papa. They should be here any minute now."

Conway picked up the *Bystander* and put it down again.

He said: "Did you mean everything you said last night—this morning?''

Simon stared out of the window.

"Every word," he said.

He said: "You see, old Roger, some queer things happen in this life of ours. You cut adrift from all ordinary rules; and then, sometimes, when you'd sell your soul for a rule, you're all at sea. And when that happens to a man he's surely damned, bar the grace of Heaven; because I only know one thing worse than swallowing every commandment that other people lay down for you, and that's having no commandments but those you lay down for yourself. None of which abstruse philosophy you will understand. . . . But I'll tell you, Roger, by way of a fact, that everything life gives you has to be paid for; also that where your life leads you, there will your heart be also. Selah. Autographed copies of that speech, on vellum, may be obtained on the installment plan at all public houses and speakeasies—one pound down, and the rest up a gum tree. . . .''

A car drove down the mews and stopped by the door. But Roger Conway was still looking at the Saint; and Roger was understanding, with a strange wild certainty, that perhaps after all he had never known the Saint, and perhaps he would never know him.

The Saint closed his book. He laid it down on the table beside him, and turned to meet Roger's eyes.

" 'For all the Saints who from their labours rest,' " he said. "Sonia has arrived, my Roger."

And he stood up, with the swift careless laugh that Roger knew, and his hand fell on Roger's shoulder, and so they went out together into the sunlight.

The Saint vs. Scotland Yard

TO
PAULINE
for happy days

Contents

Between Ourselves

NOW THAT THE last line of this, the eighth book about the Saint, has been written and blotted and passed on to its fate, I begin to wonder whether anyone has realised why I should have carried on with him so long.

Eight books, comprising some twenty adventures of the same character, is a pretty impressive sequence. I am not sure if it has yet broken the record for fictional biographies; but I'm quite sure that it's going to. For there is going to be more.

And why?

Because, in spite of the wrath of the *Gotherington Gazette and Argus,* and the patronising paragraphs of the *Tarsus (Tennessee) Tribune,* I sincerely believe that those eight books were well worth writing, and that the next eight will be even better.

Personally, I like the Saint—but maybe I'm prejudiced.

He is my protest against the miserable half-heartedness of these days. To him you may say—as has always been said to me—"One day you will settle down. One day you'll lose this youthful impetuosity and impatience, and settle down to a normal life. It is one of the things that happens." But he will not believe you. Because it will not be true.

This rubbing off of corners, this settling down, this normal life! You have tried so hard to make Youth believe you, with your specious arguments about civilisation, your weight of pot-bellied disapproval, your cheap and facile sneers!

> You have taken the wine and the laughter,
> The pride and the grace of days.

You tried to make me believe you when I was younger, but I knew better. And so you shall not shake the faith of anyone who reads a line of mine.

You are surprised? You are slightly shocked that any writer of mere "thrillers" should have the impertinence to take himself seriously?

495

I am sorry for you.

But you may still read of the Saint. He will at least entertain you. For his philosophy—and mine—is happy. You will be bored with no dreary introspections about death and doom, as in the works of your dyspeptic little Russians. You will not find him gloating interminably over the pimples on his immortal soul, as do the characters of your septic little scribblers in Bloomsbury.

Of course, if you will only admit into the sacred realms of "literature" those adventure stories in which the fighting is done with swords and the travelling on horseback, I can only amuse your idle moments. But even that is worth while. I shall be a breath of fresh air to you, and it will do you a lot of good.

Or are you of our own mettle?

Then come with us. And if your own faith is weakening, if you have begun to believe the lies or fear the mockery of the fools who have never been young, the Saint and I will inspire you.

We will go out and find more and more adventures. We will swagger and swashbuckle and laugh at the half-hearted. We will boast and sing and throw our weight about. We will put the paltry little things to derision, and dare to be angry about the things that are truly evil. And we shall refuse to grow old.

Being wise, we shall not rail against the days into which we have been born. We shall see stumbling blocks, but we shall find them dragons meet for our steel. And we shall not mourn the trappings and accoutrements of fancy dress. What have they to do with us? Men wore cloaks and ruffles because they were the fashionable things to wear; but it was the way they wore them. Men rode horses because they had nothing else to ride; but it was the way they rode. Men fought with swords because they knew no better weapons; but it was the way they fought. So it shall be with us.

We shall learn that romance lies not in the things we do, but in the way we do them. We shall discover that catching a bus can be no less of an adventure than capturing a galleon, and that if a man loves a lady he need not weep because the pillion of his motor-cycle is not the saddlebow of an Arab steed. We shall find that love and hate can still be more than empty words. We shall speak with fire in our eyes and in our voices; and which of us will care whether we are discussing the destiny of nations or the destination of the Ashes? For we shall know that nothing else counts beside the vision.

Hasta la vista, companeros valientes! Y vayan con Dios!

LESLIE CHARTERIS

Part I
The Inland Revenue

1

BEFORE THE WORLD at large had heard even one lonely rumour about the gentleman who called himself, among other things, The Scorpion, there were men who knew him in secret. They knew him only as the Scorpion, and by no other name; and where he came from and where he lived were facts that certain of them would have given much to learn.

It is merely a matter of history that one of these men had an unassailable legal right to the name of Montgomery Bird, which everyone will agree was a very jolly sort of name for a bloke to have.

Mr. Montgomery Bird was a slim and very dapper little man; and although it is true that he wore striped spats there were even more unpleasant things about him which were not so noticeable but which it is the chronicler's painful duty to record. He was, for instance, the sole proprietor of a night club officially intituled The Eyrie, but better and perhaps more appropriately known as The Birds' Nest, which was a very low night club. And in this club, on a certain evening, he interviewed the Scorpion.

That Simon Templar happened to be present was almost accidental.

Simon Templar, in fact, having for some time past cherished a purely businesslike interest in the affairs of Mr. Montgomery Bird, had decided that the time was ripe for that interest to bear its fruit.

The means by which he became a member of the Eyrie are not known. Simon Templar had his own private ways of doing these things. It is enough that he was able to enter the premises unchallenged. He was saluted by the doorkeeper, climbed the steep stairs to the converted loft in which the Eyrie had its being, collected and returned the welcoming smile of the girl at the reception desk, delivered his hat into the keeping

499

of a liveried flunkey, and passed on unquestioned. Outside the glass doors that separated the supperroom from the lounge he paused for a moment, lighting a cigarette, while his eyes wandered lazily over the crowd. He already knew that Mr. Bird was in the habit of spending the evening among his guests, and he just wanted to make sure about that particular evening. He made sure; but his subsequent and consequent movements were forced to diverge slightly from schedule, as will be seen.

Mr. Bird had met the Scorpion before. When a waiter came through and informed him that a gentleman who would give no name was asking to speak to him, Mr. Bird showed no surprise. He went out to the reception desk, nodded curtly to the visitor, signed him in under the name of J. N. Jones, and led the way into his private office without comment.

He walked to his desk; and there he stopped and turned.

"What is it now?" he asked shortly, and the visitor shrugged his broad shoulders.

"Must I explain?"

Mr. Bird sat down in his swivel chair, rested his right ankle on his left knee, and leaned back. The fingers of one carefully manicured hand played a restless tattoo on the desk.

"You had a hundred pounds only last week," he said.

"And since then you have probably made at least three hundred," replied the visitor calmly.

He sat on the arm of another chair, and his right hand remained in the pocket of his overcoat. Mr. Bird, gazing at the pocket, raised one cynical eyebrow.

"You look after yourself well."

"An elementary precaution."

"Or an elementary bluff."

The visitor shook his head.

"You might test it—if you are tired of life."

Mr. Bird smiled, stroking his small moustache.

"With that—and your false beard and smoked glasses—you're an excellent imitation of a blackguard," he said.

"The point is not up for discussion," said the visitor smoothly. "Let us confine ourselves to the object of my presence here. Must I repeat that I know you to be a trader in illicit drugs? In this very room, probably, there is enough material evidence to send you to penal servitude for five years. The police, unaided, might search for it in vain. The secret of your ingenious little hiding-place under the floor in that corner might defy their best efforts. They do not know that it will only open when the door of this room is locked and the third and fifth sections of the wainscoting on that wall are slid upwards. But suppose they were anonymously informed—"

"And then found nothing there," said Montgomery Bird, with equal suavity.

"There would still be other suggestions that I could make," said the visitor.

He stood up abruptly.

"I hope you understand me," he said. "Your offences are no concern of mine, but they would be a great concern of yours if you were placed in the dock to answer for them. They are also too profitable for you to be ready to abandon them—yet. You will therefore pay me one hundred pounds a week for as long as I choose to demand it. Is that sufficiently plain?"

"You—"

Montgomery Bird came out of his chair with a rush.

The bearded man was not disturbed. Only his right hand, in his overcoat pocket, moved slightly.

"My—er—elementary bluff is still awaiting your investigation," he said dispassionately, and the other stopped dead.

With his head thrust a little forward, he stared into the tinted lenses that masked the big man's eyes.

"One day I'll get you—you swine—"

"And until that day, you will continue to pay me one hundred pounds a week, my dear Mr. Bird," came the gentle response. "Your next contribution is already due. If it is not troubling you too much—"

He did not bother to complete the sentence. He simply waited.

Bird went back to the desk and opened a drawer. He took out an envelope and threw it on the blotter.

"Thank you," said the visitor.

His fingers had just touched the envelope when the shrill scream of a bell froze him into immobility. It was not an ordinary bell. It had a vociferous viciousness about it that stung the eardrums—something like the magnified buzzing of an infuriated wasp.

"What is that?"

"My private alarm."

Bird glanced at the illuminated clock on the mantelpiece; and the visitor, following the glance, saw that the dial had turned red.

"A police raid?"

"Yes."

The big man picked up the envelope and thrust it into his pocket.

"You will get me out of here," he said.

Only a keen ear would have noticed the least fraying of the edges of his measured accents; but Montgomery Bird noticed it, and looked at him curiously.

"If I didn't—"

"You would be foolish—very foolish," said the visitor quietly.

Bird moved back, with murderous eyes. Set in one wall was a large mirror; he put his hands to the frame of it and pushed it bodily sideways in invisible grooves, revealing a dark rectangular opening.

And it was at that moment that Simon Templar, for his own inscrutable reasons, tired of his voluntary exile.

"Stand clear of the lift gates, please," he murmured.

To the two men, wheeling round at the sound of his voice like a pair of marionettes whose control wires have got mixed up with a dynamo, it seemed as if he had appeared out of the fourth dimension. Just for an instant. And then they saw the open door of the capacious cupboard behind him.

"Pass right down the car, gents," he murmured encouragingly.

He crossed the room. He appeared to cross it slowly, but that, again, was an illusion. He had reached the two men before either of them could move. His left hand shot out and fastened on the lapels of the bearded man's coat—and the bearded man vanished. It was the most startling thing that Mr. Montgomery Bird had ever seen; but the Saint did not seem to be aware that he was multiplying miracles with an easy grace that would have made a Grand Lama look like a third-rate three-card man. He calmly pulled the sliding mirror back into place, and turned round again.

"No—not you, Montgomery," he drawled. "We may want you again this evening. Backpedal, comrade."

His arm telescoped languidly outwards, and the hand at the end of it seized the retreating Mr. Bird by one ear, fetching him up with a jerk that made him squeak in muted anguish.

Simon steered him firmly but rapidly towards the open cupboard.

"You can cool off in there," he said; and the next sensations that impinged upon Montgomery Bird's delirious consciousness consisted of a lot of darkness and the sound of a key turning in the cupboard lock.

The Saint straightened his coat and returned to the centre of the room.

He sat down in Mr. Bird's chair, put his feet on Mr. Bird's desk, lighted one of Mr. Bird's cigars, and gazed at the ceiling with an expression of indescribable beatitude on his face; and it was thus that Chief Inspector Claud Eustace Teal found him.

Some seconds passed before the detective recovered the use of his voice; but when he had done this, he made up for lost time.

"What," he snarled, "the blankety blank blanking blank-blanked blank—"

"Hush," said the Saint.

"Why?" snarled Teal, not unreasonably.

Simon held up his hand.

"Listen."

There was a moment's silence; and then Teal's glare re-calorified.

"What am I supposed to be listening to?" he demanded violently; and the saint beamed at him.

"Down in the forest something stirred—it was only the note of a bird," he explained sweetly.

The detective centralised his jaw with a visible effort.

"Is Montgomery Bird another of your fancy names?" he inquired, with a certain lusciousness. "Because if it is—"

"Yes, old dear?"

"If it is," said Chief Inspector Teal grimly, "you're going to see the inside of a prison at last."

Simon regarded him imperturbably.

"On what charge?"

"You're going to get as long as I can get you for allowing drinks to be sold in your club after hours—"

"And then?"

The detective's eyes narrrowed.

"What do you mean?"

Simon flourished Mr. Bird's cigar airily.

"I always understood that the police were pretty bone-headed," he remarked genially, "but I never knew before that they'd been reduced to employing Chief Inspectors for ordinary drinking raids."

Teal said nothing.

"On the other hand, a dope raid is quite a different matter," said the Saint.

He smiled at the detective's sudden stillness, and stood up, knocking an inch of ash from his cigar.

"I must be toddling along," he murmured. "If you really want to find some dope, and you've any time to spare after you've finished cleaning up the bar, you ought to try locking the door of this room and pulling up bits of wainscoting. The third and fifth sections—I can't tell you which wall. Oh, and if you want Montgomery he's simmering down in the Frigidaire . . . See you again soon.''

He patted the crown of Mr. Teal's bowler hat affectionately, and was gone before the detective had completely grasped what was happening.

The Saint could make those well-oiled exits when he chose; and he chose to make one then, for he was a fundamentally tactful man. Also, he had in one pocket an envelope purporting to contain one hundred pounds, and in another pocket the entire contents of Mr. Montgomery Bird's official safe; and at such times the Saint did not care to be detained.

2

SIMON TEMPLAR PUSHED back his plate.

"Today," he announced, "I have reaped the first-fruits of virtue."

He raised the letter he had received, and adjusted an imaginary pair of pince-nez. Patricia waited expectantly.

The Saint read:

> *"Dear Mr. Templar,*
> *"Having come across a copy of your book 'The Pirate' and having nothing to do I sat down to read it. Well the impression it gave me was that you are a writer with no sense of proportion. The reader's sympathy owing to the faulty setting of the first chapter naturally goes all the way with Kerrigan, even though he is a crook. It is not surprising that this book has not gone to a second edition. You do not evidently understand the mentality of an English reading public. If instead of Mario you had selected for your hero an Englishman or an American, you would have written a fairly readable and a passable tale— but a lousy Dago who works himself out of impossible difficulties and situations is too much. It is not convincing. It does not appeal. In a word it is puerile.*

"I fancy you yourself must have a fair amount of Dago blood in you—"

He stopped, and Patricia Holm looked at him puzzledly.

"Well?" she prompted.

"There is no more," explained the Saint. "No address—no signature—no closing peroration—nothing. Apparently words failed him. At that point, he probably uttered a short sharp yelp of intolerable agony and began to chew pieces out of the furniture. We may never know his fate. Possibly, in some distant asylum—"

He elaborated his theory.

During a brief spell of virtue some time before, the Saint had beguiled himself with the writing of a novel. Moreover, he had actually succeeded in finding a home for it; and the adventures of Mario, a super-brigand of South America, could be purchased at any bookstall for three half-crowns. And the letter that he had just read was part of his reward.

Another part of the reward had commenced six months previously.

"Nor is this all," said the Saint, taking another document from the table. "The following *billet-doux* appears to close some entertaining correspondence:

> Previous applications for payment of the undermentioned instalment for the year 1931–1932, *due from you on the 1st day of January, 1932,* having been made to you without effect, PERSONAL DEMAND is now made for payment, and I HEREBY GIVE YOU FINAL NOTICE that if the amount be not paid or remitted to me at the above address within SEVEN DAYS from this date, steps will be taken for recovery by DISTRAINT, with costs.   LIONEL DELBORN, Collector."

In spite of the gloomy prognostications of the anonymous critic, *The Pirate* had not passed utterly unnoticed in the spate of sensational fiction. The Intelligence Department ("A beautiful name for them," said the Saint) of the Inland Revenue had observed its appearance, had consulted their records, and had discovered that the author, the notorious Simon Templar, was not registered as a contributor towards the expensive extravagances whereby a modern boobocracy does its share in encouraging the survival of the fattest. The Saint's views about his liabilities in this cause were not invited; he simply received an assessment which presumed his income to be six thousand pounds per annum, and he was invited to

appeal against it if he thought fit. The Saint thought fit, and declared that
the assessment was bad in law, erroneous in principle, excessive in
amount, and malicious in intent. The discussion that followed was lengthy
and diverting; the Saint, conducting his own case with remarkable forensic
ability and eloquence, pleaded that he was a charitable institution and
therefore not taxable.

"If," said the Saint, in his persuasive way, "you will look up the
delightful words of Lord Macnaghten, in *Income Tax Commissioners v.
Pemsel*, 1891, A. C. at p. 583, you will find that charitable purposes are
there defined in four principal divisions, of which the fourth is *'trusts for
purposes beneficial to the community, not falling under any of the pre-
ceding heads.'* I am simply and comprehensively beneficial to the community, which the face of the third Commissioner from the left definitely
is not."

We find from the published record of the proceedings that he was
overruled; and the epistle he had just quoted was final and conclusive
proof of the fact.

"And that," said the Saint, gazing at the formidable red lettering
gloomily, "is what I get for a lifetime of philanthropy and self-denial."

"I suppose you'll have to pay," said Patricia.

"Someone will," said the Saint significantly.

He propped the printed buff envelope that had accompanied the Final
Demand against the coffeepot, and his eyes rested on it for a space with
a gentle thoughtfulness—amazingly clear, devil-may-care blue eyes with
a growing glimmer of mischief lurking somewhere behind the lazily
drooping lids. And slowly the old Saintly smile came to his lips as he
contemplated the address.

"*Someone* will have to pay," repeated the Saint thoughtfully; and
Patricia Holm sighed, for she knew the signs.

And suddenly the Saint stood up, with his swift soft laugh, and took
the Final Demand and the envelope over to the fireplace. On the wall
close by hung a plain block calendar, and on the mantelpiece lay an old
Corsican stiletto. "*Che le mia ferita sia mortale,*" said the inscription
on the blade.

The Saint rapidly flicked over the pages of the calendar and tore out
the sheet which showed in solid red figures the day on which Mr. Lionel
Delborn's patience would expire. He placed the sheet on top of the other
papers, and with one quick thrust he drove the stiletto through the collection and speared it deep into the panelled overmantel.

"Lest we forget," he said, and turned with another laugh to smile seraphically into Patricia's outraged face. "I just wasn't born to be respectable, lass, and that's all there is to it. And the time has come for us to remember the old days."

As a matter of fact, he had made that decision two full weeks before, and Patricia had known it; but not until then had he made his open declaration of war.

At eight o'clock that evening he was sallying forth in quest of an evening's innocent amusement, and a car that had been standing in the darkness at the end of the cul-de-sac of Upper Berkeley Mews suddenly switched on its headlights and roared towards him. The Saint leapt back and fell on his face in the doorway, and he heard the *plop* of a silenced gun and the thud of a bullet burying itself in the woodwork above his head. He slid out into the mews again as the car went past, and fired twice at it as it swung into Berkeley Square, but he could not tell whether he did any damage.

He returned to brush his clothes, and then continued calmly on his way; and when he met Patricia later he did not think it necessary to mention the incident that had delayed him. But it was the third time since the episode *chez* Bird that the Scorpion had tried to kill him, and no one knew better than Simon Templar that it would not be the last attempt.

3

FOR SOME DAYS past, the well-peeled eye might at intervals have observed a cadaverous and lantern-jawed individual protruding about six and a half feet upwards from the cobbled paving of Upper Berkeley Mews. Simon Templar, having that sort of eye, had in fact noticed the apparition on its first and in all its subsequent visits; and anyone less well-informed than himself might pardonably have suspected some connection between the lanky boulevardier and the recent disturbances of the peace. Simon Templar, however, was not deceived.

"That," he said once, in answer to Patricia's question, "is Mr. Harold Garrot, better known as Long Harry. He is a moderately proficient burglar; and we have met before, but not professionally. He is trying to make up

his mind to come and tell me something, and one of these days he will
take the plunge.''

The Saint's deductions were vindicated twenty-four hours after the last
firework display.

Simon was alone. The continued political activities of a certain newspaper proprietor had driven him to verse, and he was covering a sheet
of foolscap with the beginning of a minor epic expressing his own views
on the subject:

> *Charles Charleston Charlemagne St. Charles*
> *Was wont to utter fearful snarls*
> *When by professors he was pressed*
> *To note how England had progressed*
> *Since the galumptious, gory days*
> *Immortalised in Shakespeare's plays*
> *For him, no Transatlantic flights,*
> *Ford motor-cars, electric lights,*
> *Or radios at less than cost*
> *Could compensate for what he lost*
> *By chancing to coagulate*
> *About five hundred years too late.*
> *Born in the old days for him*
> *He would have swung a sword with vim,*
> *Grown ginger whiskers on his face,*
> *And mastered, with a knobbly mace,*
> *Men who wore hauberks on their chests*
> *Instead of little woollen vests,*
> *And drunk strong wine among his peers*
> *Instead of pale synthetic beers.*

At this point, the trend of his inspiration led the Saint on a brief
excursion to the barrel in one corner of the room. He replenished his
tankard, drank deeply. And there, for the moment, he stuck; and he was
cogitating the possible developments of the next stanza when he was
interrupted by the *zing!* of the front door bell.

As he stepped out into the hall, he glanced up through the fanlight
above the door at the mirror that was cunningly fixed to the underneath
of the hanging lantern outside. He recognised the caller at once, and
opened the door without hesitation.

"Come in, Harry," invited the Saint cordially, and led the way back to the sitting-room. "I was busy with a work of art that is going to make Milton look like a distant relative of the gargle, but I can spare you a few minutes."

Long Harry glanced at the sheet half-covered with the Saint's neat handwriting.

"Poetry, Mr. Templar? We used to learn poetry at school," he said reminiscently.

Simon looked at him thoughtfully for two or three seconds, and then he beamed.

"Harry, you hit the nail on the head. For the suggestion, I pray that your shadow may always be jointed at the elbows. Excuse me one moment."

He plumped himself back in his chair and wrote at speed. Then he cleared his throat, and read aloud:

> *"Eton and Oxford failed to floor*
> *The spirit of the warrior:*
> *Though ragged and bullied, teased and hissed,*
> *Charles stayed a Medievalist*
> *And even when his worldly Pa*
> *(Regarding him with nausea)*
> *Condemned him to the dismal cares*
> *Of sordid trade in stocks and shares,*
> *Charles, in top-hat and Jaeger drawers,*
> *Clung like a limpet to his Cause,*
> *Believing, in a kind of trance,*
> *That one day he would have his Chance."*

He laid the sheet down reverently.

"A mere pastime for me, but I believe Milton used to sweat blood over it," he remarked complacently. "Soda or water, Harry?"

"Neat, please, Mr. Templar."

Simon brought over the glass of Highland cream; and Long Harry sipped it, and crossed and uncrossed his legs awkwardly.

"I hope you don't mind my coming to see you, sir," he ventured at last.

"Not at all," responded the Saint heartily. "Always glad to see any Eton boys here. What's the trouble?"

Long Harry fidgeted, twiddling his fingers and corrugating his brow. He was the typical "old lag," or habitual criminal, which is to say that outside of business hours he was a perfectly ordinary man of slightly less than average intelligence and rather more than average cunning. On this occasion he was plainly and ordinarily ill at ease, and the Saint surmised that he had only begun to solve his worries when he mustered up the courage to give that single, brief, and symptomatic ring at the front door bell.

Simon lighted a cigarette and waited impassively, and presently his patience reaped its harvest.

"I wondered—I thought maybe I could tell you something that might interest you, Mr. Templar."

"Sure." The Saint allowed a thin jet of smoke to trickle through his lips, and continued to wait.

"It's about . . . it's about the Scorpion, Mr. Templar."

Instantaneously the Saint's eyes narrowed, the merest fraction of a millimetre, and the inhalation that he drew from his cigarette was long and deep and slow. And then the stare that he swivelled round in the direction of Long Harry was wide blue innocence itself.

"What Scorpion?" he inquired blandly.

Long Harry frowned.

"I thought you'd've known about the Scorpion, of course, Mr. Templar, you being—"

"Yeah?"

Simon drawled out the prompting diphthong in a honeyed slither up a gently persuasive G-string; and Long Harry shuffled his feet uncomfortably.

"Well, you remember what you used to be, Mr. Templar. There wasn't much you didn't know in those days."

"Oh, yes—once upon a time. But now—"

"Last time we met, sir—"

The Saint's features relaxed, and he smiled.

"Forget it, Harold," he advised quietly. "I'm now a respectable citizen. I was a respectable citizen the last time we met, and I haven't changed. You may tell me anything you like, Harry—as one respectable citizen to another—but I'd recommend you to forget the interview as you step over the front door mat. I shall do the same—it's safer."

Long Harry nodded.

"If you forget it, sir, it'll be safer for me," he said seriously.

"I have a hopeless memory," said the Saint carefully. "I've already forgotten your name. In another minute, I shan't be sure that you're here at all. Now shoot the dope, son."

"You've got nothing against me, sir?"

"Nothing. You're a professional burglar, housebreaker, and petty larcenist, but that's no concern of mine. Teal can attend to your little mistakes."

"And you'll forget what I'm going to say—soon as ever I've said it?"

"You heard me."

"Well, Mr. Templar—" Long Harry cleared his throat, took another pull at his drink, and blinked nervously for some seconds. "I've worked for the Scorpion, Mr. Templar," he said suddenly.

Simon Templar never moved a muscle.

"Yes?"

"Only once, sir—so far." Once having left the diving-board, Long Harry floundered on recklessly. "And there won't be a second time— not if I can help it. He's dangerous. You ain't never safe with him. I know. Sent me a message he did, through the post. Knew where I was staying, though I'd only been there two days, an' everything about me. There was five one-pound notes in the letter, and he said if I met a car that'd be waiting at the second milestone north of Hatfield at nine o'clock last Thursday night there'd be another fifty for me to earn."

"What sort of car was it?"

"I never had a chance to notice it properly, Mr. Templar. It was a big, dark car, I think. It hadn't any lights. I was going to tell you—I was a bit suspicious at first. I thought it must be a plant, but it was that talk of fifty quid that tempted me. The car was waiting for me when I got there. I went up and looked in the window, and there was a man there at the wheel. Don't ask me what he looked like—he kept his head down, and I never saw more than the top of his hat. 'Those are your instructions,' he says, pushing an envelope at me, he says, 'and there's half your money. I'll meet you here at the same time tomorrow.' And then he drove off. I struck a match, and found he'd given me the top halves of fifty pound notes."

"And then?"

"Then—I went an' did the job, Mr. Templar."

"What job?"

"I was to go to a house at St. Albans and get some papers. There was a map, an' a plan, an' all about the locks an' everything. I had my tools— I forgot to tell you the first letter said I was to bring them—and it was as easy as the orders said it would be. Friday night, I met the car as arranged, and handed over the papers, and he gave me the other halves of the notes."

Simon extended a lean brown hand.

"The orders?" he inquired briefly.

He took the cheap yellow envelope, and glanced through the contents. There was, as Long Harry had said, a neatly-drawn map and plan; and the other information, in a studiously characterless copperplate writing, covered two more closely written sheets.

"You've no idea whose house it was you entered?"

"None at all, sir."

"Did you look at these papers?"

"Yes." Long Harry raised his eyes and looked at the Saint sombrely. "That's one reason why I came to you, sir."

"What were they?"

"They were love-letters, sir. There was an address—64, Half Moon Street. And they were signed—'Mark.' "

Simon passed a hand over his sleekly perfect hair.

"Oh, yes?" he murmured.

"You saw the Sunday papers, sir?"

"I did."

Long Harry emptied his glass, and put it down with clumsy fingers.

"Sir Mark Deverest shot 'imself at 64, 'Alf Moon Street, on Saturday night," he said huskily.

When he was agitated, he occasionally lost an aspirate, and it was an index of his perturbation that he actually dropped two in that one sentence.

"That's the Scorpion's graft, Mr. Templar—blackmail. I never touched black in my life, but I'd heard that was his game. An' when he sent for me, I forgot it. Even when I was looking through those letters, it never seemed to come into my head why he wanted them. But I see it all now. He wanted 'em to put the black on Deverest, an' Deverest shot himself instead of paying up. And—I 'elped to murder 'im, Mr. Templar. Murder, that's what it was. Nothing less. An' I 'elped!" Long Harry's voice fell to a throaty whisper, and his dull eyes shifted over the clear-etched contours of the Saint's tanned face in a kind of anxiety. "I never knew what I was doing, Mr. Templar, sir—strike me dead if I did—"

Simon reached forward and crushed out his cigarette in an ashtray.

"Is that all you came to tell me?" he asked, dispassionately; and Long Harry gulped.

"I thought you'd be laying for the Scorpion, sir, knowing you always used to be—"

"Yeah?"

Again that mellifluous dissyllable, in a voice that you could have carved up with a wafer of butter.

"Well, sir, what I mean is, if you *were* the Saint, sir, and if you hadn't forgotten that you might ever have been him, you might—"

"Be hunting scorpions?"

"That's the way I thought it out, sir."

"And?"

"I was hanging around last night, Mr. Templar, trying to make up my mind to come and see you, and I saw the shooting."

"And?"

"That car—it was just like the car that met me out beyond Hatfield, sir."

"And?"

"I thought p'raps it *was* the same car."

"And?"

Simon prompted him for the fourth time from the corner table where he was replenishing Long Harry's glass. His back was turned, but there was an inconspicuous little mirror just above the level of his eyes—the room was covered from every angle by those inconspicuous little mirrors. And he saw the twitching of Long Harry's mouth.

"I came because I thought you might be able to stop the Scorpion getting me, Mr. Templar," said Long Harry, in one jerk.

"Ah!" The Saint swung round. "That's more like it! So you're on the list, are you?"

"I think so." Long Harry nodded. "There was a shot aimed at me last night, too, but I suppose you wouldn't've noticed it."

Simon Templar lighted another cigarette.

"I see. The Scorpion spotted you hanging around here, and tried to bump you off. That's natural. But, Harry, you never even started hanging around here until you got the idea you might like to tell me the story of your life—and still you haven't told me where that idea came from. Sing on, Harry—I'm listening, and I'm certainly patient."

Long Harry absorbed a gill of Maison Dewar in comparative silence, and wiped his lips on the back of his hand.

"I had another letter on Monday morning, telling me to be at the same place at midnight to-morrow."

"And?"

"Monday afternoon I was talking to some friends. I didn't tell 'em anything, but I sort of steered the conversation around, not bringing myself in personal. You remember Wilbey?"

"Found full of bullets on the Portsmouth Road three months ago? Yes—I remember."

"I heard—it's just a story, but I heard the last job he did was for the Scorpion. He talked about it. The bloke shot himself that time, too. An' I began thinking. It may surprise you, Mr. Templar, but sometimes I'm very si-chick."

"You worked it out that so long as the victims paid up, everything was all right. But if they did anything desperate, there was always a chance of trouble; and the Scorpion wouldn't want anyone who could talk running about without a muzzle. That right?"

Long Harry nodded, and his prominent Adam's-apple flickered once up and down.

"Yes, I think if I keep that appointment tomorrow I'll be—what's the American word?—on the spot. Even if I don't go—" The man broke off with a shrug that made a feeble attempt at bravado. "I couldn't take that story of mine to the police, Mr. Templar, as you'll understand, and I wondered—"

Simon Templar settled a little deeper into his chair, and sent a couple of perfect smoke-rings chasing each other up towards the ceiling.

He understood Long Harry's thought processes quite clearly. Long Harry was a commonplace and more or less peaceful yegg, and violence was not among the most prominent interests of his life. Long Harry, as the Saint knew, had never even carried so much as a life-preserver. . . . The situation was obvious.

But how the situation was to be turned to account—that required a second or two's meditation. Perhaps two seconds'. And then the little matter of spoon-feeding that squirming young pup of a plan up to a full-sized man-eating carnivore hopping around on its own pads . . . maybe five seconds more. And then—

"We deduce," said the Saint dreamily, "that our friend has arranged for you to die tomorrow; but when he found you on the outskirts of the scenery last night, he thought he might save himself a journey."

"That's the way I see it, Mr. Templar."

"From the evidence before us, we deduce that he isn't the greatest snap shot in the world. And so—"

"Yes, Mr. Templar?"

"It looks to me, Harry," said the Saint pleasantly, "as if you'll have to die tomorrow after all."

4

SIMON WAS LINGERING over a cigarette and his last breakfast cup of coffee when Mr. Teal dropped in at half-past eleven the next morning.

"Have you breakfasted?" asked the Saint hospitably. "I can easily hash you up an egg or something—"

"Thanks," said Teal, "I had breakfast at eight."

"A positively obscene hour," said the Saint.

He went to an inlaid smoking-cabinet, and solemnly transported a new and virginal packet of spearmint into the detective's vicinity.

"Make yourself at home, Claud Eustace. And why are we thus honoured?"

There was a gleaming automatic, freshly cleaned and oiled, beside the breakfast-tray, and Teal's sleepy eyes fell on it as he undressed some Wrigley. He made no comment at that point, and continued his somnambulation round the room. Before the papers pinned to the overmantel, he paused.

"You going to contribute your just share towards the expenses of the nation?" he inquired.

"Someone is going to," answered the Saint calmly.

"Who?"

"Talking of Scorpions, Teal—"

The detective revolved slowly, and his baby eyes suddenly drooped as if in intolerable ennui.

"What scorpions?" he demanded, and the Saint laughed.

"Pass it up, Teal, old stoat. That one's my copyright."

Teal frowned heavily.

"Does this mean the old game again, Saint?"

"Teal! Why bring that up?"

The detective gravitated into a pew.

"What have you got to say about scorpions?"

"They have stings in their tails."

Teal's chewing continued with rhythmic monotonousness.

"When did you become interested in the Scorpion?" he questioned casually.

"I've been interested for some time," murmured the Saint. "Just recently, though, the interest's become a shade too mutual to be healthy. Did you know the Scorpion was an amateur?'' he added abruptly.

"Why do you think that?''

"I don't think it—I know it. The Scorpion is raw. That's one reason why I shall have to tread on him. I object to being shot up by amateurs— I feel it's liable to lower my stock. And as for being finally killed by an amateur . . . Teal, put it to yourself!''

"How do you know this?''

The Saint renewed his cigarette at leisure.

"Deduction. The Sherlock Holmes stuff again. I'll teach you the trick one day, but I can give you this result out flat. Do you want chapter and verse?''

"I'd be interested.''

"O.K.'' The Saint leaned back. "A man came and gave me some news about the Scorpion last night, after hanging around for three days— and he's still alive. I was talking to him on the phone only half an hour ago. If the Scorpion had been a real professional, that man would never even have seen me—let alone have been alive to ring me up this morning. That's one point.''

"What's the next?''

"You remember the Portsmouth Road murder?''

"Yes.''

"Wilbey had worked for the Scorpion, and he was a possible danger. If you'll consult your records, you'll find that Wilbey was acquitted on a charge of felonious loitering six days before he died. It was exactly the same with the bird who came to see me last night. He had also worked for the Scorpion, and he was discharged at Bow Street only two days before the Scorpion sent for him. Does that spell anything to you?''

Teal crinkled his forehead.

"Not yet, but I'm trying.''

"Let me save you the trouble.''

"No—just a minute. The Scorpion was in court when the charges were dismissed—''

"Exactly. And he followed them home. It's obvious. If you or I wanted someone to do a specialised bit of crime—say burglary, for instance— in thirty hours we could lay our hands on thirty men we could commission. But the genuine aged-in-the-wood amateur hasn't got those advantages, however clever he may be. He simply hasn't got the connections. You can't apply for cracksmen to the ordinary labour exchange, or advertise for them in *The Times,* and if you're a respectable amateur you haven't any among your intimate friends. What's the only way you can get hold of them?''

Teal nodded slowly.

"It's an idea," he admitted. "I don't mind telling you we've looked over all the regulars long ago. The Scorpion doesn't come into the catalogue. There isn't a nose on the pay-roll who can get a whiff of him. He's something right outside our register of established clients.''

The name of the Scorpion had first been mentioned nine months before, when a prominent Midland cotton-broker had put his head in a gas-oven and forgotten to turn off the gas. In a letter that was read at the inquest occurred the words: *"I have been bled for years, and now I can endure no more. When the Scorpion stings, there is no antidote but death."*

And in the brief report of the proceedings:

The Coroner: Have you any idea what the deceased meant by that reference to a scorpion?

Witness: No.

Is there any professional blackmailer known to the police by that name?

—I have never heard it before.

And thereafter, for the general run of respectable citizens from whom the Saint expressly dissociated Teal and himself, the rest had been a suavely expanding blank . . .

But through that vast yet nebulous area popularly called "the underworld" began to voyage vague rumours, growing more and more wild and fantastic as they passed from mouth to mouth, but still coming at last to the receptive ears of Scotland Yard with enough credible vitality to be interesting. Kate Allfield, "the Mug," entered a railway carriage in which a Member of Parliament was travelling alone on a flying visit to his constituency: he stopped the train at Newbury and gave her in charge, and when her counter-charge of assault broke down under ruthless cross-examination she "confessed" that she had acted on the instigation of an unknown accomplice. Kate had tried many ways of making easy money, and the fact that the case in question was a new one in her history meant little. But round the underworld travelled two words of comment and explanation, and those two words said simply "The Scorpion."

"Basher" Tope—thief, motor-bandit, brute, and worse—was sent for. He boasted in his cups of how he was going to solve the mystery of the Scorpion, and went alone to his appointment. What happened there he never told; he was absent from his usual haunts for three weeks, and when he was seen again he had a pink scar on his temple and a surly disinclination to discuss the matter. Since he had fully earned his nick-

name, questions were not showered upon him; but once again the word
went round. . . .

And so it was with half a dozen subsequent incidents; and the legend
of the Scorpion grew up and was passed from hand to hand in queer
places, unmarked by sensation-hunting journalists, a mystery for police
and criminals alike. Jack Wilbey, ladder larcenist, died and won his niche
in the structure; but the newspapers noted his death only as another
unsolved crime on which to peg their personal criticisms of police efficiency, and only those who had heard other chapters of the story linked
up that murder with the suicide of a certain wealthy peer. Even Chief
Inspector Teal, whose finger was on the pulse of every unlawful activity
in the Metropolis, had not visualised such a connecting link as the Saint
had just forged before his eyes; and he pondered over it in a ruminative
silence before he resumed his interrogation.

"How much else do you know?" he asked at length, with the mere
ghost of a quickening of interest in his perpetually weary voice.

The Saint picked up a sheet of paper.

"Listen," he said.

> *"His faith was true: though once misled*
> *By an appeal that he had read*
> *To honour with his patronage*
> *Crusades for better Auction Bridge*
> *He was not long deceived; he found*
> *No other paladins around*
> *Prepared to perish, sword in hand,*
> *While storming in one reckless band*
> *Those strongholds of Beelzebub*
> *The portals of the Portland Club.*
> *His chance came later: one fine day*
> *Another paper blew his way:*
> *Charles wrote; Charles had an interview;*
> *And Charles, an uncrowned jousting Blue,*
> *Still spellbound by the word Crusade,*
> *Espoused the cause of Empire Trade."*

"What on earth's that?" demanded the startled detective.

"A little masterpiece of mine," said the Saint modestly. "There's
rather an uncertain rhyme in it, if you noticed. Do you think the Poet
Laureate would pass *patronage* and *Bridge?* I'd like your opinion."

Teal's eyelids lowered again.

"Have you stopped talking?" he sighed.

"Very nearly, Teal," said the Saint, putting the paper down again. "In case that miracle of tact was too subtle for you, let me explain that I was changing the subject."

"I see."

"Do you?"

Teal glanced at the automatic on the table and then again at the papers on the wall, and sighed a second time.

"I think so. You're going to ask the Scorpion to pay your income tax."

"I am."

"How?"

The Saint laughed. He pointed to the desecrated overmantel.

"One thousand three hundred and thirty-seven pounds, nineteen *and* fivepence," he said. "That's my sentence for being a useful wage-earning citizen instead of a prolific parasite, according to the laws of this spavined country. Am I supposed to pay you and do your work as well? If so, I shall emigrate on the next boat and become a naturalised Venezuelan."

"I wish you would," said Teal, from his heart.

He picked up his hat.

"Do you know the Scorpion?" he asked suddenly.

Simon shook his head.

"Not yet. But I'm going to. His donation is not yet assessed, but I can tell you where one thousand three hundred and thirty-eight pounds of it are going to travel. And that is towards the offices of Mr. Lionel Delborn, collector of extortions—may his teeth fall out and his legs putrefy! I'll stand the odd sevenpence out of my own pocket."

"And what do you think you're going to do with the man himself?"

The Saint smiled.

"That's a little difficult to say," he murmured. "Accidents sort of— er—happen, don't they? I mean, I don't want you to start getting back any of your naughty old ideas about me, but—"

Teal nodded; then he met the Saint's mocking eyes seriously.

"They'd have the coat off my back if it ever got round," he said, "but between you and me and these four walls, I'll make a deal—if you'll make one too."

Simon settled on the edge of the table, his cigarette slanting quizzically upwards between his lips, and one whimsically sardonic eyebrow arched.

"What is it?"

"Save the Scorpion for me, and I won't ask how you paid your income tax."

For a few moments the Saint's noncommittal gaze rested on the detective's round red face; then it wandered back to the impaled memorandum above the mantelpiece. And then the Saint looked Teal in the eyes again and smiled.

"O.K.," he drawled. "That's O.K. with me, Claud."

"It's a deal?"

"It is. There's a murder charge against the Scorpion, and I don't see why the hangman shouldn't earn his fiver. I guess it's about time you had a break Claud Eustace. Yes—you can have the Scorpion. Any advance on fourpence?"

Teal nodded, and held out his hand.

"Fourpence halfpenny—I'll buy you a glass of beer at any pub inside the three-mile radius on the day you bring him in," he said.

5

PATRICIA HOLM CAME in shortly after four-thirty. Simon Templar had lunched at where he always referred to as "the pub round the corner"— the Berkeley—and had ambled elegantly about the purlieus of Piccadilly for an hour thereafter; for he had scarcely learned to walk two consecutive steps when his dear old grandmother had taken him on her knee and enjoined him to "eat, drink, and be merry, for tomorrow is Stove Tuesday."

He was writing when she arrived, but he put down his pen and surveyed her solemnly.

"Oh, there you are," he remarked. "I thought you were dead, but Teal said he thought you might only have taken a trip to Vladivostok."

"I've been helping Eileen Wiltham—her wedding's only five days away. Haven't you any more interest in her?"

"None," said the Saint callously. "The thought of the approaching crime makes my mind feel unbinged—unhinged. I've already refused three times to assist Charles to select pyjamas for the bridal chamber. I told him that when he'd been married as often as I have—"

"That'll do," said Patricia.

"It will, very nearly," said the Saint.

He cast an eye over the mail that she had brought in with her from the letter-box.

"Those two envelopes with halfpenny stamps you may exterminate forthwith. On the third, in spite of the deceptive three-halfpenny *Briefmarke*, I recognise the clerkly hand of Anderson and Sheppard. Add it to the holocaust. Item four"—he picked up a small brown-paper package and weighed it calculatingly in his hand—"is much too light to contain high explosve. It's probably the new gold-mounted sock-suspenders I ordered from Asprey's. Open it, darling, and tell me what you think of them. And I will read you some more of the Hideous History of Charles."

He took up his manuscript.

> *"With what a zest did he prepare*
> *for the first meeting (open-air)!*
> *With what a glee he fastened on*
> *His bevor and his morion,*
> *His greaves, his ventail, every tace,*
> *His pauldrons and his rerebrace!*
> *He sallied forth with martial eye,*
> *Prepared to do, prepared to die,*
> *But not prepared—by Bayard! not*
> *For the reception that he got.*
> *Over that chapter of the tale*
> *It would be kind to draw a veil:*
> *Let it suffice that, in disdain,*
> *Some hecklers threw him in a drain,*
> *And plodding home—*

"Excuse me," said the Saint.

His right hand moved like lightning, and the detonation of his heavy automatic in the confined space was like a vindictive thunderclap. It left the girl with a strange hot sting of powder on her wrist and a dull buzzing in her ears. And through the buzzing drifted the Saint's unruffled accents:

> *"And plodding home, all soaked inside,*
> *He caught pneumonia—and died."*

Patricia looked at him, white-faced.

"What was it?" she asked, with the faintest tremor in her voice.

"Just an odd spot of scorpion," answered Simon Templar gently. "An unpleasant specimen of the breed—the last time I saw one like that was up in the hills north of Puruk-jahu. Looks like a pal of mine has been doing some quick travelling, or . . . Yes." The Saint grinned. "Get on the phone to the Zoo, old dear, and tell 'em they can have their property back if they care to send round and scrape it off the carpet. I don't think we shall want it any more, shall we?"

Patricia shuddered.

She had stripped away the brown paper and found a little cardboard box such as cheap jewellery is sometimes packed in. When she raised the lid, the tiny blue-green horror, like a miniature deformed lobster, had been lying there in a nest of cotton-wool; while she stared at it, it had rustled on to her hand. . . .

"It—wasn't very big," she said, in a tone that tried to match the Saint's for lightness.

"Scorpions run to all sizes," said the Saint cheerfully, "and as often as not their poisonousness is in inverse ratio to their size in boots. Mostly, they're very minor troubles—I've been stung myself, and all I got was a sore and swollen arm. But the late lamented was a member of the one and only sure-certain and no-hokum family of homicides in the species. Pity I bumped it off so stickily—it might have been really valuable stuffed."

Patricia's finger-tips slid mechanically around the rough edges of the hole that the nickel-cased .45 bullet had smashed through the polished mahogany table before ruining the carpet and losing itself somewhere in the floor. Then she looked steadily at the Saint.

"Why should anyone send you a scorpion?" she said.

Simon Templar shrugged.

"It was the immortal Paragot who said: 'In this country the expected always happens, which paralyses the brain.' And if a real man-sized Scorpion can't be expected to send his young brothers to visit his friends as a token of esteem, what can he be expected to do?"

"Is that all?"

"All what?"

"All you propose to tell me."

The Saint regarded her for a moment. He saw the tall slim lines of reposeful strength in her body, the fine moulding of the chin, the eyes as blue and level as his own. And slowly he screwed the cap on his fountain pen; and he stood up and came round the table.

"I'll tell you as much more as you want to know," he said.

"Just like in the mad old days?"

"They had their moments, hadn't they?"

She nodded.

"Sometimes I wish we were back in them," she said wistfully. "I didn't fall in love with you in a pair of Anderson and Sheppard trousers—"

"They were!" cried the Saint indignantly. "I distinctly remember—"

Patricia laughed suddenly. Her hands fell on his shoulders.

"Give me a cigarette, boy," she said, "and tell me what's been happening."

And he did so—though what he had to tell was little enough. And Chief Inspector Teal himself knew no more. The Scorpion had grown up in darkness, had struck from darkness, and crawled back deeper into the dark. Those who could have spoken dared not speak, and those who might have spoken died too soon. . . .

But as he told his tale, the Saint saw the light of all the mad old days awakening again in Patricia's eyes, and it was in a full and complete understanding of that light that he came to the one thing that Chief Inspector Teal would have given his ears to know.

"To-night, at nine—"

"You'll be there?"

"I shall," said the Saint, with the slightest tightening of his lips. "Shot up by a bloody amateur—Good God! Suppose he'd hit me! Pat, believe papa—when I pass out, there's going to be a first-class professional, hall-marked on every link, at the thick end of the gun."

Patricia, in the deep arm-chair, settled her sweet golden head among the cushions.

"What time do we start?" she asked calmly.

For a second, glancing at him sidelong, she saw the old stubborn hardening of the line of his jaw. It happened instinctively, almost without his knowing it; and then suddenly he swung off the arm of the chair in the breath of an even older Saintly laughter.

"Why not?" he said. "It's impossible—preposterous—unthinkable—but why not? The old gang have gone—Dicky, Archie, Roger—gone and got spliced on to women and come over all bowler-hat. There's only you left. It'd made the vicar's wife let out one piercing squawk and swallow her knitting-needles, but who cares? If you'd really like to have another sniff at the old brew—"

"Give me the chance!"

Simon grinned.

"And you'd flop after it like a homesick walrus down a water-chute, wouldn't you?"

"Faster," she said.

"And so you shall," said the Saint. "The little date I've got for tonight will be all the merrier for an extra soul on the side of saintliness and soft drinks. And if things don't turn out exactly according to schedule, there may be an encore for your special entertainment. Pat, I have a feeling that this is going to be our week!"

6

IT WAS ONE of the Saint's most charming characteristics that he never hurried and never worried. He insisted on spending an idle hour in the cocktail bar of the Mayfair Hotel, and seventy-thirty had struck before he collected his car, inserted Patricia, and turned the Hirondel's long silver nose northwards at an unwontedly moderate speed. They dined at Hatfield, after parking the Hirondel in the hotel garage, and after dinner the Saint commanded coffee and liqueurs and proceeded to incinerate two enormous cigars of a plutocratically delicate bouquet. He had calculated exactly how long it would take to walk out to location, and he declined to start one moment before his time-table demanded it.

"I am a doomed man," he said sombrely, "and I have my privileges. If necessary, the Scorpion will wait for me."

Actually he had no intention of being late, for the plan of campaign that he had spent the nicotinised interval after dinner adapting to Patricia's presence required them to be at the rendezvous a shade in advance of the rest of the party.

But this the Scorpion did not know.

He drove up slowly, with his headlights dimmed, scanning the dark shadows at the side of the road. Exactly beside the point where his shaded lights picked up the gray-white blur of the appointed milestone, he saw the tiny red glow of a cigarette-end, and applied his brakes gently. The cigarette-end dropped and vanished under an invisible heel, and out of the gloom a tall dark shape stretched slowly upwards.

The Scorpion's right hand felt the cold bulk of the automatic pistol in his pocket as his other hand lowered the near-side window. He leaned over toward the opening.

"Garrot?"

The question came in a whisper to the man at the side of the road and he stepped slowly forward and answered in a throaty undertone.

"Yes, sir?"

The Scorpion's head was bent low, so that the man outside the car could only see the shape of his hat.

"You obeyed your orders. That is good. Come closer. . . ."

The gun slipped silently out of the Scorpion's pocket, his forefinger curling quickly round the trigger as he drew it. He brought it up without a sound, so that the tip of the barrel rested on the ledge of the open window directly in line with the chest of the man twelve inches away. One lightning glance to left and right told him that the road was deserted.

"Now there is just one thing more—"

"There is," agreed Patricia Holm crisply. "Don't move!"

The Scorpion heard, and the glacial concentration of dispassionate unfriendliness in her voice froze him where he sat. He had not heard the noiseless turning of the handle of the door behind him, nor noticed the draught of cooler air that trickled through the car; but he felt the chilly hardness of the circle of steel that pressed into the base of his skull, and for a second he was paralysed. And in in that second his target vanished.

"Drop that gun—outside the car. And let me hear it go!"

Again that crisp, commanding voice, as inclemently smooth as an arctic sea, whisked into his eardrums like a thin cold needle. He hesistated for a moment, and then, as the muzzle of the gun behind his neck increased its pressure by one warning ounce, he moved his hand obediently and relaxed his fingers. His automatic rattled on to the runningboard, and almost immediately the figure that he had taken for Long Harry rose into view again, and was framed in the square space of window.

But the voice that acknowledged receipt of *item,* Colts, automatic, scorpions, for the use of, one, was not the voice of Long Harry. It was the most cavalier, the most mocking, the most cheerful voice that the Scorpion had ever heard—he noted those qualities about it subconsciously, for he was not in a position to revel in the discovery with any hilariously whole-hearted abandon.

"O.K. . . . And how are you, my Scorpion?"

"Who are you?" asked the man in the car.

He still kept his head lowered, and under the brim of his hat his eyes were straining into the gloom for a glimpse of the man who had spoken;

but the Saint's face was in shadow. Glancing away to one side, the Scorpion could focus the head of the girl whose gun continued to impress his cervical vertebrae with the sense of its rocklike steadiness; but a dark close-fitting hat covered the upper part of her head, and a scarf that was loosely knotted about her neck had been pulled up to veil her face from the eyes downwards.

The Saint's light laugh answered the question.

"I am the world's worst gunman, and the lady behind you is the next worst, but at this range we can say that we never miss. And that's all you need to worry about just now. The question that really arises is—who are you?"

"That is what you have still to discover," replied the man in the car impassively. "Where is Garrot?"

"Ah! That's what whole synods of experts are still trying to discover. Some would say that he was simply rotting, and others would say that that was simply rot. He might be floating around the glassy sea, clothed in white samite, mystic, wonderful, with his new regulation nightie flying in the breeze behind; or he might be attending to the central heating plant in the basement. I was never much of a theologian myself—"

"Is he dead?"

"Very," said the Saint cheerfully. "I organised the decease myself."

"You killed him?"

"Oh, no! Nothing like that about me. I merely arranged for him to die. If you survive to read your morning paper tomorrow, you may be informed that the body of an unknown man has been fished out of the Thames. That will be Long Harry. Now come out and take your curtain, sweetheart!"

The Saint stepped back and twitched open the door, pocketing the Scorpion's gun as he did so.

And at the same moment he had a queer feeling of futility. He knew that that was not the moment when he was destined to lay the Scorpion by the heels.

Once or twice before, in a life which had only lasted as long as it had by reason of a vigilance that never blinked for one split second, and a forethought that was accustomed to skid along half a dozen moves ahead of the opposition performers in every game with the agility of a startled streak of lightning zipping through space on ball bearings with the wind behind it, he had experienced the same sensation—of feeling as if an intangible shutter had guillotined down in front of one vitally receptive lens in his alertness. Something was going to happen—his trained intuition told him what would be the general trend of that forthcoming event, equally beyond all possibility of argument—but exactly what shape that event would take was more than any faculty of his could divine.

A tingling stillness settled upon the scene, and in the stillness some fact that he should have been reckoning with seemed to hammer frantically upon that closed window in his mind. He knew that that was so, but his brain produced no other response. Just for that fractional instant of time a cog slipped one pinion, and the faultless machine was at fault. The blind spot that roams around somewhere in every human cerebral system suddenly broke its moorings, and drifted down over the one minute of co-ordinating apparatus of which Simon Templar had most need; and no effort of his could dislodge it.

"Step out, Cuthbert," snapped the Saint, with a slight rasp in his voice.

In the darkness inside the car, a slight blur of white caught and interested Simon's eye. It lay on the seat beside the driver. With that premonition of failure dancing about in his subconscious and making faces at his helpless stupidity, the Saint grabbed at the straw. He got it away— a piece of paper—and the Scorpion, seeing it go, snatched wildly but not soon enough.

Simon stuffed the paper into his coat pocket, and with his other hand he took the Scorpion by the neck.

"Step!" repeated the Saint crisply.

And then his forebodings were fulfilled—simply and straightforwardly, as he had known they would be.

The Scorpion had never stopped the engine of his car—that was the infinitesimal yet sufficient fact that had been struggling ineffectively to register itself upon the Saint's brain. The sound was scarcely anything at all, even to the Saint's hypersensitive ears—scarcely more than a rhythmic pulsing disturbance of the stillness of the night. Yet all at once— too late—it seemed to rise and racket in his mind like the thunder of a hundred dynamos; and it was then that he saw his mistake.

But that was after the Scorpion had let in the clutch.

In the blackness, his left hand must have been stealthily engaging the gears; and then, as a pair of swiftly growing lights pin-pointed in his driving mirror, he unleashed the car with a bang.

The Saint, with one foot in the road and the other on the runningboard, was flung off his balance. As he stumbled, the jamb of the door crashed agonisingly into the elbow of the arm that reached out to the driver's collar, and something like a thousand red-hot needles prickled right down his forearm to the tip of his little finger and numbed every muscle through which it passed.

As he dropped back into the road, he heard the crack of Patricia's gun.

The side of the car slid past him, gathering speed, and he whipped out the Scorpion's own automatic. Quite casually, he plugged the off-side back tyre; and then a glare of light came into the tail of his eye, and he stepped quickly across to Patricia.

"Walk on," he said quietly.

They fell into step and sauntered slowly on, and the headlights of the car behind threw their shadows thirty yards ahead.

"That jerk," said Patricia ruefully—"my shot missed him by a yard. I'm sorry."

Simon nodded.

"I know. It was my fault. I should have switched his engine off."

The other car flashed past them, and Simon cursed it fluently.

"The real joy of having the country full of automobiles," he said, "is that it makes gunning so easy. You can shoot anyone up anywhere, and everyone except the victim will think it was only a backfire. But it's when people can see the gun that the deception kind of disintegrates." He gazed gloomily after the dwindling tail light of the unwelcome interruption. "If only that four-wheeled gas-crocodile had burst a blood-vessel two miles back, we mightn't have been on our way home yet."

"I heard you shoot once——"

"And he's still going—on the other three wheels. I'm not expecting he'll stop to mend that leak."

Patricia sighed.

"It was short and sweet, anyhow," she said. "Couldn't you have stopped tht other car and followed?"

He stook his head.

"Teal could have stopped it, but I'm not a policeman. I think this is a bit early for us to start gingering up our publicity campaign."

"I wish it had been a better show, boy," said Patricia wistfully, slipping her arm through his; and the Saint stopped to stare at her.

In the darkness, this was not effective; but he did it.

"You bloodthirsty child!" he said.

And then he laughed.

"But that wasn't the final curtain," he said. "If you like to note it down, I'll make you a prophecy: the mortality among Scorpions is going to rise one unit, and for once it will not be my fault."

They were back in Hatfield before she had made up her mind to ask him if he was referring to Long Harry, and for once the Saint did not look innocently outraged at the suggestion.

"Long Harry is alive and well, to the best of my knowledge and belief," he said, "but I arranged the rough outline of his decease with Teal over the telephone. If we didn't kill Long Harry, the Scorpion would; and I figure our method will be less fatal. But as for the Scorpion himself— well, Pat, I'm dreadfully afraid I've promised to let them hang him according to the law. I'm getting so respectable these days that I feel I may be removed to Heaven in a fiery chariot at any moment."

He examined his souvenir of the evening in a corner of the deserted hotel smoking-room a little later, over a final and benedictory tankard of beer. It was an envelope, postmarked in the South-Western district at 11 a.m. that morning, and addressed to Wilfred Garniman Esq., 28, Mallaby Road, Harrow. From it the Saint extracted a single sheet of paper, written in a feminine hand.

> *Dear Mr. Garniman,*
> *Can you come round for dinner and a game of bridge on Tuesday next? Colonel Barnes will be making a fourth.*
>
> > *Yours sincerely,*
> >
> > *(Mrs.) R. Venables.*

For a space he contemplated the missive with an exasperated scowl darkening the beauty of his features; then he passed it to Patricia, and reached out for the consolation of draught Bass with one hand and a cigarette with the other. The scowl continued to darken.

Patricia read, and looked at him perplexedly.

"It looks perfectly ordinary," she said.

"It looks a damned sight too ordinary!" exploded the Saint. "How the devil can you blackmail a man for being invited to play bridge?"

The girl frowned.

"But—I don't see. Why should this be anyone else's letter?"

"And why shouldn't Mr. Wilfred Garniman be the man I want?"

"Of course. Didn't you get it from that man in the car?"

"I saw it on the seat beside him—it must have come out of his pocket when he pulled his gun."

"Well?" she prompted.

"Why shouldn't this be the beginning of the Scorpion's triumphal march towards the high jump?" asked the Saint.

"That's what I want to know."

Simon surveyed her in silence. And, as he did so, the scowl faded slowly from his face. Deep in his eyes a pair of little blue devils roused up, executed a tentative double-shuffle, and paused with their heads on one side.

"Why not?" insisted Patricia.

Slowly, gently, and with tremendous precision, the Saintly smile twitched at the corners of Simon's lips, expanded, grew, and irradiated his whole face.

"I'm blowed if I know why not," said the Saint seraphically. "It's just that I have a weakness for getting both feet on the bus before I tell the world I'm travelling. And the obvious deduction seemed too good to be true."

7

MALLABY ROAD, HARROW, as the Saint discovered, was one of those jolly roads in which ladies and gentlemen live. Lords and ladies may be found in such places as Mayfair, Monte Carlo, and St. Moritz; men and women may be found almost anywhere; but Ladies and Gentlemen blossom in their full beauty only in such places as Mallaby Road, Harrow. This was a road about two hundred yards long, containing thirty of the stately homes of England, each of them a miraculously preserved specimen of Elizabethan architecture, each of them exactly the same as the other twenty-nine, and each of them surrounded by identical lawns, flower-beds, and atmospheres of overpowering gentility.

Simon Templar, entering Mallaby Road at nine o'clock—an hour of the morning at which his vitality was always rather low—felt slightly stunned.

There being no other visible distinguishing marks or peculiarities about it, he discovered No. 28 by the simple process of looking at the figures on the garden gates, and found it after inspecting fourteen other numbers which were not 28. He started on the wrong side of the road.

To the maid who opened the door he gave a card bearing the name of Mr. Andrew Herrick and the official imprint of the *Daily Record*. Simon Templar had no right whatever to either of these decorations, which were the exclusive property of a reporter whom he had once interviewed, but a little thing like that never bothered the Saint. He kept every visiting card that was ever given him and a few that had not been consciously donated, and drew appropriately upon his stock in time of need.

"Mr. Garniman is just finishing breakfast, sir," said the maid doubtfully, "but I'll ask him if he'll see you."

"I'm sure he will," said the Saint, and he said it so winningly that if the maid's name has been Mrs. Garniman the prophecy would have passed automatically into the realm of sublimely concrete certainties.

As it was, the prophecy merely proved to be correct.

Mr. Garniman saw the Saint, and the Saint saw Mr. Garniman. These things happened simultaneously, but the Saint won on points. There was a lot of Mr. Garniman.

"I'm afraid I can't spare you very long, Mr. Herrick," he said. "I have to go out in a few minutes. What did you want to see me about?"

His restless gray eyes flitted shrewdly over the Saint as he spoke, but Simon endured the scrutiny with the peaceful calm which only the man who wears the suits of Anderson and Sheppard, the shirts of Harman, the shoes of Lobb, and self-refrigerating conscience, can achieve.

"I came to ask you if you could tell us anything about the Scorpion," said the Saint calmly.

Well, that is one way of putting it. On the other hand, one could say with equal truth that his manner would have made a sheet of plate glass look like a futurist sculptor's impression of a bit of the Pacific Ocean during a hurricane. And the innocence of the Saintly face would have made a Botticelli angel look positively sinister in comparison.

His gaze rested on Mr. Wilfred Garniman's fleshy prow with no more than a reasonable directness; but he saw the momentary flicker of expression that preceeded Mr. Garniman's blandly puzzled frown, and wistfully wondered whether, if he unsheathed his swordstick and prodded it vigorously into Mr. Garniman's immediate future, there would be a loud pop, or merely a faint sizzling sound. That he overcame this insidious temptation, and allowed no sign of the soul-shattering struggle to register itself on his face, was merely a tribute to the persistently sobering influence of Mr. Lionel Delborn's official proclamation and the Saint's sternly practical devotion to Business.

"Scorpion?" repeated Mr. Garniman, frowning. "I'm afraid I don't quite—"

"Understand. Exactly. Well, I expected I should have to explain."

"I wish you would. I really don't know—"

"Why we should consider you an authority on scorpions. Precisely. The Editor told me you'd say that."

"If you'd—"

"Tell you the reason for this rather extraordinary procedure—"

"I should certainly see if I could help you in any way, but at the same time—"

"You don't see what use you could be. Absolutely. Now, shall we go on like this or shall we sing the rest in chorus?"

Mr. Garniman blinked.

"Do you want to ask me some questions?"

"I should love to," said the Saint heartily. "You don't think Mrs. Garniman will object?"

"Mrs. Garniman?"

"Mrs. Garniman."

Mr. Garniman blinked again.

"Are you—"

"Certain—"

"Are you certain you haven't made a mistake? There is no Mrs. Garniman."

"Don't mention it," said the Saint affably.

He turned the pages of an enormous notebook.

" 'Interviewed Luis Cartaro. Diamond rings and Marcel wave. Query—Do Pimples Make Good Mothers? Said—' Sorry, wrong page. . . . Here we are: '*Memo*. See Wilfred Garniman and ask the big—ask him about scorpions, 28, Mallaby Road, Harrow.' That's right, isn't it?"

"That is my name and address," said Garniman shortly. "But I have still to learn the reason for this—er—"

"Visit," supplied the Saint. He was certainly feeling helpful that morning.

He closed his book and returned it to his pocket.

"As a matter of fact," he said, "we heard that the Saint was interested in you."

He was not even looking at Garniman as he spoke. But the mirror over the mantelpiece was in the tail of his eye, and thus he saw the other's hands, which were clasped behind his back, close and unclose—once.

"The Saint?" said Garniman. "Really—"

"Are you sure I'm not detaining you?" asked the Saint, suddenly very brisk and solicitous. "If your staff will be anxious . . ."

"My staff can wait a few minutes."

"That's very good of you. But if we telephoned them—"

"I assure you—that is quite unnecessary."

"I shouldn't like to think of your office being disorganised—"

"You need not trouble," said Garniman. He moved across the room. "Will you smoke?"

"Thanks," said the Saint.

He had just taken the first puff from a cigarette when Garniman turned round with a carved ebony box open in his hand.

"Oh," said Mr. Garniman, a trifle blankly.

"Not at all," said the Saint, who was never embarrassed. "Have one of mine?"

He extended his case, but Garniman shook his head.

"I never smoke during the day. Would it be too early to offer you a drink?"

"I'm afraid so—much too early," agreed Simon blandly.

Garniman returned the ebony box to the side table from which he had taken it. Then he swung round abruptly.

"Well?" he demanded. "What's the idea?"

The Saint appeared perplexed.

"What's what idea?" he inquired innocently.

Garniman's eyebrows came down a little.

"What's all this about scorpions—and the Saint?"

"According to the Saint—"

"I don't understand you. I thought the Saint had disappeared long ago."

"Then you were grievously in error, dear heart," murmured Simon Templar coolly. "Because I am myself the Saint."

He lounged against a book-case, smiling and debonair, and his lazy blue eyes rested mockingly on the other's pale plump face.

"And I'm afraid you're the Scorpion, Wilfred," he said.

For a moment Mr. Garniman stood quite still. And then he shrugged.

"I believe I read in the newspapers that you had been pardoned, and had retired from business," he said, "so I suppose it would be useless for me to communicate your confession to the police. As for this scorpion that you have referred to several times—"

"Yourself," the Saint corrected him gently, and Garniman shrugged again.

"Whatever delusion you are suffering from—"

"Not a delusion, Wilfred."

"It is immaterial to me what you call it."

The Saint seemed to lounge even more languidly, his hands deep in his pockets, a thoughtful and reckless smile playing lightly about his lips.

"I call it a fact," he said softly. "And you will keep your hands away from that bell until I've finished talking. . . . You are the Scorpion, Wilfred, and you're probably the most successful blackmailer of the age. I grant you that—your technique is novel and thorough. But blackmail is a nasty crime. Your ingenuity has already driven two men to suicide. That was stupid of them, but it was also very naughty of you. In fact, it would really give me great pleasure to peg you out in your front garden and push this highly desirable residence over on top of you; but for one thing I've promised to reserve you for the hangman, and for another thing I've got my income tax to pay, so—Excuse me one moment."

Something like a flying chip of frozen quicksilver flashed across the room and plonked crisply into the wooden panel around the bell-push towards which Garniman's fingers were sidling. It actually passed between his second and third fingers, so that he felt the swift chill of its passage and snatched his hand away as if it had received an electric shock. But the Saint continued his languid propping up of the *Encyclopaedia Britannica,* and he did not appear to have moved.

"Just do what you're told, Wilfred, and everything will be quite all right—but I've got lots more of those missiles packed in my pants," murmured the Saint, soothingly, warningly, and untruthfully—though Mr. Garniman had no means of perceiving this last adverb. "What was I saying? . . . Oh yes, I have my income tax to pay—"

Garniman took a sudden step forward, and his lips twisted up in a snarl.

"Look here—"

"Where?" asked the Saint excitedly.

Mr. Garniman swallowed. The Saint heard him distinctly.

"You thrust yourself in here under a false name—you behave like a raving lunatic—then you make the most wild and fantastic accusations—you—"

"Throw knives about the place—"

"What the devil," bellowed Mr. Garniman, "do you mean by it?"

"Sir," suggested the Saint, mildly.

"What the devil," bellowed Mr. Garniman, "do you mean—'sir'?"

"Thank you," said the Saint.

Mr. Garniman glared.

"What the—"

"O.K.," said the Saint pleasantly. "I heard you the second time. So long as you go on calling me 'sir,' I shall know that everything is perfectly respectable and polite. And now we've lost the place again. Half a minute. . . . Here we are: 'I have my income tax to pay—' "

"Will you get out at once," asked Garniman, rather quietly, "or must I send for the police?"

Simon considered the question.

"I should send for the police," he suggested at length.

He hitched himself off the book-case and sauntered leisurely across the room. He detached his little knife from the bell panel, tested the point deliberately on his thumb, and restored the weapon to the sheath under his left sleeve; and Wildred Garniman watched him without speaking. And then the Saint turned.

"Certainly—I should send for the police," he drawled. "They will be interested. It's quite true that I had a pardon for some old offences; but whether I've gone out of business, or whether I'm simply just a little cleverer than Chief Inspector Teal, is a point that is often debated at Scotland Yard. I think that any light you could throw on the problem would be welcomed."

Garniman was still silent; and the Saint looked at him, and laughed caressingly.

"On the other hand—if you're bright enough to see a few objections to that idea—you might prefer to push quietly on to your beautiful office and think over some of the other things I've said. Particularly those pregnant words about my income tax."

"Is that all you have to say?" asked Garniman in the same low voice; and the Saint nodded.

"It'll do for now," he said lightly. "And since you seem to have decided against the police, I think I'll beetle off and concentrate on the method by which you're going to be induced to contribute to the Inland Revenue."

The slightest glitter of expression came to Wilfred Garniman's eyes for a moment, and was gone again. He walked to the door and opened it.

"I'm obliged," he said.

"After you, dear old reed-warbler," said the Saint courteously.

Her permitted Garniman to precede him out of the room, and stood in the hall adjusting the piratical slant of his hat.

"I presume we shall meet again?" Garniman remarked.

His tone was level and conversational. And the Saint smiled.

"You might bet on it," he said.

"Then—*au revoir*."

The Saint tilted back his hat and watched the other turn on his heel and go up the stairs.

Then he opened the door and stepped out; and the heavy ornamental stone flower-pot that began to gravitate earthwards at the same moment actually flicked the brim of his Stetson before it split thunderously on the flagged path an inch behind his right heel.

Simon revolved slowly, his hands still in his pockets, and cocked an eyebrow at the debris; and then he strolled back under the porch and applied his forefinger to the bell.

Presently the maid answered the door.

"I think Mr. Garniman has dropped the aspidistra," he murmured chattily, and resumed his interrupted exit before the bulging eyes of an audience of one.

8

"BUT WHAT ON earth," asked Patricia helplessly, "was the point of that?"

"It was an exercise in tact," said the Saint modestly.

The girl stared.

"If I could only see it," she began; and then the Saint laughed.

"You will, old darling," he said.

He leaned back and lighted another cigarette.

"Mr. Wilfred Garniman," he remarked, "is a surprisingly intelligent sort of cove. There was very little nonsense—and most of what there was was my own free gift to the nation. I grant you he added to his present charge-sheet by offering me a cigarette and then a drink; but that's only because, as I've told you before, he's an amateur. I'm afraid he's been reading too many thrillers, and they've put ideas into his head. But on the really important point he was most professionally bright. The way

the calm suddenly broke out in the middle of the storm was quite astonishing to watch.''

"And by this time,'' said Patricia, ''he's probably going on being calm
a couple of hundred miles away.''

Simon shook his head.

"Not Wilfred,'' he said confidently. "Except when he's loosing off
six-shooters and throwing architecture about, Wilfred is a really first-
class amateur. And he is so rapid on the uptake that if he fell off the
fortieth floor of the Empire State Building he would be sitting on the roof
before he knew what had happened. Without any assistance from me, he
divined that I had no intention of calling in the police. So he knew he
wasn't very much worse off than he was before.''

"Why?''

"He may be an amateur, as I keep telling you, but he's efficient. Long
before his house started to fall to pieces on me, he'd begun to make
friendly attempts to bump me off. That was because he'd surveyed all
the risks before he started in business, and he figured that his graft was
exactly the kind of graft that would make me sit up and take notice. In
which he was darned right. I just breezed in and proved it to him. He
told me himself that he was unmarried; I wasn't able to get him to tell
me anything about his lawful affairs, but the butcher told me that he was
supposed to be 'something in the City'—so I acquired two items of
information. I also verified his home address, which was the most important thing; and I impressed him with my own brilliance and charm of
personality, which was the next most important. I played the perfect
clown, because that's the way these situations always get me, but in the
intervals between laughs I did everything that I set out to do. And he
knew it—as I meant him to.''

"And what happens next?''

"The private war will go on,'' said the Saint comfortably.

His deductions, as usual, were precisely true; but there was one twist
in the affairs of Wilfred Garniman of which he did not know, and if he
had known of it he might not have taken life quite so easily as he did for
the next few days. That is just possible.

On the morning of that first interview, he had hung around in the
middle distances of Mallaby Road with intent to increase his store of
information; but Mr. Garniman had driven off to his righteous labours
in a car which the Saint knew at a glance it would be useless to attempt
to follow in a taxi. One the second morning, the Saint decorated the same
middle distances at the wheel of his own car, but a traffic jam at Marble

Arch baulked him of his quarry. On the third morning he tried again, and collected two punctures in the first half-mile; and when he got out to inspect the damage he found sharp steel spikes strewn all over the road. Then, fearing that four consecutive seven-o'clock breakfasts might affect his health, the Saint stayed in bed on the fourth morning and did some thinking.

One error in his own technique he perceived quite clearly.

"If I'd sleuthed him on the first morning, and postponed the backchat till the second, I should have been a bright lad," he said. "My genius seems to have gone off the boil."

That something of the sort had happened was also evidenced by the fact that during those four days the problem of evolving a really agile method of inducing Mr. Garniman to part with a proportion of his ill-gotten gains continued to elude him.

Chief Inspector Teal heard the whole story when he called in on the evening of that fourth day to make inquiries, and was almost offensive.

The Saint sat at his desk after the detective had gone, and contemplated the net result of his ninety-six hours' cerebration moodily. This consisted of a twelve-line epilogue to the Epic History of Charles.

> *His will was read. His father learned*
> *Charles wished his body to be burned*
> *With huge heroic flames of fire*
> *Upon a Roman funeral pyre.*
> *But Charles's pa, sole legatee,*
> *Adverse to such publicity,*
> *Thought that this bidding might be done*
> *Without disturbing anyone,*
> *And, in a highly touching scene,*
> *Cremated him at Kensal Green.*
>
> *And so Charles has his little shrine*
> *With cavalier and concubine.*

Simon Templar scowled sombrely at the sheet for some time; and then, with a sudden impatience, he heaved the ink-pot out of the window and stood up.

"Pat," he said, "I feel that the time is ripe for us to push into a really wicked night club and drown our sorrows in iced ginger-beer."

The girl closed her book and smiled at him.

"Where shall we go?" she asked; and then the Saint suddenly shot across the room as if he had been touched with a hot iron.

"Holy Pete!" he yelled. "Pat—old sweetheart—old angel—"

Patricia blinked at him.

"My dear old lad—"

"Hell to all dear old lads!" cried the Saint recklessly.

He took her by the arms, swung her bodily out of her chair, put her down, rumpled her hair, and kissed her.

"Paddle on," he commanded breathlessly. "Go on—go and have a bath—dress—undress—glue your face on—anything. Sew a gun into the camiwhatnots, find a butterfly net—and let's go!"

"But what's the excitement about?"

"We're going entomo-botanising. We're going to prowl around the West End fishing for beetles. We're going to look at every night club in London—I'm a member of them all. If we don't catch anything, it won't be my fault. We're going to knock the L out of London and use it to tie the Home Secretary's ears together. The voice of the flat-footed periwinkle shall be heard in the land—"

He was still burbling foolishly when Patricia fled; but when she returned he was resplendent in Gents' Evening Wear and wielding a cocktail-shaker with a wild exuberance that made her almost giddy to watch.

"For Heaven's sake," she said, catching his arm, "pull yourself together and tell me something!"

"Sure," said the Saint daftly. "The nightie of yours is a dream. Or is it meant to be a dress? You can never tell, with these long skirts. And I don't want to be personal, but are you sure you haven't forgotten to put on the back or posterior part? I can see all your spine. Not that I mind, but . . . Talking of swine—swine—there was a very fine specimen at the Embassy the other night. Must have measured at least thirty-two inches from snout to—They say that the man who landed it played for three weeks. Ordinary trout line and gaff, you know. . . ."

Patricia Holm was almost hysterical by the time they reached the Carlton, where the Saint had decided to dine. And it was not until he had ordered an extravagant dinner, with appropriate wines, that she was able to make him listen to a sober question. And then he became the picture of innocent amazement.

"But didn't you get me?" he asked. "Hadn't you figured it out for yourself? I thought you were there long ago. Have you forgotten my little exploit at the Birds' Nest? Who d'you think paid for that bit of coloured mosquito-net you're wearing? Who brought these studs I'm wearing?

Who, if it comes to that, is standing us this six-course indigestion?
. . . Well, some people might say it was Montgomery Bird, but
personally—''

The girl gasped.

''You mean that other man at the Birds' Nest was the Scorpion?''

''Who else? . . . But I never tumbled to it till tonight! I told you he
was busy putting the black on Montgomery when Teal and I butted in.
I overheard the whole conversation, and I was certainly curious. I made
a mental note at the time to investigate that bearded battleship, but it
never came into my head that it must have been Wilfred himself—I'm
damned if I know why!''

Patricia nodded.

''I'd forgotten to think of it myself,'' she said.

''And I must have been fast asleep the whole time! Of course it was
the Scorpion—and his graft's a bigger one than I ever dreamed. He's got
organisation, that guy. He probably has his finger in half the wicked pies
that are being cooked in this big city. If he was on to Montgomery,
there's no reason why he shouldn't have got on to a dozen others that
you and I can think of; and he'll be drawing his percentage from the
whole bunch. I grant you I put Montgomery out of business, but—''

''If you're right,'' said Patricia, ''and the Scorpion hasn't done a bunk,
we may find him anywhere.''

''Tonight,'' said the Saint. ''Or, if not tonight, some other night. And
I'm prepared to keep on looking. But my income tax has got to be paid
tomorrow, and so I want the reunion to be tonight.''

''Have you got an idea?''

''I've got a dozen,'' said the Saint. ''And one of them says that Wilfred
is going to have an Evening!''

His brain had suddenly picked up its stride again. In a few minutes he
had sketched out a plan of campaign as slick and agile as anything his
fertile genius had ever devised. And once again he proved a true prophet,
though the proceedings took a slight twist which he had not foreseen.

For at a quarter past eleven they ran Wilfred Garniman to earth at the
Golden Apple Club. And Wilfred Garniman certainly had an Evening.

He was standing at the door of the ballroom, sardonically surveying
the clientele, when a girl walked in and stopped beside him. He glanced
round at her almost without thinking. Having done which, he stayed
glancing—and thought a lot.

She was young, slim, fair-haired, and exquisite. Even Wilfred Garniman knew that. His rather tired eyes, taking in other details of her

appearance, recognized the simple perfection of a fifty-guinea gown. And her face was utterly innocent of guile—Wilfred Garniman had a shrewd perception of these things also. She scanned the crowd anxiously, as though looking for someone, and in due course it became apparent that the someone was not present. Wilfred Garniman was the last man she looked at. Their glances met, and held for some seconds; and then the faintest ripple of a smile touched her lips. . . .

And exactly one hour later, Simon Templar was ringing the bell of 28, Mallaby Road, Harrow.

He was not expecting a reply, but he always liked to be sure of his ground. He waited ten minutes, ringing the bell at intervals; and then he went in by a ground-floor window. It took him straight into Mr. Garniman's study. And there, after carefully drawing the curtains, the Saint was busy for some time. For thirty-five minutes by his watch, to be exact.

And then he sat down in a chair and lighted a cigarette.

"Somewhere," he murmured thoughtfully, "there is a catch in this."

For the net result of a systematic and expert search had panned out at precisely nil.

And this the Saint was not expecting. Before he left the Carlton, he had propounded one thoery with all the force of an incontestable fact.

"Wilfred may have decided to take my intrusion calmly, and trust that he'll be able to put me out of the way before I manage to strafe him good and proper; but he'd never leave himself without at least one line of retreat. And that implies being able to take his booty with him. He'd never have put it in a bank, because there'd always be the chance that someone might notice things and get curious. It will have been in a safe deposit; but it won't be there now."

Somewhere or other—somewhere within Wilfred Garniman's easy reach—there was a large quantity of good solid cash, ready and willing to be converted into all manner of music by anyone who picked it up and offered it a change of address. It might have been actually on Wilfred Garniman's person; but the Saint didn't think so. He had decided that it would most probably be somewhere in the house at Harrow; and as he drove out there he had prepared to save time by considering the potential hiding-places in advance. He had thought of many, and discarded them one by one, for various reasons; and his final judgment had led him unhesitatingly into the very room where he had spent thirty-five fruitless minutes . . . and where he was now getting set to spend some more.

"This is the Scorpion's sacred lair," he figured, "and Wilfred wouldn't let himself forget it. He'd play it up to himself for all it was worth. It's the inner sanctum of the great ruthless organisation that doesn't exist. He'd sit in that chair in the evenings—at that desk—there—thinking what a wonderful man he was. And he'd look at whatever innocent bit of interior decoration hides his secret cache, and gloat over the letters and dossiers that he's got hidden there, and the money they've brought in or are going to bring in—the fat, slimy, wallowing slug. . . .''

Again his eyes travelled slowly round the room. The plainly papered walls could have hidden nothing, except behind the pictures, and he had tried every one of those. Dummy books he had ruled out at once, for a servant may always take down a book; but he had tested the back of every shelf—and found nothing. The whole floor was carpeted, and he gave that no more than a glance: his analysis of Wilfred Garniman's august meditations did not harmonise with the vision of the same gentleman crawling about on his hands and knees. And every drawer of the desk was already unlocked, and not one of them contained anything of compromising interest.

And that appeared to exhaust the possibilities. He stared speculatively at the fireplace—but he had done that before. It ignored the exterior architecture of the building and was a plain modern affair of blue tiles and tin, and it would have been difficult to work any grisly gadgets into its bluntly bourgeois lines. Or, it appeared, into the lines of anything else in that room.

"Which," said the Saint drowsily, "is absurd."

There remained, of course, Wilfred Garniman's bedroom—the Saint had long since listed that as the only feasible alternative. But, somehow, he didn't like it. Plunder and pink poplin pyjamas didn't seem a psychologically satisfactory combination—particularly when the pyjamas must be presumed to surround something like Wilfred Garniman must have looked like without his Old Harrovian tie. The idea did not ring a bell. And yet, if the boodle and etceteral appurtenances thereof and howsoever were not in the bedroom, they must be in the study—some blistered whereabouts or what not. . . .

"Which," burbled the Saint, "is *ab*-sluly *'pos*-rous. . . ."

The situation seemed less and less annoying. . . . It really didn't matter very much. . . . Wilfred Garniman, if one came to think of it, was even fatter than Teal . . . and one made allowances for detectives. . . . Teal was fat, and Long Harry was long, and Patricia played around with Scorpions; which was all very odd and amusing, but nothing to get worked up about before breakfast, old dear. . . .

9

SOMEWHERE IN THE infinite darkness appeared a tiny speck of white. It came hurtling towards him; and as it came it grew larger and whiter and more terrible, until it seemed as if it must smash and smother and pulp him into the squashed wreckage of the whole universe at his back. He let out a yell, and the upper half of the great white sky fell back like a shutter, sending a sudden blaze of dazzling light into his eyes. The lower bit of white touched his nose and mouth damply, and an acrid stinging smell stabbed right up into the top of his head and trickled down his throat like a thin stream of condensed fire. He gasped, coughed, choked— and saw Wilfred Garniman.

"Hulloa, old toad," said the Saint weakly.

He breathed deeply, fanning out of his nasal passages the fiery tingle of the restorative that Garniman had made him inhale. His head cleared magically, so completely that for a few minutes it felt as if a cold wind had blown clear through it; and the dazzle of the light dimmed out of his eyes. But he looked down, and saw that his wrists and ankles were securely bound.

"That's a useful line of dope, Wilfred," he murmured huskily. "How did you do it?"

Garniman was folding up his handkerchief and returning it to his pocket, working with slow meticulous hands.

"The pressure of your head on the back of the chair released the gas," he replied calmly. "It's an idea of my own—I have always been prepared to have to entertain undesirable visitors. The lightest pressure is sufficient."

Simon nodded.

"It certainly is a great game," he remarked. "I never noticed a thing, though I remember now that I was blithering to myself rather inanely just before I went under. And so the little man works off his own bright ideas. . . . Wilfred, you're coming on."

"I brought my dancing partner with me," said Garniman, quite casually.

He waved a fat indicative hand; and the Saint, squirming over to follow the gesture, saw Patricia in another chair. For a second or two he looked at her; then he turned slowly round again.

"There's no satisfying you jazz fiends, is there?" he drawled. "Now I suppose you'll wind up the gramophone and start again. . . . But the girl seems to have lost the spirit of the thing . . ."

Garniman sat down at the desk and regarded the Saint with the heavy inscrutable face of a gross image.

"I had seen her before, dancing with you at the Jericho, long before we first met—I never forget a face. After she had succeeded in planting herself on me, I spent a little time assuring myself that I was not mistaken; and then the solution was simple. A few drops from a bottle that I am never without—in her champagne—and the impression was that she became helplessly drunk. She will recover without our assistance, perhaps in five minutes, perhaps in half an hour—according to her strength." Wilfred Garniman's fleshy lips loosened in the travesty of a smile. "You underestimated me, Templar."

"That," said the Saint, "remains to be seen."

Mr. Garniman shrugged.

"Need I explain that you have come to the end of your interesting and adventurous life?"

Simon twitched an eyebrow, and slid his mouth mockingly sideways.

"What—not again?" he sighed, and Garniman's smooth forehead crinkled.

"I don't understand."

"But you haven't seen so many of these situations through as I have, old horse," said the Saint lightly. "What's the programme this time— do you sew me up in the bath and light the geyser, or am I run through the mangle and buried under the billiard-table? Or can you think of something really original?"

Garniman inclined his head ironically.

"I trust you will find my method satisfactory," he said.

He lighted a cigarette, and rose from the desk again; and as he picked up a length of rope from the floor and moved across to Patricia, the Saint warbled on in the same tone of gentle weariness.

"Mind how you fix those ankles, Wilfred. That gauzy silk stuff you see on the limbs costs about five pounds a leg, and it ladders if a fly settles on it. Oh, and while we're on the subject: don't let's have any nonsense about death or dishonour. The child mightn't want to die. And besides, that stuff is played out, anyway. . . ."

Gerniman made no reply.

He continued with his task in his ponderous methodical way, making every movement with immensely phlegmatic deliberation. The Saint, who had known many criminals, and who was making no great exaggeration when he said that this particular situation had long since lost all its pristine charm for him, could recall no one in his experience who had ever been so dispassionate. Cold-blooded ruthlessness, a granite impassivity, he had met before; but through it all, deep as it might be, there had always run a perceptible taut thread of vindictive purpose. In Wilfred Garniman there showed nothing of this. He went about his work in the same way that he might have gone about the setting of a mouse-trap—with elephantine efficiency, and a complete blank in the teleological compartment of his brain. And Simon Templar knew with an eerie intuition that this was no pose, as it might have been in others. And then he knew that Wilfred Garniman was mad.

Garniman finished, and straightened up. And then, still without speaking, he picked Patricia up in his arms and carried her out of the room.

The Saint braced his muscles.

His whole body tightened to the effort like a tempered steel spring, and his arms swelled and corded up until the sleeves were stretched and strained around them. For an instant he was absolutely motionless, except for the tremors of titanic tension that shuddered down his frame like wind-ripples over a quiet pool. . . . And then he relaxed and went limp, loosing his breath in a great gasp. And the Saintly smile crawled a trifle crookedly over his face.

"Which makes things difficult," he whispered—to the four unanswering walls.

For the cords about his wrists still held him firmly.

Free to move as he chose, he could have broken those ropes with his hands; but bound as he was he could apply scarcely a quarter of his strength. And the ropes were good ones—new, half-inch, three-ply Manila. He had made the test; and he relaxed. To have struggled longer would have wasted valuable strength to no purpose. And he had come out without Belle, the little knife that ordinarily went with him everywhere, in a sheath strapped to his left forearm—the knife that had saved him on countless other occasions such as this.

Clumsily he pulled himself out of the chair, and rolled the few yards to the desk. There was a telephone there; he dragged himself to his knees and lifted the receiver. The exchange took an eternity to answer. He gave Teal's private number, and heard the preliminary buzz in the receiver as he was connected up; and then Wilfred Garniman spoke behind him, from the doorway.

"Ah! You are still active, Templar?"

He crossed the room with quick lumbering strides, and snatched the instrument away. For a second or two he listened with the receiver at his ear; then he hung it up and put the telephone down at the far end of the desk.

"You have not been at all successful this evening," he remarked stolidly.

"But you must admit we keep on trying," said the Saint cheerfully.

Wilfred Garniman took the cigarette from his mouth. His expressionless eyes contemplated the Saint abstractedly.

"I am beginning to believe that your prowess was overrated. You came here hoping to find documents or money—perhaps both. You were unsuccessful."

"Er—temporarily."

"Yet a little ingenuity would have saved you from an unpleasant experience—and shown you quite another function of this piece of furniture."

Garniman pointed to the armchair. He tilted it over on its back, prised up a couple of tacks, and allowed the canvas finishing of the bottom to fall away. Underneath was a dark steel door, secured by three swivel catches.

"I made the whole chair myself—it was a clever piece of work," he said; and then he dismissed the subject almost as if it had never been raised. "I shall now require you to rejoin your friend, Templar. Will you be carried, or would you prefer to walk?"

"How far are we going?" asked the Saint cautiously.

"Only a few yards."

"I'll walk—thanks."

Garniman knelt down and tugged at the ankle ropes. A strand slipped under his manipulations, giving an eighteen-inch hobble.

"Stand up."

Simon obeyed. Garniman gripped his arm and led him out of the room. They went down the hall, and passed through a low door under the stairs. They stumbled down a flight of narrow stone steps. At the bottom, Garniman picked up a candlestick from a niche in the wall and steered the Saint along a short flagged passage.

"You know, Wilf," murmured the Saint conversationally, "this has happened to me twice before in the last six months. And each time it was gas. Is it going to be gas again this time, or are you breaking away from the rules?''

"It will not be gas," replied Garniman flatly.

He was as heavily passionless as a contented animal. And the Saint chattered on blithely.

The other made no response, and the Saint sighed. In the matter of cross-talk comedy, Wilfred Garniman was a depressingly feeble performer. In the matter of murder, on the other hand, he was probably depressingly efficient; but the Saint couldn't help feeling that he made death a most gloomy business.

And then they came into a small low vault; and the Saint saw Patricia again.

Her eyes were open, and she looked at him steadily, with the faintest of smiles on her lips.

"Hullo, boy."

"Hullo, lass."

That was all.

Simon glanced round. In the centre of the floor there was a deep hole, and beside it was a great mound of earth. There was a dumpy white sack in one corner, and a neat conical heap of sand beside it.

Wilfred Garniman explained, in his monotonously apathetic way.

"We tried to sink a well here, but we gave it up. The hole is only about ten feet deep—it was not filled up again. I shall fill it up tonight."

He picked up the girl and took her to the hole in the floor. Dropping on one knee at the edge, he lowered her to the stretch of his arms and let go. . . . He came back to the Saint, dusting his trousers.

"Will you continue to walk?" he inquired.

Simon stepped to the side of the pit, and turned. For a moment he gazed into the other man's eyes—the eyes of a man empty of the bowels of compassion. But the Saint's blue gaze was as cold and still as a polar sea.

"You're an overfed, pot-bellied swamp-hog," he said; and then Garniman pushed him roughly backwards.

Quite unhurriedly, Wilfred Garniman took off his coat, unfastened his cuff-links, and rolled his sleeves up above his elbows. He opened the sack of cement and tipped out its contents into a hole that he trampled in the heap of sand. He picked up a spade, looked about him, and put it down again. Without the least variation of his heavily sedate stride he left the cellar, leaving the candle burning on the floor. In three or four minutes he was back again, carrying a brimming pail of water in either hand; and with the help of these he continued his unaccustomed labour, splashing gouts of water on his materials and stirring them carefully with the spade.

It took him over half an hour to reduce the mixture to a consistency smooth enough to satisfy him, for he was an inexperienced worker and yet he could afford to make no mistake. At the end of that time he was streaming with sweat, and his immaculate white collar and shirt-front were grubbily wilting rags; but those facts did not trouble him. No one will ever know what was in his mind while he did that work: perhaps he did not know himself, for his face was blank and tranquil.

His flabby muscles must have been aching, but he did not stop to rest. He took the spade over to the hole in the floor. The candle sent no light down there, but in the darkness he could see an irregular blur of white— he was not interested to gloat over it. Bending his back again, he began to shovel the earth back into the hole. It took an astonishing time, and he was breathing stertorously long before he had filled the pit up loosely level with the floor. Then he dropped the spade and tramped over the surface, packing it down tight and hard.

And then he laid over it the cement that he had prepared, finishing it off smoothly level. with the floor.

Even then he did not rest—he was busy for another hour, filling the pails with earth and carrying them up the stairs and out into the garden and emptying them over the flower-beds. He had a placidly accurate eye for detail and an enormous capacity for taking pains, had Mr. Wilfred Garniman; but it is doubtful if he gave more than a passing thought to the eternal meaning of what he had done.

10

TO MR. TEAL, who in those days knew the Saint's habits almost as well as he knew his own, it was merely axiomatic that breakfast and Simon Templar coincided somewhere between the hours of 11 a.m. and 1 p.m.; and therefore it is not surprising that the visit which he paid to 7, Upper Berkeley Mews on one historic morning resulted in a severe shock to his system. For a few moments after the door had been opened to him he stood bovinely rooted to the mat, looking like some watcher of the skies who has just seen the Great Bear turn a back-somersault and march rapidly over the horizon in column on all fours. And when he had pulled himself together, he followed the Saint into the sitting-room with the air of a man who is not at all certain that there is no basin of water balanced over the door to await his entrance.

"Have some gum, old dear," invited the Saint hospitably; and Mr. Teal stopped by the table and blinked at him.

"What's the idea?" he demanded suspiciously.

The Saint looked perplexed.

"What idea, brother?"

"Is your clock fast, or haven't you been to bed yet?"

Simon grinned.

"Neither. I'm going to travel, and Pat and I have got to push out and book passages and arrange for international overdrafts and all that sort of thing." He waved towards Patricia Holm, who was smoking a cigarette over the *Times*. "Pat, you have met Claud Eustace, haven't you? Made his pile in Consoldiated Gas. Mr. Teal, Miss Holm. Miss Holm, Mr. Teal. Consider yourselves divorced."

Teal picked up the packet of spearmint that sat sedately in the centre of the table, and put it down again uneasily. He produced another packet from his own pocket.

"Did you say you were going away?" he asked.

"I did. I'm worn out, and I feel I need a complete rest—I did a couple of hours' work yesterday, and at my time of life. . . ."

"Where were you going?"

The Saint shrugged.

"Doubtless Thomas Cook will provide. We thought of some nice warm islands. It may be the Canaries, the Balearic or Little by Little—"

"And what about the Scorpion?"

"Oh, yes, the Scorpion! . . . Well, you can have him all to yourself now, Claud."

Simon glanced towards the mantelpiece, and the detective followed his gaze. There was a raw puncture in the panelling where a stiletto had recently reposed, but the papers that had been pinned there were gone. The Saint took the sheaf from his pocket.

"I was just going to beetle along and pay my income tax," he said airily. "Are you walking Hanover Square way?"

Teal looked at him thoughtfully, and it may be recorded to the credit of the detective's somnolently cyclopean self-control that not a muscle of his face moved.

"Yes, I'll go with you—I expect you'll be wanting a drink," he said; and then his eyes fell on the Saint's wrist.

He motioned fractionally at it.

"Did you sprain that trying to get the last drops out of the barrel?" he inquired.

Simon pulled down his sleeve.

"As a matter of fact, it was a burn," he said.

"The Scorpion?"

"Patricia."

Teal's eyelids descended one millimetre. He looked at the girl, and she smiled at him in a seraphic way which made the detective's internal organs wriggle. Previously, he had been wont to console himself with the reflection that that peculiarly exasperating kind of sweetness in the smile was the original and unalienable copyright of one lone face out of the faces in the wide world. He returned his gaze to the Saint.

"Domestic strife?" he queried, and Simon assumed an expression of pained reproach.

"We aren't married," he said.

Patricia flicked her cigarette into the fireplace and came over. She tucked one hand into the belt of her plain tweed suit, and laid the other on Simon Templar's shoulder. And she continued to smile seraphically upon the detective.

"You see, we were being buried alive," she explained simply.

"All down in the—er—what's-its of the earth," said the Saint.

"Simon hadn't got his knife, but he remembered his cigarette-lighter just in time. He couldn't reach it himself, so I had to do it. And he never made a sound—I never knew till afterwards—"

"It was a minor detail," said the Saint.

He twitched a small photograph from his pocket and passed it to Teal.

"From the Scorpion's passport," he said. "I found it in a drawer of his desk. That was before he caught me with as neat a trick as I've ever come across—the armchairs in his study will repay a sleuthlike investigation, Claud. Then, if you pass on to the cellars, you'll find a piece of cement flooring that has only just begun to floor. Pat and I are supposed to be there. Which reminds me—if you decide to dig down in the hope of finding us, you'll find my second-best boiled shirt somewhere in the depths. We had to leave it behind. I don't know if you've ever noticed it, but I can give you my word that even the most pliant rubber dickey rattles like a suit of armour when you're trying to move quietly.''

For a space the detective stared at him.

Then he took out a notebook.

It was, in its way, one of the most heroic things he ever did.

"Where is this place?" he asked.

"Twenty-eight, Mallaby Road, Arrer. The name is Wilfred Garniman. And about the shirt—if you had it washed at the place where they do yours before you go toddling round the night clubs, and sent it on to me at Palma, I expect I could find a place to burn it. And I've got some old boots upstairs which I thought maybe you might like—''

Teal replaced his notebook and pencil.

"I don't want to ask too many questions," he said. "But if Garniman knows you got away—''

Simon shook his head.

"Wilfred does not know. He went out to fetch some water to dilute the concrete, and we moved while he was away. Later on I saw him carting out the surplus earth and dumping it on the gardening notes. When you were playing on the sands of Southend in a pair of pink shrimping drawers, Teal, did you ever notice that you can always dig more out of a hole than you can put back in it? Wilfred had quite enough mud left over to make him happy.''

Teal nodded.

"That's all I wanted," he said, and the Saint smiled.

"Perhaps we can give you a lift," he suggested politely.

They drove to Hanover Square in the Saint's car. The Saint was in form. Teal knew that by the way he drove. Teal was not happy about it. Teal was even less happy when the Saint insisted on being escorted into the office.

"I insist on having police protection," he said. "Scorpions I can manage, but when it comes to tax collectors . . . Not that there's a great difference. The same threatening letters, the same merciless bleeding of the honest toiler, the same bleary eyes—''

"All right," said Teal wearily.

He climbed out of the car, and followed behind Patricia; and so they climbed to the general office. At the high counter which had been erected to protect the clerks from the savage assaults of their victims the Saint halted, and clamoured in a loud voice to be ushered into the presence of Mr. Delborn.

Presently a scared little man came to the barrier.

"You wish to see Mr. Delborn, sir?"

"I do."

"Yes, sir. What is your business, sir?"

"I'm a burglar," said the Saint innocently.

"Yes, sir. What did you wish to see Mr. Delborn about, sir?"

"About the payment of my income tax, Algernon. I will see Mr. Delborn himself and nobody else; and if I don't see him at once, I shall not only refuse to pay a penny of my tax, but I shall also take this hideous office to pieces and hide it in various drains belonging to the London County Council. By the way, do you know Chief Inspector Teal? Mr. Teal, Mr. Veal. Mr. Veal—"

"Will you take a seat, sir?"

"Certainly," said the Saint.

He was half-way down the stairs when Teal caught him.

"Look here, Templar," said the detective, breathing heavily through the nose, "I don't care if you have got the Scorpion in your pocket, but if this is your idea of being funny—"

Simon put down the chair and scratched his head.

"I was only obeying instructions," he said plaintively. "I admit it seemed rather odd, but I thought maybe Lionel hadn't got a spare seat in his office."

Teal and Patricia between them got him as far as the top of the stairs, where he put the chair down, sat in it, and refused to move.

"I'm going home," said Patricia finally.

"Bring some oranges back with you," said the Saint. "And don't forget your knitting. What time do the early doors open?"

The situation was only saved by the return of the harassed clerk.

"Mr. Delborn will see you, sir."

He led the way through the general office and opened a door at the end.

"What name, sir?"

"Gandhi," said the Saint, and stalked into the room.

And there he stopped.

For the first time in his life, Simon Templar stood frozen into a kind of paralysis of sheer incredulous startlement.

In its own *genre,* that moment was the supremely flabbergasting instant of his life. Battle, murder, and sudden death of all kinds and varieties notwithstanding, the most hectic moments of the most earth-shaking cataclysms in which he had been involved paled their ineffectual fires beside the eye-shrivelling dazzle of that second. And the Saint stood utterly still, with every shadow of expression wiped from his face, momentarily robbed of even his facile power of speech, simply staring.

For the man at the desk was Wilfred Garniman.

Wilfred Garniman himself, exactly as the Saint had seen him on that very first expedition to Harrow—black-coated, black-tied, the perfect office gentleman with a fifty-two-inch waist. Wilfred Garniman sitting there in a breathless immobility that matched the Saint's, but with the prosperous colour draining from his face and his coarse lips going gray.

And then the Saint found his voice.

"Oh, it's you, Wilfred, is it?" The words trickled very softly into the deathly silence. "And this is Simon Templar speaking—not a ghost. I declined to turn into a ghost, even though I was buried. And Patricia Holm did the same. She's outside at this very moment, if you'd like to see her. And so is Chief Inspector Teal—with your photograph in his pocket. . . . Do you know that this is very tough on me, sweetheart? I've promised you to Teal, and I ought to be killing you myself. Buried Pat alive, you did—or meant to. . . . And you're the greasy swine that's been pestering me to pay yor knock-kneed taxes. No wonder you took to Scorping in your spare time. I wouldn't mind betting you began in this very office, and the capital you started with was the things you wormed out of people under the disguise of offical inquiries. . . . And I came in to give you one thousand, three hundred and thirty-seven pounds, nineteen and fivepence of your own money, all out of the strongbox under that very interesting chair, Wilfred—"

He saw the beginning of the movement that Garniman made, and hurled himself sideways. The bullet actually skinned one of his lower ribs, though he did not know it until later. He swerved into the heavy desk, and got his hands under the edge. For one weird instant he looked from a range of two yards into the eyes of Wilfred Garniman, who was in the act of rising out of his chair. Garniman's automatic was swinging round for a second shot, and the thunder of the first seemed to still be hanging in the air. And behind him Simon heard the rattle of the door.

And then—to say that he tipped the desk over would be absurd. To have done anything so feeble would have been a sentence of death pronounced simultaneously upon Patricia Holm and Claud Eustace and himself—at least. The Saint knew that.

But as the others burst into the room, it seemed as if the Saint gathered up the whole desk in his two hands, from the precarious hold that he had on it, and flung it hugely and terrifically into the wall; and Wilfred

Garniman was carried before it like a great bloated fly before a cannon-ball. . . . And, really, that was that. . . .

The story of the Old Bailey trial reached Palma about six weeks later, in an ancient newspaper which Patricia Holm produced one morning.

Simon Templar was not at all interested in the story; but he was vastly interested in an illustration thereto which he discovered at the top of the page. The press photographer had done his worst; and Chief Inspector Teal, the hero of the case, caught unawares in the very act of inserting some fresh chewing gum in his mouth as he stepped out on to the pavement of Newgate Street, was featured looking almost libellously like an in-furiated codfish afflicted with some strange uvular growth.

Simon clipped out the portrait and pasted it neatly at the head of a large plain postcard. Underneath it he wrote:

> *Claud Eustace Teal, when overjoyed,*
> *Wiggled his dexter adenoid;*
> *For well-bred policemen think it rude*
> *To show their tonsils in the nude.*

"That ought to come like a ray of sunshine into Claud's dreary life," said the Saint, surveying his handiwork.

He may have been right; for the postcard was delivered in error to an Assistant Commissioner who was gifted with a particularly acid tongue, and it is certain that Teal did not hear the last of it for many days.

Part II
The Million Pound Day

1

THE SCREAM PEALED out at such point-blank range, and was strangled so swiftly and suddenly, that Simon Templar opened his eyes and wondered for a moment whether he had dreamed it.

The darkness inside the car was impenetrable; and outside, through the thin mist that a light frost had etched upon the windows, he could distinguish nothing but the dull shadows of a few trees silhouetted against the flat pallor of the sky. A glance at the luminous dial of his wrist watch showed that it was a quarter to five: he had slept barely two hours.

A week-end visit to some friends who lived on the remote margin of Cornwall, about thirteen inches from Land's End, had terminated a little more than seven hours earlier, when the Saint, feeling slightly limp after three days in the company of two young souls who were convalescing from a recent honeymoon, had pulled out his car to make the best of a clear night road back to London. A few miles beyond Basingstoke he had backed into a side lane for a cigarette, a sandwich, and a nap. The cigarette and the sandwich he had had; but the nap should have lasted until the hands of his watch met at six-thirty and the sky was white and clear with the morning—he had fixed that time for himself, and had known that his eyes would not open one minute later.

And they hadn't. But they shouldn't have opened one minute earlier, either. . . . And the Saint sat for a second or two without moving, straining his ears into the stillness for the faintest whisper of sound that might answer the question in his mind, and driving his memory backwards into those last blank movements of sleep to recall the sound that had woken him.

555

And then, with a quick stealthy movement, he turned the handle of the door and slipped out into the road.

Before that, he had realised that that scream could never have been shaped in his imagination. The sheer shrieking horror it still rang between his eardrums and his brain: the hideous high-pitched sob on which it had died seemed still to be quivering on the air. And the muffled patter of running feet which had reached him as he listened had served only to confirm what he already knew.

He stood in the shadow of the car with the cold damp smell of the dawn in his nostrils, and heard the footsteps coming closer. They were coming towards him down the main road—now that he was outside the car, they tapped into his brain with an unmistakable clearness. He heard them so distinctly, in the utter silence that lay all around, that he felt he could almost see the man who made them. And he knew that that was the man who had screamed. The same stark terror that had gone shuddering through the very core of the scream was beating out the wild tattoo of those running feet—the same stomach-sinking dread translated into terms of muscular reaction. For the feet were not running as a man ordinarily runs. They were kicking, blinding, stumbling, hammering along in the mad muscle-binding heart-bursting flight of a man whose reason has tottered and cracked before a vision of all the tortures of the Pit. . . .

Simon felt the hairs on the nape of his neck prickling. In another instant he could hear the gasping agony of the man's breathing, but he stayed waiting where he was. He had moved a little way from the car, and now he was crouched right by the corner of the lane, less than a yard from the road, completely hidden in the blackness under the hedge.

The most elementary process of deduction told him that no man would run like that unless the terror that drove him on was close upon his heels— and no man would have screamed like that unless he had felt cold upon his shoulder the clutching hand of an intolerable doom. Therefore the Saint waited.

And then the man reached the corner of the lane.

Simon got one glimpse of him—a man of middle height and build, coatless, with his head back and his fists working. Under the feebly lightening sky his face showed thin and hollow-cheeked, pointed at the chin by a small peaked beard, the eyes starting from their sockets.

He was done in—finished. He must have been finished two hundred yards back. But as he reached the corner the ultimate end came. His feet blundered again, and he plunged as if a trip-wire had caught him across the knees. And then it must have been the last instinct of the hunted animal that made him turn and reel round into the little lane; and the Saint's strong arms caught him as he fell.

The man stared up into the Saint's face. His lips tried to shape a word, but the breath whistled voicelessly in his throat. And then his eyes closed and his body went limp, and Simon lowered him gently to the ground.

The Saint straightened up again, and vanished once more in the gloom. The slow bleaching of the sky seemed only to intensify the blackness that sheltered him, while beyond the shadows a faint light was beginning to pick out the details of the road. And Simon heard the coming of the second man.

The footfalls were so soft that he was not surprised that he had not heard them before. At the moment when he picked them up they could only have been a few yards away, and to anyone less keen of hearing they would still have been inaudible. But the Saint heard them—heard the long striding ghostly sureness of them padding over the macadam— and a second tingle of eerie understanding crawled over his scalp and glissaded down his spine like a needle-spray of ice-cold water. For the feet that made those sounds were human, but the feet were bare. . . .

And the man turned the corner.

Simon saw him as clearly as he had seen the first—more clearly.

He stood huge and straight in the opening of the lane, gazing ahead into the darkness. The wan light in the sky fell evenly across the broad black primitive-featured face, and stippled glistening silver high-lights on the gigantic ebony limbs. Except for a loosely knotted loin-cloth he was naked, and the gleaming surfaces of his tremendous chest shifted rhythmically to the mighty movements of his breathing. And the third and last thrill of comprehension slithered clammily into the small of the Saint's back as he saw all these things—as he saw the savage ruthlessness of purpose behind the mere physical presence of that magnificent brute-man, sensed the primeval lust of cruelty in the parting of the thick lips and the glitter of the eyes. Almost he seemed to smell the sickly stench of rotting jungles seeping its fetid breath into the clean cold air of that English dawn, swelling in hot stifling waves about the figure of the pursuing beast that had taken the continents and the centuries in its bare-foot loping stride.

And while Simon watched, fascinated, the eyes of the Negro fell on the sprawling figure that lay in the middle of the lane, and he stepped forward with the snarl of a beast rumbling in his throat.

And it was then that the Saint, with an effort which was as much physical as mental, tore from his mind the steely tentacles of the hypnotic spell that had held him paralysed for those few seconds—and also moved.

"Good morning," spoke the Saint politely, but that was the last polite speech he made that day. No one who had ever heard him talk had any illusions about the Saint's opinion of Simon Templar's physical prowess, and no one who had ever seen him fight had ever seriously questioned the accuracy of that opinion; but this was the kind of occasion on which the Saint knew that the paths of glory lead but to the grave. Which may help to explain why, after that single preliminary concession to the requirements of his manual of etiquette, he heaved the volume over the horizon and proceeded to lapse from grace in no uncertain manner.

After all, that encyclopaedia of all the social virtues, though it had some cheering and helpful suggestions to offer on the subject of addressing letters to archdeacons, placing Grand Lamas in the correct relation of precedence to Herzegovinian Grossherzöge, and declining invitations to open bazaars in aid of Homes for Ichthyotic Vulcanisers' Mates, had never even envisaged such a situation as that which was then up for inspection; and the Saint figured that the rules allowed him a free hand.

The Negro, crouching in the attitude in which the Saint's gentle voice had frozen him, was straining his eyes into the darkness. And out of that darkness, like a human cannon-ball, the Saint came at him.

He came in a weird kind of twisting leap that shot him out of the obscurity with no less startling a suddenness than if he had at that instant materialised out of the fourth dimension. And the Negro simply had no time to do anything about it. For that suddenness was postively the only tangible quality about the movement. It had, for instance, a very tangible momentum, which must have been one of the most painfully concrete things that the victim of it had ever encountered. That momentum started from the five toes of the Saint's left foot; it rippled up his left calf, surged up his left thigh, and gathered to itself a final wave of power from the big muscles of his hips. And then, in that twisting action of his body, it was swung on into another channel; it travelled down the tautening fibres of his right leg, gathering new force in every inch of its progress, and came right out at the end of his shoe with all the smashing violence of a ten-ton stream of water cramped down into the finest nozzle of a garden hose. And at the very instant when every molecule of shattering velocity and weight was concentrated in the point of that right shoe, the point impacted precisely in the geometrical centre of the Negro's stomach.

If there had been a football at that point of impact, a rag of shredded leather might reasonably have been expected to come to earth somewhere north of the Aberdeen Providential Society Buildings. And the effect upon the human target, colossus though it was, was just as devastating, even if a trifle less spectacular.

Simon observed the effects of his physical contact, and saw the man travel three feet backwards as if he had been caught in the full fairway of a high-speed hydraulic battering-ram. The wheezy *phe-e-ew* of electrically emptied lungs merged into the synchronised sound effects, and ended in a little grunting cough. And then the Negro seemed to dissolve on to the roadway like a statue of sculptured butter caught in the blast of a superheated furnace. . . .

Simon jerked open one of the rear doors of the car, picked the bearded man lightly off the ground, heaved him in upon the cushions, and slammed the door again.

Five seconds later he was behind the wheel, and the self-starter was whirring over the cold engine.

The headlights carved a blazing chunk of luminance out of the dimness as he touched a switch, and he saw the Negro bucking up on to his hands and knees. He let in the clutch, and the car jerked away with a spluttering exhaust. One running-board rustled in the long grass of the banking as he lashed through the narrow gap; and then he was spinning round into the wide main road.

Ten yards ahead, in the full beam of the headlights, a uniformed constable tumbled off his bicycle and ran to the middle of the road with outstretched hands; and the Saint almost gasped.

Instantaneously he realised that the scream which had woken him must have been audible for some considerable distance—the policeman's attitude could not more clearly have indicated a curiosity which the Saint was at that moment instinctively disinclined to meet.

He eased up, and the constable guilelessly fell round to the side of the car.

And then the Saint revved up his engine, let in the clutch again with a bang, and went roaring on through the dawn with the policeman's shout tattered to futile fragments in the wind behind him.

2

IT WAS FULL daylight when he turned into Upper Berkeley Mews and
stopped before his own front door, and the door opened even before he
had switched off the engine.

"Hullo, boy!" said Patricia. "I wasn't expecting you for another
hour."

"Neither was I," said the Saint.

He kissed her lightly on the lips, and stood there with his cap tilted
rakishly to the back of his head and his leather coat swinging back from
wide square shoulders, peeling off his gloves and smiling one of his most
cryptic smiles.

"I've brought you a new pet," he said.

He twitched open the door behind him, and she peered puzzledly into
the back of the car. The passenger was still unconscious, lolling back
like a limp mummy in the travelling rug which the Saint had tucked round
him, his white face turned blankly to the roof.

"But—who is he?"

"I haven't the faintest idea," said the Saint blandly. "But for the
purposes of convenient reference I have christened him Beppo. His shirt
has a Milan tab on it—Sherlock Holmes himself could deduce no more.
And up to the present, he hasn't been sufficiently compos to offer any
information."

Patricia Holm looked into his face, and saw the battle glint in his eye
and a ghost of Saintliness flickering in the corners of his smile, and tilted
her sweet fair head.

"Have you been in some more trouble?"

"It was rather a one-sided affair," said the Saint modestly. "Sambo
never had a break—and I didn't mean him to have one, either. But the
Queensberry Rules were strictly observed. There was no hitting below
belts, which were worn loosely around the ankles—"

"Who's this you're talking about now?"

"Again, we are without information. But again for the purposes of
convenient reference, you may call him His Beautitude the Negro Spiritual. And now listen."

Simon took her shoulders and swung her round.

"Somewhere between Basingstoke and Wintney," he said, "there's a gay game being played that's going to interest us a lot. And I came into it as a perfectly innocent party, for once in my life—but I haven't got time to tell you about it now. The big point at the moment is that a cop who arrived two minutes too late to be useful got my number. With Beppo in the back, I couldn't stop to hold converse with him, and you can bet he's jumped to the worst conclusions. In which he's damned right, but not in the way he thinks he is. There was a phone box twenty yards away, and unless the Negro Spiritual strangled him first he's referred my number to London most of an hour ago, and Teal will be snorting down a hot scent as soon as they can get him out of bed. Now, all you've got to know is this: I've just arrived, and I'm in my bath. Tell the glad news to anyone who rings up and anyone who calls; and if it's a call, hang a towel out of the window."

"But where are you going?"

"The Berkeley—to park the patient. I just dropped in to give you your cue." Simon Templar drew the end of a cigarette red, and snapped his lighter shut again. "And I'll be right back," he said, and wormed in behind the wheel.

A matter of seconds later the big car was in Berkeley Street, and he was pushing through the revolving doors of the hotel.

"Friend of mine had a bit of a car smash," he rapped at a sleepy reception clerk. "I wanna room for him now, and a doctor at eleven. Will you send a coupla men out to carry him in? Car at the door."

"One four eight," said the clerk, without batting an eyelid.

Simon saw the unconscious man carried upstairs, shot half-crowns into the hands of the men who performed the transportation, and closed the door on them.

Then he whipped from his pocket a thin nickelled case which he had brought from a pocket in the car. He snapped the neck of a small glass phial and drew up the colourless fluid it contained into the barrel of a hypodermic syringe. His latest protégé was still sleeping the sleep of sheer exhaustion, but Simon had no guarantee of how long that sleep would last. He proceeded to provide that guarantee himself, stabbing the needle into a limp arm and pressing home the plunger until the complete dose had been administered.

Then he closed and locked the door behind him and went quickly down the stairs.

Below, the reception clerk stopped him.

"What name shall I register, sir?"

"Teal," said the Saint, with a wry flick of humour. "Mr. C. E. Teal. He'll sign your book later."

"Yes, sir. . . . Er—has Mr. Teal no luggage, sir?"

"Nope." A new ten-pound note drifted down to the desk. "On account," said the Saint. "And see that the doctor's waiting here for me at eleven, or I'll take the roof off your hotel and crown you with it."

He pulled his cap sideways and went back to his car. As he turned into Upper Berkeley Mews for the second time, he saw that his first homecoming had only just been soon enough. But that did not surprise him, for he had figured out his chances on that schedule almost to a second. A warning blink of white from an upper window caught his expectant eye at once, and he locked the wheel hard over and pulled up broadside on across the mews. In a flash he was out of his seat unlocking a pair of garage doors right at the street end of the mews, and in another second or two the car was hissing back into that garage with the cut-out firmly closed.

The Saint, without advertising the fact, had recently become the owner of one complete side of Upper Berkeley Mews, and he was in process of making some interesting structural alterations to that block of real estate of which the London County Council had not been informed and about which the District Surveyor had not even been consulted. The great work was not yet by any means completed, but even now it was capable of serving part of its purposes.

Simon went up a ladder into the bare empty room above. In one corner, a hole had been roughly knocked through the wall; he went through it into another similar room, and on the far side of this was another hole in a wall; thus he passed in quick succession through numbers 1, 3, and 5, until the last plunge through the last hole and a curtain beyond it brought him into No. 7 and his own bedroom.

His tie was already off and his shirt unbuttoned by that time, and he took off the rest of his clothes in little more than the time it took him to stroll through to the bathroom. And the bath was already full—filled long ago by Patricia.

"Thinks of everything!" sighed the Saint, with a wide grin of pure delight.

He slid into the bath like an otter, head and all, and came out of it almost in the same movement with a mighty splash, tweaking the plug out of the waste pipe as he did so. In another couple of seconds he was hauling himself into an enormously woolly blue bath-robe and grabbing a towel . . . and he went paddling down the stairs with his feet kicking about in a pair of gorgeously dilapidated moccasins, humming the hum of a man with a copper-plated liver and not one solitary little baby sin upon his conscience.

And thus he rolled into the sitting-room.

"Sorry to have kept you waiting, old dear," he murmured; and Chief Inspector Claud Eustace Teal rose from an armchair and surveyed him heavily.

"Good morning," said Mr. Teal.

"Beautiful, isn't it?" agreed the Saint affably. Patricia was smoking a cigarette in another chair. She should, according to the book of etiquette, have been beguiling the visitor's wait with some vivacious topical chatter; but the Saint, who was sensitive to atmosphere, had perceived nothing but a glutinously expanding silence as he entered the room. The perception failed to disturb him. He lifted the silver cover from a plate of bacon and eggs, and sniffed appreciatively. "You don't mind if I eat, do you, Claud?" he murmured.

The detective swallowed. If he had never been required to interview the Saint on business, he could have enjoyed a tolerably placid life. He was not by nature an excitable man, but these interviews never seemed to take the course which he intended them to take.

"Where were you last night?" he blurted.

"In Cornwall," said the Saint. "Charming county—full of area. Know it?"

"What time did you leave?"

"Nine-fifty-two pip."

"Did anybody see you go?"

"Everyone who had stayed the course observed my departure," said the Saint carefully. "A few of the male population had retired hurt a little earlier, and others were still enthusiastic but already blind. Apart from seven who had been ruled out earlier in the week by an epidemic of measles—"

"And where were you between ten and five minutes to five this morning?"

"I was on my way."

"Were you anywhere near Wintney?"

"That would be about it."

"Notice anything peculiar around there?"

Simon wrinkled his brow.

"I recall the scene distinctly. It was the hour before the dawn. The sleeping earth, still spellbound by the magic of the night, lay quiet beneath the paling skies. Over the peaceful scene brooded the expectant hush of all the mornings since the beginning of these days. The whole world, like a bride listening for the footfall of her lover, or a breakfast sausage hoping against hope—''

The movement with which Teal clamped a battered piece of spearmint between his molars was one of sheer ferocity.

''Now listen,'' he snarled. ''Near Wintney, between ten and five minutes to five this morning, a Hirondel with your number-plates on it was called on to stop by a police officer—and it drove straight past him!''

Simon nodded.

''Sure, that was me,'' he said innocently. ''I was in a hurry. D'you mean I'm going to be summonsed?''

''I mean more than that. Shortly before you came past, the constable heard a scream—''

Simon nodded again.

''Sure, I heard it too. Weird noises owls make sometimes. Did he want me to hold his hand?''

''That was no owl screaming—''

''Yeah? You were there as well, were you?''

''I've got the constable's telephoned report—''

''You can find a use for it.'' The Saint opened his mouth, inserted egg, bacon, and buttered toast in suitable proportions, and stood up. ''And now *you* listen, Claud Eustace.'' He tapped the detective's stomach with his forefinger. ''Have you got a warrant to come round and cross-examine me at this ungodly hour of the morning—or any other hour, for that matter?''

''It's part of my duty—''

''It's part of the blunt end of the pig of the aunt of the gardener. Let that pass for a minute. Is there one single crime that even your pop-eyed imagination can think of to charge me with? There is not. But we understand the functioning of your so-called brain. Some loutish cop thought he heard someone scream in Hampshire this morning, and because I happened to be passing through the same county you think I must have had something to do with it. If somebody tells you that a dud shilling has been found in a slot machine in Blackpool, the first thing you want to know is whether I was within a hundred miles of the spot within six months of the event. A drowned man is fished out of the ocean at Boston, and if you hear a rumour that I was staying beside the same ocean at Biarritz two years before—''

''I never—''

"You invariably. And now get another earful. You haven't a search warrant, but we'll excuse that. Would you like to go upstairs and run through my wardrobe and see if you can find any bloodstains on my clothes? Because you're welcome. Would you like to push into the garage and take a look at my car and see if you can find a body under the back seat? Shove on. Make yourself absolutely at home. But digest this first.'' Again that dictatorial forefinger impressed its point on the preliminary concavity of the detective's waistcoat. "Make that search—accept my invitation—and if you can't find anything to justify it, you're going to wish your father had died a bachelor, which he may have done for all I know. You're becoming a nuisance, Claud, and I'm telling you that this is where you get off. Give me the small half of less than a quarter of a break, and I'm going to roast the hell out of you. I'm going to send you up to the sky on one big balloon; and when you come down you're not going to bounce—you're going to spread yourself out so flat that a short-sighted man will not be able to see you sideways. Got it?''

Teal gulped.

His cherubic countenance took on a slightly redder tinge, and he shuffled his feet like a truant schoolboy. But that, to do him justice, was the only childish thing about his attitude, and it was beyond Teal's power to control. For he gazed deep into the dancing, mocking, challenging, blue eyes of the Saint standing there before him, lean and reckless and debonair even in that preposterous bathrobe outfit; and he understood the issue exactly.

And Chief Inspector Claud Eustace Teal nodded.

"Of course,'' he grunted, "if that's the way you take it, there's nothing more to be said.''

"There isn't,'' agreed the Saint concisely. "And if there was, I'd say it.''

He picked up the detective's bowler hat, dusted it with his towel, and handed it over. Teal accepted it, looked at it, and sighed. And he was still sighing when the Saint took him by the arm and ushered him politely but firmly to the door.

3

"AND IF THAT," remarked the Saint, blithely returning to his interrupted breakfast, "doesn't shake up Claud Eustace from the Anzora downwards, nothing short of an earthquake will."

Patricia lighted another cigarette.

"So long as you didn't overdo it," she said. "*Qui s' excuse, s' accuse—*"

"And *honi soit qui mal y pense,*" said the Saint cheerfully. "No, old sweetheart—that outburst had been on its way for a long while. We've been seeing a great deal too much of Claud Eustace lately, and I have a feeling that the Teal-baiting season is just getting into full swing."

"But what *is* the story about Beppo?"

Simon embarked upon his second egg.

"Oh, yes! Well, Beppo. . . ."

He told her what he knew, and it is worth noting that she believed him. The recital, with necessary comment and decoration, ran out with the toast and marmalade; and at the end of it she knew as much as he did, which was not much.

"But in a little while we're going to know a whole lot more," he said.

He smoked a couple of cigarettes, glanced over the headlines of a newspaper, and went upstairs again. For several minutes he swung a pair of heavy Indian clubs with cheerful vigour; then a shave, a second and longer immersion in the bath with savon and vox humana accompaniment, and he felt ready to punch holes in three distinct and different heavyweights. None of which being available, he selected a fresh outfit of clothes, dressed himself with leisurely care, and descended once more upon the sitting-room looking like one consolidated ray of sunshine.

"Cocktail at the Bruton at a quarter of one," he murmured, and drifted out again.

By that time, which was 10:44 precisely, if that matters a damn to anyone, the floating population of Upper Berkeley Mews had increased by one conspicuous unit; but that did not surprise the Saint. Such things had happened before, they were part of the inevitable paraphernalia of the attacks of virulent detectivosis which periodically afflicted the ponderous lucubrations of Chief Inspector Teal; and after the brief but comprehensive exchange of pleasantries earlier that morning, Simon Templar would have been more disappointed than otherwise if he had seen no symptoms of fresh outbreak of the disease.

Simon was not perturbed. . . . He raised his hat politely to the sleuth, was cut dead, and remained unperturbed. . . . And he sauntered imperturbably westwards through the smaller streets of Mayfair until, in one of the very smallest streets, he was able to collar the one and only visible taxi, fluttering his handkerchief out of the window, and leaving a fuming plain-clothes man standing on the kerb glaring frantically around for another cab in which to continue the chase—and finding none.

At the Dover Street corner of Piccadilly, he paid off the driver and strolled back to the Piccadilly entrance of the Berkeley. It still wanted a few minutes to eleven, but the reception clerk, spurred on perhaps by the Saint's departing purposefulness, had a doctor already waiting for him.

Simon conducted the move to the patient's room himself, and had his first shock when he helped to remove the man's shirt.

He looked at what he saw in silence for some seconds; and then the doctor, who had also looked, turned to him with his ruddy face gone a shade paler.

"I was told that your friend had had an accident," he said bluntly, and the Saint nodded.

"Something unpleasant has certainly happened to him. Will you go on with your examination?"

He lighted a cigarette and went over to the window, where he stood gazing thoughtfully down into Berkeley Street until the doctor rejoined him.

"Your friend seems to have been given an injection of scopolamine and morphia—you have probably heard of 'twilight sleep.' His other injuries you've seen for yourself—I haven't found any more."

The Saint nodded.

"I gave him the injection myself. He should be waking up soon—he had rather less than one-hundredth of a grain of scopolamine. Will you want to move him to a nursing home?"

"I don't think that will be necessary, unless he wishes it himself, Mr.—"

"Travers."

"Mr. Travers. He should have a nurse, of course—"

"I can get one."

The doctor inclined his head.

Then he removed his pince-nez and looked the Saint directly in the eyes.

"I presume you know how your friend received his injuries?" he said.

"I can guess." The Saint flicked a short cylinder of ash from his cigarette. "I should say that he had been beaten with a raw-hide whip, and that persuasion by hot irons had also been applied."

The doctor put his finger-tips together and blinked.

"You must admit, Mr. Travers, that the circumstances are—er—somewhat unusual."

"You could say all that twice, and no one would accuse you of exaggerating," assented the Saint, with conviction. "But if that fact is bothering your professional conscience, I can only say that I'm as much in the dark as you are. The accident story was just to satisfy the birds below. As a matter of fact, I found our friend lying by the roadside in the small hours of this morning, and I sort of took charge. Doubtless the mystery will be cleared up in due course."

"Naturally, you have communicated with the police."

"I've already interviewed one detective, and I'm sure he's doing everything he can," said the Saint veraciously. He opened the door, and propelled the doctor decisively along the corridor. "Will you want to see the patient again today?"

"I hardly think it will be necessary, Mr. Travers. His dressings should be changed tonight—the nurse will see to that. I'll come in tomorrow morning—"

"Thanks very much. I shall expect you at the same time. Good-bye."

Simon shook the doctor warmly by the hand, swept him briskly into the waiting elevator, and watched him sink downwards out of view.

Then he went back to the room, poured out a glass of water, and sat down in a chair by the bedside. The patient was sleeping easily; and Simon, after a glance at his watch, prepared to await the natural working-off of the drug.

A quarter of an hour later he was extinguishing a cigarette when the patient stirred and groaned. A thin hand crawled up to the bare throat, and the man's head rolled sideways with his eyelids flickering. As Simon bent over him, a husky whisper of a word came through the relaxed lips.

"*Aqua. . . .*"

"Sure thing, brother." Simon propped up the man's head and put the glass to his mouth.

"*Mille grazie.*"

"*Prego.*"

Presently the man sank back again. And then his eyes opened, and focused on the Saint.

For a number of seconds there was not the faintest glimmer of understanding in the eyes: they stared at and through their object like the eyes of a blind man. And then, slowly, they widened into round pools of shuddering horror, and the Italian shrank away with a thin cry rattling in his throat.

Simon gripped his arm and smiled.

"Non tema. Sono un amico."

It was some time before he was able to calm the man into a dully incredulous quietness; but he won belief before he had finished, and at last the Italian sank back again among the pillows and was silent.

Simon mopped his brow and fished out his cigarette-case.

And then the man spoke again, still weakly, but in a different voice.

"Quanti ne abbiamo quest'oggi?"

"E il due ottobre."

There was a pause.

"Vuol favorire di dirmi il suo nome?"

"Templar—Simon Templar."

There was another pause. And then the man rolled over and looked at the Saint again. And he spoke in almost perfect English.

"I have heard of you. You were called—"

"Many things. But that was a long time ago."

"How did you find me?"

"Well—I rather think that you found me."

The Italian passed a hand across his eyes.

"I remember now. I was running. I fell down. Someone caught me. . . ." Suddenly he clutched the Saint's wrist. "Did you see—*him?*"

"Your gentleman friend?" murmured Simon lightly. "Sure I did. He also saw me, but not soon enough. Yes, we certainly met."

The grip of the trembling fingers loosened slowly, and the man lay still, breathing jerkily through his nose.

"Volglia scusarmi," he said at length. *"Mi vergogno."*

"Non ne val la pena."

"It is as if I had awoken from a terrible dream. Even now—" The Italian looked down at the bandages that swathed the whole of the upper part of his body, and shivered uncontrollably. "Did you put on these?" he asked.

"No—a doctor did that."

The man looked round the room.

"And this—"

"This is the Berkeley Hotel, London."

The Italian nodded. He swallowed painfully, and Simon refilled his glass and passed it back. Another silence fell, which grew so long that the Saint wondered if his patient had fallen asleep again. He rose stealthily to his feet, and the Italian roused and caught his sleeve.

"Wait." The words came quite quietly and sanely. "I must talk to you."

"Sure." Simon smiled down at the man. "But do you want to do it now? Hadn't you better rest for a bit—maybe have something to eat—"

The Italian shook his head.

"Afterwards. Will you sit down again?"

And Simon Templar sat down.

And he listened, almost without movement, while the minute hand of his watch voyaged unobserved once round the dial. He listened in a perfect trance of concentration, while the short precise sentences of the Italian's story slid into the atmosphere and built themselves up into a shape that he had never even dreamed of.

It was past one o'clock when he walked slowly down the stairs with the inside story of one of the most stupendous crimes in history whirling round in his brain like the armature of a high-powered dynamo.

Wrapped up in the rumination of what he had heard, he passed out like a sleep-walker into Berkeley Street. And it so happened that in his abstraction he almost cannoned into a man who was at that moment walking down towards Piccadilly. He stepped aside with a muttered apology, absent-mindedly registering a kind of panoramic impression of a brilliantly purple suit, lemon-coloured gloves, a gold-mounted cane, a lavender shirt, spotted tie, and—

Just for an instant, the Saint's gaze rested on the man's face. And then they were past each other, without a flicker of recognition, without the batting of an eyelid. But the Saint knew . . .

He knew that that savagely arrogant face, like a mask of black marble, was like no other black face that he had ever seen in his life before that morning. And he knew, with the same certainty, that the eyes in the black face had recognised him in the same moment as he had recognised them—and with no more betrayal of their knowledge. And as he wandered up into Berkeley Square, and the portals of the Bruton Club received him, he knew, though he had not looked back, that the black eyes were still behind him, and had seen where he went.

4

BUT THE SMILE with which the Saint greeted Patricia was as gay and carefree a smile as she had ever seen.

"I should like," said the Saint, sinking into an armchair, "three large double Martinis in a big glass. Just to line my stomach. After which, I shall be able to deal respectfully with a thirst which can only be satisfactorily slaked by two gallons of bitter beer."

"You will have one Martini, and then we'll have some lunch," said Patricia; and the Saint sighed.

"You have no soul," he complained.

Patricia put her magazine under the table.

"What's new, boy?" she asked.

"About Beppo? . . . Well, a whole heap of things are new about Beppo. I can tell you this, for instance: Beppo is no smaller a guy than the Duke of Fortezza, and he is the acting President of the Bank of Italy."

"He's—what?"

"He's the acting President of the Bank of Italy—and that's not the half of it. Pat, old girl, I told you at the start that there was some gay game being played, and, by the Lord, it's as gay a game as we may ever find!" Simon signed the chit on the waiter's tray with a flourish and settled back again, surveying his drink dreamily. "Remember reading in some paper recently that the Bank of Italy was preparing to put out an entirely new and original line of paper currency?" he asked.

"I was something about it."

"It was so. The contract was placed with Crosby Dorman, one of our own biggest printing firms—they do the thin cash and postal issues of half a dozen odd little countries. Beppo put the deal through. A while ago he brought over the plates and gave the order, and one week back he came on his second trip to take delivery of three million pounds' worth of coloured paper in a tin-lined box."

"And then?"

"I'll tell you what then. One whole extra million pounds' worth of mazuma is ordered, and that printing goes into a separate box. Ordered on official notepaper, too, with Beppo's own signature in the south-east corner. And meanwhile Beppo is indisposed. The first crate of spondulix departs in the golden galleon without him, completely surrounded by soldiers, secret service agents, and general detectives, all armed to the teeth and beyond. Another of those nice letters apologises for Beppo's absence, and instructs the guard to carry on; a third letter explains the circumstances, ditto and ditto, to the Bank—''

Patricia sat up.

"And the box is empty?"

"The box is packed tight under a hydraulic press, stiff to the sealing-wax with the genuine articles as per invoice."

"But—"

"But obviously. That box had got to go through. The new issue had to spread itself out. It's been on the market three days already. And the ground bait is now laid for the big haul—the second box, containing approximately one million hundred-lire bills convertible into equivalent sterling on sight. And the whole board of the Bank of Italy, the complete staff of cashiers, office-boys, and outside porters, the entire vigilance society of soldiers, secret service agents, and general detectives, all armed to the teeth and beyond, are as innocent of the existence of that million as the unborn daughter of the Caliph's washerwoman.''

The girl looked at him with startled eyes.

"And do you mean Beppo was in this?"

"Does it seem that way?" Simon Templar swivelled round towards her with one eyebrow inquisitorially cocked and a long wisp of smoke trailing through his lips. "I wish you could have seen him. . . . Sure he's in it. They turned him over to the Negro Spiritual, and let that big black swine pet him till he signed. If I told you what they'd done to him you wouldn't be in such a hurry for your lunch." For a moment the Saint's lips thinned fractionally. "He's just shot to pieces, and when you see him you'll know why. Sure, that bunch are like brothers to Beppo!''

Patricia sat in a thoughtful silence, and the Saint emptied his glass.

Then she said: "Who are this bunch?"

Simon slithered his cigarette round to the corner of his mouth.

"Well, the actual bunch are mostly miscellaneous, as you might say," he answered. "But the big noise seems to be a bird named Kuzela, whom we haven't met before, but, whom I'm going to meet darned soon."

"And this money—"

"Is being delivered to Kuzela's men today." The Saint glanced at his watch. "Has been, by now. And within twenty-four hours parcels of it will be burning the sky over to his agents in Paris, Berlin, Vienna, and Madrid. Within the week it will be gravitating back to him through the same channels—big bouncing wads of it, translated into authentic wads of francs, marks, and pesetas—while one million perfectly genuine hundred-lire bills whose numbers were never in the catalogue are drifting home to a Bank of Italy that will be wondering whether the whole world is falling to pieces round its ears. . . . Do you get me, Pat?''

The clear blue eyes rested on her face with the twist of mocking hell-for-leather delight that she knew so well, and she asked her next question almost mechanically.

"Is it your party?"

"It is, old Pat. And now a question asked. No living soul must ever know—there'd be a panic on the international exchanges if a word of it leaked out. But every single one of those extra million bills has got to be taken by the hand and led gently back to Beppo's tender care—and the man who's going to do it is ready for his lunch."

And lunch it was without further comment, for the Saint was like that. . . . But about his latest meeting with the Negro Spiritual he did not find it necessary to say anything at all—for, again, the Saint was that way. . . . And after lunch when Patricia was ordering coffee in the lounge, yet another incident which the Saint was inclined to regard as strictly private and personal clicked into its appointed socket in the energetic history of the day.

Simon had gone out to telephone a modest tenner on a horse for the 3:30, and he was on his way back through the hall when a porter stopped him.

"Excuse me, sir, but did you come here from the Berkeley?"

The Saint fetched his right foot up alongside his left and lowered his brows one millimetre.

"Yeah—I have been in there this morning."

"A coloured gentleman brought these for you, sir. He said he saw you drop them as you came out of the hotel, but he lost you in the crowd while he was picking them up. And then, as he was walking through Pansdowne Passage, he happened to look up and see you at one of the windows, so he brought them in. From the description he gave me it seemed as if it must have been you, sir—"

"Oh, it was certainly me."

The Saint, who had never owned a pair of lemon-colored gloves in his life, accepted the specimens gingerly, folded them, and slipped them into his pocket.

"Funny coincidence, sir, wasn't it?" said the porter chattily. "Him happening to pass by, and you happening to be in the window at that time.''

''Quite remarkable,'' agreed the Saint gravely, recalling the care he had taken to avoid all windows; and, turning back, he retired rapidly to a remote sanctuary.

There he unfolded the gloves in an empty washbasin, contriving to work them cautiously inside out with his fountain pen in one hand and his propelling pencil in the other.

He had not the vaguest idea what kind of creeping West African frightfulness might be waiting for him in those citron-hued misdemeanors, but he was certainly a trifle surprised when he saw what fell out of the first glove that he tackled.

It was simply a thin splinter of wood, pointed at both ends, and stained with some dark stain.

For a moment or two he looked at it expressionlessly.

Then he picked it up between two matches and stowed it carefully in his cigarette-case.

He turned his attention to the second glove, and extracted from it a soiled scrap of paper. He read:

> If you will come to 85, Vandermeer Avenue, Hampstead,
> at midnight tonight, we may be able to reach some mutually
> satisfactory agreement. Otherwise, I fear that the consequences
> of your interference may be infinitely regrettable.   K.

Simon Templar held the message at arm's length, well up to the light, and gazed at it wall-eyed.

''And whales do so lay eggs,'' he articulated at last, when he could find a voice sufficiently impregnated with emotion.

And then he laughed and went back to Patricia.

''If Monday's Child comes home, you shall have a new hat,'' he said, and the girl smiled.

''What else happens before that?'' she asked.

''We go on a little tour,'' said the Saint.

They left the club together, and boarded a taxi that had just been paid off at the door.

''Piccadilly Hotel,'' said the Saint.

He settled back, lighting a cigarette.

''I shook off Teal's man by Method One,'' he explained. ''You are now going to see a demonstration of Method Two. If you can go on studying under my supervision, all the shadowers you will ever meet will mean nothing to you. . . . The present performance may be a waste of energy''—he glanced back through the rear window—''or it may not. But the wise man is permanently suspicious.''

They reached the Piccadilly entrance of the hotel in a few minutes, and the Saint opened the door. The exact fare, plus bonus, was ready in the Saint's hand, and he dropped it in the driver's palm and followed Patricia across the pavement—without any appearance of haste, but very briskly. As he reached the doors, he saw in one glass panel the reflection of another taxi pulling in to the kerb behind him.

''This way.''

He steered the girl swiftly through the main hall, swung her through a short passage, across another hall, and up some steps, and brought her out through another door into Regent Street. A break in the traffic let him straight through to the taxi rank in the middle of the road.

''Berkeley Hotel,'' said the Saint.

He lounged deep in his corner and grinned at her.

''Method Two is not for use on a trained sleuth who knows you know he's after you,'' he murmured. ''Other times, it's the whelk's kneecap.'' He took her bag from her hands, slipped out the little mirror, and used it for a periscope to survey the south side pavement as they drove away. ''This is one of those whens,'' he said complacently.

''Then why are we going to the Berkeley?''

''Because you are the nurse who is going to look after Beppo. His number if 148, and 149 is already booked for you. Incidently, you might remember that he's registered in the name of Teal—C. E. Teal. I'll pack a bag and bring it along to you later; but once you're inside the Berkeley Arms you've got to stay put so long as it's daylight. The doctor's name is Branson and mine is Travers, and if anyone else applies for admission you will shoot him through the binder and ring for the bell-hop to remove the body.''

''But what will you be doing?''

''I am the proud possessor of a Clue, and I'm going to be very busy tying a knot in its tail. Also I have an ambition to be humorous, and that will mean that I've got to push round to a shop I wot of and purchase one of those mechanical jokes that are said to create roars of laughter. I've been remembering my younger days, and they've brought back to me the very thing I need. . . . And here we are.''

The cab had stopped at its destination, and they got out. Patricia hesitated in the doorway.

"When will you be back?" she asked.

"I shall be along for dinner about eight," said the Saint. "Meanwhile, you'll be able to get acquainted with Beppo. Really, you'll find him quite human. Prattle gently to him, and he'll eat out of your hand. When he's stronger, you might even be allowed to sing to him—I'll ask the doctor about that to-morrow. . . . So long, lass!"

And the Saint was gone.

And he did exactly that he had said he was going to do. He went to a shop in Regent Street and bought a little toy and took it back with him to Upper Berkeley Mews, and a certain alteration which he made to its inner functionings kept him busy for some time and afforded him considerable amusement.

For he had not the slightest doubt that there was going to be fun and games before the next dawn. The incident of those lemon-colored gloves was a distinct encouragement. It showed a certain thoroughness on the part of the opposition, and that sort of thing always gave the Saint great pleasure.

"If one glove doesn't work, the other is expected to oblige," he figured it out, as he popped studs into a snowy white dress shirt. "And it would be a pity to disappoint anyone."

He elaborated this latter idea to Patricia Holm when he rejoined her at the Berkeley, having shaken off his official watcher again by Method Three. Before he left, he told her nearly everything.

"At midnight, all the dreams of the ungodly are coming true," he said. "Picture to yourself the scene. It will be the witching hour. The menace of dark deeds will veil the stars. And up the heights of Hampstead will come toiling the pitiful figure of the unsuspecting victim, with his bleary eyes bulging and his mouth hanging open and the green moss sprouting behind his ears; and that will be Little Boy. . . ."

5

SOME MEN ENJOY trouble; others just as definitely don't. And there are some who enjoy dreaming about the things they would do if they only dared—but they need not concern us.

Simon Templar came into Category A—straight and slick, with his name in a panel all to itself, and a full stop just where it hits hardest.

For there is a price ticket on everything that puts a whiz into life, and adventure follows the rule. It's distressing, but there you are. If there was no competition, everything would be quite all right. If you could be certain that you were the strongest man in the world, the most quick-witted, the most cunning, the most keen-sighted, the most vigilant, and simultaneously the possessor of the one and only lethal weapon in the whole wide universe, there wouldn't be much difficulty about it. You would just step out of your hutch and hammer the first thing that came along.

But it doesn't always pan out like that in practice. When you try the medicine on the dog, you are apt to discover some violent reactions which were not arranged for in the prescription. And then, when the guns give tongue, and a spot of fur begins to fly, you are liable to arrive at the sudden and soul-shattering realisation that a couple of ounces of lead travelling with a given velocity will make precisely as deep an impression on your anatomical system as they will on that of the next man.

Which monumental fact the Saint had thoroughly digested a few days after mastering his alphabet. And the effect it had registered upon his unweaned peace of mind had been so near to absolute zero that a hair-line could not have been drawn between them—neither on the day of the discovery nor on any subsequent day in all his life.

In theory . . .

In theory, of course, he allowed the artillery to pop, and the fur to become volatile without permitting a single lock of his own sleek dark hair to aberrate from the patent-leather discipline in which he disposed it; and thereby he became the Saint. But it is perfectly possible to appreciate and acknowledge the penetrating unpleasantness of high-velocity lead, and forthwith to adopt a debonairly philosophical attitude towards the same, without being in a tearing hurry to offer your own carcase for the purposes of practical demonstration; this also the Saint did, and by doing it with meticulous attention contrived to be spoken of in the present tense for many years longer than the most optimistic insurance broker would have backed him to achieve.

All of which has not a little to do with 85, Vandermeer Avenue, Hampstead.

Down this road strolled the Saint, his hands deep in the pockets of knife-edged trousers, the crook of his walking-stick hooked over his left wrist, and slanting sidelong over his right eye a filibustering black felt hat which alone was something very like a breach of the peace. A little song rollicked on his lips, and was inaudible two yards away. And as he walked, his lazy eyes absorbed every interesting item of the scenery.

> *"Aspidistra, little herb,*
> *Do you think it silly*
> *When the botaniser's blurb*
> *Links you with the lily?"*

Up in one window of the house, he caught the almost imperceptible sway of a shifting curtain, and knew that his approach had already been observed. "But it is nice," thought the Saint, "to be expected." And he sauntered on.

> *"Up above your window-ledge*
> *Streatham stars are gleaming:*
> *Aspidistra, little veg,*
> *Does your soul go dreaming?"*

A low, iron gate opened from the road. He pushed it wide with his foot, and went up the steps to the porch. Beside the door was a bell-push set in a panel of polished brass tracery.

The Saint's fingers moved towards it . . . and travelled back again. He stooped and examined the filigree more closely, and a little smile lightened his face.

Then he cuddled himself into the extreme houseward corner of the porch, held his hat over the panel, and pressed the button with the ferrule of his stick. He heard a faint hiss, and turned his hat back to the light of a street lamp. A stained splinter of wood quivered in the white satin lining of the crown; and the Saint's smile became blindingly seraphic as he reached into a side pocket of his jacket for a pair of tweezers. . . .

And then the door was opening slowly.

Deep in his angle of shadow, he watched the strip of yellow light widening across the porch and down the short flagged passage to the gate. The silhouette of a man looked into it and stood motionless for a while behind the threshold.

Then it stepped out into full view—a big, heavy-shouldered, close-cropped man, with thick bunched fists hanging loosely at his sides. He peered outwards down the shaft of light, and then to right and left, his battered face creasing to the strain of probing the darkness on either side.

The Saint's white shirt-front caught his eye, and he licked his lips and spoke like an automaton.

"Comin' in?"

"Behind you, brother," said the Saint.

He stepped across the light, taking the bruiser by the elbows and spinning him adroitly round. They entered the house in the order of his own arrangement, and Simon kicked the door shut behind him.

There was no machine-gun at the far end of the hall, as he had half expected; but the Saint was unashamed.

"Windy?" sneered the bruiser, as the Saint released him; and Simon smiled.

"Never since taking soda-mint," he murmured. "Where do we go from here?"

The bruiser glanced sideways, jerking his head.

"Upstairs."

"Oh, yeah?"

Simon slanted a cigarette into his mouth and followed the glance. His eyes weaved up the banisters and down the separate steps of the stairway.

"After you again," he drawled. "Just to be certain."

The bruiser led the way, and Simon followed discreetly. They arrived in procession at the upper landing, where a second bruiser, a trifle shorter than the first, but even heavier of shoulder, lounged beside an open door with an unlighted stump of cigar in his mouth.

The second man gestured with his lower jaw and the cigar.

"In there."

"Thanks," said the Saint.

He paused for a moment in the doorway and surveyed the room, one hand ostentatiously remaining in the pocket of his coat.

Facing him, in the centre of the rich brown carpet, was a broad flat-topped desk. It harmonised with the solid simplicity of the book-cases that broke the panelling of the bare walls, and with the long austere lines of the velvet hangings that covered the windows—even, perhaps, with the squat square materialism of the safe that stood in a corner behind it. And on the far side of the desk sat the man whom the Saint had come to see, leaning forward out of a straight-backed oak chair.

Simon moved forward, and the two bruisers closed the door and ranged themselves on either side of him.

"Good evening, Kuzela," said the Saint.

"Good evening, Mr. Templar." The man behind the desk moved one white hand. "Sit down."

Simon looked at the chair that had been placed ready for him. Then he turned, and took one of the bruisers by the lapels of his coat. He shot the man into the chair, bounced him up and down a couple of times, swung him from side to side, and yanked him out again.

"Just to make *quite* certain," said the Saint sweetly. He beamed upon the glowering pugilist, felt his biceps, and patted him encouragingly on the shoulder. "You'll be a big man when you grow up, Cuthbert," he said affably.

Then he moved the chair a yard to one side and sat in it himself. "I'm sure you'll excuse all these formalities," he remarked conversationally. "I have to be so careful these days. The most extraordinary things happen to me. Only the other day, a large spotted hypotenuse, overtaking on the wrong side—"

"I have already observed that you possess a well-developed instinct of self-preservation, Mr. Templar," said Kuzela suavely.

He clasped his well-kept hands on the blotter before him, and studied the Saint interestedly.

Simon returned the compliment.

He saw a man in healthy middle age, broad-shouldered and strongly built. A high, firmly modelled forehead rose into a receding setting of clipped iron-grey hair. With his square jaw and slightly aquiline nose, he might have posed for a symbolical portrait of any successful business man. Only his eyes might have betrayed the imposture. Pale blue, deep-set and unwinking, they levelled themselves upon the object of their scrutiny in a feline stare of utter ruthlessness. . . . And the Saint looked into the eyes and laughed.

"You certainly win on the exchange," he said; and a slight frown came between the other's eyebrows.

"If you would explain—?"

"I'm good-looking," said the Saint easily, and centred his tie with elegance.

Kuzela leaned back.

"Your name is known to me, of course; but I think this is the first time we have had the pleasure of meeting."

"This is certainly the first time you've had the pleasure of meeting me," said the Saint carefully.

"Even now, the responsibility is yours. You have elected to interfere with my affairs—"

Simon shook his head sympathetically.

"It's most distressing, isn't it?" he murmured. "And your most strenuous efforts up to date have failed to dispose of the interference. Even when you sent me a pair of gloves that would have given a rhinoceros a headache to look at, I survived the shock. It must be Fate, old dear.''

Kuzela pulled himself forward again.

"You are an enterprising young man,'' he said quietly. "An unusually enterprising young man. There are not many men living who could have overcome Ngano, even by the method which you adopted. The mere fact that you were able to enter this house is another testimony to your fore-sight—or your good luck.''

"My foresight,'' said the Saint modestly.

"You moved your chair before you sat down—and that again showed remarkable intelligence. If you had sat where I intended you to sit, it would have been possible for me, by a slight movement of my foot, to send a bullet through the centre of your body.''

"So I guessed.''

"Since you arrived, your hand has been in your pocket several times. I presume you are armed—''

Simon Templar inspected the finger-nails of his two hands.

"If I had been born the day before yesterday,'' he observed mildly, "you'd find out everything you wanted to know in approximately two minutes.''

"Again, a man of your reputation would not have communicated with the police—''

"But he would take great care of himself.'' The Saint's eyes met Kuzela's steadily. "I'll talk or fight, Kuzela, just as you like. Which is it to be?''

"You are prepared to deal?''

"Within limits—yes.''

Kuzela drummed his knuckles together.

"On what terms?''

"They might be—one hundred thousand pounds.''

Kuzela shrugged.

"If you came here in a week's time—''

"I should be very pleased to have a drink with you,'' said the Saint pointedly.

"Suppose,'' said Kuzela, "I gave you a cheque which you could cash to-morrow morning—''

"Or suppose,'' said the Saint calmly, "you gave me some cash with which I could buy jujubes on my way home.''

Kuzela looked at him with a kind of admiration.

"Rumour has not lied about you, Mr. Templar," he said. "I imagine you will have no objection to receiving this sum in—er—foreign currency?"

"None whatever," said the Saint blandly.

The other stood up, taking a little key from his waistcoat pocket. And the Saint, who for the moment had been looking at the delicately painted shade of the lamp that stood on one side of the desk, which was the sole dim illumination of the room, slewed round with a sudden start.

He knew that there was going to be a catch somewhere—that, with a man of Kuzela's type, a man who had sent those gloves and who had devised that extremely ingenious bell-push on the front door, a coup could never be quite so easy. How that last catch was going to be worked he had no idea; nor was he inclined to wait and learn it. In his own way, he had done as much as he had hoped to do; and, all things considered—

"Let me see that key!" he exclaimed.

Kuzela turned puzzledly.

"Really, Mr. Templar—"

"Let me see it!" repeated the Saint excitedly.

He reached over the desk and took the key out of Kuzela's hands. For a second he gazed at it; and then he raised his eyes again with a dancing devil of mischief glinting out of their blueness.

"Sorry I must be going, souls," he said; and with one smashing sweep of his arm he sent the lamp flying off the desk and plunged the room into inky blackness.

6

THE PHRASE IS neither original nor copyright, and may be performed in public without fee or licence. It remains, however, an excellent way of describing that particular phenomenon.

With the extinction of the single source of luminance, the darkness came down in all the drenching suddenness of an unleashed cataract of Stygian gloom. For an instant, it seemed to blot out not only the sense of sight, but also every other active faculty; and a frozen, throbbing stillness settled between the four walls. And in that stillness the Saint sank down without a sound upon his toes and the tips of his fingers. . . .

He knew his bearings to the nth part of a degree, and he travelled to his destination with the noiseless precision of a cat. Around him he could hear the sounds of tensely restrained breathing, and the slithering caress of wary feet creeping over the carpet. Then, behind him, came the vibration of a violent movement, the thud of a heavy blow, a curse, a scuffle, a crashing fall, and a shrill yelp of startled anguish . . . and the Saint grinned gently.

"I got 'im," proclaimed a triumphant voice, out of the dark void. "Strike a light, Bill."

Through an undercurrent of muffled yammering sizzled the crisp kindling of a match. It was held in the hand of Kuzela himself, and by its light the two bruisers glared at each other, their reddened stares of hate aimed upwards and downwards respectively. And before the match went out the opinions of the foundation member found fervid utterance.

"You perishing bleeder," he said, in accents that literally wobbled with earnestness.

"Peep-bo," said the Saint, and heard the contortionist effects blasphemously disentangling themselves as he closed the door behind him.

A bullet splintered a panel two inches east of his neck as he shifted briskly westwards. The next door stood invitingly ajar: he went through it as the other door reopened, slammed it behind him, and turned the key.

In a few strides he was across the room and flinging up the window. He squirmed over the sill like an eel, curved his fingers over the edge, and hung at the full stretch of his arms. A foot below the level of his eyes there was a narrow stone ledge running along the side of the building: he transferred himself to it, and worked rapidly along to the nearest corner. As he rounded it, he looked down into the road, twenty feet below, and saw a car standing by the kerb.

Another window came over his head. He reached up, got a grip of the sill, and levered his elbows above the sill level with a skillful kick and an acrobatic twist of his body. From there he was able to make a grab for the top of the lower sash. . . . And in another moment he was standing upright on the sill, pushing the upper sash cautiously downwards.

A murmur of dumbfounded voices drifted to his ears.

"Where the 'ell can 'e 'ave gorn to?"

"Think 'e jumped for it?"

"Jumped for it, yer silly fat-'ead? . . ."

And then the Saint lowered himself cat-footed to the carpet on the safe side of the curtains in the room he had recently left.

Through a narrow gap in the hangings he could see Kuzela replacing the shattered bulb of the table lamp by the light of a match. The man's white efficient hands were perfectly steady; his face was without expression. He accomplished his task with the tremorless tranquillity of a patient middle-aged gentleman whom no slight accident could seriously annoy— tested the switch. . . .

And then, as the room lighted up again, he raised his eyes to the convex mirror panel on the opposite wall, and had one distorted glimpse of the figure behind him. . . .

Then the Saint took him by the neck.

Fingers like bands of steel paralysed his larynx and choked back into his chest the cry he would have uttered. He fought like a maniac; but though his strength was above the average, he was as helpless as a puppet in that relentless grip. And almost affectionately Simon Templar's thumbs sidled round to their mark—the deadly pressure on the carotid arteries which is to crude ordinary throttling what foil play is to sabre work. . . .

It was all over in a few seconds. And Kuzela was lying limply spread-eagled across the desk, and Simon Templar was fitting his key into the lock of the safe.

The plungers pistoned smoothly back, and the heavy door swung open. And the Saint sat back on his heels and gazed in rapture at what he saw.

Five small leather attaché cases stood in a neat row before his eyes. It was superb—splendiferous—it was just five times infinity more than he had ever seriously dared to hope. That one hundred million lire were lying around somewhere in London he had been as sure as a man can be of anything—Kuzela would never have wasted time transporting his booty from the departure centre to the country house where the Duke of Fortezza had been kept—but that the most extempore bluff should have led him promptly and faultlessly to the hiding-place of all that merry mazuma was almost too good to be true. And for a few precious seconds the Saint stared entranced at the vision that his everlastingly preposterous luck had ladled out for his delight. . . .

And then he was swiftly hauling the valises out on to the floor.

He did not even have to attempt to open one of them. He knew. . . .

Rapidly he ranged the bags in a happy little line across the carpet. He picked up his stick; and he was adjusting his hat at its most effective angle when the two men who had pursued him returned through the door. But there was a wicked little automatic pivoting round in his free hand, and the two men noticed it in time.

"Restrain your enthusiasm, boys," said the Saint. "We're going on a journey. Pick up your luggage, and let's be moving."

He transferred one of the bags to his left hand, and his gun continued to conduct the orchestra. And under its gentle supervision the two men obeyed his orders. The delirious progress of events during the past couple of minutes had been a shade too much for their ivorine uptakes: their faces wore two uniformly blank expressions of pained bewilderment, vaguely reminiscent of the registers of a pair of precocious goldfish photographed immediately after signing their first talking picture contract. Even the power of protest had temporarily drained out of their vocal organs. They picked up two bags apiece, and suffered themselves to be shepherded out of the room in the same bovine vacuity of acquiescence.

In the hall, Simon halted the fatigue party for a moment.

"Before we pass out into the night," he said, "I want you to be quite clear about one thing. Those bags you're carrying, as you may or may not know, are each supposed to contain the equivalent of two hundred thousand pounds in ready money; and I want you to know that anything you may be prepared to do to keep all those spondulix for yourselves is just so much tadpole-gizzard beside what I'm prepared to do to prise it off you. So you should think a long while before you do anything rash. I am the greatest gun artist in the world," said the Saint persuasively, but with a singular lack of honesty, "and I'm warning you here and now that at the first sign I see of any undue enterprise, I shall shoot each of you through the middle of the eleventh spinal vertebra, counting from the bottom. Move on, my children."

The procession moved on.

It went down the porch steps and through the iron gate to the road; and the Saint brought up the rear with his right hand in his pocket. The comedy was played without witnesses: at that hour Vandermeer Avenue, a quiet backwater even at the height of the day, was absolutely deserted. A sum total of four lighted windows was visible along the whole length of the thoroughfare, and those were too far away to provide the slightest inconvenience in any conceivable circumstances. Hampstead was being good that night. . . .

The car which Simon had observed on his prowl round the exterior of the house was parked right opposite the gate—which was where he had expected it to be. As the two men paused outside the gate, waiting for further instructions, a door of the car opened, and a slim supple figure decanted itself lightly on to the sidewalk. Patricia. . . . She came forward with her swinging long-limbed stride.

"O.K., Simon?"

"O.K., lass."

"Gee, boy, I'm glad to see you!"

"And I you. And the whole Wild West show was just a sitting rabbit, believe it or believe it not." The Saint's hand touched her arm. "Get back behind the wheel, Pat, start her up, and be ready to pull out so soon as the boodle's on board. It isn't every day we ferry a cool million across London, and I don't see why the honour of being the pilot shouldn't be your share of the act."

"Right-ho. . . ."

The girl disappeared, and Simon opened another door.

He watched the cases being stowed one by one in the back of the car, and the forefinger of his right hand curled tensely over the trigger of his gun. He had meant every word of his threat to the two men who were doing the job; and they must have known it, for they carried out his orders with commendable alacrity.

And yet Simon felt a faint electric tingle of uneasiness fanning up his back and into the roots of his hair like the march of a thousand ghostly needle-points. He could not have described it in any other way, and he was as much at a loss to account for it as if the simile had been the actual fact. It was sheer blind instinct, a seventh sense born of a hundred breathless adventures, that touched him with that single thrill of insufficient warning—and left it at that. And for once in his life he ignored the danger-sign. He heard the whine of the self-starter, followed by the low-pitched powerful pulsing of the eight cleanly balanced cylinders, and saw the door closed upon the last of the bags; and he turned smiling to the two bruisers. He pointed.

"If you keep straight on down that road," he said, "it ought to land you up somewhere near Birmingham—if you travel far enough. You might make that your next stop."

One of the men took a pace towards him.

"You just listen a minute—"

"To what?" asked the Saint politely.

"I'm tellin' yer—"

"A bad habit," said the Saint disapprovingly. "You must try and break yourself of that. And now I'm sorry, but I can't stop. I hope you'll wash the back of your neck, see that your socks are aired, say your

prayers every night, and get your face lifted at the first opportunity.
. . . Now push your ears back, my cherubs, and let your feet chase each
other.''

His right hand moved significantly in his pocket, and there was an
instant's perilous silence. And then the man who had spoken jerked his
head at the other.

"Come on," he said.

The two men turned and lurched slowly away, looking back over their
shoulders.

And the Saint put one foot on the runningboard.

And somewhere, far away, he heard the sound of his own head being
hit. It was as extraordinary an experience as any that had ever happened
to him. Patricia was looking ahead down the road, while her hand eased
the gears quietly into mesh; and the Saint himself had not heard the
slightest movement that might have put him on his guard. And the pre-
monitory crawling of his nerves which he had felt a few seconds earlier
had performed what it considered to be its duty, and had subsided.
. . . He could have believed that the whole thing was an incredibly vivid
hallucination—but for the sickening sharp stab of sudden agony that
plunged through his brain like a spurt of molten metal and paralysed
every milligram of strength in his body.

A great white light swelled up and exploded before his eyes; and after
it came a wave of whirling blackness shot with rocketing flashes of dizzy,
dazzling colour, and the blackness was filled with a thin high singing
note that drilled into his eardrums. His knees seemed to melt away beneath
him. . . .

And then, from somewhere above the vast dark gulf into which he was
sinking, he heard Patricia's voice cry out.

"Simon!"

The word seemed to spell itself into his dulled brain letter by letter,
as if his mind read it off a slowly uncoiling scroll. But it touched a nerve
centre that roused him for one fractional instant of time to fight back
titanically against the numbing oblivion that was swallowing him up.

He knew that his eyes were open, but all he could see was one blurred
segment of her face, as he might have seen her picture in a badly-focused
fade-out that had gone askew. And to that isolated scrap of vision in the
overwhelming blackness he found the blessed strength to croak two words:

"Drive on."

And then a second surge of darkness welled up around him and blotted
out every sight and sound, and he fell away into the infinite black void.

7

"So EVEN YOUR arrangements can break down, Templar—when your accomplice fails you," Kuzela remarked silkily. "My enterprising young friend, when you are older you will realise that it is always a mistake to rely upon a woman. I have never employed a woman myself for that reason."

"I'll bet that broke her heart," said the Saint.

Once again he sat in Kuzela's study, with his head still throbbing painfully from the crashing welt it had received, and a lump on the back of it feeling as if it were growing out of his skull like a great auk's egg. His hair was slightly disarranged, and the straps on his wrists prevented him from rearranging it effectively; but the Saintly smile had not lost one iota of its charm.

"It remains, however, to decide whether you are going to be permitted to profit by this experience—whether you are going to live long enough to do so. Perhaps it has not occurred to you that you may have come to the end of your promising career," continued the man on the other side of the desk dispassionately; and the Saint sighed.

"What, not again?" he pleaded brokenly, and Kuzela frowned.

"I do not understand you."

"Only a few months ago I was listening to those very words," explained the Saint. "Alas, poor Wilfred! And he meant it, too. 'Wilf, old polecat,' I said, 'don't you realise that I can't be killed before page three hundred and twenty?' He didn't believe me. And he died. They put a rope round his neck and dropped him through a hole in the floor, and the consequences to his figure were very startling. Up to the base of the neck he was not so thin—but oh, boy, from then on. . . . It was awfully sad."

And Simon Templar beamed around upon the congregation—upon Kuzela, and upon the two bruisers who loafed about the room, and upon the Negro who stood behind his chair. And the Negro he indicated with a nod.

"One of your little pets?" he inquired; and Kuzela's lips moved in the fraction of a smile.

"It was fortunate that Ngano heard some of the noise," he said. "He came out of the house just in time."

"To soak me over the head from behind?" drawled the Saint genially. "Doubtless, old dear. But apart from that—"

"Your accomplice escaped, with my property. True. But my dear Templar, need that prove to be a tragedy? We have your own invaluable self still with us—and you, I am quite sure, know not only where the lady has gone, but also were you have hidden a gentleman whom I should very much like to have restored to me."

Simon raised languid eyebrows.

"When I was the Wallachian Vice-Consul at Pfaffenhausen," he said pleasantly, "our diplomacy was governed by a picturesque little Pomeranian poem, which begins:

> *Der Steiss des Elephanten*
> *Ist nicht, ist nicht so klein.*

If you get the idea—"

Kuzela nodded without animosity. His deliberate, ruthless white hands trimmed the end of a cigar.

"You must not think that I am unused to hearing remarks like that, Templar," he said equably. "In fact, I remember listening to a precisely similar speech from our friend the Duke of Fortezza. And yet—" He paused to blow a few minute flakes of tobacco leaf from the shining top of the desk, and then his pale bland eyes flicked up again to the Saint's face. . . . "The Duke of Fortezza changed his mind," he said.

Simon blinked.

"Do you know," he said enthusiastically, "there's one of the great songs of the century there! I can just feel it. Something like this:

> *The Duke of Fortezza*
> *Quite frequently gets a*
> *Nimpulse to go blithering off on the blind,*
> *But the Duchess starts bimbling*
> *And wambling and wimbling*
> *And threatens to wallop his ducal behind;*
> *And her Ladyship's threats are*
> *So fierce that he sweats a*
> *Nd just sobs as he pets her*
> *With tearful regrets—Ah!*
> *The Duke of Fortezza*
> *Is changing his mind.*

We could polish up the idea a lot if we had time, but you must admit that for an impromptu effort—''

''You underrate my own sense of humour, Templar.'' Unemotionally Kuzela inspected the even reddening of the tip of his cigar, and waved his match slowly in the air till it went out. ''But do you know another mistake which you also make?''

''I haven't the foggiest notion,'' said the Saint cheerfully.

''You underrate my sense of proportion.''

The Saint smiled.

''In many ways,'' he murmured, ''you remind me of the late Mr. Garniman. I wonder how you'll get on together?''

The other straightened up suddenly in his chair. For a moment the mask of amiable self-possession fell from him.

''I shall be interested to bandy words with you later—if you survive, my friend.'' He spoke without raising his voice; but two little specks of red burned in the cores of his eyes, and a shimmering marrow of vitriolic savagery edged up through his unalteringly level intonation. ''For the present, our time is short, and you have already wasted more than your due allowance. But I think you understand me.'' Once again, a smooth evanescent trickle of honey glossed over the bitingly measured syllables. ''Come, now, my dear young friend, it would be a pity for us to quarrel. We have crossed swords, and you have lost. Let us reach an amicable armistice. You have only to give me a little information; and then, as soon as I have verified it, and have finished my work—say after seven days, during which time you would stay with me as an honoured guest— you would be as free as air. We would shake hands and go our ways.'' Kuzela smiled and picked up a pencil. ''Now firstly: where has your accomplice gone?''

''Naturally, she drove straight to Buckingham Palace,'' said the Saint. Kuzela continued to smile.

''But you are suspicious. Possibly you think that some harm might befall her, and perhaps you would be unwilling to accept my assurance that she will be as safe as yourself. Well, it is a human suspicion after all, and I can understand it. But suppose we ask you another question. . . . Where is the Duke of Fortezza?'' Kuzela drew a small memorandum block towards him, and poised his pencil with engaging expectancy. ''Come, come! That is not a very difficult question to answer, is it? He is nothing to you—a man whom you met a few hours ago for the first time. If, say, you had never met him, and you had read in your newspaper that some fatal accident had overtaken him, you would not have been in the least disturbed. And if it is a decision between his temporary inconvenience and your own promising young life . . .'' Kuzela shrugged. ''I have no wish to use threats. But you, with your experience and imagination, must know that death does not always come easily. And very recently you did something which has mortally offended the invaluable Ngano. It would distress me to have to deliver you into his keeping. . . . Now, now, let us make up our minds quickly. What have you done with the Duke?''

Simon dropped his chin and looked upwards across the desk.

''Nothing that I should be ashamed to tell my mother,'' he said winningly; and the other's eyes narrowed slowly.

''Do I, after all, understand you to refuse to tell me?''

The Saint crossed his left ankle over on to his right knee.

''You know, laddie,'' he remarked, ''you should be in the movies, really you should. As the strong silent man you'd be simply great, if you were a bit stronger and didn't talk so much.''

For some seconds Kuzela looked at him.

Then he threw down his pencil and pushed away the pad.

''Very well,'' he said.

He snapped his fingers without turning his head, and one of the two bruisers came to his side. Kuzela spoke without giving the man a glance.

''Yelver, you bring round the car. We shall require it very shortly.''

The man nodded and went out; and Kuzela clasped his hands again on the desk before him.

''And you, Templar, will tell us where we are going,'' he said, and Simon raised his head.

His eyes gazed full and clear into Kuzela's face, bright with the reckless light of their indomitable mockery, and a sardonically Saintly smile curved the corners of his mouth.

''You're going to hell, old dear,'' he said coolly; and then the Negro dragged him up out of his chair.

Simon went meekly down the stairs, with the Negro gripping his arm and the second bruiser following behind; and his brain was weighing up the exterior circumstances with lightning accuracy.

Patricia had got away—that was the first and greatest thing. He praised the Lord who had inspired her with the sober far-sightedness and clearness of head not to attempt any futile heroism. There was nothing she could have done, and mercifully she'd had the sense to see it. . . . But having got away, what would be her next move?

''Claud Eustace, presumably,'' thought the Saint; and a wry little twist roved across his lips, for he had always been the most incorrigible optimist in the world.

So he reached the hall, and there he was turned round and hustled along towards the back of the house. As he went, he stole a glance at his wrist watch. . . . Patricia must have been gone for the best part of an hour, and that would have been more than long enough for Teal to get busy. Half of that time would have been sufficient to get Teal on the phone from the nearest call box and have the house surrounded by enough men to wipe up a brigade—if anything of that sort were going to be done. And not a sign of any such developments had interrupted the playing of the piece. . . .

Down from the kitchen a flight of steps ran to the cellar; and as the Saint was led down them he had a vivid appreciation of another similarity between that adventure and a concluding episode in the history of the late Mr. Garniman. The subterranean prospects in each case had been decidedly uninviting; and now the Saint held his fire and wondered what treat was going to be offered him this time.

The cigar-chewing escort stopped at the foot of the steps, and the Saint was led on alone into a small bare room. From the threshold, the Negro flung him forward into a far corner, and turned to lock the door behind him. He put the key in his pocket, took off his coat, and rolled up his sleeves; and all the time his dark blazing eyes were riveted upon the Saint.

And then he picked up a great leather whip from the floor, and his thick lips curled back from his teeth in a ghastly grin.

"You will not talk, no?" he said.

He swung his arm; and the long lash whistled and crackled through the air, and snaked over the Saint's shoulders like the recoiling snap of an overstrained hawser.

8

SIMON REELED AWAY in a slash of agony that ate into his chest as if a thin jet of boiling acid had been sprayed across his back.

And he went mad.

Never, otherwise, could he have accomplished what he did. For one blinding instant, which branded itself on his optic nerves with such an eye-aching clarity that it might have stood for an eternity of frozen stillness, he saw everything there was to see in that little room. He saw the stained grey walls and ceiling and the dusty paving underfoot; he saw the locked door; he saw the towering figure of the gigantic hate-vengeful Negro before him, and the cyclopean muscles swelling and rippling under the thin texture of the lavender silk shirt; and he saw himself. Just for that instant he saw those things as he had never seen anything before, with every thought of everything else and every other living soul in the world wiped from his mind like chalk marks smeared from a smooth board. . . .

And then a red fog bellied up before his eyes, and the stillness seemed to burst inwards like the smithereening of a great glass vacuum bulb.

He felt nothing more—in that white heat of berserk fury, the sense of pain was simply blotted out. He dodged round the room by instinct, ducking and swerving mechanically, and scarcely knew when he succeeded and when he failed.

And at his wrists he felt nothing at all.

The buckle of the strap there was out of reach of his teeth, but he twisted his hands inwards, one over the other, tightening up the leather with all his strength, till his muscles ached with the strain. He saw the edges of the strap biting into his skin, and the flesh swelling whitely up on either side; the pain of that alone should have stopped him, but there was no such thing. . . . And he stood still and twisted once again, with a concentrated passion of power that writhed over the whole of his upper body like the stirring of a volcano; and the leather broke before his eyes like a strip of tissue paper. . . .

And the Saint laughed.

The whip sang around again, and he leapt in underneath it and caught it as it fell. And what he had intuitively expected happened. The Negro jerked at it savagely—and Simon Templar did not resist. But he kept his hold fast, and allowed all the vicious energy of that jerk to merge flowingly into his own unchecked rush; and it catapulted him to his mark like a stone from a sling. His right fist sogged full and square into the Negro's throat with a force that jarred the Saint's own shoulder, and Simon found the whip hanging free in his hand.

He stepped back and watched the grin melting out of the contorted black face. The Negro's chest heaved up to the encompassing of a great groaning breath, but the shattering mule-power of that pent-up super-

auxiliated swipe in the gullet has stunned his thyro-arytenoids as effectively as if a bullet had gone through them. His mouth worked wildly,
but he could produce nothing more than an inaudible whisper. And the
Saint laughed again, gathering up the whip.

"The boys will be expecting some music," he said, very gently. "And
you are going to provide it."

Then the Negro sprang at him like a tiger.

That one single punch which had reversed the situation would have
sent any living European swooning off into hours of tortured helplessness,
but in this case the Saint had never expected any such result from it. It
had done all that he had ever hoped that it would do—obliterated the
Negro's speaking voice, and given the Saint himself the advantage of the
one unwieldy weapon in the room. And with the red mists of unholy rage
still swirling across his vision, Simon Templar went grimly into the fight
of his life.

He sidestepped the Negro's first maniac charge as smoothly and easily
as a practised pedestrian evading a two-horse dray, and as he swerved
he brought the whip cracking round in a stroke that split the lavender silk
shirt as crisply as if a razor had been scored across it.

The Negro fetched up against the far wall with an animal scream, spun
round, and sprang at him again. And again the Saint swayed lightly aside,
and made the whip lick venomously home with a report like a gunshot. . . .

He knew that that was the only earthly hope he had—to keep his
opponent tearing blindly through a hazing madness of pain and fury that
would scatter every idea of scientific fighting to the four winds. There
were six feet eight inches of the Negro, most of three hundred pounds'
pitiless, clawing, blood-mad primitive malignity caged up with Simon
Templar within those blank damp-blotched walls; and Simon knew, with
a quiet cold certainty, that if once those six feet eight inches, those three
hundred odd pounds of bone and muscle, resolved themselves into the
same weight and size of logical, crafty, fighting precision, there was no
man in the world who could have stood two minutes against them. And
the Saint quietly and relentlessly crimped down his own strength and
speed and fighting madness into the one narrow channel that would give
him a fighting chance.

It was a duel between brute strength and animal ferocity on the one
hand, and on the otther hand the lithe swiftness and lightning eye of the
trickiest man alive—a duel with no referee, in which no foul was barred.
Tirelessly the Saint went round the room, flitting airily beyond, around,

even under the massive arms that grappled for him, bobbing and swooping and turning, up on his toes and supple as a dancer, as elusive as a drop of quicksilver on a plate; and always the tapered leather thong in his hand was whirling and hissing like an angry fer-de-lance, striking and coiling and striking again with a bitter deadliness of aim. Once the Negro grabbed at the whip and found it, and the Saint broke his hold with a kick to the elbow that opened the man's fingers as if the tendons had been cut; once the Saint's foot slipped, and he battered his way out of a closing trap in a desperate flurry of rib-creaking body blows that made even the Negro stagger for a sufficient moment; and the fight went on.

It went on till the Negro's half-naked torso shone with a streaming lather of sweat and blood, and a sudden kicking lurch in his step shot into Simon's taut-strung brain the wild wide knowledge that the fight was won.

And for the first time the Saint stood his ground, with his back to one wall, holding the Negro at bay by the flailing sweep of the lash alone.

Then Simon pressed forward, and the Negro went back. . . .

The Saint drove him into the opposite corner and beat him whimpering to his knees. And then, as the man spilled forward on to his face, Simon leapt in and got an ankle hold.

"Get your hands right up behind your back," he rasped incisively, "or I'll twist the leg off you!"

He applied his leverage vigorously, and the man obeyed him with a yelp. Simon locked the ankle with his knee and bent his weight over it. With quick deft fingers he knotted the tail of the whip round the Negro's wrists, and passed the stock over one shoulder, round the neck, and back over the other shoulder into a slip-knot. A draught of air gulped noisily into the Negro's straining lungs, and Simon gave the noose a yank.

"One word from you, and you graze in the Green Pastures," he stated pungently, and heard the lungful choke sibilantly out again. "And get this," said the Saint, with no increase of friendliness: "if you move the half of an inch in that hog-tie, you'll bowstring your own sweet self. That's all."

He fished the key of the door out of the Negro's pocket and stood up, breathing deeply.

He himself was starting to look as if he had recently taken a warm shower-bath in his clothes; and now that the anaesthetic red mists were thinning out, a large part of his back was beginning to stiffen itself up into an identical acreage of ache; but he was not yet ready to sit down and be sorry about such minor discomforts. With the key snapping over in the lock, he brushed the hair back off his forehead and opened the door; and the cigar-chewer at the foot of the steps crawled upright like a slow-motion picture, with his jaw sagging nervelessly and his eyes popping from their orbits, gaping at the Saint as he might have gaped at his own ghost. . . .

Smiling, and without any haste, Simon walked towards him.

And the man stood there staring at him, watching him come on, numbed with a bone-chilling superstitious terror. It was not until the Saint was within two yards of him that a sobbing little wail gurgled in his throat and he reached feebly round to his hip pocket.

And of the rest of the entertainment he knew little. He knew that a grip about which there was nothing ghostly seized upon his right wrist before he had time to draw, while another metallic clutch closed round his knees; he knew that the weight came suddenly off his feet; and then he seemed to go floating ethereally through space. Somewhere in the course of that flight an astonishingly hard quantity of concrete impinged upon his skull, but it did not seem an important incident. His soul went bimbering on, way out into the land of blissful dreams. . . .

And the Saint went on up the steps.

He was half-way up when a bell jangled somewhere overhead, and he checked voluntarily. And then a tiny skew-eyed grin skimmed over his lips.

"Claud Eustace for the hell of it," he murmured, and went upwards very softly.

Right up by the door at the top of the stairs he stopped again and listened. He heard slow and watchful footsteps going down the hall, followed by the rattle of a latch and the cautious whine of slowly turning hinges. And then he heard the most perplexing thing of all, which was nothing more or less than an expansive and omnipotent silence.

The Saint put up one hand and gently scratched his ear, with a puzzled crease chiselling in between his eyebrows. He was prepared to hear almost anything else but that. And he didn't. The silence continued for some time, and then the front door closed again and the footsteps started back solo on the return journey.

And then, in the very opposite direction, the creak of a window-sash sliding up made him blink.

Someone was wriggling stealthily over the sill. With his ear glued to a panel of the door, he could visualise every movement as clearly as if he could have seen it. He heard the faint patter of the intruder's weight coming on to the floor, and then the equally faint sound of footsteps creeping over the linoleum. They connected up in his mind with the footsteps of the man who had gone to the door like the other part of a duet. Then the second set of footsteps died away, and there was only the sound of the man returning from the hall. Another door opened. . . . And then a voice uttered a corrosively quiet command.

"Keep still!"

Simon almost fell down the steps, And then he windmilled dazedly back to his balance and hugged himself.

"Oh, Pat!" he breathed. "Mightn't I have known it? And you ring the bell to draw the fire, and sprint round and come in the back way. . . . Oh, you little treasure!"

Grinning a great wide grin, he listened to the dialogue.

"Put your hands right up. . . . That's fine. . . . And now, where's Kuzela?"

Silence.

"Where is Kuzela?"

A shifting of feet, and then the grudging answer:

"Upstairs."

"Lead on, sweetheart."

The sounds of reluctant movement. . . .

And the whole of Simon Templar's inside squirmed with ecstasy at the pure poetic Saintliness of the technique. Not for a thousand million pounds would he have butted in just then—not one second before Kuzela himself had also had time to appreciate the full ripe beauty of the situation. He heard the footsteps travelling again: they came right past his door and went on into the hall, and the Saint pointed his toes in a few movements of an improvised cachucha.

And then, after a due pause, he opened the door and followed on.

He gave the others time to reach the upper landing, and then he went whisking up the first flight. Peeking round the banisters, he was just in time to get a sight of Patricia disappearing into Kuzela's study. Then the door slammed behind her, and the Saint raced on up and halted outside it.

While after the answering of the dud front door call there had certainly been a silence, the stillness to which he listened now made all previous efforts in noiselessness sound like an artillery barrage. Against that background of devastating blankness, the clatter of a distant passing truck seemed to shake the earth, and the hoot of its klaxon sounded like the Last Trump.

And then Patricia spoke again, quite calmly, but with a lethal clearness that was hedged around on every side with the menace of every manner of murder.

"Where is the Saint?" she asked.

And upon those words Simon Templar figured that he had his cue.

He turned the handle soundlessly and pushed the door wide open.

Patricia's back was toward him. A little further on to one side the second bruiser stood by with his hands high in the air. And behind the desk sat Kuzela, with his face still frozen in an expression of dumb, incredulous stupefaction. . . . And as the door swung back, and the Saint advanced gracefully into the limelight, the eyes of the two men revolved and centred on him, and dilated slowly into petrified staring orbs of something near to panic.

"Good morning," said the Saint.

Patricia half turned. She could not help herself—the expression on the faces of the two men in front of her were far too transparently heartfelt to leave her with any mistrust that they were part of a ruse to put her off her guard.

But the result of her movement was the same; for as she turned her eyes away, the smallest part in the cast had his moment. He awoke out of his groping comatosity, saw his chance, and grabbed it with both fists.

The automatic was wrested violently out of the girl's hands, and she was thrown stumbling back into the Saint's arms. And the Saint's gentle smile never altered.

He passed Patricia to one side, and cocked a derisive eye at the gun that was turned against him. And with no more heed for it than that, he continued on toward the desk.

"So nice to see you again," he said.

9

Kuzela rose lingeringly to his feet.

There was a perceptible pause before he gained control of the faculty of speech. The two consecutive smacks that had been jolted into the very roots of his being within the space of the last forty seconds would have tottered the equilibrium of any man—of any man except, perhaps, the

Saint himself. . . . But the Saint was not at all disturbed. He waited in a genteel silence, while the other schooled the flabby startlement out of his face and dragged up his mouth into an answering smile.

"My dear young friend!"

The voice, when Kuzela found it, had the same svelte timbre as before, and Simon bowed a mocking compliment to the other's nerve.

"My dear old comrade!" he murmured, open-armed.

"You have saved us the trouble of fetching you, Templar," Kuzela said blandly. "But where is Ngano?"

"The Negro Spiritual?" The Saint aligned his eyebrows banteringly. "I'm afraid he—er—met with a slight accident."

"Ah!"

"No—not exactly. I don't think he's quite dead yet, though he may easily have strangled himself by this time. But he hasn't enjoyed himself. I think, if the circumstances had been reversed, he would have talked," said the Saint, with a glacial inclemency of quietness.

Kuzela stroked his chin.

"That is unfortunate," he said.

And then he smiled.

"But it is not fatal, my friend," he purred. "The lady has already solved one problem for us herself. And now that she is here, I am sure you would do anything rather than expose her to the slightest danger. So let us return to our previous conversation at once. Perhaps the lady will tell us herself where she went to when she drove away from here?"

Simon put his hands in his pockets.

"Why, yes," he said good-humouredly. "I should think she would."

The girl looked at him as if she could not quite believe her ears. And Simon met her puzzled gaze with blue eyes of such a blinding Saintly innocence that even she could read no enticement to deception in them.

"Do you mean that?" she asked.

"Of course," said the Saint. "There are one or two things I shouldn't mind knowing myself."

Patricia put a hand to her head.

"If you want to know—when I left here I drove straight to—"

"Buckingham Palace," drawled the Saint. "And then?"

"I had the bags taken up to Beppo's room, and I saw him myself. He was quite wide awake and sensible. I told him I was coming back here to get you out, and said that if I wasn't back by four o'clock, or one of us hadn't rung him up, he was to get in touch with Teal. I gave him Teal's private number. He didn't want me to go at all, but I insisted.

That's all there is to tell. I picked up a puncture on the second trip out here, and that held me up a bit—''

"But who cares about that?" said the Saint.

He turned back to the desk.

The man with the gun stood less than a yard away on his right front; but the Saint, ignoring his very existence, leaned a little forward and looked from the distance of another yard into the face of Kuzela. The loose poise of his body somehow centred attention even while it disarmed suspicion. But the mockery had gone out of his eyes.

"You heard?" he asked.

Kuzela nodded. His mouth went up at one corner.

"But I still see no reason for alarm, my friend," he said, in that wheedling voice of slow malevolence. "After all, there is still time for much to happen. Before your friend, Mr. Teal, arrives—"

"Before my friend Chief Inspector Teal arrives with a squad of policemen in a plain van, I shall be a long way from here," said the Saint.

Kuzela started.

"So you have invoked the police?" he snapped. And then again he recovered himself. "But that is your affair. By the time they arrive, as you say, you will have left here. But where do you think you will have gone?"

"Home, James," said the Saint.

He took one hand out of its pocket to straighten his coat, and smiled without mirth.

"Fortunately, the argument between us can be settled tonight," he said, "which will save me having to stage any reunions. Your black torturer has been dealt with. I have given him a dose of his own medicine which will, I think, put him in hospital for several weeks. But you remain. You are, after all, the man who gave Ngano his orders. I have seen what you did to the Duke of Fortezza, and I know what you wanted to have done to me. . . . I hope you will get on well with Wilfred.''

"And what do you think you are going to do to me?" asked Kuzela throatily; and Simon held him with his eyes.

"I'm going to kill you, Kuzela," he said simply.

"Ah! And how will you do that?"

Simon's fingers dipped into his pocket. They came out with an ordinary match-box, and he laid it on the desk.

"That is the answer to all questions," he said.

Kuzela stared down at the box. It sat there in the middle of his clean white blotter, yellow and oblong and angular, as commonplace a thing as any man could see on his desk—and the mystery of it seemed to leer up at him malignantly. He picked it up and shook it: it weighed light in his hand, and his mind balked at the idea that it could conceal any engine of destruction. And the Saint's manner of presenting it had been void of the most minute scintilla of excitement—and still was. He eyed Kuzela quizzically.

"Why not open it?" he suggested.

Kuzela looked at him blankly. And then, with a sudden impatience, he jabbed his thumb at the little sliding drawer. . . .

In a dead silence, the box fell through the air and flopped half-open on the desk.

"What does this mean?" asked Kuzela, almost in a whisper.

"It means that you have four minutes to live," said the Saint.

Kuzela held up his hand and stared at it.

In the centre of the ball of his right thumb a little globule of blood was swelling up in the pinky-white of the surrounding skin. He gazed stupidly from it to the match-box and back again. In imagination, he felt a second time the asp-like prick that had bitten into his thumb as he moved the drawer of the box—and understood. "The answer to all questions. . . ."

He stood there as powerless to move as a man in a nightmare, and watched the infinitely slow distension of the tiny crimson sphere under his eyes, his face going ashen with the knowledge of inescapable doom. The drop of blood hypnotised him, filled his vision till he could see nothing else but the miscroscopic reflections glistening over the surface of it—until all at once it seemed to grow magically into a coruscating red vesicle of enormous size, thrusting in upon him, bearing him down, filling the whole universe with the menace of its smothering scarlet magnitude. A roaring of mighty waters seethed up about his ears. . . .

The others saw him brace himself on his feet as if to resist falling; and he remained quite still, with his eyes fixing and going dim. And then he took one step sideways, swayed, and crumpled down on to the floor with his limbs twitching convulsively and his chest labouring. . . .

Quite calmly and casually the Saint put out a hand and clasped it on the gun wrist of the man who stood beside him.

The man seemed to come alive out of a dream. And without any noticeable interregnum of full consciousness, he seemed to pass right on into another kind of dream—the transition being effected by the contingence upon the point of his jaw of a tearing uppercut that started well below the Saint's waistline and consummated every erg of its weight and velocity at the most vital angle of the victim's face. With the results aforementioned. He went down in a heap and lay very still, even as his companion had done a little earlier; and Simon picked up the gun.

"Which finishes that," said the Saint, and found Patricia looking down again at Kuzela.

"What happened to him?" she asked, a trifle unsteadily.

"More or less what he tried to make happen to me. Ever come across those trick match-boxes that shoot a needle into you when you try to open them? I bought one last afternoon, and replaced the needle with something that was sent to me along with the message you know about. And I don't know that we shall want it again."

He took the little box of death over to the fireplace, dropped it in the grate, and raked the glowing embers over it. Then he took up his hat and stick, which he saw lying in a chair, and glanced around for the last time. Only Kuzela's fingers were twitching now, and a wet froth gleamed on his lips and dribbled down one cheek. . . . Simon put an arm round the girl's shoulders.

"I guess we can be going," he said, and led her out of the room.

It was in the hall that the expression on the face of a clock caught his eye and pulled him up with a jerk.

"What time did you say Beppo was going to get in touch with Teal?" he inquired.

"Four o'clock." Patricia followed his gaze, and then looked at her wrist. "That clock must be fast—"

"Or else you've stopped," said the Saint pithily. He turned back his sleeve and inspected his own watch. "And stopped you have, old darling. It's thirty-three minutes after four now—and to give Claud Eustace even a chance to think that he'd pulled me out of a mess would break my heart. Not to include another reason why he mustn't find us here. Where did you leave the car?"

"Just one block away."

"This is where we make greyhounds look lazy," said the Saint, and opened the front door.

They were at the gate when Simon saw the lights of a car slowing up and swinging in to the kerb on his left. Right in front of him, Kuzela's car was parked; and the Saint knew clairvoyantly that that was their only chance.

He caught Patricia's arm and flipped up the collar of her coat.

"Jump to it," he crisped.

He scudded round to the driving seat, and the girl tumbled in beside him as he let in the clutch. He shot right past the police car with his head well down and his shoulders hunched. A tattered shout reached him as he went by; and then he was bucking off down a side street with the car heeling over on two wheels as he crammed it round the corner. The police car would have to be turned right round in a narrow road before it could get after him, and he knew he was well away. He dodged hectically south-east, and kept hard at it till he was sure he had left any pursuit far behind.

Somewhere in the northern hinterlands of the Tottenham Court Road he stopped the car and made some hurried repairs to his appearance with the aid of the driving mirror, and ended up looking distinctly more presentable than he had been when they left Hampstead. He looked so presentable, in fact, that they abandoned the car on that spot, and walked boldly on until they met a taxi, which took them to Berkeley Square.

"For the night isn't nearly over yet," said the Saint, as they walked down Upper Berkeley Mews together after the taxi had chugged off out of sight.

It was one of those fool-proof prophecies which always delighted his sense of the slickness of things by the brisk promptness with which they fulfilled themselves. He had hardly closed the door of his house when the telephone bell began to ring, and he went to answer the call with a feeling of large and unalloyed contentment.

"Hullo-o? . . . Speaking. . . . That's which? . . . Teal? . . . Well, blow me, Claud Eustace, this is very late for you to be out! Does your grandmother allow you—What? . . . What have I been doing tonight? I've been drinking beer with Beppo. . . . No, not a leper—BEPPO. B for bdellium, E for eiderdown, P for psychology, P for pneumonia, O for a muse of fire that would ascend the brightest heaven of . . . I beg your pardon? . . . You were called up and told I was in trouble? . . . Someone's been pulling your leg, Claud. I'm at peace with the world. . . . Whassat? . . . Why, sure. I was just going to bed, but I guess I can stay up a few minutes longer. Will you be bringing your own gum? . . . Right-ho . . ."

He listened for a moment longer; and then he hung up the receiver and turned to Pat.

"Claud's coming right along," he said gleefully, and the laughter was lilting in his voice. "We're not to try to get away, because he'll have an armed guard at every sea and air port in the British Isles ten minutes after he gets here and finds we've done a bunk. Which will be tremendous fun for all concerned. . . . And now, get through to Beppo as fast as you can spin the dial, old sweetheart, while I sprint upstairs and change my shirt—for there's going to be a great day!''

10

CHIEF INSPECTOR CLAUD Eustace Teal fixed his pudgy hands in the belt of his overcoat, and levelled his unfriendly gaze on the superbly elegant young man who lounged against the table in front of him.

"So that message I had was a fake, was it?" he snarled.

"It must have been, Claud."

Teal nodded fatly.

"Perhaps it was," he said. "But I went to the address it gave me—and what do you think I found?"

"The Shah of Persia playing ludo," hazarded Simon Templar, intelligently; and the detective glowered.

"In the cellar I found a Negro tied up with the whip that had beaten half the hide off his back. Outside, there was a white man with a fractured skull—he's gone to hospital as well. In a room upstairs there was another man laid out with a broken jaw, and a fourth man in the same room—dead."

The Saint raised his eyebrows.

"But, my dear old sturgeon!" he protested reasonably—"what on earth do you think I am? A sort of human earthquake?"

"Both the Negro and the man with the broken jaw," Teal continued stonily, "gave me a description of the man responsible, and it fits you like a glove. The man with the broken jaw also added the description of a woman who couldn't be distinguished apart from Miss Holm."

"Then we obviously have doubles, Claud."

"He also heard the woman say: 'Where is the Saint?' "

Simon frowned.

"That's certainly odd," he admitted. "Where did you say this was?"

"You know darned well where it was! And I'll tell you some more. Just as I got there in the police car, a man and a woman dashed out of the house and got away. And who do you suppose they looked like?"

"The same doubles, obviously," said the Saint with great brilliance.

"And just one block away from that house we found a blue saloon Hirondel, which the two people I saw would have got away in if they'd had time to reach it. The number of it was ZX1257. Is that the number of your car?"

The Saint sat up.

"Claud, you're a blessing in disguise! That certainly is my car—and I was thinking I'd lost her! Pinched outside the Mayfair only yesterday afternoon, she was, in broad daylight. I was meaning to ring up Vine Street before, but what with one thing and another—"

Teal drew a deep breath—and then he exploded.

"Now would you like to know what I think of your defence?" he blurted out, in a boiling gust of righteous wrath. And he went on without waiting for encouragement. "I think it's the most weak-kneed tangle of moonshine I've ever had to listen to in my life. I think it's so drivelling that if any jury will listen to it for ten minutes, I'll walk right out of the court and have myself certified. I've got two men who'll swear to you on their dying oaths, and another one to put beside them if he recovers, and I know what I saw myself and what the men who were with me saw; and I think everything you've got to say is so maudlin that I'm going to take you straight back to Scotland Yard with me and have it put in writing before we lock you up. I think I've landed you at last, Mr. Saint, and after what you said to me this morning I'm damned glad I've done it."

The Saint took out his cigarette-case and flopped off the table into an armchair, sprawling one long leg comfortably over the arm.

"Well, that does express your point of view quite clearly," he conceded. He lighted a cigarette, and looked up brightly. "Claud, you're getting almost fluent in your old age. But you've got to mind you don't let your new-found eloquence run away with you."

"Oh, have I?" The detective took the bait right down into his oesophagus, and clinched his teeth on the line. "Very well. Then while all these extraordinary things were being done by your double—while half a dozen sober men were seeing you and listening to you and being beaten up by you and getting messages from you—maybe you'll tell me what you were doing and who else knows it besides yourself?"

Simon inhaled luxuriously, and smiled.

"Why, sure. As I told you over the phone, I was drinking beer with Beppo."

"And who's he?"

"The Duke of Fortezza."

"Oh, yes?" Teal grew sarcastic. "And where was the King of Spain and the Prime Minister of Yugoslavia?"

"Blowed if I know," said the Saint ingenuously. "But there were some other distinguished people present. The Count of Montalano, and Prince Marco d'Ombria, and the Italian Ambassador—"

"The Italian *what?*"

"Ambassador. You know. Gent with top hat and spats."

"And where was this?"

"At the Italian embassy. It was just a little private party, but it went on for a long time. We started about midnight, and didn't break up till half-past four—I hadn't been home two minutes when you phoned."

Teal almost choked.

"What sort of bluff are you trying to pull on me now?" he demanded. "Have you got hold of the idea that I've gone dotty? Are you sitting there believing that I'll soak up that story, along with everything else you've told me, and just go home and ask no questions?" Teal snorted savagely. "You must have gone daft!" he blared.

The Saint came slowly out of his chair. He posed himself before the detective, feet astraddle, his left hand on his hip, loose-limbed and smiling and dangerous; and the long dictatorial forefinger which Teal had seen and hated before drove a straight and peremptory line into the third button of the detective's waistcoat.

"And now you listen to me again, Claud," said the Saint waspily. "Do you know what you're letting yourself in for?"

"Do I know what I'm—"

"Do you know what you're letting yourself in for? You burst into my house and make wild accusations against me. You shout at me, you bully me, you tell me I'm either lying or dippy, and you threaten to arrest me. I'm very sensitive, Claud," said the Saint, "and you hurt me. You hurt me so much that I've a damned good mind to let you run me in—and then, when you'd put the rope right round your own neck and drawn it up as tight as it'd go, I'd pull such a shemozzle around your bat ears that you'd want nothing more in life than to hand in your resignation and get away to some forgotten corner of the earth where they've never seen a newspaper. That's what's coming your way so fast that you're going to have to jump like a kangaroo to get from under it. It's only because I'm of a godly and forgiving disposition," said the Saint virtuously, "that I'm giving you a chance to save your skin. I'm going to let you verify my alibi before you arrest me, instead of having it fed into you with a stomach-pump afterwards; and then you are going to apologise to me and go home,'' said the Saint.

He picked up a telephone directory, found a place, and thrust the book under Teal's oscillating eyes.

"There's the number,'' he said. "Mayfair three two three O. Check it up for yourself now, and save yourself the trouble of telling me I'm just ringing up an accomplice.

He left the detective blinking at the volume, and went to the telephone.

Teal read off the number, put down the book, and pulled at his collar.

Once again the situation had passed out of his control. He gazed at the Saint purply, and the beginnings of a despondent weariness pouched up under his eyes. It was starting to be borne in upon him, with a preposterous certitude, that he had just been listening to something more than bluff. And the irony of it made him want to burst into tears. It was unfair. It was brutal. It outraged every canon of logic and justice. He knew his case was watertight, knew that against the evidence he could put into a witness-box there could simply be no human way of escape—he would have sworn to it on the rack, and would have gone to his death still swearing it. And he knew that it wasn't going to work.

Through a haze of almost homicidal futility, he heard the Saint speaking.

"Oh, is that you, Signor Ravelli? . . . Simon Templar speaking. Listen: there's some weird eruption going on in the brains of Scotland Yard. Some crime or other was committed somewhere tonight, and for some blithering reason they seem to think I was mixed up in it. I'm sorry to have to stop you on your way to bed, but a fat policeman has just barged in here—''

"Give me that telephone!'' snarled Teal.

He snatched the instrument away and rammed the receiver up against his ear.

"Hullo!'' he barked. "This is Chief Inspector Teal, Criminal Investigation Department, speaking. I have every reason to believe that this man Templar was concerned in a murder which took place in Hampstead shortly after four o'clock this morning. He's tried to tell me some cock-and-bull story about . . . What? . . . But damn it— . . . I beg your pardon, sir, but I definitely know . . . From twelve o'clock till half-past four? . . . But . . . But . . . But oh, hell, I . . . No, sir, I said . . . But he . . . *Who?* . . .''

The diaphragm of the receiver clacked and chattered, and Teal's round red face sagged sickly.

And then:

"All right, sir. Thank you very much, sir," he said in a strangled voice, and slammed the receiver back on its bracket.

The Saint smoothed his hair.

"We might get on to Beppo next," he suggested hopefully. "He's staying at the Berkeley. Then you can have a word with Prince d'Ombria—"

"Can I?" Teal had eaten wormwood, and his voice was thick and raw with the bitterness of it. "Well, I haven't got time. I know when I'm licked. I know where I am when half a dozen princes and ambassadors will go into the witness-box and swear that you're chasing them round the equator at the very moment when I know that I'm talking to you here in this room. I don't even ask how you worked it. I expect you rang up the President of the United States and got him to fix it for you. But I'll be seeing you another time—don't worry."

He hitched his coat round, and grabbed up his hat.

"Bye-bye," sang the Saint.

"And you remember this," Teal gulped out. "I'm not through with you yet. You're not going to sit back on your laurels. You wouldn't. And that's what's going to be the finish of you. You'll be up to something else soon enough—and maybe you won't have the entire Italian Diplomatic Service primed to lie you out of it next time. From this minute, you're not even going to blow your nose unless I know it. I'll have you watched closer than the Crown Jewels, and the next mistake you make is going to be the last."

"Cheerio, dear heart," said the Saint, and heard the vicious bang of the front door before he sank back into his chair in hysterics of helpless laughter.

But the epilogue of that story was not written until some weeks later, when a registered packet bearing an Italian postmark was delivered at No. 7, Upper Berkeley Mews.

Simon opened it after breakfast.

First came a smaller envelope, which contained a draft on the Bank of Italy for a sum whose proportions made even Simon Templar blink.

And then he took out a small shagreen case, and turned it over curiously. He pressed his thumbnail into the little spring catch, and the lid flew up and left him staring.

Patricia put a hand on his shoulder.

"What is it?" she asked, and the Saint looked at her.

"It's the medallion of the Order of the Annunziatta—and I think we shall both have to have new hats on this," he said.

Part III
The Melancholy
Journey of Mr. Teal

1

Now THERE WAS a day when the Saint went quite mad.

Of course, one might with considerable justification say that he always had been mad, anyway, so that the metamorphosis suggested by that first sentence would be difficult for the ordinary observer to discover. Patricia Holm said so, quite definitely; and the Saint only smiled.

"Neverwithstanding," he said, "I am convinced that the season is ripe for Isadore to make his contribution to our bank balance."

"You must be potty," said his lady, for the second time; and the Saint nodded blandly.

"I am. That was the everlasting fact with which we started the day's philosophy and meditation. If you remember—"

Patricia looked at the calendar on the wall, and her sweet lips came together in the obstinate little line that her man knew so well.

"Exactly six months ago," she said, "Teal was in here giving such a slick imitation of the sorest man on earth that anyone might have thought it was no impersonation at all. Two of his best men have been hanging around outside for twenty-four hours a day ever since. They're out there now. If you think six months is as far as his memory will go—"

"I don't."

"Then what are you thinking?"

The Saint lighted his second cigarette, and blew a streamer of smoke towards the ceiling. His blue eyes laughed.

"I think," he answered carefully, "that Claud Eustace is just getting set for his come-back. I think he's just finished nursing the flea I shot

into his ear last time so tenderly that it's now big and blood-thirsty enough
to annihilate anything smaller than an elephant—and maybe that plus.
And I'm darned sure that if we lie low much longer, Claud Eustace will
be getting ideas into his head, which would be very bad for him indeed."

"But—"

"There are," said the Saint, "no buts. I had a look at my pass-book
yesterday, and it seems to be one of the eternal verities of this uncertain
life that I could this day write a cheque for ninety-six thousand, two
hundred and forty-seven pounds, eleven shillings, and fourpence—*and*
have it honoured. Which is very nice, but just not quite nice enough.
When I started this racket, I promised myself I wasn't coming out with
one penny less than a hundred thousand pounds. I didn't say I'd come
out even then, but I did think that when I reached that figure I might sit
down for a bit and consider the possible advantages of respectability.
And I feel that the time is getting ripe for me to have that think."

This was after a certain breakfast. Half a dozen volumes might be
written around nothing else but those after-breakfast seances in Upper
Berkeley Mews. They occupied most of the early afternoon in days of
leisure, for the Saint had his own opinions about the correct hours for
meals; and they were the times when ninety per cent of his coups were
schemed. Towards noon the Saint would arise like a giant refreshed, robe
himself in furiously patterned foulard, and enter with an immense earnestness of concentration upon the task of shattering his fast. And after
that had been accomplished in a properly solemn silence, Simon Templar
lighted a cigarette, slanted his eyebrows, shifted back his ears, and met-
aphorically rolled up his sleeves and looked around for something to
knock sideways. A new day—or what was left of it—loomed up on his
horizon like a fresh world waiting to be conquered, and the Saint stanced
himself to sail into it with an irrepressible impetuosity of hare-brained
devilment that was never too tired or short-winded to lavish itself on the
minutest detail as cheerfully and generously as it would have spread itself
over the most momentous affair in the whole solar system.

And in those moods of reckless unrepentance he smiled with shameless
Saintliness right into that stubborn alignment of his lady's mouth, challenged it, teased it, dared it, laughed it into confusion, kissed it in a way
that would have melted the mouth of a marble statue, and won her again
and again, as he always would, into his own inimitable madness. As he
did then. . . .

"There's money and trouble to be had for the asking," said the Saint,
when it was all over. "And what more could anyone want, old dear?

. . . More trouble even than that, maybe. Well, I heard last night that Claud Eustace was also interested in Isadore, though I haven't the foggiest idea how much he knows. Tell me, Pat, old sweetheart, isn't it our cue?''

And Patricia sighed.

When Frankie Hormer landed at Southampton, he figured that his arrival was as secret as human ingenuity could make it. Even Detective-Inspector Peters, who had been waiting for him for years on and off, knew nothing about it—and he was at Southampton at the time. Frankie walked straight past him, securely hidden behind a beard which had sprouted to very respectable dimensions since he last set foot in England, and showed a passport made out in a name that his godfathers and godmothers had never thought of. Admittedly, there had been a little difficulty with the tall dark man who had entered his life in Johannesburg and followed him all the way to Durban—inconspicuously, but not quite inconspicuously enough. But Frankie had dealt with that intrusion the night before he sailed. He carried two guns, and knew how to use them both.

And after that had been settled, the only man who should have known anything at all was Elberman, the genial little Jew who had financed the expedition at a staggering rate of interest, and who had personally procured the passport aforementioned, which was absolutely indistinguishable from the genuine-article although it had never been inside the Foreign Office in its life.

Frankie had made that trip a number of times before—often enough to acquire a fairly extensive knowledge of the possible pitfalls. And this time he was reckoning to clean up, and he was taking no chances. The man from Johannesburg had bothered him more than a little, but the voyage back to England had given him time to forget that. And in the train that was speeding him towards Waterloo, Frankie thought ahead into a pleasant and peaceful future—with a chalet in Switzerland, probably, and a villa on the Riviera thrown in, and an endless immunity from the anxieties that are inseparable from what those who have never tried to earn it call ''easy money.''

And so, perhaps, his vigilance relaxed a trifle on the last lap of the journey—which was a pity, because he was quite a likeable man in spite of his sins. Perrigo got him somewhere between Southampton and Waterloo—Perrigo of the big coarse hands that were so quick and skilful with the knife. Thus Frankie Hormer enters the story and departs; and two men have been killed in the first five pages, which is good going.

Of this, Simon Templar knew nothing at the moment. His absorbing

interest in Mr. Perrigo, and particularly in Mr. Perrigo's trousers, developed a little later. But he knew a whole lot of other things closely
connected with the dramatis personae already introduced, for it was part
of the Saint's business to know something about everything that was
happening in certain circles; and on the strength of that he went after
Isadore Elberman in quest of further information.

The structural alterations along the south side of Upper Berkeley Mews,
which had recently been providing the Saint with as much exercise as he
wanted, were not completed; and by means of a slight elaboration of his
original scheme, he was able to enter and leave his home without in any
way disturbing the stolid vigil of the two plain-clothes men who prowled
before his front door, day and night, in a variety of disguises which
afforded his continuous entertainment.

At nine o'clock that night he went upstairs to his bedroom, slid back
the tall pier-glass which adorned one wall, and stepped into a narrow
dimly-lighted passage, closing the panel again behind him. Thus, with
his feet making no sound on the thick felt matting that was laid over the
floor, he passed down the corridor between the back of the mews and the
dummy wall which he had built with his own hands, through numbers
5 and 3—which highly desirable residences had already been re-let to
two impeccably respectable tenants who never knew that their landlord
had a secret right-of-way through their homes. So the Saint came (through
the false back of a wardrobe) into the bedroom of No. 1, which was
occupied by the chauffeur of a Mr. Joshua Pond, who was the owner of
No. 104, Berkeley Square, which adjoined the corner of the mews. Mr.
Pond was not otherwise known to the police as Simon Templar, but he
would have been if the police had been clever enough to discover the
fact. And the Saint left No. 1, Upper Berkeley Mews through another
cupboard in the room at which he had entered it, and reappeared out of
a similar cupboard in one of the bathrooms of No. 104, Berkeley Square,
and so became a free man again, while Chief Inspector Teal's watchers
went on patrolling Upper Berkeley Mews in an ineffable magnificence
of futility which can't really have done them any harm.

This was one of the things that Perrigo didn't know; and the possibility
that the Saint might have any business with Isadore Elberman that night
was another.

Perrigo had got what he wanted. It had been easier than he had expected, for Frankie Hormer had made the mistake of occupying a reserved
compartment all by himself on the boat train. Perrigo walked in on him
with some gold braid pinned to his overcoat and a guard's cap on his

head, and took him by surprise. The trouble had started at Waterloo—
a detective had recognised him in the station, and he had only just
managed to make his getaway.

He reached Elberman's house at Regent's Park by a roundabout route,
and morsed out the prearranged signal on the bell with feverish haste.
The entrance of the house was at the back, in a little courtyard which
contained the doorways of four other houses that also overlooked the
Park. While he waited for the summons to be answered, Perrigo's eyes
searched the shadows with the unsleeping instinct of his calling. But he
did not see the Saint, for the simple reason that the Saint was at the
moment slipping through a first-floor window on the Park side.

Elberman himself opened the door, and recognised his visitor.

"You're late," he said.

His pale bird-like face, behind the owlish spectacles, expressed no
more agitation than his voice. He merely stated the fact—a perkily unemotional little man.

"I had to run for it at Waterloo," said Perrigo shortly.

He pushed into the hall, and shed his overcoat while Elberman barred
the door behind him. Divested of that voluminous garment, he seemed
even huskier than when he was wearing it. His jaw was square and
pugnacious, and his nose had been broken years ago.

Elberman came back and looked up at him inquiringly.

"You weren't followed?"

"Not far."

"Everything else all right?"

Perrigo grunted a curt affirmative. He clapped his hat on a peg and
thrust out his jaw.

"What *you're* talking about's O.K.," he said. "It's the follow-up
that's not jake. When Henderson hears about Frankie, he'll remember
the way I ran—and there's a warrant for me over that Hammersmith job
already."

"You killed Frankie?"

All Elberman's questions were phrased in the same way: they were
flat statements, with the slightest of perfunctory interrogation marks
tacked on to the last syllable.

"Had to," Perrigo said briefly. "Let's get on—I want a drink."

He was as barren of emotion as the Jew, but for a different reason.
Habit had a hand in Perrigo's callousness. In the course of his chequered
career he had been one of Chicago's star torpedoes, until a spot of trouble
that could not be squared had forced him to jump the Canadian border

and thence remove himself from the American continent. There were fourteen notches on his gun—but he was not by nature a boastful man.

Elberman led the way up the stairs, and Perrigo followed at his shoulder.

"Did you get that ticket?"

"Yes, I got you a berth. It's on the *Berengaria*. She sails tomorrow afternoon. You're in a hurry to leave?"

"I'll say I am. I guess it's safe for me to go back now, and I know a dealer in Detroit who'll give me a good price for my share. I'll get enough to give me a big start, and I'll make it grow. There's no money in this durned country."

Elberman shrugged, and opened a door.

He took two paces into the room, and Perrigo took one. And then and there the pair of them halted in their tracks like a Punch and Judy show whose operator has heard the lunch-hour siren, the muscles of their jaws going limp with sheer incredulous astonishment.

2

"COME RIGHT IN, boys," said the Saint breezily.

He reclined gracefully in Isadore Elberman's own sacrosanct armchair. Between the fingers of one hand was a freshly-lit cigarette; the fingers of the other hand curved round the butt of a .38 lead-pump that looked as if it could do everything the makers claimed for it and then some. It was as unsociable-looking a piece of armament as Perrigo had ever seen— and he knew what he was talking about. The sight of it kept his hands straight down and flaccid at his sides, as innocuous as the fists of something out of a waxwork exhibition.

If further pictorial detail is required, it may be provided by mentioning that the Saint was wearing a light grey suit and a silk shirt, both of which showed no traces of ever having been worn before; and an unwary angel might have been pardoned for turning round and hurriedly overhauling its own conscience after getting one glimpse of the radiant innocence of his face.

But most of these interesting points were wasted on the single-track minds of the two men in the doorway. Their retinas, certainly, registered a photographic impression of the general homoscape; but the spotlight of their attention merely oscillated momentarily over the broader features of the picture, and settled back in focus on the salient factor of the whole scenery—the starkly-fashioned chunk of blue steel that stared unwinkingly into the exact centre of the six-inch space between them, only too plainly ready and eager to concentrate its entire affection upon whichever of them first put in a bid for the monopoly.

"Make yourself at home, boys," murmured the Saint. "Perrigo, you may close the door—how did you leave Frankie, by the way?"

Perrigo, with one hand dumbly obedient on the knob, started as if he had received an electric shock. The casual question needled with such an uncanny precison slick into the very core of things that he stared back at the Saint in the dim beginnings of a kind of vengeful terror.

"What do you know about Frankie?" he croaked.

"This and that," said the Saint, nonchanlantly unhelpful. "Carry on shutting the door, brother, and afterwards you may keep on talking." He listened to the click of the latch, and spilled a quantity of cigarette-ash on to Mr. Elberman's priceless carpet. "It was tough on your pal being bumped off in Durban," he continued conversationally, as if had no other object but to put his victims at their ease. "Also, in my opinion, unnecessary. I know Frankie was inclined to be cagey, but I think a clever man could have found out what ship he was sailing home on without sending a man out to South Africa to spy on him. . . . Come in, boys, come in. Sit down. Have a drink. I want you to feel happy."

"Who are you?" snarled Perrigo.

Simon shifted his mocking gaze to Elberman.

"Do you know, Isadore?"

Elberman shook his head, moistening his lips mechanically.

Simon smiled, and stood up.

"Sit down," he said.

He ushered the two men forcefully into chairs, relieving Perrigo of a shooting-iron during the process. And then he put his back to the fire and leaned against the mantelpiece, spinning his gun gently round one finger hooked in the trigger-guard.

"I might deceive you," he said with disarming candour, "but I won't. I am the Saint." He absorbed the reflex ripples of expression that jerked over the seated men, and smiled again. "Yes—I'm the guy you've been wanting to meet all these years. I am the man with the load of mischief. I," said the Saint, who was partial to the personal pronoun, and apt to become loquacious when he found that it could start a good sentence, "am the Holy Terror, and the only thing for you boys to do is to try and look pleased about it. I'm on the point of taking a longish holiday, and my bank balance is just a few pounds shy of the amount I'd fixed for my pension. You may not have heard anything about it before, but you are going to make a donation to the fund."

The two men digested his speech in silence. It took them a little time, which the Saint did not begrudge them. He always enjoyed these moments. He allowed the gist of the idea to percolate deeply into their brains, timing the seconds by the regular spinning of his gun. There were six of them. Then—

"What d'you want?" snarled Perrigo.

"Diamonds," said the Saint succinctly.

"What diamonds?"

Perrigo's voice cracked on the question. The boil of belligerent animosity with him split through the thin overlay of puzzlement in which he tried to clothe his words, and tore the flimsy bluff to shreds. And the Saint's eyes danced.

"The illicit diamonds," he said, "which Frankie Hormer was bringing over by the arrangement with Isadore. The diamonds for which Isadore double-crossed Frankie and took you into partnership, my pet. The boodle that you've got on your person right now, Pretty Perrigo!"

"I don't know what you're talking about."

"No? Then perhaps Isadore will explain."

Again the Saint's bantering attention transferred itself to the owner of the house, but Elberman said nothing.

And Simon shook his head sadly.

"You may be the hell of a bright conspirator, Isadore," he remarked, "but you seem to be the odd man out of this *conversazione*. Pardon me while I do my Wild West stuff."

He unbuttoned his coat and took a length of light cord from an inside pocket. There was a running bowline ready at one end of it: he crossed to the Jew's chair and dropped the noose over Elberman's head, letting it settle down to his waist. With a brisk yank and a couple of twists he had the man's arms pinioned to his sides and the complete exhibit attached to the chair, finishing off with a pair of nonskid knots. He performed the entire operation with his left hand, and the gun in his right hand never ceased to keep the situation under effective control.

Then he turned to Perrigo.

"Where are they, sweetheart?" he inquired laconically; and the man tightened up a vicious lower lip.

"They're where you won't find them," he said.

Simon shrugged.

"This place does not exist," he said.

His glance quartered Perrigo with leisurely approbation—north to south, east to west. Somewhere in the area it covered was a hundred thousand pounds' worth of crystallised carbon, which wouldn't take up much room. A search through the man's pockets would only have taken a few seconds; but the saint rather liked being clever. And sometimes he had inspirations of uncanny brilliance.

"Your trousers and coat don't match." he said abruptly.

The inspiration grew larger, whizzing out of the back of beyond with the acceleration of something off Daytona Beach, and the jump that Perrigo gave kicked it slap into the immediate urgent present.

"And I'll bet Frankie Hormer's don't, either," said the Saint.

The words came out in a snap.

And then he laughed. He couldn't help it. His long shot had gone welting through the bull's-eye with point-blank accuracy, and the scoring of the hit was registered on Perrigo's face as plainly as if a battery of coloured lamps had lighted up and a steam organ had begun to play *Down Among the Dead Men* to celebrate the event.

"What's the joke?" demanded Perrigo harshly; and Simon pulled himself together.

"Let me reconstruct it. Diamonds are precious things—especially when they're the kind about which possession is the whole ten points of the law. If you're packing a load of that variety around you, you don't take chances with 'em. You keep 'em as close to you as they'll go. You don't even carry them in your pockets, because pockets have their dangers. You sew them into your clothes. Frankie did, anyway. Wait a minute!" The Saint was working back like lightning over the ground he knew. He grabbed another thread and hauled it out of the skein—and it matched. "Why didn't you cut the diamonds out of Frankie's clothes? If you had time to trade clothes, you had time to do that. Then it must have been because it was dangerous. Why so? Because Frankie was dead! Because you didn't want to leave a clue to your motive. You killed Frankie, and— Hold the line, Perrigo!" The gangster was coming out of his chair, but Simon's gun checked him half-way. "You killed Frankie," said the Saint, "and you changed your coat for his."

Perrigo relaxed slowly.

"I don't know what you're talking about," he said.

"You do. You're three minutes late with your bluff. The train has pulled out and left you in the gentlemen's cloak-room. Where you have no right to be. Take off that coat!"

Perrigo hesitated for a moment; and then, sullenly, he obeyed.

He threw the garment down at the Saint's feet, and Simon dropped on one knee. With the flat of his hand he went padding over every inch of the coat, feeling for the patch of tell-tale hardness that would indicate the whereabout of Frankie Hormer's half-million-dollar cargo.

That was the sort of happy harvest that it was an unadulterated pleasure for the Saint to reap—the kind in which you just winked at the ears, and they hopped down off their stalks and marched in an orderly fashion into the barn. It made him feel at peace with the world. . . . Down the sleeves he went, with tingling fingers, and over the lapels. . . . Almost like lifting shoe-laces out of a blind beggar's tray, it was. . . . He went along the bottom of the coat and up the back. He turned the pockets inside out, and investigated a wallet which he found in one of them.

And then, with a power-driven vacuum pump starting work on his interior, he turned the coat over and began again.

He wouldn't have been mistaken. He'd been as sure of his deductions as any man can be. The aptness of them had been placarded all over the place. And never in his life before had one of those moments of inspiration led him astray. He had grown to accept the conclusions they drew and the procedures they dictated as things no less inevitable and infallible then the laws of Nature that make water run downhill and mountains sit about the world with their fat ends undermost. And now, with a direct controversion of his faith right under his groping hands, he felt as if he were seeing Niagara Falls squirting upwards into Lake Ontario, while the Peak of Teneriffe perambulated about on its head with its splayed roots waving among the clouds.

For the first search had yielded nothing at all.

And the second search produced no more.

"Is—that—really—so!" drawled the Saint.

He stared at Perrigo without goodwill, and read the sneer in the other's eyes. It touched the rawest part of the Saint's most personal vanity—but he didn't tell the world.

"Thinking again?" Perrigo gibed.

"Why, yes," said the Saint mildly. "I often do it."

He stood up unconcernedly, fishing for his cigarette-case, and lighted another cigarette, still allowing nothing to distract the relentless aim of his automatic.

Somewhere there was a leak in the pipe, and his brain was humming out to locate it.

From Elberman there was nothing to be learned—the Jew sat placidly where the Saint had roped him, outwardly unperturbed by what was happening, apparently satisfied to leave what small chance there was of effective opposition in the hands of Perrigo. And Elberman probably knew no more than the Saint, anyhow.

No—the secret was locked up behind the narrowed glinting eyes of Perrigo. Somewhere in the mind of that tough baby was stored the sole living human knowledge of the fate of the biggest packet of illicit diamonds ever brought into England in one batch; and Simon Templar was going to extract that knowledge if he had to carve it out with dynamite and rock-drills.

3

"I HEARD YOU were clever." Perrigo spoke again, rasping into the breach in a voice that was jagged with spiteful triumph. "Got a reputation, haven't you? I'll say you must have earned it."

"Sure I did," assented the Saint, with a gaze like twin pin-points of blue fire.

And then a thunder of knocking on the front door drummed up through the house and froze the three of them into an instant's bewildered immobility.

It was, if the Saint had but known it at that moment, the herald of an interruption that was destined to turn that exceedingly simple adventure into the most riotous procession that the chronicler has yet been called upon to record. It was the starting gun for the wildest of all wild-goose chases. It was, in its essence, the beginning of the Melancholy Journey of Mr. Teal. If the Saint had known it, he would have chalked up the exact time on the wall and drawn a halo round it. But he did not know.

He stiffened up like a pointer, with his head cocked on one side and two short vertical lines etching in between his eyebrows. The clamorous insistence of that knocking boded no welcome visitor. There was nothing furtive or sympathetic about it—nothing that one could associate with any possible client of a receiver of stolen goods. It hammered up the stairway in an atmosphere of case-hardened determination. And then it stopped, and grimly awaited results.

Simon looked from Elberman to Perrigo, and back again. He intercepted the glances that passed between them, and gathered from them a joint nescience equal to his own. In Perrigo's eyes there was suspicion and interrogation, in Elberman's nothing but an answering blank.

"Throwing a party?" murmured the Saint.

In silence he inhaled from his cigarette, and flicked it backwards into the fire. Listening intently, he heard through the window on his left the single sharp pip of a motor-horn sounding on a peculiar note. And the knocking below started again.

There was no doubt about its intentions this time. It signified its uncompromising determination to be noticed, and added a rider to the effect that if it wasn't noticed damned quickly it was perfectly prepared to bust down the door and march in regardless.

"So you've brought the cops, have you?" grated Perrigo.

He came recklessly out of his chair.

The obvious solution had dawned upon him a second after it dawned upon the Saint, and he acted accordingly. His interpretation was all wrong, but his reasoning process was simple.

To the Saint, however, the situation remained the same, whatever Perrigo thought. With the police outside, his gun was temporarily useless as a piece of scrap-iron. And besides, he wanted further converse with Perrigo. Those three hundred carats of compact mazuma were still somewhere in Perrigo's charge, and Simon Templar was not going home without them. Therefore the bluff was called. Perrigo had got to stay alive, aesthetically distressing as his continued existence might be.

Simon pocketed his gun and stood foursquare to the fact. He slipped his head under Perrigo's smashing fist, and lammed into the gangster's solar plexus a half-arm jolt that sogged home like a battering-ram writhing, and the Saint grinned.

"Sing to him, Isadore," he instructed hopefully, and went briskly out on to the landing.

That toot on the horn outside the window had been Patricia's signal to say that something troublesome was looming up and that she was wide awake; but the first item of information was becoming increasingly self-evident. As Simon went down the stairs, the clattering on the front door broke out again, reinforced by impatient peals on the bell, and the door itself was shaking before an onslaught of ponderous shoulders as the Saint turned out the light and drew the bolts.

A small avalanche of men launched themselves at him out of the gloom. Simon hacked one of them on the shins and secured a crippling grip on the nose of another; and then someone found the switch and put the light on again, and the Saint looked along his arms and found that his fingers were firmly clamped on the proboscis of Chief Inspector Teal himself.

"Why, it's Claud Eustace!" cried the Saint, without moving.

Teal shook the hand savagely off his nose, and wiped his streaming eyes.

"What the hell are you doing here?" he brayed.

"Playing dingbat through the daisies," said the Saint.

All the debonair gay impudence that he possessed was glimmering around his presence like a sort of invisible aurora borealis, and the perception of it made something seethe up through the detective like a gush of boiling lava. His brows knitted down over a glare of actual malevolence.

"Yes? And where's Perrigo?"

"He's upstairs."

"Since when?"

"About half an hour."

"And when did you arrive?"

"Roughly simultaneous, I should say."

"What for?"

"Well, if you must know," said the Saint, "I heard a rumour that Perrigo had discovered the second rhyme to 'Putney,' which I wanted for a limerick I was trying to compose. I thought of an old retired colonel of Putney, who lived on dill pickles and chutney, till one day he tried chilis boiled with carbide, tiddy dum diddy utney. It's all very difficult."

Teal unfastened his coat and signed to one of the men who were with him.

"Take him," he ordered curtly.

Simon put his hands in his pockets and leaned against the wall with an air of injury.

"In your own words—what for?" he inquired; and a little of Chief Inspector Teal's old pose of heavy sleepiness returned. It was an affectation on which the detective had lately been losing a lot of his grip.

"A man named Hormer, a diamond smuggler, was murdered on the train between Southampton and Waterloo this evening. Perrigo was seen at Waterloo. I want him on suspicion of having commited the murder, and I'm going to take you on suspicion of being an accessory."

"Sorry," said the Saint; and something about the way he said it made Teal's baby blue eyes go dark and beady.

"Going to tell me you've got another alibi?"

"I am."

"I'll hear about that later."

"You'll hear about it now." The arrogant forefinger which Teal had learned to hate as personally as if it had a separate individual existence prodded into the gibbosity of his waistline with unequivocal emphasis. "From seven o'clock till eight-fifteen I was having dinner at Dorchester House—which includes the time that train got in. I had two friends with me. I talked to the head waiter, I discussed vintages with the wine waiter, and I gave the *maître d' hotel* a personal lesson in the art of making perfect *crêpes suzette*. Go and ask 'em. And ask your own flat-footed oaf outside my house what time he saw me come in."

Teal champed grimly on his gum.

"I didn't accuse you of committing the murder," he said. "I'm having you for an accessory, and you can prove you were in Nova Scotia at the time for all that'll help you. Tell me you're going to prove you're in Nova Scotia right now, and perhaps I'll listen."

The Saint's brain functioned at racing speed.

A neat handful of spiky little facts pickled into its machinery, graded themselves, and were dealt with. One—that Perrigo had still got the diamonds. Two—that the diamonds must be detached from Perrigo. Three—that the detaching must not be done by Claud Eustace Teal. Four—that the Saint must therefore remain a free agent. Five—that the Saint would not remain a free agent if Claud Eustace Teal could help it.

Item five was fairly crackling about in the subtler undertones of the detective's drowsy voice, and it was that item which finally administered the upward heave to the balloon. The Teal-Templar feud was blowing up to bursting point, and nobody knew it better than the Saint. But he also knew something else, which was that the burst was going to spray out into the maddest and merriest rodeo that ever was. Simon Templar proposed personally to supervise the spray.

He slipped his hands out of his pockets, and a very Saintly smile touched his lips.

"I might even prove something like that," he said.

And then he pushed Teal backwards and went away in one wild leap. He had reached the foot of the stairs before the detectives had fully grasped what was happening, and he took the steps in flights of four at a pace that no detective in England could have approached. He made the upper landing before they were properly started. There was a big oak chest on that landing—Simon had noticed it on his way down—and he hulked it off the wall and ran it to the top of the stairs.

"Watch your toes, boys," he sang out, and shoved.

The three men below looked up and saw the chest hurtling down upon them. Having no time to get from under, they braced themselves and took the shock. And there they stuck, half-way up and half-way down. The huge iron-bound coffer tobogganed massively into them, two hundredweight of it if there was an ounce, and jammed them in their tracks. They couldn't go round, they couldn't go over, and it was several seconds before some incandescent intellect conceived the idea of going back.

Which was some time after the Saint had renewed his hectic acquaintance with Gunner Perrigo.

He found the gangster on his feet by a side table, cramming some papers into a shabby wallet. Perrigo's face was still contorted with agony, but he turned and crouched for a fight as the Saint burst in. As a matter of fact, the Saint was the last person he had ever expected to see again that night, and his puzzled amazement combined with the gesture of the Saint's up-raised hand to check him where he was.

"Hold everything, Beautiful," said the Saint. "The police are in, and you and I are pulling our freight together."

He locked the door and strode coolly past the dumbfounded hoodlum. Flinging the window wide, he looked down into the private gardens that adjoined Gloucester Terrace and the park beyond. He saw shadows that moved, and knew that the house was surrounded. Simon waved a cheery hand to the cordon and closed the window again.

He turned back to Perrigo.

"Is there a way over the roof, or a back staircase?" he asked.

The man looked at him, his underlip jutting.

"What's the idea, Templar?"

"The idea is to get to hell out of here," said the Saint crisply. "Tell me what you know—and tell it quick!"

Perrigo glowered at him uncertainly, and in the silence they heard Teal's invading contingent arriving profanely on the landing.

And Perrigo made up his mind.

"There's no way out," he said.

He spoke the truth as far as he knew it; but the Saint laughed.

"Then we'll go out that way!"

The door-handle rattled, and the woodwork creaked under an impacting weight; and Elberman suddenly roused out of his long retirement.

"And vot happens to me?" he squeaked, with his laboriously cultivated accent scattering to the four winds. "Vot do I say ven dey com' in?"

Simon walked to the mantelpiece and picked up a large globular vase, from which he removed the artificial flowers.

"You stay here and sing," he said, and forced the pot down firmly over the receiver's ears.

Outside, Chief Inspector Teal settled his hat and stepped back a pace. The casket that had delayed him was at the bottom of the stairs then, but if Teal could have had his way with it it would have been at the bottom of the nethermost basement in Gehenna.

"All together," he snapped.

Three brawny shoulders moved as one, and the door splintered inwards.

Except for Isadore Elberman, struggling like a maniac to shake the porcelain cowl off his head, the room was empty of humanity.

Teal's glance scorched round it. There was plenty of furniture, but not a thing that would have given cover to a full-grown man. Then he saw a communicating door in another wall, and swore.

He dashed through, leaving his men to deal with the easy prisoner. Curtains flapping before an open window caught his eye, and instinctively he went over and stuck his head out. A man standing by a bush below looked up.

"Seen anyone?" Teal shouted.

"No, sir."

Teal withdrew his head and noticed a second door standing ajar. He went through it and found himself back on the landing he had just left, and his language became lurid.

Simon Templar and Perrigo stopped for a moment in the hall. Perrigo was a tough guy from the Uskides upwards, but Simon felt personally responsible for his safety and he took the responsibility seriously. There were irrefutable financial reasons for his solicitude—one hundred thousand of them. And for the duration of that fast-travelling episode he had got Perrigo's confidence. He tapped the gangster's bosom impressively.

"In case we should get separated, 7, Upper Berkeley Mews is the address," he stated. "See you remember it."

Perrigo gloomed sidelong at him, still fuddled with suspicious perplexity.

"I don't want to see you again," he growled.

"You will," said the Saint, and pushed him onwards.

Chief Inspector Teal floundered to the top of the stairs, and two of his men pressed closely behind him. They looked down and saw Simon Templar alone in the hall, hands on hips, with his back to the door and an angelic smile on his upturned face.

"About that rhyme," said the Saint. "I've thought of something. Suppose the old colonel 'went up in smoke for his gluttony'? Would the Poet Laureate pass it? Would Wilhelmina Stitch approve?"

"Get him!" snapped Teal.

The detectives swept down in a bunch.

They saw the Saint open the door, and heard outside the sharp pipping of a motor-horn. Patricia Holm was cruising round. But this they did not know. The door slammed shut again, and as a kind of multiple echo to the slam came the splattering crackle of an automatic. It fired four times, and then Teal got the door open.

he faced a considerable volume of pitchy darkness, out of which spoke the voice of one of the men he had posted to guard the courtyard.

"I'm sorry, sir—they got away."

"What happened?"

"Shot out the lights and slipped us in the dark, sir."

Way down the road, a horn tooted seven times, derisively.

4

A TINGE OF old beetroot suffused Mr. Teal's rubicund complexion.

To say that his goat was completely and omnipotently got conveys nothing at all. In the last ten minutes his goat had been utterly annihilated, and the remains spirited away to the exact point in space where (so Einstein says) eternity changes its socks and starts back on the return journey. He was as comprehensively de-goated as a man can be.

With a foaming cauldron of fury bubbling just below his collar, he stood and watched his two out-posts come up the steps towards him.

"Did you see Perrigo?" he rasped.

"Yes, sir. He came out first, and waited. I didn't recognise him at once—thought it was one of our own men. Then another bloke came out—"

Teal turned on the men behind him.

"And what are you loafing about here for?" he stormed. "D'you want your nannies to hold your hands when you go out at night? Get after them!"

He left the pursuit in their hands, and fumed back up the stairs. There he found a bedraggled Isadore Elberman, released at last from his eccentric headgear, in charge of a plain-clothes constable. The receiver was as loquacious as Teal allowed him to be.

"You can't hold me for nothing, Mr. Teal. Those men attacked me and tied me up. You saw how I was fixed when you came in."

"I know all about you," said Teal unpleasantly.

Elberman blinked rapidly.

"Now you listen and I tell you somethings, Mr. Teal. I don't like Perrigo. He's stole some tickets and never pay me for them, nor nothing else vot he owes me. You catch him and I'll tell you all about him. I'm an innocent man vot's been robbed. Now I'll tell you."

"You can tell the magistrate in the morning," said Teal.

He was in no mood to listen patiently to anyone. His temper had been jagged over with a cross-cut saw. Simon Templar had tweaked his nose for the umpteenth time, literally and figuratively; and the realisation of it was making Teal's palms sweat. It mattered nothing that a warrant to arrest the Saint could be obtained for the trouble of asking for it, and that the Saint could probably be located in fifteen minutes by the elementary process of going to No. 7, Upper Berkeley Mews and ringing the bell. Time after time Teal had thought his task was just as easy, and time after time he had found a flourishing colony of bluebottles using his ointment for a breeding ground. It had gone on until Teal was past feeling the faintest tremour of optimism over anything less than a capture of the Saint red-handed, with stereoscopic cameras trained on the scene and a board of bishops standing by for witnesses. And something dimly approaching that ideal had offered itself that night—only to slither through his fingers and flip him in the eye with its departing tail.

He had no real enthusiasm for the arrest of Elberman, and even his interest in Perrigo had waned. The Saint filled his horizon to the exclusion of everything else. With a morose detachment he watched the Jew removed in a taxi, and stayed on in the same spirit to receive the reports of the men who had been down the road.

These were not helpful.

"We went as far as Euston Road in the squad car, sir, but it wasn't any use. They had too long a start."

Teal had expected no better. He gave his subordinates one crowded minute of the caustic edge of his tongue for not having got on the job more promptly, and was mad with himself for doing it. Then he dismissed them.

"And give my love to your Divisional Inspector." he said. "Tell him I like his officers. And when I want some dumb-bell exericse, I'll send for you again."

He made his exit on that line, and was sourly aware that their surprised and reproachful glances followed him out of the house.

He realised that the Saint had got under his skin more deeply than he knew. Never in any ordinary circumstances could the stoical and even-tempered Mr. Teal have been moved to pass the buck to his helpless underlings in such a fashion.

And Teal didn't care. As he climbed into his car, the broiling crucibles of fury within him were simmering down to a steady white-hot calidity of purpose. By the time he got to grips with his man again, the Saint would probably have another peck of dust ready to throw in his eyes, some new smooth piece of hokum laid out for him to skate over. Teal was prepared for it. It made no difference to him. His whole universe at that moment comprised but one ambition—to hound Simon Templar into a corner form which there could be no escape, corral him there, and proceed to baste into him every form of discourtesy and dolour permitted by the laws of England. And he was going to do it if it took him forty years and travelled him four thousand miles.

Some of which it did—but this prophecy was hidden from him.

The most inexorably wrathful detective in the British Isles, Chief Inspector Claud Eustace Teal stepped on the gas and walloped into the second lap of his odyssey, heading for Upper Berkeley Mews.

5

SIMON TEMPLAR GARAGED his gat in a side pocket and leapt into the darkness. The men outside were on their toes for concerted action, but the dousing of the lights beat them. Simon swerved nimbly round the noises of their blundering, and sprinted for the square patch of twilight that indicated the way out of the courtyard.

His fingers hooked on the brickwork at the side of the opening as he reached it, and he fetched round into the road on a tight hair-pin turn that brought him up with his back to the wall outside. A yard or two to his left he saw the parking lights of a car gliding along the kerb.

Then Perrigo came plunging out. He skidded round the same turn and picked up his stride again without a pause. Simon shot off the wall and closed alongside him. He grabbed Perrigo's arm.

"The car—you won't make it on foot!"

He sprang for the running-board as he spoke—Patricia was keeping level, with the Hirondel dawdling easily along in second. Perrigo looked round hesitantly, making the pace flat-footed. Then he also hauled himself aboard.

"Right away, lass," said the Saint.

The great car surged forward, sprawling Perrigo head over heels on to the cushions of the back seat. Patricia changed up without a click, and Simon swung himself lightly over into place beside her.

"Well?" she asked calmly; and the Saint laughed.

"Oh, we had quite a jolly little party."

"What happened?"

Simon lighted a cigarette, and inhaled with deep satisfaction.

"Claud Eustace Teal's stomach walked in, closely followed by Claud Eustace. It was most extraordinary. Subsequently, I walked out. Claud Eustace is now thinking that that was even more extraordinary."

Patricia nodded.

"I saw the men getting into the gardens, and then I drove round to the back and saw the squad car. Did you have much trouble?"

"Nothing to speak of." The Saint was slewed round in his seat, his keen eyes searching back up the road. "I pulled Teal's nose, told him a perfectly drawing-room limerick, and left him to think it over. . . . I should turn off again here, old darling—they're certain to be after us."

The girl obeyed.

And then she flashed the Saint a smile, and she said: "Boy, I was all set to crash that squad car if they'd tried to take you away in it."

The Saint started.

"You were which?"

"Sure, I'd have wrecked that car all right."

"And then?"

"I'd have got you out somehow."

"Pat, have you gone loco?"

She laughed, and shook her head, hustling the car recklessly down the long clear street.

Simon gazed at her thoughtfully.

It was typical of him that even then he was able to do that—and do it with his whole attention on the job. But the longer you knew him, the more amazing did that characteristic of light-hearted insouciance become. The most tempestuous incidents of his turbulent life occupied just as much of his mind as he allotted to them, and no more. And their claims were repudiated altogether by such a mood of scapegrace devilment as descended upon him at that instant.

He took in the features that he knew even better than his own with a new sense of delight. They stood out fair and clean-cut against the speeding background of sombre buildings—the small nose, the finely modelled forehead, the firm chin, the red lips slightly parted, the eyes gay and shining. The wind whipped a faint flush into her cheeks and swept back her hair like a golden mane.

She turned to him, knowing his eyes were on her.

"What are you thinking, lad?"

"I'm thinking that I shall always want to remember you as I'm seeing you now," said the Saint.

One of the small strong hands came off the wheel and rested on his knee. He covered it with his own.

"I'm glad I was never a gentleman," he said.

They raced on, carving a wide circle out of the map of London. Traffic crossing delayed them here and there, but they kept as much as possible to unfrequented side streets, and moved fast. Perrigo sat in the back and brooded, with his coat collar turned up over his ears. His cosmos was still in a dizzy whirl, which he was trying to reduce to some sort of coherence. The vicissitudes that had somersaulted upon him from all angles during the past forty-five minutes had hopelessly dislocated his bearings. One minute the Saint was thumping him in the stomach, the next minute he was helping him on with his hat. One minute the Saint was preparing to hoist him, the next minute he was yanking him out of a splice. One minute the Saint seemed to have a direct hook-up with the police, the next minute he was leading the duck-out with all the zeal of an honest citizen avoiding contact with a member of Parliament. It was a bit too much for Gunner Perrigo, a simple soul for whom the solution of all reasonable problems lay in the breech of a Smith-Wesson.

But out of the chaos one imperishable thought emerged to the forefront of his consciousness, and it was that which motivated his eventual decision. One bifurcated fact stood indefeasible amid the maelstrom. The Saint knew too much, and the Saint had at one time announced his intention of hijacking a certain parcel of diamonds. And the two prongs of that fact linked up and pointed to a single certainty: that the safest course for Gunner Perrigo was to get the hell out of any place where the Saint might be—and to make the voyage alone.

The car was held up at an Oxford Street crossing, and the Saint's back was towards him. Perrigo thought he had it all his own way.

But he had reckoned without the driving mirror. For several minutes past the Saint had been doing a lot of Perrigo's thinking for him, and the imminence of some such manoeuvre as that had been keeping him on the tip-toe of alertness. Throughout that time the driving mirror had never been out of the tail of his eye, and he spotted Perrigo's stealthy movement almost before it had begun.

He turned his head and smiled sweetly.

"No," he said.

Perrigo squinted at him, sinking back a trifle.

"I can look after myself now," he grunted.

"You can't," said the Saint.

He was turning round again when Perrigo set his teeth, jumped up, and wrenched at the handle of the door.

It flew open; and then the Saint put one foot on the front seat and went over into the tonneau in a flying tackle.

He took Perrigo with him. They pelted over into the back seat in a lashing welter of legs and arms, fighting like savages. Perrigo had the weight and brute strength, but Simon had the speed and cunning. The car lurched forward again while they rolled over and over in a flailing thudding tangle. After a few seconds of it, the Saint got an arm loose and whipped in a couple of pile-driving rib-binders; the effects of them put him on top of the mess, and he wedged Perrigo vigorously into a corner and held him there with a knee in his chest.

Then he looked up at the familiar helmet of a police contable, and found that the car had stopped.

They were in one of the narrow streets in the triangle of which Regent and Oxford form two sides. A heavy truck and a brace of taxis had combined to put a temporary plug in the meagre passage, and the constable happened to be standing by. Patricia was looking round helplessly.

"Wot's this?" demanded the Law, and Simon smiled winningly.

"We are secret emissaries of the Sheik Ali ben Dova, and we have sworn to place the sacred domestic utensil of the Caliph on top of the Albert Memorial.''

"Wot?''

"Well, what I mean is that my friend is rather drunk, and that's his idea.''

The Law produced a notebook.

"Any 'ow,'' he said, "you got no right to be treating 'im like that.''

Perrigo's mouth opened, and Simon shifted some more weight on to his knee. Perrigo choked and went red in the face.

"Ah, but you've no idea how violent he gets when he's had a few,'' said the Saint. "Goes quite bats. I'm trying to get him home now before he does any damage.''

"Help!'' yapped Perrigo feebly.

"Gets delusions, and all that sort of thing,'' said the Saint. "Thinks people are trying to kidnap him and murder him and so forth. Fancies everyone he meets is a notorious criminal. Doesn't even recognise his own wife—this is his wife, officer. Leads her an awful life. I don't know why she married the fool. And yet if you met him when he was sober, you'd take him for the most respectable gentleman you ever saluted. And he is, too. Man with a big diamond business. Right now, he's worth more money than you could save out of your salary if you were in the Force another three hundred years and lived on air.''

Patricia leaned over pleadingly.

"Oh, officer, it's dreadful!'' she cried. "Please try to understand—please help me to save a scandal! Last time, the magistrate said he'd send my husband to prison if it happened again.''

"I'm not your husband!'' howled Perrigo. "I'm being robbed! Officer—''

"You see?'' said the Saint. "Just what I told you. Three weeks ago he fired a shot-gun at the postman because he said he was trying to put a bomb in the letter-box.''

The policeman looked doubtfully from his to the lovely anxious face of Patricia, and was visibly moved. And then Perrigo heaved up again.

"Don't you know who this guy is?'' he blurted. "He's the Sglooglphwf—''

This was not what Perrigo meant to say, but Simon clapped a hand over his mouth.

"Uses the most frightful language, too, when he's like this,'' said the Saint confidentially. "I couldn't even repeat what he called the cook when he thought she was sprinkling arsenic on the potatoes. If I had my way he'd be locked up. He's a dangerous lunatic, that's what he is—''

Suddenly the policeman's eyes glazed.

"Wot's that?" he barked.

Simon glanced round. His automatic lay in a corner of the seat, clear to view—it must have fallen out of his pocket during the scramble. It gleamed up accusingly from the glossy green leather upholstery, and every milligram of the accusation was reflected in the constable's fixed and goggling eyes. . . .

Simon drew a deep breath.

"Oh, that's just one of the props. We've been to a rehearsal of one of these amateur dramatic shows—"

The constable's head ducked with unexpected quickness. It pressed down close to the face of Perrigo, and when it raised itself again there was blunt certitude written all over it.

"*That* man ain't bin drinking," it pronounced.

"Deodorised gin," explained the Saint easily. "A new invention for the benefit of A.W.O.L. matrimoniates. Wonderful stuff. No longer can it be said that the wages of gin is breath."

The policeman straightened up.

"Ho, yus? Well, I think you better come round to the station, and let's 'ear some more about this."

The Saint shook his head.

He looked over the front of the car, and saw that the jam ahead had sorted itself out, and the road was clear. One hand touched Patricia's shoulder. And he smiled very seraphically.

"Sorry," he said. "We've got that date with the Albert Memorial."

He struck flat-handed at the policeman's shoulder, sending him staggering back; and as he did so Patricia engaged the gears and the Hirondel rocketed off the mark again like a shell from a howitzer.

Simon and Perrigo spilled over in another wild flurry. This time the objective was the gun on the seat. Simon got it. He also got Perrigo effectively screwed down to the mat, and knelt heavily on his biceps. The cold muzzle of the automatic rammed up under Perrigo's chin.

"That will be the end of your bonehead act, brother," said the Saint tersely. "You'd better understand that the only chance you've got is with me. You're a stranger over here. If I left you on your own, Teal would have you behind bars in record time. You wouldn't last twenty-four hours. And if you'd been able to make that cop take notice of you the way you wanted, you wouldn't have lasted twenty-four minutes—he'd have lugged you off to the station with the rest of us, and that would have been your finale. Get that up under your skull. And then put this beside it: you can't make your getaway now without consulting me. I've got your passport and your ticket to New York right next to my heart—dipped them out of your pocket before we left Isadore's. Which is why you're going to stick as close to me as you know how. When I'm through with you, I'll give you the bum's rush quick enough—but not before!''

6

THE HIRONDEL SKIMMED round a corner and flashed out into Regent Street. The bows of an omnibus loomed up, bearing down upon them. Patricia spun the wheel coolly; they swerved round the wrong side of an island, dodged a taxi and a private car, and dived off the main road again.

Perrigo, on the floor of the tonneau, digested the fresh set of facts that the Saint had streamed into him. However apocryphal the first sheaf that he had meditated had been, these new ones were definitely concise and concrete—as was the circle of steel that bored steadily into his dewlap. He assimilated them in a momentous silence, while the stars gyrated giddily above him.

"All right," he said at length. "Let me up."

Simon hitched himself on to the seat; his gun went into his pocket, but retained command of the situation. As they entered Berkeley Square he watched Perrigo looking out to left and right, and was prompted to utter an additional warning.

"Stepping off moving vehicles," he said, "is the cause of umpteen street accidents per annum. If you left us now, it would be the cause of umpteen plus one. Ponder the equation, brother. . . . And besides," said the Saint, who was starting to feel expansive again, "we've only just begun to know each other. The warbling and the woofling dies, so to speak, and we settle down to get acquainted. We approach the peaceful interlude

> *When the cakes and ale are over*
> *And the buns and beer run dry,*
> *And the pigs are all in clover*
> *Up above the bright blue sky—*

as the poet hath it. Do you ever write poetry?''

Perrigo said nothing.

"He does not write poetry," said the Saint.

The car stopped a few yards from the entrance of Upper Berkeley Mews, and Simon leaned forward and put his elbows on the back of the front seat. He rested his chin on his hands.

"When we were interrupted, darling," he said, "I was on the point of making some remarks about your mouth. It is, bar none, the most bewitching, alluring, tempting, maddening, seductive mouth I've ever kiss—set eyes on. The idea that it should ever be used for eating kippers is sacreligious. You will oblige me by eating no more kippers. The way your lips curl at the corners when you're not sure whether you'll smile or not—''

Patricia turned with demure eyes.

"What do we do now?" she asked; and the Saint sighed.

"Teal's bloodhound saw you go out?"

"Yes."

"Then he'd better see you go in again. It'll set his mind at rest. Bertie and I will go our ways.''

He opened the door and stepped out. Perrigo followed, being constrained to do so by a grip which the Saint had fastened on the scruff of his neck. Maintaining possession of Perrigo, Simon leaned on the side of the car.

"When we get a minute or two to ourselves, Pat," he said, "remind me that my discourse on your eyes, which occupies about two hundred and fifty well-chosen words—''

"Is to be continued in our next," said Patricia happily, and let in the clutch.

Simon stood for a moment where she had left him, watching the car swing round into the mews.

And he was realising that the warbling and the woofling were very near their end. His flippant parody had struck home into the truth.

It was a queer moment for that blithe young cavalier of fortune. Out of the clear sky of the completely commonplace, it had flashed down upon him with a blinding brightness. The lights pointed to the end. No tremendous battle had done it, no breathless race for life, no cataclysmic instant of vision when all the intangible battlements of Paradise were shown up under the shadow of the sword. Fate, in the cussedness of its own inscrutable designs, had ordained that the revelation should be otherwise. Something simple and startling, a thing seen so often and grown so tranquilly familiar that the sudden unmasking of its inner portent would sweep away all the foundations of his belief like a tidal wave; something that would sheer ruthlessly through all sophistries and lies. A girl's profile against the streaking backcloth of smoke-stained stone. Yellow lamplight rippling on a flying mane of golden hair. *Commedia.*

On the night of the 3rd of April, at 10:30 p.m., Simon Templar stood on the pavement of Berkeley Square and looked life squarely in the eyes.

Just for that moment. And then the Hirondel was gone, and the moment was past. But all that there was to be done was done. The High Gods had spoken.

Simon turned. There was a new light in his eyes.

"Let's go," he said.

They went. His step was light and swift, and the blood laughed in his veins. He had drunk the magic wine of the High Gods at one draught, down to the last dregs. It is a brave man who can do that, and he has his reward.

Perrigo walked tamely by his side. Simon had less than no idea what was passing in the gangster's mind just then. And he cared less than nothing. He would have taken on a hundred Perrigos that night, one after another or in two squads of fifty, just as they pleased—blipped them, bounced them, boned them, rolled them, trussed them up, wrapped them in grease-proof paper, and laid them out in a row to be called for by the corporation scavengers. And if Perrigo didn't believe it, Perrigo had only got to start something and see what happened. Simon thought less of Perrigo than a resolute rhinoceros would think of a small worm.

He ran up the steps of 104, Berkeley Square, turned his key in the lock, and switched on the lights. He made way for Perrigo with a courtly gesture.

"In," he said.

Perrigo walked in very slowly. Some fresh plan of campaign was formulating behind the gangster's sullen compliance. Simon knew it. He knew that the ice was very thin—that only the two trump cards of passport and tickets, and the superb assurance with which they had been played, had driven Perrigo so far without a third bid for freedom. And he was not interested. As Perrigo's rearward foot lifted over the threshold, Simon shoved him on, followed him in a flash, and put his back to the closed door.

"You're thinking," he murmured, "that this is where you slug me over the head with the umbrella-stand, recover your property, and fade out. You're wrong."

He pushed Perrigo backwards. It seemed quite an effortless push, but there was an unsuspected kick of strength behind it. It flung Perrigo three paces towards the stairs; and then the hoodlum stopped on his heels and returned in a savage recoil. Simon slipped the gun out of his pocket, and Perrigo reined in.

"You daren't shoot," he blustered.

"Again you're wrong," said the Saint metallically. "It would give me great pleasure to shoot. I haven't shot anyone for months. Perhaps you're thinking I'll be scared of the noise. Once more you're wrong. This gun isn't silenced, but the first three cartridges are only half charged. No one in the street would hear a sound." For a tense second the Saint's gaze snapped daggers across the space between them. "You still think I'm bluffing. You've half a mind to test it out. Right. This is your chance. You've only to take one step towards me. One little step. . . . I'm waiting for you!"

And Perrigo took the step.

The automatic slanted up, and hiccoughed. It made less noise than opening up a bottle of champagne, but Perrigo's hat whisked off his head and floated down to the carpet behind him. The gunman looked round stupidly at it, his face going a shade paler.

"Of course," said the Saint, relapsing into the conversational style, "I'm not a very good shot. I've been practising a bit lately, but I've a long way to go yet before I get into your class. Another time, I might sort of kill you accidental like, and that would be very distressing. And then the question arises, Perrigo: would you go to Heaven? I doubt it. They're so particular about the people they let in. I don't think they'd like that check suit you're wearing. And can you play a harp? Do you know your psalms? Have you got a white nightie?"

Perrigo's fists clenched.

"What game are you playing?" he snarled.

"You know me," said the Saint rhetorically. "I am the man who knocked the L out of London, and at any moment I may become the man who knocked the P out of Perrigo. My game hasn't changed since we first met. It's a private party, and the police seemed to want to interfere, so we commuted to another site. That's the only reason why we're here, and why I took the trouble to get you away from Regent's Park. In short, if you haven't guessed it already, I'm still after those diamonds, my pet. They mean the beginning of a new chapter in my career, and a brief interlude of peace for Chief Inspector Teal. They are my old-age pension. I want that packet of boodle more than I've ever wanted any loot before;

and if you imagine I'm not going to have them, your name is Mug. And now you can pass on—this hall's getting draughty.''

"I'll see you in hell first," grated Perrigo.

"You won't see me in hell at all," said the Saint. "I like warm climates, but I'm very musical, and I think the harps have it. Forward march!"

He propelled Perrigo down the hall to a door which opened on to a flight of stone steps. At the bottom of these steps there was a small square cellar furnished with a chair and a camp bed. The door, Perrigo noticed, was of three-inch oak, and a broad iron bar slid in grooves across it. Simon pointed, and Perrigo went in and sat on the bed.

"When you know me better," said the Saint, "you'll discover that I have a cellar complex. So many people have taken me into cellars in order to do me grievous bodily harm that the infection has got into my system. There's something very sinister and thrilling about a cellar, don't you think?"

Perrigo hazarded no opinion.

"How long do I stay here?" he asked.

"Until to-morrow," Simon told him. "You'll find the place rather damp and stuffy, but there's enough ventilation to save you from suffocating. If you decide to strangle yourself with your braces, you might do it under that loose flagstone in the corner, which conceals a deep grave already dug for any corpses I might have on my hands. And in the morning I'll be along with some breakfast and a pair of thumbscrews, and we'll have a little chat. Night-night, old dear.''

He left Perrigo with those cheering thoughts to chew over, and went out, bolting the iron bar into place and securing it with a steel staple.

A silver-noted buzzer was purring somewhere above him as he ran up the stairs, and he knew that the next development was already on its way. He was not surprised—he had been expecting it—but the promptitude with which his expectations had been realised argued a tenacious implacability on the part of Chief Inspector Teal that would have unsettled the serenity of anyone but a Simon Templar. But the Saint was lining up to the starting-gate of an odyssey quite different from that of Mr. Teal. He let himself through the linen cupboard of the first-floor bathroom into No. 1, Upper Berkeley Mews, and went quickly down the runway to No. 7; and he was smiling as he stepped out of it into his own bedroom and slid the mirror panel shut behind him.

Patricia was waiting for him there.

"Teal's on his way," she said.

"Alone?"

"He was talking to his sleuth-hound when I gave you the signal. There wasn't anyone else with him."

"Splendid."

His coat off, the Saint was over at the dressing table, putting a lightning polish on his hair with brush and comb. Under Patricia's eyes, the traces of his recent rough-and-tumble in the car disappeared miraculously. In a matter of seconds he was his old spruce self, lean and immaculate and alert, a laughing storm-centre of hell-for-leather mischief, flipping into a blue velvet smoking gown. . . .

"Darling—"

She stopped him, with a hand on his arm. She was quite serious.

"Listen, boy. I've never questioned you before, but this time there's no Duke of Fortezza to frame you out."

"Maybe not."

"Are you sure there isn't going to be real trouble?"

"I'm sure there is. For one thing, our beautiful little bolt-hole has done its stuff. Never again will it make that sleuth-hound outside my perfect alibi. After tonight, Claud Eustace will know that I've got a spare exit, and he'll come back with a search warrant and a gang of navvies to find it. But we'll have had our money's worth out of it. Sure, there's going to be trouble. I asked for it—by special delivery!"

"And what then?"

Simon clapped his hands on her shoulders, smiling the old Saintly smile.

"Have you ever known any trouble that I couldn't get out of?" he demanded. "Have you ever seen me beaten?"

She thrilled to his madcap buoyancy—she did not know why.

"Never!" she cried.

Downstairs, the front door bell rang. The Saint took no notice. He held her with his eyes, near to laughing, vibrant with impetuous audacity, magnificently mad.

"Is there anything that can put me down?"

"I can't imagine it."

He swept her to him and kissed her red lips.

The bell rang again. Simon pointed, with one of his wide gestures.

"Down there," he said, "there's an out-size detective whose one aim in life is to spike the holiday that's coming to us. Our own Claud Eustace Teal, with his mouth full of gum and his wattles crimsoning, paying us his last professional call. Let's go and swipe him on the jaw."

7

IN THE SITTING room, Patricia closed her book and looked up as Chief Inspector Teal waddled in. Simon followed the visitor. It was inevitable that he should dramatise himself—that he should extract the last molecule of diversion from the scene by playing his part as strenuously as if life and death depended on it. He was an artist. And that night the zest of his self-appointed task tingled electrically in all his fibres. Teal, chewing stolidly through a few seconds' portentous pause, thought that he had never seen the Saint so debonair and dangerous.

"I hope I don't intrude," he said at last, heavily.

"Not at all," murmured the Saint. "You see before you a scene of domestic repose. Have some beer?"

Teal took a tight hold on himself. He knew that there was a toe-to-toe scrap in front of him, and he wasn't going to put himself at a disadvantage sooner than he could help. The searing vials of righteous indignation within him had simmered down still further doing the drive from Regent's Park, and out of the travail caution had been born. His purpose hadn't weakened in the least, but he wasn't going to trip over his own feet in the attempt to achieve it. The lights of battle glittering about in the Saint's blue eyes augured a heap of snags along the route that was to be paddled, and for once Chief Inspector Teal was trying to take the hint.

"Coming quietly?" he asked.

The feeler went out, gruffly noncommittal; and Simon smiled.

"You're expecting me to ask why," he drawled, "but I refuse to do anything that's expected of me. Besides, I know."

"How do you know?"

"My spies are everywhere. Sit down, Claud. That's a collapsible chair we bought specially for you, and the cigars in that box explode when you light them. Oh, and would you mind taking off your hat?—it doesn't go with the wallpaper."

Teal removed his bowler with savage tenderness. He realised that he was going to have an uphill fight to keep the promise he had made to himself. There was the faintest thickening in his lethargic voice as he repeated his question.

"How do you know what I want you for?"

"My dear soul, how else could I have known except by being with you when you first conceived the idea of wanting me?" answered the Saint blandly.

"So you're going to admit it really was you I was talking to at Regent's Park?"

"Between ourselves—it was."

"Got some underground way out of here, haven't you?"

"The place is a rabbit-warren."

"And where's Perrigo?"

"He's playing bunny."

Teal twiddled a button, and his eyelids lowered. The leading tentacles of a nasty cold sensation were starting to weave clammily up his spine. It was something akin to the sensation experienced by a man who, in the prelude to a nightmare, has been cavorting happily about in the middle of a bridge over a fathomless abyss, and who suddenly discovers that the bridge has turned into a thin slab of toffee and the temperature is rising.

Something was springing a leak. He hadn't the ghost of a presentiment of what the leak was going to be, but the symptoms of its approach were bristling all over the situation like the quills on a porcupine.

"You helped Perrigo to escape at Regent's Park, didn't you?" He tried to make his voice sleepier and more bored than it had ever been before, but the strain clipped minute snippets off the ends of the syllables. "You're admitting that you caused a wilful breach of the peace by discharging firearms in a public thoroughfare, that you obstructed and assaulted the police in the execution of their duty, and that you became an accessory to wilful murder?"

"Between these four walls," said the Saint, "and in these trousers, I cannot tell a lie."

"Very well." Teal's knuckles whitened over the brim of his hat. "Templar, I arrest you—"

"Oh, no," said the Saint. "Oh, no, Claud, you don't."

The detective tautened up as if he had received a blow. But Simon Templar wasn't even looking at him. He was selecting a cigarette from a box on the centre table. He flicked it into the air and caught it between his lips, with his hands complacently outspread. "My only parlour trick," he remarked, changing the subject.

Teal spoke through his teeth.

"And why?" he flared.

"Only one I ever learnt," explained the Saint naively.

"Why don't I arrest you?"

Simon ranged himself side-saddle on the table. He stroked the cog of an automatic lighter and put his cigarette in the flame.

"Because, Claud, what I say to you now, between these four walls and in these trousers, and what I'd say in the witness-box, are two things so totally different you'd hardly believe they came from the same rosebud mouth."

Teal snorted.

"Perjury, eh? I thought something cleverer than that was coming from you, Saint."

"You needn't be disappointed."

"Got a speech that you think'll let you out?"

"I have, Claud. I've got a peach of a speech. Put me in the dock, and I'll lie like a newspaper proprietor. Any idea what that means?"

The detective shrugged.

"That's your affair," he grunted. "If you want to be run for perjury as well as the other things, I'm afraid I can't stop you."

Simon leaned forward, his left hand on his hip and his right hand on his knee. The deep blue danger lights were glinting more brightly than ever in his eyes, and there was fight in every line of him. A back-to-the-wall, buccaneering fight, rollicking out to damn the odds.

"Claud, did you think you'd got me at last?"

"I did. And I still think so."

"Thought that the great day had dawned when my name was coming out of the Unfinished Business ledger, and you were going to sleep nights?"

"I did."

"That's too bad, Claud," said the Saint.

Teal pursed his lips tolerantly, but there were pin-points of red luminance darting about in his gaze.

"I'm still waiting to hear why," he said flatly.

Simon stood up.

"O.K.," he said, and a new indefinable timbre of menace was pulsing into his easy drawl. "I'll tell you why. You asked for the showdown. I'll tell you what you've been thinking. There was a feather you wanted for that hat of yours; you tried all manner of ways to get it, but it wasn't having you. You were too dumb. And then you thought you'd got it. Tonight was your big night. You were going to collect the Saint on the most footling break he ever made. I've got away with everything from murder downwards under your bloodshot eyes, but you were going to run me for stealing four-pence out of the Bank of England."

"That's not what I said."

"It goes for what you meant. You get what you asked for, Claud. Thought I was the World's Wet Smack, did you? Figured that I was so busy crashing the mountains that I'd never have time to put a tab on all the mole-hills? Well, you asked for something. Now would you like to know what I've really been doing tonight?"

"I'll hear it."

"I've been entertaining a dozen friends, and I'll give you from now till Kingdom Come to prove it's a lie!"

The detective glared.

"D'you think I was born yesterday?" he yelped.

"I don't know," said the Saint lazily. "Maybe you weren't born at all. Maybe you were just dug up. What's that got to do with it?"

Teal choked. His restraint split into small pieces, and the winds of his wrath began to twitch the bits out of his grasp, one by one.

"What's the idea?" he demanded heatedly; and the Saint smiled.

"Only the usual alibi, old corpuscle. Like it?"

"Alibi?" Teal rent the word with sadistic violence. "Oh, yes, you've got an alibi! Six men saw you at Regent's Park alone, but you've got twelve men to give you an alibi. And where was this alibi?"

"In the house that communicates with this one by the secret passage you wot of."

"You aren't going to change your mind about that passage?"

"Why should I? It may be eccentric, but there's nothing in the Statute Book to say it's illegal."

"And that's the alibi you're going to try and put over on me?"

"It's more," said the Saint comfortably. "It's the alibi that's going to dish you."

"Is it?"

Simon dropped his cigarette into an ashtray and put his hands in his pockets. He stood in front of the detective, six feet two inches of hair-trigger disorder—with a smile.

"Claud," he said, "you're missing the opportunity of a lifetime. I'm letting you in on the ground floor. Out of the kindness of my heart I'm presenting you with a low-down on the organisation of a master criminal that hundreds would give their ears to get. I'm not doing it without expense to myself, either. I'm giving away my labyrinth of secret passages, which means that if I want to be troublesome again I shall have to look for a new headquarters. I'm showing you the works of my emergency alibi, guaranteed to rescue anyone from any predicament: there are four lords, a knight, and three officers of field dank in it—they've taken me years to collect, and now I shall have to fossick around for a new bunch. But what are trifles like that between friends? . . . Now be sensible, Claud. It becomes increasingly evident that someone is impersonating me.''

'Yes, and I know who it is!''

"But it was bound to happen, wasn't it?'' said the Saint, continuing in that philosophically persuasive strain under which the razor-keen knife-edges were gliding about like hungry sharks in a smooth tropical sea. "In my misguided efforts to do good, I once made myself so notorious that someone or other was bound to think of hanging his sins on me. The wonder is that it wasn't thought of years ago. Now look at that recent affair in Hampstead—''

"I don't want to know any more about the affair in Hampstead,'' said Teal torridly. "I want to know how you're going to swing it on me this time. Come on. Let me have the names and addresses of these twelve liars. I'll run them for perjury at the same time as I'm running you.''

"You won't. But I'll tell you what *I'll* do—''

The Saint's forefinger shot out. Teal struck it aside.

"Don't do that!'' he yapped.

"I have to,'' said the Saint. "I love the way your tummy dents in and pops out again. Talking of tummies—''

"You tell me what you think you're going to do.''

"I'll run you for bribery, corruption, and blackmail!'' said the Saint.
His languid voice tightened up on the sentence with a sudden crispness that had the effect of a gunshot. It rocked the atmosphere like an exploding bomb. And it was followed by a silence that was ear-splitting.

The detective gaped at him with goggling eyes, while a substratum of dull scarlet sapped up under the skin of his face. It was the most flabbergasting utterance that Chief Inspector Teal had ever listened to. He blinked as if he had been smitten with doubts of his own sanity.

"Have you gone off your head?'' he hooted.

"Not that I know of.''

"And who's supposed to have been bribing me?''

"I have.''

"You?"

"Yeah.'' The Saint took another cigarette from the box and lighted it composedly. "Haven't seen your pass-book lately, have you? You'd better ask for it to-morrow morning. You'll discover that in the last six weeks alone you've taken eight hundred and fifty pounds off me. Two hundred pounds on February the sixteenth, two-fifty on March the sixth, four hundred on March the twenty-second—apart from smaller regular payments extending over the previous six months. All the cheques have got your endorsement on 'em, and they've all been passed through your account: they're back in my bank now, available for inspection by an authorized person. It's quite a tidy sum, Claud—eighteen hundred quid altogether. You'll have a grand time explaining it away."

Some of the colour ebbed slowly out of Teal's plump cheeks, and he seemed to sag inside his overcoat. Only the expression in his eyes remained the same—a stare of blank, frozen, incredulous stupefaction.

"You framed me for that?" he got out.

"I'm afraid I did." Simon inhaled, and blew a smoke-ring. "It was just another of my brilliant ideas. Are you thinking you can deny the endorsements? It won't be easy. Eight hundred and fifty pounds in six weeks is real money. I wrote it off as insurance, but I still hated parting with it. And how many juries would believe that I paid a detective eighteen hundred pounds inside six months just with the idea of being funny? It'd be a steep gamble for you if we had to go through the courts, old dear. I admit it was very naughty of me to bribe you, but there it is. . . . Unfortunately, you couldn't be content with what I gave you. You wanted more, and you tried all sorts of persecutions to get it. First that Hampstead affair, and then this show tonight. . . . Oh, well, Claud, it looks as if we shall have to swing together."

8

THE DETECTIVE SEEMED to have shrunk. His complexion had gone lined and blotchy, and there was a dazed look in his eyes that stabbed the Saint with a twinge of pity.

Teal was a man facing the end. The bombshell that the Saint had flung at him had knocked the underpinning from the very foundation of his universe. The fight and bluster had gone out of him. He knew, better than anyone, the full and devastating significance of the trap that had been laid for him. There was no way out of it—no human bluff or subterfuge that would let him out. He could stick to his guns and give battle to the last ditch—arrest the Saint as he had intended, take his chance with the threatened alibi, fight out the counter-charge of bribery and corruption when it came along, perhaps even win an acquittal—but it would still be the end of his career. Even if he won, he would be a ruined man. A police officer must be above suspicion. And those endorsed and cancelled cheques of which the Saint had spoken, produced in court, would be damning evidence. Acquitted, Teal would still be under a cloud. Even afterwards, there would be gossips to point to him and whisper that he was a man who had broken the eleventh commandment and escaped the consequences by the skin of his teeth. And he was not so young as he had been—not so young that he could snap his fingers at the gossips and buckle grimly back into the task of making good again. He would have to resign. He would be through.

He stood there, going paler, but not flinching; and the Saint blew two more smoke-rings.

Teal was trying to think, but he couldn't. The suddenness with which the blow had fallen had pulverised his wits. He felt himself going mentally and physically numb. Under the surveillance of those devilishly bleak blue eyes, and in the vivid presence of what they stood for, he couldn't do any consecutive and sober thinking.

Abruptly, he settled his belt and shook down his coat.

"I'll see you in the morning," he said, in a sort of gulp, and walked jerkily out of the room.

Simon heard the front door close, and listened to the detective's footsteps clumping past the window and dying away towards Berkeley Square. Something seemed to have paralysed their ordinary ponderous self-reliance. There was the least little telltale drag in them. . . . And the Saint turned and found Patricia watching him.

"A notable triumph," he said quietly.

The girl stood up.

"Were you bluffing?" she asked.

"Of course not. I knew that Teal and I were certain to have that showdown sooner or later, and I was prepared for it. I'd got half a dozen more shocks waiting for him, if he'd stayed to hear them. I just wanted to put the wind up him. But I'd no idea it'd be such a smash."

Patricia looked away.

"It was pathetic," she said. "Oh, I could see him go ten years older while you were talking."

Simon nodded. The fruits of victory were strangely bitter.

"Pat, did you know that an hour or so ago I was planning for this to be the sorriest show Teal ever stuck his nose into? The noble game of Teal-baiting was going to be played as it had never been played before. That's all I've got to say. . . . What a damn-fool racket it is!''

He turned on his heel, and left her without another word.

His mind was too full to talk. Upstairs, he threw off his clothes and tumbled into bed, and almost instantly he fell asleep. That gift of sleep is one that all great adventurers have shared—a sleep that heals the mind and solves all problems. Patricia, coming up later, found his face as peaceful as a child's.

He must have slept very soundly, for the sound of a stealthy rustle only half roused him. Then he heard a click, and was wide awake.

He opened his eyes and glanced round the room. There was enough light for him to see that there was no unusual shadow anywhere. He looked at his watch, and saw that it was nearly seven o'clock in the morning. For some moments he lay still, gazing at the indicator panel on the opposite wall. An ingenious system of invisible alarms connected up with that panel from every part of the house, and it was impossible for anyone to move about inside No. 7, Upper Berkeley Mews at night without every yard of his progress being charted by winking little coloured bulbs on the panel. But not one bulb was flickering, and the auxiliary buzzer under the Saint's pillow was silent.

Simon frowned puzzledly, wondering if his imagination had deceived him. And then a breath-taking duet of inspirations whirled into his brain, and he wriggled noiselessly from between the sheets.

He pushed the pier-glass aside, and touched a switch that illuminated the secret passage. Right at his feet, he saw a charred match-end lying on the felt matting, and his lips tightened. He sped down the corridor, and entered the end house. In front of him, the door of a cupboard, and its false back communicating with the bathroom in 104, Berkeley Square, were both wide open; and he remembered that he had left them ajar behind him on the previous night, in his haste to get home and resume the feud with Chief Inspector Teal. The bathroom door was also ajar; he slipped through it, and emerged on the landing. A tiny glow of light further down the stairs caught his eye, and vanished immediately.

Then he established a second link between the two parts of the duet that had brought him to where he was, and wished he had delayed the chase while he picked up his gun. He crept downwards, and saw a shadow that moved.

"Stay where you are," he rapped. "I've got you covered!"

The shadow leapt away, and Simon hurled himself after it. He was still four steps behind when he sprang through the air and landed on the man's shoulders. They crashed down together, rolled down the remaining treads, and reached the bottom with a bump. The Saint groped for a stranglehold. He had found it with one hand when he saw a dull gleam of steel in the light of the street lamp that flung a faint nimbus of rays through the transom above the front door. He squirmed aside, and the point ripped his pyjamas and thudded into the floor. Then a bony knee kicked up into his stomach, and he gasped and went limp with agony. The front door banged while he lay there twisting helplessly.

It was ten minutes before he was able to stagger to his feet and go on a tour of investigation. Down in the basement, he found the cellar door wide open. A hole big enough for a man's arm to pass through had been carved out of it a foot above the massive bolt, and the flagstones were littered with chips of wood. Simon realised that he had been incredibly careless.

He returned to his bedroom and looked at the coat he had been wearing. It had been moved from where he had thrown it down—that had been the cause of the soft rustling that had first disturbed his slumbers. A further investigation showed that Perrigo's passport and tickets were missing from the pocket where Simon had left them. This was no worse than the Saint had expected.

Aching, he went back to bed and slept again. And this time he dreamed a dream.

He was running up the wrong side of a narrow moving stairway. Patricia was in front of him, and he couldn't go fast enough: he had to keep pushing her. He wanted to get past her and catch Perrigo, who was dancing about just out of his grasp. Perrigo was dressed something like an organ-grinder's monkey, in a ridiculous straw hat, a tail coat, and a pair of white flannel trousers. There was an enormous diamond necklace over his collar; and he jeered and grimaced and bawled: "Not in these trousers." Then the scene changed, and Teal came riding by on a giraffe, wearing a pair of plus fours; and he also said: "Not in these trousers."

Then the Saint woke up, and saw that it was half-past eight. He jumped out of bed, lighted a cigarette, and made for the bathroom. He soaped his face and shaved, haunted by his dream for some reason that he could not nail down; and he was wallowing in bath salts when the interruption of it flashed upon him with an aptness that made him erupt out of the water with an almighty splash.

Ten minutes later, gorgeously apparalled in his new spring suit, he tore down the stairs and found bacon and eggs on the table and Patricia reading a newspaper.

"Perrigo has left us," he said.

The girl looked up with startled eyes, but Simon was laughing.

"He's left us, but I know where he's gone," said the Saint. "He collected his papers before he went. I forgot that he carried a knife, and locked him up without fanning him—he spent the night digging his way through the door, and came through here for his passport in the early morning. I was just too slow to catch him. We'll meet him again on the boat train—it leaves at ten o'clock."

"How do you know he'll be on it?"

"If he didn't mean to do that, why did he come back for his ticket? No—I know exactly what's in his head. He knows that he's only got one way out, now that he's bereaved of Isadore, and he's going to try to make the grade. He's made up his mind that I'm not helping the police, and he's going to take his chance on a straight duck with me—and I'll bet he'll park himself in the most crowded compartment he can find, just to give himself the turn of the odds. And I'll say some more: I know where those diamonds are now?"

"Have you got them?"

"Not yet. But up at Isadore's I spotted that Perrigo's costume was assorted. I thought he'd changed jackets with Frankie Hormer, and I went over his jacket twice before Teal buzzed in. Naturally, I didn't find anything. I must have been half-witted. It wasn't coats he'd swapped—it was trousers. Those diamonds are sewn up somewhere in Bertie's leg draperies!"

Patricia came over to the table.

"Have you thought any more about Teal?" she asked.

Simon strode across to a book-case and took down a small leather-bound volume. There were months of painstaking work in its unassuming compass—names, addresses, personal data, means of approach, sources of evidence, all the laboriously perfected groundwork that enabled the Saint's raids upon the underworld to be carried through so smoothly and made their meteoric audacity possible.

"Pat," said the Saint, "I'm going to make Teal a great man. It may be extravagant, but what the hell? Can you have the whole earth for ten cents? This party has already cost us our home, our prize alibi, and one of our shrewdest counter-attacks—but who cares? Let's finish the thing in style. I'm the cleverest man in the world. Can't I find six more homes, work out fourteen bigger and better alibis, and invent seventy-nine more stratagems and spoils? Can't I fell two more books like this if I want to?''

Patricia put her arms round his neck.

''Are you going to give Teal that book?''

The Saint nodded. He was radiant.

''I'm going to steal Perrigo's pants, Claud Eustace is going to smile again, and you and I are going away together.''

9

THE SAINT WAS in a thaumaturgical mood. He performed a minor sorcery on a Pullman attendant that materialised seats where none had been before, and ensconced himself with the air of a wizard taking his ease. After a couple of meditative cigarettes, he produced a pencil and commenced a metrical composition in the margins of the wine list.

He was still scribbling with unalloyed enthusiasm when Patricia got up and went for a walk down the train. She was away for several minutes; and when she returned, the Saint looked up and deliberately disregarded the confusion in her eyes.

''Give ear,'' he said. ''This is the Ballad of the Bold Bad Man, another Precautionary Tale:

> *Daniel Dinwiddie Gigsworth-Glue*
> *Was warranted by those who knew*
> *To be a perfect paragon*
> *With or without his trousers on;*
> *An upright man (the Gigsworths are*
> *Peerlessly perpendicular)*
> *Staunch to the old mortality,*
> *Who would have rather died than be*
> *Observed at Slumpton-under-Slop*
> *In bathing drawers without the top.*

''Simon,'' said the girl, ''Perrigo isn't on the train.''

The Saint put down his pencil.

"He is, old darling. I saw him when we boarded it at Waterloo, and I think he saw me."

"But I've looked in every carriage—"

"Did you take everyone's finger-prints?"

"A man like Perrigo wouldn't find it easy to disguise himself."

Simon smiled.

"Disguises are tricky things," he said. "It isn't the false whiskers and the putty nose that get you down—it's the little details. Did I ever tell you about a friend of mine who thought he'd get the inside dope about Chelsea? He bought a pink shirt and a velvet coat, grew a large semi-circular beard, rented a studio, and changed his name to Prmnlovcwz; and he had a great time until one day they caught him in an artist's colourman's trying to buy a tube of Golder's Green. . . . Now you must hear some more about Daniel:

> *How lovely, oh, how luminous*
> *His spotless virtue seemed to us*
> *Who sat among the cherubim*
> *Reserving Daniel's pew for him!*
> *Impossible to indispose,*
> *His honour, shining like his nose,*
> *Blazed through an age of sin and strife*
> *The beacon of a blameless life. . . .*
> *And then he fell. . . .*
>   *The Tempter, who*
> *Was mortified by Daniel Glue,*
> *Played his last evil card; and Dan*
> *Who, like a perfect gentleman,*
> *Had scorned strong drink and wicked oaths*
> *And blondes with pink silk underclothes,*
> *Bought (Oh, we saw the angels weep!)*
> *A ticket in the Irish Sweep."*

Patricia reached across the table and captured the Saint's hands.

"Simon, I won't be out of it! Where *is* Perrigo?"

"If you talk much louder, he'll hear you."

"Hs isn't in this coach!"

"He's in the next one."

The girl stared.

"What does he look like?"

Simon smiled, lighting a cigarette.

"He's chosen the simplest and nearly the most effective disguise there is. He's got himself up as a very fair imitation of our old pal the Negro Spiritual." The Saint looked at her with merry eyes. "He's done it well, too; but I spotted him at once. Hence my parable. Did you ever see a Negro with light yellow eyes? They may exist, but I've never met one. There used to be a blue-eyed Sikh in Hong Kong who became quite famous, but that's the only similar freak I've met. So when I got a glimpse of those eyes I took another peek at the face—and Perrigo it was. Remember him now?"

Patricia nodded breathlessly.

"Why couldn't I see it?" she exclaimed.

"You've got to have a brain for that sort of thing," said the Saint modestly.

"But—yes, I remember now—the carriage he's in is full—"

"And you're wondering how I'm going to get his trousers off him? Well, the problem certainly has its interesting angles. How does one steal a man's trousers on a crowded train? You mayn't believe it, but I've seen difficulties about that myself."

An official came down the train, checking up visas and issuing embarkation vouchers. Simon obtained a couple of passes, and smoked thoughtfully for some minutes. And then he laughed and stood up.

"Why worry?" he wanted to know. "I've thought of a much better thing to do. One of my really wonderful inspirations."

"What's that?"

Simon tapped her on the shoulder.

"I'm going to beguile the time by baiting Bertie," he said, with immense solemnity. "C'mon!"

He hurtled off in his volcanic way, with a long-striding swing of lean impetuous limbs, as if a gale of wind swept him on.

And Patricia Holm was smiling as she ran to catch him up—the unfathomable and infinitely tender smile of all the women who have been doomed to love romantic men. For she knew the Saint better than he knew himself. He could not grow old. Oh, yes, he would grow in years, would feel more deeply, would think more deeply, would endeavour with spasmodic soberness to fall in line with the common facts of life; but the mainsprings of his character could not change. He would deceive himself, but he would never deceive her. Even now, she knew what was in his mind. He was trying to brace himself to march down the road that all his friends had taken. He was daring himself to take up the glove that the

High Gods had thrown at his feet, and to take it up as he would have taken up any other challenge—with a laugh and a flourish, and the sound of trumpets in his ears. And already she knew how she would answer him.

She came up behind him and caught his elbow.

"But is this going to help you, lad?"

"It will amuse me," said the Saint. "And it's an act of piety. It's our sacred duty to see that Bertie has a journey he'll never forget. I shall open the ball by trying to touch him for a subscription to the funds of the Society for Distributing Woollen Vests to the Patriarchs of the Upper Dogsboddi. Speaking emotionally and in a loud voice, I shall wax eloquent on the work that has already been done among his black brothers, and invite him to make a contribution. If he doesn't, you'll barge in and ask him for his autograph. Address him as Al Jolson, and ask him to sing something. After that—"

"After that," said Patricia firmly, "he'll pull the communication cord, and we shall both be thrown off the train. Lead on, boy!"

Simon nodded, and went to the door of the compartment he had marked down.

And there he stopped, statuesquely, while the skyward-slanting cigarette between his lips sank slowly through the arc of a circle and ended up at a comically contrasting droop.

After a few seconds, Patricia stepped to his side and also looked into the compartment. And the Saint took the cigarette from his mouth and exhaled smoke in a long expiring whistle.

Perrigo was gone.

There wasn't a doubt about that. The corner seat that he had occupied was as innocent of human habitation as any corner seat has ever been since George Stephenson hitched up his wagons and went rioting down to Stockton-upon-Tees. If not more so. As for the other seats, they were occupied respectively by a portly matron with a wart on her chin, a small boy in a sailor suit, and a thin-flanked female with pimples and a camouflaged copy of *The Well of Loneliness,* into none of whom could Gunner Perrigo by any conceivable miracle of make-up have transformed himself. . . . Those were the irrefutable facts about the scene, pithily and systematically recorded; and the longer one looked at them, the more grisly they became.

Simon singed the inoffensive air with a line of oratory that would have scorched the hide of a salamander. He did it as if his heart was in the job, which it was. Carefully and comprehensively, he covered every aspect and detail of the situation with a calorific lavishness of imagery that would have warmed the cockles of a sergeant-major's heart. Nobody and nothing, however remotely connected with the incident, was left outside the wide embrace of his oration. He started with the paleolithic progenitors of the said George Stephenson, and worked steadily down to the back teeth of Isadore Elberman's grandchildren. At which point Patricia interrupted him.

"He might be having a wash, or something," she said.

"Yeah!" The Saint was scathing. "Sure, he might be having a wash. And he took his bag with him in case the flies laid eggs on it. Did you notice that bag? I did. It was brand new—hadn't a scratch on it. He'd been doing some early morning shopping before he caught the train, hustling up some kit for the voyage. All his own stuff was at Isadore's, and he wouldn't risk going back there. And his bag's gone!"

The embarkation officer passed them, and opened the door of the compartment.

"Miss Lovedew?" The pimply female acknowledged it. "Your papers are quite in order—"

Simon took Patricia's arm and steered her gently away.

"Her name is Lovedew," he said sepulchrally. "Let us go and find somewhere to die."

They tottered a few steps down the corridor; and then Patricia said: "He must be still on the train! We haven't slowed up once since we started, and he couldn't have jumped off without breaking his neck—"

The Saint gripped her hands.

"You're right!" he whooped. "Pat, you're damn right! I said you wanted a brain for this sort of thing. Bertie must be on the train still, and if he's on the train we'll find him—it we have to take the whole outfit to pieces. Now, you go that way and I'll go this way, and you keep your eyes peeled. And if you see a man with a huge tufted beard, you take hold of it and give it a good pull!"

"Right-o, Saint!"

"Then let's go!"

He went flying down the alley, lurching from side to side for the rocking of the train, and contriving to light another cigarette as he went.

He did his share thoroughly. In the space of ten minutes, he reviewed a selection of passengers so variegated that his brain began to reel. Before his eyes passed an array of physiognomies that would have made Cesare Lombrosco chirrup ecstatically and reach for his tape measure. Americans of all shapes and sizes, Englishmen in plus fours, flannel bags, and natty

suitings, male children, female children, ambiguous children, large
women, small women, three cosmopolitan millionaires—one fat, one
thin, one sozzled—three cosmopolitan millionaires' wives—ditto, but
shuffled—a novelist, an actor, a politician, four Parsees, three Hindus,
two Chinese, and a wild man from Borneo. Simon Templar inspected
every one of them who could by any stretch of the imagination have
come within the frame of the picture, and acquired sufficient data to write
three books or six hundred and eighty-seven modern novels. But he did
not find Gunner Perrigo.

He came to the end of the last coach, and stood gazing moodily out
of a window before starting back on the return journey.

And it was while he was there that he saw a strange sight.

The first manifestation of it did not impress him immediately. It was
simply a scrap of white that went drifting past the window. His eyes
followed it abstractedly, and then reverted to their gloomy concentration
on the scenery. Then two more scraps of white flittered past his nose,
and a second later he saw a spread of red stuff fluttering feebly on the
wire fence beside the line.

The Saint frowned, and watched more attentively. And a perfect cataract of whatnots began to aviate past his eyes and distribute themselves
about the route. Big whatnots and little whatnots, in divers formations
and half the colours of the rainbow, went wafting by the window and
scattered over the fields and hedges. A mass of green taffeta flapped past,
looking like a bilious vulture after an argument with a stream hammer,
and was closely followed by a jaundiced cotton seagull that seemed to
have suffered a similar experience. A covey of miscellaneous bits and
pieces drove by in hot pursuit. No less than eight palpitating banners of
assorted hues curveted down the breeze and perched on railings and
telegraph poles by the wayside. It went on until the entire landscape
seemed to be littered with the loot of all the emporia of Knightsbridge
and the Brompton Road.

And suddenly the meaning of it flashed upon the Saint—so suddenly
and lucidly that he threw back his head and bowed before a gust of
helpless mirth.

He spun round to the door beside him. He had made sure that it was
locked, but he must have been mistaken. He heaved his shoulder at it,
and it burst open—it had been temporarily secured with a gimlet, as he
discovered later. He hadn't a doubt in his head that his latest and most
sudden inspiration was right, and he knew exactly what he was going to
do about it.

Five minutes later, after a brief interlude for wash and brush-up purposes, he was careering blissfully back along the corridor on one of the most supremely joyous journeys of his life.

At the compartment in which Perrigo had been, he stopped, and opened the door.

"Miss Lovedew," he said pensively, and again the impetiginous female looked and acknowledged the charge. "Is your luggage insured?"

"Of course," said the woman. "Why?"

"You should begin making out your claim immediately," said the Saint.

The woman stared.

"I don't understand you. What's happened? Are you one of the company's servants?"

"I am the head cook and bottle-washer," said the Saint gravely, "and I did not like your red flannel nighties."

He closed the door again and passed on, carolling hilariously to himself, and leaving the lady to suffer from astounded fury as well as acne.

In the Pullman he found Patricia gazing disconsolately in front of her. Her face lighted up as he arrived.

"Did you find him?"

Simon sat down.

"What luck did you have?"

"Just sweet damn-all," said the girl wryly. "I've been over my part of the train four times, and I wouldn't have missed Perrigo if he'd disguised himself as a mosquito."

"I am inspired," said the Saint.

He took the wine list and his pencil, and wrote rapidly. Then he held up the sheet and read:

> *"The mountains shook, the thunders came,*
> *The very heavens wept for shame;*
> *A Gigsworth in a white chemise*
> *Visibly vortexed at the knees,*
> *While Dan's defection turned quite giddy*
> *The ghost of Ancestor Dinwiddie.*
> *If Dan had been a common cad*
> *It wouldn't have been half so bad;*
> *If he had merely robbed a bank,*
> *Or floated companies that sank,*
> *Or, with a piece of sharp bamboo,*

Bashfully bumped off Mrs. Blue;
They might have understood his whim
And, in the end, forgiven him:
Such things, though odd, have now and then
Been done by perfect gentlemen;
But Daniel's foul iniquity
Could scarcely have been worse if he
Had bought (or so it seemed to them)
A chocolate after 9 p.m.''

Patricia smiled.

"Will you always be mad?'' she asked.

"Until the day I die, please God,'' said the Saint.

"But if you didn't find Perrigo—''

"But I did find him!''

The girl gasped.

"You found him?''

Simon nodded; and she saw then that his eyes were laughing.

"I did. He was in the luggage van at the end, heaving mentionables and unmentionables out of a wardrobe trunk. And just for the glory of it, Pat, the trunk was labelled with the immortal name of Lovedew—I found that out afterwards and tried to break the news to her, but I don't think she believed me. Anyway, I whaled into him, and there was a breezy exchange of pleasantries. And the long and the short of it is—''

"Is—''

"That Perrigo is locked up in that trunk, just where he wanted to be; but there's an entirely new set of labels on it that are going to cause no small stir on board the *Berengaria* if Claud Eustace arrives in time. Which I expect he will—Isadore is almost certain to have squealed. And all we've got to do is wait for the orchestra to tune up.'' Simon looked at his watch. "There's half an hour to go yet, old Pat, and I think we might stand ourselves a bottle!''

10

A CLOCK WAS booming the half-hour after twelve when Chief Inspector Teal climbed stiffly out of his special police car at the gates of the Ocean Dock. It had been half-past ten when he left Albany Street Police Station, and that single chime indicated that the Flying Squad driver had made a very creditable run of it from London to Southampton.

For Isadore Elberman had duly squealed, as the Saint had expected, and it had been no mean squeal. Considerably stewed down after a sleepless night in the cells, he had reiterated to the Divisional Inspector the story with which he had failed to gain Teal's ear the evening before; and the tale had come through with a wealth of embellishments in the way of circumstantial detail that had made the Inspector reach hastily for the telephone and call for Mr. Teal to lend his personal patronage to the squeak.

Isadore Elberman was not the only member of the cast who had spent a sleepless night. Teal had been waiting on the doorstep of his bank when it opened in the morning. He asked casually for his balance, and in a few minutes the cashier passed a slip of paper across the counter. It showed exactly one thousand eight hundred pounds more to his credit than it should have done, and he had no need to make further inquiries. He took a taxi from the bank to Upper Berkeley Mews; but a prolonged assault on the front door elicited no response, and the relief watcher told him that Templar and the girl had gone out at nine-thirty and had not returned. Teal went back to New Scotland Yard, and it was there that the call from Albany Street found him.

And on the way down to Southampton the different fragments of the jigsaw in which he had involved himself had fitted themselves together in his head, dovetailing neatly into one another without a gap or a protuberance anywhere, and producing a shape with one coherent outline and a sickeningly simply picture lithographed upon it in three colours. So far as the raw stark facts of the case were concerned, there wasn't a leak or a loose end in the whole copper-bottomed consolidation of them. It was as puerile and patent as the most elementary exercise in kindergarten arithmetic. It sat up on its hind legs and leered at him.

Slowly and stolidly, with clenched fists buried deep in the pockets of his overcoat, Chief Inspector Teal went up the gangway of the *Berengaria* to see the story through.

And down in the well-deck aft, Simon Templar was sitting on a wardrobe trunk discoursing genially to two stewards, a porter, an irate lady with pimples, and a small group of fascinated passengers.

"I agree," the Saint was saying. "It is an outrage. But you must blame Bertie for that. I can only conclude that he doesn't like red flannel nighties either. So far as can be deduced from the circumstances, the sight of your eminently respectable robes filled him with such an uncontrollable frenzy that he began to empty the whole contents of your trunk out of the window. But am I to blame? Am I Bertie's keeper? At a moment when my back was turned—"

"I don't believe you!" stormed the irate lady. "You're a common thief, that's what you are! I should know that trunk anywhere. I can describe everything that's in it—"

"I'll bet you can't," said the Saint.

The lady appealed to the assembled spectators.

"This is unbearable!" she raved. "It's the most barefaced imposture I ever heard of! This man has stolen my clothes and put his own labels on the trunk—"

"Madam," said the Saint, "I've never disputed that the trunk, as a trunk, was yours. The labels refer to the destination of the contents. As a strictly law-abiding citizen—"

"Where," demanded the pimply female hysterically, "is the Captain?"

And at that point Teal shouldered himself into the front rank of the crowd.

Just for a second he stood looking at the Saint, and Simon saw that there were shadows under his eyes and the faintest trace of flabbiness about his cheeks. But the eyes themselves were hard and expressionless, and the lips below them were pressed up into a dour line.

"I thought I should find you here," he said.

The last of the Lovedews whirled round.

"Do you know this man?"

"Yes," said Teal rigidly. "I know him."

The Saint crossed his legs and took out a cigarette-case. He indicated the detective with a wave of his hand.

"Ladies and gentlemen," he murmured, "allow me to introduce the *deus ex machina,* or whizzbang out of the works. This is Mr. Claud Eustace Teal, who is going to tell us about his wanderings in Northern Euthanasia. Mr. Teal, Miss Lovedew. Miss Lovedew—"

"Teal?" The infuriated lady leapt back as though she had been stung. "Are you Teal?"

"That is my name," said the slightly startled detective.

"You stand there and admit that to me?"

"Yes—of course."

The woman reeled back into the arms of one of the bystanders.

"Has everyone gone mad?" she wailed. "I'm being robbed in broad daylight! That is this man's accomplice—he hasn't denied it! Can nobody do anything to stop them?"

Teal blinked.

"I'm a police officer," he said.

"You're a liar!" screamed the woman.

"My good lady—"

"Don't you dare speak to me like that! You're a low, mean, impertinent thief—"

"But—"

"I want my trunk! I'm going to have my trunk! How can I go to New York without my trunk? That is my own trunk—"

"But, Claud," said the Saint earnestly, "have you seen the trunk of the butler of her uncle? That is a trunk of the most colossal."

Miss Lovedew gazed wildly about her.

"Will no one help me?" she moaned.

Simon removed the cigarette from his mouth and stood up. He placed one foot on the trunk, rested his right forearm on his knee, and raised a hand for silence.

"May I be allowed to explain?" he said.

The woman clutched her forehead.

"Is anybody going to listen to this—this—this—"

"Gentleman?" suggested the Saint, tentatively.

Teal stepped forward and took a grip of his belt.

"I am a police officer," he repeated trenchantly, "and I should certainly like to hear his explanation."

This time he made the statement of his identity with such a bald authoritativeness that the buzz of surrounding comment died down to a tense hush. Even the pimply protagonist gaped at him in silence, with her assurance momentarily shaken. The stillness piled up with almost theatrical effect.

"Well?" said Teal.

The Saint gestured airily with his cigarette.

"You arrive," he said, "in time to arbitrate over a serious misunderstanding. Let me give you the facts. I travelled down by the boat train from Waterloo this morning in order to keep an eye on a friend of ours whom we'll call Bertie. During the journey I lost sight of him. I tooled around to find out what was happening to him, and eventually located him in the luggage van in the very act of throwing the last of Miss Lovedew's what's-its out of the window."

"It's a lie!" bleated the lady, faint but pursuing. "He stole my clothes, insulted me in my carriage—"

"We come to that in a minute," said the Saint imperturbably. "As

I was saying, I found Bertie just crawling into the trunk he had so unceremoniously emptied. At great personal peril and inconvenience, Claud, I helped him towards his objective and locked him up for delivery to yourself. In order to do this, I was compelled to make a temporary alteration to the labels on the trunk, which I admit I borrowed for the good cause without Miss Lovedew's permission. I made one attempt to explain the circumstances to her, but was rejected with contumely. Then, while I was waiting for you to arrive, this argument about the rightful ownership of the property began. The trunk, as I've never denied, belongs to Miss Lovedew. The dispute seems to be about Bertie.''

Miss Lovedew goggled at him.

"Do you mean to say that there's a *man* in that trunk?" she demanded hideously.

"Madam," said the Saint, "there is. Would you like him? Mr. Teal has the first claim, but I'm open to competitive offers. The specimen is in full running order, suffering at the moment from a black eye and an aching jaw, but otherwise complete and ready for the road. He is highly-strung and sensitive, but extremely virile. Fed on a diet of rye whisky and caviar—"

Teal bent over the trunk and examined the labels. The name on them was his own. He straightened up and levelled his gaze inflexibly upon the Saint.

"I'll talk to you alone for a moment," he said.

"Pleasure," said the Saint briefly.

The detective looked round.

"That trunk is not to be touched without my permission," he said.

He walked over to the rail, and Simon Templar strolled along by his side. They passed out of earshot of the crowd, and stopped. For a few seconds they eyed each other steadily.

"Is that Perrigo you've got in that trunk?" Teal asked presently.

"None other."

"We've had a full confession from Elberman. Do you know what the penalty is for being in possession of illicit diamonds?"

"I know what the penalty is for being caught in possession of illicit diamonds," said the Saint circumspectly.

"Do you know where those diamonds are now?"

Simon nodded.

"They are sewn into the seat of Perrigo's pants," he said.

"Is that what you wanted Perrigo for?"

The Saint leaned on the rail.

"You know, Claud," he remarked, "you're the damnedest fool."
Teal's eyes hardened.
"Why?"
Because you're playing the damnedest fool game with me. Have you ever known me to be an accessory to wanton murder?"
"I've known you to be mixed up in some darned funny things."
"You've never known me to be mixed up in anything as darned unfunny as that. But you work yourself up to the point where you're ready to believe anything you want to believe. It's the racket. It's dog eating dog. I beat you to something, and you get mad. When you get mad, I have to bait you. The more I bait you, the madder you get. And the madder you get, the more I have to bait you. We get so's nothing's too bad for us to do to each other." The Saint smiled. "Well, Claud, I'm taking a little holiday, and before I go I'm giving you a break."
Teal shrugged mountainously, but for a moment he said nothing. And the Saint balanced his cigarette on his thumbnail and flipped it far and wide.
"Let me do some thinking for you," he said. "I'm great on doing other people's thinking for them these days. . . . Overnight you thought over what I said to you last evening. This morning you verified that I hadn't been bluffing. And you knew there was only one thing for you to do. Your conscience wouldn't let you lie down under what I'd done. You'd got to take what was coming to you—arrest me, and face the music. You'd got to play square with yourself, even if it broke you. I know just how you felt. I admire you for it. But I'm not going to let you do it."
"No?"
"Not in these trousers," said the Saint. "Why should you? You've got Perrigo, and I'm ready for a short rest. And here's your surprise packet. Get busy on what it tells you, and you may be a superintendent before the end of the season."
Teal glanced at the book which the Saint had thrust into his hands, and turned it over thoughtfully.
Then he looked again at the Saint. His face was still as impassive as the face of a graven image, but a little of the chilled steel had gone out of his eyes. And, as he looked, he saw that the Saint was laughing again— the old, unchangeable, soundless, impudent Saintly laughter. And the blue imps in the Saint's eyes danced.
"I play the game by my own rules, Claud," said the Saint. "Don't you forget it. That profound philosophy covers the craziest things I do.

It also makes me the only man in this bleary age who enjoys every minute of his life. And''—for the last time in that story, the Saintly forefinger drove gaily and debonairly to its mark—''if you take a leaf out of my book, Claud, one day, Claud, you will have fun and games for ever.''

And then the Saint was gone.

He departed in the Saintly way, with a last Saintly smile and the clap of a hand on the detective's shoulder; and Teal watched him go without a word.

Patricia was waiting for him further along the deck. He fell into step beside her, and they went down the gangway and crossed the quay. At the corner of a warehouse Simon stopped. Quite quietly he looked at her, propping up the building with one hand.

And the girl knew what his silence meant. For him, the die was cast; and, being the man he was, he was ready to pay cash. His hand was in his pocket, and the smile hadn't wavered on his lips. But just for that moment he was taking his unflinching farewell of the fair fields of irresponsible adventure, understanding just what it would mean to him to pay the score, scanning the road ahead with the steady eyes that had never feared anything in this life. And he was ready to start the journey there and then.

And Patricia smiled. She had never loved him more than she did at that moment; but she smiled with nothing but the smile behind her eyes. And she answered before he had spoken.

''Boy,'' she said, ''I couldn't be happier than I am now.''

He did not move. She went on, quickly:

''Don't say it, Simon! I don't want you to. Haven't we both got everything we want as it is? Isn't life splendid enough? Aren't we going to have more adventures, and—and—''

''Fun and games for ever?''

''Yes! Aren't we? Why spoil the magic? I won't listen to you. Even if we've missed out on this adventure—''

Suddenly he laughed. His hands went to his hips. She had been waiting for that laugh. She had put all that she was into the task of winning it. And, with that laugh, the spell that had held his eyes so quiet and steady was broken. She saw the leap of the old mirth and glamour lighting them again. She was happy.

''Pat, is that really what you want?''

''It's everything I want.''

''To go on with the fighting and the fun? To go on racketing around the world, doing everything that's utterly and gloriously mad—swaggering, swashbuckling, singing—showing all these dreary old dogs what can be done with life—not giving a damn for anyone—robbing the rich, helping the poor—plaguing the pompous, killing dragons, pulling policemen's legs—"

"I'm ready for it all!"

He caught her hands.

"Are you sure?"

"Positive."

"Not one tiny little doubt about it?"

"Not one."

"Then we can start this minute."

She stared.

"What do you mean?" she asked.

The Saint loosened his belt and pointed downwards. Even then, she didn't understand.

"Remember how I found Bertie? He was halfway into the Lovedew's wardrobe trunk. We had a short but merry scrap. And then he went on in. Well, during the tumult and the shouting, and the general excitement, in the course of which Bertie soaked up one of the juciest K.O.'s I've ever distributed—"

He broke off, and the girl turned round in amazed perplexity.

From somewhere on the *Berengaria* had pealed out the wild and frantic shriek of an irreparably outraged camel collapsing under the last intolerable straw.

Patricia turned again, her face blank with bewilderment.

"What on earth was that?" she asked.

The Saint smiled seraphically.

"That was the death-cry of old Pimply-face. They've just opened her trunk and discovered Bertie. And he has no trousers on. We can begin our travels right now," said the Saint.